The Best Military Science Fiction of the 20th Century

THE BEST MILITARY SCIENCE FICTION OF THE 20TH CENTURY

EDITED BY HARRY TURTLEDOVE
WITH MARTIN H. GREENBERG

A Del Rey® Book
THE BALLANTINE PUBLISHING GROUP
NEW YORK

A Del Rey® Book
Published by The Ballantine Publishing Group

Introduction and compilation copyright © 2001 by Harry Turtledove

www.randomhouse.com/delrey/

Library of Congress Cataloging-in-Publication Data
The best military science fiction of the twentieth century / edited by Harry
Turtledove with Martin Greenberg.— 1st ed.
    p.   cm.
  "A Del Rey book."
  ISBN 0-345-43989-9
  1. Science fiction, American. 2. Imaginary wars and battles—
Fiction. 3. Military art and science—Fiction. 4. Space warfare—
Fiction. 5. Science fiction, English. 6. War stories, American.
7. War stories, English. I. Turtledove, Harry. II. Greenberg, Martin
Harry.
PS648.S3 B494 2001
813'.0876208358—dc21   00-068066

Manufactured in the United States of America

Cover design by David Stevenson
Cover photograph © Jeff Corwin/Tony Stone Images

First Edition: May 2001

10 9 8 7 6 5 4 3 2 1

# CONTENTS

 **INTRODUCTION**

Harry Turtledove

Sing, goddess, of the accursed rage of Akhilleus
Son of Peleus, which gave pain to countless Akhaioi,
Sent the many sturdy souls of warriors to
Hades, and left their bodies as spoil for all the dogs
And birds of prey. . . .
—HOMER, ILIAD 1.1–5

It is well that war is so terrible, or we should grow too fond of it.
—ROBERT E. LEE

HERE AT THE DAWN of the third millennium C.E., we don't like to think about actually fighting wars. We hope we've outgrown them. For more than half a century, we've had the chance to wreck our civilization, and we haven't taken it. This says something good about us as a species, maybe even something surprisingly good. Perhaps—just perhaps—we aren't really so stupid as we often give signs of being.

Mankind has always hated war. And yet, it has always fascinated us, too. As long as we've written, we've written about it. This is quite literally true. *The Epic of Gilgamesh* goes back to the earliest days of our literacy and is, among other things, the story of warfare. The *Iliad*, the foundation stone of all Greek literature, centers on the siege of Troy and the great struggle between Akhilleus and Hektor. The *Aeneid*, *Beowulf*, the Norse sagas, the *Chanson de Roland* . . . all stories of battle, of warriors. And we're still writing fiction about war, in and out of science fiction, to this day.

Why?

For the two cents it's worth, here's my answer. Fiction is about character under stress. What we do when the heat is on reveals far more about us than how we behave in ordinary times. What comes close to putting so much stress on the character, fictional or otherwise, as nearly getting killed? As Samuel Johnson said, "When a man knows he is to be hanged in a fortnight, it concentrates his mind wonderfully."

Well, I admit there is one other stress that does the same thing: love. And, of course, what passes between man and woman (or, less often, between man and man or between woman and woman) is the other enduringly popular theme of fiction.

And to this mix science fiction adds a couple of other interesting riffs: gadgetry as interesting as the writer can come up with and, sometimes, alien beings also as interesting as the writer can likewise. The granddaddy of stories of this type, H. G. Wells's *The War of the Worlds*, actually saw print in 1898, but since it set the stage for so much that came afterward, I don't see how I can possibly neglect mentioning it here.

Wells was far from the only author interested in the effects of the Industrial Revolution on warfare yet to come. In the late nineteenth and early twentieth centuries, there was, in fact, a small boom in what we would now call technothrillers, stories examining near-future wars with emphasis on the newfangled machines that would make it different from anything that had gone before: ancestors of Tom Clancy, one might say. A fair number of these tales are collected in a fascinating volume called *The Tale of the Next Great War, 1871–1914*, edited by I. F. Clarke. In 1907, in his story "The Trenches," a British army officer, Capt. C. E. Vickers, foretold the invention of the tank. His colleague, Major (later Major General) Sir Ernest Swinton—also a writer of such tales—must surely have seen this piece; when World War I broke out, he was one of the people who helped devise the actual armored fighting vehicle. Here fiction may well have influenced later fact. Others of that period who worked in this subgenre include Sir Arthur Conan Doyle, Jack London, and A. A. Milne, who is better known—and deservedly so—for *Winnie-the-Pooh* than for tales such as his 1909 story "The Secret of the Army Aeroplane."

Drawing a hard and fast line between technothrillers and science fiction proper has never been easy, and probably never will be. The one I'd try to make is that technothrillers tend to be interested in gadgetry for its own sake, while science fiction examines not only the machinery but its influence on the society that's invented it. And if people are now lining up to tear me rhetorical limb from limb, well, so be it.

After the experience of World War I, far fewer people were interested in predicting what a second world war might be like. The short answer—*dreadful*—seemed obvious to everyone: and, indeed, everyone was right. Instead, conflicts set in distant times and against strange aliens took pride of place for a while. John W. Campbell, later the tremendously influential editor of *Astounding* and its later incarnation, *Analog,* was one of the champions of this invent a weapon today, mass produce it tomorrow, and use it to beat the enemy the day after school of writing.

A writer who stuck closer to home, and one whose influence on the entire field of science fiction was also incalculably large, was Robert A. Heinlein. His novellas "If This Goes On . . ." and "Solution Unsatisfactory" and his novel *Sixth Column,* all written before the American entry into World War II (*Sixth Column* springing in part from a Campbell idea), remain readable—and in print—today, while so much of the fiction of two generations ago has fallen by the wayside. "Solution Unsatisfactory" is an early and remarkably prescient attempt to define a problem that has plagued us ever since: How do you deal with the specter of atomic weaponry? The solutions we have worked out are as unsatisfactory as the one Heinlein proposed—but, as I said before, so far we've been both smarter and luckier than we might have been. As a graduate of the Naval Academy, Heinlein spoke with peculiar authority on matters military.

The brute fact of the atomic bomb hit popular consciousness hard after 1945. Nuclear war and its aftermath became a common theme in science fiction. Two early examples were Poul Anderson's stories later collected in the paste-up novel *Twilight World,* and those of Henry Kuttner collected as *Mutant.* Anderson in particular would go on to have a long and amazingly successful career, frequently revisiting military themes in a variety of contexts: most often in his future history peopled by such swashbucklers as Nicholas van Rijn and Dominic Flandry.

Another writer who did likewise was H. Beam Piper, till his unfortunate and premature death in the mid 1960s. His series of paratime stories of alternate history, particularly his fine last work *Lord Kalvan of Otherwhen,* revolve around matters military. So does the elaborate future history he built up, including such novels as *The Cosmic Computer* and *Space Viking,* which combines themes from medieval European warfare and the rise of Hitler in a most striking way.

Heinlein, of course, did not disappear after the war, either. In his juvenile novels (what would now be known as YAs), such as *Between Planets*, *Space Cadet*, *Citizen of the Galaxy*, and *Red Planet*, military themes either dominate or play a strong subordinate role. And in *Starship Troopers*, he produced a novel of military fiction that remains intensely controversial more than forty years after its publication, was made into an extraordinarily bad movie, and spawned at least two fine novels of direct rebuttal, Gordon R. Dickson's *Soldier, Ask Not* and Joe W. Haldeman's *The Forever War*: no mean feat.

Another work from about the same period that should not pass unmentioned is Christopher Anvil's novella "Pandora's Planet," later expanded into a novel of the same name. Anvil, most often published in *Astounding* and *Analog*, took a contrarian, sardonic, and often very funny look at things, and "Pandora's Planet" shows him at the top of his form, with bumbling invading aliens trying to deal with humans who are both smarter than they are and, except for lacking starships, more technologically advanced, too.

During the 1960s and 1970s, no doubt under the influence of the Vietnam War, interest in military science fiction waned. The military generally came under a cloud during those turbulent decades. One interesting exception to the rule here is the rise in those same decades of fantasy series chronicling enormous wars, most often against the power of evil. The archetype, of course, is J. R. R. Tolkien's The Lord of the Rings. I think such works became popular for a couple of reasons: first, who was good and who was not was very explicitly defined—which was not always the case in either the real world or the more realistic forms of science fiction—and, second, the stories were set in worlds so far removed from our own as to distance the readers from the everyday mundanities of life.

Fred Saberhagen's Berserker series of science-fiction adventure tales solved the problem of good guys and bad guys by making the enemy a fleet of robot starships programmed to root out life wherever it might be encountered (a theme also used earlier, not long after the end of World War II, by Theodore Sturgeon in "There Is No Defense"). In *The Men in the Jungle*, Norman Spinrad solved it by not solving it; as far as anyone can tell, there are no heroes in the story, only villains of one stripe or another—again, a motif disturbingly close to real life.

There is a certain irony in the fact that, in the 1970s, military science fiction revived not so much in book form but in the movies—irony be-

cause Hollywood, a traditionally liberal place, has not always taken kindly
to soldiers and their trade. But blood and thunder have played very important roles in both the Star Wars and Star Trek sagas, not least because
matters military tend to create strong blacks and whites without shades
of gray, and also because they lend themselves to spectacular special
effects. Written science fiction is often thought-provoking; filmed sci-fi is
more often jaw-dropping. The two usually appeal to different audiences,
which aficionados of the written variety sometimes forget to their peril —
and frustration.

The last two decades of the twentieth century saw a revival of written
military science fiction. Jerry Pournelle, a Korean War veteran, has written a number of stirring novels with strong military themes, both with
Larry Niven (notably in *The Mote in God's Eye*, a first-contact story, and
Footfall, a fine tale of alien invasion) and by himself.

David Drake (who, like Joe W. Haldeman, saw the elephant in Vietnam) has contributed a gritty realism to the field in his future-history stories, such as *Hammer's Slammers*, and, thanks to his strong background
in ancient history and classics, with tales such as *Ranks of Bronze* and
Birds of Prey.

Drake and S. M. Stirling have also collaborated on a series of novels
set in the far future but based on the career of the Byzantine emperor
Justinian's great marshal, Belisarius. On his own hook, Stirling special-
izes in alternate histories with a strong military flavor: the Draka universe, surely as unpleasant a dystopia as has burst from anyone's word
processor; and the stories begun with *Island in the Sea of Time*, which
drop the island of Nantucket back to 1250 B.C.E. and involve the inhabitants in military affairs up to their necks.

Lois McMaster Bujold's series of novels, mostly based on the fragile
(both in ego and in corpus) hero Miles Vorkosigan, have deservedly attracted a large following. Miles subverts hierarchies and discipline but is
remarkably effective in spite of—or because of—that. His adventures
also have in them a strong humorous strain not often seen in military science fiction.

Where Drake and Stirling have projected the career of an actual his-
torical figure into the future, David Weber's series of novels about Honor
Harrington has many analogies to the fictional seafaring adventures of
Horatio Hornblower set in Napoleonic times. Many fans of military sci-
ence fiction are also passionate aficionados of the tales penned by C. S.
Forester, Patrick O'Brian, and others who work in the small, crowded

world of the late eighteenth and early nineteenth centuries. I don't pre-cisely know why this should be so, but that it's so seems indisputable; it's an enthusiasm I share myself.

One of the advantages of writing an introduction such as this is that I can also subject my readers to a two-paragraph commercial for my own work. As an escaped Byzantine historian, I've used Byzantium as a base for my Videssos universe, with the Time of Troubles series being based on the eventful career of the Emperor Herakleios, The Tale of Krispos on the reigns of Basil the Macedonian and John Tzimiskes (an advantage to fiction is that one can mix and match to suit one-self), and The Videssos Cycle on the chaos surrounding the Battle of Manzikert.

Switching from fantasy to science fiction, I've imagined time-traveling South Africans interfering in the American Civil War in *The Guns of the South*, an alien invasion during World War II in the Worldwar series, and the United States and Confederate States on opposite sides of the European alliance system during the late nineteenth century and World War I in *How Few Remain* and the books of the Great War series.

Elizabeth Moon is a former member of the Marine Corps who has made a name for herself with both military-oriented fantasy and science fiction. Her worlds combine gritty realism and striking wit; no one else currently working in the field has a similar voice.

The Sten novels from the team of Allan Cole and Chris Bunch com-bine military affairs and political intrigue. The team—unfortunately no longer working together—had a striking mix of talents, Bunch hav-ing served as a member of a long-range reconnaissance patrol in Viet-nam and Cole being the son of a prominent CIA official. Their hero, named for a British submachine gun of World War II vintage, is every bit as deadly as his prototype, and much less likely to go to pieces in action.

Technothrillers are vulnerable to events in the world around them. With the collapse of the Soviet Union, truly world-shattering ones be-came much harder to write; indeed, the entire genre suffered something of a collapse. However pleasant a much-reduced likelihood of armaged-don may be for the world at large, it's not far from hell for those who made a living with stories about such catastrophes.

Military science fiction seems less vulnerable to events in the world around it. Technothrillers, by their very nature, are limited to the near future, while military science fiction can and does span all of space and time. If the near future looks peaceful, there's always the further future to explore—either that or a twisted past in which things went differently from the way they turned out in real history.

One area where written military science fiction differs from what vast audiences see on the silver screen is that it demands more from those who pursue it.

Poul Anderson

A winner of multiple Hugo and Nebula Awards, Poul Anderson has written dozens of novels and hundreds of short stories since his science fiction debut in 1947. His long-running Technic History saga, a multibook chronicle of interstellar exploration and empire building, covers fifty centuries of future history and includes the acclaimed novels War of the Wing-Men, The Day of Their Return, and The Game of Empire. Anderson has tackled many of science fiction's classic themes, including human evolution in Brain Wave (1954), near-light-speed space travel in Tau Zero (1970), and the time-travel paradox in his series of Time Patrol stories collected as Guardians of Time. He is renowned for his interweaving of science fiction and mythology, notably in his alien-contact novel The High Crusade. He also has produced distinguished fantasy fiction, including the heroic sagas Three Hearts and Three Lions and The Broken Sword, and an alternate history according to Shakespeare, Midsummer Tempest. He received the Tolkien Memorial Award in 1978. With his wife, Karen, he wrote The King of Ys Celtic fantasy quartet. With Gordon R. Dickson, he has authored the popular comic Hoka series. His short story "Call Me Joe" was chosen for inclusion in the Science Fiction Hall of Fame in 1974, and his short fiction has been collected in several volumes, notably The Queen of Air and Darkness and Other Stories, All One Universe, and The Best of Poul Anderson.

AMONG THIEVES

Poul Anderson

HIS EXCELLENCY M'KATZE UNDUMA, Ambassador of the Terrestrial Federation to the Double Kingdom, was not accustomed to being kept waiting. But as the minutes dragged into an hour, anger faded before a chill deduction.

In this bleakly clock-bound society a short delay was bad manners, even if it were unintentional. But if you kept a man of rank cooling his heels for an entire sixty minutes, you offered him an unforgivable insult. Rusch was a barbarian but he was too canny to humiliate Earth's representative without reason.

Which bore out everything that Terrestrial Intelligence had discovered. From a drunken junior officer, weeping in his cups because Old Earth, Civilization, was going to be attacked and the campus where he had once learned and loved would be scorched to ruin by *his* fire guns—to the battle plans and annotations thereon, which six men had died to smuggle out of the Royal War College—and now, this degradation of the ambassador himself—everything fitted.

The Margrave of Drakenstane had sold out Civilization.

Unduma shuddered, beneath the iridescent cloak, embroidered robe, and ostrich-plume headdress of his rank. He swept the antechamber with the eyes of a trapped animal.

This castle was ancient, dating back some eight hundred years to the first settlement of Norstad. The grim square massiveness of it, fused stone piled into a turreted mountain, was not much relieved by modern fittings. Tableservs, loungers, drapes, jewel mosaics, and biomurals only clashed with those fortress walls and ringing flagstones; fluorosheets did not light up all the dark corners, there was perpetual dusk up among the rafters where the old battle banners hung.

A dozen guards were posted around the room, in breastplate and plumed helmet but with very modern blast rifles. They were identical seven-foot blonds, and none of them moved at all, you couldn't even see them breathe. It was an unnerving sight for a Civilized man.

Unduma snubbed out his cigar, swore miserably to himself, and wished he had at least brought along a book.

The inner door opened on noiseless hinges and a shavepate officer emerged. He clicked his heels and bowed at Unduma. "His Lordship will be honored to receive you now, excellency."

The ambassador throttled his anger, nodded, and stood up. He was a tall thin man, the relatively light skin and sharp features of Bantu stock predominant in him. Earth's emissaries were normally chosen to approximate a local ideal of beauty—hard to do for some of those weird little cultures scattered through the galaxy—and Norstad-Ostarik had been settled by a rather extreme Caucasoid type which had almost entirely emigrated from the home planet.

The aide showed him through the door and disappeared. Hans von Thoma Rusch, Margrave of Drakenstane, Lawman of the Western Folkmote, Hereditary Guardian of the White River Gates, et cetera, et cetera, et cetera, sat waiting behind a desk at the end of an enormous black-and-red tile floor. He had a book in his hands, and didn't close it till Unduma, sandals whispering on the great chessboard squares, had come near. Then he stood up and made a short ironic bow.

"How do you do, your excellency," he said. "I am sorry to be so late. Please sit." Such curtness was no apology at all, and both of them knew it.

Unduma lowered himself to a chair in front of the desk. He would *not* show temper, he thought, he was here for a greater purpose. His teeth clamped together.

"Thank you, your lordship," he said tonelessly. "I hope you will have time to talk with me in some detail. I have come on a matter of grave importance."

Rusch's right eyebrow tilted up, so that the archaic monocle he affected beneath it seemed in danger of falling out. He was a big man, stiffly and solidly built, yellow hair cropped to a wiry brush around the long skull, a scar puckering his left cheek. He wore Army uniform, the gray high-collared tunic and old-fashioned breeches and shiny boots of his planet; the trident and suns of a primary general; a sidearm, its handle worn smooth from much use. If ever the iron barbarian with the iron brain had an epitome, thought Unduma, here he sat!

"Well, your excellency," murmured Rusch—though the harsh Norron language did not lend itself to murmurs—"of course I'll be glad to hear you out. But after all, I've no standing in the Ministry, except as unofficial advisor, and—"

"Please." Unduma lifted a hand. "Must we keep up the fable? You not only speak for all the landed warloads—and the Nor-Samurai are still the most powerful single class in the Double Kingdom—but you have the General Staff in your pouch and, ah, you are well thought of by the royal family. I think I can talk directly to you."

Rusch did not smile, but neither did he trouble to deny what everyone knew, that he was the leader of the fighting aristocracy, friend of the widowed Queen Regent, virtual step-father of her eight-year-old son King Hjalmar—in a word, that he was the dictator. If he preferred to keep a small title and not have his name unnecessarily before the public, what difference did that make?

"I'll be glad to pass on whatever you wish to say to the proper authorities," he answered slowly. "Pipe." That was an order to his chair, which produced a lit briar for him.

Unduma felt appalled. This series of—informalities—was like one savage blow after another. Till now, in the three-hundred-year history of relations between Earth and the Double Kingdom, the Terrestrial ambassador had ranked everyone but God and the royal family.

No human planet, no matter how long sundered from the main stream, no matter what strange ways it had wandered, failed to remember that Earth was Earth, the home of man and the heart of Civilization. No *human* planet—had Norstad-Ostarik, then, gone the way of Kolresh?

Biologically, no, thought Unduma with an inward shudder. Nor culturally—yet. But it shrieked at him, from every insolent movement and twist of words, that Rusch had made a political deal.

"Well?" said the Margrave.

Unduma cleared his throat, desperately, and leaned forward. "Your lordship," he said, "my embassy cannot help taking notice of certain public statements, as well as certain military preparations and other matters of common knowledge—"

"And items your spies have dug up," drawled Rusch.

Unduma started. "My lord!"

"My good ambassador," grinned Rusch, "it was you who suggested a straightforward talk. I know Earth has spies here. In any event, it's impossible to hide so large a business as the mobilization of two planets for war."

Unduma felt sweat trickle down his ribs.

"There is . . . you . . . your Ministry has only announced it is a . . . a defense measure," he stammered. "I had hoped . . . frankly, yes, till the last minute I hoped you . . . your people might see fit to join us against Kolresh."

There was a moment's quiet. So quiet, thought Unduma. A redness crept up Rusch's cheeks, the scar stood livid and his pale eyes were the coldest thing Unduma had ever seen.

Then, slowly, the Margrave got it out through his teeth: "For a number of centuries, your excellency, our people hoped Earth might join them."

"What do you mean?" Unduma forgot all polished inanities. Rusch didn't seem to notice. He stood up and went to the window.

"Come here," he said. "Let me show you something."

THE WINDOW WAS a modern inset of clear, invisible plastic, a broad sheet high in the castle's infamous Witch Tower. It looked out on a black sky, the sun was down and the glacial forty-hour darkness of northern Norstad was crawling toward midnight.

Stars glittered mercilessly keen in an emptiness which seemed like crystal, which seemed about to ring thinly in contracting anguish under the cold. Ostarik, the companion planet, stood low to the south, a gibbous moon of steely blue; it never moved in that sky, the two worlds forever faced each other, the windy white peaks of one glaring at the warm lazy seas of the other. Northward, a great curtain of aurora flapped halfway around the cragged horizon.

From this dizzy height, Unduma could see little of the town Drakenstane: a few high-peaked roofs and small glowing windows, lamps lonesome above frozen streets. There wasn't much to see anyhow—no big cities on either planet, only the small towns which had grown from scattered thorps, each clustered humbly about the manor of its lord. Beyond lay winter fields, climbing up the valley walls to the hard green blink of glaciers. It must be blowing out there, he saw snowdevils chase ghostly across the blue-tinged desolation.

Rusch spoke roughly: "Not much of a planet we've got here, is it? Out on the far end of nowhere, a thousand light-years from your precious Earth, and right in the middle of a glacial epoch. Have you ever wondered why we don't set up weather-control stations and give this world a decent climate?"

"Well," began Unduma, "of course, the exigencies of—"

"Of war." Rusch sent his hand upward in a chopping motion, to sweep around the alien constellations. Among them burned Polaris, less than thirty parsecs away, huge and cruelly bright. "We never had a chance. Every time we thought we could begin, there would be war, usually with Kolresh, and the labor and materials would have to go for that. Once, about two centuries back, we did actually get stations established, it was even beginning to warm up a little. Kolresh blasted them off the map.

"Norstad was settled eight hundred years ago. For seven of those centuries, we've had Kolresh at our throats. Do you wonder if we've grown tired?"

"My lord, I . . . I can sympathize," said Unduma awkwardly. "I am not ignorant of your heroic history. But it would seem to me . . . after all, Earth has also fought—"

"At a range of a thousand light-years!" jeered Rusch. "The forgotten war. A few underpaid patrolmen in obsolete rustbucket ships to defend unimportant outposts from sporadic Kolreshite raids. We live on their borders!"

"It would certainly appear, your lordship, that Kolresh is your natural enemy," said Unduma. "As indeed it is of all Civilization of Homo sapiens himself. What I cannot credit are the, ah, the rumors of an, er, alliance—"

"And why shouldn't we?" snarled Rusch. "For seven hundred years we've held them at bay, while your precious so-called Civilization grew fat behind a wall of our dead young men. The temptation to recoup some of our losses by helping Kolresh conquer Earth is very strong!"

"You don't mean it!" The breath rushed from Unduma's lungs.

The other man's face was like carved bone. "Don't jump to conclusions," he answered. "I merely point out that from our side there's a good deal to be said for such a policy. Now if Earth is prepared to make a different policy worth our while—do you understand? Nothing is going to happen in the immediate future. You have time to think about it."

"I would have to . . . communicate with my government," whispered Unduma.

"Of course," said Rusch. His bootheels clacked on the floor as he went back to his desk. "I've had a memorandum prepared for you, an unofficial informal sort of protocol, points which his majesty's government would like to make the basis of negotiations with the Terrestrial Federation. Ah, here!" He picked up a bulky folio. "I suggest you take a leave of absence, your excellency, go home and show your superiors this, ah—"

"Ultimatum," said Unduma in a sick voice.

Rusch shrugged. "Call it what you will." His tone was empty and remote, as if he had already cut himself and his people out of Civilization.

As he accepted the folio, Unduma noticed the book beside it, the one Rusch had been reading: a local edition of Schakspier, badly printed on sleazy paper, but in the original Old Anglic. Odd thing for a barbarian dictator to read. But then, Rusch was a bit of an historical scholar, as well as an enthusiastic kayak racer, meteor polo player, chess champion, mountain climber, and . . . and all-around scoundrel!

NORSTAD LAY IN the grip of a ten-thousand-year winter, while Ostarik was a heaven of blue seas breaking on warm island sands. Nevertheless, because Ostarik harbored a peculiarly nasty plague virus, it remained an unattainable paradise in the sky till a bare two hundred fifty years ago. Then a research team from Earth got to work, found an effective vaccine, and saw a mountain carved into their likeness by the Norron folk.

It was through such means—and the sheer weight of example, the liberty and wealth and happiness of its people—that the Civilization centered on Earth had been propagating itself among colonies isolated for centuries. There were none which lacked reverence for Earth the Mother, Earth the Wise, Earth the Kindly: none but Kolresh, which had long ceased to be human.

Rusch's private speedster whipped him from the icicle walls of Festning Drakenstane to the rose gardens of Sorgenlos in an hour of hell-bat haste across vacuum. But it was several hours more until he and the queen could get away from their courtiers and be alone.

They walked through geometric beds of smoldering blooms under songbirds and fronded trees, while the copper spires of the little palace reached up to the evening star and the hours-long sunset of Ostarik blazed gold across great quiet waters. The island was no more than a royal retreat, but lately it had known agonies.

Queen Ingra stooped over a mutant rose, tiger striped and a foot across; she plucked the petals from it and said close to weeping: "But I liked Unduma. I don't want him to hate us."

"He's not a bad sort," agreed Rusch. He stood behind her in a black dress uniform with silver insignia, like a formal version of death.

"He's more than that, Hans. He stands for decency—Norstad froze our souls, and Ostarik hasn't thawed them. I thought Earth might—" Her voice trailed off. She was slender and dark, still young, and her folk came from the rainy dales of Norstad's equator, a farm race with gentler ways than the miners and fishermen and hunters of the red-haired ice ape who had bred Rusch. In her throat, the Norron language softened to a burring music; the Drakenstane men spat their words out rough-edged.

"Earth might what?" Rusch turned a moody gaze to the west. "Lavish more gifts on us? We were always proud of paying our own way."

"Oh, no," said Ingra wearily. "After all, we could trade with them, furs and minerals and so on, if ninety per cent of our production didn't have to go into defense. I only thought they might teach us how to be human."

"I had assumed we were still classified Homo sapiens," said Rusch in a parched tone.

"Oh, you know what I mean!" She turned on him, violet eyes suddenly aflare. "Sometimes I wonder if you're human, Margrave Hans von Thoma Rusch. I mean free, free to be something more than a robot, free to raise children knowing they won't have their lungs shoved out their mouths when a Kolreshite cruiser hulls one of our spaceships. What is our whole culture, Hans? A layer of brutalized farmhands and factory workers—serfs! A top crust of heel-clattering aristocrats who live for nothing but war. A little folk art, folk music, folk saga, full of blood and treachery. Where are our symphonies, novels, cathedrals, research laboratories . . . where are people who can say what they wish and make what they will of their lives and be happy?"

RUSCH DIDN'T ANSWER for a moment. He looked at her, unblinking behind his monocle, till she dropped her gaze and twisted her hands together. Then he said only: "You exaggerate."

"Perhaps. It's still the basic truth." Rebellion rode in her voice. "It's what all the other worlds think of us."

"Even if the democratic assumption—that the eternal verities can be discovered by counting enough noses—were true," said Rusch, "you cannot repeal eight hundred years of history by decree."

"No. But you could work toward it," she said. "I think you're wrong in despising the common man, Hans . . . when was he ever given a chance, in this kingdom? We could make a beginning now, and Earth could send psychotechnic advisors, and in two or three generations—"

"What would Kolresh be doing while we experimented with forms of government?" he laughed.

"Always Kolresh." Her shoulders, slim behind the burning-red cloak, slumped. "Kolresh turned a hundred hopeful towns into radioactive craters and left the gnawed bones of children in the fields. Kolresh killed my husband, like a score of kings before him. Kolresh blasted your family to ash, Hans, and scarred your face and your soul—" She whirled back on him, fists aloft, and almost screamed: "Do you want to make an ally of Kolresh?"

The Margrave took out his pipe and began filling it. The saffron sundown, reflected off the ocean to his face, gave him a metal look.

"Well," he said, "we've been at peace with them for all of ten years now. Almost a record."

"Can't we find allies? Real ones? I'm sick of being a figurehead! I'd befriend Ahuramazda, New Mars, Lagrange— We could raise a crusade against Kolresh, wipe every last filthy one of them out of the universe!"

"Now who's a heel-clattering aristocrat?" grinned Rusch.

He lit his pipe and strolled toward the beach. She stood for an angry moment, then sighed and followed him.

"Do you think it hasn't been tried?" he said patiently. "For generations we've tried to build up a permanent alliance directed at Kolresh. What temporary ones we achieved have always fallen apart. Nobody loves us enough—and, since we've always taken the heaviest blows, nobody hates Kolresh enough."

He found a bench on the glistening edge of the strand, and sat down and looked across a steady march of surf, turned to molten gold by the low sun and the incandescent western clouds. Ingra joined him.

"I can't really blame the others for not liking us," she said in a small voice. "We are overmechanized and undercultured, arrogant, tactless, undemocratic, hard-boiled . . . oh, yes. But their own self-interest—"

"They don't imagine it can happen to them," replied Rusch contemptuously. "And there are even pro-Kolresh elements, here and there." He raised his voice an octave: "Oh, my dear sir, my dear Margrave, what are you *saying*? Why, of *course* Kolresh would never attack us! They made a *treaty* never to attack us!"

Ingra sighed, forlornly. Rusch laid an arm across her shoulders. They sat for a while without speaking.

"ANYWAY," SAID THE man finally, "Kolresh is too strong for any combination of powers in this part of the galaxy. We and they are the only ones with a military strength worth mentioning. Even Earth would have a hard time defeating them, and Earth, of course, will lean backward before undertaking a major war. She has too much to lose; it's so much more comfortable to regard the Kolreshite raids as mere piracies, the skirmishes as 'police actions.' She just plain will not pay the stiff price of an army and a navy able to whip Kolresh and occupy the Kolreshite planets."

"And so it is to be war again." Ingra looked out in desolation across the sea.

"Maybe not," said Rusch. "Maybe a different kind of war, at least—no more black ships coming out of *our* sky."

He blew smoke for a while, as if gathering courage, then spoke in a quick, impersonal manner: "Look here. We Norrons are not a naval power. It's not in our tradition. Our navy has always been inadequate and always will be. But we can breed the toughest soldiers in the known galaxy, in unlimited numbers; we can condition them into fighting machines, and equip them with the most lethal weapons living flesh can wield.

"Kolresh, of course, is just the opposite. Space nomads, small population, able to destroy anything their guns can reach but not able to dig in and hold it against us. For seven hundred years, we and they have been the elephant and the whale. Neither could ever win a real victory over the other; war became the normal state of affairs, peace a breathing spell. Because of the mutation, there will always be war, as long as one single Kolreshite lives. We can't kill them, we can't befriend them—all we can do is to be bled white to stop them."

A wind sighed over the slow thunder on the beach. A line of sea birds crossed the sky, thin and black against glowing bronze.

"I know," said Ingra. "I know the history, and I know what you're leading up to. Kolresh will furnish transportation and naval escort; Norstad-Ostarik will furnish men. Between us, we may be able to take Earth."

"We will," said Rusch flatly. "Earth has grown plump and lazy. She can't possibly rearm enough in a few months to stop such a combination."

"And all the galaxy will spit on our name."

"All the galaxy will lie open to conquest, once Earth has fallen."

"How long do you think we would last, riding the Kolresh tiger?"

"I have no illusions about them, my dear. But neither can I see any way to break this eternal deadlock. In a fluid situation, such as the collapse of Earth would produce, we might be able to create a navy as good as theirs. They've never yet given us a chance to build one, but perhaps—"

"Perhaps not! I doubt very much it was a meteor which wrecked my husband's ship, five years ago. I think Kolresh knew of his hopes, of the shipyard he wanted to start, and murdered him."

"It's probable," said Rusch.

"And you would league us with them." Ingra turned a colorless face on him. "I'm still the queen. I forbid any further consideration of this . . . this obscene alliance!"

Rusch sighed. "I was afraid of that, your highness." For a moment he looked gray, tired. "You have a veto power, of course. But I don't think the Ministry would continue in office a regent who used it against the best interests of—"

She leaped to her feet. "You wouldn't!"

"Oh, you'd not be harmed," said Rusch with a crooked smile. "Not even deposed. You'd be in a protective custody, shall we say. Of course, his majesty, your son, would have to be educated elsewhere, but if you wish—"

Her palm cracked on his face. He made no motion.

"I . . . won't veto—" Ingra shook her head. Then her back grew stiff. "Your ship will be ready to take you home, my lord. I do not think we shall require your presence here again."

"As you will, your highness," mumbled the dictator of the Double Kingdom.

THOUGH HE RETURNED with a bitter word in his mouth, Unduma felt the joy, the biological rightness of being home, rise warm within him. He sat on a terrace under the mild sky of Earth, with the dear bright flow of the Zambezi River at his feet and the slim towers of Capital City rearing as far as he could see, each gracious, in its own green park. The people on the clean quiet streets wore airy blouses and colorful kilts—not the trousers for men, ankle-length skirts for women, which muffled the sad folk of Norstad. And there was educated conversation in the gentle Tierrans language, music from an open window, laughter on the verandas and children playing in the parks: freedom, law, and leisure.

The thought that this might be rubbed out of history, that the robots of Norstad and the snake-souled monsters of Kolresh might tramp between broken spires where starved Earthmen hid, was a tearing in Unduma.

He managed to lift his drink and lean back with the proper casual elegance. "No, sir," he said, "they are not bluffing."

Ngu Chilongo, Premier of the Federation Parliament, blinked unhappy eyes. He was a small grizzled man, and a wise man, but this lay beyond everything he had known in a long lifetime and he was slow to grasp it.

"But surely—" he began. "Surely this . . . this Rusch person is not insane. He cannot think that his two planets, with a population of, what is it, perhaps one billion, can overcome four billion Terrestrials!"

"There would also be several million Kolreshites to help," reminded Unduma. "However, they would handle the naval end of it entirely—and their navy *is* considerably stronger than ours. The Norron forces would be the ones which actually landed, to fight the air and ground battles. And out of those paltry one billion, Rusch can raise approximately one hundred million soldiers."

Chilongo's glass crashed to the terrace. "What!"

"It's true, sir." The third man present, Mustafa Lefarge, Minister of Defense, spoke in a miserable tone. "It's a question of every able-bodied citizen, male and female, being a trained member of the armed forces. In time of war, virtually everyone not in actual combat is directly contributing to some phase of the effort—a civilian economy virtually ceases to exist. They're used to getting along for years at a stretch with no comforts and a bare minimum of necessities." His voice grew sardonic. "By necessities, they mean things like food and ammunition—not, say, entertainment or cultural activity, as we assume."

"A hundred million," whispered Chilongo. He stared at his hands. "Why, that's ten times our *total* forces!"

"Which are ill-trained, ill-equipped, and ill-regarded by our own civilians," pointed out Lefarge bitterly.

"In short, sir," said Unduma, "while we could defeat either Kolresh or Norstad-Ostarik in an all-out war—though with considerable difficulty—between them they can defeat us."

Chilongo shivered. Unduma felt a certain pity for him. You had to get used to it in small doses, this fact which Civilization screened from Earth: that the depths of hell are found in the human soul. That no law of nature guards the upright innocent from malice.

"But they wouldn't dare!" protested the Premier. "Our friends . . . everywhere—"

"All the human-colonized galaxy will wring its hands and send stiff notes of protest," said Lefarge. "Then they'll pull the blankets back over their heads and assure themselves that now the big bad aggressor has been sated."

"This note—of Rusch's." Chilongo seemed to be grabbing out after support while the world dropped from beneath his feet. Sweat glistened on his wrinkled brown forehead. "Their terms . . . surely we can make some agreement?"

"Their terms are impossible, as you'll see for yourself when you read," said Unduma flatly. "They want us to declare war on Kolresh, accept a joint command under Norron leadership, foot the bill and— No!"

"But if we have to fight anyway," began Chilongo, "it would seem better to have at least one ally—"

"Has Earth changed that much since I was gone?" asked Unduma in astonishment. "Would our people really consent to this . . . this extortion . . . letting those hairy barbarians write our foreign policy for us— Why, jumping into war, making the first declaration ourselves, it's unconstitutional! It's un-Civilized!"

Chilongo seemed to shrink a little. "No," he said. "No, I don't mean that. Of course it's impossible; better to be honestly defeated in battle. I only thought, perhaps we could bargain—"

"We can try," said Unduma skeptically, "but I never heard of Hans Rusch yielding an angstrom without a pistol at his head."

Lefarge struck a cigar, inhaled deeply, and took another sip from his glass. "I hardly imagine an alliance with Kolresh would please his own people," he mused.

"Scarcely!" said Unduma. "But they'll accept it if they must."

"Oh? No chance for us to get him overthrown—assassinated, even?"

"Not to speak of. Let me explain. He's only a petty aristocrat by birth, but during the last war with Kolresh he gained high rank and a personal following of fanatically loyal young officers. For the past few years, since the king died, he's been the dictator. He's filled the key posts with his men: hard, able, and unquestioning. Everyone else is either admiring or cowed. Give him credit, he's no megalomaniac—he shuns publicity—

but that simply divorces his power all the more from responsibility. You can measure it by pointing out that everyone knows he will probably ally with Kolresh, and everyone has a nearly physical loathing of the idea—but there is not a word of criticism for Rusch himself, and when he orders it they will embark on Kolreshite ships to ruin the Earth they love."

"It could almost make you believe in the old myths," whispered Chilongo. "About the Devil incarnate."

"Well," said Unduma, "this sort of thing has happened before, you know."

"Hm-m-m?" Lefarge sat up.

Unduma smiled sadly. "Historical examples," he said. "They're of no practical value today, except for giving the cold consolation that we're not uniquely betrayed."

"What do you mean?" asked Chilongo.

"Well," said Unduma, "consider the astropolitics of the situation. Around Polaris and beyond lies Kolresh territory, where for a long time they sharpened their teeth preying on backward autochthones. At last they started expanding toward the richer human-settled planets. Norstad happened to lie directly on their path, so Norstad took the first blow—and stopped them.

"Since then, it's been seven hundred years of stalemated war. Oh, naturally Kolresh outflanks Norstad from time to time, seizes this planet in the galactic west and raids that one to the north, fights a war with one to the south and makes an alliance with one to the east. But it has never amounted to anything important. It can't, with Norstad astride the most direct line between the heart of Kolresh and the heart of Civilization. If Kolresh made a serious effort to by-pass Norstad, the Norrons could—and would—disrupt everything with an attack in the rear.

"In short, despite the fact that interstellar space is three-dimensional and enormous, Norstad guards the northern marches of Civilization."

He paused for another sip. It was cool and subtle on his tongue, a benediction after the outworld rotgut.

"Hm-m-m, I never thought of it just that way," said Lefarge. "I assumed it was just a matter of barbarians fighting each other for the usual barbarian reasons."

"Oh, it is, I imagine," said Unduma, "but the result is that Norstad acts as the shield of Earth.

"Now if you examine early Terrestrial history—and Rusch, who has a remarkable knowledge of it, stimulated me to do so—you'll find that this is a common thing. A small semicivilized state, out on the marches, holds off the enemy while the true civilization prospers behind it. Assyria warded Mesopotamia, Rome defended Greece, the Welsh border lords kept England safe, the Transoxanian Tartars were the shield of Persia, Prussia blocked the approaches to western Europe . . . oh, I could add a good many examples. In every instance, a somewhat backward people on the distant frontier of a civilization receive the worst hammer-blows of the really alien races beyond, the wild men who would leave nothing standing if they could get at the protected cities of the inner society."

He paused for breath. "And so?" asked Chilongo.

"Well, of course, suffering isn't good for people," shrugged Unduma. "It tends to make them rather nasty. The marchmen react to incessant war by becoming a warrior race, uncouth peasants with an absolute government of ruthless militarists. Nobody loves them, neither the outer savages nor the inner polite nations.

"And in the end, they're all too apt to turn inward. Their military skill and vigor need a more promising outlet than this grim business of always fighting off an enemy who always comes back and who has even less to steal than the sentry culture.

"So Assyria sacks Babylon; Rome conquers Greece; Percy rises against King Henry; Tamerlane overthrows Bajazet; Prussia clanks into France—"

"And Norstad-Ostarik falls on Earth," finished Lefarge.

"Exactly," said Unduma. "It's not even unprecedented for the border state to join hands with the very tribes it fought so long. Percy and Owen Glendower, for instance . . . though in that case, I imagine both parties were considerably more attractive than Hans Rusch or Klerak Belug."

"What are we going to do?" Chilongo whispered it toward the blue sky of Earth, from which no bombs had fallen for a thousand years.

Then he shook himself, jumped to his feet, and faced the other two. "I'm sorry, gentlemen. This has taken me rather by surprise, and I'll naturally require time to look at this Norron protocol and evaluate the other data. But if it turns out you're right"—he bowed urbanely—"as I'm sure it will—"

"Yes?" said Unduma in a tautening voice.

"Why, then, we appear to have some months, at least, before anything drastic happens. We can try to gain more time by negotiation. We do have the largest industrial complex in the known universe, and four billion people who have surely not had courage bred out of them. We'll build up our armed forces, and if those barbarians attack we'll whip them back into their own kennels and kick them through the rear walls thereof!"

"I hoped you'd say that," breathed Unduma.

"*I* hope we'll be granted time," Lefarge scowled. "I assume Rusch is not a fool. We cannot rearm in anything less than a glare of publicity. When he learns of it, what's to prevent him from cementing the Kolresh alliance and attacking at once, before we're ready?"

"Their mutual suspiciousness ought to help," said Unduma. "I'll go back there, of course, and do what I can to stir up trouble between them."

He sat still for a moment, then added as if to himself: "Till we do finish preparing, we have no resources but hope."

THE KOLRESHITE MUTATION was a subtle thing. It did not show on the surface: physically, they were a handsome people, running to white skin and orange hair. Over the centuries, thousands of Norron spies had infiltrated them, and frequently gotten back alive; what made such work unusually difficult was not the normal hazards of impersonation, but an ingrained reluctance to practice cannibalism and worse.

The mutation was a psychic twist, probably originating in some obscure gene related to the endocrine system. It was extraordinarily hard to describe—every categorical statement about it had the usual quota of exceptions and qualifications. But one might, to a first approximation, call it extreme xenophobia. It is normal for Homo sapiens to be somewhat wary of outsiders till he has established their bona fides; it was normal for Homo Kolreshi to *hate* all outsiders, from first glimpse to final destruction.

Naturally, such an instinct produced a tendency to inbreeding, which lowered fertility, but systematic execution of the unfit had so far kept the stock vigorous. The instinct also led to strongarm rule within the nation; to nomadism, where a planet was only a base like the oasis of the ancient Bedouin, essential to life but rarely seen; to a cult of secrecy and cruelty, a religion of abominations; to an ultimate goal of conquering the accessible universe and wiping out all other races.

Of course, it was not so simple, nor so blatant. Among themselves, the Kolreshites doubtless found a degree of tenderness and fidelity. Visiting on neutral planets—i.e., planets which it was not yet expedient to attack—they were very courteous and had an account of defending themselves against one unprovoked aggression after another, which some found plausible. Even their enemies stood in awe of their personal heroism.

Nevertheless, few in the galaxy would have wept if the Kolreshites all died one rainy night.

Hans von Thoma Rusch brought his speedster to the great whale-back of the battleship. It lay a light-year from his sun, hidden by cold emptiness; the co-ordinates had been given him secretly, together with an invitation which was more like a summons.

He glided into the landing cradle, under the turrets of guns that could pound a moon apart, and let the mechanism suck him down below decks. When he stepped out into the high, coldly lit debarkation chamber, an honor guard in red presented arms and pipes twittered for him.

He walked slowly forward, a big man in black and silver, to meet his counterpart, Klerak Belug, the Overman of Kolresh, who waited rigid in a blood-colored tunic. The cabin bristled around him with secret police and guns.

Rusch clicked heels. "Good day, your dominance," he said. A faint echo followed his voice. For some unknown reason, this folk liked echoes and always built walls to resonate.

Belug, an aging giant who topped him by a head, raised shaggy brows. "Are you alone, your lordship?" he asked in atrociously accented Norron. "It was understood that you could bring a personal bodyguard."

Rusch shrugged. "I would have needed a personal dreadnought to be quite safe," he replied in fluent Kolra, "so I decided to trust your safe conduct. I assume you realize that any harm done to me means instant war with my kingdom."

The broad, wrinkled lion-face before him split into a grin. "My representatives did not misjudge you, your lordship. I think we can indeed do business. Come."

The Overman turned and led the way down a ramp toward the guts of the ship. Rusch followed, enclosed by guards and bayonets. He kept a hand on his own sidearm—not that it would do him much good, if matters came to that.

Events were approaching their climax, he thought in a cold layer of his brain. For more than a year now, negotiations had dragged on, hemmed in by the requirement of secrecy, weighted down by mutual suspicion. There were only two points of disagreement remaining, but discussion had been so thoroughly snagged on those that the two absolute rulers must meet to settle it personally. It was Belug who had issued the contemptuous invitation.

And he, Rusch, had come. Tonight the old kings of Norstad wept worms in their graves.

The party entered a small, luxuriously chaired room. There were the usual robots, for transcription and reference purposes, and there were guards, but Overman and Margrave were essentially alone.

Belug wheezed his bulk into a seat. "Smoke? Drink?"

"I have my own, thank you." Rusch took out his pipe and a hip flask.

"That is scarcely diplomatic," rumbled Belug.

Rusch laughed. "I'd always understood that your dominance had no use for the mannerisms of Civilization. I daresay we'd both like to finish our business as quickly as possible."

The Overman snapped his fingers. Someone glided up with wine in a glass. He sipped for a while before answering: "Yes. By all means. Let us reach an executive agreement now and wait for our hirelings to draw up a formal treaty. But it seems odd, sir, that after all these months of delay, you are suddenly so eager to complete the work."

"Not odd," said Rusch. "Earth is rearming at a considerable rate. She's had almost a year now. We can still whip her, but in another six months we'll no longer be able to; give her automated factories half a year beyond *that*, and she'll destroy us!"

"It must have been clear to you, sir, that after the Earth Ambassador— what's his name, Unduma—after he returned to your planets last year, he was doing all he could to gain time."

"Oh, yes," said Rusch. "Making offers to me, and then haggling over them—brewing trouble elsewhere to divert our attention—a gallant effort. But it didn't work. Frankly, your dominance, you've only yourself to blame for the delays. For example, your insisting that Earth be administered as Kolreshite territory—"

"My dear sir!" exploded Belug. "It was a talking point. Only a talking point. Any diplomatist would have understood. But you took six weeks to study it, then offered that preposterous counter-proposal that everything should revert to *you*, loot and territory both— Why, if you had been truly willing to co-operate, we could have settled the terms in a month!"

"As you like, your dominance," said Rusch carelessly. "It's all past now. There are only these questions of troop transport and prisoners, then we're in total agreement."

Klerak Belug narrowed his eyes and rubbed his chin with one outsize hand. "I do not comprehend," he said, "and neither do my naval officers. We have regular transports for your men, nothing extraordinary in the way of comfort, to be sure, but infinitely more suitable for so long a voyage than . . . than the naval units you insist we use. Don't you understand? A transport is for carrying men or cargo; a ship of the line is to fight or convoy. You do *not* mix the functions!"

"I do, your dominance," said Rusch. "As many of my soldiers as possible are going to travel on regular warships furnished by Kolresh, and there are going to be Double Kingdom naval personnel with them for liaison."

"But—" Belug's fist closed on his wineglass as if to splinter it. "Why?" he roared.

"My representatives have explained it a hundred times," said Rusch wearily. "In blunt language, I don't trust you. If . . . oh, let us say there should be disagreement between us while the armada is en route . . . well, a transport ship is easily replaced, after its convoy vessels have blown it up. The fighting craft of Kolresh are a better hostage for your good behavior." He struck a light to his pipe. "Naturally, you can't take our whole fifty-million-man expeditionary force on your battle wagons; but I want soldiers on every warship as well as in the transports."

Belug shook his ginger head. "No."

"Come now," said Rusch. "Your spies have been active enough on Norstad and Ostarik. Have you found any reason to doubt my intentions? Bearing in mind that an army the size of ours cannot be alerted for a given operation without a great many people knowing the fact—"

"Yes, yes," grumbled Belug. "Granted." He smiled, a sharp flash of teeth. "But the upper hand is mine, your lordship. I can wait indefinitely to attack Earth. You can't."

"Eh?" Rusch drew hard on his pipe.

"In the last analysis, even dictators rely on popular support. My Intelligence tells me you are rapidly losing yours. The queen has not spoken to you for a year, has she? And there are many Norrons whose first loyalty is to the Crown. As the thought of war with Earth seeps in, as men have time to comprehend how little they like the idea, time to see through your present anti-Terrestrial propaganda—they grow angry. Already they mutter about you in the beer halls and the officers' clubs, they whisper in ministry cloakrooms. My agents have heard.

"Your personal cadre of young key officers are the only ones left with unquestioning loyalty to you. Let discontent grow just a little more, let open revolt break out, and your followers will be hanged from the lamp posts.

"You can't delay much longer."

Rusch made no reply for a while. Then he sat up, his monocle glittering like a cold round window on winter.

"I can always call off this plan and resume the normal state of affairs," he snapped.

Belug flushed red. "War with Kolresh again? It would take you too long to shift gears—to reorganize."

"It would not. Our war college, like any other, has prepared military plans for all foreseeable combinations of circumstances. If I cannot come to terms with you, Plan No. So-and-So goes into effect. And obviously *it* will have popular enthusiasm behind it!"

He nailed the Overman with a fish-pale eye and continued in frozen tones: "After all, your dominance, I would prefer to fight you. The only thing I would enjoy more would be to hunt you with hounds. Seven hundred years have shown this to be impossible. I opened negotiations to make the best of an evil bargain—since you cannot be conquered, it will pay better to join with you on a course of mutually profitable imperialism.

"But if your stubbornness prevents an agreement, I can declare war on you in the usual manner and be no worse off than I was. The choice is, therefore, yours."

Belug swallowed. Even his guards lost some of their blankness. One does not speak in that fashion across the negotiators' table.

Finally, only his lips stirring, he said: "Your frankness is appreciated, my lord. Some day I would like to discuss that aspect further. As for now, though . . . yes, I can see your point. I am prepared to admit some of your troops to our ships of the line." After another moment, still sitting like a stone idol: "But this question of returning prisoners of war. We have never done it. I do not propose to begin."

"*I* do not propose to let poor devils of Norrons rot any longer in your camps," said Rusch. "I have a pretty good idea of what goes on there. If we're to be allies, I'll want back such of my countrymen as are still alive."

"Not many are still sane," Belug told him deliberately.

Rusch puffed smoke and made no reply.

"If I give in on the one item," said Belug, "I have a right to test your sincerity by the other. We keep our prisoners."

Rusch's own face had gone quite pale and still. It grew altogether silent in the room.

"Very well," he said after a long time. "Let it be so."

WITHOUT A WORD, Major Othkar Graaborg led his company into the black cruiser. The words came from the spaceport, where police held off a hooting, hissing, rock-throwing mob. It was the first time in history that Norron folk had stoned their own soldiers.

His men tramped stolidly behind him, up the gangway and through the corridors. Among the helmets and packs and weapons, racketing boots and clashing body armor, their faces were lost, they were an army without faces.

Graaborg followed a Kolreshite ensign, who kept looking back nervously at these hereditary foes, till they reached the bunkroom. It had been hastily converted from a storage hold, and was scant cramped comfort for a thousand men.

"All right, boys," he said when the door had closed on his guide. "Make yourselves at home."

They got busy, opening packs, spreading bedrolls on bunks. Immediately thereafter, they started to assemble heavy machine guns, howitzers, even a nuclear blaster.

"You, there!" The accented voice squawked indignantly from a loudspeaker in the wall. "I see that. I got video. You not put guns together here."

Graaborg looked up from his inspection of a live fission shell. "Obscenity you," he said pleasantly. "Who are you, anyway?"

"I executive officer. I tell captain."

"Go right ahead. My orders say that according to treaty, as long as we stay in our assigned part of the ship, we're under our own discipline. If your captain doesn't like it, let him come down here and talk to us." Graaborg ran a thumb along the edge of his bayonet. A wolfish chorus from his men underlined the invitation.

No one pressed the point. The cruiser lumbered into space, rendezvoused with her task force, and went into nonspatial drive. For several days, the Norron army contingent remained in its den, more patient with such stinking quarters than the Kolreshites could imagine anyone being. Nevertheless, no spaceman ventured in there; meals were fetched at the galley by Norron squads.

Graaborg alone wandered freely about the ship. He was joined by

Commander von Brecca of Ostarik, the head of the Double Kingdom's naval liaison on this ship: a small band of officers and ratings, housed elsewhere. They conferred with the Kolreshite officers as the necessity arose, on routine problems, rehearsal of various operations to be performed when Earth was reached a month hence—but they did not mingle socially. This suited their hosts.

The fact is, the Kolreshites were rather frightened of them. A spaceman does not lack courage, but he is a gentleman among warriors. His ship either functions well, keeping him clean and comfortable, or it does not function at all and he dies quickly and mercifully. He fights with machines, at enormous ranges.

The ground soldier, muscle in mud, whose ultimate weapon is whetted steel in bare hands, has a different kind of toughness.

Two weeks after departure, Graaborg's wrist chronometer showed a certain hour. He was drilling his men in full combat rig, as he had been doing every "day" in spite of the narrow quarters.

"Ten-SHUN!" The order flowed through captains, lieutenants, and sergeants; the bulky mass of men crashed to stillness.

Major Graaborg put a small pocket amplifier to his lips. "All right, lads," he said casually, "assume gas masks, radiation shields, all gun squads to weapons. Now let's clean up this ship."

He himself blew down the wall with a grenade.

Being perhaps the most thoroughly trained soldiers in the universe, the Norron men paused for only one amazed second. Then they cheered, with death and hell in their voices, and crowded at his heels.

Little resistance was met until Graaborg had picked up von Brecca's naval command, the crucial ones, who could sail and fight the ship. The Kolreshites were too dumbfounded. Thereafter the nomads rallied and fought gamely. Graaborg was handicapped by not having been able to give his men a battle plan. He split up his forces and trusted to the intelligence of the noncoms.

His faith was not misplaced, though the ship was in poor condition by the time the last Kolreshite had been machine-gunned.

Graaborg himself had used a bayonet, with vast satisfaction.

M'KATZE UNDUMA ENTERED the office in the Witch Tower. "You sent for me, your lordship?" he asked. His voice was as cold and bitter as the gale outside.

"Yes. Please be seated." Margrave Hans von Thoma Rusch looked tired. "I have some news for you."

"What news? You declared war on Earth two weeks ago. Your army can't have reached her yet." Unduma leaned over the desk. "Is it that you've found transportation to send me home?"

"Somewhat better news, your excellency." Rusch leaned over and tuned a telescreen. A background of clattering robots and frantically busy junior officers came into view.

Then a face entered the screen, young, and with more life in it than Unduma had ever before seen on this sullen planet. "Central Data headquarters— Oh, yes, your lordship." Boyishly, against all rules: "We've got her! The *Bheoka* just called in . . . she's ours!"

"Hm-m-m. Good." Rusch glanced at Unduma. "The *Bheoka* is the superdreadnought accompanying Task Force Two. Carry on with the news."

"Yes, sir. She's already reducing the units we failed to capture. Admiral Sorrens estimates he'll control Force Two entirely in another hour. Bulletin just came in from Force Three. Admiral Gundrup killed in fighting, but Vice Admiral Smitt has assumed command and reports three-fourths of the ships in our hands. He's delaying fire until he sees how it goes aboard the rest. Also—"

"Never mind," said Rusch. "I'll get the comprehensive report later. Remind Staff that for the next few hours all command decisions had better be made by officers on the spot. After that, when we see what we've got, broader tactics can be prepared. If some extreme emergency doesn't arise, it'll be a few hours before I can get over to HQ."

"Yes, sir. Sir, I . . . may I say—" So might the young Norron have addressed a god.

"All right, son, you've said it." Rusch turned off the screen and looked at Unduma. "Do you realize what's happening?"

The ambassador sat down; his knees seemed all at once to have melted. "What have you done?" It was like a stranger speaking.

"What I planned quite a few years ago," said the Margrave.

He reached into his desk and brought forth a bottle. "Here, your excellency. I think we could both use a swig. Authentic Terrestrial Scotch. I've saved it for this day."

But there was no glory leaping in him. It is often thus, you reach a dream and you only feel how tired you are.

Unduma let the liquid fire slide down his throat.

"You understand, don't you?" said Rusch. "For seven centuries, the

Elephant and the Whale fought, without being able to get at each other's vitals. I made this alliance against Earth solely to get our men aboard their ships. But a really large operation like that can't be faked. It has to be genuine—the agreements, the preparations, the propaganda, everything. Only a handful of officers, men who could be trusted to . . . to infinity"—his voice cracked over, and Unduma thought of war prisoners sacrificed, hideous casualties in the steel corridors of spaceships, Norron gunners destroying Kolreshite vessels and the survivors of Norron detachments which failed to capture them—"only a few could be told, and then only at the last instant. For the rest, I relied on the quality of our troops. They're good lads, every one of them and, therefore adaptable. They're especially adaptable when suddenly told to fall on the men they'd most like to kill."

He tilted the bottle afresh. "It's proving expensive," he said in a slurred, hurried tone. "It will cost us as many casualties, no doubt, as ten years of ordinary war. But if I hadn't done this, there could easily have been another seven hundred years of war. Couldn't there? Couldn't there have been? As it is, we've already broken the spine of the Kolreshite fleet. She has plenty of ships yet, to be sure, still a menace, but crippled. I hope Earth will see fit to join us. Between them, Earth and Norstad-Ostarik can finish off Kolresh in a hurry. And after all, Kolresh *did* declare war on you, had every intention of destroying you. If you won't help, well, we can end it by ourselves, now that the fleet is broken. But I hope you'll join us."

"I don't know," said Unduma. He was still wobbling in a new cosmos. "We're not a . . . a hard people."

"You ought to be," said Rusch. "Hard enough, anyway, to win a voice for yourselves in what's going to happen around Polaris. Important frontier, Polaris."

"Yes," said Unduma slowly. "There is that. It won't cause any hosannahs in our streets, but . . . yes, I think we will continue the war, as your allies, if only to prevent you from massacring the Kolreshites. They can be rehabilitated, you know."

"I doubt that," grunted Rusch. "But it's a detail. At the very least, they'll never be allowed weapons again." He raised a sardonic brow. "I suppose we, too, can be rehabilitated, once you get your peace groups and psychotechs out here. No doubt you'll manage to demilitarize us and turn us into good plump democrats. All right, Unduma, send your Civilizing missionaries. But permit me to give thanks that I won't live to see their work completed!"

The Earthman nodded, rather coldly. You couldn't blame Rusch for treachery, callousness, and arrogance—he was what his history had made him—but he remained unpleasant company for a Civilized man. "I shall communicate with my government at once, your lordship, and recommend a provisional alliance, the terms to be settled later," he said. "I will report back to you as soon as . . . ah, where will you be?"

"How should I know?" Rusch got out of his chair. The winter night howled at his back. "I have to convene the Ministry, and make a public telecast, and get over to Staff, and— No. The devil with it! If you need me inside the next few hours, I'll be at Sorgenlos on Ostarik. But the matter had better be urgent!"

Philip K. Dick

Regarded as one of the most important writers of science fiction in the twentieth century, Philip K. Dick built his reputation on subtly complex tales of intersecting alternate realities. His novel The Man in the High Castle, set in a future where Japan and Germany emerged victorious from World War II, won the Hugo Award for best novel in 1963 and is regarded as one of the best alternate history tales in science fiction. Dr. Bloodmoney offers a vision of American society in the aftermath of nuclear war. The Three Stigmata of Palmer Eldritch and Ubik, both set in worlds where time slips and reality shifts are the norm, crystallize the mood of paranoia and often comically chaotic instability that characterizes much of his writing. His Valis trilogy, comprised of the novels Valis, The Divine Invasion, and The Transmigration of Timothy Archer, has been praised for its use of science fiction and fantasy tropes in the service of philosophic and cosmologic inquiry. Several of his best-known stories have been successfully adapted for the screen: his novel Do Androids Dream of Electric Sheep? was filmed as the blockbuster movie Blade Runner in 1982, and his short story "We Can Remember It for You Wholesale" was adapted as Total Recall in 1990. Revival of interest in Dick's work after his death in 1982 led to the publication of his many mainstream novels, several volumes of his collected letters, and the five-volume Collected Stories of Philip K. Dick.

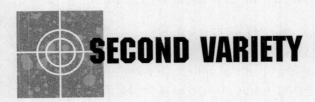

SECOND VARIETY

Philip K. Dick

THE RUSSIAN SOLDIER made his way nervously up the ragged side of the hill, holding his gun ready. He glanced around him, licking his dry lips, his face set. From time to time he reached up a gloved hand and wiped perspiration from his neck, pushing down his coat collar.

Eric turned to Corporal Leone. "Want him? Or can I have him?" He adjusted the view sight so the Russian's features squarely filled the glass, the lines cutting across his hard, somber features.

Leone considered. The Russian was close, moving rapidly, almost running. "Don't fire. Wait." Leone tensed. "I don't think we're needed."

The Russian increased his pace, kicking ash and piles of debris out of his way. He reached the top of the hill and stopped, panting, staring around him. The sky was overcast, with drifting clouds of gray particles. Bare trunks of trees jutted up occasionally; the ground was level and bare, rubble-strewn, with the ruins of buildings standing out here and there like yellowing skulls.

The Russian was uneasy. He knew something was wrong. He started down the hill. Now he was only a few paces from the bunker. Eric was getting fidgety. He played with his pistol, glancing at Leone.

"Don't worry," Leone said. "He won't get here. They'll take care of him."

"Are you sure? He's got damn far."

"They hang around close to the bunker. He's getting into the bad part. Get set!"

The Russian began to hurry, sliding down the hill, his boots sinking into the heaps of gray ash, trying to keep his gun up. He stopped for a moment, lifting his field glasses to his face.

"He's looking right at us," Eric said.

The Russian came on. They could see his eyes, like two blue stones. His mouth was open a little. He needed a shave; his chin was stubbled. On one bony cheek was a square of tape, showing blue at the edge. A fungoid spot. His coat was muddy and torn. One glove was missing. As he ran, his belt counter bounced up and down against him.

Leone touched Eric's arm. "Here one comes."

Across the ground something small and metallic came, flashing in the dull sunlight of midday. A metal sphere. It raced up the hill after the Russian, its treads flying. It was small, one of the baby ones. Its claws were out, two razor projections spinning in a blur of white steel. The Russian heard it. He turned instantly, firing. The sphere dissolved into particles. But already a second had emerged and was following the first. The Russian fired again.

A third sphere leaped up the Russian's leg, clicking and whirring. It jumped to the shoulder. The spinning blades disappeared into the Russian's throat.

Eric relaxed. "Well, that's that. God, those damn things give me the creeps. Sometimes I think we were better off before."

"If we hadn't invented them, they would have." Leone lit a cigarette shakily. "I wonder why a Russian would come all this way alone. I didn't see anyone covering him."

Lieutenant Scott came slipping up the tunnel, into the bunker. "What happened? Something entered the screen."

"An Ivan."

"Just one?"

Eric brought the viewscreen around. Scott peered into it. Now there were numerous metal spheres crawling over the prostrate body, dull metal globes clicking and whirring, sawing up the Russian into small parts to be carried away.

"What a lot of claws," Scott murmured.

"They come like flies. Not much game for them anymore."

Scott pushed the sight away, disgusted. "Like flies. I wonder why he was out there. They know we have claws all around."

A larger robot had joined the smaller spheres. A long blunt tube with projecting eyepieces, it was directing operations. There was not much left of the soldier. What remained was being brought down the hillside by the host of claws.

"Sir," Leone said. "If it's all right, I'd like to go out there and take a look at him."

"Why?"

"Maybe he came with something."

Scott considered. He shrugged. "All right. But be careful."

"I have my tab." Leone patted the metal band at his wrist. "I'll be out of bounds."

He picked up his rifle and stepped carefully up to the mouth of the bunker, making his way between blocks of concrete and steel prongs, twisted and bent. The air was cold at the top. He crossed over the ground toward the remains of the soldier, striding across the soft ash. A wind blew around him, swirling gray particles up in his face. He squinted and pushed on.

The claws retreated as he came close, some of them stiffening into immobility. He touched his tab. The Ivan would have given something for that! Short hard radiation emitted from the tab neutralized the claws, put them out of commission. Even the big robot with its two waving eye-stalks retreated respectfully as he approached.

He bent down over the remains of the soldier. The gloved hand was closed tightly. There was something in it. Leone pried the fingers apart. A sealed container, aluminum. Still shiny.

He put it in his pocket and made his way back to the bunker. Behind him the claws came back to life, moving into operation again. The procession resumed, metal spheres moving through the gray ash with their loads. He could hear their treads scrabbling against the ground. He shuddered.

Scott watched intently as he brought the shiny tube out of his pocket. "He had that?"

"In his hand." Leone unscrewed the top. "Maybe you should look at it, sir."

Scott took it. He emptied the contents out in the palm of his hand. A small piece of silk paper, carefully folded. He sat down by the light and unfolded it.

"What's it say, sir?" Eric said. Several officers came up the tunnel. Major Hendricks appeared.

"Major," Scott said. "Look at this."

Hendricks read the slip. "This just come?"

"A single runner. Just now."

"Where is he?" Hendricks asked sharply.

"The claws got him."

Major Hendricks grunted. "Here." He passed it to his companions. "I think this is what we've been waiting for. They certainly took their time about it."

"So they want to talk terms," Scott said. "Are we going along with them?"

"That's not for us to decide." Hendricks sat down. "Where's the communications officer? I want the Moon Base."

Leone pondered as the communications officer raised the outside antenna cautiously, scanning the sky above the bunker for any sign of a watching Russian ship.

"Sir," Scott said to Hendricks. "It's sure strange they suddenly came around. We've been using the claws for almost a year. Now all of a sudden they start to fold."

"Maybe claws have been getting down in their bunkers."

"One of the big ones, the kind with stalks, got into an Ivan bunker last week," Eric said. "It got a whole platoon of them before they got their lid shut."

"How do you know?"

"A buddy told me. The thing came back with—with remains."

"Moon Base, sir," the communications officer said.

On the screen the face of the lunar monitor appeared. His crisp uniform contrasted to the uniforms in the bunker. And he was cleanshaven. "Moon Base."

"This is forward command L-Whistle. On Terra. Let me have General Thompson."

The monitor faded. Presently General Thompson's heavy features came into focus. "What is it, Major?"

"Our claws got a single Russian runner with a message. We don't know whether to act on it—there have been tricks like this in the past."

"What's the message?"

"The Russians want us to send a single officer on policy level over to their lines. For a conference. They don't state the nature of the conference. They say that matters of—" He consulted the slip: "—matters of grave urgency make it advisable that discussion be opened between a representative of the UN forces and themselves."

He held the message up to the screen for the general to scan. Thompson's eyes moved.

"What should we do?" Hendricks said.

"Send a man out."

"You don't think it's a trap?"

"It might be. But the location they give for their forward command is correct. It's worth a try, at any rate."

"I'll send an officer out. And report the results to you as soon as he returns."

"All right, Major." Thompson broke the connection. The screen died. Up above, the antenna came slowly down.

Hendricks rolled up the paper, deep in thought.

"I'll go," Leone said.

"They want somebody at policy level." Hendricks rubbed his jaw. "Policy level. I haven't been outside in months. Maybe I could use a little air."

"Don't you think it's risky?"

Hendricks lifted the view sight and gazed into it. The remains of the Russian were gone. Only a single claw was in sight. It was folding itself back, disappearing into the ash, like a crab. Like some hideous metal crab . . . "That's the only thing that bothers me." Hendricks rubbed his wrist. "I know I'm safe as long as I have this on me. But there's something about them. I hate the damn things. I wish we'd never invented them. There's something wrong with them. Relentless little—"

"If we hadn't invented them, the Ivans would have."

Hendricks pushed the sight back. "Anyhow, it seems to be winning the war. I guess that's good."

"Sounds like you're getting the same jitters as the Ivans."

Hendricks examined his wristwatch. "I guess I had better get started, if I want to be there before dark."

HE TOOK A deep breath and then stepped out onto the gray rubbled ground. After a minute he lit a cigarette and stood gazing around him. The landscape was dead. Nothing stirred. He could see for miles, endless ash and slag, ruins of buildings. A few trees without leaves or branches, only the trunks. Above him the eternal rolling clouds of gray, drifting between Terra and the sun.

Major Hendricks went on. Off to the right something scuttled, something round and metallic. A claw, going lickety-split after something. Probably after a small animal, a rat. They got rats, too. As a sort of sideline.

He came to the top of the little hill and lifted his field glasses. The Russian lines were a few miles ahead of him. They had a forward command post there. The runner had come from it.

A squat robot with undulating arms passed by him, its arms weaving inquiringly. The robot went on its way, disappearing under some debris. Hendricks watched it go. He had never seen that type before. There were getting to be more and more types he had never seen, new varieties and sizes coming up from the underground factories.

Hendricks put out his cigarette and hurried on. It was interesting, the use of artificial forms in warfare. How had they got started? Necessity. The Soviet Union had gained great initial success, usual with the side that got the war going. Most of North America had been blasted off the map. Retaliation was quick in coming, of course. The sky was full of circling diskbombers long before the war began; they had been up there for years. The disks began sailing down all over Russia within hours after Washington got it.

But that hadn't helped Washington.

The American bloc governments moved to the Moon Base the first year. There was not much else to do. Europe was gone, a slag heap with dark weeds growing from the ashes and bones. Most of North America was useless, nothing could be planted, no one could live. A few million people kept going up in Canada and down in South America. But during the second year Soviet parachutists began to drop, a few at first, then more and more. They wore the first really effective antiradiation equipment; what was left of American production moved to the Moon along with the governments.

All but the troops. The remaining troops stayed behind as best they could, a few thousand here, a platoon there. No one knew exactly where they were; they stayed where they could, moving around at night, hiding in ruins, in sewers, cellars, with the rats and snakes. It looked as if the Soviet Union had the war almost won. Except for a handful of projectiles fired off from the Moon daily, there was almost no weapon in use against them. They came and went as they pleased. The war, for all practical purposes, was over. Nothing effective opposed them.

And then the first claws appeared. And overnight the complexion of the war changed.

The claws were awkward, at first. Slow. The Ivans knocked them off almost as fast as they crawled out of their underground tunnels. But then they got better, faster and more cunning. Factories, all on Terra, turned them out. Factories a long way underground, behind the Soviet lines, factories that had once made atomic projectiles, now almost forgotten.

The claws got faster, and they got bigger. New types appeared, some with feelers, some that flew. There were a few jumping kinds. The best technicians on the Moon were working on designs, making them more and more intricate, more flexible. They became uncanny; the Ivans were having a lot of trouble with them. Some of the little claws were learning to hide themselves, burrowing down into the ash, lying in wait.

And then they started getting into the Russian bunkers, slipping down when the lids were raised for air and a look around. One claw inside a bunker, a churning sphere of blades and metal—that was enough. And when one got in others followed. With a weapon like that the war couldn't go on much longer.

Maybe it was already over.

Maybe he was going to hear the news. Maybe the Politburo had decided to throw in the sponge. Too bad it had taken so long. Six years. A long time for war like that, the way they had waged it. The automatic retaliation disks, spinning down all over Russia, hundreds of thousands of them. Bacteria crystals. The Soviet guided missiles, whistling through the air. The chain bombs. And now this, the robots, the claws—

The claws weren't like other weapons. They were *alive*, from any practical standpoint, whether the Governments wanted to admit it or not. They were not machines. They were living things, spinning, creeping, shaking themselves up suddenly from the gray ash and darting toward a man, climbing up him, rushing for his throat. And that was what they had been designed to do. Their job.

They did their job well. Especially lately, with the new designs coming up. Now they repaired themselves. They were on their own. Radiation tabs protected the UN troops, but if a man lost his tab he was fair game for the claws, no matter what his uniform. Down below the surface automatic machinery stamped them out. Human beings stayed a long way off. It was too risky; nobody wanted to be around them. They were left to themselves. And they seemed to be doing all right. The new designs were faster, more complex. More efficient.

Apparently they had won the war.

MAJOR HENDRICKS LIT a second cigarette. The landscape depressed him. Nothing but ash and ruins. He seemed to be alone, the only living thing in the whole world. To the right the ruins of a town rose up, a few walls and heaps of debris. He tossed the dead match away, increasing his pace. Suddenly he stopped, jerking up his gun, his body tense. For a minute it looked like—

From behind the shell of a ruined building a figure came, walking slowly toward him, walking hesitantly.

Hendricks blinked. "Stop!"

The boy stopped. Hendricks lowered his gun. The boy stood silently, looking at him. He was small, not very old. Perhaps eight. But it was hard to tell. Most of the kids who remained were stunted. He wore a faded blue sweater ragged with dirt, and short pants. His hair was long and matted. Brown hair. It hung over his face and around his ears. He held something in his arms.

"What's that you have?" Hendricks said sharply.

The boy held it out. It was a toy, a bear. A teddy bear. The boy's eyes were large, but without expression.

Hendricks relaxed. "I don't want it. Keep it."

The boy hugged the bear again.

"Where do you live?" Henricks said.

"In there."

"The ruins?"

"Yes."

"Underground?"

"Yes."

"How many are there?"

"How—how many?"

"How many of you. How big's your settlement?"

The boy did not answer.

Hendricks frowned. "You're not all by yourself, are you?"

The boy nodded.

"How do you stay alive?"

"There's food."

"What kind of food?"

"Different."

Hendricks studied him. "How old are you?"

"Thirteen."

It wasn't possible. Or was it? The boy was thin, stunted. And probably sterile. Radiation exposure, years straight. No wonder he was so small. His arms and legs were like pipe cleaners, knobby and thin. Hendricks touched the boy's arm. His skin was dry and rough; radiation skin. He bent down, looking into the boy's face. There was no expression. Big eyes, big and dark.

"Are you blind?" Henricks said.

"No. I can see some."

"How do you get away from the claws?"

"The claws?"

"The round things. That run and burrow."

"I don't understand."

Maybe there weren't any claws around. A lot of areas were free. They collected mostly around bunkers, where there were people. The claws had been designed to sense warmth, warmth of living things.

"You're lucky." Hendricks straightened up. "Well? Which way are you going? Back—back there?"

"Can I come with you?"

"With *me*?" Hendricks folded his arms. "I'm going a long way. Miles. I have to hurry." He looked at his watch. "I have to get there by nightfall."

"I want to come."

Hendricks fumbled in his pack. "It isn't worth it. Here." He tossed down the food cans he had with him. "You take these and go back. Okay?"

The boy said nothing.

"I'll be coming back this way. In a day or so. If you're around here when I come back you can come along with me. All right?"

"I want to go with you now."

"It's a long walk."

"I can walk."

Hendricks shifted uneasily. It made too good a target, two people walking along. And the boy would slow him down. But he might not come back this way. And if the boy were really all alone—

"Okay. Come along."

The boy fell in beside him. Hendricks strode along. The boy walked silently, clutching his teddy bear.

"What's your name?" Hendricks said, after a time.

"David Edward Derring."

"David? What—what happened to your mother and father?"

"They died."

"How?"

"In the blast."

"How long ago?"

"Six years."

Hendricks slowed down. "You've been alone six years?"

"No. There were other people for a while. They went away."

"And you've been alone since?"

"Yes."

Hendricks glanced down. The boy was strange, saying very little. Withdrawn. But that was the way they were, the children who had survived. Quiet. Stoic. A strange kind of fatalism gripped them. Nothing came as a surprise. They accepted anything that came along. There was no longer any *normal*, any natural course of things, moral or physical, for them to expect. Custom, habit, all the determining forces of learning were gone; only brute experience remained.

"Am I walking too fast?" Hendricks said.

"No."

"How did you happen to see me?"

"I was waiting."

"Waiting?" Hendricks was puzzled. "What were you waiting for?"

"To catch things."

"What kind of things?"

"Things to eat."

"Oh." Hendricks set his lips grimly. A thirteen-year-old boy, living on rats and gophers and half-rotten canned food. Down in a hole under the ruins of a town. With radiation pools and claws, and Russian dive-mines up above, coasting around in the sky.

"Where are we going?" David asked.

"To the Russian lines."

"Russian?"

"The enemy. The people who started the war. They dropped the first radiation bombs. They began all this."

The boy nodded. His face showed no expression.

"I'm an American," Hendricks said.

There was no comment. On they went, the two of them, Hendricks walking a little ahead, David trailing behind him, hugging his dirty teddy bear against his chest.

About four in the afternoon they stopped to eat. Hendricks built a fire in a hollow between some slabs of concrete. He cleared the weeds away and heaped up bits of wood. The Russians' lines were not very far ahead. Around him was what had once been a long valley, acres of fruit trees and grapes. Nothing remained now but a few bleak stumps and the mountains that stretched across the horizon at the far end. And the clouds of rolling ash that blew and drifted with the wind, settling over the weeds and remains of buildings, walls here and there, once in a while what had been a road.

Hendricks made coffee and heated up some boiled mutton and bread. "Here." He handed bread and mutton to David. David squatted by the edge of the fire, his knees knobby and white. He examined the food and then passed it back, shaking his head.

"No."

"No? Don't you want any?"

"No."

Hendricks shrugged. Maybe the boy was a mutant, used to special food. It didn't matter. When he was hungry he would find something to eat. The boy was strange. But there were many strange changes coming over the world. Life was not the same anymore. It would never be the same again. The human race was going to have to realize that.

"Suit yourself," Hendricks said. He ate the bread and mutton by himself, washing it down with coffee. He ate slowly, finding the food hard to digest. When he was done he got to his feet and stamped the fire out.

David rose slowly, watching him with his young-old eyes.

"We're going," Hendricks said.

"All right."

Hendricks walked along, his gun in his arms. They were close; he was tense, ready for anything. The Russians should be expecting a runner, an answer to their own runner, but they were tricky. There was always the possibility of a slip-up. He scanned the landscape around him. Nothing but slag and ash, a few hills, charred trees. Concrete walls. But some place ahead was the first bunker of the Russian lines, the forward command. Underground, buried deep, with only a periscope showing, a few gun muzzles. Maybe an antenna.

"Will we be there soon?" David asked.

"Yes. Getting tired?"

"No."

"Why, then?"

David did not answer. He plodded carefully along behind, picking his way over the ash. His legs and shoes were gray with dust. His pinched face was streaked, lines of gray ash in riverlets down the pale white of his skin. There was no color to his face. Typical of the new children, growing up in cellars and sewers and underground shelters.

Hendricks slowed down. He lifted his field glasses and studied the ground ahead of him. Were they there, some place, waiting for him? Watching him, the way his men had watched the Russian runner? A chill went up his back. Maybe they were getting their guns ready, preparing to fire, the way his men had prepared, made ready to kill.

Hendricks stopped, wiping perspiration from his face. "Damn." It made him uneasy. But he should be expected. The situation was different.

He strode over the ash, holding his gun tightly with both hands. Behind him came David. Hendricks peered around, tight-lipped. Any second it might happen. A burst of white light, a blast, carefully aimed from inside a deep concrete bunker.

He raised his arm and waved it around in a circle.

Nothing moved. To the right a long ridge ran, topped with dead tree trunks. A few wild vines had grown up around the trees, remains of arbors. And the eternal dark weeds. Hendricks studied the ridge. Was anything up there? Perfect place for a lookout. He approached the ridge warily, David coming silently behind. If it were his command he'd have a sentry up there, watching for troops trying to infiltrate into the command area. Of course, if it were his command there would be the claws around the area for full protection.

He stopped, feet apart, hands on his hips.

"Are we there?" David said.

"Almost."

"Why have we stopped?"

"I don't want to take any chances." Hendricks advanced slowly. Now the ridge lay directly beside him, along his right. Overlooking him. His uneasy feeling increased. If an Ivan was up there he wouldn't have a chance. He waved his arm again. They should be expecting someone in the UN uniform, in response to the note capsule. Unless the whole thing was a trap.

"Keep up with me." He turned toward David. "Don't drop behind."

"With you?"

"Up beside me! We're close. We can't take any chances. Come on."

"I'll be all right." David remained behind him, in the rear, a few paces away, still clutching his teddy bear.

"Have it your way." Hendricks raised his glasses again, suddenly tense. For a moment—had something moved? He scanned the ridge carefully. Everything was silent. Dead. No life up there, only tree trunks and ash. Maybe a few rats. The big black rats that had survived the claws. Mutants—built their own shelters out of saliva and ash. Some kind of plaster. Adaptation. He started forward again.

A tall figure came out on the ridge above him, cloak flapping. Gray-green. A Russian. Behind him a second soldier appeared, another Russian. Both lifted their guns, aiming.

Hendricks froze. He opened his mouth. The soldiers were kneeling, sighting down the side of the slope. A third figure had joined them on the ridge top, a smaller figure in gray-green. A woman. She stood behind the other two.

Hendricks found his voice. "Stop!" He waved up at them frantically. "I'm—"

The two Russians fired. Behind Hendricks there was a faint *pop*. Waves of heat lapped against him, throwing him to the ground. Ash tore at his face, grinding into his eyes and nose. Choking, he pulled himself to his knees. It was all a trap. He was finished. He had come to be killed, like a steer. The soldiers and the woman were coming down the side of the ridge toward him, sliding down through the soft ash. Hendricks was numb. His head throbbed. Awkwardly, he got his rifle up and took aim. It weighed a thousand tons; he could hardly hold it. His nose and cheeks stung. The air was full of the blast smell, a bitter acrid stench.

"Don't fire," the first Russian said, in heavily accented English.

The three of them came up to him, surrounding him. "Put down your rifle, Yank," the other said.

Hendricks was dazed. Everything had happened so fast. He had been caught. And they had blasted the boy. He turned his head. David was gone. What remained of him was strewn across the ground.

The three Russians studied him curiously. Hendricks sat, wiping blood from his nose, picking out bits of ash. He shook his head, trying to clear it. "Why did you do it?" he murmured thickly. "The boy."

"Why?" One of the soldiers helped him roughly to his feet. He turned Hendricks around. "Look."

Hendricks closed his eyes.

"Look!" The two Russians pulled him forward. "See. Hurry up. There isn't much time to spare, Yank!"

Hendricks looked. And gasped.

"See now? Now do you understand?"

From the remains of David a metal wheel rolled. Relays, glinting metal. Parts, wiring. One of the Russians kicked at the heap of remains. Parts popped out, rolling away, wheels and springs and rods. A plastic section fell in, half charred. Hendricks bent shakily down. The front of the head had come off. He could make out the intricate brain, wires and relays, tiny tubes and switches, thousands of minute studs—

"A robot," the soldier holding his arm said. "We watched it tagging you."

"Tagging me?"

"That's their way. They tag along with you. Into the bunker. That's how they get in."

Hendricks blinked, dazed. "But—"

"Come on." They led him toward the ridge. "We can't stay here. It isn't safe. There must be hundreds of them all around here."

The three of them pulled him up the side of the ridge, sliding and slipping on the ash. The woman reached the top and stood waiting for them.

"The forward command," Hendricks muttered. "I came to negotiate with the Soviet—"

"There is no more forward command. *They* got in. We'll explain." They reached the top of the ridge. "We're all that's left. The three of us. The rest were down in the bunker."

"This way. Down this way." The woman unscrewed a lid, a gray man-hole cover set in the ground. "Get in."

Hendricks lowered himself. The two soldiers and the woman came behind him, following him down the ladder. The woman closed the lid after them, bolting it tightly into place.

"Good thing we saw you," one of the two soldiers grunted. "It had tagged you about as far as it was going to."

"Give me one of your cigarettes," the woman said. "I haven't had an American cigarette for weeks."

Hendricks pushed the pack to her. She took a cigarette and passed the pack to the two soldiers. In the corner of the small room the lamp gleamed fitfully. The room was low-ceilinged, cramped. The four of them sat around a small wood table. A few dirty dishes were stacked to one side. Behind a ragged curtain a second room was partly visible. Hendricks saw the corner of a coat, some blankets, clothes hung on a hook.

"We were here," the soldier beside him said. He took off his helmet, pushing his blond hair back. "I'm Corporal Rudi Maxer. Polish. Impressed in the Soviet Army two years ago." He held out his hand.

Hendricks hesitated and then shook. "Major Joseph Hendricks."

"Klaus Epstein." The other soldier shook with him, a small dark man with thinning hair. Epstein plucked nervously at his ear. "Austrian. Impressed God knows when. I don't remember. The three of us were here, Rudi and I, with Tasso." He indicated the woman. "That's how we escaped. All the rest were down in the bunker."

"And—and *they* got in?"

Epstein lit a cigarette. "First just one of them. The kind that tagged you. Then it let others in."

Hendricks became alert. "The *kind*? Are there more than one kind?"

"The little boy. David. David holding his teddy bear. That's Variety Three. The most effective."

"What are the other types?"

Epstein reached into his coat. "Here." He tossed a packet of photographs onto the table, tied with a string. "Look for yourself."

Hendricks untied the string.

"You see," Rudi Maxer said, "that was why we wanted to talk terms. The Russians, I mean. We found out about a week ago. Found out that your claws were beginning to make up new designs on their own. New types of their own. Better types. Down in your underground factories behind our lines. You let them stamp themselves, repair themselves. Made them more and more intricate. It's your fault this happened."

Hendricks examined the photos. They had been snapped hurriedly; they were blurred and indistinct. The first few showed—David. David walking along a road, by himself. David and another David. Three Davids. All exactly alike. Each with a ragged teddy bear.

All pathetic.

"Look at the others," Tasso said.

The next pictures, taken at a great distance, showed a towering wounded soldier sitting by the side of a path, his arm in a sling, the stump of one leg extended, a crude crutch on his lap. Then two wounded soldiers, both the same, standing side by side.

"That's Variety One. The Wounded Soldier." Klaus reached out and took the pictures. "You see, the claws were designed to get to human beings. To find them. Each kind was better than the last. They got farther, closer, past most of our defenses, into our lines. But as long as they were merely *machines*, metal spheres with claws and horns, feelers, they could be picked off like any other object. They could be detected as lethal robots as soon as they were seen. Once we caught sight of them—"

"Variety One subverted our whole north wing," Rudi said. "It was a long time before anyone caught on. Then it was too late. They came in, wounded soldiers, knocking and begging to be let in. So we let them in. And as soon as they were in they took over. We were watching out for machines. . . ."

"At that time it was thought there was only the one type," Klaus Epstein said. "No one suspected there were other types. The pictures were flashed to us. When the runner was sent to you, we knew of just one type. Variety One. The big Wounded Soldier. We thought that was all."

"Your line fell to—"

"To Variety Three. David and his bear. That worked even better." Klaus smiled bitterly. "Soldiers are suckers for children. We brought them in and tried to feed them. We found out the hard way what they were after. At least, those who were in the bunker."

"The three of us were lucky," Rudi said. "Klaus and I were—were visiting Tasso when it happened. This is her place." He waved a big hand around. "This little cellar. We finished and climbed the ladder to start back. From the ridge we saw that they were all around the bunker. Fighting was still going on. David and his bear. Hundreds of them. Klaus took the pictures."

Klaus tied up the photographs again.

"And it's going on all along your line?" Hendricks said.

"Yes."

"How about *our* lines?" Without thinking, he touched the tab on his arm. "Can they—"

"They're not bothered by your radiation tabs. It makes no difference to them, Russian, American, Pole, German. It's all the same. They're doing what they were designed to do. Carrying out the original idea. They track down life, wherever they find it."

"They go by warmth," Klaus said. "That was the way you constructed them from the very start. Of course, those you designed were kept back by the radiation tabs you wear. Now they've got around that. These new varieties are lead-lined."

"What's the other variety?" Hendricks asked. "The David type, the Wounded Soldier—what's the other?"

"We don't know." Klaus pointed up at the wall. On the wall were two metal plates, ragged at the edges. Hendricks got up and studied them. They were bent and dented.

"The one on the left came off a Wounded Soldier," Rudi said. "We got one of them. It was going along toward our old bunker. We got it from the ridge, the same way we got the David tagging you."

The plate was stamped: *I-V*. Hendricks touched the other plate. "And this came from the David type?"

"Yes." The plate was stamped: *III-V*.

Klaus took a look at them, leaning over Hendricks's broad shoulder. "You can see what we're up against. There's another type. Maybe it was abandoned. Maybe it didn't work. But there must be a Second Variety. There's One and Three."

"You were lucky," Rudi said. "The David tagged you all the way here and never touched you. Probably thought you'd get it into a bunker, somewhere."

"One gets in and it's all over," Klaus said. "They move fast. One lets all the rest inside. They're inflexible. Machines with one purpose. They were built for only one thing." He rubbed sweat from his lip. "We saw."

They were silent.

"Let me have another cigarette, Yank," Tasso said. "They are good. I almost forgot how they were."

It WAS NIGHT. The sky was black. No stars were visible through the rolling clouds of ash. Klaus lifted the lid cautiously so that Hendricks could look out.

Rudi pointed into the darkness. "Over that way are the bunkers. Where we used to be. Not over half a mile from us. It was just chance Klaus and I were not there when it happened. Weakness. Saved by our lusts."

"All the rest must be dead," Klaus said in a low voice. "It came quickly. This morning the Politburo reached their decision. They notified us—forward command. Our runner was sent out at once. We saw him start toward the direction of your lines. We covered him until he was out of sight."

"Alex Radrivsky. We both knew him. He disappeared about six o'clock. The sun had just come up. About noon Klaus and I had an hour relief. We crept off, away from the bunkers. No one was watching. We came here. There used to be a town here, a few houses, a street. This cellar was part of a big farmhouse. We knew Tasso would be here, hiding down in her little place. We had come here before. Others from the bunkers came here. Today happened to be our turn."

"So we were saved," Klaus said. "Chance. It might have been others. We—we finished, and then we came up to the surface and started back along the ridge. That was when we saw them, the Davids. We understood right away. We had seen the photos of the First Variety, the Wounded Soldier. Our Commissar distributed them to us with an explanation. If we had gone another step they would have seen us. As it was we had to blast two Davids before we got back. There were hundreds of them, all around. Like ants. We took pictures and slipped back here, bolting the lid tight."

"They're not so much when you catch them alone. We moved faster than they did. But they're inexorable. Not like living things. They came right at us. And we blasted them."

Major Hendricks rested against the edge of the lid, adjusting his eyes to the darkness. "Is it safe to have the lid up at all?"

"If we're careful. How else can you operate your transmitter?"

Hendricks lifted the small belt transmitter slowly. He pressed it against his ear. The metal was cold and damp. He blew against the mike, raising up the short antenna. A faint hum sounded in his ear. "That's true, I suppose."

But he still hesitated.

"We'll pull you under if anything happens," Klaus said.

"Thanks." Hendricks waited a moment, resting the transmitter against his shoulder. "Interesting, isn't it?"

"What?"

"This, the new types. The new varieties of claws. We're completely at their mercy, aren't we? By now they've probably gotten into the UN lines, too. It makes me wonder if we're not seeing the beginning of a new species. *The* new species. Evolution. The race to come after man."

Rudi grunted. "There is no race after man."

"No? Why not? Maybe we're seeing it now, the end of human beings, the beginning of the new society."

"They're not a race. They're mechanical killers. You made them to destroy. That's all they can do. They're machines with a job."

"So it seems now. But how about later on? After the war is over. Maybe, when there aren't any humans to destroy, their real potentialities will begin to show."

"You talk as if they were alive!"

"Aren't they?"

There was silence. "They're machines," Rudi said. "They look like people, but they're machines."

"Use your transmitter, Major," Klaus said. "We can't stay up here forever."

Holding the transmitter tightly, Hendricks called the code of the command bunker. He waited, listening. No response. Only silence. He checked the leads carefully. Everything was in place.

"Scott!" he said into the mike. "Can you hear me?"

Silence. He raised the gain up full and tried again. Only static.

"I don't get anything. They may hear me but they may not want to answer."

"Tell them it's an emergency."

"They'll think I'm being forced to call. Under your direction." He tried again, outlining briefly what he had learned. But still the phone was silent, except for the faint static.

"Radiation pools kill most transmission," Klaus said, after a while. "Maybe that's it."

Hendricks shut the transmitter up. "No use. No answer. Radiation pools? Maybe. Or they hear me, but won't answer. Frankly, that's what I would do, if a runner tried to call from the Soviet lines. They have no reason to believe such a story. They may hear everything I say—"

"Or maybe it's too late."

Hendricks nodded.

"We better get the lid down," Rudi said nervously. "We don't want to take unnecessary chances."

They climbed slowly back down the tunnel. Klaus bolted the lid carefully into place. They descended into the kitchen. The air was heavy and close around them.

"Could they work that fast?" Hendricks said. "I left the bunker this noon. Ten hours ago. How could they move so quickly?"

"It doesn't take them long. Not after the first one gets in. It goes wild. You know what the little claws can do. Even *one* of these is beyond belief. Razors, each finger. Maniacal."

"All right." Hendricks moved away impatiently. He stood with his back to them.

"What's the matter?" Rudi said.

"The Moon Base. God, if they've gotten there—"

"The Moon Base?"

Hendricks turned around. "They couldn't have got to the Moon Base. How would they get there? It isn't possible. I can't believe it."

"What is this Moon Base? We've heard rumors, but nothing definite. What is the actual situation? You seem concerned."

"We're supplied from the Moon. The governments are there, under the lunar surface. All our people and industries. That's what keeps us going. If they should find some way of getting off Terra, onto the Moon—"

"It only takes one of them. Once the first one gets in it admits the others. Hundreds of them, all alike. You should have seen them. Identical. Like ants."

"Perfect socialism," Tasso said. "The ideal of the communist state. All citizens interchangeable."

Klaus grunted angrily. "That's enough. Well? What next?"

Hendricks paced back and forth, around the small room. The air was full of smells of food and perspiration. The others watched him. Presently Tasso pushed through the curtain, into the other room. "I'm going to take a nap."

The curtain closed behind her. Rudi and Klaus sat down at the table, still watching Hendricks. "It's up to you," Klaus said. "We don't know your situation."

Hendricks nodded.

"It's a problem." Rudi drank some coffee, filling his cup from a rusty pot. "We're safe here for a while, but we can't stay here forever. Not enough food or supplies."

"But if we go outside—"

"If we go outside they'll get us. Or probably they'll get us. We couldn't go very far. How far is your command bunker, Major?"

"Three or four miles."

"We might make it. The four of us. Four of us could watch all sides. They couldn't slip up behind us and start tagging us. We have three rifles, three blast rifles. Tasso can have my pistol." Rudi tapped his belt. "In the Soviet army we didn't have shoes always, but we had guns. With all four of us armed one of us might get to your command bunker. Preferably you, Major."

"What if they're already there?" Klaus said.

Rudi shrugged. "Well, then we come back here."

Hendricks stopped pacing. "What do you think the chances are they're already in the American lines?"

"Hard to say. Fairly good. They're organized. They know exactly what they're doing. Once they start they go like a horde of locusts. They have to keep moving, and fast. It's secrecy and speed they depend on. Surprise. They push their way in before anyone has any idea."

"I see," Hendricks murmured.

From the other room Tasso stirred. "Major?"

Hendricks pushed the curtain back. "What?"

Tasso looked up at him lazily from the cot. "Have you any more American cigarettes left?"

Hendricks went into the room and sat down across from her, on a wood stool. He felt in his pockets. "No. All gone."

"Too bad."

"What nationality are you?" Hendricks asked her after a while.

"Russian."

"How did you get here?"

"Here?"

"This used to be France. This was part of Normandy. Did you come with the Soviet army?"

"Why?"

"Just curious." He studied her. She had taken off her coat, tossing it over the end of the cot. She was young, about twenty. Slim. Her long hair stretched out over the pillow. She was staring at him silently, her eyes dark and large.

"What's on your mind?" Tasso said.

"Nothing. How old are you?"

"Eighteen." She continued to watch him, unblinking, her arms behind her head. She had on Russian army pants and shirt. Gray-green. Thick leather belt with counter and cartridges. Medicine kit.

"You're in the Soviet army?"

"No."

"Where did you get the uniform?"

She shrugged. "It was given to me," she told him.

"How—how old were you when you came here?"

"Sixteen."

"That young?"

Her eyes narrowed. "What do you mean?"

Hendricks rubbed his jaw. "Your life would have been a lot different if there had been no war. Sixteen. You came here at sixteen. To live this way."

"I had to survive."

"I'm not moralizing."

"Your life would have been different, too," Tasso murmured. She reached down and unfastened one of her boots. She kicked the boot off, onto the floor. "Major, do you want to go in the other room? I'm sleepy."

"It's going to be a problem, the four of us here. It's going to be hard to live in these quarters. Are there just the two rooms?"

"Yes."

"How big was the cellar originally? Was it larger than this? Are there other rooms filled up with debris? We might be able to open one of them."

"Perhaps. I really don't know." Tasso loosened her belt. She made herself comfortable on the cot, unbuttoning her shirt. "You're sure you have no more cigarettes?"

"I had only one pack."

"Too bad. Maybe if we get back to your bunker we can find some." The other boot fell. Tasso reached up for the light cord. "Good night."

"You're going to sleep?"

"That's right."

The room plunged into darkness. Hendricks got up and made his way past the curtain, into the kitchen. And stopped, rigid.

Rudi stood against the wall, his face white and gleaming. His mouth opened and closed but no sounds came. Klaus stood in front of him, the muzzle of his pistol in Rudi's stomach. Neither of them moved. Klaus, his hand tight around the gun, his features set. Rudi, pale and silent, spread-eagled against the wall.

"What—" Hendricks muttered, but Klaus cut him off.

"Be quiet, Major, Come over here. Your gun. Get out your gun."

Hendricks drew his pistol. "What is it?"

"Cover him." Klaus motioned him forward. "Beside me. Hurry!"

Rudi moved a little, lowering his arms. He turned to Hendricks, licking his lips. The whites of his eyes shone wildly. Sweat dripped from his forehead, down his cheeks. He fixed his gaze on Hendricks. "Major, he's gone insane. Stop him." Rudi's voice was thin and hoarse, almost inaudible.

"What's going on?" Hendricks demanded.

Without lowering his pistol Klaus answered. "Major, remember our discussion? The Three Varieties? We knew about One and Three. But we didn't know about Two. At least, we didn't know before." Klaus's fingers tightened around the gun butt. "We didn't know before, but we know now."

He pressed the trigger. A burst of white heat rolled out of the gun, licking around Rudi.

"Major, this is the Second Variety."

Tasso swept the curtain aside. "Klaus! What did you do?"

Klaus turned from the charred form, gradually sinking down the wall onto the floor. "The Second Variety, Tasso. Now we know. We have all three types identified. The danger is less. I—"

Tasso stared past him at the remains of Rudi, at the blackened, smoldering fragments and bits of cloth. "You killed him."

"Him? *It*, you mean. I was watching. I had a feeling but I wasn't sure. At least, I wasn't sure before. But this evening I was certain." Klaus rubbed his pistol butt nervously. "We're lucky. Don't you understand? Another hour and it might—"

"You were *certain*?" Tasso pushed past him and bent down, over the steaming remains on the floor. Her face became hard. "Major, see for yourself. Bones. Flesh."

Hendricks bent down beside her. The remains were human remains. Seared flesh, charred bone fragments, part of a skull. Ligaments, viscera, blood. Blood forming a pool against the wall.

"No wheels," Tasso said calmly. She straightened up. "No wheels, no parts, no relays. Not a claw. Not the Second Variety." She folded her arms. "You're going to have to be able to explain this."

Klaus sat down at the table, all the color drained suddenly from his face. He put his head in his hands and rocked back and forth.

"Snap out of it." Tasso's fingers closed over his shoulder. "Why did you do it? Why did you kill him?"

"He was frightened," Hendricks said. "All this, the whole thing, building up around us."

"Maybe."

"What, then? What do you think?"

"I think he may have had a reason for killing Rudi. A good reason."

"What reason?"

"Maybe Rudi learned something."

Hendricks studied her bleak face. "About what?" he asked.

"About him. About Klaus."

Klaus looked up quickly. "You can see what she's trying to say. She thinks I'm the Second Variety. Don't you see, Major? Now she wants you to believe I killed him on purpose. That I'm—"

"Why did you kill him, then?" Tasso said.

"I told you." Klaus shook his head wearily. "I thought he was a claw. I thought I knew."

"Why?"

"I had been watching him. I was suspicious."

"Why?"

"I thought I had seen something. Heard something. I thought I—" He stopped.

"Go on."

"We were sitting at the table. Playing cards. You two were in the other room. It was silent. I thought I heard him—*whirr*."

There was silence.

"Do you believe that?" Tasso said to Hendricks.

"Yes. I believe what he says."

"I don't. I think he killed Rudi for a good purpose." Tasso touched the rifle resting in the corner of the room. "Major—"

"No." Hendricks shook his head. "Let's stop it right now. One is enough. We're afraid, the way he was. If we kill him we'll be doing what he did to Rudi."

Klaus looked gratefully up at him. "Thanks. I was afraid. You understand, don't you? Now she's afraid, the way I was. She wants to kill me."

"No more killing." Hendricks moved toward the end of the ladder. "I'm going above and try the transmitter once more. If I can't get them we're moving back toward my lines tomorrow morning."

Klaus rose quickly. "I'll come up with you and give you a hand."

THE NIGHT AIR was cold. The earth was cooling off. Klaus took a deep breath, filling his lungs. He and Hendricks stepped onto the ground, out of the tunnel. Klaus planted his feet wide apart, the rifle up, watching and listening. Hendricks crouched by the tunnel mouth, tuning the small transmitter.

"Any luck?" Klaus asked presently.

"Not yet."

"Keep trying. Tell them what happened."

Hendricks kept trying. Without success. Finally he lowered the antenna. "It's useless. They can't hear me. Or they hear me and won't answer. Or—"

"Or they don't exist."

"I'll try once more." Hendricks raised the antenna. "Scott, can you hear me? Come in!"

He listened. There was only static. Then, still very faintly—

"This is Scott."

His fingers tightened. "Scott! Is it you?"

"This is Scott."

Klaus squatted down. "Is it your command?"

"Scott, listen. Do you understand? About them, the claws. Did you get my message? Did you hear me?"

"Yes." Faintly. Almost inaudible. He could hardly make out the word.

"You got my message? Is everything all right at the bunker? None of them have got in?"

"Everything is all right."

"Have they tried to get in?"

The voice was weaker.

"No."

Hendricks turned to Klaus. "They're all right."

"Have they been attacked?"

"No." Hendricks pressed the phone tighter to his ear. "Scott, I can hardly hear you. Have you notified the Moon Base? Do they know? Are they alerted?"

No answer.

"Scott! Can you hear me?"

Silence.

Hendricks relaxed, sagging. "Faded out. Must be radiation pools."

Hendricks and Klaus looked at each other. Neither of them said anything. After a time Klaus said, "Did it sound like any of your men? Could you identify the voice?"

"It was too faint."

"You couldn't be certain?"

"No."

"Then it could have been—"

"I don't know. Now I'm not sure. Let's go back down and get the lid closed."

They climbed back down the ladder slowly, into the warm cellar. Klaus bolted the lid behind them. Tasso waited for them, her face expressionless.

"Any luck?" she asked.

Neither of them answered. "Well?" Klaus said at last. "What do you think, Major? Was it your officer, or was it one of *them*?"

"I don't know."

"Then we're just where we were before."

Hendricks stared down at the floor, his jaw set. "We'll have to go. To be sure."

"Anyhow, we have food here for only a few weeks. We'd have to go up after that, in any case."

"Apparently so."

"What's wrong?" Tasso demanded. "Did you get across to your bunker? What's the matter?"

"It may have been one of my men," Hendricks said slowly. "Or it may have been one of *them*. But we'll never know standing here." He examined his watch. "Let's turn in and get some sleep. We want to be up early tomorrow."

"Early?"

"Our best chance to get through the claws should be early in the morning," Hendricks said.

THE MORNING WAS crisp and clear. Major Hendricks studied the countryside through his field glasses.

"See anything?" Klaus said.

"No."

"Can you make out our bunkers?"

"Which way?"

"Here." Klaus took the glasses and adjusted them. "I know where to look." He looked a long time, silently.

Tasso came to the top of the tunnel and stepped up onto the ground. "Anything?"

"No." Klaus passed the glasses back to Hendricks. "They're out of sight. Come on. Let's not stay here."

The three of them made their way down the side of the ridge, sliding in the soft ash. Across a flat rock a lizard scuttled. They stopped instantly, rigid.

"What was it?" Klaus muttered.

"A lizard."

The lizard ran on, hurrying through the ash. It was exactly the same color as the ash.

"Perfect adaptation," Klaus said. "Proves we were right. Lysenko, I mean."

They reached the bottom of the ridge and stopped, standing close together, looking around them.

"Let's go." Hendricks started off. "It's a good long trip, on foot."

Klaus fell in beside him. Tasso walked behind, her pistol held alertly. "Major, I've been meaning to ask you something," Klaus said. "How did you run across the David? The one that was tagging you."

"I met it along the way. In some ruins."

"What did it say?"

"Not much. It said it was alone. By itself."

"You couldn't tell it was a machine? It talked like a living person? You never suspected?"

"It didn't say much. I noticed nothing unusual."

"It's strange, machines so much like people that you can be fooled. Almost alive. I wonder where it'll end."

"They're doing what you Yanks designed them to do," Tasso said. "You designed them to hunt out life and destroy. Human life. Wherever they find it."

Hendricks was watching Klaus intently. "Why did you ask me? What's on your mind?"

"Nothing," Klaus answered.

"Klaus thinks you're the Second Variety," Tasso said calmly, from behind them. "Now he's got his eye on you."

Klaus flushed. "Why not? We sent a runner to the Yank lines and *he* comes back. Maybe he thought he'd find some good game here."

Hendricks laughed harshly. "I came from the UN bunkers. There were human beings all around me."

"Maybe you saw an opportunity to get into the Soviet lines. Maybe you saw your chance. Maybe you—"

"The Soviet lines had already been taken over. Your lines had been invaded before I left my command bunker. Don't forget that."

Tasso came up beside him. "That proves nothing at all, Major."

"Why not?"

"There appears to be little communication between the varieties. Each is made in a different factory. They don't seem to work together. You might have started for the Soviet lines without knowing anything about the work of the other varieties. Or even what the other varieties were like."

"How do you know so much about the claws?" Hendricks said.

"I've seen them. I've observed them take over the Soviet bunkers."

"You know quite a lot," Klaus said. "Actually, you saw very little. Strange that you should have been such an acute observer."

Tasso laughed. "Do you suspect me, now?"

"Forget it," Hendricks said. They walked on in silence.

"Are we going the whole way on foot?" Tasso said, after a while. "I'm not used to walking." She gazed around at the plain of ash, stretching out on all sides of them, as far as they could see. "How dreary."

"It's like this all the way," Klaus said.

"In a way I wish you had been in your bunker when the attack came."

"Somebody else would have been with you, if not me," Klaus muttered.

Tasso laughed, putting her hands in her pockets. "I suppose so."

They walked on, keeping their eyes on the vast plain of silent ash around them.

THE SUN WAS setting. Hendricks made his way forward slowly, waving Tasso and Klaus back. Klaus squatted down, resting his gun butt against the ground.

Tasso found a concrete slab and sat down with a sigh. "It's good to rest."

"Be quiet," Klaus said sharply.

Hendricks pushed up to the top of the rise ahead of them. The same rise the Russian runner had come up, the day before. Hendricks dropped down, stretching himself out, peering through his glasses at what lay beyond.

Nothing was visible. Only ash and occasional trees. But there, not more than fifty yards ahead, was the entrance of the forward command bunker. The bunker from which he had come. Hendricks watched silently. No motion. No sign of life. Nothing stirred.

Klaus slithered up beside him. "Where is it?"

"Down there." Hendricks passed him the glasses. Clouds of ash rolled across the evening sky. The world was darkening. They had a couple of hours of light left, at the most. Probably not that much.

"I don't see anything," Klaus said.

"That tree there. The stump. By the pile of bricks. The entrance is to the right of the bricks."

"I'll have to take your word for it."

"You and Tasso cover me from here. You'll be able to sight all the way to the bunker entrance."

"You're going down alone?"

"With my wrist tab I'll be safe. The ground around the bunker is a living field of claws. They collect down in the ash. Like crabs. Without tabs you wouldn't have a chance."

"Maybe you're right."

"I'll walk slowly all the way. As soon as I know for certain—"

"If they're down inside the bunker you won't be able to get back up here. They go fast. You don't realize."

"What do you suggest?"

Klaus considered. "I don't know. Get them to come up to the surface. So you can see."

Hendricks brought his transmitter from his belt, raising the antenna. "Let's get started."

Klaus signaled to Tasso. She crawled expertly up the side of the rise to where they were sitting.

"He's going down alone," Klaus said. "We'll cover him from here. As soon as you see him start back, fire past him at once. They come quick."

"You're not very optimistic," Tasso said.

"No, I'm not."

Hendricks opened the breech of his gun, checking it carefully. "Maybe things are all right."

"You didn't see them. Hundreds of them. All the same. Pouring out like ants."

"I should be able to find out without going down all the way." Hendricks locked his gun, gripping it in one hand, the transmitter in the other. "Well, wish me luck."

Klaus put out his hand. "Don't go down until you're sure. Talk to them from up here. Make them show themselves."

Hendricks stood up. He stepped down the side of the rise.

A moment later he was walking slowly toward the pile of bricks and debris beside the dead tree stump. Toward the entrance of the forward command bunker.

Nothing stirred. He raised the transmitter, clicking it on. "Scott? Can you hear me?"

Silence.

"Scott! This is Hendricks. Can you hear me? I'm standing outside the bunker. You should be able to see me in the view sight."

He listened, the transmitter gripped tightly. No sound. Only static. He walked forward. A claw burrowed out of the ash and raced toward him. It halted a few feet away and then slunk off. A second claw appeared, one of the big ones with feelers. It moved toward him, studied him intently, and then fell in behind him, dogging respectfully after him, a few paces away. A moment later a second big claw joined it. Silently, the claws trailed him as he walked slowly toward the bunker.

Hendricks stopped, and behind him, the claws came to a halt. He was close now. Almost to the bunker steps.

"Scott! Can you hear me? I'm standing right above you. Outside. On the surface. Are you picking me up?"

He waited, holding his gun against his side, the transmitter tightly to his ear. Time passed. He strained to hear, but there was only silence. Silence, and faint static.

Then, distantly, metallically—

"This is Scott."

The voice was neutral. Cold. He could not identify it. But the earphone was minute.

"Scott! Listen. I'm standing right above you. I'm on the surface, looking down into the bunker entrance."

"Yes."

"Can you see me?"

"Yes."

"Through the view sight? You have the sight trained on me?"

"Yes."

Hendricks pondered. A circle of claws waited quietly around him, gray-metal bodies on all sides of him. "Is everything all right in the bunker? Nothing unusual has happened?"

"Everything is all right."

"Will you come up to the surface? I want to see you for a moment." Hendricks took a deep breath. "Come up here with me. I want to talk to you."

"Come down."

"I'm giving you an order."

Silence.

"Are you coming?" Hendricks listened. There was no response. "I order you to come to the surface."

"Come down."

Hendricks set his jaw. "Let me talk to Leone."

There was a long pause. He listened to the static. Then a voice came, hard, thin, metallic. The same as the other. "This is Leone."

"Hendricks. I'm on the surface. At the bunker entrance. I want one of you to come up here."

"Come down."

"Why come down? I'm giving you an order!"

Silence. Hendricks lowered the transmitter. He looked carefully around him. The entrance was just ahead. Almost at his feet. He lowered the antenna and fastened the transmitter to his belt. Carefully, he gripped his gun with both hands. He moved forward, a step at a time. If they could see him they knew he was starting toward the entrance. He closed his eyes a moment.

Then he put his foot on the first step that led downward.

Two Davids came up at him, their faces identical and expressionless. He blasted them into particles. More came rushing silently up, a whole pack of them. All exactly the same.

Hendricks turned and raced back, away from the bunker, back toward the rise.

At the top of the rise Tasso and Klaus were firing down. The small claws were already streaking up toward them, shining metal spheres going fast, racing frantically through the ash. But he had no time to think about that. He knelt down, aiming at the bunker entrance, gun against his cheek. The Davids were coming out in groups, clutching their teddy bears, their thin knobby legs pumping as they ran up the steps to the surface. Hendricks fired into the main body of them. They burst apart, wheels and springs flying in all directions. He fired again, through the mist of particles.

A giant lumbering figure rose up in the bunker entrance, tall and swaying. Hendricks paused, amazed. A man, a soldier. With one leg, supporting himself with a crutch.

"Major!" Tasso's voice came. More firing. The huge figure moved forward, Davids swarming around it. Hendricks broke out of his freeze. The First Variety. The Wounded Soldier. He aimed and fired. The soldier burst into bits, parts and relays flying. Now many Davids were out on the flat ground, away from the bunker. He fired again and again, moving slowly back, half-crouching and aiming.

From the rise, Klaus fired down. The side of the rise was alive with claws making their way up. Hendricks retreated toward the rise, running and crouching. Tasso had left Klaus and was circling slowly to the right, moving away from the rise.

A David slipped up toward him, its small white face expressionless, brown hair hanging down in its eyes. It bent over suddenly, opening its arms. Its teddy bear hurtled down and leaped across the ground, bounding toward him. Hendricks fired. The bear and the David both dissolved. He grinned, blinking. It was like a dream.

"Up here!" Tasso's voice. Hendricks made his way toward her. She was over by some columns of concrete, walls of a ruined building. She was firing past him, with the hand pistol Klaus had given her.

"Thanks." He joined her, gasping for breath. She pulled him back, behind the concrete, fumbling at her belt.

"Close your eyes!" She unfastened a globe from her waist. Rapidly, she unscrewed the cap, locking it into place. "Close your eyes and get down."

She threw the bomb. It sailed in an arc, an expert, rolling and bouncing to the entrance of the bunker. Two Wounded Soldiers stood uncertainly by the brick pile. More Davids poured from behind them, out onto the plain. One of the Wounded Soldiers moved toward the bomb, stooping awkwardly down to pick it up.

The bomb went off. The concussion whirled Hendricks around, throwing him on his face. A hot wind rolled over him. Dimly he saw Tasso standing behind the columns, firing slowly and methodically at the Davids coming out of the raging clouds of white fire.

Back along the rise Klaus struggled with a ring of claws circling around him. He retreated, blasting at them and moving back, trying to break through the ring.

Hendricks struggled to his feet. His head ached. He could hardly see. Everything was licking at him, raging and whirling. His right arm would not move.

Tasso pulled back toward him. "Come on. Let's go."

"Klaus—he's still up there."

"Come on!" Tasso dragged Hendricks back, away from the columns. Hendricks shook his head, trying to clear it. Tasso led him rapidly away, her eyes intense and bright, watching for claws that had escaped the blast.

One David came out of the rolling clouds of flame. Tasso blasted it. No more appeared.

"But Klaus. What about him?" Hendricks stopped, standing unsteadily. "He—"

"Come on!"

They retreated, moving farther and farther away from the bunker. A few small claws followed them for a little while and then gave up, turning back and going off.

At last Tasso stopped. "We can stop here and get our breaths."

Hendricks sat down on some heaps of debris. He wiped his neck, gasping. "We left Klaus back there."

Tasso said nothing. She opened her gun, sliding a fresh round of blast cartridges into place.

Hendricks stared at her, dazed. "You left him back there on purpose."

Tasso snapped the gun together. She studied the heaps of rubble around them, her face expressionless. As if she were watching for something.

"What is it?" Hendricks demanded. "What are you looking for? Is something coming?" He shook his head, trying to understand. What was she doing? What was she waiting for? He could see nothing. Ash lay all around them, ash and ruins. Occasional stark tree trunks, without leaves or branches. "What—"

Tasso cut him off. "Be still." Her eyes narrowed. Suddenly her gun came up. Hendricks turned, following her gaze.

Back the way they had come a figure appeared. The figure walked unsteadily toward them. Its clothes were torn. It limped as it made its way along, going very slowly and carefully. Stopping now and then, resting and getting its strength. Once it almost fell. It stood for a moment, trying to steady itself. Then it came on.

Klaus.

Hendricks stood up. "Klaus!" He started toward him. "How the hell did you—"

Tasso fired. Hendricks swung back. She fired again, the blast passing him, a searing line of heat. The beam caught Klaus in the chest. He exploded, gears and wheels flying. For a moment he continued to walk. Then he swayed back and forth. He crashed to the ground, his arms flung out. A few more wheels rolled away.

Silence.

Tasso turned to Hendricks. "Now you understand why he killed Rudi."

Hendricks sat down again slowly. He shook his head. He was numb. He could not think.

"Do you see?" Tasso said. "Do you understand?"

Hendricks said nothing. Everything was slipping away from him, faster and faster. Darkness, rolling and plucking at him.

He closed his eyes.

HENDRICKS OPENED HIS eyes slowly. His body ached all over. He tried to sit up but needles of pain shot through his arm and shoulder. He gasped.

"Don't try to get up," Tasso said. She bent down, putting her cold hand against his forehead.

It was night. A few stars glinted above, shining through the drifting clouds of ash. Hendricks lay back, his teeth locked. Tasso watched him impassively. She had built a fire with some wood and weeds. The fire licked feebly, hissing at a metal cup suspended over it. Everything was silent. Unmoving darkness, beyond the fire.

"So he was the Second Variety," Hendricks murmured.

"I had always thought so."

"Why didn't you destroy him sooner?" He wanted to know.

"You held me back." Tasso crossed to the fire to look into the metal cup. "Coffee. It'll be ready to drink in a while."

She came back and sat down beside him. Presently she opened her pistol and began to disassemble the firing mechanism, studying it intently.

"This is a beautiful gun," Tasso said, half aloud. "The construction is superb."

"What about them? The claws."

"The concussion from the bomb put most of them out of action. They're delicate. Highly organized, I suppose."

"The Davids, too?"

"Yes."

"How did you happen to have a bomb like that?"

Tasso shrugged. "We designed it. You shouldn't underestimate our technology, Major. Without such a bomb you and I would no longer exist."

"Very useful."

Tasso stretched out her legs, warming her feet in the heat of the fire. "It surprised me that you did not seem to understand, after he killed Rudi. Why did you think he—"

"I told you. I thought he was afraid."

"Really? You know, Major, for a little while I suspected you. Because you wouldn't let me kill him. I thought you might be protecting him." She laughed.

"Are we safe here?" Hendricks asked presently.

"For a while. Until they get reinforcements from some other area." Tasso began to clear the interior of the gun with a bit of rag. She finished and pushed the mechanism back into place. She closed the gun, running her finger along the barrel.

"We were lucky," Hendricks murmured.

"Yes. Very lucky."

"Thanks for pulling me away."

Tasso did not answer. She glanced up at him, her eyes bright in the firelight. Hendricks examined his arm. He could not move his fingers. His whole side seemed numb. Down inside him was a dull steady ache.

"How do you feel?" Tasso asked.

"My arm is damaged."

"Anything else?"

"Internal injuries."

"You didn't get down when the bomb went off."

Hendricks said nothing. He watched Tasso pour the coffee from the cup into a flat metal pan. She brought it over to him.

"Thanks." He struggled up enough to drink. It was hard to swallow. His insides turned over and he pushed the pan away. "That's all I can drink now."

Tasso drank the rest. Time passed. The clouds of ash moved across the dark sky above them. Hendricks rested, his mind blank. After a while he became aware that Tasso was standing over him, gazing down at him.

"What is it?" he murmured.

"Do you feel any better?"

"Some."

"You know, Major, if I hadn't dragged you away they would have got you. You would be dead. Like Rudi."

"I know."

"Do you want to know why I brought you out? I could have left you. I could have left you there."

"Why did you bring me out?"

"Because we have to get away from here." Tasso stirred the fire with a stick, peering calmly down into it. "No human being can live here. When their reinforcements come we won't have a chance. I've pondered about it while you were unconscious. We have perhaps three hours before they come."

"And you expect me to get us away?"

"That's right. I expect you to get us out of here."

"Why me?"

"Because I don't know any way." Her eyes shone at him in the light, bright and steady. "If you can't get us out of here they'll kill us within three hours. I see nothing else ahead. Well, Major? What are you going to do? I've been waiting all night. While you were unconscious I sat here, waiting and listening. It's almost dawn. The night is almost over."

Hendricks considered. "It's curious," he said at last.

"Curious?"

"That you should think I can get us out of here. I wonder what you think I can do."

"Can you get us to the Moon Base?"

"The Moon Base? How?"

"There must be some way."

Hendricks shook his head. "No. There's no way that I know of."

Tasso said nothing. For a moment her steady gaze wavered. She ducked her head, turning abruptly away. She scrambled to her feet. "More coffee?"

"No."

"Suit yourself." Tasso drank silently. He could not see her face. He lay back against the ground, deep in thought, trying to concentrate. It was hard to think. His head still hurt. And the numbing daze still hung over him.

"There might be one way," he said suddenly.

"Oh?"

"How soon is dawn?"

"Two hours. The sun will be coming up shortly."

"There's supposed to be a ship near here. I've never seen it. But I know it exists."

"What kind of a ship?" Her voice was sharp.

"A rocket cruiser."

"Will it take us off? To the Moon Base?"

"It's supposed to. In case of emergency." He rubbed his forehead.

"What's wrong?"

"My head. It's hard to think. I can hardly—hardly concentrate. The bomb."

"Is the ship near here?" Tasso slid over beside him, settling down on her haunches. "How far is it? Where is it?"

"I'm trying to think."

Her fingers dug into his arm. "Nearby?" Her voice was like iron. "Where would it be? Would they store it underground? Hidden underground?"

"Yes. In a storage locker."

"How do we find it? Is it marked? Is there a code marker to iden-tify it?"

Hendricks concentrated. "No. No markings. No code symbol."

"What, then?"

"A sign."

"What sort of sign?"

Hendricks did not answer. In the flickering light his eyes were glazed, two sightless orbs. Tasso's fingers dug into his arm.

"What sort of sign? What is it?"

"I — I can't think. Let me rest."

"All right." She let go and stood up. Hendricks lay back against the ground, his eyes closed. Tasso walked away from him, her hands in her pockets. She kicked a rock out of her way and stood staring up at the sky. The night blackness was already beginning to fade into gray. Morning was coming.

Tasso gripped her pistol and walked around the fire in a circle, back and forth. On the ground Major Hendricks lay, his eyes closed, unmoving. The grayness rose in the sky, higher and higher. The landscape became visible, fields of ash stretching out in all directions. Ash and ruins of buildings, a wall here and there, heaps of concrete, the naked trunk of a tree.

The air was cold and sharp. Somewhere a long way off a bird made a few bleak sounds.

Hendricks stirred. He opened his eyes. "Is it dawn? Already?"

"Yes."

Hendricks sat up a little. "You wanted to know something. You were asking me."

"Do you remember now?"

"Yes."

"What is it?" She tensed. "What?" she repeated sharply.

"A well. A ruined well. It's in a storage locker under a well."

"A well." Tasso relaxed. "Then we'll find a well." She looked at her watch. "We have about an hour, Major. Do you think we can find it in an hour?"

"Give me a hand up," Hendricks said.

Tasso put her pistol away and helped him to his feet. "This is going to be difficult."

"Yes, it is." Hendricks set his lips tightly. "I don't think we're going to go very far."

They began to walk. The early sun cast a little warmth down on them. The land was flat and barren, stretching out gray and lifeless as far as they could see. A few birds sailed silently, far above them, circling slowly.

"See anything?" Hendricks said. "Any claws?"

"No. Not yet."

They passed through some ruins, upright concrete and bricks. A cement foundation. Rats scuttled away. Tasso jumped back warily.

"This used to be a town," Hendricks said. "A village. Provincial village. This was all grape country, once. Where we are now."

They came onto a ruined street, weeds and cracks criss-crossing it. Over to the right a stone chimney stuck up.

"Be careful," he warned her.

A pit yawned, an open basement. Ragged ends of pipes jutted up, twisted and bent. They passed part of a house, a bathtub turned on its side. A broken chair. A few spoons and bits of china dishes. In the center of the street the ground had sunk away. The depression was filled with weeds and debris and bones.

"Over here," Hendricks murmured.

"This way?"

"To the right."

They passed the remains of a heavy-duty tank. Hendricks's belt counter clicked ominously. The tank had been radiation-blasted. A few feet from the tank a mumified body lay sprawled out, mouth open. Beyond the road was a flat field. Stones and weeds, and bits of broken glass.

"There," Hendricks said.

A stone well jutted up, sagging and broken. A few boards lay across it. Most of the well had sunk into rubble. Hendricks walked unsteadily toward it, Tasso beside him.

"Are you certain about this?" Tasso said. "This doesn't look like anything."

"I'm sure." Hendricks sat down at the edge of the well, his teeth locked. His breath came quickly. He wiped perspiration from his face. "This was arranged so the senior command officer could get away. If anything happened. If the bunker fell."

"That was you?"

"Yes."

"Where is the ship? Is it here?"

"We're standing on it." Hendricks ran his hands over the surface of the well stones. "The eye-lock responds to me, not to anybody else. It's my ship. Or it was supposed to be."

There was a sharp click. Presently they heard a low grating sound from below them.

"Step back," Hendricks said. He and Tasso moved away from the well.

A section of the ground slid back. A metal frame pushed slowly up through the ash, shoving bricks and weeds out of the way. The action ceased as the ship nosed into view.

"There it is," Hendricks said.

The ship was small. It rested quietly, suspended in its mesh frame like a blunt needle. A rain of ash sifted down into the dark cavity from which the ship had been raised. Hendricks made his way over to it. He mounted the mesh and unscrewed the hatch, pulling it back. Inside the ship the control banks and the pressure seat were visible.

Tasso came and stood beside him, gazing into the ship. "I'm not accustomed to rocket piloting," she said after a while.

Hendricks glanced at her. "I'll do the piloting."

"Will you? There's only one seat, Major, I can see it's built to carry only a single person."

Hendricks's breathing changed. He studied the interior of the ship intently. Tasso was right. There was only one seat. The ship was built to carry only one person. "I see," he said slowly. "And the one person is you."

She nodded. "Of course."

"Why?"

"You can't go. You might not live through the trip. You're injured. You probably wouldn't get there."

"An interesting point. But you see, I know where the Moon Base is. And you don't. You might fly around for months and not find it. It's well hidden. Without knowing what to look for—"

"I'll have to take my chances. Maybe I won't find it. Not by myself. But I think you'll give me all the information I need. Your life depends on it."

"How?"

"If I find the Moon Base in time, perhaps I can get them to send a ship back to pick you up. If I find the Base in time. If not, then you haven't a chance. I imagine there are supplies on the ship. They will last me long enough—"

Hendricks moved quickly. But his injured arm betrayed him. Tasso ducked, sliding lithely aside. Her hand came up, lightning fast. Hendricks saw the gun butt coming. He tried to ward off the blow, but she was too fast. The metal butt struck against the side of his head, just above his ear. Numbing pain rushing through him. Pain and rolling clouds of blackness. He sank down, sliding to the ground.

Dimly, he was aware that Tasso was standing over him, kicking him with her toe.

"Major! Wake up."

He opened his eyes, groaning.

"Listen to me." She bent down, the gun pointed at his face. "I have to hurry. There isn't much time left. The ship is ready to go, but you must give me the information I need before I leave."

Hendricks shook his head, trying to clear it.

"Hurry up! Where is the Moon Base? How do I find it? What do I look for?"

Hendricks said nothing.

"Answer me!"

"Sorry."

"Major, the ship is loaded with provisions. I can coast for weeks. I'll find the Base eventually. And in a half-hour you'll be dead. Your only chance of survival—" She broke off.

Along the slope, by some crumbling ruins, something moved. Something in the ash. Tasso turned quickly, aiming. She fired. A puff of flame leaped. Something scuttled away, rolling across the ash. She fired again. The claw burst apart, wheels flying.

"See?" Tasso said. "A scout. It won't be long."

"You'll bring them back here to get me?"

"Yes. As soon as possible."

Hendricks looked up at her. He studied her intently. "You're telling the truth?" A strange expression had come over his face, an avid hunger. "You will come back for me? You'll get me to the Moon Base?"

"I'll get you to the Moon Base. But tell me where it is! There's only a little time left."

"All right." Hendricks picked up a piece of rock, pulling himself to a sitting position. "Watch."

Hendricks began to scratch in the ash. Tasso stood by him, watching the motion of the rock. Hendricks was sketching a crude lunar map.

"This is the Appenine range. Here is the Crater of Archimedes, the Moon Base is beyond the end of the Appenine, about two hundred miles. I don't know exactly where. No one on Terra knows. But when you're over the Appenine, signal with one red flare and a green flare, followed by two red flares in quick succession. The Base monitor will record your signal. The Base is under the surface, of course. They'll guide you down with magnetic grapples."

"And the controls? Can I operate them?"

"The controls are virtually automatic. All you have to do is give the right signal at the right time."

"I will."

"The seat absorbs most of the takeoff shock. Air and temperature are automatically controlled. The ship will leave Terra and pass out into free space. It'll line itself up with the Moon, falling into an orbit around it, about a hundred miles above the surface. The orbit will carry you over the Base. When you're in the region of the Appenine, release the signal rockets."

Tasso slid into the ship and lowered herself into the pressure seat. The arm locks folded automatically around her. She fingered the controls. "Too bad you're not going, Major. All this put here for you, and you can't make the trip."

"Leave me the pistol."

Tasso pulled the pistol from her belt. She held it in her hand, weighing it thoughtfully. "Don't go too far from this location. It'll be hard to find you, as it is."

"No. I'll stay here by the well."

Tasso gripped the takeoff switch, running her fingers over the smooth metal. "A beautiful ship, Major. Well built. I admire your workmanship. You people have always done good work. You build fine things. Your work, your creations, are your greatest achievement."

"Give me the pistol," Hendricks said impatiently, holding out his hand. He struggled to his feet.

"Good-bye, Major." Tasso tossed the pistol past Hendricks. The pistol clattered against the ground, bouncing and rolling away. Hendricks hurried after it. He bent down, snatching it up.

The hatch of the ship clanged shut. The bolts fell into place. Hendricks made his way back. The inner door was being sealed. He raised the pistol unsteadily.

There was a shattering roar. The ship burst up from its metal cage, fusing the mesh behind it. Hendricks cringed, pulling back. The ship shot up into the rolling clouds of ash, disappearing into the sky.

Hendricks stood watching a long time, until even the streamer had dissipated. Nothing stirred. The morning air was chill and silent. He began to walk aimlessly back the way they had come. Better to keep moving around. It would be a long time before help came—if it came at all.

He searched his pockets until he found a package of cigarettes. He lit one grimly. They had all wanted cigarettes from him. But cigarettes were scarce.

A lizard slithered by him, through the ash. He halted, rigid. The lizard disappeared. Above, the sun rose higher in the sky. Some flies landed on a flat rock to one side of him. Hendricks kicked at them with his foot.

It was getting hot. Sweat trickled down his face, into his collar. His mouth was dry.

Presently he stopped walking and sat down on some debris. He unfastened his medicine kit and swallowed a few narcotic capsules. He looked around him. Where was he?

Something lay ahead. Stretched out on the ground. Silent and unmoving.

Hendricks drew his gun quickly. It looked like a man. Then he remembered. It was the remains of Klaus. The Second Variety. Where Tasso had blasted him. He could see wheels and relays and metal parts, strewn around on the ash. Glittering and sparkling in the sunlight.

Hendricks got to his feet and walked over. He nudged the inert form with his foot, turning it over a little. He could see the metal hull, the aluminum ribs and struts. More wiring fell out. Like viscera. Heaps of wiring, switches and relays. Endless motors and rods.

He bent down. The brain was visible. He gazed at it. A maze of circuits. Miniature tubes. Wires as fine as hair. He touched the brain cage. It swung aside. The type plate was visible. Hendricks studied the plate.

And blanched.

IV—IV.

For a long time he stared at the plate. Fourth Variety. Not the Second. They had been wrong. There were more types. Not just three. Many more, perhaps. At least four. And Klaus wasn't the Second Variety.

But if Klaus wasn't the Second Variety—

Suddenly he tensed. Something was coming, walking through the ash beyond the hill. What was it? He strained to see. Figures coming slowly along, making their way through the ash.

Coming toward him.

Hendricks crouched quickly, raising his gun. Sweat dripped down into his eyes. He fought down rising panic, as the figures neared.

The first was a David. The David saw him and increased its pace. The others hurried behind it. A second David. A third. Three Davids, all alike, coming toward him silently, without expression, their thin legs rising and falling. Clutching their teddy bears.

He aimed and fired. The first two Davids dissolved into particles. The third came on. And the figure behind it. Climbing silently toward him across the gray ash. A Wounded Soldier, towering over the David. And—

AND BEHIND THE Wounded Soldier came two Tassos, walking side by side. Heavy belt, Russian army pants, shirt, long hair. The familiar figure, as he had seen her only a little while before. Sitting in the pressure seat of the ship. Two slim, silent figures, both identical.

They were very near. The David bent down suddenly, dropping its teddy bear. The bear raced across the ground. Automatically, Hendricks's fingers tightened around the trigger. The bear was gone, dissolved into mist. The two Tasso Types moved on, expressionless, walking side by side, through the gray ash.

When they were almost to him, Hendricks raised the pistol waist high and fired.

The two Tassos dissolved. But already a new group was starting up the rise, five or six Tassos, all identical, a line of them coming rapidly toward him.

And he had given her the ship and the signal code. Because of him she was on her way to the moon, to the Moon Base. He had made it possible.

He had been right about the bomb, after all. It had been designed with knowledge of the other types, the David Type and the Wounded Soldier Type. And the Klaus Type. Not designed by human beings. It had been designed by one of the underground factories, apart from all human contact.

The line of Tassos came up to him. Hendricks braced himself, watching them calmly. The familiar face, the belt, the heavy shirt, the bomb carefully in place.

The bomb—

As the Tassos reached for him, a last ironic thought drifted through Hendricks's mind. He felt a little better, thinking about it. The bomb. Made by the Second Variety to destroy the other varieties. Made for that end alone.

They were already beginning to design weapons to use against each other.

Joe W. Haldeman

Praised for its authentic portrayal of the emotional detachment and psychological dislocation of soldiers in a millennium-long future war, Joe Haldeman's first science fiction novel, The Forever War, won both the Hugo and Nebula Awards when it was published in 1974 and was later adapted into a three-part graphic-novel series. Since then, Haldeman has returned to the theme of future war several times, notably in his trilogy Worlds, Worlds Apart, and Worlds Enough and Time, about a future Earth facing nuclear extinction, and Forever Peace, a further exploration of the dehumanizing potential of armed conflict. Haldeman's other novels include Mindbridge, All My Sins Remembered, and the alternate-world opus The Hemingway Hoax, expanded from his Nebula Award–winning novella of the same name. Haldeman's stories have been collected in Infinite Dreams and Dealing in Futures, and several of his essays are mixed with fiction in Vietnam and Other Alien Worlds. His powerful non–science fiction writing includes War Year, drawn from experiences during his tour of duty in Vietnam, and 1968, a portrait of America in the Vietnam era. He has also coedited the anthologies Body Armor 2000, Space-fighters, and Supertanks.

HERO

Joe W. Haldeman

1

"Tonight we're going to show you eight silent ways to kill a man." The guy who said that was a sergeant who didn't look five years older than I. Ergo, as they say, he couldn't possibly ever have killed a man, not in combat, silently or otherwise.

I already knew eighty ways to kill people, though most of them were pretty noisy. I sat up straight in my chair and assumed a look of polite attention and fell asleep with my eyes open. So did most everybody else. We'd learned that they never schedule anything important for these after-chop classes.

The projector woke me up and I sat through a short movie showing the "eight silent ways." Some of the actors must have been brainwipes, since they were actually killed.

After the movie a girl in the front row raised her hand. The sergeant nodded at her and she rose to parade rest. Not bad-looking, but kind of chunky about the neck and shoulders. Everybody gets that way after carrying a heavy pack around for a couple of months.

"Sir"—we had to call sergeants "sir" until graduation—"most of those methods, really, they looked . . . kind of silly."

"For instance?"

"Like killing a man with a blow to the kidneys, from an entrenching tool. I mean, when would you *actually* just have an entrenching tool, and no gun or knife? And why not just bash him over the head with it?"

"He might have a helmet on," he said reasonably.

"Besides, Taurans probably don't even *have* kidneys!"

He shrugged. "Probably they don't." This was 1997, and we'd never seen a Tauran: hadn't even found any pieces of Taurans bigger than a scorched chromosome. "But their body chemistry is similar to ours, and we have to assume they're similarly complex creatures. They *must* have weaknesses, vulnerable spots. You have to find out where they are.

"That's the important thing." He stabbed a finger at the screen. "That's why those eight convicts got caulked for your benefit . . . you've got to find out how to kill Taurans, and be able to do it whether you have a megawatt laser or just an emery board."

She sat back down, not looking too convinced.

"Any more questions?" Nobody raised a hand.

"O.K.—tench-hut!" We staggered upright and he looked at us expectantly.

"Screw you, sir," came the tired chorus.

"Louder!"

"SCREW YOU, SIR!"

One of the army's less-inspired morale devices.

"That's better. Don't forget, predawn maneuvers tomorrow. Chop at 0330, first formation, 0400. Anybody sacked after 0340 gets one stripe. Dismissed."

I zipped up my coverall and went across the snow to the lounge for a cup of soya and a joint. I'd always been able to get by on five or six hours of sleep, and this was the only time I could be by myself, out of the army for a while. Looked at the newsfax for a few minutes. Another ship got caulked, out by Aldebaran sector. That was four years ago. They were mounting a reprisal fleet, but it'll take four years more for them to get out there. By then, the Taurans would have every portal planet sewed up tight.

Back at the billet, everybody else was sacked and the main lights were out. The whole company'd been dragging ever since we got back from the two-week lunar training. I dumped my clothes in the locker, checked the roster and found out I was in bunk 31. Damn it, right under the heater.

I slipped through the curtain as quietly as possible so as not to wake up my bunkmate. Couldn't see who it was, but I couldn't have cared less. I slipped under the blanket.

"You're late, Mandella," a voice yawned. It was Rogers.

"Sorry I woke you up," I whispered.

" 'Sallright." She snuggled over and clasped me spoon-fashion. She was warm and reasonably soft. I patted her hip in what I hoped was a brotherly fashion. "Night, Rogers."

"G'night, Stallion." She returned the gesture, a good deal more pointedly.

Why do you always get the tired ones when you're ready and the randy ones when you're tired? I bowed to the inevitable.

2

"Awright, let's get some *back* inta that! Stringer team! Move it up—move up!"

A warm front had come in about midnight and the snow had turned to sleet. The permaplast stringer weighed five hundred pounds and was a bitch to handle, even when it wasn't covered with ice. There were four of us, two at each end, carrying the plastic girder with frozen fingertips. Rogers and I were partners.

"Steel!" the guy behind me yelled, meaning that he was losing his hold. It wasn't steel, but it was heavy enough to break your foot. Everybody let go and hopped away. It splashed slush and mud all over us.

"Damn it, Petrov," Rogers said, "why didn't you go out for Star Fleet or maybe the Red Cross? This damn thing's not that damn heavy." Most of the girls were a little more circumspect in their speech.

"Awright, get a *move* on, stringers—Epoxy team! Dog 'em! Dog 'em!"

Our two epoxy people ran up, swinging their buckets. "Let's go, Mandella. I'm freezin'."

"Me, too," the girl said earnestly.

"One—two—heave!" We got the thing up again and staggered toward the bridge. It was about three-quarters completed. Looked as if the Second Platoon was going to beat us. I wouldn't give a damn, but the platoon that got their bridge built first got to fly home. Four miles of muck for the rest of us, and no rest before chop.

We got the stringer in place, dropped it with a clank, and fitted the static clamps that held it to the rise-beams. The female half of the epoxy team started slopping glue on it before we even had it secured. Her partner was waiting for the stringer on the other side. The floor team was waiting at the foot of the bridge, each one holding a piece of the light stressed permaplast over his head, like an umbrella. They were dry and clean. I wondered aloud what they had done to deserve it, and Rogers suggested a couple of colorful, but unlikely possibilities.

We were going back to stand by the next stringer when the Field First—he was named Dougelstein, but we called him "Awright"—blew a whistle and bellowed, "Awright, soldier boys and girls, ten minutes. Smoke 'em if you got 'em." He reached into his pocket and turned on the control that heated our coveralls.

Rogers and I sat down on our end of the stringer and I took out my weed box. I had lots of joints, but we weren't allowed to smoke them until after night-chop. The only tobacco I had was a cigarro butt about three inches long. I lit it on the side of the box; it wasn't too bad after the first couple of puffs. Rogers took a puff to be sociable, but made a face and gave it back.

"Were you in school when you got drafted?" she asked.

"Yeah. Just got a degree in Physics. Was going after a teacher's certificate."

She nodded soberly. "I was in Biology. . . ."

"Figures." I ducked a handful of slush. "How far?"

"Six years, bachelor's and technical." She slid her boot along the ground, turning up a ridge of mud and slush the consistency of freezing ice milk. "Why the hell did this have to happen?"

I shrugged. It didn't call for an answer, least of all the answer that the UNEF kept giving us. Intellectual and physical elite of the planet, going out to guard humanity against the Tauran menace. It was all just a big experience. See whether we could goad the Taurans into ground action.

Awright blew the whistle two minutes early, as expected, but Rogers and I and the other two stringers got to sit for a minute while the epoxy and floor teams finished covering our stringer. It got cold fast, sitting there with our suits turned off, but we remained inactive, on principle.

I really didn't see the sense of us having to train in the cold. Typical army half-logic. Sure, it was going to be cold where we were going; but not ice-cold or snow-cold. Almost by definition, a portal planet remained within a degree or two of absolute zero all the time, since collapsars don't shine—and the first chill you felt would mean that you were a dead man.

TWELVE YEARS BEFORE, when I was ten years old, they had discovered the collapsar jump. Just fling an object at a collapsar with sufficient speed, and it pops out in some other part of the galaxy. It didn't take long to figure out the formula that predicted where it would come out; it just traveled along the same "line"—actually an Einsteinian geodesic—it would have followed if the collapsar hadn't been in the way—until it reaches another collapsar field, whereupon it reappears, repelled with the same speed it had approaching the original collapsar. Travel time between the two collapsars is exactly zero.

It made a lot of work for mathematical physicists, who had to redefine simultaneity, then tear down general relativity and build it back up again. And it made the politicians very happy, because now they could send a shipload of colonists to Fomalhaut for less than it once cost to put a brace of men on the Moon. There were a lot of people the politicians would just love to see on Fomalhaut, implementing a glorious adventure instead of stirring up trouble at home.

The ships were always accompanied by an automated probe that followed a couple of million miles behind. We knew about the portal planets, little bits of flotsam that whirled around the collapsars; the purpose of the drone was to come back and tell us in the event that a ship had smacked into a portal planet at .999 of the speed of light.

That particular catastrophe never happened, but one day a drone did come limping back alone. Its data were analyzed, and it turned out that the colonists' ship had been pursued by another vessel and destroyed. This happened near Aldebaran, in the constellation Taurus, but since "Aldebaranian" is a little hard to handle, they named the enemy Taurans.

Colonizing vessels thenceforth went out protected by an armed guard. Often the armed guard went out alone, and finally the colonization effort itself slowed to a token trickle. The United Nations Exploratory and Colonization Group got shortened to UNEF, United Nations Exploratory Force, emphasis on the "force."

Then some bright lad in the General Assembly decided that we ought to field an army of footsoldiers to guard the portal planets of the nearer collapsars. This led to the Elite Conscription Act of 1996 and the most rigorously selected army in the history of warfare.

So here we are, fifty men and fifty women, with IQ's over 150 and bodies of unusual health and strength, slogging elitely through the mud and slush of central Missouri, reflecting on how useful our skill in building bridges will be, on worlds where the only fluid will be your occasional standing pool of liquid helium.

3

About a month later, we left for our final training exercise; maneuvers on the planet Charon. Though nearing perihelion, it was still more than twice as far from the sun as Pluto.

The troopship was a converted "cattlewagon," made to carry two hundred colonists and assorted bushes and beasts. Don't think it was roomy, though, just because there were half that many of us. Most of the excess space was taken up with extra reaction mass and ordnance.

The whole trip took three weeks, accelerating at 2 Gs halfway; decelerating the other half. Our top speed, as we roared by the orbit of Pluto, was around one twentieth of the speed of light—not quite enough for relativity to rear its complicated head.

Three weeks of carrying around twice as much weight as normal . . . it's no picnic. We did some cautious exercises three times a day, and remained horizontal as much as possible. Still, we had several broken bones and serious dislocations. The men had to wear special supporters. It was almost impossible to sleep, what with nightmares of choking and being crushed, and the necessity of rolling over periodically to prevent blood pooling and bedsores. One girl got so fatigued that she almost slept through the experience of having a rib rub through to the open air.

I'd been in space several times before, so when we finally stopped decelerating and went into free fall, it was nothing but a relief. But some people had never been out, except for our training on the Moon, and succumbed to the sudden vertigo and disorientation. The rest of us cleaned up after them, floating through the quarters with sponges and inspirators to suck up globules of partly-digested "Concentrate, High-protein, Low-residue, Beef Flavor (Soya)."

A shuttle took us down to the surface in three trips. I waited for the last one, along with everybody else who wasn't bothered by free fall.

We had a good view of Charon, coming down from orbit. There wasn't much to see, though. It was just a dim, off-white sphere with a few smudges on it. We landed about two hundred meters from the base. A pressurized crawler came out and mated with the ferry, so we didn't have to suit up. We clanked and squeaked up to the main building, a featureless box of grayish plastic.

Inside, the walls were the same inspired color. The rest of the company was sitting at desks, chattering away. There was a seat next to Freeland.

"Jeff—feeling better?" He still looked a little pale.

"If the gods had meant for man to survive in free fall, they would have given him a cast-iron glottis. Somewhat better. Dying for a smoke."

"Yeah."

"*You* seemed to take it all right. Went up in school, didn't you?"

"Senior thesis in vacuum welding, yeah, three weeks in Earth orbit." I sat back and reached for my weed box, for the thousandth time. It still wasn't there, of course. The Life Support Unit didn't want to handle nicotine and THC.

"Training was bad enough," Jeff groused, "but *this* crap—"

"I don't know." I'd been thinking about it. "It might just all be worth it."

"Hell, no—this is a *space* war, let Star Fleet take care of it . . . they're just going to send us out and either we sit for fifty years on some damn ice cube of a portal planet, or we get. . . ."

"Well, Jeff, you've got to look at it the other way, too. Even if there's only one chance in a thousand that we'll be doing some good, keeping the Taurans. . . ."

"TENCH-HUT!" WE stood up in a raggety-ass fashion, by twos and threes. The door opened and a full major came in. I stiffened a little. He was the highest-ranking officer I'd ever seen. He had a row of ribbons stitched into his coveralls, including a purple strip meaning he'd been wounded in combat, fighting in the old American army. Must have been that Indochina thing, but it had fizzled out before I was born. He didn't look that old.

"Sit, sit." He made a patting motion with his hand. Then he put his hands on his hips and scanned the company with a small smile on his face. "Welcome to Charon. You picked a lovely day to land; the temperature outside is a summery eight point one five degrees Absolute. We expect little change for the next two centuries or so." Some of us laughed half-heartedly.

"You'd best enjoy the tropical climate here at Miami Base, enjoy it while you can. We're on the center of sunside here, and most of your training will be on darkside. Over there, the temperature drops to a chilly two point zero eight.

"You might as well regard all the training you got on Earth and the Moon as just a warm-up exercise, to give you a fair chance of surviving

Charon. You'll have to go through your whole repertory here: tools, weapons, maneuvers. And you'll find that, at these temperatures, tools don't work the way they should, weapons don't want to fire. And people move v-e-r-y cautiously."

He studied the clipboard in his hand. "Right now, you have forty-nine women and forty-eight men. Two deaths, one psychiatric release. Having read an outline of your training program, I'm frankly surprised that so many of you pulled through.

"But you might as well know that I won't be displeased if as few as fifty of you graduate from this final phase. And the only way not to graduate is to die. Here. The only way anybody gets back to Earth—including me—is after a combat tour.

"You will complete your training in one month. From here you go to Stargate collapsar, a little over two lights away. You will stay at the settlement on Stargate I, the largest portal planet, until replacements arrive. Hopefully, that will be no more than a month; another group is due here as soon as you leave.

"When you leave Stargate, you will be going to a strategically important collapsar, set up a military base there, and fight the enemy, if attacked. Otherwise, maintain the base until further orders.

"The last two weeks of your training will consist of constructing such a base, on darkside. There you will be totally isolated from Miami Base: no communication, no medical evacuation, no resupply. Sometime before the two weeks are up, your defense facilities will be evaluated in an attack by guided drones. They will be armed.

"All of the permanent personnel here on Charon are combat veterans. Thus, all of us are forty to fifty years of age, but I think we can keep up with you. Two of us will be with you at all times, and will accompany you at least as far as Stargate. They are Captain Sherman Stott, your company commander, and Sergeant Octavio Cortez, your first sergeant. Gentlemen?"

Two men in the front row stood easily and turned to face us. Captain Stott was a little smaller than the major, but cut from the same mold; face hard and smooth as porcelain, cynical half-smile, a precise centimeter of beard framing a large chin, looking thirty at the most. He wore a large, gunpowder-type pistol on his hip.

Sergeant Cortez was another story. His head was shaved and the wrong shape; flattened out on one side where a large piece of skull had obviously been taken out. His face was very dark and seamed with wrinkles and scars. Half his left ear was missing and his eyes were as expressive as buttons on a machine. He had a moustache-and-beard combination that looked like a skinny white caterpillar taking a lap around his mouth. On anybody else, his schoolboy smile might look pleasant, but he was about the ugliest, meanest-looking creature I'd ever seen. Still, if you didn't look at his head and considered the lower six feet or so, he could pose as the "after" advertisement for a body-building spa. Neither Stott nor Cortez wore any ribbons. Cortez had a small pocket-laser suspended in a magnetic rig, sideways, under his left armpit. It had wooden grips that were worn very smooth.

"Now, before I turn you over to the tender mercies of these two gentlemen, let me caution you again.

"Two months ago there was not a living soul on this planet, a working force of forty-five men struggled for a month to erect this base. Twenty-four of them, more than half, died in the construction of it. This is the most dangerous planet men have ever tried to live on, but the places you'll be going will be this bad and worse. Your cadre will try to keep you alive for the next month. Listen to them . . . and follow their example; all of them have survived here for longer than you'll have to. Captain?" The captain stood up as the major went out the door.

"Tench-*hut!*" The last syllable was like an explosion and we all jerked to our feet.

"Now, I'm only gonna say this *once* so you better listen," he growled. "We *are* in a combat situation here and in a combat situation there is only *one* penalty for disobedience and insubordination." He jerked the pistol from his hip and held it by the barrel, like a club. "This is an Army model 1911 automatic *pistol* caliber .45 and it is a primitive, but effective, weapon. The sergeant and I are authorized to use our weapons to kill to enforce discipline, don't make us do it because we will. We *will*." He put the pistol back. The holster snap made a loud crack in the dead quiet.

"Sergeant Cortez and I between us have killed more people than are sitting in this room. Both of us fought in Vietnam on the American side and both of us joined the United Nations International Guard more than ten years ago. I took a break in grade from major for the privilege of commanding this company, and First Sergeant Cortez took a break from sub-major, because we are both *combat* soldiers and this is the first *combat* situation since 1974.

"Keep in mind what I've said while the First Sergeant instructs you more specifically in what your duties will be under this command. Take over, Sergeant." He turned on his heel and strode out of the room, with the little smile on his face that hadn't changed one millimeter during the whole harangue.

The First Sergeant moved like a heavy machine with lots of ball bearings. When the door hissed shut he swiveled ponderously to face us and said, "At ease, siddown," in a surprisingly gentle voice. He sat on a table in the front of the room. It creaked—but held.

"Now, the captain talks scary and I look scary, but we both mean well. You'll be working pretty closely with me, so you better get used to this thing I've got hanging in front of my brain. You probably won't see the captain much, except on maneuvers."

He touched the flat part of his head. "And speaking of brains, I still have just about all mine, in spite of Chinese efforts to the contrary. All of us old vets who mustered into UNEF had to pass the same criteria that got you drafted by the Elite Conscription Act. So I suspect all of you are smart and tough—but just keep in mind that the captain and I are smart and tough *and* experienced."

He flipped through the roster without really looking at it. "Now, as the captain said, there'll be only one kind of disciplinary action on maneuvers. Capital punishment. But normally *we* won't have to kill you for disobeying. Charon'll save us the trouble.

"Back in the billeting area, it'll be another story. We don't much care what you do inside, but once you suit up and go outside, you've gotta have discipline that would shame a Centurian. There will be situations where one stupid act could kill us all.

"Anyhow, the first thing we've gotta do is get you fitted to your fighting suits. The armorer's waiting at your billet; he'll take you one at a time. Let's go."

4

"Now, I know you got lectured and lectured on what a fighting suit can do, back on Earth." The armorer was a small man, partially bald, with no insignia of rank on his coveralls. Sergeant Cortez told us to call him "sir," since he was a lieutenant.

"But I'd like to reinforce a couple of points, maybe add some things your instructors Earthside weren't clear about, or couldn't know. Your

First Sergeant was kind enough to consent to being my visual aid. Sergeant?"

Cortez slipped out of his coveralls and came up to the little raised platform where a fighting suit was standing, popped open like a man-shaped clam. He backed into it and slipped his arms into the rigid sleeves. There was a click and the thing swung shut with a sigh. It was bright green with CORTEZ stenciled in white letters on the helmet.

"Camouflage, Sergeant."

The green faded to white, then dirty gray. "This is good camouflage for Charon, and most of your portal planets," said Cortez, from a deep well. "But there are several other combinations available." The gray dappled and brightened to a combination of greens and browns: "Jungle." Then smoothed out to a hard light ochre: "Desert." Dark brown, darker, to a deep flat black: "Night or space."

"Very good, Sergeant. To my knowledge, this is the only feature of the suit which was perfected after your training. The control is around your left wrist and is admittedly awkward. But once you find the right combination, it's easy to lock in.

"Now, you didn't get much in-suit training Earthside because we didn't want you to get used to using the thing in a friendly environment. The fighting suit is the deadliest personal weapon ever built, and with no weapon it is easier for the user to kill himself through carelessness. Turn around, Sergeant.

"Case in point." He tapped a square protuberance between the shoulders. "Exhaust fins. As you know, the suit tries to keep you at a comfortable temperature no matter what the weather's like outside. The material of the suit is as near to a perfect insulator as we could get, consistent with mechanical demands. Therefore, these fins get *hot*—especially hot, compared to darkside temperatures—as they bleed off the body's heat.

"All you have to do is lean up against a boulder of frozen gas; there's lots of it around. The gas will sublime off faster than it can escape from the fins; in escaping, it will push against the surrounding 'ice' and fracture it . . . and in about one hundredth of a second, you have the equivalent of a hand grenade going off right below your neck. You'll never feel a thing.

"Variations on this theme have killed eleven people in the past two months. And they were just building a bunch of huts.

"I assume you know how easily the waldo capabilities can kill you or your companions. Anybody want to shake hands with the sergeant?" He stepped over and clasped his glove. "He's had lots of practice. Until *you* have, be extremely careful. You might scratch an itch and wind up bleeding to death. Remember, semi-logarithmic repose: two pounds' pressure exerts five pounds' force; three pounds gives ten; four pounds, twenty-three; five pounds, forty-seven. Most of you can muster up a grip of well over a hundred pounds. Theoretically, you could rip a steel girder in two with that, amplified. Actually, you'd destroy the material of your gloves and, at least on Charon, die very quickly. It'd be a race between decompression and flash-freezing. You'd be the loser.

"The leg waldos are also dangerous, even though the amplification is less extreme. Until you're really skilled, don't try to run, or jump. You're likely to trip, and that means you're likely to die.

"Charon's gravity is three-fourths of Earth normal, so it's not too bad. But on a really small world, like Luna, you could take a running jump and not come down for twenty minutes, just keep sailing over the horizon. Maybe bash into a mountain at eighty meters per second. On a small asteroid, it'd be no trick at all to run up to escape velocity and be off on an informal tour of intergalactic space. It's a slow way to travel.

"Tomorrow morning, we'll start teaching you how to stay alive inside of this infernal machine. The rest of the afternoon and evening, I'll call you one at a time to be fitted. That's all, Sergeant."

Cortez went to the door and turned the stopcock that let air into the air lock. A bank of infrared lamps went on to keep the air from freezing inside it. When the pressures were equalized, he shut the stopcock, unclamped the door and stepped in, clamping it shut behind him. A pump hummed for about a minute, evacuating the air lock, then he stepped out and sealed the outside door. It was pretty much like the ones on Luna.

"First I want Private Omar Almizar. The rest of you can go find your bunks. I'll call you over the squawker."

"Alphabetical order, sir?"

"Yep. About ten minutes apiece. If your name begins with Z, you might as well get sacked."

That was Rogers. She probably *was* thinking about getting sacked.

5

The sun was a hard white point directly overhead. It was a lot brighter than I had expected it to be; since we were eighty AUs out, it was only

1/6400th as bright as it is on Earth. Still, it was putting out about as much light as a powerful streetlamp.

"This is considerably more light than you'll have on a portal planet," Captain Stott's voice crackled in our collective ear. "Be glad that you'll be able to watch your step."

We were lined up, single file, on a permaplast sidewalk connecting the billet and the supply hut. We'd practiced walking inside, all morning, and this wasn't any different except for the exotic scenery. Though the light was rather dim, you could see all the way to the horizon quite clearly, with no atmosphere in the way. A black cliff that looked too regular to be natural stretched from one horizon to the other, passing within a kilometer of us. The ground was obsidian-black, mottled with patches of white, or bluish, ice. Next to the supply hut was a small mountain of snow in a bin marked OXYGEN.

The suit was fairly comfortable, but it gave you the odd feeling of being simultaneously a marionette and a puppeteer. You apply the impulse to move your leg and the suit picks it up and magnifies it and moves your leg for you.

"Today we're only going to walk around the company area and nobody will *leave* the company area." The captain wasn't wearing his .45, but he had a laser-finger like the rest of us. And his was probably hooked up.

Keeping an interval of at least two meters between each person, we stepped off the permaplast and followed the captain over the smooth rock. We walked carefully for about an hour, spiraling out, and finally stopped at the far edge of the perimeter.

"Now everybody pay close attention. I'm going out to that blue slab of ice"—it was a big one, about twenty meters away—"and show you something that you'd better know if you want to live."

He walked out a dozen confident steps. "First I have to heat up a rock—filters down." I slapped the stud under my armpit and the filter slid into place over my image converter. The captain pointed his finger at a black rock the size of a basketball and gave it a short burst. The glare rolled a long shadow of the captain over us and beyond. The rock shattered into a pile of hazy splinters.

"It doesn't take long for these to cool down." He stooped and picked up a piece. "This one is probably twenty or twenty-five degrees. Watch." He tossed the "warm" rock on the ice slab. It skittered around in a crazy pattern and shot off the side. He tossed another one, and it did the same.

"As you know, you are not quite *perfectly* insulated. These rocks are about the temperature of the soles of your boots. If you try to stand on a slab of hydrogen the same thing will happen to you. Except that the rock is *already* dead.

"The reason for this behavior is that the rock makes a slick interface with the ice—a little puddle of liquid hydrogen—and rides a few molecules above the liquid on a cushion of hydrogen vapor. This makes the rock, or *you*, a frictionless bearing as far as the ice is concerned and you *can't* stand up without any friction under your boots.

"After you have lived in your suit for a month or so you *should* be able to survive falling down, but right *now* you just don't know enough. Watch."

The captain flexed and hopped up onto the slab. His feet shot out from under him and he twisted around in midair, landing on hands and knees. He slipped off and stood on the ground.

"The idea is to keep your exhaust fins from making contact with the frozen gas. Compared to the ice they are as hot as a blast furnace and contact with any weight behind it will result in an explosion."

AFTER THAT DEMONSTRATION, we walked around for another hour or so, and returned to the billet. Once through the air lock, we had to mill around for a while, letting the suits get up to something like room temperature. Somebody came up and touched helmets with me.

"William?" She had MC COY stenciled above her faceplate.

"Hi, Sean. Anything special?"

"I just wondered if you had anyone to sleep with tonight."

That's right; I'd forgotten, there wasn't any sleeping roster here. Everybody just chose his own partner. "Sure, I mean, uh, no . . . no, I haven't asked anybody, sure, if you want to. . . ."

"Thanks, William. See you later." I watched her walk away and thought that if anybody could make a fighting suit look sexy, it'd be Sean. But even Sean couldn't.

Cortez decided we were warm enough and led us to the suit room where we backed the things into place and hooked them up to the charging plates—each suit had a little chunk of plutonium that would power it for several years, but we were supposed to run on fuel cells as much as possible. After a lot of shuffling around, everybody finally got plugged in and we were allowed to unsuit, ninety-seven naked chickens squirming out of bright green eggs. It was *cold*—the air, the floor, and especially the suits—and we made a pretty disorderly exit toward the lockers.

I slipped on tunic, trousers and sandals and was still cold. I took my cup and joined the line for soya, everybody jumping up and down to keep warm.

"How c-cold, do you think, it is, M-Mandella?" That was McCoy.

"I don't, even want, to think, about it." I stopped jumping and rubbed myself as briskly as possible, while holding a cup in one hand. "At least as cold as Missouri was."

"Ung . . . wish they'd, get some damn heat in, this place." It always affects the small girls more than anybody else. McCoy was the littlest one in the company, a waspwaist doll barely five feet high.

"They've got the airco going. It can't be long now."

"I wish I, was a big, slab of, meat like, you."

I was glad she wasn't.

6

We had our first casualty on the third day, learning how to dig holes.

With such large amounts of energy stored in a soldier's weapons, it wouldn't be practical for him to hack out a hole in the frozen ground with the conventional pick and shovel. Still, you can launch grenades all day and get nothing but shallow depressions—so the usual method is to bore a hole in the ground with the hand laser, drop a timed charge in after it's cooled down and, ideally, fill the hole with stuff. Of course, there's not much loose rock on Charon, unless you've already blown a hole nearby.

The only difficult thing about the procedure is getting away. To be safe, we were told, you've got to either be behind something really solid, or be at least a hundred meters away. You've got about three minutes after setting the charge, but you can't just spring away. Not on Charon.

The accident happened when we were making a really deep hole, the kind you want for a large underground bunker. For this, we had to blow a hole, then climb down to the bottom of the crater and repeat the procedure again and again until the hole was deep enough. Inside the crater we used charges with a five-minute delay, but it hardly

seemed enough time—you really had to go slow, picking your way up
the crater's edge.

Just about everybody had blown a double hole; everybody but me and
three others. I guess we were the only ones paying really close attention
when Bovanovitch got into trouble. All of us were a good two hundred
meters away. With my image converter turned up to about forty power, I
watched her disappear over the rim of the crater. After that I could only
listen in on her conversation with Cortez.

"I'm on the bottom, Sergeant." Normal radio procedure was suspended
for these maneuvers; only the trainee and Cortez could broadcast.

"O.K., move to the center and clear out the rubble. Take your time.
No rush until you pull the pin."

"Sure, Sergeant." We could hear small echoes of rocks clattering;
sound conduction through her boots. She didn't say anything for several
minutes.

"Found bottom." She sounded a little out of breath.

"Ice, or rock?"

"Oh, it's rock, Sergeant. The greenish stuff."

"Use a low setting, then. One point two, dispersion four."

"God darn it, Sergeant, that'll take forever."

"Yeah, but that stuff's got hydrated crystals in it—heat it up too fast
and you might make it fracture. And we'd just have to leave you there,
girl."

"O.K., one point two dee four." The inside edge of the crater flickered
red with reflected laser light.

"When you get about half a meter deep, squeeze it up to dee two."

"Roger." It took her exactly seventeen minutes, three of them at dispersion two. I could imagine how tired her shooting arm was.

"Now rest for a few minutes. When the bottom of the hole stops glowing, arm the charge and drop it in. Then *walk* out. Understand? You'll
have plenty of time."

"I understand, Sergeant. Walk out." She sounded nervous. Well, you
don't often have to tiptoe away from a twenty microton tachyon bomb.
We listened to her breathing for a few minutes.

"Here goes." Faint slithering sound of the bomb sliding down.

"Slow and easy now, you've got five minutes."

"Y-yeah. Five." Her footsteps started out slow and regular. Then, after
she started climbing the side, the sounds were less regular; maybe a
little frantic. And with four minutes to go—

"Crap!" A loud scraping noise, then clatters and bumps.

"What's wrong, Private?"

"Oh, crap." Silence. "Crap!"

"Private, you don't wanna get shot, you *tell me what's wrong!*"

"I . . . I'm stuck, damn rockslide . . . DO SOMETHING I can't move. I can't move I, I—"

"Shut up! How deep?"

"Can't move my crap, my damn legs HELP ME—"

"Then damn it use your arms—push!—you can move a ton with each hand." Three minutes.

Then she stopped cussing and started to mumble, in Russian, I guess, a low monotone. She was panting and you could hear rocks tumbling away.

"I'm free." Two minutes.

"Go as fast as you can." Cortez's voice was flat, emotionless.

At ninety seconds she appeared crawling over the rim. "Run, girl . . . you better run." She ran five or six steps and fell, skidded a few meters and got back up, running; fell again, got up again—

It looked like she was going pretty fast, but she had only covered about thirty meters when Cortez said, "All right, Bovanovitch, get down on your stomach and lie still." Ten seconds, but she didn't hear him, or she wanted to get just a little more distance, and she kept running, careless leaping strides and at the high point of one leap there was a flash and a rumble and something big hit her below the neck and her headless body spun off end over end through space, trailing a red-black spiral of flash-frozen blood that settled gracefully to the ground, a path of crystal powder that nobody disturbed while we gathered rocks to cover the juiceless thing at the end of it.

That night Cortez didn't lecture us, didn't even show up for night-chop. We were all very polite to each other and everybody was afraid to talk about it.

I sacked with Rogers; everybody sacked with a good friend, but all she wanted to do was cry, and she cried so long and so hard that she got me doing it, too.

7

"Fire team A—move out!" The twelve of us advanced in a ragged line toward the simulated bunker. It was about a kilometer away, across a carefully prepared obstacle course. We could move pretty fast, since all of the ice had been cleared from the field, but even with ten days' experience we weren't ready to do more than an easy jog.

I carried a grenade launcher, loaded with tenth-microton practice grenades. Everybody had their laser-fingers set at point oh eight dee one; not much more than a flashlight. This was a *simulated* attack—the bunker and its robot defender cost too much to be used once and thrown away.

"Team B follow. Team leaders, take over."

We approached a clump of boulders at about the halfway mark, and Potter, my team leader, said "Stop and cover." We clustered behind the rocks and waited for team B.

Barely visible in their blackened suits, the dozen men and women whispered by us. As soon as they were clear, they jogged left, out of our line of sight.

"Fire!" Red circles of light danced a half-click downrange, where the bunker was just visible. Five hundred meters was the limit for these practice grenades; but I might luck out, so I lined the launcher up on the image of the bunker, held it at a 45° angle and popped off a salvo of three.

Return fire from the bunker started before my grenades even landed. Its automatic lasers were no more powerful than the ones we were using, but a direct hit would deactivate your image converter, leaving you blind. It was setting down a random field of fire, not even coming close to the boulders we were hiding behind.

Three magnesium-bright flashes blinked simultaneously, about thirty meters short of the bunker. "Mandella! I thought you were supposed to be *good* with that thing."

"Damn it, Potter—it only throws half a click. Once we get closer, I'll lay 'em right on top, every time."

"*Sure* you will." I didn't say anything. She wouldn't be team leader forever. Besides, she hadn't been such a bad girl before the power went to her head.

Since the grenadier is the assistant team leader, I was slaved into Potter's radio and could hear B team talk to her.

"Potter, this is Freeman. Losses?"

"Potter here—no, looks like they were concentrating on you."

"Yeah, we lost three. Right now we're in a depression about eighty, a hundred meters down from you. We can give cover whenever you're ready."

"O.K., start." Soft click: "A team follow me." She slid out from behind the rock and turned on the faint pink beacon beneath her powerpack. I turned on mine and moved out to run alongside of her and the rest of the team fanned out in a trailing wedge. Nobody fired while B team laid down a cover for us.

All I could hear was Potter's breathing and the soft *crunch-crunch* of my boots. Couldn't see much of anything, so I tongued the image converter up to a log two intensification. That made the image kind of blurry but adequately bright. Looked like the bunker had B team pretty well pinned down; they were getting quite a roasting. All of their return fire was laser; they must have lost their grenadier.

"Potter, this is Mandella. Shouldn't we take some of the heat off B team?"

"Soon as I can find us good enough cover. Is that all right with you? Private?" She'd been promoted to corporal for the duration of the exercise.

We angled to the right and laid down behind a slab of rock. Most of the others found cover nearby, but a few had to just hug the ground.

"Freeman, this is Potter."

"Potter, this is Smithy. Freeman's out; Samuels is out. We only have five men left. Give us some cover so we can get. . . ."

"Roger, Smithy."—*click*—"Open up, A team. The B's are really hurtin'."

I PEEKED OUT over the edge of the rock. My rangefinder said that the bunker was about three hundred fifty meters away, still pretty far. I aimed just a smidgeon high and popped three, then down a couple of degrees and three more. The first ones overshot by about twenty meters, then the second salvo flared up directly in front of the bunker. I tried to hold on that angle and popped fifteen, the rest of the magazine, in the same direction.

I should have ducked down behind the rock to reload, but I wanted to see where the fifteen would land, so I kept my eyes on the bunker while I reached back to unclip another magazine. . . .

When the laser hit my image converter there was a red glare so intense it seemed to go right through my eyes and bounce off the back of my skull. It must have been only a few milliseconds before the converter overloaded and went blind, but the bright green afterimage hurt my eyes for several minutes.

Since I was officially "dead," my radio automatically cut off and I had to remain where I was until the mock battle was over. With no sensory input besides the feel of my own skin—and it ached where the image converter had shone on it—and the ringing in my ears, it seemed like an awfully long time. Finally, a helmet clanked against mine:

"You O.K., Mandella?" Potter's voice.

"Sorry, I died of boredom twenty minutes ago."

"Stand up and take my hand." I did so and we shuffled back to the billet. It must have taken over an hour. She didn't say anything more, all the way back—it's a pretty awkward way to communicate—but after we'd cycled through the air lock and warmed up, she helped me undo my suit. I got ready for a mild tongue-lashing, but when the suit popped open, before I could even get my eyes adjusted to the light, she grabbed me around the neck and planted a wet kiss on my mouth.

"Nice shooting, Mandella."

"Huh?"

"The last salvo before you got hit—four direct hits; the bunker decided it was knocked out, and all we had to do was walk the rest of the way."

"Great." I scratched my face under the eyes and some dry skin flaked off. She giggled.

"You should see yourself, you look like. . . ."

"All personnel report to the assembly area." That was the captain's voice. Bad news.

She handed me a tunic and sandals. "Let's go."

The assembly area/chop hall was just down the corridor. There was a row of roll-call buttons at the door; I pressed the one beside my name. Four of the names were covered with black tape. That was good, we hadn't lost anybody else during today's maneuvers.

The captain was sitting on the raised dais, which at least meant we didn't have to go through the tench-hut bullshit. The place filled up in less than a minute; a soft chime indicated the roll was complete.

Captain Stott didn't stand up. "You did *fairly* well today, nobody got killed and I expected some to. In that respect you exceeded my expectations but in *every* other respect you did a poor job.

"I am glad you're taking good care of yourselves because each of you represents an investment of over a million dollars and one-fourth of a human life.

"But in this simulated battle against a *very* stupid robot enemy, thirty-seven of you managed to walk into laser fire and be killed in a *simulated* way and since dead people require no food *you* will require no food, for the next three days. Each person who was a casualty in this battle will be allowed only two liters of water and a vitamin ration each day."

We knew enough not to groan or anything, but there were some pretty disgusted looks, especially on the faces that had singed eyebrows and a pink rectangle of sunburn framing their eyes.

"Mandella."

"Sir?"

"You are far and away the worst burned casualty. Was your image converter set on normal?"

Oh, crap. "No, sir. Log two."

"I see. Who was your team leader for the exercise?"

"Acting Corporal Potter, sir."

"Private Potter, did you order him to use image intensification?"

"Sir, I . . . I don't remember."

"You don't. Well, as a memory exercise you may join the dead people. Is that satisfactory?"

"Yes, sir."

"Good. Dead people get one last meal tonight, and go on no rations starting tomorrow. Are there any questions?" He must have been kidding. "All right. Dismissed."

I SELECTED THE meal that looked as if it had the most calories and took my tray over to sit by Potter.

"That was a quixotic damn thing to do. But thanks."

"Nothing. I've been wanting to lose a few pounds anyway." I couldn't see where she was carrying any extra.

"I know a good exercise," I said. She smiled without looking up from her tray. "Have anybody for tonight?"

"Kind of thought I'd ask Jeff. . . ."

"Better hurry, then. He's lusting after Uhuru." Well, that was mostly true. Everybody did.

"I don't know. Maybe we ought to save our strength. That third day. . . ."

"Come on." I scratched the back of her hand lightly with a fingernail. "We haven't sacked since Missouri. Maybe I've learned something new."

"Maybe you have." She tilted her head up at me in a sly way. "O.K."

Actually, she was the one with the new trick. The French corkscrew, she called it. She wouldn't tell me who taught it to her, though. I'd like to shake his hand.

8

The two weeks' training around Miami Base eventually cost us eleven lives. Twelve, if you count Dahlquist. I guess having to spend the rest of your life on Charon, with a hand and both legs missing, is close enough to dying.

Little Foster was crushed in a landslide and Freeland had a suit malfunction that froze him solid before we could carry him inside. Most of the other deaders were people I didn't know all that well. But they all hurt. And they seemed to make us more scared rather than more cautious.

Now darkside. A flier brought us over in groups of twenty, and set us down beside a pile of building materials, thoughtfully immersed in a pool of helium II.

We used grapples to haul the stuff out of the pool. It's not safe to go wading, since the stuff crawls all over you and it's hard to tell what's underneath; you could walk out onto a slab of hydrogen and be out of luck.

I'd suggested that we try to boil away the pool with our lasers, but ten minutes of concentrated fire didn't drop the helium level appreciably. It didn't boil, either; helium II is a "superfluid," so what evaporation there was had to take place evenly, all over the surface. No hot spots, so no bubbling.

We weren't supposed to use lights, to "avoid detection." There was plenty of starlight, with your image converter cranked up to log three or four, but each stage of amplification meant some loss of detail. By log four, the landscape looked like a crude monochrome painting, and you couldn't read the names on people's helmets unless they were right in front of you.

The landscape wasn't all that interesting, anyhow. There were half a dozen medium-sized meteor craters—all with exactly the same level of helium II in them—and the suggestion of some puny mountains just over the horizon. The uneven ground was the consistency of frozen spiderwebs; every time you put your foot down, you'd sink half an inch with a squeaking crunch. It could get on your nerves.

It took most of a day to pull all the stuff out of the pool. We took shifts napping, which you could do either standing up, sitting, or lying on your stomach. I didn't do well in any of those positions, so I was anxious to get the bunker built and pressurized.

We could build the thing underground—it'd just fill up with helium II—so the first thing to do was to build an insulating platform, a permaplast-vacuum sandwich three layers tall.

I was an acting corporal, with a crew of ten people. We were carrying the permaplast layers to the building site—two people can carry one easily—when one of "my" men slipped and fell on his back.

"Damn it, Singer, watch your step." We'd had a couple of deaders that way.

"Sorry, Corporal. I'm bushed, just got my feet tangled up."

"Yeah, just watch it." He got back up all right, and with his partner placed the sheet and went back to get another.

I kept my eye on him. In a few minutes he was practically staggering, not easy to do with that suit of cybernetic armor.

"Singer! After you set that plank, I want to see you."

"O.K." He labored through the task and mooched over.

"Let me check your readout." I opened the door on his chest to expose the medical monitor. His temperature was two degrees high; blood pressure and heart rate both elevated. Not up to the red line, though.

"You sick or something?"

"Hell, Mandella, I feel O.K., just tired. Since I fell I've been a little dizzy."

I CHINNED THE medic's combination. "Doc, this is Mandella. You wanna come over here for a minute?"

"Sure, where are you?" I waved and he walked over from poolside.

"What's the problem?" I showed him Singer's readout.

He knew what all the other little dials and things meant, so it took him a while. "As far as I can tell, Mandella . . . he's just hot."

"Hell, I coulda told you that," said Singer.

"Maybe you better have the armorer take a look at his suit." We had two people who'd taken a crash course in suit maintenance; they were our "armorers."

I chinned Sanchez and asked him to come over with his tool kit.

"Be a couple of minutes, Corporal. Carryin' a plank."

"Well, put it down and get on over here." I was getting an uneasy feeling. Waiting for him, the medic and I looked over Singer's suit.

"Uh-oh," Doc Jones said. "Look at this." I went around to the back and looked where he was pointing. Two of the fins on the heat exchanger were bent out of shape.

"What is wrong?" Singer asked.

"You fell on your heat exchanger, right?"

"Sure, Corporal—that's it, it must not be working right."

"I don't think it's working at *all*," said Doc.

Sanchez came over with his diagnostic kit and we told him what had happened. He looked at the heat exchanger, then plugged a couple of jacks into it and got a digital readout from a little monitor in his kit. I didn't know what it was measuring, but it came out zero to eight decimal places.

Heard a soft click, Sanchez chinning my private frequency. "Corporal, this guy's a deader."

"What? Can't you fix the damn thing?"

"Maybe . . . maybe I could, if I could take it apart. But there's no way. . . ."

"Hey! Sanchez?" Singer was talking on the general freak. "Find out what's wrong?" He was panting.

Click. "Keep your pants on, man, we're working on it." *Click.* "He won't last long enough for us to get the bunker pressurized. And I can't work on that heat exchanger from outside of the suit."

"You've got a spare suit, haven't you?"

"Two of 'em, the fit-anybody kind. But there's no place . . . say. . . ."

"Right. Go get one of the suits warmed up." I chinned the general freak. "Listen, Singer, we've gotta get you out of that thing. Sanchez has a spare unit, but to make the switch, we're gonna have to build a house around you. Understand?"

"Huh-uh."

"Look, we'll just make a box with you inside, and hook it up to the life-support unit. That way you can breathe while you make the switch."

"Soun's pretty compis . . . complicated t'me."

"Look, just come along. . . ."

"I'll be all right, man, jus' lemme res'. . . ."

I grabbed his arm and led him to the building site. He was really weaving. Doc took his other arm, and between us we kept him from falling over.

"Corporal Ho, this is Corporal Mandella." Ho was in charge of the life-support unit.

"Go away, Mandella, I'm busy."

"You're going to be busier." I outlined the problem to her. While her group hurried to adapt the LSU—for this purpose, it need only be an air hose and heater—I got my crew to bring around six slabs of permaplast, so we could build a big box around Singer and the extra suit. It would look like a huge coffin, a meter square and six meters long.

We set the suit down on the slab that would be the floor of the coffin. "O.K., Singer, let's go."

No answer.

"Singer!" He was just standing there. Doc Jones checked his readout. "He's out, man, unconscious."

MY MIND RACED. There might just be room for another person in the box. "Give me a hand here." I took Singer's shoulders and Doc took his feet, and we carefully laid him out at the feet of the empty suit.

Then I laid down myself, above the suit. "O.K., close 'er up."

"Look, Mandella, if anybody goes in there, it oughta be me."

"No, Doc. *My* job. My man." That sounded all wrong. William Mandella, boy hero.

They stood a slab up on edge—it had two openings for the LSU input and exhaust—and proceeded to weld it to the bottom plank with a narrow laser beam. On Earth, we'd just use glue, but here the only fluid was helium, which has lots of interesting properties, but is definitely not sticky.

After about ten minutes we were completely walled up. I could feel the LSU humming. I switched on my suit light—the first time since we landed on darkside—and the glare made purple blotches dance in front of my eyes.

"Mandella, this is Ho. Stay in your suit at least two or three minutes. We're putting hot air in, but it's coming back just this side of liquid." I lay and watched the purple fade.

"O.K., it's still cold, but you can make it." I popped my suit. It wouldn't open all the way, but I didn't have too much trouble getting out. The suit was still cold enough to take some skin off my fingers and butt as I wiggled out.

I had to crawl feet-first down the coffin to get to Singer. It got darker fast, moving away from my light. When I popped his suit a rush of hot stink hit me in the face. In the dim light his skin was dark red and splotchy. His breathing was very shallow and I could see his heart palpitating.

FIRST I UNHOOKED the relief tubes—an unpleasant business—then the bio sensors, and then I had the problem of getting his arms out of their sleeves.

It's pretty easy to do for yourself. You twist this way and turn that way and the arm pops out. Doing it from the outside is a different matter: I had to twist his arm and then reach under and move the suit's arm to match—and it takes muscle to move a suit around from the outside.

Once I had one arm out it was pretty easy: I just crawled forward, putting my feet on the suit's shoulders, and pulled on his free arm. He slid out of the suit like an oyster slipping out of its shell.

I popped the spare suit and, after a lot of pulling and pushing, managed to get his legs in. Hooked up the bio sensors and the front relief tube. He'd have to do the other one himself, it's too complicated. For the nth time I was glad not to have been born female; they have to have two of those damned plumber's friends, instead of just one and a simple hose.

I left his arms out of the sleeves. The suit would be useless for any kind of work, anyhow; waldos have to be tailored to the individual.

His eyelids fluttered. "Man . . . della. Where . . . the hell. . . ."

I explained, slowly, and he seemed to get most of it. "Now I'm gonna close you up and go get into my suit. I'll have the crew cut the end off this thing and I'll haul you out. Got it?"

He nodded. Strange to see that—when you nod or shrug in a suit, it doesn't communicate anything.

I crawled into my suit, hooked up the attachments and chinned the general freak. "Doc, I think he's gonna be O.K. Get us out of here now."

"Will do." Ho's voice. The LSU hum was replaced by a chatter, then a throb; evacuating the box to prevent an explosion.

One corner of the seam grew red, then white, and a bright crimson beam lanced through, not a foot away from my head. I scrunched back as far as I could. The beam slid up the seam and around three corners, back to where it started. The end of the box fell away slowly, trailing filaments of melted 'plast.

"Wait for the stuff to harden, Mandella."

"Sanchez, I'm not that stupid."

"Here you go." Somebody tossed a line to me. That *would* be smarter than dragging him out by myself. I threaded a long bight under his arms and tied it behind his neck. Then I scrambled out to help them pull, which was silly—they had a dozen people already lined up to haul.

Singer got out all right and was actually sitting up while Doc Jones checked his readout. People were asking me about it and congratulating me when suddenly Ho said "Look!" and pointed toward the horizon.

It was a black ship, coming in fast. I just had time to think it wasn't fair, they weren't supposed to attack until the last few days, and then the ship was right on top of us.

9

We all flopped to the ground instinctively, but the ship didn't attack. It blasted braking rockets and dropped to land on skids. Then it skied around to come to a rest beside the building site.

Everybody had it figured out and was standing around sheepishly when the two suited figures stepped out of the ship.

A familiar voice crackled over the general freak. "Every *one* of you saw us coming in and not *one* of you responded with laser fire. It wouldn't have done any good but it would have indicated a certain amount of fighting spirit. You have a week or less before the real thing and since the sergeant and *I* will be here *I* will insist that you show a little more will to live. Acting Sergeant Potter."

"Here, sir."

"Get me a detail of twelve men to unload cargo. We brought a hundred small robot drones for *target* practice so that you might have at least a fighting chance, when a live target comes over.

"Move *now*; we only have thirty minutes before the ship returns to Miami."

I checked, and it was actually more like forty minutes.

HAVING THE CAPTAIN and sergeant there didn't really make much difference; we were still on our own, they were just observing.

Once we got the floor down, it only took one day to complete the bunker. It was a gray oblong, featureless except for the air-lock blister and four windows. On top was a swivel-mounted bevawatt laser. The operator—you couldn't call him a "gunner"—sat in a chair holding dead-man switches in both hands. The laser wouldn't fire as long as he was holding one of those switches. If he let go, it would automatically aim for any moving aerial object and fire at will. Primary detection and aiming was by means of a kilometer-high antenna mounted beside the bunker.

It was the only arrangement that could really be expected to work, with the horizon so close and human reflexes so slow. You couldn't have the thing fully automatic, because in theory, friendly ships might also approach.

The aiming computer could choose up to twelve targets, appearing simultaneously—firing at the largest ones first. And it would get all twelve in the space of half a second.

The installation was partly protected from enemy fire by an efficient ablative layer that covered everything except the human operator. But then they *were* dead-man switches. One man above guarding eighty inside. The army's good at that kind of arithmetic.

Once the bunker was finished, half of us stayed inside at all times—feeling very much like targets—taking turns operating the laser, while the other half went on maneuvers.

About four clicks from the base was a large "lake" of frozen hydrogen; one of our most important maneuvers was to learn how to get around on the treacherous stuff.

It really wasn't too difficult. You couldn't stand up on it, so you had to belly down and slide.

If you had somebody to push you from the edge, getting started was no problem. Otherwise, you had to scrabble with your hands and feet, pushing down as hard as was practical, until you started moving, in a series of little jumps. Once started, you would keep going until you ran out of ice. You could steer a little bit by digging in, hand and foot, on the appropriate side, but you couldn't slow to a stop that way. So it was a good idea not to go too fast, and to be positioned in such a way that your helmet didn't absorb the shock of stopping.

We went through all the things we'd done on the Miami side; weapons practice, demolition, attack patterns. We also launched drones at irregular intervals, toward the bunker. Thus, ten or fifteen times a day, the operators got to demonstrate their skill in letting go of the handles as soon as the proximity light went on.

I had four hours of that, like everybody else. I was nervous until the first "attack," when I saw how little there was to it. The light went on, I let go, the gun aimed and when the drone peeped over the horizon—*zzt!* Nice touch of color, the molten metal spraying through space. Otherwise not too exciting.

So none of us were worried about the upcoming "graduation exercise," thinking it would be just more of the same.

MIAMI BASE ATTACKED on the thirteenth day with two simultaneous missiles streaking over opposite sides of the horizon at some forty kilometers per second. The laser vaporized the first one with no trouble, but the second got within eight clicks of the bunker before it was hit.

We were coming back from maneuvers, about a click away from the bunker. I wouldn't have seen it happen if I hadn't been looking directly at the bunker the moment of the attack.

The second missile sent a shower of molten debris straight toward the bunker. Eleven pieces hit, and, as we later reconstructed it, this is what happened.

The first casualty was Uhuru, pretty Uhuru inside the bunker, who was hit in the back and head and died instantly. With the drop in pressure, the LSU went into high gear. Friedman was standing in front of the main airco outlet and was blown into the opposite wall hard enough to knock him unconscious; he died of decompression before the others could get him to his suit.

Everybody else managed to stagger through the gale and get into their suits, but Garcia's suit had been holed and didn't do him any good.

By the time we got there, they had turned off the LSU and were welding up the holes in the wall. One man was trying to scrape up the unrecognizable mess that had been Uhuru. I could hear him sobbing and retching. They had already taken Garcia and Friedman outside for burial. The captain took over the repair detail from Potter. Sergeant Cortez led the sobbing man over to a corner and came back to work on cleaning up Uhuru's remains, alone. He didn't order anybody to help and nobody volunteered.

10

As a graduation exercise, we were unceremoniously stuffed into a ship—*Earth's Hope*, the same one we rode to Charon—and bundled off to Stargate at a little more than 1 G.

The trip seemed endless, about six months subjective time, and boring, but not as hard on the carcass as going to Charon had been. Captain Stott made us review our training orally, day by day, and we did exercises every day until we were worn to a collective frazzle.

Stargate I was like Charon's darkside, only more so. The base on Stargate I was smaller than Miami Base—only a little bigger than the one we constructed on darkside—and we were due to lay over a week to help expand the facilities. The crew there was very glad to see us; especially the two females, who looked a little worn around the edges.

We all crowded into the small dining hall, where Submajor Williamson, the man in charge of Stargate I, gave us some disconcerting news:

"Everybody get comfortable. Get off the tables, though, there's plenty of floor.

"I have some idea of what you just went through, training on Charon. I won't say it's all been wasted. But where you're headed, things will be quite different. Warmer."

He paused to let that soak in.

"Aleph Aurigae, the first collapsar ever detected, revolves around the normal star Epsilon Aurigae, in a twenty-seven-year orbit. The enemy has a base of operations, not on a regular portal planet of Aleph, but on a planet in orbit around Epsilon. We don't know much about the planet: just that it goes around Epsilon once every seven hundred forty-five days, is about three-fourths the size of Earth, and has an albedo of 0.8, meaning it's probably covered with clouds. We can't say precisely how hot it will be, but judging from its distance from Epsilon, it's probably rather hotter than Earth. Of course, we don't know whether you'll be work-ing . . . fighting on lightside or darkside, equator or poles. It's highly unlikely that the atmosphere will be breathable—at any rate, you'll stay inside your suits.

"Now you know exactly as much about where you're going as I do. Questions?"

"Sir," Stein drawled, "now we know where we're goin' . . . anybody know what we're goin' to do when we get there?"

Williamson shrugged. "That's up to your captain—and your sergeant, and the captain of *Earth's Hope*, and *Hope*'s logistic computer. We just don't have enough data yet, to project a course of action for you. It may be a long and bloody battle, it may be just a case of walking in to pick up the pieces. Conceivably, the Taurans might want to make a peace offer"—Cortez snorted—"in which case you would simply be part of our muscle, our bargaining power." He looked at Cortez mildly. "No one can say for sure."

THE ORGY THAT night was kind of amusing, but it was like trying to sleep in the middle of a raucous beach party. The only area big enough to sleep all of us was the dining hall; they draped a few bedsheets here and there for privacy, then unleashed Stargate's eighteen sex-starved men on our women, compliant and promiscuous by military custom— and law—but desiring nothing so much as sleep on solid ground.

The eighteen men acted as if they were compelled to try as many permutations as possible, and their performance was impressive—in a strictly quantitative sense, that is.

The next morning—and every other morning we were on Star-gate I—we staggered out of bed and into our suits, to go outside and work on the "new wing." Eventually, Stargate would be tactical and logistic headquarters for the war, with thousands of permanent per-sonnel, guarded by half-a-dozen heavy cruisers in *Hope*'s class. When we started, it was two shacks and twenty people; when we left, it was four shacks and twenty people. The work was a breeze, compared to darkside, since we had all the light we needed, and got sixteen hours inside for every eight hours' work. And no drone attacks for a final exam.

When we shuttled back up to the *Hope*, nobody was too happy about leaving—though some of the more popular females declared it'd be good to get some rest—Stargate was the last easy, safe assignment we'd have before taking up arms against the Taurans. And as Williamson had pointed out the first day, there was no way of predicting what that would be like.

Most of us didn't feel too enthusiastic about making a collapsar jump, either. We'd been assured that we wouldn't even feel it happen, just free fall all the way.

I wasn't convinced. As a physics student, I'd had the usual courses in general relativity and theories of gravitation. We only had a little direct data at that time—Stargate was discovered when I was in grade school—but the mathematical model seemed clear enough.

The collapsar Stargate was a perfect sphere about three kilometers in radius. It was suspended forever in a state of gravitational collapse that should have meant its surface was dropping toward its center at nearly the speed of light. Relativity propped it up, at least gave it the illusion of being there . . . the way all reality becomes illusory and observer-oriented when you study general relativity, or Buddhism.

At any rate, there would be a theoretical point in spacetime when one end of our ship was just above the surface of the collapsar, and the other end was a kilometer away—in our frame of reference. In any sane universe, this would set up tidal stresses and tear the ship apart, and we would be just another million kilograms of degenerate matter on the theoretical surface, rushing headlong to nowhere for the rest of eternity; or dropping to the center in the next trillionth of a second. You pays your money and you takes your frame of reference.

But they were right. We blasted away from Stargate I, made a few course corrections and then just dropped, for about an hour.

Then a bell rang and we sank into our cushions under a steady two gravities of deceleration. We were in enemy territory.

11

We'd been decelerating at two gravities for almost nine days when the battle began. Lying on our couches being miserable, all we felt were two soft bumps, missiles being released. Some eight hours later, the squawk-box crackled: "Attention, all crew. This is the captain." Quinsana, the pilot, was only a lieutenant, but was allowed to call himself captain aboard the vessel, where he outranked all of us, even Captain Stott. "You grunts in the cargo hold can listen, too.

"We just engaged the enemy with two fifty-bevaton tachyon missiles, and have destroyed both the enemy vessel and another object which it had launched approximately three microseconds before.

"The enemy has been trying to overtake us for the past one hundred seventy-nine hours, ship time. At the time of the engagement, the enemy was moving at a little over half the speed of light, relative to Aleph, and was only about thirty AU's from *Earth's Hope*. It was moving at .47c relative to us, and thus we would have been coincident in spacetime"—rammed!—"in a little more than nine hours. The missiles were launched at 0719 ship's time, and destroyed the enemy at 1540, both tachyon bombs detonating within a thousand clicks of the enemy objects."

The two missiles were a type whose propulsion system itself was only a barely-controlled tachyon bomb. They accelerated at a constant rate of 100 Gs, and were traveling at a relativistic speed by the time the nearby mass of the enemy ship detonated them.

"We expect no further interference from enemy vessels. Our velocity with respect to Aleph will be zero in another five hours; we will then begin to journey back. The return will take twenty-seven days." General moans and dejected cussing. Everybody knew all that already, of course; but we didn't care to be reminded of it.

So AFTER ANOTHER month of logycalisthenics and drill, at a constant 2 Gs, we got our first look at the planet we were going to attack. Invaders from outer space, yes, sir.

It was a blinding white crescent basking two AU's from Epsilon. The captain had pinned down the location of the enemy base from fifty AU's out, and we had jockeyed in on a wide arc, keeping the bulk of the planet between them and us. That didn't mean we were sneaking up on them—quite the contrary; they launched three abortive attacks—but it put us in a stronger defensive position. Until we had to go to the surface, that is. Then only the ship and its Star Fleet crew would be reasonably safe.

Since the planet rotated rather slowly—once every ten and one-half days—a "stationary" orbit for the ship had to be one hundred fifty thousand clicks out. This made the people in the ship feel quite secure,

with six thousand miles of rock and ninety thousand miles of space between them and the enemy. But it meant a whole second's time lag in
communication between us on the ground and the ship's battle computer. A person could get awful dead while that neutrino pulse crawled
up and back.

Our vague orders were to attack the base and gain control while damaging a minimum of enemy equipment. We were to take at least one
enemy alive. We were under no circumstances to allow *ourselves* to be
taken alive, however. And the decision wasn't up to us; one special pulse
from the battle computer, and that speck of plutonium in your power
plant would fission with all of .01% efficiency, and you'd be nothing but
a rapidly expanding, very hot plasma.

They strapped us into six scoutships—one platoon of twelve people in
each—and we blasted away from *Earth's Hope* at 8 Gs. Each scoutship
was supposed to follow its own carefully random path to our rendezvous
point, one hundred eight clicks from the base. Fourteen drone ships
were launched at the same time, to confound the enemy's antispacecraft
system.

The landing went off almost perfectly. One ship suffered minor damage, a near miss boiling away some of the ablative material on one side
of the hull, but it'd still be able to make it and return, as long as it kept
its speed down while in the atmosphere.

We zigged and zagged and wound up first ship at the rendezvous
point. There was only one trouble. It was under four kilometers of water.

I could almost hear that machine, ninety thousand miles away, grinding its mental gears, adding this new bit of data. We proceeded just as if
we were landing on solid ground: braking rockets, falling, skids out, hit
the water, skip, hit the water, skip, hit the water, sink.

It would have made sense to go ahead and land on the bottom—we
were streamlined, after all, and water just another fluid—but the hull
wasn't strong enough to hold up a four-kilometer column of water.
Sergeant Cortez was in the scoutship with us.

"Sarge, tell that computer to *do* something! We're gonna get. . . ."

"Oh, shut up, Mandella. Trust in th' lord." "Lord" was definitely
lower-case when Cortez said it.

There was a loud bubbly sigh, then another and a slight increase in
pressure on my back that meant the ship was rising. "Flotation bags?"
Cortez didn't deign to answer, or didn't know.

That must have been it. We rose to within ten or fifteen meters of the surface and stopped, suspended there. Through the port I could see the surface above, shimmering like a mirror of hammered silver. I wondered what it could be like, to be a fish and have a definite roof over your world.

I watched another ship splash in. It made a great cloud of bubbles and turbulence, then fell—slightly tailfirst—for a short distance before large bags popped out under each delta wing. Then it bobbed up to about our level and stayed.

Soon all of the ships were floating within a few hundred meters of us, like a school of ungainly fish.

"This is Captain Stott. Now listen carefully. There is a beach some twenty-eight clicks from your present position, in the direction of the enemy. You will be proceeding to this beach by scoutship and from there will mount your assault on the Tauran position." That was *some* improvement; we'd only have to walk eighty clicks.

WE DEFLATED THE bags, blasted to the surface and flew in a slow, spread-out formation to the beach. It took several minutes. As the ship scraped to a halt I could hear pumps humming, making the cabin pressure equal to the air pressure outside. Before it had quite stopped moving, the escape slot beside my couch slid open. I rolled out onto the wing of the craft and jumped to the ground. Ten seconds to find cover—I sprinted across loose gravel to the "treeline," a twisty bramble of tall sparse bluish-green shrubs. I dove into the briar path and turned to watch the ships leave. The drones that were left rose slowly to about a hundred meters, then took off in all directions with a bone-jarring roar. The real scoutships slid slowly back into the water. Maybe that was a good idea.

It wasn't a terribly attractive world, but certainly would be easier to get around in than the cryogenic nightmare we were trained for. The sky was a uniform dull silver brightness that merged with the mist over the ocean so completely as to make it impossible to tell where water ended and air began. Small wavelets licked at the black gravel shore, much too slow and graceful in the three-quarters Earth normal gravity. Even from fifty meters away, the rattle of billions of pebbles rolling with the tide was loud in my ears.

The air temperature was 79° Centigrade, not quite hot enough for the sea to boil, even though the air pressure was low compared to Earth's.

Wisps of steam drifted quickly upward from the line where water met land. I wondered how long a man would survive, exposed here without a suit. Would the heat or the low oxygen—partial pressure one-eighth Earth normal—kill him first? Or was there some deadly microorganism that would beat them both. . . .

"This is Cortez. Everybody come over and assemble by me." He was standing on the beach a little to the left of me, waving his hand in a circle over his head. I walked toward him through the shrubs. They were brittle, unsubstantial, seemed paradoxically dried-out in the steamy air. They wouldn't offer much in the way of cover.

"We'll be advancing on a heading .05 radians east of north. I want Platoon One to take point. Two and Three follow about twenty meters behind, to the left and right. Seven, command platoon, is in the middle, twenty meters behind Two and Three. Five and Six, bring up the rear, in a semicircular closed flank. Everybody straight?" Sure, we could do that "arrowhead" maneuver in our sleep. "O.K., let's move out."

I was in Platoon Seven, the "command group." Captain Stott put me there not because I was expected to give any commands, but because of my training in physics.

The command group was supposedly the safest place, buffered by six platoons: people were assigned to it because there was some tactical reason for them to survive at least a little longer than the rest. Cortez was there to give orders. Chavez was there to correct suit malfuncts. The senior medic, Doc Wilson—the only medic who actually had an MD—was there and so was Theodopolis, the radio engineer: our link with the captain, who had elected to stay in orbit.

The rest of us were assigned to the command group by dint of special training or aptitude that wouldn't normally be considered of a "tactical" nature. Facing a totally unknown enemy, there was no way of telling what might prove important. Thus I was there because I was the closest the company had to a physicist. Rogers was biology. Tate was chemistry. He could crank out a perfect score on the Rhine extrasensory perception test, every time. Bohrs was a polyglot, able to speak twenty-one languages fluently, idiomatically. Petrov's talent was that he had tested out to have not one molecule of xenophobia in his psyche. Keating was a skilled acrobat. Debby Hollister—"Lucky" Hollister—showed a remarkable aptitude for making money, and also had a consistently high Rhine potential.

12

When we first set out, we were using the "jungle" camouflage combination on our suits. But what passed for jungle in these anemic tropics was too sparse; we looked like a band of conspicuous harlequins trooping through the woods. Cortez had us switch to black, but that was just as bad, as the light from Epsilon came evenly from all parts of the sky, and there were no shadows except us. We finally settled on the dun-colored desert camouflage.

The nature of the countryside changed slowly as we walked north, away from the sea. The throned stalks, I guess you could call them trees, came in fewer numbers but were bigger around and less brittle; at the base of each was a tangled mass of vine with the same blue-green color, which spread out in a flattened cone some ten meters in diameter. There was a delicate green flower the size of a man's head near the top of each tree.

Grass began to appear some five clicks from the sea. It seemed to respect the trees' "property rights," leaving a strip of bare earth around each cone of vine. At the edge of such a clearing, it would grow as timid blue-green stubble; then, moving away from the tree, would get thicker and taller until it reached shoulder-high in some places, where the separation between two trees was unusually large. The grass was a lighter, greener shade than the trees and vines. We changed the color of our suits to the bright green we had used for maximum visibility on Charon. Keeping to the thickest part of the grass, we were fairly inconspicuous.

I couldn't help thinking that one week of training in a South American jungle would have been worth a hell of a lot more than all those weeks on Charon. We wouldn't be so understrength, either.

We covered over twenty clicks each day, buoyant after months under 2 Gs. Until the second day, the only form of animal life we saw was a kind of black worm, finger-sized with hundreds of cilium legs like the bristles of a stiff brush. Rogers said that there obviously had to be some sort of larger creature around, or there would be no reason for the trees to have thorns. So we were doubly on guard, expecting trouble both from the Taurans and the unidentified "large creatures."

Potter's Second Platoon was on point; the general freak was reserved for her, since point would likely be the first platoon to spot any trouble.

"Sarge, this is Potter," we all heard. "Movement ahead."

"Get down, then!"

"We are. Don't think they see us."

"First Platoon, go up to the right of point. Keep down. Fourth, get up to the left. Tell me when you get in position. Sixth Platoon, stay back and guard the rear. Fifth and Third, close with the command group."

Two dozen people whispered out of the grass, to join us. Cortez must have heard from the Fourth Platoon.

"Good. How about you, First . . . O.K., fine. How many are there?"

"Eight we can see." Potter's voice.

"Good. When I give the word, open fire. Shoot to kill."

"Sarge . . . they're just animals."

"Potter—if you've known all this time what a Tauran looks like, you should've told us. Shoot to kill."

"But we need. . . ."

"We need a prisoner, but we don't need to escort him forty clicks to his home base and keep an eye on him while we fight. Clear?"

"Yes. Sergeant."

"O.K. Seventh, all you brains and weirds, we're going up and watch. Fifth and Third, come along to guard."

We crawled through the meter-high grass to where the Second Platoon had stretched out in a firing line.

"I don't see anything," Cortez said.

"Ahead and just to the left. Dark green."

THEY WERE ONLY a shade darker than the grass. But after you saw the first one, you could see them all, moving slowly around some thirty meters ahead.

"Fire!" Cortez fired first, then twelve streaks of crimson leaped out and the grass wilted back, disappeared and the creatures convulsed and died trying to scatter.

"Hold fire, hold it!" Cortez stood up. "We want to have something left—Second Platoon, follow me." He strode out toward the smoldering corpses, laser finger pointed out front, obscene divining rod pulling him toward the carnage . . . I felt my gorge rising and knew that all the lurid training tapes, all the horrible deaths in training accidents, hadn't prepared me for this sudden reality . . . that I had a magic wand that I could point at a life and make it a smoking piece of half-raw meat; I wasn't a soldier nor even wanted to be one nor ever would want. . . .

"O.K., Seventh, come on up."

While we were walking toward them, one of the creatures moved, a tiny shudder, and Cortez flicked the beam of his laser over it with an almost negligent gesture. It made a hand-deep gash across the creature's middle. It died, like the others, without emitting a sound.

They were not quite as tall as humans, but wider in girth. They were covered with dark green, almost black fur; white curls where the laser had singed. They appeared to have three legs and an arm. The only ornament to their shaggy heads was a mouth, wet black orifice filled with flat black teeth. They were thoroughly repulsive but their worst feature was not a difference from human beings but a similarity . . . wherever the laser had opened a body cavity, milk-white glistening veined globes and coils of organs spilled out, and their blood was dark clotting red.

"Rogers, take a look. Taurans or not?"

Rogers knelt by one of the disemboweled creatures and opened a flat plastic box, filled with glistening dissecting tools. She selected a scalpel. "One way we might be able to find out." Doc Wilson watched over her shoulder as she methodically slit the membrane covering several organs.

"Here." She held up a blackish fibrous mass between two fingers, parody of daintiness through all that armor.

"So?"

"It's grass, Sergeant. If the Taurans can eat grass and breathe the air, they certainly found a planet remarkably like their home." She tossed it away. "They're animals, Sergeant, just damn animals."

"I don't know," Doc Wilson said. "Just because they walk around on all fours, threes maybe, and are able to eat grass. . . ."

"Well, let's check out the brain." She found one that had been hit on the head and scraped the superficial black char from the wound. "Look at that."

It was almost solid bone. She tugged and ruffled the hair all over the head of another one. "What the hell does it use for sensory organs? No eyes, or ears, or. . . ." She stood up. "Nothing in that head but a mouth and ten centimeters of skull. To protect nothing, not a damn thing."

"If I could shrug, I'd shrug," the doctor said. "It doesn't prove anything—a brain doesn't have to look like a mushy walnut and it doesn't have to be in the head. Maybe that skull isn't bone, maybe *that's* the brain, some crystal lattice. . . ."

"Yeah, but the stomach's in the right place, and if those aren't intestines I'll eat—"

"Look," Cortez said, "this is all real interesting, but all we need to know is whether that thing's dangerous, then we've gotta move on, we don't have all. . . ."

"They aren't dangerous," Rogers began. "They don't. . . ."

"MEDIC! DOC!" SOMEBODY was waving his arms, back at the firing line. Doc sprinted back to him, the rest of us following.

"What's wrong?" He had reached back and unclipped his medical kit on the run.

"It's Ho, she's out."

Doc swung open the door on Ho's biomedical monitor. He didn't have to look far. "She's dead."

"Dead?" Cortez said. "What the hell. . . ."

"Just a minute." Doc plugged a jack into the monitor and fiddled with some dials on his kit. "Everybody's biomed readout is stored for twelve hours. I'm running it backwards, should be able to—there!"

"What?"

"Four and a half minutes ago—must have been when you opened fire. . . ."

"Well?"

"Massive cerebral hemorrhage. No. . . ." He watched the dials. "No . . . warning, no indication of anything out of the ordinary; blood pressure up, pulse up, but normal under the circumstances . . . nothing to . . . indicate. . . ." He reached down and popped her suit. Her fine oriental features were distorted in a horrible grimace, both gums showing. Sticky fluid ran from under her collapsed eyelids and a trickle of blood still dripped from each ear. Doc Wilson closed the suit back up.

"I've never seen anything like it. It's as if a bomb went off in her skull."

"Oh crap," Rogers said, "she was Rhine-sensitive, wasn't she."

"That's right." Cortez sounded thoughtful. "All right, everybody listen. Platoon leaders, check your platoons and see if anybody's missing, or hurt. Anybody else in Seventh?"

"I . . . I've got a splitting headache, Sarge," Lucky said.

Four others had bad headaches. One of them affirmed that he was slightly Rhine-sensitive. The others didn't know.

"Cortez, I think it's obvious," Doc Wilson said, "that we should give these . . . monsters wide berth, especially shouldn't harm any more of them. Not with five people susceptible to whatever apparently killed Ho."

"Of course, damn it, I don't need anybody to tell me that. We'd better get moving. I just filled the captain in on what happened; he agrees that we'd better get as far away from here as we can, before we stop for the night.

"Let's get back in formation and continue on the same bearing. Fifth Platoon, take over point; Second, come back to the rear. Everybody else, same as before."

"What about Ho?" Lucky asked.

"She'll be taken care of. From the ship."

After we'd gone half a click, there was a flash and rolling thunder. Where Ho had been, came a wispy luminous mushroom cloud boiling up to disappear against the gray sky.

13

We stopped for the "night"—actually, the sun wouldn't set for another seventy hours—atop a slight rise some ten clicks from where we had killed the aliens. But they weren't aliens, I had to remind myself—we were.

Two platoons deployed in a ring around the rest of us, and we flopped down exhausted. Everybody was allowed four hours' sleep and had two hours' guard duty.

Potter came over and sat next to me. I chinned her frequency.

"Hi, Marygay."

"Oh, William," her voice over the radio was hoarse and cracking. "God, it's so horrible."

"It's over now. . . ."

"I killed one of them, the first instant, I shot it right in the, in the . . ."

I put my hand on her knee. The contact made a plastic click and I jerked it back, visions of machines embracing, copulating. "Don't feel singled out, Marygay, whatever guilt there is belongs evenly to all of us . . . but a triple portion for Cor. . . ."

"You privates quit jawin' and get some sleep. You both pull guard in two hours."

"O.K., Sarge." Her voice was so sad and tired I couldn't bear it. I felt if I could only touch her I could drain off the sadness like a ground wire draining current but we were each trapped in our own plastic world.

"G'night, William."

"Night." It's almost impossible to get sexually excited inside a suit, with the relief tube and all the silver chloride sensors poking you, but somehow this was my body's response to the emotional impotence, maybe remembering more pleasant sleeps with Marygay, maybe feeling that in the midst of all this death, personal death could be soon, cranking up the pro-creative derrick for one last try . . . lovely thoughts like this, and I fell asleep and dreamed that I was a machine, mimicking the functions of life, creaking and clanking my clumsy way through the world, people too polite to say anything but giggling behind my back, and the little man who sat inside my head pulling the levers and clutches and watching the dials, he was hopelessly mad and was storing up hurts for the day. . . .

"Mandella—wake up, damn it, your shift!"

I shuffled over to my place on the perimeter to watch for God knows what . . . but I was so weary I couldn't keep my eyes open. Finally I tongued a stimtab, knowing I'd pay for it later.

For over an hour I sat there, scanning my sector left, right, near, far; the scene never changing, not even a breath of wind to stir the grass.

Then suddenly the grass parted and one of the three-legged creatures was right in front of me. I raised my finger but didn't squeeze.

"Movement!"

"Movement!"

"HOLD YOUR FIRE. Don't shoot!"

"Movement."

"Movement." I looked left and right and as far as I could see, every perimeter guard had one of the blind dumb creatures standing right in front of him.

Maybe the drug I'd taken to stay awake made me more sensitive to whatever they did. My scalp crawled and I felt a formless *thing* in my mind, the feeling you get when somebody has said something and you didn't quite hear it, want to respond but the opportunity to ask him to repeat it is gone.

The creature sat back on its haunches, leaning forward on the one front leg. Big green bear with a withered arm. Its power threaded through my mind, spiderwebs, echo of night terrors, trying to communicate, trying to destroy me, I couldn't know.

"ALL RIGHT, EVERYBODY on the perimeter, fall back, slow. Don't make any quick gestures . . . anybody got a headache or anything?"

"Sergeant, this is Hollister." Lucky.

"They're trying to say something . . . I can almost . . . no, just. . . ."

"Well?"

"All I can get is that they think we're . . . think we're . . . well, *funny*. They aren't afraid."

"You mean the one in front of you isn't. . . ."

"No, the feeling comes from all of them, they're all thinking the same thing. Don't ask me how I know, I just do."

"Maybe they thought it was funny, what they did to Ho."

"Maybe. I don't feel like they're dangerous. Just curious about us."

"Sergeant, this is Bohrs."

"Yeah."

"The Taurans have been here at least a year—maybe they've learned how to communicate with these . . . overgrown teddy-bears. They might be spying on us, might be sending back. . . ."

"I don't think they'd show themselves, if that were the case," Lucky said. "They can obviously hide from us pretty well when they want to."

"Anyhow," Cortez said, "if they're spies, the damage has been done. Don't think it'd be smart to take any action against them. I know you'd all like to see 'em dead for what they did to Ho, so would I, but we'd better be careful."

I didn't want to see them dead, but I'd just as soon not see them in any condition. I was walking backwards slowly, toward the middle of camp. The creature didn't seem disposed to follow. Maybe he just knew we were surrounded. He was pulling up grass with his arm and munching.

"O.K., all of you platoon leaders, wake everybody up, get a roll count. Let me know if anybody's been hurt. Tell your people we're moving out in one minute."

I don't know what Cortez expected, but of course the creatures just followed right along. They didn't keep us surrounded; just had twenty or thirty following us all the time. Not the same ones, either. Individuals would saunter away, new ones would join the parade. It was pretty obvious that *they* weren't going to tire out.

We were each allowed one stimtab. Without it, no one could have marched an hour. A second pill would have been welcome after the edge started to wear off, but the mathematics of the situation forbade it: we were still thirty clicks from the enemy base; fifteen hours' marching at the least. And though one could stay awake and energetic for a hundred hours on the 'tabs, aberrations of judgment and perception snowballed after the second 'tab, until *in extremis* the most bizarre hallucinations would be taken at face value, and a person would fidget for hours, deciding whether to have breakfast.

Under artificial stimulation, the company traveled with great energy for the first six hours, was slowing by the seventh, and ground to an exhausted halt after nine hours and nineteen kilometers. The teddy-bears had never lost sight of us and, according to Lucky, had never stopped "broadcasting." Cortez's decision was that we would stop for seven hours, each platoon taking one hour of perimeter guard. I was never so glad to have been in the Seventh Platoon, as we stood guard the last shift and thus were the only ones to get six hours of uninterrupted sleep.

In the few moments I lay awake after finally lying down, the thought came to me that the next time I closed my eyes could well be the last. And partly because of the drug hangover, mostly because of the past day's horrors, I found that I really just didn't give a damn.

14

Our first contact with the Taurans came during my shift.

The teddy-bears were still there when I woke up and replaced Doc Jones on guard. They'd gone back to their original formation, one in front of each guard position. The one who was waiting for me seemed a little larger than normal, but otherwise looked just like all the others. All the grass had been cropped where he was sitting, so he occasionally made forays to the left or right. But he always returned to sit right in front of me, you would say staring if he had had anything to stare with.

We had been facing each other for about fifteen minutes when Cortez's voice rumbled:

"Awright, everybody wake up and get hid!"

I followed instinct and flopped to the ground and rolled into a tall stand of grass.

"Enemy vessel overhead." His voice was almost laconic.

Strictly speaking, it wasn't really overhead, but rather passing somewhat east of us. It was moving slowly, maybe a hundred clicks per hour, and looked like a broomstick surrounded by a dirty soap bubble. The creature riding it was a little more human-looking than the teddy-bears, but still no prize. I cranked my image amplifier up to forty log two for a closer look.

He had two arms and two legs, but his waist was so small you could encompass it with both hands. Under the tiny waist was a large horseshoe-shaped pelvic structure nearly a meter wide, from which dangled two long skinny legs with no apparent knee joint. Above that waist his body swelled out again, to a chest no smaller than the huge pelvis. His arms looked surprisingly human, except that they were too long and under-muscled. There were too many fingers on his hands. Shoulderless, neck-less; his head was a nightmarish growth that swelled like a goiter from his massive chest. Two eyes that looked like clusters of fish eggs, a bundle of tassles instead of a nose, and a rigidly open hole that might have been a mouth sitting low down where his Adam's apple should have been. Evidently the soap bubble contained an amenable environment, as he was wearing absolutely nothing except a ridged hide that looked like skin submerged too long in hot water, then dyed a pale orange. "He" had no external genitalia, nor anything that might hint of mammary glands.

Obviously, he either didn't see us, or thought we were part of the herd of teddy-bears. He never looked back at us, but just continued in the same direction we were headed, .05 rad east of north.

"Might as well go back to sleep now, if you can sleep after looking at *that* thing. We move out at 0435." Forty minutes.

Because of the planet's opaque cloud cover, there had been no way to tell, from space, what the enemy base looked like or how big it was. We only knew its position, the same way we knew the position the scoutships were supposed to land on. So it could easily have been underwater too, or underground.

But some of the drones were reconnaissance ships as well as decoys; and in their mock attacks on the base, one managed to get close enough to take a picture. Captain Stott beamed down a diagram of the place to Cortez—the only one with a visor in his suit—when we were five clicks from the base's "radio" position. We stopped and he called all of the platoon leaders in with the Seventh Platoon to confer. Two teddy-bears loped in, too. We tried to ignore them.

"O.K., the captain sent down some pictures of our objective. I'm going to draw a map; you platoon leaders copy." They took pads and styli out of their leg pockets, while Cortez unrolled a large plastic mat. He gave it a shake to randomize any residual charge, and turned on his stylus.

"Now, we're coming from this direction." He put an arrow at the bottom of the sheet. "First thing we'll hit is this row of huts, probably billets, or bunkers, but who the hell knows . . . our initial objective is to destroy these buildings—the whole base is on a flat plain; there's no way we could really sneak by them."

"Potter here. Why can't we jump over them?"

"Yeah, we could do that, and wind up completely surrounded, cut to ribbons. We take the buildings.

"After we do that . . . all I can say is that we'll have to think on our feet. From the aerial reconnaissance, we can figure out the function of only a couple of buildings—and that stinks. We might wind up wasting a lot of time demolishing the equivalent of an enlisted man's bar, ignoring a huge logistic computer because it looks like . . . a garbage dump or something."

"Mandella here," I said. "Isn't there a spaceport of some kind—seems to me we ought to. . . ."

"I'll *get* to that, damn it. There's a ring of these huts all around the camp, so we've got to break through somewhere. This place'll be closest, less chance of giving away our position before we attack.

"There's nothing in the whole place that actually looks like a weapon. That doesn't mean anything, though; you could hide a bevawatt laser in each of those huts.

"Now, about five hundred meters from the huts, in the middle of the base, we'll come to this big flower-shaped structure." Cortez drew a large symmetrical shape that looked like the outline of a flower with seven petals. "What the hell this is, your guess is as good as mine. There's only one of them, though, so we don't damage it any more than we have to. Which means . . . we blast it to splinters if I think it's dangerous.

"Now, as far as your spaceport, Mandella, is concerned—there just isn't one. Nothing.

"That cruiser the *Hope* caulked had probably been left in orbit, like ours has to be. If they have any equivalent of a scoutship, or drone missiles, they're either not kept here or they're well hidden."

"Bohrs here. Then what did they attack with, while we were coming down from orbit?"

"I wish we knew, Private.

"Obviously, we don't have any way of estimating their numbers, not directly. Recon pictures failed to show a single Tauran on the grounds of the base. Meaning nothing, because it *is* an alien environment. Indirectly, though . . . we can count the number of broomsticks.

"There are fifty-one huts, and each has at most one broomstick. Four don't have one parked outside, but we located three at various other parts of the base. Maybe this indicates that there are fifty-one Taurans, one of whom was outside the base when the picture was taken."

"Keating here. Or fifty-one officers."

"That's right—maybe fifty thousand infantrymen stacked in one of these buildings. No way to tell. Maybe ten Taurans, each with five broomsticks, to use according to his mood.

"We've got one thing in our favor, and that's communications. They evidently use a frequency modulation of megahertz electromagnetic radiation."

"Radio!"

"That's right, whoever you are. Identify yourself when you speak. So, it's quite possible that they can't detect our phased-neutrino communications. Also, just prior to the attack, the *Hope* is going to deliver a nice dirty fission bomb; detonate it in the upper atmosphere right over the base. That'll restrict them to line-of-sight communication for some time; even those will be full of static."

"Why don't . . . Tate here . . . why don't they just drop the bomb right in their laps? Would save us a lot of. . . ."

"That doesn't even deserve an answer, Private. But the answer is, they might. And you better hope they don't. If they caulk the base, it'll be for the safety of the *Hope*. *After* we've attacked, and probably before we're far enough away for it to make much difference.

"We keep that from happening by doing a good job. We have to reduce the base to where it can no longer function; at the same time, leave as much intact as possible. And take one prisoner."

"Potter here. You mean, at least one prisoner."

"I mean what I say. One only. Potter . . . you're relieved of your platoon. Send Chavez up."

"All right, Sergeant." The relief in her voice was unmistakable.

CORTEZ CONTINUED WITH his map and instructions. There was one other building whose function was pretty obvious; it had a large steerable dish antenna on top. We were to destroy it as soon as the grenadiers got in range.

The attack plan was very loose. Our signal to begin would be the flash of the fission bomb. At the same time, several drones would converge on the base, so we could see what their antispacecraft defenses were. We would try to reduce the effectiveness of those defenses without destroying them completely.

Immediately after the bomb and the drones, the grenadiers would vaporize a line of seven huts. Everybody would break through the hole into the base . . . and what would happen after that was anybody's guess.

Ideally, we'd sweep from that end of the base to the other, destroying certain targets, caulking all but one Tauran. But that was unlikely to happen, as it depended on the Taurans' offering very little resistance.

On the other hand, if the Taurans showed obvious superiority from the beginning, Cortez would give the order to scatter: everybody had a different compass bearing for retreat—we'd blossom out in all directions, the survivors to rendezvous in a valley some forty clicks east of the base. Then we'd see about a return engagement, after the *Hope* softened the base up a bit.

"One last thing," Cortez rasped. "Maybe some of you feel the way Potter evidently does, maybe some of your men feel that way . . . that we ought to go easy, not make this so much of a bloodbath. Mercy is a luxury, a weakness we can't afford to indulge in at this stage of the war. *All* we know about the enemy is that they have killed seven hundred and ninety-eight humans. They haven't shown any restraint in attacking our cruisers, and it'd be foolish to expect any this time, this first ground action.

"*They* are responsible for the lives of all of your comrades who died in training, and for Ho, and for all the others who are surely going to die today. I can't *understand* anybody who wants to spare them. But that doesn't make any difference. You have your orders, and what the hell, you might as well know, all of you have a posthypnotic suggestion that I will trigger by a phrase, just before the battle. It will make your job easier."

"Sergeant. . . ."

"Shut up. We're short on time; get back to your platoons and brief them. We move out in five minutes."

The platoon leaders returned to their men, leaving Cortez and the ten of us, plus three teddy-bears, milling around, getting in the way.

15

We took the last five clicks very carefully, sticking to the highest grass, running across occasional clearings. When we were five hundred meters from where the base was supposed to be, Cortez took the Third Platoon forward to scout, while the rest of us laid low.

Cortez's voice came over the general freak: "Looks pretty much like we expected. Advance in a file, crawling. When you get to the Third Platoon, follow your squad leader to the left, or right."

We did that and wound up with a string of eighty-three people in a line roughly perpendicular to the direction of attack. We were pretty well hidden, except for the dozen or so teddy-bears that mooched along the line munching grass.

There was no sign of life inside the base. All of the buildings were windowless, and a uniform shiny white. The huts that were our first objective were large featureless half-buried eggs, some sixty meters apart. Cortez assigned one to each grenadier.

We were broken into three fire teams: Team A consisted of platoons Two, Four, and Six; Team B was One, Three, and Five; the command platoon was Team C.

"Less than a minute now—filters down!—when I say 'fire,' grenadiers take out your targets. God help you if you miss."

There was a sound like a giant's belch and a stream of five or six iridescent bubbles floated up from the flower-shaped building. They rose with increasing speed to where they were almost out of sight, then shot off to the south, over our heads. The ground was suddenly bright and for the first time in a long time, I saw my shadow, a long one pointed north. The bomb had gone off prematurely. I just had time to think that it didn't make too much difference; it'd still make alphabet soup out of their communications. . . .

"Drones!" A ship came screaming in just above tree level, and a bubble was in the air to meet it. When they contacted, the bubble popped and the drone exploded into a million tiny fragments. Another one came from the opposite side and suffered the same fate.

"FIRE!" Seven bright glares of 500-microton grenades and a sustained concussion that I'm sure would have killed an unprotected man.

"Filters up." Gray haze of smoke and dust. Clods of dirt falling with a sound like heavy raindrops.

"Listen up:

" 'Scots, wha hae wi' Wallace bled;
Scots, wham Bruce has aften led,
Welcome to your gory bed,
Or to victory!' "

I hardly heard him, for trying to keep track of what was going on in my skull. I knew it was just posthypnotic suggestion, even remembered the session in Missouri when they'd implanted it, but that didn't make it any less compelling. My mind reeled under the strong pseudo-memories; shaggy hulks that were Taurans—not at all what we now knew they looked like—boarding a colonist's vessel, eating babies while mothers watched in screaming terror—the colonists never took babies; they wouldn't stand the acceleration—then raping the women to death with huge veined purple members—ridiculous that they would feel desire for humans—holding the men down while they plucked flesh from their living bodies and gobbled it . . . a hundred grisly details as sharply remembered as the events of a minute ago, ridiculously overdone and logically absurd; but while my conscious mind was reflecting the silliness, somewhere much deeper, down in that sleeping giant where we keep our real motives and morals, something was thirsting for alien blood, secure in the conviction that the noblest thing a man could do would be to die killing one of those horrible monsters. . . .

I knew it was all purest soya, and I hated the men who had taken such obscene liberties with my mind, but still I could hear my teeth grinding, feel cheeks frozen in a spastic grin, bloodlust . . . a teddy-bear walked in front of me, looking dazed. I started to raise my laserfinger, but somebody beat me to it and the creature's head exploded in a cloud of gray splinters and blood.

Lucky groaned, half-whining, "Dirty . . . filthy bastards." Lasers flared and crisscrossed and all of the teddy-bears fell dead.

"*Watch* it, damn it," Cortez screamed. "*Aim* those things; they aren't toys!

"Team A, move out—into the craters to cover B."

Somebody was laughing and sobbing. "What the crap is wrong with *you*, Petrov?" First time I could remember Cortez cussing.

I twisted around and saw Petrov, behind and to my left, lying in a shallow hole, digging frantically with both hands, crying and gurgling.

"Crap," Cortez said. "Team B! past the craters ten meters, get down in a line. Team C—into the craters with A."

. . .

I scrambled up and covered the hundred meters in twelve amplified strides. The craters were practically large enough to hide a scoutship, some ten meters in diameter. I jumped to the opposite side of the hole and landed next to a fellow named Chin. He didn't even look around when I landed, just kept scanning the base for signs of life.

"Team A—past Team B ten meters, down in line." Just as he finished, the building in front of us burped and a salvo of the bubbles fanned out toward our lines. Most people saw it coming and got down, but Chin was just getting up to make his rush and stepped right into one.

It grazed the top of his helmet, and disappeared with a faint pop. He took one step backwards and toppled over the edge of the crater, trailing an arc of blood and brains. Lifeless, spreadeagled, he slid halfway to the bottom, shoveling dirt into the perfectly symmetrical hole where the bubble had chewed through plastic, hair, skin, bone and brain indiscriminately.

"Everybody hold it. Platoon leaders, casualty report . . . check . . . check, check . . . check, check, check . . . check. We have three deaders. Wouldn't be *any* if you'd have kept low. So everybody grab dirt when you hear that thing go off. Team A, complete the rush."

They completed the maneuver without incident. "O.K. Team C, rush to where B . . . hold it! Down!"

Everybody was already hugging the ground. The bubbles slid by in a smooth arc about two meters off the ground. They went serenely over our heads and, except for one that made toothpicks out of a tree, disappeared in the distance.

"B, rush past A ten meters. C, take over B's place. You B grenadiers see if you can reach the Flower."

Two grenades tore up the ground thirty or forty meters from the structure. In a good imitation of panic, it started belching out a continuous stream of bubbles—still, none coming lower than two meters off the ground. We kept hunched down and continued to advance.

Suddenly, a seam appeared in the building, widened to the size of a large door, and Taurans came swarming out.

"Grenadiers, hold your fire. B team, laser fire to the left and right, keep 'em bunched up. A and C, rush down the center."

One Tauran died trying to turn through a laser beam. The others stayed where they were.

In a suit, it's pretty awkward to run and try to keep your head down, at the same time. You have to go from side to side, like a skater getting started; otherwise you'll be airborne. At least one person, somebody in A team, bounced too high and suffered the same fate as Chin.

I was feeling pretty fenced-in and trapped, with a wall of laser fire on each side and a low ceiling that meant death to touch. But in spite of myself, I felt happy, euphoric at finally getting the chance to kill some of those villainous baby-eaters.

They weren't fighting back, except for the rather ineffective bubbles—obviously not designed as an antipersonnel weapon—and they didn't retreat back into the building, either. They just milled around, about a hundred of them, and watched us get closer. A couple of grenades would caulk them all, but I guess Cortez was thinking about the prisoner.

"O.K., when I say 'go,' we're going to flank 'em. B team will hold fire . . . Second and Fourth to the right, Sixth and Seventh to the left. B team will move forward in line to box them in.

"Go!" We peeled off to the left. As soon as the lasers stopped, the Taurans bolted, running in a group on a collision course with our flank.

"A Team, down and fire! Don't shoot until you're sure of your aim—if you miss you might hit a friendly. And fer Chris'sake save me one!"

It was a horrifying sight, that herd of monsters bearing down on us. They were running in great leaps—the bubbles avoiding them—and they all looked like the one we saw earlier, riding the broomstick; naked except for an almost transparent sphere around their whole bodies, that moved along with them. The right flank started firing, picking off individuals in the rear of the pack.

Suddenly a laser flared through the Taurans from the other side, somebody missing his mark. There was a horrible scream and I looked down the line to see someone, I think it was Perry, writhing on the ground, right hand over the smoldering stump of his left arm, seared off just below the elbow. Blood sprayed through his fingers and the suit, its camouflage circuits scrambled, flickered black-white-jungle-desert-green-gray. I don't know how long I stared—long enough for the medic to run over and start giving aid—but when I looked up the Taurans were almost on top of me.

My first shot was wild and high, but it grazed the top of the leading Tauran's protective bubble. The bubble disappeared and the monster stumbled and fell to the ground, jerking spasmodically. Foam gushed out of his mouth-hole, first white, then streaked with red. With one last jerk he became rigid and twisted backwards, almost to the shape of a horseshoe. His long scream, a high-pitched whistle, stopped just as his comrades trampled over him and I hated myself for smiling.

It was slaughter, even though our flank was outnumbered five to one. They kept coming without faltering, even when they had to climb over the drift of bodies and parts of bodies that piled up high, parallel to our flank. The ground between us was slick red with Tauran blood—all God's children got hemoglobin—and, like the teddy-bears, their guts looked pretty much like guts to my untrained eye. My helmet reverberated with hysterical laughter while we cut them to gory chunks. I almost didn't hear Cortez.

"Hold your fire—I said HOLD IT damn it! *Catch* a couple of the bastards, they won't hurt you."

I stopped shooting and eventually so did everybody else. When the next Tauran jumped over the smoking pile of meat in front of me, I dove to tackle him around those spindly legs.

It was like hugging a big, slippery balloon. When I tried to drag him down, he just popped out of my arms and kept running.

We managed to stop one of them by the simple expedient of piling half-a-dozen people on top of him. By that time the others had run through our line and were headed for the row of large cylindrical tanks that Cortez had said were probably for storage. A little door had opened in the base of each one.

"We've *got* our prisoner," Cortez shouted. "*Kill!*"

They were fifty meters away and running hard, difficult targets. Lasers slashed around them, bobbing high and low. One fell, sliced in two, but the others, about ten of them, kept going and were almost to the doors when the grenadiers started firing.

They were still loaded with 500-mike bombs, but a near miss wasn't enough—the concussion would just send them flying, unhurt in their bubbles.

"The buildings! Get the damn buildings!" The grenadiers raised their aim and let fly, but the bombs only seemed to scorch the white outside of the structures until, by chance, one landed in a door. That split the building just as if it had a seam; the two halves popped away and a cloud of machinery flew into the air, accompanied by a huge pale flame that rolled up and disappeared in an instant. Then the others all concentrated on the doors, except for potshots at some of the Taurans; not so much to get them as to blow them away before they could get inside. They seemed awfully eager.

ALL THIS TIME, we were trying to get the Taurans with laser fire, while they weaved and bounced around trying to get into the structures. We moved in as close to them as we could without putting ourselves in danger from the grenade blasts—that was still too far away for good aim.

Still, we were getting them one by one, and managed to destroy four of the seven buildings. Then, when there were only two aliens left, a nearby grenade blast flung one of them to within a few meters of a door. He dove in and several grenadiers fired salvos after him, but they all fell short, or detonated harmlessly on the side. Bombs were falling all around, making an awful racket, but the sound was suddenly drowned out by a great sigh, like a giant's intake of breath, and where the building had been was a thick cylindrical cloud of smoke, solid-looking, dwindling away into the stratosphere, straight as if laid down by a ruler. The other Tauran had been right at the base of the cylinder; I could see pieces of him flying. A second later, a shock wave hit us and I rolled helplessly, pinwheeling, to smash into the pile of Tauran bodies and roll beyond.

I picked myself up and panicked for a second when I saw there was blood all over my suit—when I realized it was only alien blood, I relaxed but felt unclean.

"*Catch* the bastard! Catch him!" In the confusion, the Tauran—now the only one left alive—had got free and was running for the grass. One platoon was chasing after him, losing ground, but then all of B team ran over and cut him off. I jogged over to join in the fun.

There were four people on top of him, and fifty people watching.

"Spread out, damn it! There might be a thousand more of them waiting to get us in one place." We dispersed, grumbling. By unspoken agreement we were all sure that there were no more live Taurans on the face of the planet.

Cortez was walking toward the prisoner while I backed away. Suddenly the four men collapsed in a pile on top of the creature . . . even from my distance I could see the foam spouting from his mouth-hole. His bubble had popped. Suicide.

"Damn!" Cortez was right there. "Get off that bastard." The four men got off and Cortez used his laser to slice the monster into a dozen quivering chunks. Heartwarming sight.

"That's all right, though, we'll find another one—everybody! Back in the arrowhead formation. Combat assault, on the Flower."

Well, we assaulted the Flower, which had evidently run out of ammunition—it was still belching, but no bubbles—and it was empty. We just scurried up ramps and through corridors, fingers at the ready, like kids playing soldier. There was nobody home.

The same lack of response at the antenna installation, the "Salami," and twenty other major buildings, as well as the forty-four perimeter huts still intact. So we had "captured" dozens of buildings, mostly of incomprehensible purpose, but failed in our main mission; capturing a Tauran for the xenologists to experiment with. Oh, well, they could have all the bits and pieces of the creatures they'd ever want. That was something.

After we'd combed every last square centimeter of the base, a scout-ship came in with the real exploration crew, Star Fleet scientists. Cortez said, "All right, snap out of it," and the hypnotic compulsion fell away.

At first it was pretty grim. A lot of the people, like Lucky and Mary-gay, almost went crazy with the memories of bloody murder multiplied a hundred times. Cortez ordered everybody to take a sedtab, two for the ones most upset. I took two without being specifically ordered to do so.

Because it *was* murder, unadorned butchery—once we had the anti-spacecraft weapon doped out, we weren't in any danger. The Taurans didn't seem to have any conception of person-to-person fighting. We just herded them up and slaughtered them, in the first encounter between mankind and another intelligent species. What might have happened if we had sat down and tried to communicate? Maybe it was the second encounter, counting the teddy-bears. But they got the same treatment.

I spent a long time after that telling myself over and over that it hadn't been *me* who so gleefully carved up those frightened, stampeding creatures. Back in the Twentieth Century, they established to everybody's satisfaction that "I was just following orders" was an inadequate excuse for inhuman conduct . . . but what can you do when the orders come from deep down in that puppet master of the unconscious?

Worst of all was the feeling that perhaps my actions weren't all that inhuman. Ancestors only a few generations back would have done the same thing, even to their fellowmen, without any hypnotic conditioning.

So I was disgusted with the human race, disgusted with the army, and horrified at the prospect of living with myself for another century or so . . . well, there was always brainwipe.

The ship that the lone Tauran survivor had escaped in had got away, clean, the bulk of the planet shielding it from *Earth's Hope* while it dropped into Aleph's collapsar field. Escaped to home, I guessed, wherever that was, to report what twenty men with hand-weapons could do to a hundred fleeing on foot, unarmed.

I suspected that the next time humans met Taurans in ground combat, we would be more evenly matched. And I was right.

Arthur C. Clarke

Arthur C. Clarke's lengthy publishing credentials include articles in mid-century scientific journals that laid the groundwork for the development of telecommunications satellites. Among his many influential works of science fiction are the visionary novel of man's future in the universe, Childhood's End, *and the now legendary film and fiction that grew out of its concepts:* 2001: A Space Odyssey, 2010: Odyssey Two, 2061: Odyssey Three, *and* 3001: The Final Odyssey. *Clarke is regarded as one of the masters of hard science fiction, and his novels* Prelude to Space, A Fall of Moondust, *and* The Fountains of Paradise *have all been praised for their meticulous scientific accuracy. At the same time, he has explored the metaphysical and cosmological implications of science and space exploration in such works as the Hugo and Nebula Award–winning novel* Rendezvous with Rama *and the oft-reprinted title story of* The Nine Billion Names of God, *one of the many collections of his short fiction, which include* Reach for Tomorrow, Tales from the White Hart, The Other Side of the Sky, *and* Tales of Ten Worlds. *Clarke's bestselling books of popular science include* The Exploration of Space, Profiles of the Future, *and* The View from Serendip. *He has also authored the young adult novels* Islands in the Sky *and* Dolphin Island, *and the autobiographical volume* Astounding Days.

SUPERIORITY

Arthur C. Clarke

IN MAKING THIS STATEMENT—which I do of my own free will—I wish first to make it perfectly clear that I am not in any way trying to gain sympathy, nor do I expect any mitigation of whatever sentence the Court may pronounce. I am writing this in an attempt to refute some of the lying reports broadcast over the prison radio and published in the papers I have been allowed to see. These have given an entirely false picture of the true cause of our defeat, and as the leader of my race's armed forces at the cessation of hostilities I feel it my duty to protest against such libels upon those who served under me.

I also hope that this statement may explain the reasons for the application I have twice made to the Court, and will now induce it to grant a favor for which I can see no possible grounds of refusal.

The ultimate cause of our failure was a simple one: despite all statements to the contrary, it was not due to lack of bravery on the part of our men, or to any fault of the Fleet's. We were defeated by one thing only— by the inferior science of our enemies. I repeat—by the *inferior* science of our enemies.

When the war opened we had no doubt of our ultimate victory. The combined fleets of our allies greatly exceeded in number and armament those which the enemy could muster against us, and in almost all branches of military science we were their superiors. We were sure that we could maintain this superiority. Our belief proved, alas, to be only too well founded.

At the opening of the war our main weapons were the long-range homing torpedo, dirigible ball-lightning and the various modifications of the Klydon beam. Every unit of the Fleet was equipped with these and though the enemy possessed similar weapons their installations were generally of lesser power. Moreover, we had behind us a far greater military Research Organization, and with this initial advantage we could not possibly lose.

The campaign proceeded according to plan until the Battle of the Five Suns. We won this, of course, but the opposition proved stronger than we had expected. It was realized that victory might be more difficult, and more delayed, than had first been imagined. A conference of supreme commanders was therefore called to discuss our future strategy.

Present for the first time at one of our war conferences was Professor-General Norden, the new Chief of the Research Staff, who had just been appointed to fill the gap left by the death of Malvar, our greatest scientist. Malvar's leadership had been responsible, more than any other single factor, for the efficiency and power of our weapons. His loss was a very serious blow, but no one doubted the brilliance of his successor—though many of us disputed the wisdom of appointing a theoretical scientist to fill a post of such vital importance. But we had been overruled.

I can well remember the impression Norden made at that conference. The military advisers were worried, and as usual turned to the scientists for help. Would it be possible to improve our existing weapons, they asked, so that our present advantage could be increased still further?

Norden's reply was quite unexpected. Malvar had often been asked such a question—and he had always done what we requested.

"Frankly, gentlemen," said Norden, "I doubt it. Our existing weapons have practically reached finality. I don't wish to criticize my predecessor, or the excellent work done by the Research Staff in the last few generations, but do you realize that there has been no basic change in armaments for over a century? It is, I am afraid, the result of a tradition that has become conservative. For too long, the Research Staff has devoted itself to perfecting old weapons instead of developing new ones. It is fortunate for us that our opponents have been no wiser: we cannot assume that this will always be so."

Norden's words left an uncomfortable impression, as he had no doubt intended. He quickly pressed home the attack.

"What we want are *new* weapons—weapons totally different from any that have been employed before. Such weapons can be made: it will take time, of course, but since assuming charge I have replaced some of the older scientists with young men and have directed research into several unexplored fields which show great promise. I believe, in fact, that a revolution in warfare may soon be upon us."

We were skeptical. There was a bombastic tone in Norden's voice that made us suspicious of his claims. We did not know, then, that he never promised anything that he had not already almost perfected in the laboratory. *In the laboratory*—that was the operative phrase.

Norden proved his case less than a month later, when he demonstrated the Sphere of Annihilation, which produced complete disintegration of matter over a radius of several hundred meters. We were intoxicated by the power of the new weapon, and were quite prepared to overlook one fundamental defect—the fact that it *was* a sphere and hence destroyed its rather complicated generating equipment at the instant of formation. This meant, of course, that it could not be used on warships but only on guided missiles, and a great program was started to convert all homing torpedoes to carry the new weapon. For the time being all further offensives were suspended.

We realize now that this was our first mistake. I still think that it was a natural one, for it seemed to us then that all our existing weapons had become obsolete overnight, and we already regarded them as almost primitive survivals. What we did not appreciate was the magnitude of the task we were attempting, and the length of time it would take to get the revolutionary super-weapon into battle. Nothing like this had happened for a hundred years and we had no previous experience to guide us.

The conversion problem proved far more difficult than anticipated. A new class of torpedo had to be designed, as the standard model was too small. This meant in turn that only the larger ships could launch the weapon, but we were prepared to accept this penalty. After six months, the heavy units of the Fleet were being equipped with the Sphere. Training maneuvers and tests had shown that it was operating satisfactorily and we were ready to take it into action. Norden was already being hailed as the architect of victory, and had half promised even more spectacular weapons.

Then two things happened. One of our battleships disappeared completely on a training flight, and an investigation showed that under certain conditions the ship's long-range radar could trigger the Sphere immediately after it had been launched. The modification needed to overcome this defect was trivial, but it caused a delay of another month and was the source of much bad feeling between the naval staff and the scientists. We were ready for action again—when Norden announced that the radius of effectiveness of the Sphere had now been increased by ten, thus multiplying by a thousand the chances of destroying an enemy ship.

So the modifications started all over again, but everyone agreed that the delay would be worth it. Meanwhile, however, the enemy had been emboldened by the absence of further attacks and had made an unexpected onslaught. Our ships were short of torpedoes, since none had been coming from the factories, and were forced to retire. So we lost the systems of Kyrane and Floranus, and the planetary fortress of Rhamsandron.

It was an annoying but not a serious blow, for the recaptured systems had been unfriendly, and difficult to administer. We had no doubt that we could restore the position in the near future, as soon as the new weapon became operational.

These hopes were only partially fulfilled. When we renewed our offensive, we had to do so with fewer of the Spheres of Annihilation than had been planned, and this was one reason for our limited success. The other reason was more serious.

While we had been equipping as many of our ships as we could with the irresistible weapon, the enemy had been building feverishly. His ships were of the old pattern with the old weapons—but they now outnumbered ours. When we went into action, we found that the numbers ranged against us were often 100 percent greater than expected, causing target confusion among the automatic weapons and resulting in higher losses than anticipated. The enemy losses were higher still, for once a Sphere had reached its objective, destruction was certain, but the balance had not swung as far in our favor as we had hoped.

Moreover, while the main fleets had been engaged, the enemy had launched a daring attack on the lightly held systems of Eriston, Duranus, Carmanidora and Pharanidon—recapturing them all. We were thus faced with a threat only fifty light-years from our home planets.

There was much recrimination at the next meeting of the supreme commanders. Most of the complaints were addressed to Norden—Grand Admiral Taxaris in particular maintaining that thanks to our admittedly irresistible weapon we were now considerably worse off than before. We should, he claimed, have continued to build conventional ships, thus preventing the loss of our numerical superiority.

Norden was equally angry and called the naval staff ungrateful bunglers. But I could tell that he was worried—as indeed we all were—by the unexpected turn of events. He hinted that there might be a speedy way of remedying the situation.

We now know that Research had been working on the Battle Analyzer for many years, but at the time it came as a revelation to us and perhaps we were too easily swept off our feet. Norden's argument, also, was seductively convincing. What did it matter, he said, if the enemy had twice as many ships as we—if the efficiency of ours could be doubled or even trebled? For decades the limiting factor in warfare had been not mechanical but biological—it had become more and more difficult for any single mind, or group of minds, to cope with the rapidly changing complexities of battle in three-dimensional space. Norden's mathematicians had analyzed some of the classic engagements of the past, and had shown that even when we had been victorious we had often operated our units at much less than half of their theoretical efficiency.

The Battle Analyzer would change all this by replacing the operations staff with electronic calculators. The idea was not new, in theory, but until now it had been no more than a utopian dream. Many of us found it difficult to believe that it was still anything but a dream: after we had run through several very complex dummy battles, however, we were convinced.

It was decided to install the Analyzer in four of our heaviest ships, so that each of the main fleets could be equipped with one. At this stage, the trouble began—though we did not know it until later.

The Analyzer contained just short of a million vacuum tubes and needed a team of five hundred technicians to maintain and operate it. It was quite impossible to accommodate the extra staff aboard a battleship, so each of the four units had to be accompanied by a converted liner to carry the technicians not on duty. Installation was also a very slow and tedious business, but by gigantic efforts it was completed in six months.

Then, to our dismay, we were confronted by another crisis. Nearly five thousand highly skilled men had been selected to serve the Analyzers and had been given an intensive course at the Technical Training Schools. At the end of seven months, 10 per cent of them had had nervous breakdowns and only 40 per cent had qualified.

Once again, everyone started to blame everyone else. Norden, of course, said that the Research Staff could not be held responsible, and so incurred the enmity of the Personnel and Training Commands. It was finally decided that the only thing to do was to use two instead of four

Analyzers and to bring the others into action as soon as men could be trained. There was little time to lose, for the enemy was still on the offensive and his morale was rising.

The first Analyzer fleet was ordered to recapture the system of Eriston. On the way, by one of the hazards of war, the liner carrying the technicians was struck by a roving mine. A warship would have survived, but the liner with its irreplaceable cargo was totally destroyed. So the operation had to be abandoned.

The other expedition was, at first, more successful. There was no doubt at all that the Analyzer fulfilled its designers' claims, and the enemy was heavily defeated in the first engagements. He withdrew, leaving us in possession of Saphran, Leucon and Hexanerax. But his Intelligence Staff must have noted the change in our tactics and the inexplicable presence of a liner in the heart of our battlefleet. It must have noted, also, that our first fleet had been accompanied by a similar ship—and had withdrawn when it had been destroyed.

In the next engagement, the enemy used his superior numbers to launch an overwhelming attack on the Analyzer ship and its unarmed consort. The attack was made without regard to losses—both ships were, of course, very heavily protected—and it succeeded. The result was the virtual decapitation of the Fleet, since an effectual transfer to the old operational methods proved impossible. We disengaged under heavy fire, and so lost all our gains and also the systems of Lormyia, Ismarnus, Beronis, Alphanidon and Sideneus.

At this stage, Grand Admiral Taxaris expressed his disapproval of Norden by committing suicide, and I assumed supreme command.

The situation was now both serious and infuriating. With stubborn conservatism and complete lack of imagination, the enemy continued to advance with his old-fashioned and inefficient but now vastly more numerous ships. It was galling to realize that if we had only continued building, without seeking new weapons, we would have been in a far more advantageous position. There were many acrimonious conferences at which Norden defended the scientists while everyone else blamed them for all that had happened. The difficulty was that Norden had proved every one of his claims: he had a perfect excuse for all the disasters that had occurred. And we could not now turn back—the search for an irresistible weapon must go on. At first it had been a luxury that would shorten the war. Now it was a necessity if we were to end it victoriously.

We were on the defensive, and so was Norden. He was more than ever determined to reestablish his prestige and that of the Research Staff. But we had been twice disappointed, and would not make the same mistake again. No doubt Norden's twenty thousand scientists would produce many further weapons: we would remain unimpressed.

We were wrong. The final weapon was something so fantastic that even now it seems difficult to believe that it ever existed. Its innocent, noncommittal name—The Exponential Field—gave no hint of its real potentialities. Some of Norden's mathematicians had discovered it during a piece of entirely theoretical research into the properties of space, and to everyone's great surprise their results were found to be physically realizable.

It seems very difficult to explain the operation of the Field to the layman. According to the technical description, it "produces an exponential condition of space, so that a finite distance in normal, linear space may become infinite in pseudo-space." Norden gave an analogy which some of us found useful. It was as if one took a flat disk of rubber—representing a region of normal space—and then pulled its center out to infinity. The circumference of the disk would be unaltered—but its "diameter" would be infinite. That was the sort of thing the generator of the Field did to the space around it.

As an example, suppose that a ship carrying the generator was surrounded by a ring of hostile machines. If it switched on the Field, *each* of the enemy ships would think that it—and the ships on the far side of the circle—had suddenly receded into nothingness. Yet the circumference of the circle would be the same as before: only the journey to the center would be of infinite duration, for as one proceeded, distances would appear to become greater and greater as the "scale" of space altered.

It was a nightmare condition, but a very useful one. Nothing could reach a ship carrying the Field: it might be englobed by an enemy fleet yet would be as inaccessible as if it were at the other side of the Universe. Against this, of course, it could not fight back without switching off the Field, but this still left it at a very great advantage, not only in defense but in offense. For a ship fitted with the Field could approach an enemy fleet undetected and suddenly appear in its midst.

This time there seemed to be no flaws in the new weapon. Needless to say, we looked for all the possible objections before we committed ourselves again. Fortunately the equipment was fairly simple and did not require a large operating staff. After much debate, we decided to rush it into production, for we realized that time was running short and the war was going against us. We had now lost about the whole of our initial gains and enemy forces had made several raids into our own solar system.

We managed to hold off the enemy while the Fleet was reequipped and the new battle techniques were worked out. To use the Field operationally it was necessary to locate an enemy formation, set a course that would intercept it, and then switch on the generator for the calculated period of time. On releasing the Field again—if the calculations had been accurate—one would be in the enemy's midst and could do great damage during the resulting confusion, retreating by the same route when necessary.

The first trial maneuvers proved satisfactory and the equipment seemed quite reliable. Numerous mock attacks were made and the crews became accustomed to the new technique. I was on one of the test flights and can vividly remember my impressions as the Field was switched on. The ships around us seemed to dwindle as if on the surface of an expanding bubble: in an instant they had vanished completely. So had the stars—but presently we could see that the Galaxy was still visible as a faint band of light around the ship. The virtual radius of our pseudo-space was not really infinite, but some hundred thousand light-years, and so the distance to the farthest stars of our system had not been greatly increased—though the nearest had of course totally disappeared.

These training maneuvers, however, had to be canceled before they were completed, owing to a whole flock of minor technical troubles in various pieces of equipment, notably the communications circuits. These were annoying, but not important, though it was thought best to return to Base to clear them up.

At that moment the enemy made what was obviously intended to be a decisive attack against the fortress planet of Iton at the limits of our Solar System. The Fleet had to go into battle before repairs could be made.

The enemy must have believed that we had mastered the secret of invisibility—as in a sense we had. Our ships appeared suddenly out of nowhere and inflicted tremendous damage—for a while. And then something quite baffling and inexplicable happened.

I was in command of the flagship *Hircania* when the trouble started. We had been operating as independent units, each against assigned objectives. Our detectors observed an enemy formation at medium range and the navigating officers measured its distance with great accuracy. We set course and switched on the generator.

The Exponential Field was released at the moment when we should have been passing through the center of the enemy group. To our consternation, we emerged into normal space at a distance of many hundred miles—and when we found the enemy, he had already found us. We retreated, and tried again. This time we were so far away from the enemy that he located us first.

Obviously, something was seriously wrong. We broke communicator silence and tried to contact the other ships of the Fleet to see if they had experienced the same trouble. Once again we failed—and this time the failure was beyond all reason, for the communication equipment appeared to be working perfectly. We could only assume, fantastic though it seemed, that the rest of the Fleet had been destroyed.

I do not wish to describe the scenes when the scattered units of the Fleet struggled back to Base. Our casualties had actually been negligible, but the ships were completely demoralized. Almost all had lost touch with one another and had found that their ranging equipment showed inexplicable errors. It was obvious that the Exponential Field was the cause of the troubles, despite the fact that they were only apparent when it was switched off.

The explanation came too late to do us any good, and Norden's final discomfiture was small consolation for the virtual loss of the war. As I have explained, the Field generators produced a radial distortion of space, distances appearing greater and greater as one approached the center of the artificial pseudo-space. When the Field was switched off, conditions returned to normal.

But not quite. It was never possible to restore the initial state *exactly*. Switching the Field on and off was equivalent to an elongation and contraction of the ship carrying the generator, but there was a hysteretic effect, as it were, and the initial condition was never quite reproducible, owing to all the thousands of electrical changes and movements of mass aboard the ship while the Field was on. These asymmetries and distortions were cumulative, and though they seldom amounted to more than a fraction of one per cent, that was quite enough. It meant that the precision ranging equipment and the tuned circuits in the communication apparatus were thrown completely out of adjustment. Any single ship could never detect the change—only when it compared its equipment with that of another vessel, or tried to communicate with it, could it tell what had happened.

It is impossible to describe the resultant chaos. Not a single component of one ship could be expected with certainty to work aboard another. The very nuts and bolts were no longer interchangeable, and the supply position became quite impossible. Given time, we might even have overcome these difficulties, but the enemy ships were already attacking in thousands with weapons which now seemed centuries behind those that we had invented. Our magnificent Fleet, crippled by our own science, fought on as best it could until it was overwhelmed and forced to surrender. The ships fitted with the Field were still invulnerable, but as fighting units they were almost helpless. Every time they switched on their generators to escape from enemy attack, the permanent distortion of their equipment increased. In a month, it was all over.

THIS IS THE true story of our defeat, which I give without prejudice to my defense before this Court. I make it, as I have said, to counteract the libels that have been circulating against the men who fought under me, and to show where the true blame for our misfortunes lay.

Finally, my request, which as the Court will now realize I make in no frivolous manner and which I hope will therefore be granted.

The Court will be aware that the conditions under which we are housed and the constant surveillance to which we are subjected night and day are somewhat distressing. Yet I am not complaining of this: nor do I complain of the fact that shortage of accommodation has made it necessary to house us in pairs.

But I cannot be held responsible for my future actions if I am compelled any longer to share my cell with Professor Norden, late Chief of the Research Staff of my armed forces.

Orson Scott Card

Orson Scott Card's landmark novels Ender's Game and its sequel, Speaker for the Dead, made science fiction history when they became the first books ever to win both the Hugo and Nebula Awards in successive years. With Xenocide and Children of the Mind, they make up one of the most celebrated sagas of modern science fiction, a richly imagined and morally complex inquiry into issues of war, genocide, and human responsibility. Much of Card's fantasy and science fiction interconnects to form inventive extended series, including The Worthing Chronicle, a linked group of stories related as the experiences as a messianic leader of a space colony, and his lengthy Hatrick River sequence, a folk history of an alternate United States whose individual volumes include Seventh Son, Prentice Alvin, and Heartfire. Card's eloquent short fiction has been collected in Maps in a Mirror. He is also the author of the historical novel A Woman of Destiny, the dark fantasy novels Lost Boys, Treasure Box, and Homebody, and the Hugo Award–winning guide How to Write Science Fiction and Fantasy.

ENDER'S GAME

Orson Scott Card

"WHATEVER YOUR GRAVITY is when you get to the door, remember—the enemy's gate is *down*. If you step through your own door like you're out for a stroll, you're a big target and you deserve to get hit. With more than a flasher." Ender Wiggins paused and looked over the group. Most were just watching him nervously. A few understanding. A few sullen and resisting.

First day with this army, all fresh from the teacher squads, and Ender had forgotten how young new kids could be. He'd been in it for three years, they'd had six months—nobody over nine years old in the whole bunch. But they were his. At eleven, he was half a year early to be a commander. He'd had a toon of his own and knew a few tricks, but there were forty in his new army. Green. All marksmen with a flasher, all in top shape, or they wouldn't be here—but they were all just as likely as not to get wiped out first time into battle.

"Remember," he went on, "they can't see you till you get through that door. But the second you're out, they'll be on you. So hit that door the way you want to be when they shoot at you. Legs go under you, going straight *down*." He pointed at a sullen kid who looked like he was only seven, the smallest of them all. "Which way is down, greenoh!"

"Toward the enemy door." The answer was quick. It was also surly, as if to say, Yeah, yeah, now get on with the important stuff.

"Name, kid?"

"Bean."

"Get that for size or for brains?"

Bean didn't answer. The rest laughed a little. Ender had chosen right. The kid *was* younger than the rest, must have been advanced because he was sharp. The others didn't like him much, they were happy to see him taken down a little. Like Ender's first commander had taken him down.

"Well, Bean, you're right onto things. Now I tell you this, nobody's gonna get through that door without a good chance of getting hit. A lot of you are going to be turned into cement somewhere. Make sure it's your legs. Right? If only your legs get hit, then only your legs get frozen, and in nullo that's no sweat." Ender turned to one of the dazed ones. "What're legs for? Hmmm?"

Blank stare. Confusion. Stammer.

"Forget it. Guess I'll have to ask Bean here."

"Legs are for pushing off walls." Still bored.

"Thanks, Bean. Get that, everybody?" They all got it, and didn't like getting it from Bean. "Right. You can't *see* with legs, you can't *shoot* with legs, and most of the time they just get in the way. If they get frozen sticking straight out you've turned yourself into a blimp. No way to hide. So how do legs go?"

A few answered this time, to prove that Bean wasn't the only one who knew anything. "Under you. Tucked up under."

"Right. A shield. You're kneeling on a shield, and the shield is your own legs. And there's a trick to the suits. Even when your legs are flashed you can *still* kick off. I've never seen anybody do it but me—but you're all gonna learn it."

Ender Wiggins turned on his flasher. It glowed faintly green in his hand. Then he let himself rise in the weightless workout room, pulled his legs under him as though he were kneeling, and flashed both of them. Immediately his suit stiffened at the knees and ankles, so that he couldn't bend at all.

"Okay, I'm frozen, see?"

He was floating a meter above them. They all looked up at him, puzzled. He leaned back and caught one of the handholds on the wall behind him, and pulled himself flush against the wall.

"I'm stuck at a wall. If I had legs, I'd use legs, and string myself out like a string *bean*, right?"

They laughed.

"But I don't have legs, and that's *better*, got it? Because of this." Ender jackknifed at the waist, then straightened out violently. He was across the workout room in only a moment. From the other side he called to them. "Got that? I didn't use hands, so I still had use of my flasher. *And* I didn't have my legs floating five feet behind me. Now watch it again."

He repeated the jackknife, and caught a handhold on the wall near them. "Now, I don't just want you to do that when they've flashed your legs. I want you to do that when you've still got legs, because it's better. And because they'll never be expecting it. All right now, everybody up in the air and kneeling."

Most were up in a few seconds. Ender flashed the stragglers, and they dangled, helplessly frozen, while the others laughed. "When I give an order, you move. Got it? When we're at a door and they clear it, I'll be giving you orders in two seconds, as soon as I see the setup. And when I give the order you better be out there, because whoever's out there first is going to win, unless he's a fool. I'm not. And you better not be, or I'll have you back in the teacher squads." He saw more than a few of them gulp, and the frozen ones looked at him with fear. "You guys who are hanging there. You watch. You'll thaw out in about fifteen minutes, and let's see if you can catch up to the others."

For the next half hour Ender had them jackknifing off walls. He called a stop when he saw that they all had the basic idea. They were a good group, maybe. They'd get better.

"Now you're warmed up," he said to them, "we'll start working."

ENDER WAS THE last one out after practice, since he stayed to help some of the slower ones improve on technique. They'd had good teachers, but like all armies they were uneven, and some of them could be a real drawback in battle. Their first battle might be weeks away. It might be tomorrow. A schedule was never printed. The commander just woke up and found a note by his bunk, giving him the time of his battle and the name of his opponent. So for the first while he was going to drive his boys until they were in top shape—all of them. Ready for anything, at any time. Strategy was nice, but it was worth nothing if the soldiers couldn't hold up under the strain.

He turned the corner into the residence wing and found himself face to face with Bean, the seven-year-old he had picked on all through practice that day. Problems. Ender didn't want problems right now.

"Ho, Bean."

"Ho, Ender."

Pause.

"Sir," Ender said softly.

"We're not on duty."

"In my army, Bean, we're always on duty." Ender brushed past him.

Bean's high voice piped up behind him. "I know what you're doing, Ender, sir, and I'm warning you."

Ender turned slowly and looked at him. "Warning me?"

"I'm the best man you've got. But I'd better be treated like it."

"Or what?" Ender smiled menacingly.

"Or I'll be the worst man you've got. One or the other."

"And what do you want? Love and kisses?" Ender was getting angry now.

Bean was unworried. "I want a toon."

Ender walked back to him and stood looking down into his eyes. "I'll give a toon," he said, "to the boys who prove they're worth something. They've got to be good soldiers, they've got to know how to take orders, they've got to be able to think for themselves in a pinch, and they've got to be able to keep respect. That's how I got to be a commander. That's how you'll get to be a toon leader. Got it?"

Bean smiled. "That's fair. *If* you actually work that way, I'll be a toon leader in a month."

Ender reached down and grabbed the front of his uniform and shoved him into the wall. "When I say I work a certain way, Bean, then that's the way I work."

Bean just smiled. Ender let go of him and walked away, and didn't look back. He was sure, without looking, that Bean was still watching, still smiling, still just a little contemptuous. He might make a good toon leader at that. Ender would keep an eye on him.

CAPTAIN GRAFF, SIX foot two and a little chubby, stroked his belly as he leaned back in his chair. Across his desk sat Lieutenant Anderson, who was earnestly pointing out high points on a chart.

"Here it is, Captain," Anderson said. "Ender's already got them doing a tactic that's going to throw off everyone who meets it. Doubled their speed."

Graff nodded.

"And you know his test scores. He thinks well, too."

Graff smiled. "All true, all true, Anderson, he's a fine student, shows real promise."

They waited.

Graff sighed. "So what do you want me to do?"

"Ender's the one. He's got to be."

"He'll never be ready in time, Lieutenant. He's eleven, for heaven's sake, man, what do you want, a miracle?"

"I want him into battles, every day starting tomorrow. I want him to have a year's worth of battles in a month."

Graff shook his head. "That would have his army in the hospital."

"No, sir. He's getting them into form. And we need Ender."

"Correction, Lieutenant. We need somebody. You think it's Ender."

"All right, I think it's Ender. Which of the commanders if it isn't him?"

"I don't know, Lieutenant." Graff ran his hands over his slightly fuzzy bald head. "These are children, Anderson. Do you realize that? Ender's army is nine years old. Are we going to put them against the older kids? Are we going to put them through hell for a month like that?"

Lieutenant Anderson leaned even farther over Graff's desk. "Ender's test scores, Captain!"

"I've seen his bloody test scores! I've watched him in battle, I've listened to tapes of his training sessions. I've watched his sleep patterns, I've heard tapes of his conversations in the corridors and in the bathrooms, I'm more aware of Ender Wiggins than you could possibly imagine! And against all the arguments, against his obvious qualities, I'm weighing one thing. I have this picture of Ender a year from now, if you have your way. I see him completely useless, worn down, a failure, because he was pushed farther than he or any living person could go. But it doesn't weigh enough, does it, Lieutenant, because there's a war on, and our best talent is gone, and the biggest battles are ahead. So give Ender a battle every day this week. And then bring me a report."

Anderson stood and saluted. "Thank you, sir."

He had almost reached the door when Graff called his name. He turned and faced the captain.

"Anderson," Captain Graff said. "Have you been outside, lately I mean?"

"Not since last leave, six months ago."

"I didn't think so. Not that it makes any difference. But have you ever been to Beaman Park, there in the city? Hmm? Beautiful park. Trees. Grass. No nullo, no battles, no worries. Do you know what else there is in Beaman Park?"

"What, sir?" Lieutenant Anderson asked.

"Children," Graff answered.

"Of course, children," said Anderson.

"I mean children. I mean kids who get up in the morning when their mothers call them and they go to school and then in the afternoons they go to Beaman Park and play. They're happy, they smile a lot, they laugh, they have fun. Hmmm?"

"I'm sure they do, sir."

"Is that all you can say, Anderson?"

Anderson cleared his throat. "It's good for children to have fun, I think, sir. I know I did when I was a boy. But right now the world needs soldiers. And this is the way to get them."

Graff nodded and closed his eyes. "Oh, indeed, you're right, by statistical proof and by all the important theories, and dammit they work and the system is right but all the same Ender's older than I am. He's not a child. He's barely a person."

"If that's true, sir, then at least we all know that Ender is making it possible for the others of his age to be playing in the park."

"And Jesus died to save all men, of course." Graff sat up and looked at Anderson almost sadly. "But we're the ones," Graff said, "we're the ones who are driving in the nails."

ENDER WIGGINS LAY on his bed staring at the ceiling. He never slept more than five hours a night—but the lights went off at 2200 and didn't come on again until 0600. So he stared at the ceiling and thought.

He'd had his army for three and a half weeks. Dragon Army. The name was assigned, and it wasn't a lucky one. Oh, the charts said that about nine years ago a Dragon Army had done fairly well. But for the next six years the name had been attached to inferior armies, and finally, because of the superstition that was beginning to play about the name, Dragon Army was retired. Until now. And now, Ender thought, smiling, Dragon Army was going to take them by surprise.

The door opened quietly. Ender did not turn his head. Someone stepped softly into his room, then left with the sound of the door shutting. When soft steps died away Ender rolled over and saw a white slip of paper lying on the floor. He reached down and picked it up.

"Dragon Army against Rabbit Army, Ender Wiggins and Carn Carby, 0700."

The first battle. Ender got out of bed and quickly dressed. He went rapidly to the rooms of each of his toon leaders and told them to rouse their boys. In five minutes they were all gathered in the corridor, sleepy and slow. Ender spoke softly.

"First battle, 0700 against Rabbit Army. I've fought them twice before but they've got a new commander. Never heard of him. They're an older group, though, and I know a few of their old tricks. Now wake up. Run, doublefast, warmup in workroom three."

For an hour and a half they worked out, with three mock battles and calisthenics in the corridor out of the nullo. Then for fifteen minutes they all lay up in the air, totally relaxing in the weightlessness. At 0650 Ender roused them and they hurried into the corridor. Ender led them down the corridor, running again, and occasionally leaping to touch a light panel on the ceiling. The boys all touched the same light panel. And at 0658 they reached their gate to the battleroom.

The members of toons C and D grabbed the first eight handholds in the ceiling of the corridor. Toons A, B, and E crouched on the floor. Ender hooked his feet into two handholds in the middle of the ceiling, so he was out of everyone's way.

"Which way is the enemy's door?" he hissed.

"Down!" they whispered back, and laughed.

"Flashers on." The boxes in their hands glowed green. They waited for a few seconds more, and then the grey wall in front of them disappeared and the battleroom was visible.

Ender sized it up immediately. The familiar open grid of most early games, like the monkey bars at the park, with seven or eight boxes scattered through the grid. They called the boxes *stars*. There were enough of them, and in forward enough positions, that they were worth going for. Ender decided this in a second, and he hissed, "Spread to near stars. E hold!"

The four groups in the corners plunged through the forcefield at the doorway and fell down into the battleroom. Before the enemy even appeared through the opposite gate Ender's army had spread from the door to the nearest stars.

Then the enemy soldiers came through the door. From their stance Ender knew they had been in a different gravity, and didn't know enough to disorient themselves from it. They came through standing up, their entire bodies spread and defenseless.

"Kill 'em, E!" Ender hissed, and threw himself out the door knees first, with his flasher between his legs and firing. While Ender's group flew across the room the rest of Dragon Army lay down a protecting fire, so that E group reached a forward position with only one boy frozen completely, though they had all lost the use of their legs—which didn't impair them in the least. There was a lull as Ender and his opponent, Carn Carnby, assessed their positions. Aside from Rabbit Army's losses at the gate, there had been few casualties, and both armies were near full strength. But Carn had no originality—he was in a four-corner spread that any five-year-old in the teacher squads might have thought of. And Ender knew how to defeat it.

He called out, loudly, "E covers A, C down. B, D angle east wall." Under E toon's cover, B and D toons lunged away from their stars. While they were still exposed, A and C toons left their stars and drifted toward the near wall. They reached it together, and together jackknifed off the wall. At double the normal speed they appeared behind the enemy's stars, and opened fire. In a few seconds the battle was over, with the enemy almost entirely frozen, including the commander, and the rest scattered to the corners. For the next five minutes, in squads of four, Dragon Army cleaned out the dark corners of the battleroom and shepherded the enemy into the center, where their bodies, frozen at impossible angles, jostled each other. Then Ender took three of his boys to the enemy gate and went through the formality of reversing the one-way field by simultaneously touching a Dragon Army helmet at each corner. Then Ender assembled his army in vertical files near the knot of frozen Rabbit Army soldiers.

Only three of Dragon Army's soldiers were immobile. Their victory margin—38 to 0—was ridiculously high, and Ender began to laugh. Dragon Army joined him, laughing long and loud. They were still laughing when Lieutenant Anderson and Lieutenant Morris came in from the teachergate at the south end of the battleroom.

Lieutenant Anderson kept his face stiff and unsmiling, but Ender saw him wink as he held out his hand and offered the stiff, formal congratulations that were ritually given to the victor in the game.

Morris found Carn Carby and unfroze him, and the thirteen-year-old came and presented himself to Ender, who laughed without malice and held out his hand. Carn graciously took Ender's hand and bowed his head over it. It was that or be flashed again.

Lieutenant Anderson dismissed Dragon Army, and they silently left the battleroom through the enemy's door—again part of the ritual. A light was blinking on the north side of the square door, indicating where the gravity was in that corridor. Ender, leading his soldiers, changed his orientation and went through the forcefield and into gravity on his feet. His army followed him at a brisk run back to the workroom. When they got there they formed up into squads, and Ender hung in the air, watching them.

"Good first battle," he said, which was excuse enough for a cheer, which he quieted. "Dragon Army did all right against Rabbits. But the enemy isn't always going to be that bad. And if that had been a good army we would have been smashed. We still would have won, but we would have been smashed. Now let me see B and D toons out here. Your takeoff from the stars was way too slow. If Rabbit Army knew how to aim a flasher, you all would have been frozen solid before A and C even got to the wall."

They worked out for the rest of the day.

That night Ender went for the first time to the commanders' mess hall. No one was allowed there until he had won at least one battle, and Ender was the youngest commander ever to make it. There was no great stir when he came in. But when some of the other boys saw the Dragon on his breast pocket, they stared at him openly, and by the time he got his tray and sat at an empty table, the entire room was silent, with the other commanders watching him. Intensely self-conscious, Ender wondered how they all knew, and why they all looked so hostile.

Then he looked above the door he had just come through. There was a huge scoreboard across the entire wall. It showed the win/loss record for the commander of every army; that day's battles were lit in red. Only four of them. The other three winners had barely made it—the best of them had only two men whole and eleven mobile at the end of the game. Dragon Army's score of thirty-eight mobile was embarrassingly better.

Other new commanders had been admitted to the commanders' mess hall with cheers and congratulations. Other new commanders hadn't won thirty-eight to zero.

Ender looked for Rabbit Army on the scoreboard. He was surprised to find that Carn Carby's score to date was eight wins and three losses. Was he that good? Or had he only fought against inferior armies? Whichever, there was still a zero in Carn's mobile and whole columns, and Ender looked down from the scoreboard grinning. No one smiled back, and Ender knew that they were afraid of him, which meant that they would hate him, which meant that anyone who went into battle against Dragon Army would be scared and angry and less competent. Ender looked for

Carn Carby in the crowd, and found him not too far away. He stared at Carby until one of the other boys nudged the Rabbit commander and pointed to Ender. Ender smiled again and waved slightly. Carby turned red, and Ender, satisfied, leaned over his dinner and began to eat.

AT THE END of the week Dragon Army had fought seven battles in seven days. The score stood 7 wins and 0 losses. Ender had never had more than five boys frozen in any game. It was no longer possible for the other commanders to ignore Ender. A few of them sat with him and quietly conversed about game strategies that Ender's opponents had used. Other much larger groups were talking with the commanders that Ender had defeated, trying to find out what Ender had done to beat them.

In the middle of the meal the teacher door opened and the groups fell silent as Lieutenant Anderson stepped in and looked over the group. When he located Ender he strode quickly across the room and whispered in Ender's ear. Ender nodded, finished his glass of water, and left with the lieutenant. On the way out, Anderson handed a slip of paper to one of the older boys. The room became very noisy with conversation as Anderson and Ender left.

Ender was escorted down corridors he had never seen before. They didn't have the blue glow of the soldier corridors. Most were wood paneled, and the floors were carpeted. The doors were wood, with nameplates on them, and they stopped at one that said "Captain Graff, supervisor." Anderson knocked softly, and a low voice said, "Come in."

They went in. Captain Graff was seated behind a desk, his hands folded across his pot belly. He nodded, and Anderson sat. Ender also sat down. Graff cleared his throat and spoke.

"Seven days since your first battle, Ender."

Ender did not reply.

"Won seven battles, one every day."

Ender nodded.

"Scores unusually high, too."

Ender blinked.

"Why?" Graff asked him.

Ender glanced at Anderson, and then spoke to the captain behind the desk. "Two new tactics, sir. Legs doubled up as a shield, so that a flash doesn't immobilize. Jackknife takeoffs from the walls. Superior strategy, as Lieutenant Anderson taught, think places, not spaces. Five toons of eight instead of four of ten. Incompetent opponents. Excellent toon leaders, good soldiers."

Graff looked at Ender without expression. Waiting for what, Ender wondered. Lieutenant Anderson spoke up.

"Ender, what's the condition of your army?"

Do they want me to ask for relief? Not a chance, he decided. "A little tired, in peak condition, morale high, learning fast. Anxious for the next battle."

Anderson looked at Graff. Graff shrugged slightly and turned to Ender.

"Is there anything you want to know?"

Ender held his hands loosely in his lap. "When are you going to put us up against a good army?"

Graff's laughter rang in the room, and when it stopped, Graff handed a piece of paper to Ender.

"Now," the captain said, and Ender read the paper: "Dragon Army against Leopard Army, Ender Wiggins and Pol Slattery, 2000."

Ender looked up at Captain Graff. "That's ten minutes from now, sir."

Graff smiled. "Better hurry, then, boy."

As Ender left he realized Pol Slattery was the boy who had been handed his orders as Ender left the mess hall.

He got to his army five minutes later. Three toon leaders were already undressed and lying naked on their beds. He sent them all flying down the corridors to rouse their toons, and gathered up their suits himself. When all his boys were assembled in the corridor, most of them still getting dressed, Ender spoke to them.

"This one's hot and there's no time. We'll be late to the door, and the enemy'll be deployed right outside our gate. Ambush, and I've never heard of it happening before. So we'll take our time at the door. A and B toons, keep your belts loose, and give your flashers to the leaders and seconds of the other toons."

Puzzled, his soldiers complied. By then all were dressed, and Ender led them at a trot to the gate. When they reached it the forcefield was already on one-way, and some of his soldiers were panting. They had had one battle that day and a full workout. They were tired.

Ender stopped at the entrance and looked at the placement of the enemy soldiers. Some of them were grouped not more than twenty feet out from the gate. There was no grid, there were no stars. A big empty space. Where were most of the enemy soldiers? There should have been thirty more.

"They're flat against this wall," Ender said, "where we can't see them."

He took A and B toons and made them kneel, their hands on their hips. Then he flashed them, so that their bodies were frozen rigid.

"You're shields," Ender said, and then had boys from C and D kneel on their legs and hook both arms under the frozen boys' belts. Each boy was holding two flashers. Then Ender and the members of E toon picked up the duos, three at a time, and threw them out the door.

Of course, the enemy opened fire immediately. But they mainly hit the boys who were already flashed, and in a few moments pandemonium broke out in the battleroom. All the soldiers of Leopard Army were easy targets as they lay pressed flat against the wall or floated, unprotected, in the middle of the battleroom; and Ender's soldiers, armed with two flashers each, carved them up easily. Pol Slattery reacted quickly, ordering his men away from the wall, but not quickly enough—only a few were able to move, and they were flashed before they could get a quarter of the way across the battleroom.

When the battle was over Dragon Army had only twelve boys whole, the lowest score they had ever had. But Ender was satisfied. And during the ritual of surrender Pol Slattery broke form by shaking hands and asking, "Why did you wait so long getting out of the gate?"

Ender glanced at Anderson, who was floating nearby. "I was informed late," he said. "It was an ambush."

Slattery grinned, and gripped Ender's hand again. "Good game."

Ender didn't smile at Anderson this time. He knew that now the games would be arranged against him, to even up the odds. He didn't like it.

IT WAS 2150, nearly time for lights out, when Ender knocked at the door of the room shared by Bean and three other soldiers. One of the others opened the door, then stepped back and held it wide. Ender stood for a moment, then asked if he could come in. They answered, of course, of course, come in, and he walked to the upper bunk, where Bean had set down his book and was leaning on one elbow to look at Ender.

"Bean, can you give me twenty minutes?"

"Near lights out," Bean answered.

"My room," Ender answered. "I'll cover for you."

Bean sat up and slid off his bed. Together he and Ender padded silently down the corridor to Ender's room. Bean entered first, and Ender closed the door behind them.

"Sit down," Ender said, and they both sat on the edge of the bed, looking at each other.

"Remember four weeks ago, Bean? When you told me to make you a toon leader?"

"Yeah."

"I've made five toon leaders since then, haven't I? And none of them was you."

Bean looked at him calmly.

"Was I right?" Ender asked.

"Yes, sir," Bean answered.

Ender nodded. "How have you done in these battles?"

Bean cocked his head to one side. "I've never been immobilized, sir, and I've immobilized forty-three of the enemy. I've obeyed orders quickly, and I've commanded a squad in mop-up and never lost a soldier."

"Then you'll understand this." Ender paused, then decided to back up and say something else first.

"You know you're early, Bean, by a good half year. I was, too, and I've been made a commander six months early. Now they've put me into battles after only three weeks of training with my army. They've given me eight battles in seven days. I've already had more battles than boys who were made commander four months ago. I've won more battles than many who've been commanders for a year. And then tonight. You know what happened tonight."

Bean nodded. "They told you late."

"I don't know what the teachers are doing. But my army is getting tired, and I'm getting tired, and now they're changing the rules of the game. You see, Bean, I've looked in the old charts. No one has ever destroyed so many enemies and kept so many of his own soldiers whole in the history of the game. I'm unique—and I'm getting unique treatment."

Bean smiled. "You're the best, Ender."

Ender shook his head. "Maybe. But it was no accident that I got the soldiers I got. My worst soldier could be a toon leader in another army. I've got the best. They've loaded things my way—but now they're loading it all against me. I don't know why. But I know I have to be ready for it. I need your help."

"Why mine?"

"Because even though there are some better soldiers than you in Dragon Army—not many, but some—there's nobody who can think better and faster than you." Bean said nothing. They both knew it was true.

Ender continued, "I need to be ready, but I can't retrain the whole army. So I'm going to cut every toon down by one, including you. With four others you'll be a special squad under me. And you'll learn to do some new things. Most of the time you'll be in the regular toons just like you are now. But when I need you. See?"

Bean smiled and nodded. "That's right, that's good, can I pick them myself?"

"One from each toon except your own, and you can't take any toon leaders."

"What do you want us to do?"

"Bean, I don't know. I don't know what they'll throw at us. What would you do if suddenly our flashers didn't work, and the enemy's did? What would you do if we had to face two armies at once? The only thing I know is—there may be a game where we don't even try for score. Where we just go for the enemy's gate. That's when the battle is technically won—four helmets at the corners of the gate. I want you ready to do that any time I call for it. Got it? You take them for two hours a day during regular workout. Then you and I and your soldiers, we'll work at night after dinner."

"We'll get tired."

"I have a feeling we don't know what tired is." Ender reached out and took Bean's hand, and gripped it. "Even when it's rigged against us, Bean. We'll win."

Bean left in silence and padded down the corridor.

DRAGON ARMY WASN'T the only army working out after hours now. The other commanders had finally realized they had some catching up to do. From early morning to lights out soldiers all over Training and Command Center, none of them over fourteen years old, were learning to jackknife off walls and use each other as living shields.

But while other commanders mastered the techniques that Ender had used to defeat them, Ender and Bean worked on solutions to problems that had never come up.

There were still battles every day, but for a while they were normal, with grids and stars and sudden plunges through the gate. And after the battles, Ender and Bean and four other soldiers would leave the main group and practice strange maneuvers. Attacks without flashers, using feet to physically disarm or disorient an enemy. Using four frozen soldiers to reverse the enemy's gate in less than two seconds. And one day Bean came to workout with a 300-meter cord.

"What's that for?"

"I don't know yet." Absently Bean spun one end of the cord. It wasn't more than an eighth of an inch thick, but it could have lifted ten adults without breaking.

"Where did you get it?"

"Commissary. They asked what for. I said to practice tying knots."

Bean tied a loop in the end of the rope and slid it over his shoulders.

"Here, you two, hang on to the wall here. Now don't let go of the rope. Give me about fifty yards of slack." They complied, and Bean moved about ten feet from them along the wall. As soon as he was sure they were ready, he jackknifed off the wall and flew straight out, fifty yards. Then the rope snapped taut. It was so fine that it was virtually invisible, but it was strong enough to force Bean to veer off at almost a right angle. It happened so suddenly that he had inscribed a perfect arc and hit the wall hard before most of the other soldiers knew what had happened. Bean did a perfect rebound and drifted quickly back to where Ender and the others waited for him.

Many of the soldiers in the five regular squads hadn't noticed the rope, and were demanding to know how it was done. It was impossible to change direction that abruptly in nullo. Bean just laughed.

"Wait till the next game without a grid! They'll never know what hit them."

They never did. The next game was only two hours later, but Bean and two others had become pretty good at aiming and shooting while they flew at ridiculous speeds at the end of the rope. The slip of paper was delivered, and Dragon Army trotted off to the gate, to battle with Griffin Army. Bean coiled the rope all the way.

When the gate opened, all they could see was a large brown star only fifteen feet away, completely blocking their view of the enemy's gate.

Ender didn't pause. "Bean, give yourself fifty feet of rope and go around the star." Bean and his four soldiers dropped through the gate and in a moment Bean was launched sideways away from the star. The rope snapped taut, and Bean flew forward. As the rope was stopped by each edge of the star in turn, his arc became tighter and his speed greater, until when he hit the wall only a few feet away from the gate, he was barely able to control his rebound to end up behind the star. But he immediately moved all his arms and legs so that those waiting inside the gate would know that the enemy hadn't flashed him anywhere.

Ender dropped through the gate, and Bean quickly told him how Griffin Army was situated. "They've got two squares of stars, all the way around the gate. All their soldiers are under cover, and there's no way to hit any of them until we're clear to the bottom wall. Even with shields, we'd get there at half strength and we wouldn't have a chance."

"They moving?" Ender asked.

"Do they need to?"

"I would." Ender thought for a moment. "This one's tough. We'll go for the gate, Bean."

Griffin Army began to call out to them.

"Hey, is anybody there!"

"Wake up, there's a war on!"

"We wanna join the picnic!"

They were still calling when Ender's army came out from behind their star with a shield of fourteen frozen soldiers. William Bee, Griffin Army's commander, waited patiently as the screen approached, his men waiting at the fringes of their stars for the moment when whatever was behind the screen became visible. About ten yards away the screen suddenly exploded as the soldiers behind it shoved the screen north. The momentum carried them south twice as fast, and at the same moment the rest of Dragon Army burst from behind their star at the opposite end of the room, firing rapidly.

William Bee's boys joined battle immediately, of course, but William Bee was far more interested in what had been left behind when the shield disappeared. A formation of four frozen Dragon Army soldiers was moving headfirst toward the Griffin Army gate, held together by another frozen soldier whose feet and hands were hooked through their belts. A sixth soldier hung to his waist and trailed like the tail of a kite. Griffin Army was winning the battle easily, and William Bee concentrated on the formation as it approached the gate. Suddenly the soldier trailing in back moved — he wasn't frozen at all! And even though William Bee flashed him immediately, the damage was done. The formation drifted to the Griffin Army gate, and their helmets touched all four corners simultaneously. A buzzer sounded, the gate reversed, and the frozen soldier in the middle was carried by momentum right through the gate. All the flashers stopped working, and the game was over.

The teachergate opened and Lieutenant Anderson came in. Anderson stopped himself with a slight movement of his hands when he reached the center of the battleroom. "Ender," he called, breaking protocol. One of the frozen Dragon soldiers near the south wall tried to call through jaws that were clamped shut by the suit. Anderson drifted to him and unfroze him.

Ender was smiling.

"I beat you again, sir," Ender said.

Anderson didn't smile. "That's nonsense, Ender," Anderson said softly. "Your battle was with William Bee of Griffin Army."

Ender raised an eyebrow.

"After that maneuver," Anderson said, "the rules are being revised to require that all of the enemy's soldiers must be immobilized before the gate can be reversed."

"That's all right," Ender said. "It could only work once, anyway." Anderson nodded, and was turning away when Ender added, "Is there going to be a new rule that armies be given equal positions to fight from?"

Anderson turned back around. "If you're in one of the positions, Ender, you can hardly call them equal, whatever they are."

William Bee counted carefully and wondered how in the world he had lost when not one of his soldiers had been flashed and only four of Ender's soldiers were even mobile.

And that night as Ender came into the commanders' mess hall, he was greeted with applause and cheers, and his table was crowded with respectful commanders, many of them two or three years older than he was. He was friendly, but while he ate he wondered what the teachers would do to him in his next battle. He didn't need to worry. His next two battles were easy victories, and after that he never saw the battleroom again.

It was 2100 and Ender was a little irritated to hear someone knock at his door. His army was exhausted, and he had ordered them all to be in bed after 2030. The last two days had been regular battles, and Ender was expecting the worst in the morning.

It was Bean. He came in sheepishly, and saluted.

Ender returned his salute and snapped, "Bean, I wanted everybody in bed."

Bean nodded but didn't leave. Ender considered ordering him out. But as he looked at Bean it occurred to him for the first time in weeks just how young Bean was. He had turned eight a week before, and he was still small and—no, Ender thought, he wasn't young. Nobody was young. Bean had been in battle, and with a whole army depending on him he had come through and won. And even though he was small, Ender could never think of him as young again.

Ender shrugged and Bean came over and sat on the edge of the bed. The younger boy looked at his hands for a while, and finally Ender grew impatient and asked, "Well, what is it?"

"I'm transferred. Got orders just a few minutes ago."

Ender closed his eyes for a moment. "I knew they'd pull something new. Now they're taking—where are you going?"

"Rabbit Army."

"How can they put you under an idiot like Carn Carby!"

"Carn was graduated. Support squads."

Ender looked up. "Well, who's commanding Rabbit then?"

Bean held his hands out helplessly.

"Me," he said.

Ender nodded, and then smiled. "Of course. After all, you're only four years younger than the regular age."

"It isn't funny," Bean said. "I don't know what's going on here. First all the changes in the game. And now this. I wasn't the only one transferred, either, Ender. Ren, Peder, Brian, Wins, Younger. All commanders now."

Ender stood up angrily and strode to the wall. "Every damn toon leader I've got!" he said, and whirled to face Bean. "If they're going to break up my army, Bean, why did they bother making me a commander at all?"

Bean shook his head. "I don't know. You're the best, Ender. Nobody's ever done what you've done. Nineteen battles in fifteen days, sir, and you won every one of them, no matter what they did to you."

"And now you and the others are commanders. You know every trick I've got, I trained you, and who am I supposed to replace you with? Are they going to stick me with six greenohs?"

"It stinks, Ender, but you know that if they gave you five crippled midgets and armed you with a roll of toilet paper you'd win."

They both laughed, and then they noticed that the door was open.

Lieutenant Anderson stepped in. He was followed by Captain Graff. "Ender Wiggins," Graff said, holding his hands across his stomach.

"Yes, sir," Ender answered.

"Orders."

Anderson extended a slip of paper. Ender read it quickly, then crumpled it, still looking at the air where the paper had been. After a few moments he asked, "Can I tell my army?"

"They'll find out," Graff answered. "It's better not to talk to them after orders. It makes it easier."

"For you or for me?" Ender asked. He didn't wait for an answer. He turned quickly to Bean, took his hand for a moment, and then headed for the door.

"Wait," Bean said. "Where are you going? Tactical or Support School?"

"Command School," Ender answered, and then he was gone and Anderson closed the door.

Command School, Bean thought. Nobody went to Command School until they had gone through three years of Tactical. But then, nobody went to Tactical until they had been through at least five years of Battle School. Ender had only had three.

The system was breaking up. No doubt about it, Bean thought. Either somebody at the top was going crazy, or something was going wrong with the war—the real war, the one they were training to fight in. Why else would they break down the training system, advance somebody—even somebody as good as Ender—straight to Command School? Why else would they ever have an eight-year-old greenoh like Bean command an army?

Bean wondered about it for a long time, and then he finally lay down on Ender's bed and realized that he'd never see Ender again, probably. For some reason that made him want to cry. But he didn't cry, of course. Training in the preschools had taught him how to force down emotions like that. He remembered how his first teacher, when he was three, would have been upset to see his lip quivering and his eyes full of tears.

Bean went through the relaxing routine until he didn't feel like crying anymore. Then he drifted off to sleep. His hand was near his mouth. It lay on his pillow hesitantly, as if Bean couldn't decide whether to bite his nails or suck on his fingertips. His forehead was creased and furrowed. His breathing was quick and light. He was a soldier, and if anyone had asked him what he wanted to be when he grew up, he wouldn't have known what they meant.

. . .

THERE'S A WAR on, they said, and that was excuse enough for all the hurry in the world. They said it like a password and flashed a little card at every ticket counter and customs check and guard station. It got them to the head of every line.

Ender Wiggins was rushed from place to place so quickly he had no time to examine anything. But he did see trees for the first time. He saw men who were not in uniform. He saw women. He saw strange animals that didn't speak, but that followed docilely behind women and small children. He saw suitcases and conveyor belts and signs that said words he had never heard of. He would have asked someone what the words meant, except that purpose and authority surrounded him in the persons of four very high officers who never spoke to each other and never spoke to him.

Ender Wiggins was a stranger to the world he was being trained to save. He did not remember ever leaving Battle School before. His earliest memories were of childish war games under the direction of a teacher, of meals with other boys in the grey and green uniforms of the armed forces of his world. He did not know that the grey represented the sky and the green represented the great forests of his planet. All he knew of the world was from vague references to "outside."

And before he could make any sense of the strange world he was seeing for the first time, they enclosed him again within the shell of the military, where nobody had to say "There's a war on" anymore because no one within the shell of the military forgot it for a single instant of a single day.

They put him in a spaceship and launched him to a large artificial satellite that circled the world.

This space station was called Command School. It held the ansible.

On his first day Ender Wiggins was taught about the ansible and what it meant to warfare. It meant that even though the starships of today's battles were launched a hundred years ago, the commanders of the starships were men of today, who used the ansible to send messages to the computers and the few men on each ship. The ansible sent words as they were spoken, orders as they were made. Battleplans as they were fought. Light was a pedestrian.

For two months Ender Wiggins didn't meet a single person. They came to him namelessly, taught him what they knew, and left him to other teachers. He had no time to miss his friends at Battle School. He only had time to learn how to operate the simulator, which flashed battle patterns around him as if he were in a starship at the center of the battle. How to command mock ships in mock battle by manipulating the keys on the simulator and speaking words into the ansible. How to recognize instantly every enemy ship and the weapons it carried by the pattern that the simulator showed. How to transfer all that he learned in the nullo battles at Battle School to the starship battles at Command School.

He had thought the game was taken seriously before. Here they hurried him through every step, were angry and worried beyond reason every time he forgot something or made a mistake. But he worked as he had always worked, and learned as he had always learned. After a while he didn't make any more mistakes. He used the simulator as if it were a part of himself. Then they stopped being worried and gave him a teacher.

MAEZR RACKHAM WAS sitting cross-legged on the floor when Ender awoke. He said nothing as Ender got up and showered and dressed, and Ender did not bother to ask him anything. He had long since learned that when something unusual was going on, he would often find out more information faster by waiting than by asking.

Maezr still hadn't spoken when Ender was ready and went to the door to leave the room. The door didn't open. Ender turned to face the man sitting on the floor. Maezr was at least forty, which made him the oldest man Ender had ever seen close up. He had a day's growth of black and white whiskers that grizzled his face only slightly less than his close-cut hair. His face sagged a little and his eyes were surrounded by creases and lines. He looked at Ender without interest.

Ender turned back to the door and tried again to open it.

"All right," he said, giving up. "Why's the door locked?"

Maezr continued to look at him blankly.

Ender became impatient. "I'm going to be late. If I'm not supposed to be there until later, than tell me so I can go back to bed." No answer. "Is it a guessing game?" Ender asked. No answer. Ender decided that maybe the man was trying to make him angry, so he went through a relaxing exercise as he leaned on the door, and soon he was calm again. Maezr didn't take his eyes off Ender.

For the next two hours the silence endured, Maezr watching Ender constantly, Ender trying to pretend he didn't notice the old man. The boy became more and more nervous, and finally ended up walking from one end of the room to the other in a sporadic pattern.

He walked by Maezr as he had several times before, and Maezr's hand shot out and pushed Ender's left leg into his right in the middle of a step. Ender fell flat on the floor.

He leaped to his feet immediately, furious. He found Maezr sitting calmly, cross-legged, as if he had never moved. Ender stood poised to fight. But the other's immobility made it impossible for Ender to attack, and he found himself wondering if he had only imagined the old man's hand tripping him up.

The pacing continued for another hour, with Ender Wiggins trying the door every now and then. At last he gave up and took off his uniform and walked to his bed.

As he leaned over to pull the covers back, he felt a hand jab roughly between his thighs and another hand grab his hair. In a moment he had been turned upside down. His face and shoulders were being pressed into the floor by the old man's knee, while his back was excruciatingly bent and his legs were pinioned by Maezr's arm. Ender was helpless to use his arms, and he couldn't bend his back to gain slack so he could use his legs. In less than two seconds the old man had completely defeated Ender Wiggins.

"All right," Ender gasped. "You win."

Maezr's knee thrust painfully downward.

"Since when," Maezr asked in a soft, rasping voice, "do you have to tell the enemy when he has won?"

Ender remained silent.

"I surprised you once, Ender Wiggins. Why didn't you destroy me immediately afterward? Just because I looked peaceful? You turned your back on me. Stupid. You have learned nothing. You have never had a teacher."

Ender was angry now. "I've had too many damned teachers, how was I supposed to know you'd turn out to be a—" Ender hunted for a word. Maezr supplied one.

"An enemy, Ender Wiggins," Maezr whispered. "I am your enemy, the first one you've ever had who was smarter than you. There is no teacher but the enemy, Ender Wiggins. No one but the enemy will ever tell you what the enemy is going to do. No one but the enemy will ever teach you how to destroy and conquer. I am your enemy, from now on. From now on I am your teacher."

Then Maezr let Ender's legs fall to the floor. Because the old man still held Ender's head to the floor, the boy couldn't use his arms to compensate, and his legs hit the plastic surface with a loud crack and a sickening pain that made Ender wince. Then Maezr stood and let Ender rise.

Slowly the boy pulled his legs under him, with a faint groan of pain, and he knelt on all fours for a moment, recovering. Then his right arm flashed out. Maezr quickly danced back and Ender's hand closed on air as his teacher's foot shot forward to catch Ender on the chin.

Ender's chin wasn't there. He was lying flat on his back, spinning on the floor, and during the moment that Maezr was off balance from his kick Ender's feet smashed into Maezr's other leg. The old man fell on the ground in a heap.

What seemed to be a heap was really a hornet's nest. Ender couldn't find an arm or a leg that held still long enough to be grabbed, and in the meantime blows were landing on his back and arms. Ender was smaller— he couldn't reach past the old man's flailing limbs.

So he leaped back out of the way and stood poised near the door.

The old man stopped thrashing about and sat up, cross-legged again, laughing. "Better, this time, boy. But slow. You will have to be better with a fleet than you are with your body or no one will be safe with you in command. Lesson learned?"

Ender nodded slowly.

Maezr smiled. "Good. Then we'll never have such a battle again. All the rest with the simulator. I will program your battles, I will devise the strategy of your enemy, and you will learn to be quick and discover what tricks the enemy has for you. Remember, boy. From now on the enemy is more clever than you. From now on the enemy is stronger than you. From now on you are always about to lose."

Then Maezr's face became serious again. "You will be about to lose, Ender, but you will win. You will learn to defeat the enemy. He will teach you how."

Maezr got up and walked toward the door. Ender stepped back out of the way. As the old man touched the handle of the door, Ender leaped into the air and kicked Maezr in the small of the back with both feet. He hit hard enough that he rebounded onto his feet, as Maezr cried out and collapsed on the floor.

Maezr got up slowly, holding on to the door handle, his face contorted with pain. He seemed disabled, but Ender didn't trust him. He waited warily. And yet in spite of his suspicion he was caught off guard by Maezr's speed. In a moment he found himself on the floor near the opposite wall, his nose and lip bleeding where his face had hit the bed. He was able to turn enough to see Maezr open the door and leave. The old man was limping and walking slowly.

Ender smiled in spite of the pain, then rolled over onto his back and laughed until his mouth filled with blood and he started to gag. Then he got up and painfully made his way to the bed. He lay down and in a few minutes a medic came and took care of his injuries.

As the drug had its effect and Ender drifted off to sleep he remembered the way Maezr limped out of his room and laughed again. He was still laughing softly as his mind went blank and the medic pulled the blanket over him and snapped off the light. He slept until the pain woke him in the morning. He dreamed of defeating Maezr.

THE NEXT DAY Ender went to the simulator room with his nose bandaged and his lip still puffy. Maezr was not there. Instead, a captain who had worked with him before showed him an addition that had been made. The captain pointed to a tube with a loop at one end. "Radio. Primitive, I know, but it loops over your ear and we tuck the other end into your mouth like this."

"Watch it," Ender said as the captain pushed the end of the tube into his swollen lip.

"Sorry. Now you just talk."

"Good. Who to?"

The captain smiled. "Ask and see."

Ender shrugged and turned to the simulator. As he did a voice reverberated through his skull. It was too loud for him to understand, and he ripped the radio off his ear.

"What are you trying to do, make me deaf?"

The captain shook his head and turned a dial on a small box on a nearby table. Ender put the radio back on.

"Commander," the radio said in a familiar voice.

Ender answered, "Yes."

"Instructions, sir?"

The voice was definitely familiar. "Bean?" Ender asked.

"Yes, sir."

"Bean, this is Ender."

Silence. And then a burst of laughter from the other side. Then six or seven more voices laughing, and Ender waited for silence to return. When it did, he asked, "Who else?"

A few voices spoke at once, but Bean drowned them out. "Me, I'm Bean, and Peder, Wins, Younger, Lee, and Vlad."

Ender thought for a moment. Then he asked what the hell was going on. They laughed again.

"They can't break up the group," Bean said. "We were commanders for maybe two weeks, and here we are at Command School, training with the simulator, and all of a sudden they told us we were going to form a fleet with a new commander. And that's you."

Ender smiled. "Are you boys any good?"

"If we aren't, you'll let us know."

Ender chuckled a little. "Might work out. A fleet."

For the next ten days Ender trained his toon leaders until they could maneuver their ships like precision dancers. It was like being back in the battleroom again, except that now Ender could always see everything, and could speak to his toon leaders and change their orders at any time.

One day as Ender sat down at the control board and switched on the simulator, harsh green lights appeared in the space—the enemy.

"This is it," Ender said. "X, Y, bullet, C, D, reserve screen, E, south loop, Bean, angle north."

The enemy was grouped in a globe, and outnumbered Ender two to one. Half of Ender's force was grouped in a tight, bulletlike formation, with the rest in a flat circular screen—except for a tiny force under Bean that moved off the simulator, heading behind the enemy's formation. Ender quickly learned the enemy's strategy: whenever Ender's bullet formation came close, the enemy would give way, hoping to draw Ender inside the globe where he would be surrounded. So Ender obligingly fell into the trap, bringing his bullet to the center of the globe.

The enemy began to contract slowly, not wanting to come within range until all their weapons could be brought to bear at once. Then Ender began to work in earnest. His reserve screen approached the outside of the globe, and the enemy began to concentrate his forces there. Then Bean's force appeared on the opposite side, and the enemy again deployed ships on that side.

Which left most of the globe only thinly defended. Ender's bullet attacked, and since at the point of attack it outnumbered the enemy over-whelmingly, he tore a hole in the formation. The enemy reacted to try to plug the gap, but in the confusion the reserve force and Bean's small force attacked simultaneously, with the bullet moved to another part of the globe. In a few more minutes the formation was shattered, most of the enemy ships destroyed, and the few survivors rushing away as fast as they could go.

Ender switched the simulator off. All the lights faded. Maezr was standing beside Ender, his hands in his pockets, his body tense. Ender looked up at him.

"I thought you said the enemy would be smart," Ender said.

Maezr's face remained expressionless. "What did you learn?"

"I learned that a sphere only works if your enemy's a fool. He had his forces so spread out that I outnumbered him whenever I engaged him."

"And?"

"And," Ender said, "you can't stay committed to one pattern. It makes you too easy to predict."

"Is that all?" Maezr asked quietly.

Ender took off his radio. "The enemy could have defeated me by breaking the sphere earlier."

Maezr nodded. "You had an unfair advantage."

Ender looked up at him coldly. "I was outnumbered two to one."

Maezr shook his head. "You have the ansible. The enemy doesn't. We include that in the mock battles. Their messages travel at the speed of light."

Ender glanced toward the simulator. "Is there enough space to make a difference?"

"Don't you know?" Maezr asked. "None of the ships was ever closer than thirty thousand kilometers to any other."

Ender tried to figure the size of the enemy's sphere. Astronomy was beyond him. But now his curiosity was stirred.

"What kind of weapons are on those ships? To be able to strike so fast?"

Maezr shook his head. "The science is too much for you. You'd have to study many more years than you've lived to understand even the basics. All you need to know is that the weapons work."

"Why do we have to come so close to be in range?"

"The ships are all protected by forcefields. A certain distance away the weapons are weaker and can't get through. Closer in the weapons are stronger than the shields. But the computers take care of all that. They're constantly firing in any direction that won't hurt one of our ships. The computers pick targets, aim; they do all the detail work. You just tell them when and get them in a position to win. All right?"

"No." Ender twisted the tube of the radio around his fingers. "I have to know how the weapons work."

"I told you, it would take—"

"I can't command a fleet—not even on the simulator—unless I know." Ender waited a moment, then added, "Just the rough idea."

Maezr stood up and walked a few steps away. "All right, Ender. It won't make any sense, but I'll try. As simply as I can." He shoved his hands into his pockets. "It's this way, Ender. Everything is made up of atoms, little particles so small you can't see them with your eyes. These atoms, there are only a few different types, and they're all made up of even smaller particles that are pretty much the same. These atoms can be broken, so that they stop being atoms. So that this metal doesn't hold together anymore. Or the plastic floor. Or your body. Or even the air. They just seem to disappear, if you break the atoms. All that's left is the pieces. And they fly around and break more atoms. The weapons on the ships set up an area where it's impossible for atoms of anything to stay together. They all break down. So things in that area—they disappear."

Ender nodded. "You're right, I don't understand it. Can it be blocked?"

"No. But it gets wider and weaker the farther it goes from the ship, so that after a while a forcefield will block it. OK? And to make it strong at all, it has to be focused, so that a ship can only fire effectively in maybe three or four directions at once."

Ender nodded again, but he didn't really understand, not well enough. "If the pieces of the broken atoms go breaking more atoms, why doesn't it just make everything disappear?"

"Space. Those thousands of kilometers between the ships, they're empty. Almost no atoms. The pieces don't hit anything, and when they finally do hit something, they're so spread out they can't do any harm." Maezr cocked his head quizzically. "Anything else you need to know?"

"Do the weapons on the ships—do they work against anything besides ships?"

Maezr moved in close to Ender and said firmly, "We only use them against ships. Never anything else. If we used them against anything else, the enemy would use them against us. Got it?"

Maezr walked away, and was nearly out the door when Ender called to him.

"I don't know your name yet," Ender said blandly.

"Maezr Rackham."

"Maezr Rackham," Ender said, "I defeated you."

Maezr laughed.

"Ender, you weren't fighting me today," he said. "You were fighting the stupidest computer in the Command School, set on a ten-year-old program. You don't think I'd use a sphere, do you?" He shook his head. "Ender, my dear little fellow, when you fight me you'll know it. Because you'll lose." And Maezr left the room.

ENDER STILL PRACTICED ten hours a day with his toon leaders. He never saw them, though, only heard their voices on the radio. Battles came every two or three days. The enemy had something new every time, something harder—but Ender coped with it. And won every time. And after every battle Maezr would point out mistakes and show Ender that he had really lost. Maezr only let Ender finish so that he would learn to handle the end of the game.

Until finally Maezr came in and solemnly shook Ender's hand and said, "That, boy, was a good battle."

Because the praise was so long in coming, it pleased Ender more than praise had ever pleased him before. And because it was so condescending, he resented it.

"So from now on," Maezr said, "we can give you hard ones."

From then on Ender's life was a slow nervous breakdown.

He began fighting two battles a day, with problems that steadily grew more difficult. He had been trained in nothing but the game all his life, but now the game began to consume him. He woke in the morning with new strategies for the simulator and went fitfully to sleep at night with the mistakes of the day preying on him. Sometimes he would wake up in the middle of the night crying for a reason he didn't remember. Sometimes he woke with his knuckles bloody from biting them. But every day he went impassively to the simulator and drilled his toon leaders until the battles, and drilled his toon leaders after the battles, and endured and studied the harsh criticism that Maezr Rackham piled on him. He noted that Rackham perversely criticized him more after his hardest battles. He noted that every time he thought of a new strategy the enemy was using it within a few days. And he noted that while his fleet always stayed the same size, the enemy increased in numbers every day.

He asked his teacher.

"We are showing you what it will be like when you really command. The ratios of enemy to us."

"Why does the enemy always outnumber us?"

Maezr bowed his grey head for a moment, as if deciding whether to answer. Finally he looked up and reached out his hand and touched Ender on the shoulder. "I will tell you, even though the information is secret. You see, the enemy attacked us first. He had good reason to attack us, but that is a matter for politicians, and whether the fault was ours or his, we could not let him win. So when the enemy came to our worlds, we fought back, hard, and spent the finest of our young men in the fleets. But we won, and the enemy retreated."

Maezr smiled ruefully. "But the enemy was not through, boy. The enemy would never be through. They came again, with more numbers, and it was harder to beat them. And another generation of young men was spent. Only a few survived. So we came up with a plan—the big men came up with the plan. We knew that we had to destroy the enemy once and for all, totally, eliminate his ability to make war against us. To do that we had to go to his home worlds—his home world, really, since the enemy's empire is all tied to his capital world."

"And so?" Ender asked.

"And so we made a fleet. We made more ships than the enemy ever had. We made a hundred ships for every ship he had sent against us. And we launched them against his twenty-eight worlds. They started leaving a hundred years ago. And they carried on them the ansible, and only a few men. So that someday a commander could sit on a planet somewhere far from the battle and command the fleet. So that our best minds would not be destroyed by the enemy."

Ender's question had still not been answered. "Why do they outnumber us?"

Maezr laughed. "Because it took a hundred years for our ships to get there. They've had a hundred years to prepare for us. They'd be fools, don't you think, boy, if they waited in old tugboats to defend their harbors. They have new ships, great ships, hundreds of ships. All we have is the ansible, that and the fact that they have to put a commander with every fleet, and when they lose—and they will lose—they lose one of their best minds every time."

Ender started to ask another question.

"No more, Ender Wiggins. I've told you more than you ought to know as it is."

Ender stood angrily and turned away. "I have a right to know. Do you think this can go on forever, pushing me through one school and another and never telling me what my life is for? You use me and the others as a tool, someday we'll command your ships, someday maybe we'll save your lives, but I'm not a computer, and I have to *know!*"

"Ask me a question, then, boy," Maezr said, "and if I can answer, I will."

"If you use your best minds to command the fleets, and you never lose any, then what do you need me for? Who am I replacing, if they're all still there?"

Maezr shook his head. "I can't tell you the answer to that, Ender. Be content that we will need you, soon. It's late. Go to bed. You have a battle in the morning."

Ender walked out of the simulator room. But when Maezr left by the same door a few moments later, the boy was waiting in the hall.

"All right, boy," Maezr said impatiently, "what is it? I don't have all night and you need to sleep."

Ender wasn't sure what his question was, but Maezr waited. Finally Ender asked softly, "Do they live?"

"Does who live?"

"The other commanders. The ones now. And before me."

Maezr snorted. "Live. Of course they live. He wonders if they live." Still chuckling, the old man walked off down the hall. Ender stood in the corridor for a while, but at last he was tired and he went off to bed. They live, he thought. They live, but he can't tell me what happens to them.

That night Ender didn't wake up crying. But he did wake up with blood on his hands.

MONTHS WORE ON with battles every day, until at last Ender settled into the routine of the destruction of himself. He slept less every night, dreamed more, and he began to have terrible pains in his stomach. They put him on a very bland diet, but soon he didn't even have an appetite for that. "Eat," Maezr said, and Ender would mechanically put food in his mouth. But if nobody told him to eat he didn't eat.

One day as he was drilling his toon leaders the room went black and he woke up on the floor with his face bloody where he had hit the controls.

They put him to bed then, and for three days he was very ill. He remembered seeing faces in his dreams, but they weren't real faces, and he knew it even while he thought he saw them. He thought he saw Bean sometimes, and sometimes he thought he saw Lieutenant Anderson and Captain Graff. And then he woke up and it was only his enemy Maezr Rackham.

"I'm awake," he said to Maezr.

"So I see," Maezr answered. "Took you long enough. You have a battle today."

So Ender got up and fought the battle and he won it. But there was no second battle that day, and they let him go to bed earlier. His hands were shaking as he undressed.

During the night he thought he felt hands touching him gently, and he dreamed he heard voices saying, "How long can he go on?"

"Long enough."

"So soon?"

"In a few days, then he's through."

"How will he do?"

"Fine. Even today, he was better than ever."

Ender recognized the last voice as Maezr Rackham's. He resented Rackham's intruding even in his sleep.

He woke up and fought another battle and won.

Then he went to bed.

He woke up and won again.

And the next day was his last day in Command School, though he didn't know it. He got up and went to the simulator for the battle.

MAEZR WAS WAITING for him. Ender walked slowly into the simulator room. He step was slightly shuffling, and he seemed tired and dull. Maezr frowned.

"Are you awake, boy?" If Ender had been alert, he would have cared more about the concern in his teacher's voice. Instead, he simply went to the controls and sat down. Maezr spoke to him.

"Today's game needs a little explanation, Ender Wiggins. Please turn around and pay strict attention."

Ender turned around, and for the first time he noticed that there were people at the back of the room. He recognized Graff and Anderson from Battle School, and vaguely remembered a few of the men from Command School—teachers for a few hours at some time or another. But most of the people he didn't know at all.

"Who are they?"

Maezr shook his head and answered, "Observers. Every now and then we let observers come in to watch the battle. If you don't want them, we'll send them out."

Ender shrugged. Maezr began his explanation. "Today's game, boy, has a new element. We're staging this battle around a planet. This will complicate things in two ways. The planet isn't large, on the scale we're using, but the ansible can't detect anything on the other side of it—so there's a blind spot. Also, it's against the rules to use weapons against the planet itself. All right?"

"Why, don't the weapons work against planets?"

Maezr answered coldly, "There are rules of war, Ender, that apply even in training games."

Ender shook his head slowly. "Can the planet attack?"

Maezr looked nonplussed for a moment, then smiled. "I guess you'll have to find that one out, boy. And one more thing. Today, Ender, your opponent isn't the computer. I am your enemy today, and today I won't be letting you off so easily. Today is a battle to the end. And I'll use any means I can to defeat you."

Then Maezr was gone, and Ender expressionlessly led his toon leaders through maneuvers. Ender was doing well, of course, but several of the observers shook their heads, and Graff kept clasping and unclasping his hands, crossing and uncrossing his legs. Ender would be slow today, and today Ender couldn't afford to be slow.

A warning buzzer sounded, and Ender cleared the simulator board, waiting for today's game to appear. He felt muddled today, and wondered why people were there watching. Were they going to judge him today? Decide if he was good enough for something else? For another two years of grueling training, another two years of struggling to exceed his best? Ender was twelve. He felt very old. And as he waited for the game to appear, he wished he could simply lose it, lose the battle badly and completely so that they would remove him from the program, punish him however they wanted, he didn't care, just so he could sleep.

Then the enemy formation appeared, and Ender's weariness turned to desperation.

The enemy outnumbered him a thousand to one, the simulator glowed green with them, and Ender knew that he couldn't win.

And the enemy was not stupid. There was no formation that Ender could study and attack. Instead the vast swarms of ships were constantly moving, constantly shifting from one momentary formation to another, so that a space that for one moment was empty was immediately filled with formidable enemy force. And even though Ender's fleet was the largest he had ever had, there was no place he could deploy it where he would outnumber the enemy long enough to accomplish anything.

And behind the enemy was the planet. The planet, which Maezr had warned him about. What difference did a planet make, when Ender couldn't hope to get near it? Ender waited, waited for the flash of insight that would tell him what to do, how to destroy the enemy. And as he waited, he heard the observers behind him begin to shift in their seats, wondering what Ender was doing, what plan he would follow. And finally it was obvious to everyone that Ender didn't know what to do, that there was nothing to do, and a few of the men at the back of the room made quiet little sounds in their throats.

Then Ender heard Bean's voice in his ear. Bean chuckled and said, "Remember, the enemy's gate is *down*." A few of the other toon leaders laughed and Ender thought back to the simple games he had played and won in Battle School. They had put him against hopeless odds there, too. And he had beaten them. And he'd be damned if he'd let Maezr Rackham beat him with a cheap trick like outnumbering him a thousand to one. He had won a game in Battle School by going for something against the rules—he had won by going against the enemy's gate.

And the enemy's gate was down.

Ender smiled, and realized that if he broke this rule they'd probably kick him out of school, and that way he'd win for sure: He would never have to play a game again.

He whispered into the microphone. His six commanders each took a part of the fleet and launched themselves against the enemy. They pursued erratic courses, darting off in one direction and then another. The enemy immediately stopped his aimless maneuvering and began to group around Ender's six fleets.

Ender took off his microphone, leaned back in his chair, and watched. The observers murmured out loud now. Ender was doing nothing—he had thrown the game away.

But a pattern began to emerge from the quick confrontations with the enemy. Ender's six groups lost ships constantly as they brushed with each enemy force—but they never stopped for a fight, even when for a moment they could have won a small tactical victory. Instead they continued on their erratic course that led, eventually, down. Toward the enemy planet.

And because of their seemingly random course the enemy didn't realize it until the same time that the observers did. By then it was too late, just as it had been too late for William Bee to stop Ender's soldiers from activating the gate. More of Ender's ships could be hit and destroyed, so that of the six fleets only two were able to get to the planet, and those were decimated. But those tiny groups *did* get through, and they opened fire on the planet.

Ender leaned forward now, anxious to see if his guess would pay off. He half expected a buzzer to sound and the game to be stopped, because he had broken the rule. But he was betting on the accuracy of the simulator. If it could simulate a planet, it could simulate what would happen to a planet under attack.

It did.

The weapons that blew up little ships didn't blow up the entire planet at first. But they did cause terrible explosions. And on the planet there was no space to dissipate the chain reaction. On the planet the chain reaction found more and more fuel to feed it.

The planet's surface seemed to be moving back and forth, but soon the surface gave way in an immense explosion that sent light flashing in all directions. It swallowed up Ender's entire fleet. And then it reached the enemy ships.

The first simply vanished in the explosion. Then, as the explosion spread and became less bright, it was clear what happened to each ship. As the light reached them they flashed brightly for a moment and disappeared. They were all fuel for the fire of the planet.

It took more than three minutes for the explosion to reach the limits of the simulator, and by then it was much fainter. All the ships were gone, and if any had escaped before the explosion reached them, they were few and not worth worrying about. Where the planet had been there was nothing. The simulator was empty.

Ender had destroyed the enemy by sacrificing his entire fleet and breaking the rule against destroying the enemy planet. He wasn't sure whether to feel triumphant at his victory or defiant at the rebuke he was certain would come. So instead he felt nothing. He was tired. He wanted to go to bed and sleep.

He switched off the simulator, and finally heard the noise behind him.

There were no longer two rows of dignified military observers. Instead there was chaos. Some of them were slapping each other on the back; some of them were bowed, head in hands; others were openly weeping. Captain Graff detached himself from the group and came to Ender. Tears streamed down his face, but he was smiling. He reached out his arms, and to Ender's surprise he embraced the boy, held him tightly, and whispered, "Thank you, thank you, thank you, Ender."

Soon all the observers were gathered around the bewildered child, thanking him and cheering him and patting him on the shoulder and shaking his hand. Ender tried to make sense of what they were saying. Had he passed the test after all? Why did it matter so much to them?

Then the crowd parted and Maezr Rackham walked through. He came straight up to Ender Wiggins and held out his hand.

"You made the hard choice, boy. But heaven knows there was no other way you could have done it. Congratulations. You beat them, and it's all over."

All over. Beat them. "I beat *you*, Maezr Rackham."

Maezr laughed, a loud laugh that filled the room. "Ender Wiggins, you never played me. You never played a *game* since I was your teacher."

Ender didn't get the joke. He had played a great many games, at a terrible cost to himself. He began to get angry.

Maezr reached out and touched his shoulder. Ender shrugged him off. Maezr then grew serious and said, "Ender Wiggins, for the last months you have been the commander of our fleets. There were no games. The battles were real. Your only enemy was *the* enemy. You won every battle. And finally today you fought them at their home world, and you destroyed their world, their fleet, you destroyed them completely, and they'll never come against us again. You did it. You."

Real. Not a game. Ender's mind was too tired to cope with it all. He walked away from Maezr, walked silently through the crowd that still whispered thanks and congratulations to the boy, walked out of the simulator room and finally arrived in his bedroom and closed the door.

HE WAS ASLEEP when Graff and Maezr Rackham found him. They came in quietly and roused him. He awoke slowly, and when he recognized them he turned away to go back to sleep.

"Ender," Graff said. "We need to talk to you."

Ender rolled back to face them. He said nothing.

Graff smiled. "It was a shock to you yesterday, I know. But it must make you feel good to know you won the war."

Ender nodded slowly.

"Maezr Rackham here, he never played against you. He only analyzed your battles to find out your weak spots, to help you improve. It worked, didn't it?"

Ender closed his eyes tightly. They waited. He said, "Why didn't you tell me?"

Maezr smiled. "A hundred years ago, Ender, we found out some things. That when a commander's life is in danger he becomes afraid, and fear slows down his thinking. When a commander knows that he's killing people, he becomes cautious or insane, and neither of those help him do well. And when he's mature, when he has responsibilities and an understanding of the world, he becomes cautious and sluggish and can't do his job. So we trained children, who didn't know anything but the game, and never knew when it would become real. That was the theory, and you proved that the theory worked."

Graff reached out and touched Ender's shoulder. "We launched the ships so that they would all arrive at their destination during these few months. We knew that we'd probably have only one good commander, if we were lucky. In history it's been very rare to have more than one genius in a war. So we planned on having a genius. We were gambling. And you came along and we won."

Ender opened his eyes again and they realized that he was angry. "Yes, you won."

Graff and Maezr Rackham looked at each other. "He doesn't understand," Graff whispered.

"I understand," Ender said. "You needed a weapon, and you got it, and it was me."

"That's right," Maezr answered.

"So tell me," Ender went on, "how many people lived on that planet that I destroyed."

They didn't answer him. They waited awhile in silence, and then Graff spoke. "Weapons don't need to understand what they're pointed at, Ender. We did the pointing, and so we're responsible. You just did your job."

Maezr smiled. "Of course, Ender, you'll be taken care of. The government will never forget you. You served us all very well."

Ender rolled over and faced the wall, and even though they tried to talk to him, he didn't answer them. Finally they left.

Ender lay in his bed for a long time before anyone disturbed him again. The door opened softly. Ender didn't turn to see who it was. Then a hand touched him softly.

"Ender, it's me, Bean."

Ender turned over and looked at the little boy who was standing by his bed.

"Sit down," Ender said.

Bean sat. "That last battle, Ender. I didn't know how you'd get us out of it."

Ender smiled. "I didn't. I cheated. I thought they'd kick me out."

"Can you believe it! We won the war. The whole war's over, and we thought we'd have to wait till we grew up to fight in it, and it was us fighting it all the time. I mean, Ender, we're little kids. I'm a little kid, anyway." Bean laughed and Ender smiled. Then they were silent for a little while, Bean sitting on the edge of the bed, Ender watching him out of half-closed eyes.

Finally Bean thought of something else to say.

"What will we do now that the war's over?" he said.

Ender closed his eyes and said, "I need some sleep, Bean."

Bean got up and left and Ender slept.

GRAFF AND ANDERSON walked through the gates into the park. There was a breeze, but the sun was hot on their shoulders.

"Abba Technics? In the capital?" Graff asked.

"No, in Biggock County. Training division," Anderson replied. "They think my work with children is good preparation. And you?"

Graff smiled and shook his head. "No plans. I'll be here for a few more months. Reports, winding down. I've had offers. Personnel development for DCIA, executive vice-president for U and P, but I said no. Publisher wants me to do memoirs of the war. I don't know."

They sat on a bench and watched leaves shivering in the breeze. Children on the monkey bars were laughing and yelling, but the wind and the distance swallowed their words. "Look," Graff said, pointing. A little boy jumped from the bars and ran near the bench where the two men sat. Another boy followed him, and holding his hands like a gun he made an explosive sound. The child he was shooting at didn't stop. He fired again.

"I got you! Come back here!"

The other little boy ran on out of sight.

"Don't you know when you're dead?" The boy shoved his hands in his pockets and kicked a rock back to the monkey bars. Anderson smiled and shook his head. "Kids," he said. Then he and Graff stood up and walked on out of the park.

David Drake

David Drake's multivolume series of novels and short fiction featuring
Hammer's Slammers (Hammer's Slammers, Cross the Stars, At Any
Price, Counting the Cost, Rolling Hot, The Warrior, The Sharp End), a
team of interstellar mercenaries, has helped to establish him as one of the
leading exponents of modern military science fiction. With Bill Fawcett,
he coedited the six-book shared world Fleet series of future war fiction, as
well as both volumes of its sequel, the Battlestation series. Other anthology
credits include Space Gladiators, Space Dreadnoughts, Space Infantry,
and two volumes in tribute to Rudyard Kipling and his influence on science fiction, Heads to the Storm and A Separate Star. Ancient Rome
serves as a setting for some of Drake's most inventive science fiction and
fantasy, in the time travel tale Birds of Prey, the alien contact story Ranks
of Bronze, and the fantasy collection Vettius and His Friends. His many
other books include the Arthurian fantasy The Dragon Lord and an out-
standing collection of horror, fantasy, and science fiction short stories,
From the Heart of Darkness, many of which have war-based themes.

HANGMAN

David Drake

THE LIGHT IN the kitchen alcove glittered on Lt. Schilling's blond curls; glittered also on the frost-spangled window beside her and from the armor of the tank parked outside. All the highlights looked cold to Capt. Danny Pritchard as he stepped closer to the infantry lieutenant.

"Sal—" Pritchard began. From the orderly room behind them came the babble of the radios ranked against one wall and, less muted, the laughter of soldiers waiting for action. "You can't think like a Dutchman anymore. We're Hammer's Slammers, all of us. We're mercs. Not Dutch, not Frisians—"

"You're not," Lt. Schilling snapped, looking up from the cup of bitter chocolate she had just drawn from the urn. She was a short woman and lightly built, but she had the unerring instinct of a bully who is willing to make a scene for a victim who is not willing to be part of one. "You're a farmer from Dunstan, what d'you care about Dutch miners, whatever these bleeding French do to them. But a lot of us do care, Danny, and if you had a little compassion—"

"But Sal—" Pritchard repeated, only his right arm moving as he touched the blond girl's shoulder.

"Get your hands off me, Captain!" she shouted. "That's over!" She shifted the mug of steaming chocolate in her hand. The voices in the orderly room stilled. Then, simultaneously, someone turned up the volume of the radios and at least three people began to talk loudly on unconnected subjects.

Pritchard studied the back of his hand, turned it over to examine the calloused palm as well. He smiled. "Sorry, I'll remember that," he said in a normal voice. He turned and stepped back into the orderly room, a brown-haired man of 34 with a good set of muscles to cover his moderate frame and nothing at all to cover his heart. Those who knew Danny Pritchard slightly thought him a relaxed man, and he looked relaxed even now. But waiting around the electric grate were three troopers who knew Danny very well indeed: the crew of The Plow, Pritchard's command tank.

Kowie drove the beast, a rabbit-eyed man whose fingers now flipped cards in another game of privy solitaire. His deck was so dirty that only familiarity allowed him to read the pips. Kowie's hands and eyes were just as quick at the controls of the tank, sliding its bulbous hundred and fifty metric tons through spaces that were only big enough to pass it. When he had to, he drove nervelessly through objects instead of going around. Kowie would never be more than a tank driver; but he was the best tank driver in the Regiment.

Rob Jenne was big and as blond as Lt. Schilling. He grinned up at Pritchard, his expression changing from embarrassment to relief as he saw that his captain was able to smile also. Jenne had transferred from combat cars to tanks three years back, after the Slammers had pulled out of Squire's World. He was sharp-eyed and calm in a crisis. Twice after his transfer Jenne had been offered a blower of his own to command if he would return to combat cars. He had refused both promotions, saying he would stay with tanks or buy back his contract, that there was no way he was going back to those open-topped coffins again. When a tank commander's slot came open, Jenne got it; and Pritchard had made the blond sergeant his own blower chief when a directional mine had retired the previous man. Now Jenne straddled a chair backwards, his hands flexing a collapsible torsion device that kept his muscles as dense and hard as they had been the day he was recruited from a quarry on Burlage.

Line tanks carry only a driver and the blower chief who directs the tank and its guns when they are not under the direct charge of the Regiment's computer. In addition to those two and a captain, command tanks have a Communications Technician to handle the multiplex burden of radio traffic focused on the vehicle. Pritchard's commo tech was Margritte DiManzo, a slender widow who cropped her lustrous hair short so that it would not interfere with the radio helmet she wore most of her waking hours. She was off duty now, but she had not removed the bulky headgear which linked her to the six radios in the tank parked outside. Their simultaneous sound would have been unintelligible babbling to most listeners. The black-haired woman's training, both conscious and hypnotic, broke that babbling into a set of discrete conversations. When Pritchard reentered the room, Margritte was speaking to Jenne. She did not look up at her commander until Jenne's brightening expression showed her it was safe to do so.

Two commo people and a sergeant with Intelligence tabs were at consoles in the orderly room. They were from the Regiment's HQ Battalion, assigned to Sector Two here on Kobold but in no sense a part of the sector's combat companies: Capt. Riis' S Company—infantry—and Pritchard's own tanks.

Riis was the senior captain and in charge of the sector, a matter which neither he nor Pritchard ever forgot. Sally Schilling led his first platoon. Her aide, a black-haired corporal, sat with his huge boots up, humming as he polished the pieces of his field-stripped powergun. Its barrel gleamed orange in the light of the electric grate. Electricity was more general on Kobold than on some wealthier worlds, since mining and copper smelting made fusion units a practical necessity. But though the copper in the transmission cable might well have been processed on Kobold, the wire had probably been drawn off-world and shipped back here. Aurore and Friesland had refused to allow even such simple manufactures here on their joint colony. They had kept Kobold a market and a supplier of raw materials, but never a rival.

"Going to snow tonight?" Jenne asked.

"Umm, too cold," Pritchard said, walking over to the grate. He pretended he did not hear Lt. Schilling stepping out of the alcove. "I figure—"

"Hold it," said Margritte, her index finger curling out for a volume control before the duty man had time to react. One of the wall radios boomed loudly to the whole room. Prodding another switch, Margritte patched the signal separately through the link implanted in Pritchard's right mastoid.

"—guns and looks like satchel charges. There's only one man in each truck, but they've been on the horn too and we can figure on more Frenchies here any—"

"Red Alert," Pritchard ordered, facing his commo tech so that she could read his lips. "Where is this?"

The headquarters radiomen stood nervously, afraid to interfere but unwilling to let an outsider run their equipment, however ably. "Red Alert,"

Margritte was repeating over all bands. Then, through Pritchard's implant, she said, "It's Patrol Sigma three-nine, near Haacin. Dutch civilians've stopped three outbound provisions trucks from Barthe's Company."

"Scramble First Platoon," Pritchard said, "but tell 'em to hold for us to arrive." As Margritte coolly passed on the order, Pritchard picked up the commo helmet he had laid on his chair when he followed Lt. Schilling into the kitchen. The helmet gave him automatic switching and greater range than the bio-electric unit behind his ear.

The wall radio was saying, "—need some big friendlies fast or it'll drop in the pot for sure."

"Sigma three-niner," Pritchard said, "this is Michael One."

"Go ahead, Michael One," replied the distant squad leader. Pritchard's commo helmet added an airy boundlessness to his surroundings without really deadening the ambient noise.

"Hold what you've got, boys," the tank captain said. "There's help on the way."

The door of the orderly room stood ajar the way Pritchard's crewmen had left it. The captain slammed it shut as he too ran for his tank. Behind in the orderly room, Lt. Schilling was snapping out quick directions to her own platoon and to her awakened commander.

The Plow was already floating when Danny reached it. Ice crystals, spewed from beneath the skirts by the lift fans, made a blue-white dazzle in the vehicle's running lights. Frost whitened the ladder up the high side of the tank's plenum chamber and hull. Pritchard paused to pull on his gloves before mounting. Sgt. Jenne, anchoring himself with his left hand on the turret's storage rack, reached down and lifted his captain aboard without noticeable effort. Side by side, the two men slid through the hatches to their battle stations.

"Ready," Pritchard said over the intercom.

"Movin' on," replied Kowie, and with his words the tank slid forward over the frozen ground like grease on a hot griddle.

The command post had been a district road-maintenance center before all semblance of central government on Kobold had collapsed. The orderly room and officers' quarters were in the supervisor's house, a comfortable structure with shutters and mottoes embroidered in French on the walls. Some of the hangings had been defaced by short-range gunfire. The crew barracks across the road now served the troopers on headquarters duty. Many of the Slammers could read the Dutch periodicals abandoned there in the break-up. The equipment shed beside the barracks garaged the infantry skimmers because the battery-powered platforms could not shrug off the weather like the huge panzers of M Company. The shed doors were open, pluming the night with heated air as the duty platoon ran for its mounts. Some of the troopers had not yet donned their helmets and body armor. Jenne waved as the tank swept on by; then the road curved and the infantry was lost in the night.

Kobold was a joint colony of Aurore and Friesland. When eighty years of French oppression had driven the Dutch settlers to rebellion, their first act was to hire Hammer's Slammers. The break between Hammer and Friesland had been sharp, but time has a way of blunting anger and letting old habits resume. The Regimental language was Dutch, and many of the Slammers' officers were Frisians seconded from their own service. Friesland gained from the men's experience when they returned home; Hammer gained company officers with excellent training from the Gröningen Academy.

To counter the Slammers, the settlers of Auroran descent had hired three Francophone regiments. If either group of colonists could have afforded to pay its mercenaries unaided, the fighting would have been immediate and brief. Kobold had been kept deliberately poor by its home worlds, however; so in their necessities the settlers turned to those home worlds for financial help.

And neither Aurore nor Friesland wanted a war on Kobold.

Friesland had let its settlers swing almost from the beginning, sloughing their interests for a half share of the copper produced and concessions elsewhere in its sphere of influence. The arrangement was still satisfactory to the Council of State, if Frisian public opinion could be mollified by apparent activity. Aurore was on the brink of war in the Zemla System. Her Parlement feared another proxy war which could in a moment explode full-fledged, even though Friesland had been weakened by a decade of severe internal troubles. So Aurore and Friesland reached a compromise. Then, under threat of abandonment, the warring parties were forced to transfer their mercenaries' contracts to the home worlds. Finally, Aurore and Friesland mutually hired the four regiments: the Slammers; Compagnie de Barthe; the Alaudae; and Phenix Moirots. Mercs from either side were mixed and divided among eight sectors imposed on a map of inhabited Kobold. There the contract ordered them to keep peace between the factions; prevent the importation of modern weapons to either side; and — wait.

But Col. Barthe and the Auroran leaders had come to a further, secret agreement; and although Hammer had learned of it, he had informed only two men—Maj. Steuben, his aide and bodyguard; and Capt. Daniel Pritchard.

Pritchard scowled at the memory. Even without the details a traitor had sold Hammer, it would have been obvious that Barthe had his own plans. In the other sectors, Hammer's men and their French counterparts ran joint patrols. Both sides scattered their camps throughout the sectors, just as the villages of either nationality were scattered. Barthe had split his sectors in halves, brusquely ordering the Slammers to keep to the west of the River Aillet because his own troops were mining the east of the basin heavily. Barthe's Company was noted for its minefields. That skill was one of the reasons they had been hired by the French. Since most of Kobold was covered either by forests or by rugged hills, armor was limited to roads where well-placed mines could stack tanks like crushed boxes.

Hammer listened to Barthe's pronouncement and laughed, despite the anger of most of his staff officers. Beside him, Joachim Steuben had grinned and traced the line of his cut-away holster. When Danny Pritchard was informed, he had only shivered a little and called a vehicle inspection for the next morning. That had been three months ago. . . .

The night streamed by like smoke around the tank. Pritchard lowered his face shield, but he did not drop his seat into the belly of the tank. Vision blocks within gave a 360° view of the tank's surroundings, but the farmer in Danny could not avoid the feeling of blindness within the impenetrable walls. Jenne sat beside his captain in a cupola fitted with a three-barrelled automatic weapon. He too rode with his head out of the hatch, but that was only for comradeship. The sergeant much preferred to be inside. He would button up at the first sign of hostile action. Jenne was in no sense a coward; it was just that he had quirks. Most combat veterans do.

Pritchard liked the whistle of the black wind past his helmet. Warm air from the tank's resistance heaters jetted up through the hatch and kept his body quite comfortable. The vehicle's huge mass required the power of a fusion plant to drive its lift motors, and the additional burden of climate control was inconsequential.

The tankers' face shields automatically augmented the light of the moon, dim and red because the sun it reflected was dim and red as well. The boosted light level displayed the walls of forest, the boles snaking

densely to either side of the road. At Kobold's perihelion, the thin stems
grew in days to their full six-meter height and spread a ceiling of red-
brown leaves the size of blankets. Now, at aphelion, the chilled, sapless
trees burned with almost explosive intensity. The wood was too dangerous to use for heating, even if electricity had not been common; but it
fueled the gasogene engines of most vehicles on the planet.

Jenne gestured ahead. "Blowers," he muttered on the intercom. His
head rested on the gun switch though he knew the vehicles must be
friendly. The Plow slowed.

Pritchard nodded agreement. "Michael First, this is Michael One,"
he said. "Flash your running lights so we can be sure it's you."

"Roger," replied the radio. Blue light flickered from the shapes hulking at the edge of the forest ahead. Kowie throttled the fans up to cruise,
then chopped them and swung expertly into the midst of the four tanks
of the outlying platoon.

"Michael One, this is Sigma One," Capt. Riis' angry voice demanded
in the helmet.

"Go ahead."

"Barthe's sent a battalion across the river. I'm moving Lt. Schilling
into position to block 'em and called Central for artillery support. You
hold your first platoon at Haacin for reserve and any partisans up from
Portela. I'll take direct command of the rest of—"

"Negative, negative, Sigma One!" Pritchard snapped. The Plow was
accelerating again, second in the line of five tanks. They were beasts of
prey sliding across the landscape of snow and black trees at 80 kph and
climbing. "Let the French through, Captain. There won't be fighting,
repeat, negative fighting."

"There damned well *will* be fighting, Michael One, if Barthe tries to
shove a battalion into my sector!" Riis thundered back. "Remember, this
isn't your command or a joint command. *I'm* in charge here."

"Margritte, patch me through to Battalion," Pritchard hissed on intercom. The Plow's turret was cocked 30° to the right. It covered the forest sweeping by to that side and anything which might be hiding there.
Pritchard's mind was on Sally Schilling, riding a skimmer through forest
like that flanking the tanks, hurrying with her fifty men to try to stop a
battalion's hasty advance.

The commo helmet popped quietly to itself. Pritchard tensed, groping
for the words he would need to convince Lt. Col. Miezierk. Miezierk,
under whom command of Sectors One and Two was grouped, had been

a Frisian regular until five years ago. He was supposed to think like a
merc now, not like a Frisian; but. . . .

The voice that suddenly rasped, "Override, override!" was not
Miezierk's. "Sigma One, Michael One, this is Regiment."

"Go ahead," Pritchard blurted. Capt. Riis, equally rattled, said, "Yes,
sir!" on the three-way link.

"Sigma, your fire order is cancelled. Keep your troops on alert, but
keep 'em the hell out of Barthe's way."

"But Col. Hammer—"

"Riis, you're not going to start a war tonight. Michael One, can
your panzers handle whatever's going on at Haacin without violating the
contract?"

"Yes, sir." Pritchard flashed a map briefly on his face shield to check
his position. "We're almost there now."

"If you can't handle it, Captain, you'd better hope you're killed in
action," Col. Hammer said bluntly. "I haven't nursed this regiment
for twenty-three years to lose it because somebody forgets what his job
is." Then, more softly—Pritchard could imagine the colonel flicking
his eyes side to side to gauge bystanders' reactions—he added, "There's
support if you need it, Captain—if they're the ones who breach the
contract."

"Affirmative."

"Keep the lid on, boy. Regiment out."

The trees had drunk the whine of the fans. Now the road curved and
the tanks banked greasily to join the main highway from Dimo to
Portela. The tailings pile of the Haacin Mine loomed to the right and
hurled the drive noise back redoubled at the vehicles. The steel skirts of
the lead tank touched the road metal momentarily, showering the night
with orange sparks. Beyond the mine were the now-empty wheat fields
and then the village itself.

Haacin, the largest Dutch settlement in Sector Two, sprawled to
either side of the highway. Its houses were two- and three-story lumps of
cemented mine tailings. They were roofed with tile or plastic rather than
shakes of native timber, because of the wood's lethal flammability. The
highway was straight and broad. It gave Pritchard a good view of the
three cargo vehicles pulled to one side. Men in local dress swarmed
about them. Across the road were ten of Hammer's khaki-clad infantry,
patrol S-39, whose ported weapons half-threatened, half-protected the
trio of drivers in their midst. Occasionally a civilian turned to hurl a

curse at Barthe's men, but mostly the Dutch busied themselves with off-loading cartons from the trucks.

Pritchard gave a brief series of commands. The four line tanks grounded in a hedgehog at the edge of the village. Their main guns and automatics faced outward in all directions. Kowie swung the command vehicle around the tank which had been leading it. He cut the fans' angle of attack, slowing The Plow without losing the ability to accelerate quickly. The command vehicle eased past the squad of infantry, then grounded behind the rearmost truck. Pritchard felt the fans' hum through the metal of the hull.

"Who's in charge here?" the captain demanded, his voice booming through the command vehicle's public address system.

The Dutch unloading the trucks halted silently. A squat man in a parka of feathery native fur stepped forward. Unlike many of the other civilians, he was not armed. He did not flinch when Pritchard pinned him with the spotlight of the tank. "I am Paul van Oosten," the man announced in the heavy Dutch of Kobold. "I am Mayor of Haacin. But if you mean who leads us in what we are doing here, well . . . perhaps Justice herself does. Klaus, show them what these trucks were carrying to Portela."

Another civilian stepped forward, ripping the top off the box he carried. Flat plastic wafers spilled from it, glittering in the cold light: power-gun ammunition, intended for shoulder weapons like those the infantry carried.

"They were taking powerguns to the beasts of Portela to use against us," van Oosten said. He used the slang term "skepsels" to name the Francophone settlers. The mayor's shaven jaw was jutting out in anger.

"Captain!" called one of Barthe's truck drivers, brushing forward through the ring of Hammer's men. "Let me explain."

One of the civilians growled and lifted his heavy musket. Rob Jenne rang his knuckles twice on the receiver of his tribarrel, calling attention to the muzzles as he swept them down across the crowd. The Dutchman froze. Jenne smiled without speaking.

"We were sent to pick up wheat the regiment had purchased," Barthe's man began. Pritchard was not familiar with Barthe's insigniae, but from the merc's age and bearing he was a senior sergeant. An unlikely choice to be driving a provisions truck. "One of the vehicles happened to be partly loaded. We didn't take the time to empty it because we were in a hurry to finish the run and go off duty—there was enough room and lift to handle that little bit of gear and the grain besides.

"In any case—" and here the sergeant began pressing, because the tank captain had not cut him off at the first sentence as expected—"you do not, and these fools *surely* do not, have the right to stop Col. Barthe's transport. If you have questions about the way we pick up wheat, that's between your CO and ours, sir."

Pritchard ran his gloved index finger back and forth below his right eyesocket. He was ice inside, bubbling ice that tore and chilled him and had nothing to do with the weather. He turned back to Mayor van Oosten. "Reload the trucks," he said, hoping that his voice did not break.

"You can't!" van Oosten cried. "These powerguns are the only chance my village, my *people* have to survive when you leave. You know that'll happen, don't you? Friesland and Aurore, they'll come to an agreement, a *trade-off*, they'll call it, and all the troops will leave. It's our lives they're trading! The beasts in Dimo, in Portela if you let these go through, they'll have powerguns that *their* mercenaries gave them. And we—"

Pritchard whispered a prepared order into his helmet mike. The rearmost of the four tanks at the edge of the village fired a single round from its main gun. The night flared cyan as the 200 mm bolt struck the middle of the tailings pile a kilometer away. Stone, decomposed by the enormous energy of the shot, recombined in a huge gout of flame. Vapor, lava, and cinders spewed in every direction. After a moment, bits of high-flung rock began pattering down on the roofs of Haacin.

The bolt caused a double thunder-clap, that of the heated air followed by the explosive release of energy at the point of impact. When the reverberations died away there was utter silence in Haacin. On the distant jumble of rock, a dying red glow marked where the charge had hit. The shot had also ignited some saplings rooted among the stones. They had blazed as white torches for a few moments but they were already collapsing as cinders.

"The Slammers are playing this by the rules," Pritchard said. Loudspeakers flung his quiet words about the village like the echoes of the shot; but he was really speaking for the recorder in the belly of the tank, preserving his words for a later Bonding Authority hearing. "There'll be no powerguns in civilian hands. Load every bit of this gear back in the truck. Remember, there's satellites up there—" Pritchard waved generally at the sky—"that see everything that happens on Kobold. If one powergun is fired by a civilian in this sector, I'll come for him. I promise you."

The mayor sagged within his furs. Turning to the crowd behind him, he said, "Put the guns back on the truck. So that the Portelans can kill us more easily."

"Are you mad, van Oosten?" demanded the gunman who had earlier threatened Barthe's sergeant.

"Are *you* mad, Kruse?" the mayor shouted back without trying to hide his fury. "D'ye doubt what those tanks would do to Haacin? And do you doubt this butcher—" his back was to Pritchard but there was no doubt as to whom the mayor meant—"would use them on us? Perhaps tomorrow we could have. . . ."

There was motion at the far edge of the crowd, near the corner of a building. Margritte, watching the vision blocks within, called a warning. Pritchard reached for his panic bar—Rob Jenne was traversing the tribarrel. All three of them were too late. The muzzle flash was red and it expanded in Pritchard's eyes as a hammer blow smashed him in the middle of the forehead.

The bullet's impact heaved the tanker up and backwards. His shattered helmet flew off into the night. The unyielding hatch coaming caught him in the small of the back, arching his torso over it as if he were being broken on the wheel. Pritchard's eyes flared with sheets of light. As reaction flung him forward again, he realized he was hearing the reports of Jenne's powergun and that some of the hellish flashes were real.

If the tribarrel's discharges were less brilliant than that of the main gun, then they were more than a hundred times as close to the civilians. The burst snapped within a meter of one bystander, an old man who stumbled backwards into a wall. His mouth and staring eyes were three circles of empty terror. Jenne fired seven rounds. Every charge but one struck the sniper or the building he sheltered against. Powdered concrete sprayed from the wall. The sniper's body spun backwards, chest gobbled away by the bolts. His right arm still gripped the musket he had fired at Pritchard. The arm had been flung alone onto the snowy pavement. The electric bite of ozone hung in the air with the ghostly afterimages of the shots. The dead man's clothes were burning, tiny orange flames that rippled into smoke an inch from their bases.

Jenne's big left hand was wrapped in the fabric of Pritchard's jacket, holding the dazed officer upright. "There's another rule you play by," the sergeant roared to the crowd. "You shoot at Hammer's Slammers and you get your balls kicked between your ears. Sure as God, boys; sure as death." Jenne's right hand swung the muzzles of his weapon across the faces of the civilians. "Now, load the bleeding trucks like the captain said, heroes."

For a brief moment, nothing moved but the threatening powergun. Then a civilian turned and hefted a heavy crate back aboard the truck from which he had just taken it. Empty-handed, the colonist began to sidle away from the vehicle—and from the deadly tribarrel. One by one the other villagers reloaded the hijacked cargo, the guns and ammunition they had hoped would save them in the cataclysm they awaited. One by one they took the blower chief's unspoken leave to return to their houses. One who did not leave was sobbing out her grief over the mangled body of the sniper. None of her neighbors had gone to her side. They could all appreciate—now—what it would have meant if that first shot had led to a general firefight instead of Jenne's selective response.

"Rob, help me get him inside," Pritchard heard Margritte say.

Pritchard braced himself with both hands and leaned away from his sergeant's supporting arm. "No, I'm all right," he croaked. His vision was clear enough, but the landscape was flashing bright and dim with vari-colored light.

The side hatch of the turret clanked. Margritte was beside her captain. She had stripped off her cold weather gear in the belly of the tank and wore only her khaki uniform. "Get back inside there," Pritchard muttered. "It's not safe." He was afraid of falling if he raised a hand to fend her away. He felt an injector prick the swelling flesh over his cheekbones. The flashing colors died away though Pritchard's ears began to ring.

"They carried some into the nearest building," the non-com from Barthe's Company was saying. He spoke in Dutch, having sleep-trained in the language during the transit to Kobold just as Hammer's men had in French.

"Get it," Jenne ordered the civilians still near the trucks. Three of them were already scurrying toward the house the merc had indicated. They were back in moments, carrying the last of the arms chests.

Pritchard surveyed the scene. The cargo had been reloaded, except for the few spilled rounds winking from the pavement. Van Oosten and the furious Kruse were the only villagers still in sight. "All right," Pritchard said to the truck drivers, "get aboard and get moving. And come back by way of Bitzen, not here. I'll arrange an escort for you."

The French non-com winked, grinned, and shouted a quick order to his men. The infantrymen stepped aside silently to pass the truckers.

The French mercenaries mounted their vehicles and kicked them to life. Their fans whined and the trucks lifted, sending snow crystals dancing. With gathering speed, they slid westward along the forest-rimmed highway.

Jenne shook his head at the departing trucks, then stiffened as his helmet spat a message. "Captain," he said, "we got company coming."

Pritchard grunted. His own radio helmet had been smashed by the bullet, and his implant would only relay messages on the band to which it had been verbally keyed most recently. "Margritte, start switching for me," he said. His slender commo tech was already slipping back inside through the side hatch. Pritchard's blood raced with the chemicals Margritte had shot into it. His eyes and mind worked perfectly, though all his thoughts seemed to have razor edges on them.

"Use mine," Jenne said, trying to hand the captain his helmet.

"I've got the implant," Pritchard said. He started to shake his head and regretted the motion instantly. "That and Margritte's worth a helmet any day."

"It's a whole battalion," Jenne explained quietly, his eyes scanning the Bever Road down which Command Central had warned that Barthe's troops were coming. "All but the artillery—that's back in Dimo, but it'll range here easy enough. Brought in anti-tank battery and a couple calliopes, though."

"Slide us up ahead of Michael First," Pritchard ordered his driver. As The Plow shuddered, then spun on its axis, the captain dropped his seat into the turret to use the vision blocks. He heard Jenne's seat whirr down beside him and the cupola hatch snick closed. In front of Pritchard's knees, pale in the instrument lights, Margritte DiManzo sat still and open-eyed at her communications console.

"Little friendlies," Pritchard called through his loudspeakers to the ten infantrymen, "find yourselves a quiet alley and hope nothing happens. The Lord help you if you fire a shot without me ordering it." The Lord help us all, Pritchard thought to himself.

Ahead of the command vehicle, the beetle shapes of First Platoon began to shift position. "Michael First," Pritchard ordered sharply, "get back as you were. We're not going to engage Barthe, we're going to meet him." Maybe.

Kowie slid them alongside, then a little forward of the point vehicle of the defensive lozenge. They set down. All of the tanks were buttoned up, save for the hatch over Pritchard's head. The central vision block was a meter by 30 cm panel. It could be set for anything from a 360° view of the tank's surroundings to a one-to-one image of an object a kilometer away. Pritchard focused and ran the gain to ten magnifications, then thirty. At the higher power, motion curling along the snow-smoothed grainfields between Haacin and its mine resolved into men. Barthe's troops were clad in sooty-white coveralls and battle armor. The leading elements were hunched low on the meager platforms of their skimmers. Magnification and the augmented light made the skittering images grainy, but the tanker's practiced eye caught the tubes of rocket launchers clipped to every one of the skimmers. The skirmish line swelled at two points where self-propelled guns were strung like beads on the cord of men: anti-tank weapons, 50 mm powerguns firing high-intensity charges. They were supposed to be able to burn through the heaviest armor. Barthe's boys had come loaded for bear; oh yes. They thought they knew just what they were going up against. Well, the Slammers weren't going to show them they were wrong. Tonight.

"Running lights, everybody," Pritchard ordered. Then, taking a deep breath, he touched the lift on his seat and raised himself head and shoulders back into the chill night air. There was a hand light clipped to Pritchard's jacket. He snapped it on, aiming the beam down onto the turret top so that the burnished metal splashed diffused radiance up over him. It bathed his torso and face plainly for the oncoming infantry. Through the open hatch, Pritchard could hear Rob cursing. Just possibly Margritte was mumbling a prayer.

"Batteries at Dimo and Harfleur in Sector One have received fire orders and are waiting for a signal to execute," the implant grated. "If Barthe opens fire, Command Central will not, repeat, negative, use Michael First or Michael One to knock down the shells. Your guns will be clear for action, Michael One."

Pritchard grinned starkly. His face would not have been pleasant even if livid bruises were not covering almost all of it. The Slammers' central fire direction computer used radar and satellite reconnaissance to track shells in flight. Then the computer took control of any of the Regiment's vehicle-mounted powerguns and swung them onto the target. Central's message notified Pritchard that he would have full control of his weapons at all times, while guns tens or hundreds of kilometers away kept his force clear of artillery fire.

Margritte had blocked most of the commo traffic, Pritchard realized.

She had let through only this message that was crucial to what they were about to do. A good commo tech; a very good person indeed.

The skirmish line grounded. The nearest infantrymen were within fifty meters of the tanks and their fellows spread off into the night like lethal wings. Barthe's men rolled off their skimmers and lay prone. Pritchard began to relax when he noticed that their rocket launchers were still aboard the skimmers. The anti-tank weapons were in instant reach, but at least they were not being leveled for an immediate salvo. Barthe didn't want to fight the Slammers. His targets were the Dutch civilians, just as Mayor van Oosten had suggested.

An air cushion jeep with a driver and two officers aboard drew close. It hissed slowly through the line of infantry, then stopped nearly touching the command vehicle's bow armor. One of the officers dismounted. He was a tall man who was probably very thin when he was not wearing insulated coveralls and battle armor. He raised his face to Pritchard atop the high curve of the blower, sweeping up his reflective face shield as he did so. He was Lt. Col. Benoit, commander of the French mercenaries in Sector Two; a clean-shaven man with sharp features and a splash of gray hair displaced across his forehead by his helmet. Benoit grinned and waved at the muzzle of the 200 mm powergun pointed at him. Nobody had ever said Barthe's chief subordinate was a coward.

Pritchard climbed out of the turret to the deck, then slid down the bow slope to the ground. Benoit was several inches taller than the tanker, with a force of personality which was daunting in a way that height alone could never be. It didn't matter to Pritchard. He worked with tanks and with Col. Hammer; nothing else was going to face down a man who was accustomed to those.

"Sgt. Major Oberlie reported how well and . . . firmly you handled their little affair, Captain," Benoit said, extending his hand to Pritchard. "I'll admit that I was a little concerned that I would have to rescue my men myself."

"Hammer's Slammers can be depended on to keep their contracts," the tanker replied, smiling with false warmth. "I told these squareheads that any civilian caught with a powergun was going to have to answer to me for it. Then we made sure nobody thinks we were kidding."

Benoit chuckled. Little puffs of vapor spurted from his mouth with the sounds. "You've been sent to the Gröningen Academy, have you not, Capt. Pritchard?" the older man asked. "You understand that I take an interest in my opposite numbers in this sector."

Pritchard nodded. "The Old Man picked me for the two year crash course on Friesland, yeah. Now and again he sends non-coms he wants to promote."

"But you're not a Frisian, though you have Frisian military training," the other mercenary continued, nodding to himself. "As you know, Captain, promotion in some infantry regiments comes much faster than it does in the . . . Slammers. If you feel a desire to speak to Col. Barthe some time in the future, I assure you this evening's business will not be forgotten."

"Just doing my job, Colonel," Pritchard simpered. Did Benoit think a job offer would make a traitor of him? Perhaps. Hammer had bought Barthe's plans for very little, considering their military worth. "Enforcing the contract, just like you'd have done if things were the other way around."

Benoit chuckled again and stepped back aboard his jeep. "Until we meet again, Capt. Pritchard," he said. "For the moment, I think we'll just proceed on into Portela. That's permissible under the contract, of course."

"Swing wide around Haacin, will you?" Pritchard called back. "The folks there're pretty worked up. Nobody wants more trouble, do we?"

Benoit nodded. As his jeep lifted, he spoke into his helmet communicator. The skirmish company rose awkwardly and set off in a counterclockwise circuit of Haacin. Behind them, in a column re-formed from their support positions at the base of the tailings heap, came the truck-mounted men of the other three companies. Pritchard stood and watched until the last of them whined past.

Air stirred by the tank's idling fans leaked out under the skirts. The jets formed tiny deltas of the snow which winked as Pritchard's feet caused eddy currents. In their cold precision, the tanker recalled Col. Benoit's grin.

"Command Central," Pritchard said as he climbed his blower, "Michael One. Everything's smooth here. Over." Then, "Sigma One, this is Michael One. I'll be back as quick as fans'll move me, so if you have anything to say we can discuss it then." Pritchard knew that Capt. Riis must have been burning the net up, trying to raise him for a report or to make demands. It wasn't fair to make Margritte hold the bag now that Pritchard himself was free to respond to the sector chief; but neither did the Dunstan tanker have the energy to argue with Riis just at the moment. Already this night he'd faced death and Col. Benoit. Riis could wait another ten minutes.

. . .

THE PLOW'S ARMOR was a tight fit for its crew, the radios, and the central bulk of the main gun with its feed mechanism. The command vehicle rode glass-smooth over the frozen roadway, with none of the jouncing that a rougher surface might bring even through the air cushion. Margritte faced Pritchard over her console, her seat a meter lower than his so that she appeared a suppliant. Her short hair was the lustrous purple-black of a grackle's throat in sunlight. Hidden illumination from the instruments brought her face to life.

"Gee, Captain," Jenne was saying at Pritchard's side, "I wish you'd a let me pick up that squarehead's rifle. I know those groundpounders. They're just as apt as not to claim the kill credit themselves, and if I can't prove I stepped on the body they might get away with it. I remember on Paradise, me and Piet de Hagen—he was left wing gunner, I was right— both shot at a partisan. And then damned if Central didn't decide the slope had blown herself up with a hand grenade after we'd wounded her. So *neither* of us got the credit. You'd think—"

"Lord's *blood*, Sergeant," Pritchard snarled, "are you so damned proud of killing one of the poor bastards who hired us to protect them?"

Jenne said nothing. Pritchard shrank up inside, realizing what he had said and unable to take the words back. "Oh, Lord, Rob," he said without looking up, "I'm sorry. It . . . I'm shook, that's all."

After a brief silence, the blond sergeant laughed. "Never been shot in the head myself, Captain, but I can see it might shake a fellow, yeah." Jenne let the whine of the fans stand for a moment as the only further comment while he decided whether he would go on. Then he said, "Captain, for a week after I first saw action I meant to get out of the Slammers, even if I had to sweep floors on Curwin for the rest of my life. Finally I decided I'd stick it. I didn't like the . . . rules of the game, but I could learn to play by them.

"And I did. And one rule is that you get to be as good as you can at killing the people Col. Hammer wants killed. Yeah, I'm proud about that one just now. It was a tough snap shot and I made it. I don't care why we're on Kobold or who brought us here. But I know I'm supposed to kill anybody who shoots at us, and I will."

"Well, I'm glad you did," Pritchard said evenly as he looked the sergeant in the eyes. "You pretty well saved things from getting out of hand by the way you reacted."

As if he had not heard his captain, Jenne went on, "I was afraid if I stayed in the Slammers I'd turn into an animal, like the dogs we trained back home to kill rats in the quarries. And I was right. But it's the way I am now, so I don't seem to mind."

"You do care about those villagers, don't you?" Margritte asked Pritchard unexpectedly.

The captain looked down and found her eyes on him. They were the rich powder-blue of chicory flowers. "You're probably the only person in the Regiment who thinks that," he said bitterly. "Except for me. And maybe Col. Hammer. . . ."

Margritte smiled, a quick flash and as quickly gone. "There're rule-book soldiers in the Slammers," she said, "captains who'd never believe Barthe was passing arms to the Auroran settlements since he'd signed a contract that said he wouldn't. You aren't that kind. And the Lord knows Col. Hammer isn't, and he's backing you. I've been around you too long, Danny, to believe you like what you see the French doing."

Pritchard shrugged. His whole face was stiff with bruises and the drugs Margritte had injected to control them. If he'd locked the helmet's chin strap, the bullet's impact would have broken his neck even though the lead itself did not penetrate. "No, I don't like it," the brown-haired captain said. "It reminds me too much of the way the Combine kept us so poor on Dunstan that a thousand of us signed on for birdseed to fight off-planet. Just because it *was* off-planet. And if Kobold only gets cop from the worlds who settled her, then the French skim the best of that. . . . Sure, I'll tell the Lord I feel sorry for the Dutch here."

Pritchard held the commo tech's eyes with his own as he continued, "But it's just like Rob said, Margritte: I'll do my job, no matter who gets hurt. We can't do a thing to Barthe or the French until they step over the line in a really obvious way. That'll mean a lot of people get hurt too. But that's what I'm waiting for."

Margritte reached up and touched Pritchard's hand where it rested on his knee. "You'll do something when you can," she said quietly.

He turned his palm up so that he could grasp the woman's fingers. What if she knew he was planning an incident, not just waiting for one? "I'll do something, yeah," he said. "But it's going to be too late for an awful lot of people."

.   .   .

KOWIE KEPT THE Plow at cruising speed until they were actually in the yard of the command post. Then he cocked the fan shafts forward, lifting the bow and bringing the tank's mass around in a curve that killed its velocity and blasted an arc of snow against the building. Someone inside had started to unlatch the door as they heard the vehicle approach. The air spilling from the tank's skirts flung the panel against the inner wall and skidded the man within on his back.

The man was Capt. Riis, Pritchard noted without surprise. Well, the incident wouldn't make the infantry captain any angrier than the rest of the evening had made him already.

Riis had regained his feet by the time Pritchard could jump from the deck of his blower to the fan-cleared ground in front of the building. The Frisian's normally pale face was livid now with rage. He was of the same somatotype as Lt. Col. Benoit, his French counterpart in the sector: tall, thin, and proudly erect. Despite the fact that Riis was only 27, he was Pritchard's senior in grade by two years. He had kept the rank he held in Friesland's regular army when Col. Hammer recruited him. Many of the Slammers were like Riis, Frisian soldiers who had transferred for the action and pay of a fighting regiment in which their training would be appreciated.

"You cowardly filth!" the infantryman hissed as Pritchard approached. A squad in battle gear stood within the orderly room beyond Riis. He pursed his fine lips to spit.

"Hey Captain!" Rob Jenne called. Riis looked up. Pritchard turned, surprised that the big tank commander was not right on his heels. Jenne still smiled from The Plow's cupola. He waved at the officers with his left hand. His right was on the butterfly trigger of the tribarrel.

The threat, unspoken as it was, made a professional of Riis again. "Come on into my office," he muttered to the tank captain, turning his back on the armored vehicle as if it were only a part of the landscape.

The infantrymen inside parted to pass the captains. Sally Schilling was there. Her eyes were as hard as her porcelain armor as they raked over Pritchard. That didn't matter, he lied to himself tiredly.

Riis' office was at the top of the stairs, a narrow cubicle which had once been a child's bedroom. The sloping roof pressed in on the occupants, though a dormer window brightened the room during daylight. One wall was decorated with a regimental battle flag—not Hammer's rampant lion but a pattern of seven stars on a white field. It had probably come from the unit in which Riis had served on Friesland. Over the door hung another souvenir, a big-bore musket of local manufacture. Riis threw himself into the padded chair behind his desk. "Those bastards were carrying powerguns to Portela!" he snarled at Pritchard.

The tanker nodded. He was leaning with his right shoulder against the door jamb. "That's what the folks at Haacin thought," he agreed. "If they'll put in a complaint with the Bonding Authority, I'll testify to what I saw."

"Testify, *testify!*" Riis shouted. "We're not lawyers, we're soldiers! You should've seized the trucks right then and—"

"No I should *not* have, Captain!" Pritchard shouted back, holding up a mirror to Riis' anger. "Because if I had, Barthe would've complained to the Authority himself, and we'd at least've been fined. At least! The contract says the Slammers'll cooperate with the other three units in keeping peace on Kobold. Just because we suspect Barthe is violating the contract doesn't give us a right to violate it ourselves. Especially in a way any *simpleton* can see is a violation."

"If Barthe can get away with it, we can," Riis insisted, but he settled back in his chair. He was physically bigger than Pritchard, but the tanker had spent half his life with the Slammers. Years like those mark men; death is never very far behind their eyes.

"I don't think Barthe can get away with it," Pritchard lied quietly, remembering Hammer's advice on how to handle Riis and calm the Frisian without telling him the truth. Barthe's officers had been in on his plans; and one of them had talked. Any regiment might have one traitor.

The tanker lifted down the musket on the wall behind him and began turning it in his fingers. "If the Dutch settlers can prove to the Authority that Barthe's been passing out powerguns to the French," the tanker mused aloud, "well, they're responsible for half Barthe's pay, remember. It's about as bad a violation as you'll find. The Authority'll forfeit his whole bond and pay it over to whoever they decide the injured parties are. That's about three years' gross earnings for Barthe, I'd judge—he won't be able to replace it. And without a bond posted, well, he may get jobs, but they'll be the kind nobody else'd touch for the risk and the pay. His best troops'll sign on with other people. In a year or so, Barthe won't have a regiment anymore."

"He's willing to take the chance," said Riis.

"Col. Hammer isn't!" Pritchard blazed back.

"You don't know that. It isn't the sort of thing the colonel could say—"

"Say?" Pritchard shouted. He waved the musket at Riis. Its breech was triple-strapped to take the shock of the industrial explosive it used for propellant. Clumsy and large, it was the best that could be produced on a mining colony whose home worlds had forbidden local manufacturing. "Say? I bet my life against one of these tonight that the colonel wanted us to obey the contract. Do you have the guts to ask him flat out if he wants us to run guns to the Dutch?"

"I don't think that would be proper, Captain," said Riis coldly as he stood up again.

"Then try not to 'think it proper' to go do some bloody stupid stunt on your own—sir," Pritchard retorted. So much for good intentions. Hammer—and Pritchard—had expected Riis' support of the Dutch civilians. They had even planned on it. But the man seemed to have lost all his common sense. Pritchard laid the musket on the desk because his hands were trembling too badly to hang it back on the hooks.

"If it weren't for you, Captain," Riis said, "there's not a Slammer in this sector who'd object to our helping the only decent people on this planet the way we ought to. You've made your decision, and it sickens me. But I've made decisions too."

Pritchard went out without being dismissed. He blundered into the jamb, but he did not try to slam the door. That would have been petty, and there was nothing petty in the tanker's rage.

Blank-faced, he clumped down the stairs. His bunk was in a parlor which had its own door to the outside. Pritchard's crew was still in The Plow. There they had listened intently to his half of the argument with Riis, transmitted by the implant. If Pritchard had called for help, Kowie would have sent the command vehicle through the front wall buttoned up, with Jenne ready to shoot if he had to, to rescue his CO. A tank looks huge when seen close-up. It is all howling steel and iridium, with black muzzles ready to spew death across a planet. On a battlefield, when the sky is a thousand shrieking colors no god ever made and the earth beneath trembles and gouts in sudden mountains, a tank is a small world indeed for its crew. Their loyalties are to nearer things than an abstraction like "The Regiment."

Besides, tankers and infantrymen have never gotten along well together.

No one was in the orderly room except two radiomen. They kept their backs to the stairs. Pritchard glanced at them, then unlatched his door. The room was dark, as he had left it, but there was a presence. Pritchard said, "Sal—" as he stepped within and the club knocked him forward into the arms of the man waiting to catch his body.

The first thing Pritchard thought as his mind slipped toward oblivion was that the cloth rubbing his face was homespun, not the hard synthetic from which uniforms were made. The last thing Pritchard thought was that there could have been no civilians within the headquarters perimeter unless the guards had allowed them; and that Lt. Schilling was officer of the guard tonight.

PRITCHARD COULD NOT be quite certain when he regained consciousness. A heavy felt rug covered and hid his trussed body on the floor of a clattering surface vehicle. He had no memory of being carried to the truck, though presumably it had been parked some distance from the command post. Riis and his confederates would not have been so open as to have civilians drive to the door to take a kidnapped officer, even if Pritchard's crew could have been expected to ignore the breach of security.

Kidnapped. Not for later murder, or he would already be dead instead of smothering under the musty rug. Thick as it was, the rug was still inadequate to keep the cold from his shivering body. The only lights Pritchard could see were the washings of icy color from the night's doubled shock to his skull.

That bone-deep ache reminded Pritchard of the transceiver implanted in his mastoid. He said in a husky whisper which he hoped would not penetrate the rug, "Michael One to any unit, any unit at all. Come in please, any Slammer."

Nothing. Well, no surprise. The implant had an effective range of less than twenty meters, enough for relaying to and from a base unit, but unlikely to be useful in Kobold's empty darkness. Of course, if the truck happened to be passing one of M Company's night defensive positions. . . . "Michael One to any unit," the tanker repeated more urgently.

A boot slammed him in the ribs. A voice in guttural Dutch snarled, "Shut up, you, or you get what you gave Henrik."

So he'd been shopped to the Dutch, not that there had been much question about it. And not that he might not have been safer in French hands, the way everybody on this cursed planet thought he was a traitor to his real employers. Well, it wasn't fair; but Danny Pritchard had grown up a farmer, and no farmer is ever tricked into believing that life is fair.

The truck finally jolted to a stop. Gloved hands jerked the cover from Pritchard's eyes. He was not surprised to recognize the concrete angles of Haacin as men passed him hand to hand into a cellar. The attempt to hijack Barthe's powerguns had been an accident, an opportunity seized; but the crew which had kidnapped Pritchard must have been in position before the call from S-39 had intervened.

"Is this wise?" Pritchard heard someone demand from the background. "If they begin searching, surely they'll begin in Haacin."

The two men at the bottom of the cellar stairs took Pritchard's shoulders and ankles to carry him to a spring cot. It had no mattress. The man at his feet called, "There won't be a search, they don't have enough men. Besides, the beast'll be blamed—as they should be for so many things. If Pauli won't let us kill the turncoat, then we'll all have to stand the extra risk of him living."

"You talk too much," Mayor van Oosten muttered as he dropped Pritchard's shoulders on the bunk. Many civilians had followed the captive into the cellar. The last of them swung the door closed. It lay almost horizontal to the ground. When it slammed, dust sprang from the ceiling. Someone switched on a dim incandescent light. The scores of men and women in the storage room were as hard and fell as the bare walls. There were three windows at street level, high on the wall. Slotted shutters blocked most of their dusty glass.

"Get some heat in this hole or you may as well cut my throat," Pritchard grumbled.

A woman with a musket cursed and spat in his face. The man behind her took her arm before the gunbutt could smear the spittle. Almost in apology, the man said to Pritchard, "It was her husband you killed."

"You're being kept out of the way," said a husky man—Kruse, the hothead from the hijack scene. His facial hair was pale and long, merging indistinguishably with the silky fringe of his parka. Like most of the others in the cellar, he carried a musket. "Without your meddling, there'll be a chance for us to . . . get ready to protect ourselves, after the tanks leave and the beasts come to finish us with their powerguns."

"Does Riis think I won't talk when this is over?" Pritchard asked.

"I told you—" one of the men shouted at van Oosten. The heavy-set mayor silenced him with a tap on the chest and a bellowed, "Quiet!" The rising babble hushed long enough for van Oosten to say, "Captain, you will be released in a very few days. If you—cause trouble, then, it will only be an embarrassment to yourself. Even if your colonel believes you were doing right, he won't be the one to bring to light a violation which was committed with—so you will claim—the connivance of his own officers."

The mayor paused to clear his throat and glower around the room. "Though in fact we had no help from any of your fellows, either in seizing you or in arming ourselves for our own protection."

"Are you all blind?" Pritchard demanded. He struggled with his elbows and back to raise himself against the wall. "Do you think a few lies will cover it all up? The only ships that've touched on Kobold in three months are the ones supplying us and the other mercs. Barthe maybe's smuggled in enough guns in cans of lube oil and the like to arm some civilians. He won't be able to keep that a secret, but maybe he can keep the Authority from proving who's responsible.

"That's with three months and pre-planning. If Riis tries to do anything on his own, that many of his own men are going to be short sidearms—they're all issued by serial number, Lord take it!—and a blind Mongoloid could get enough proof to sink the Regiment."

"You think we don't understand," said Kruse in a quiet voice. He transferred his musket to his left hand, then slapped Pritchard across the side of the head. "We understand very well," the civilian said. "All the mercenaries will leave in a few days or weeks. If the French have powerguns and we do not, they will kill us, our wives, our children. . . . There's a hundred and fifty villages on Kobold like this one, Dutch, and as many French ones scattered between. It was bad before, with no one but the beasts allowed any real say in the government; but now if they win, there'll be French villages and French mines—and slave pens. Forever."

"You think a few guns'll save you?" Pritchard asked. Kruse's blow left no visible mark in the tanker's livid flesh, though a better judge than Kruse might have noted that Pritchard's eyes were as hard as his voice was mild.

"They'll help us save ourselves when the time comes," Kruse retorted.

"If you'd gotten powerguns from French civilians instead of the mercs directly, you might have been all right," the captain said. He was coldly aware that the lie he was telling was more likely to be believed in this situation than it would have been in any setting he might deliberately have contrived. There had to be an incident, the French civilians *had* to think they were safe in using their illegal weapons. . . . "The Portelans, say, couldn't admit to having guns to lose. But anything you take from mercs—us or Barthe, it doesn't matter—we'll take back the hard way. You don't know what you're buying into."

Kruse's face did not change, but his fist drew back for another blow. The mayor caught the younger man's arm and snapped, "Franz, we're here to show him that it's not a few of us, it's every family in the village behind . . . our holding him," van Oosten nodded around the room. "More of us than your colonel could dream of trying to punish," he added naively to Pritchard. Then he flashed back at Kruse, "If you act like a fool, he'll want revenge anyway."

"You may never believe this," Pritchard interjected wearily, "but I just want to do my job. If you let me go now, it—may be easier in the long run."

"Fool," Kruse spat, and turned his back on the tanker.

A trap door opened in the ceiling, spilling more light into the cellar. "Pauli!" a woman shouted down the opening, "Hals is on the radio. There's tanks coming down the road, just like before!"

"The Lord's wounds!" van Oosten gasped. "We must—"

"They can't know!" Kruse insisted. "But we've got to get everybody out of here and back to their own houses. Everybody but me and him"— a nod at Pritchard—"and this." The musket lowered so that its round black eye pointed straight into the bound man's face.

"No, by the side door!" van Oosten called to the press of conspirators clumping up toward the street. "Don't run right out in front of them." Cursing and jostling, the villagers climbed the ladder to the ground floor, there presumably to exit on an alley.

Able only to twist his head and legs, Pritchard watched Kruse and the trembling muzzle of his weapon. The village must have watchmen with radios at either approach through the forests. If Hals was atop the heap of mine tailings—where Pritchard would have placed his outpost if he were in charge, certainly—then he'd gotten a nasty surprise when the main gun splashed the rocks with Hell. The captain grinned at the thought. Kruse misunderstood and snarled, "If they *are* coming for you, you're dead, you treacherous bastard!" To the backs of his departing fellows, the young Dutchman called, "Turn out the light here, but leave the trap door open. That won't show on the street, but it'll give me enough light to shoot by."

The tanks weren't coming for him, Pritchard knew, because they couldn't have any idea where he was. Perhaps his disappearance had stirred up some patrolling, for want of more directed action; perhaps a platoon was just changing ground because of its commander's whim. Pritchard had encouraged random motion. Tanks that freeze in one place are sitting targets, albeit hard ones. But whatever the reason tanks were approaching Haacin, if they whined by in the street outside they would be well within range of his implanted transmitter.

The big blowers were audible now, nearing with an arrogant lack of haste as if bears headed for a beehive. They were moving at about 30 kph, more slowly than Pritchard would have expected even for a contact patrol. From the sound there were four or more of them, smooth and gray and deadly.

"Kruse, I'm serious," the Slammer captain said. Light from the trap door back-lit the civilian into a hulking beast with a musket. "If you—"

"Shut up!" Kruse snarled, prodding his prisoner's bruised forehead with the gun muzzle. "One more word, any word, and—"

Kruse's right hand was so tense and white that the musket might fire even without his deliberate intent.

The first of the tanks slid by outside. Its cushion of air was so dense that the ground trembled even though none of the blower's 170 tonnes was in direct contact with it. Squeezed between the pavement and the steel curtain of the plenum chamber, the air spurted sideways and rattled the cellar windows. The rattling was inaudible against the howling of the fans themselves, but the trembling shutters chopped facets in the play of the tank's running lights. Kruse's face and the far wall flickered in blotched abstraction.

The tank moved on without pausing. Pritchard had not tried to summon it.

"That power," Kruse was mumbling to himself, "that should be for us to use to sweep the beasts—" The rest of his words were lost in the growing wail of the second tank in the column.

Pritchard tensed within. Even if a passing tank picked up his implant's transmission, its crew would probably ignore the message. Unless Pritchard identified himself, the tankers would assume it was babbling thrown by the ionosphere. And if he did identify himself, Kruse—

Kruse thrust his musket against Pritchard's skull again, banging the tanker's head back against the cellar wall. The Dutchman's voice was lost in the blower's howling, but his blue-lit lips clearly were repeating, "One word. . . ."

The tank moved on down the highway toward Portela.

". . . and maybe I'll shoot you anyway," Kruse was saying. "That's the way to serve traitors, isn't it? *Mercenary!*"

The third blower was approaching. Its note seemed slightly different, though that might be the aftereffect of the preceding vehicles' echoing din. Pritchard was cold all the way to his heart, because in a moment he was going to call for help. He knew that Kruse would shoot him, knew also that he would rather die now than live after hope had come so near but passed on, passed on. . . .

The third tank smashed through the wall of the house.

The Plow's skirts were not a bulldozer blade, but they were thick steel and backed with the mass of a 150 tonne command tank. The slag wall repowdered at the impact. Ceiling joists buckled into pretzel shape and ripped the cellar open to the floor above. Kruse flung his musket up and fired through the cascading rubble. The boom and red flash were lost in the chaos, but the blue-green fire stabbing back across the cellar laid the Dutchman on his back with his parka aflame. Pritchard rolled to the floor at the first shock. He thrust himself with corded legs and arms back under the feeble protection of the bunk. When the sound of falling objects had died away, the captain slitted his eyelids against the rock dust and risked a look upward.

The collision had torn a gap ten feet long in the house wall, crushing it from street level to the beams supporting the second story. The tank blocked the hole with its gray bulk. Fresh scars brightened the patina of corrosion etched onto its skirts by the atmospheres of a dozen planets. Through the buckled flooring and the dust whipped into arabesques by the idling fans, Pritchard glimpsed a slight figure clinging lefthanded to the turret. Her right hand still threatened the wreckage with a submachinegun. Carpeting burned on the floor above, ignited by the burst that killed Kruse. Somewhere a woman was screaming in Dutch.

"Margritte!" Pritchard shouted. "Margritte! Down here!"

The helmeted woman swung up her face shield and tried to pierce the cellar gloom with her unaided eyes. The tank-battered opening had sufficed for the exchange of shots, but the tangle of structural members and splintered flooring was too tight to pass a man—or even a small woman. Sooty flames were beginning to shroud the gap. Margritte jumped to the ground and struggled for a moment before she was able to heave open the door. The Plow's turret swung to cover her, though neither the main gun nor the tribarrel in the cupola could depress enough to rake the cellar. Margritte ran down the steps to Pritchard.

Coughing in the rock dust, he rolled out over the rubble to meet her. Much of the smashed sidewall had collapsed onto the street when the tank backed after the initial impact. Still, the crumpled beams of the ground floor sagged further with the additional weight of the slag on them. Head-sized pieces had splanged on the cot above Pritchard.

Margritte switched the submachinegun to her left hand and began using a clasp knife on her captain's bonds. The cord with which he was tied bit momentarily deeper at the blade's pressure.

Pritchard winced, then began flexing his freed hands. "You know, Margi," he said, "I don't think I've ever seen you with a gun before."

The commo tech's face hardened as if the polarized helmet shield had slipped down over it again. "You hadn't," she said. The ankle bindings parted and she stood, the dust graying her helmet and her foam-filled coveralls. "Captain, Kowie had to drive and we needed Rob in the cupola at the gun. That left me to—do anything else that had to be done. I did what had to be done."

Pritchard tried to stand, using the technician as a post on which to draw himself upright. Margritte looked frail, but with her legs braced she stood like a rock. Her arm around Pritchard's back was as firm as a man's.

"You didn't ask Capt. Riis for help, I guess," Pritchard said, pain making his breath catch. The line tanks had two-man crews with no one to spare for outrider, of course.

"We didn't report you missing," Margritte said, "even to First Platoon. They just went along like before, thinking you were in The Plow giving orders." Together, captain and technician shuffled across the floor to the stairs. As they passed Kruse's body, Margritte muttered cryptically, "That's four."

Pritchard assumed the tremors beginning to shake the woman's body were from physical strain. He took as much weight off her as he could and found his numbed feet were beginning to function reasonably well. He would never have been able to board The Plow without Sgt. Jenne's grip on his arm, however.

The battered officer settled in the turret with a groan of comfort. The seat cradled his body with gentle firmness, and the warm air blown across him was just the near side of heaven.

"Captain," Jenne said, "what d'we do about the slopes who grabbed you? Shall we call in an interrogation team and—"

"We don't do anything," Pritchard interrupted. "We just pretend none of this happened and head back to. . . ." He paused. His flesh wavered both hot and cold as Margritte sprayed his ankles with some of the apparatus from the medical kit. "Say, how did you find me, anyway?"

"We shut off coverage when you—went into your room," Jenne said, seeing that the commo tech herself did not intend to speak. He meant, Pritchard knew, they had shut off the sound when their captain had said, "Sal." None of the three of them were looking either of the other two in the eyes. "After a bit, though, Margi noticed the carrier line from your implant had dropped off her oscilloscope. I checked your room, didn't find you. Didn't see much point talking it over with the remfs on duty, either.

"So we got satellite recce and found two trucks'd left the area since we got back. One was Riis', and the other was a civvie junker before that. It'd been parked in the woods out of sight, half a kay up the road from the buildings. Both trucks unloaded in Haacin. We couldn't tell which load was you, but Margi said if we got close, she'd home on your carrier even though you weren't calling us on the implant. Some girl we got here, hey?"

Pritchard bent forward and squeezed the commo tech's shoulder. She did not look up, but she smiled. "Yeah, always knew she was something," he agreed, "but I don't think I realized quite what a person she was until just now."

Margritte lifted her smile. "Rob ordered First Platoon to fall in with us," she said. "He set up the whole rescue." Her fine-fingered hands caressed Pritchard's calves.

But there was other business in Haacin, now. Riis had been quicker to act than Pritchard had hoped. He asked, "You say one of the infantry's trucks took a load here a little bit ago?"

"Yeah, you want the off-print?" Jenne agreed, searching for the flimsy copy of the satellite picture. "What the hell would they be doing, anyhow?"

"I got a suspicion," his captain said grimly, "and I suppose it's one we've got to check out."

"Michael First-Three to Michael One," the radio broke in. "Vehicles approaching from the east on the hardball."

"Michael One to Michael First," Pritchard said, letting the search for contraband arms wait for this new development. "Reverse and form a line abreast beyond the village. Twenty meter intervals. The Plow'll take the road." More weapons from Riis? More of Barthe's troops when half his sector command was already in Portela? Pritchard touched switches beneath the vision blocks as Kowie slid the tank into position. He split the screen between satellite coverage and a ground-level view at top magnification. Six vehicles, combat cars, coming fast. Pritchard swore. Friendly, because only the Slammers had armored vehicles on Kobold, not that cars were a threat to tanks anyway. But no combat cars were assigned to this sector; and the unexpected is always bad news to a company commander juggling too many variables already.

"Platoon nearing Tango Sigma four-two, three-two, please identify to Michael One," Pritchard requested, giving Haacin's map coordinates.

Margritte turned up the volume of the main radio while she continued to bandage the captain's rope cuts. The set crackled, "Michael One, this is Alpha One and Alpha First. Stand by."

"God's bleeding cunt!" Rob Jenne swore under his breath. Pritchard was nodding in equal agitation. Alpha was the Regiment's special duty company. Its four combat car platoons were Col. Hammer's bodyguards and police. The troopers of A Company were nicknamed the White Mice, and they were viewed askance even by the Slammers of other companies—men who prided themselves on being harder than any other combat force in the galaxy. The White Mice in turn feared their commander, Maj. Joachim Steuben; and if that slightly-built killer feared anyone, it was the man who was probably traveling with him this night. Pritchard sighed and asked the question. "Alpha One, this is Michael One. Are you flying a pennant, sir?"

"Affirmative, Michael One."

Well, he'd figured Col. Hammer was along as soon as he heard what the unit was. What the Old Man was doing here was another question, and one whose answer Pritchard did not look forward to learning.

The combat cars glided to a halt under the guns of their bigger brethren. The tremble of their fans gave the appearance of heat ripples despite the snow. From his higher vantage point, Pritchard watched the second car slide out of line and fall alongside The Plow. The men at the nose and right wing guns were both short, garbed in nondescript battle gear. They differed from the other troopers only in that their helmet shields were raised and that the faces visible beneath were older than those of most Slammers: Col. Alois Hammer and his hatchetman.

"No need for radio, Captain," Hammer called in a husky voice. "What are you doing here?"

Pritchard's tongue quivered between the truth and a lie. His crew had been covering for him, and he wasn't about to leave them holding the bag. All the breaches of regulations they had committed were for their captain's sake. "Sir, I brought First Platoon back to Haacin to check whether any of the powerguns they'd hijacked from Barthe were still in civvie hands." Pritchard could feel eyes behind the cracked shutters of every east-facing window in the village.

"And have you completed your check?" the colonel pressed, his voice mild but his eyes as hard as those of Maj. Steuben beside him; as hard as the iridium plates of the gun shields.

Pritchard swallowed. He owed nothing to Capt. Riis, but the young fool *was* his superior—and at least he hadn't wanted the Dutch to kill Pritchard. He wouldn't put Riis' ass in the bucket if there were neutral ways to explain the contraband. Besides, they were going to need Riis and his Dutch contacts for the rest of the plan. "Sir, when you approached I was about to search a building where I suspect some illegal weapons are stored."

"And instead you'll provide back-up for the major here," said Hammer, the false humor gone from his face. His words rattled like shrapnel. "He'll retrieve the twenty-four powerguns which Capt. Riis saw fit to turn over to civilians tonight. If Joachim hadn't chanced, *chanced* onto that requisition. . . ." Hammer's left glove shuddered with the strength of his grip on the forward tribarrel. Then the colonel lowered his eyes and voice, adding, "The quartermaster who filled a requisition for twenty-four pistols from Central Supply is in the infantry again tonight. And Capt. Riis is no longer with the Regiment."

Steuben tittered, loose despite the tension of everyone around him. The cold was bitter, but Joachim's right hand was bare. With it he traced the baroque intaglios of his holstered pistol. "Mr. Riis is lucky to be alive," the slight Newlander said pleasantly. "Luckier than some would have wished. But Colonel, I think we'd best go pick up the merchandise before anybody nerves themself to use it on us."

Hammer nodded, calm again. "Interfile your blowers with ours, Captain," he ordered. "Your panzers watch street level while the cars take care of upper floors and roofs."

Pritchard saluted and slid down into the tank, relaying the order to the rest of his platoon. Kowie blipped The Plow's throttles, swinging the turreted mass in its own length and sending it back into the village behind the lead combat car. The tank felt light as a dancer, despite the constricting sidestreet Kowie followed the car into. Pritchard scanned the full circuit of the vision blocks. Nothing save the wind and armored vehicles moved in Haacin. When Steuben had learned a line company was requisitioning two dozen extra sidearms, the major had made the same deductions as Pritchard had and had inspected the same satellite tape of a truck unloading. Either Riis was insane or he really thought Col. Hammer was willing to throw away his life's work to arm a village — inadequately. Lord and Martyrs! Riis would have *had* to be insane to believe that!

Their objective was a nondescript two-story building separated from its neighbors by narrow alleys. Hammer directed the four rearmost blowers down a parallel street to block the rear. The searchlights of the vehicles chilled the flat concrete and glared back from the windows of the building. A battered surface truck was parked in the street outside. It was empty. Nothing stirred in the house.

Hammer and Steuben dismounted without haste. The major's helmet was slaved to a loudspeaker in the car. The speaker boomed, "Everyone out of the building. You have thirty seconds. Anyone found inside after that'll be shot. Thirty seconds!"

Though the residents had not shown themselves earlier, the way they boiled out of the doors proved they had expected the summons. All told, there were eleven of them. From the front door came a well-dressed man and woman with their three children: a sexless infant carried by its mother in a zippered cocoon; a girl of eight with her hood down and her hair coiled in braids about her forehead; and a twelve-year-old boy who looked nearly as husky as his father. Outside staircases disgorged an aged couple on the one hand and four tough-looking men on the other.

Pritchard looked at his blower chief. The sergeant's right hand was near the gun switch and he mumbled an old ballad under his breath. Chest tightening, Pritchard climbed out of his hatch. He jumped to the ground and paced quietly over to Hammer and his aide.

"There's twenty-four pistols in this building," Joachim's amplified voice roared, "or at least you people know where they are. I want somebody to save trouble and tell me."

The civilians tensed. The mother half-turned to swing her body between her baby and the officers.

Joachim's pistol was in his hand, though Pritchard had not seen him draw it. "Nobody to speak?" Joachim queried. He shot the eight-year-old in the right knee. The spray of blood was momentary as the flesh exploded. The girl's mouth pursed as her buckling leg dropped her facedown in the street. The pain would come later. Her parents screamed, the father falling to his knees to snatch up the child as the mother pressed her forehead against the door jamb in blind panic.

Pritchard shouted, "You son of a bitch!" and clawed for his own sidearm. Steuben turned with the precision of a turret lathe. His pistol's muzzle was a white-hot ring from its previous discharge. Pritchard knew only that and the fact that his own weapon was not clear of its holster. Then he realized that Col. Hammer was shouting, "No!" and that his open hand had rocked Joachim's head back.

Joachim's face went pale except for the handprint burning on his cheek. His eyes were empty. After a moment, he holstered his weapon and turned back to the civilians. "Now, who'll tell us where the guns are?" he asked in a voice like breaking glassware.

The tear-blind woman, still holding her infant, gurgled, "Here! In the basement!" as she threw open the door. Two troopers followed her within at a nod from Hammer. The father was trying to close the girl's wounded leg with his hands, but his palms were not broad enough.

Pritchard vomited on the snowy street.

Margritte was out of the tank with a medikit in her hand. She flicked the civilian's hands aside and began freezing the wound with a spray. The front door banged open again. The two White Mice were back with their submachineguns slung under their arms and a heavy steel weapons-chest between them. Hammer nodded and walked to them.

"You could have brought in an interrogation team!" Pritchard shouted at the backs of his superiors. "You don't shoot children!"

"Machine interrogation takes time, Captain," Steuben said mildly. He did not turn to acknowledge the tanker. "This was just as effective."

"That's a little girl!" Pritchard insisted with his hand clenched. The child was beginning to cry, though the local anesthetic in the skin-sealer had probably blocked the physical pain. The psychic shock of a body that would soon end at the right knee would be worse, though. The child was old enough to know that no local doctor could save the limb. "This isn't something that human beings *do*!"

"Captain," Steuben said, "they're lucky I haven't shot all of them."

Hammer closed the arms chest. "We've got what we came for," he said. "Let's go."

"Stealing guns from my colonel," the Newlander continued as if Hammer had not spoken. The handprint had faded to a dull blotch. "I really ought to—"

"Joachim, shut it off!" Hammer shouted. "We're going to talk about

what happened tonight, you and I. I'd rather do it when we were alone—
but I'll tell you now if I have to. Or in front of a court martial."

Steuben squeezed his forehead with the fingers of his left hand. He
said nothing.

"Let's go," the colonel repeated.

Pritchard caught Hammer's arm. "Take the kid back to Central's
medics," he demanded.

Hammer blinked. "I should have thought of that," he said simply.
"Sometimes I lose track of . . . things that aren't going to shoot at me. But
we don't need this sort of reputation."

"I don't care cop for public relations," Pritchard snapped. "Just save
that little girl's leg."

Steuben reached for the child, now lying limp. Margritte had used a
shot of general anesthetic. The girl's father went wild-eyed and swung at
Joachim from his crouch. Margritte jabbed with the injector from behind the civilian. He gasped as the drug took hold, then sagged as if his
bones had dissolved. Steuben picked up the girl.

Hammer vaulted aboard the combat car and took the child from his
subordinate's arms. Cutting himself into the loudspeaker system, the
stocky colonel thundered to the street, "Listen you people. If you take
guns from mercs—either Barthe's men or my own—we'll grind you to
dust. Take 'em from civilians if you think you can. You may have a
chance then. If you rob mercs, you just get a chance to die."

Hammer nodded to the civilians, nodded again to the brooding buildings to either side. He gave an unheard command to his driver. The
combat cars began to rev their fans.

Pritchard gave Margritte a hand up and followed her. "Michael One
to Michael First," he said. "Head back with Alpha First."

PRITCHARD RODE INSIDE the turret after they left Haacin, glad for once
of the armor and the cabin lights. In the writhing tree-limbs he had seen
the Dutch mother's face as the shot maimed her daughter.

Margritte passed only one call to her commander. It came shortly
after the combat cars had separated to return to their base camp near
Midi, the planetary capital. The colonel's voice was as smooth as it ever
got. It held no hint of the rage which had blazed out in Haacin. "Capt.
Pritchard," Hammer said, "I've transferred command of Sigma Company to the leader of its First Platoon. The sector, of course, is in your

hands now. I expect you to carry out your duties with the ability you've already shown."

"Michael One to Regiment," Pritchard replied curtly. "Acknowledged."

Kowie drew up in front of the command post without the furious caracole which had marked their most recent approach. Pritchard slid his hatch open. His crewmen did not move. "I've got to worry about being sector chief for a while," he said, "but you three can rack out in the barracks now. You've put in a full tour in my book."

"Think I'll sleep here," Rob said. He touched a stud, rotating his seat into a couch alongside the receiver and loading tube of the main gun.

Pritchard frowned. "Margritte?" he asked.

She shrugged. "No, I'll stay by my set for a while." Her eyes were blue and calm.

On the intercom, Kowie chimed in with, "Yeah, you worry about the sector, we'll worry about ourselves. Say, don't you think a tank platoon'd be better for base security than these pongoes?"

"Shut up, Kowie," Jenne snapped. The blond Burlager glanced at his captain. "Everything'll be fine, so long as we're here," he said from one elbow. He patted the breech of the 200 mm gun.

Pritchard shrugged and climbed out into the cold night. He heard the hatch grind shut behind him.

Until Pritchard walked in the door of the building, it had not occurred to him that Riis' replacement was Sally Schilling. The words "First Platoon leader" had not been a name to the tanker, not in the midst of the furor of his mind. The little blonde glanced up at Pritchard from the map display she was studying. She spat cracklingly on the electric stove and faced around again. Her aide, the big corporal, blinked in some embarrassment. None of the headquarters staff spoke.

"I need the display console from my room," Pritchard said to the corporal.

The infantryman nodded and got up. Before he had taken three steps, Lt. Schilling's voice cracked like pressure-heaved ice, "Cpl. Webbert!"

"Sir?" The big man's face went tight as he found himself a pawn in a game whose stakes went beyond his interest.

"Go get the display console for our new commander. It's in his room."

Licking his lips with relief, the corporal obeyed. He carried the heavy four-legged console back without effort.

Sally was making it easier for him, Pritchard thought. But how he wished that Riis hadn't made so complete a fool of himself that he had to be removed. Using Riis to set up a double massacre would have been a lot easier to justify when Danny awoke in the middle of the night and found himself remembering. . . .

Pritchard positioned the console so that he sat with his back to the heater. It separated him from Schilling. The top of the instrument was a slanted, 40 cm screen which glowed when Pritchard switched it on. "Sector Two display," he directed. In response to his words the screen sharpened into a relief map. "Population centers," he said. They flashed on as well, several dozen of them ranging from a few hundred souls to the several thousand of Haacin and Dimo. Portela, the largest Francophone settlement west of the Aillet, was about twenty kilometers west of Haacin.

And there were now French mercenaries on both sides of that division line. Sally had turned from her own console and stood up to see what Pritchard was doing. The tanker said, "All mercenary positions, confirmed and calculated."

The board spangled itself with red and green symbols, each of them marked in small letters with a unit designation. The reconnaissance satellites gave unit strengths very accurately, and computer analysis of radio traffic could generally name the forces. In the eastern half of the sector, Lt. Col. Benoit had spread out one battalion in platoon-strength billets. The guardposts were close enough to most points to put down trouble immediately. A full company near Dimo guarded the headquarters and two batteries of rocket howitzers.

The remaining battalion in the sector, Benoit's own, was concentrated in positions blasted into the rocky highlands ten kays west of Portela. It was not a deployment that would allow the mercs to effectively police the west half of the sector, but it was a very good defensive arrangement. The forest that covered the center of the sector was ideal for hit-and-run sniping by small units of infantry. The tree boles were too densely woven for tanks to plow through them. Because the forest was so flammable at this season, however, it would be equally dangerous to ambushers. Benoit was wise to concentrate in the barren high-ground.

Besides the highlands, the fields cleared around every settlement were the only safe locations for a modern firefight. The fields, and the broad swathes cleared for roads through the forest. . . .

"Incoming traffic for Sector Chief," announced a radioman. "It's from the skepsel colonel, sir." He threw his words into the air, afraid to direct them at either of the officers in the orderly room.

"Voice only, or is there visual?" Pritchard asked. Schilling held her silence.

"Visual component, sir."

"Patch him through to my console," the tanker decided. "And son—watch your language. Otherwise, you say 'beast' when you shouldn't."

The map blurred from the display screen and was replaced by the hawk features of Lt. Col. Benoit. A pick-up on the screen's surface threw Pritchard's own image onto Benoit's similar console.

The Frenchman blinked. "Capt. Pritchard? I'm very pleased to see you, but my words must be with Capt. Riis directly. Could you wake him?"

"There've been some changes," the tanker said. In the back of his mind, he wondered what had happened to Riis. Pulled back under arrest, probably. "I'm in charge of Sector Two now. Co-charge with you, that is."

Benoit's face steadied as he absorbed the information without betraying an opinion about it. Then he beamed like a feasting wolf and said, "Congratulations, Captain. Some day you and I will have to discuss the . . . events of the past few days. But what I was calling about is far less pleasant, I'm afraid."

Benoit's image wavered on the screen as he paused. Pritchard touched his tongue to the corner of his mouth. "Go ahead, Colonel," he said. "I've gotten enough bad news today that a little more won't signify."

Benoit quirked his brow in what might or might not have been humor. "When we were proceeding to Portela," he said, "some of my troops mistook the situation and set up passive tank interdiction points. Mines, all over the sector. They're booby-trapped, of course. The only safe way to remove them is for the troops responsible to do it. They will of course be punished later."

Pritchard chuckled. "How long do you estimate it'll take to clear the roads, Colonel?" he asked.

The Frenchman spread his hands, palms up. "Weeks, perhaps. It's much harder to clear mines safely than to lay them, of course."

"But there wouldn't be anything between *here* and Haacin, would there?" the tanker prodded. It was all happening just as Hammer's informant had said Barthe planned it. First, hem the tanks in with nets of forest and minefields; then, break the most important Dutch stronghold while your mercs were still around to back you up. . . . "The spur road to our HQ here wasn't on your route; and besides, we just drove tanks over it a few minutes ago."

Behind Pritchard, Sally Schilling was cursing in a sharp, carrying voice. Benoit could probably hear her, but the colonel kept his voice as smooth as milk as he said, "Actually, I'm afraid there *is* a field—gas, shaped charges, and glass-shard antipersonnel mines—somewhere on that road, yes. Fortunately, the field was signal activated. It wasn't primed until after you had passed through. I assure you, Capt. Pritchard, that all the roads west of the Aillet may be too dangerous to traverse until I have cleared them. I warn you both as a friend and so that we will not be charged with damage to any of your vehicles—and men. You have been fully warned of the danger; anything that happens now is your responsibility."

Pritchard leaned back in the console's integral seat, chuckling again. "You know, Colonel," the tank captain said, "I'm not sure that the Bonding Authority wouldn't find those mines were a hostile act justifying our retaliation." Benoit stiffened, more an internal hardness than anything that showed in his muscles. Pritchard continued to speak through a smile. "We won't, of course. Mistakes happen. But one thing, Col. Benoit—"

The Frenchman nodded, waiting for the edge to bite. He knew as well as Pritchard did that, at best, if there were an Authority investigation, Barthe would have to throw a scapegoat out. A high-ranking scapegoat.

"Mistakes happen," Pritchard repeated, "but they can't be allowed to happen twice. You've got my permission to send out a ten-man team by daylight—only by daylight—to clear the road from Portela to Bever. That'll give you a route back to your side of the sector. If any other troops leave their present position, for any reason, I'll treat it as an attack."

"Captain, this demarcation within the sector was not part of the contract—"

"It was at the demand of Col. Barthe," Pritchard snapped, "and agreed to by the demonstrable practice of both regiments over the past three months." Hammer had briefed Pritchard very carefully on the words to use here, to be recorded for the benefit of the Bonding Authority. "You've heard the terms, Colonel. You can either take them or we'll put the whole thing—the minefields and some other matters that've come up recently—before the Authority right now. Your choice."

Benoit stared at Pritchard, apparently calm but tugging at his upper lip with thumb and forefinger. "I think you are unwise, Captain, in taking full responsibility for an area in which your tanks cannot move; but that is your affair, of course. I will obey your mandate. We should have the Portela-Haacin segment cleared by evening; tomorrow we'll proceed to Bever. Good day."

The screen segued back to the map display. Pritchard stood up. A spare helmet rested beside one of the radiomen. The tank captain donned it—he had forgotten to requisition a replacement from stores—and said, "Michael One to all Michael units." He paused for the acknowledgment lights from his four platoons and the command vehicle. Then, "Hold your present position. Don't attempt to move by road, any road, until further notice. The roads have been mined. There are probably safe areas, and we'll get you a map of them as soon as Command Central works it up. For the time being, just stay where you are. Michael One, out."

"Are you really going to take that?" Lt. Schilling demanded in a low, harsh voice.

"Pass the same orders to your troops, Sally," Pritchard said. "I know they can move through the woods where my tanks can't, but I don't want any friendlies in the forest right now either." To the intelligence sergeant on watch, Pritchard added, "Samuels, get Central to run a plot of all activity by any of Benoit's men. That won't tell us where they've laid mines, but it'll let us know where they can't have."

"What happens if the bleeding skepsels ignore you?" Sally blazed. "You've bloody taught them to ignore you, haven't you? Knuckling under every time somebody whispers 'contract'? You can't move a tank to stop them if they do leave their base, and *I've* got 198 effectives. A battalion'd laugh at me, *laugh!*"

Schilling's arms were akimbo, her face as pale with rage as the snow outside. Speaking with deliberate calm, Pritchard said, "I'll call in artillery if I need to. Benoit only brought two calliopes with him, and they can't stop all the shells from three firebases at the same time. The road between his position and Portela's just a snake-track cut between rocks. A couple firecracker rounds going off above infantry, strung out there—Via, it'll be a butcher shop."

Schilling's eyes brightened. "Then for tonight, the sector's just like it was before we came," she thought out loud. "Well, I suppose you know best," she added in false agreement, with false nonchalance. "I'm going back to the barracks. I'll brief First Platoon in person and radio the others from there. Come along, Webbert."

The corporal slammed the door behind himself and his lieutenant.

The gust of air that licked about the walls was cold, but Pritchard was already shivering at what he had just done to a woman he loved.

It was daylight by now, and the frosted windows turned to flame in the ruddy sun. Speaking to no one but his console's memory, Pritchard began to plot tracks from each tank platoon. He used a topographic display, ignoring the existence of the impenetrable forest which covered the ground.

Margritte's resonant voice twanged in the implant, "Captain, would you come to the blower for half a sec?"

"On the way," Pritchard said, shrugging into his coat. The orderly room staff glanced up at him.

Margritte poked her head out of the side hatch. Pritchard climbed onto the deck to avoid some of the generator whine. The skirts sang even when the fans were cut off completely. Rob Jenne, curious but at ease, was visible at his battle station beyond the commo tech. "Sir," Margritte said, "we've been picking up signals from—there." The blue-eyed woman thumbed briefly at the infantry barracks without letting her pupils follow the gesture.

Pritchard nodded. "Lt. Schilling's passing on my orders to her company."

"Danny, the transmission's in code, and it's not a code of ours." Margritte hesitated, then touched the back of the officer's gloved left hand. "There's answering signals, too. I can't triangulate without moving the blower, of course, but the source is in line with the tailings pile at Haacin."

It was what he had planned, after all. Someone the villagers could trust had to get word of the situation to them. Otherwise they wouldn't draw the Portelans and their mercenary backers into a fatal mistake. Hard luck for the villagers who were acting as bait, but very good for every other Dutchman on Kobold. . . . Pritchard had no reason to feel anything but relief that it had happened. He tried to relax the muscles which were crushing all the breath out of his lungs. Margritte's fingers closed over his hand and squeezed it.

"Ignore the signals," the captain said at last. "We've known all along they were talking to the civilians, haven't we?" Neither of his crewmen spoke. Pritchard's eyes closed tightly. He said, "We've known for months, Hammer and I, every damned thing that Barthe's been plotting with the skepsels. They want a chance to break Haacin now, while they're around to cover for the Portelans. We'll give them their chance and ram it up their ass crosswise. The Old Man hasn't spread the word for fear the story'd get out, the same way Barthe's plans did. We're all mercenaries, after all. But I want you three to know. And I'll be glad when the only thing I have to worry about is the direction the shots are coming from."

Abruptly, the captain dropped back to the ground. "Get some sleep," he called. "I'll be needing you sharp tonight."

BACK AT HIS console, Pritchard resumed plotting courses and distances. After he figured each line, he called in a series of map coordinates to Command Central. He knew his radio traffic was being monitored and probably unscrambled by Barthe's intelligence staff; knew also that even if he had read the coordinates out in clear, the French would have assumed it was a code. The locations made no sense unless one knew they were ground zero for incendiary shells.

As Pritchard worked, he kept close watch on the French battalions. Benoit's own troops held their position, as Pritchard had ordered. They used the time to dig in. At first they had blasted slit trenches in the rock. Now they dug covered bunkers with the help of mining machinery tracked from Portela by civilians. Five of the six anti-tank guns were sited atop the eastern ridge of the position. They could rake the highway as it snaked and switched back among the foothills west of Portela.

Pritchard chuckled grimly again when Sgt. Samuels handed him high-magnification offprints from the satellites. Benoit's two squat, bulky calliopes were sited in defilade behind the humps of the eastern ridge line. There the eight-barrelled powerguns were safe from the smashing fire of M Company's tanks, but their ability to sweep artillery shells from the sky was degraded by the closer horizon. The Slammers did not bother with calliopes themselves. Their central fire director did a far better job by working through the hundreds of vehicle-mounted weapons. How much better, Benoit might learn very shortly.

The mine-sweeping team cleared the Portela-Haacin road, as directed. The men returned to Benoit's encampment an hour before dusk. The French did not come within five kilometers of the Dutch village.

Pritchard watched the retiring mine sweepers, then snapped off the console. He stood. "I'm going out to my blower," he said.

His crew had been watching for him. A hatch shot open, spouting condensate, as soon as Pritchard came out the door. The smooth bulk of the tank blew like a restive whale. On the horizon, the sun was so low that the treetops stood out in silhouette like a line of bayonets.

Wearily, the captain dropped through the hatch into his seat. Jenne and Margritte murmured greeting and waited, noticeably tense. "I'm going to get a couple hours' sleep," Pritchard said. He swung his seat out and up, so that he lay horizontal in the turret. His legs hid Margritte's oval face from him. "Punch up coverage of the road west of Haacin, would you?" he asked. "I'm going to take a tab of Glirine. Slap me with the antidote when something moves there."

"If something moves," Jenne amended.

"When." Pritchard sucked down the pill. "The squareheads think they've got one last chance to smack Portela and hijack the powerguns again. Thing is, the Portelans'll have already distributed the guns and be waiting for the Dutch to come through. It'll be a damn short fight, that one. . . ." The drug took hold and Pritchard's consciousness began to flow away like a sugar cube in water. "Damn short. . . ."

AT FIRST PRITCHARD felt only the sting on the inside of his wrist. Then the narcotic haze ripped away and he was fully conscious again.

"There a line of trucks, looks like twenty, moving west out of Haacin, sir. They're blacked out, but the satellite has 'em on infra-red."

"Red alert," Pritchard ordered. He locked his seat upright into its combat position. Margritte's soft voice sounded the general alarm. Pritchard slipped on his radio helmet. "Michael One to all Michael units. Check off." Five green lights flashed their silent acknowledgements across the top of the captain's face-shield display. "Michael One to Sigma One," Pritchard continued.

"Go ahead, Michael One." Sally's voice held a note of triumph.

"Sigma One, pull all your troops into large, clear areas—the fields around the towns are fine, but stay the hell away from Portela and Haacin. Get ready to slow down anybody coming this way from across the Aillet. Over."

"Affirmative, Danny, affirmative!" Sally replied. Couldn't she use the satellite reconnaissance herself and see the five blurred dots halfway between the villages? They were clearly the trucks which had brought the Portelans into their ambush positions. What would she say when she realized how she had set up the villagers she was trying to protect? Lambs to the slaughter. . . .

The vision block showed the Dutch trucks more clearly than the camouflaged Portelans. The crushed stone of the roadway was dark on the screen, cooler than the surrounding trees and the vehicles upon it. Pritchard patted the breech of the main gun and looked across it to his blower chief. "We got a basic load for this aboard?" he asked.

"Do bears cop in the woods?" Jenne grinned. "We gonna get a chance to bust caps tonight, Captain?"

Pritchard nodded. "For three months we've been here, doing nothing but selling rope to the French. Tonight they've bought enough that we can hang 'em with it." He looked at the vision block again. "You alive, Kowie?" he asked on intercom.

"Ready to slide any time you give me a course," said the driver from his closed cockpit.

The vision block sizzled with bright streaks that seemed to hang on the screen though they had passed in microseconds. The leading blobs expanded and brightened as trucks blew up.

"Michael One to Fire Central," Pritchard said.

"Go ahead, Michael One," replied the machine voice.

"Prepare Fire Order Alpha."

"Roger, Michael One."

"Margritte, get me Benoit."

"Go ahead, Captain."

"Slammers to Benoit. Pritchard to Benoit. Come in please, Colonel."

"Capt. Pritchard, Michel Benoit here." The colonel's voice was smooth but too hurried to disguise the concern underlying it. "I assure you that none of my men are involved in the present fighting. I have a company ready to go out and control the disturbance immediately, however."

The tanker ignored him. The shooting had already stopped for lack of targets. "Colonel, I've got some artillery aimed to drop various places in the forest. It's coming nowhere near your troops or any other human beings. If you interfere with this necessary shelling, the Slammer'll treat it as an act of war. I speak with my colonel's authority."

"Captain, I don't—"

Pritchard switched manually. "Michael One to Fire Central. Execute Fire Order Alpha."

"On the way, Michael One."

"Michael One to Michael First, Second, Fourth. Command Central has fed movement orders into your map displays. Incendiary clusters are going to burst over marked locations to ignite the forest. Use your own main guns to set the trees burning in front of your immediate positions. One round ought to do it. Button up and you can move through the fire—the trees just fall to pieces when they've burned."

The turret whined as it slid under Rob's control. "Michael Third, I'm attaching you to the infantry. More Frenchmen're apt to be coming this way from the east. It's up to you to see they don't slam a door on us."

The main gun fired, its discharge so sudden that the air rang like a solid thing. Seepage from the ejection system filled the hull with the reek of superheated polyurethane. The side vision blocks flashed cyan, then began to flood with the mounting white hell-light of the blazing trees. In the central block, still set on remote, all the Dutch trucks were burning, as were patches of forest which the ambush had ignited. The Portelans had left the concealment of the trees and swept across the road, mopping up the Dutch.

"Kowie, let's move," Jenne was saying on intercom, syncopated by the mild echo of his voice in the turret. Margritte's face was calm, her lips moving subtly as she handled some traffic that she did not pass on to her captain. The tank slid forward like oil on a lake. From the far distance came the thumps of incendiary rounds scattering their hundreds of separate fireballs high over the trees.

Pritchard slapped the central vision block back on direct; the tank's interior shone white with transmitted fire. The Plow's bow slope sheared into a thicket of blazing trees. The wood tangled and sagged, then gave in a splash of fiery splinters whipped aloft by the blower's fans. The tank was in hell on all sides, Kowie steering by instinct and his inertial compass. Even with his screens filtered all the way down, the driver would not be able to use his eyes effectively until more of the labyrinth had burned away.

Benoit's calliopes had not tried to stop the shelling. Well, there were other ways to get the French mercs to take the first step over the line. For instance—

"Punch up Benoit again," Pritchard ordered. Even through the dense iridium plating, the roar of the fire was a subaural presence in the tank.

"Go ahead," Margritte said, flipping a switch on her console. She had somehow been holding the French officer in conversation all the time Pritchard was on other frequencies.

"Colonel," Pritchard said, "we've got clear running through this fire. We're going to chase down everybody who used a powergun tonight; then we'll shoot them. We'll shoot everybody in their families, everybody with them in this ambush, and we'll blow up every house that anybody involved lived in. That's likely to be every house in Portela, isn't it?"

More than the heat and ions of the blazing forest distorted Benoit's face. He shouted, "Are you mad? You can't think of such a thing, Pritchard!"

The tanker's lips parted like a wolf's. He could think of mass murder, and there were plenty of men in the Slammers who would really be willing to carry out the threat. But Pritchard wouldn't have to, because Benoit was like Riis and Schilling: too much of a nationalist to remember his first duty as a merc. . . . "Col. Benoit, the contract demands we keep the peace and stay impartial. The record shows how we treated people in Haacin for *having* powerguns. For what the Portelans did tonight—don't worry, we'll be impartial. And they'll never break the peace again."

"Captain, I will not allow you to massacre French civilians," Benoit stated flatly.

"Move a man out of your present positions and I'll shoot him dead," Pritchard said. "It's your choice, Colonel. Over and out."

The Plow bucked and rolled as it pulverized fire-shattered trucks, but the vehicle was meeting nothing solid enough to slam it to a halt. Pritchard used a side block on remote to examine Benoit's encampment. The satellite's enhanced infra-red showed a stream of sparks flowing from the defensive positions toward the Portela road: infantry on skimmers. The pair of larger, more diffuse blobs were probably anti-tank guns. Benoit wasn't moving his whole battalion, only a reinforced company in a show of force to make Pritchard back off.

The fool. Nobody was going to back off now.

"Michael One to all Michael and Sigma units," Pritchard said in a voice as clear as the white flames around his tank. "We're now in a state of war with Barthe's Company and its civilian auxiliaries. Michael First, Second, and Fourth, we'll rendezvous at the ambush site as plotted on your displays. Anybody between there and Portela is fair game. If we take any fire from Portela, we go down the main drag in line and blow the cop out of it. If any of Barthe's people are in the way, we keep on sliding west. Sigma One, mount a fluid defense, don't push, and wait for help.

It's coming. If this works, it's Barthe against Hammer—and that's wheat against the scythe. Acknowledged?"

As Pritchard's call board lit green, a raspy new voice broke into the sector frequency. "Wish I was with you, panzers. We'll cover your butts and the other sectors—if anybody's dumb enough to move. Good hunting!"

"I wish you *were* here and not me, Colonel," Pritchard whispered, but that was to himself . . . and perhaps it was not true even in his heart. Danny's guts were very cold, and his face was as cold as death.

To Pritchard's left, a lighted display segregated the area of operations. It was a computer analog, not direct satellite coverage. Doubtful images were brightened and labeled—green for the Slammers, red for Barthe; blue for civilians unless they were fighting on one side or the other. The green dot of The Plow converged on the ambush site at the same time as the columns of First and Fourth Platoons. Second was a minute or two farther off. Pritchard's breath caught. A sheaf of narrow red lines was streaking across the display toward his tanks. Barthe had ordered his Company's artillery to support Benoit's threatened battalion.

The salvo frayed and vanished more suddenly than it had appeared. Other Slammers' vehicles had ripped the threat from the sky. Green lines darted from Hammer's own three firebases, offscreen at the analog's present scale. The fighting was no longer limited to Sector Two. If Pritchard and Hammer had played their hand right, though, it would stay limited to only the Slammers and Compagnie de Barthe. The other Francophone regiments would fear to join an unexpected battle which certainly resulted from someone's contract violation. If the breach were Hammer's, the Dutch would not be allowed to profit by the fighting. If the breach were Barthe's, anybody who joined him was apt to be punished as sternly by the Bonding Authority.

So violent was the forest's combustion that the flames were already dying down into sparks and black ashes. The command tank growled out into the broad avenue of the road west of Haacin. Dutch trucks were still burning—fabric, lubricants, and the very paint of their frames had been ignited by the powerguns. Many of the bodies sprawled beside the vehicles were smouldering also. Some corpses still clutched their useless muskets. The dead were victims of six centuries of progress which had come to Kobold pre-packaged, just in time to kill them. Barthe had given the Portelans only shoulder weapons, but even that meant the world here. The powerguns were repeaters with awesome destruction in every bolt. Without answering fire to rattle them, even untrained gunmen could be effective with weapons which shot line-straight and had no recoil. Certainly the Portelans had been effective.

Throwing ash and fire like sharks in the surf, the four behemoths of First Platoon slewed onto the road from the south. Almost simultaneously, Fourth joined through the dying hellstorm to the other side. The right of way was fifty meters wide and there was no reason to keep to the center of it. The forest, ablaze or glowing embers, held no ambushes anymore.

The Plow lurched as Kowie guided it through the bodies. Some of them were still moving. Pritchard wondered if any of the Dutch had lived through the night, but that was with the back of his mind. The Slammers were at war, and nothing else really mattered. "Triple line ahead," he ordered. "First to the left, Fourth to the right; The Plow'll take the center alone till Second joins. Second, wick up when you hit the hardball and fall in behind us. If it moves, shoot it."

At 100 kph, the leading tanks caught the Portelans three kilometers east of their village. The settlers were in the trucks that had been hidden in the forest fringe until the fires had been started. The ambushers may not have known they were being pursued until the rearmost truck exploded. Rob Jenne had shredded it with his tribarrel at five kilometers' distance. The cyan flicker and its answering orange blast signalled the flanking tanks to fire. They had just enough parallax to be able to rake the four remaining trucks without being blocked by the one which had blown up. A few snapping discharges proved that some Portelans survived to use their new powerguns on tougher meat than before. Hits streaked ashes on the tanks' armor. No one inside noticed.

From Portela's eastern windows, children watched their parents burn.

A hose of cyan light played from a distant roof top. It touched the command tank as Kowie slewed to avoid a Portelan truck. The burst was perfectly aimed, an automatic weapon served by professionals. Professionals should have known how useless it would be against heavy armor. A vision block dulled as a few receptors fused. Jenne cursed and trod the foot-switch of the main gun. A building leaped into dazzling prominence in the microsecond flash. Then it and most of the block behind collapsed into internal fires, burying the machinegun and everything else in the neighborhood. A moment later, a salvo of Hammer's high explosive got through the calliopes' inadequate screen. The village began to spew skyward in white flashes.

The Portelans had wanted to play soldier, Pritchard thought. He had dammed up all pity for the villagers of Haacin; he would not spend it now on these folk.

"Line ahead—First, Fourth, and Second," Pritchard ordered. The triple column slowed and re-formed, with The Plow the second vehicle in the new line. The shelling lifted from Portela as the tanks plunged into the village. Green trails on the analog terminated over the road crowded with Benoit's men and over the main French position, despite anything the calliopes could do. The sky over Benoit's bunkers rippled and flared as firecracker rounds sleeted down their thousands of individual bomblets. The defensive fire cut off entirely. Pritchard could imagine the carnage among the unprotected calliope crews when the shrapnel whirred through them.

The tanks were firing into the houses on either side, using tribarrels and occasional wallops from their main guns. The blue-green flashes were so intense they colored even the flames they lit among the wreckage. At 50 kph the thirteen tanks swept through the center of town, hindered only by the rubble of houses spilled across the street. Barthe's men were skittering white shadows who burst when powerguns hit them point blank.

The copper mine was just west of the village and three hundred meters north of the highway. As the lead tank bellowed out around the last houses, a dozen infantrymen rose from where they had sheltered in the pit head and loosed a salvo of buzzbombs. The tank's automatic defense system was live. White fire rippled from just above the skirts as the charges there flailed pellets outward to intersect the rockets. Most of the buzzbombs exploded ten meters distant against the steel hail. One missile soared harmlessly over its target, its motor a tiny flare against the flickering sky. Only one of the shaped charges burst alongside the turret, forming a bell of light momentarily bigger than the tank. Even that was only a near miss. It gouged the iridium armor like a misthrust rapier which tears skin but does not pierce the skull.

Main guns and tribarrels answered the rockets instantly. Men dropped, some dead, some reloading. "Second Platoon, go put some HE down the shaft and rejoin," Pritchard ordered. The lead tank now had expended half its defensive charges. "Michael First-Three, fall in behind First-One. Michael One leads," he went on.

Kowie grunted acknowledgement. The Plow revved up to full honk. Benoit's men were on the road, those who had not reached Portela when the shooting started or who had fled when the artillery churned the houses to froth. The infantry skimmers were trapped between sheer rocks and sheer drop-offs, between their own slow speed and the on-rushing frontal slope of The Plow. There were trees where the rocks had given them purchase. Scattered incendiaries had made them blazing cressets lighting a charnel procession.

Jenne's tribarrel scythed through body armor and dismembered men in short bursts. One of the anti-tank guns—was the other buried in Portela?—lay skewed against a rock wall, its driver killed by a shell fragment. Rob put a round from the main gun into it. So did each of the next two tanks. At the third shot, the ammunition ignited in a blinding secondary explosion.

The anti-tank guns still emplaced on the ridge line had not fired, though they swept several stretches of the road. Perhaps the crews had been rattled by the shelling, perhaps Benoit had held his fire for fear of hitting his own men. A narrow defile notched the final ridge. The Plow heaved itself up the rise, and at the top three bolts slapped it from different angles.

Because the bow was lifted, two of the shots vaporized portions of the skirt and the front fans. The tank nosed down and sprayed sparks with half its length. The third bolt grazed the left top of the turret, making the iridium ring as it expanded. The interior of the armor streaked white though it was not pierced. The temperature inside the tank rose 30°. Even as The Plow skidded, Sgt. Jenne was laying his main gun on the hot spot that was the barrel of the leftmost anti-tank weapon. The Plow's shot did what heavy top cover had prevented Hammer's rocket howitzers from accomplishing with shrapnel. The anti-tank gun blew up in a distance-muffled flash. One of its crewmen was silhouetted high in the air by the vaporizing metal of his gun.

Then the two remaining weapons ripped the night and the command blower with their charges.

The bolt that touched the right side of the turret spewed droplets of iridium across the interior of the hull. Air pistoned Pritchard's eardrums. Rob Jenne lurched in his harness, right arm burned away by the shot. His left hand blackened where it touched bare metal that sparked and sang as circuits shorted. Margritte's radios were exploding one by one under the overloads. The vision blocks worked and the

turret hummed placidly as Pritchard rotated it to the right with his duplicate controls.

"Cut the power! Rob's burning!" Margritte was shrieking. She had
torn off her helmet. Her thick hair stood out like tendrils of bread mold
in the gathering charge. Then Pritchard had the main gun bearing and
it lit the ridge line with another secondary explosion.

"Danny, our ammunition! It'll—"

Benoit's remaining gun blew the tribarrel and the cupola away deaf-
eningly. The automatic's loading tube began to gang-fire down into the
bowels of the tank. It reached a bright tendril up into the sky. But the turret still rolled.

Electricity crackled around Pritchard's boot and the foot trip as he
fired again. The bolt stabbed the night. There was no answering blast.
Pritchard held down the switch, his nostrils thick with ozone and superheated plastic and the sizzling flesh of his friend. There was still no explosion from the target bunker. The rock turned white between the cyan
flashes. It cracked and flowed away like sun-melted snow, and the anti-
tank gun never fired again.

The loading tube emptied. Pritchard slapped the main switch and cut
off the current. The interior light and the dancing arcs died, leaving only
the dying glow of the bolt-heated iridium. Tank after tank edged by the
silent command vehicle and roared on toward the ridge. Benoit's demoralized men were already beginning to throw down their weapons
and surrender.

Pritchard manually unlatched Jenne's harness and swung it horizontal. The blower chief was breathing but unconscious. Pritchard switched
on a battery-powered handlight. He held it steady as Margritte began to
spray sealant on the burns. Occasionally she paused to separate clothing
from flesh with a stylus.

"It had to be done," Pritchard whispered. By sacrificing Haacin, he
had mousetrapped Benoit into starting a war the infantry could not
win. Hammer was now crushing Barthe's Company, one on one, in an
iridium vise. Friesland's Council of State would not have let Hammer
act had they known his intentions, but in the face of a stunning victory
they simply could not avoid dictating terms to the French.

"It had to be done. But I look at *what* I did—" Pritchard swung
his right hand in a gesture that would have included both the fuming
wreck of Portela and the raiders from Haacin, dead on the road beyond.
He struck the breech of the main gun instead. Clenching his fist, he

slammed it again into the metal in self-punishment. Margritte cried out and blocked his arm with her own.

"Margi," Pritchard repeated in anguish, "it isn't something that human beings *do* to each other."

But soldiers do.

And hangmen.

Harry Turtledove

Harry Turtledove first came to prominence as a writer of alternate world fantasy with The Misplaced Legion, *the first novel in his multibook Videssos Cycle about the experiences of a Roman legion transferred to a world that runs on magic. Since then, he has explored the impact of altered historical events in a variety of works, including* Agent of Byzantium, *set in medieval times; the acclaimed* The Guns of the South, *in which time travelers manipulate a southern victory in the American Civil War; and the first two volumes of the Great War saga,* American Front *and* Walk in Hell, *which envisions an America in which the United States and the Confederate States support opposing sides in World War I. His ambitious Worldwar series—which includes* In the Balance, Tilting the Balance, Striking the Balance, *and* Upsetting the Balance—*projects an alternate World War II in which an alien invasion forges alliances between Axis and Allied opponents. Turtledove has also coedited the anthology* Alternate Generals. *His many other works include the short-fiction collection* Departures, *the comic fantasy* The Case of the Toxic Spell Dump, *and the linked novels* Into the Darkness *and* Darkness Descending, *epic tales of empire building set in a fantasy world where cataclysmic wars are fought with magic.*

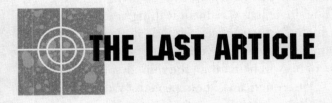

THE LAST ARTICLE

Harry Turtledove

Nonviolence is the first article of my faith. It is also the last article of my creed.
—MOHANDAS GANDHI

The one means that wins the easiest victory over reason: terror and force.
—ADOLF HITLER, *Mein Kampf*

THE TANK RUMBLED DOWN the Rajpath, past the ruins of the Memorial Arch, toward the India Gate. The gateway arch was still standing, although it had taken a couple of shell hits in the fighting before New Delhi fell. The Union Jack fluttered above it.

British troops lined both sides of the Rajpath, watching silently as the tank rolled past them. Their khaki uniforms were filthy and torn; many wore bandages. They had the weary, past-caring stares of beaten men, though the Army of India had fought until flesh and munitions gave out.

The India Gate drew near. A military band, smartened up for the occasion, began to play as the tank went past. The bagpipes sounded thin and lost in the hot, humid air.

A single man stood waiting in the shadow of the Gate. Field Marshal Walther Model leaned down into the cupola of the Panzer IV. "No one can match the British at ceremonies of this sort," he said to his aide.

Major Dieter Lasch laughed, a bit unkindly. "They've had enough practice, sir," he answered, raising his voice to be heard over the flatulent roar of the tank's engine.

"What is that tune?" the field marshal asked. "Does it have a meaning?"

"It's called 'The World Turned Upside Down,' " said Lasch, who had been involved with his British opposite number in planning the formal surrender. "Lord Cornwallis's army musicians played it when he yielded to the Americans at Yorktown."

"Ah, the Americans." Model was for a moment so lost in his own thoughts that his monocle threatened to slip from his right eye. He screwed it back in. The single lens was the only thing he shared with the clichéd image of a high German officer. He was no lean, hawk-faced Prussian. But his rounded features were unyielding, and his stocky body sustained the energy of his will better than the thin, dyspeptic frames of so many aristocrats. "The Americans," he repeated. "Well, that will be the next step, won't it? But enough. One thing at a time."

The panzer stopped. The driver switched off the engine. The sudden quiet was startling. Model leaped nimbly down. He had been leaping down from tanks for eight years now, since his days as a staff officer for the IV Corps in the Polish campaign.

The man in the shadows stepped forward, saluted. Flashbulbs lit his long, tired face as German photographers recorded the moment for history. The Englishman ignored cameras and cameramen alike. "Field Marshal Model," he said politely. He might have been about to discuss the weather.

Model admired his sangfroid. "Field Marshal Auchinleck," he replied, returning the salute and giving Auchinleck a last few seconds to remain his equal. Then he came back to the matter at hand. "Field Marshal, have you signed the instrument of surrender of the British Army of India to the forces of the Reich?"

"I have," Auchinleck replied. He reached into the left blouse pocket of his battledress, removed a folded sheet of paper. Before handing it to Model, though, he said, "I should like to request your permission to make a brief statement at this time."

"Of course, sir. You may say what you like, at whatever length you like." In victory, Model could afford to be magnanimous. He had even granted Marshal Zhukov leave to speak in the Soviet capitulation at Kuibyshev, before the marshal was taken out and shot.

"I thank you." Auchinleck stiffly dipped his head. "I will say, then, that I find the terms I have been forced to accept to be cruelly hard on the brave men who have served under my command."

"That is your privilege, sir." But Model's round face was no longer kindly, and his voice had iron in it as he replied, "I must remind you, however, that my treating with you at all under the rules of war is an act of mercy for which Berlin may yet reprimand me. When Britain surrendered in 1941, all Imperial forces were also ordered to lay down their arms. I daresay you did not expect us to come so far, but I would be within my rights in reckoning you no more than so many bandits."

A slow flush darkened Auchinleck's cheeks. "We gave you a bloody good run, for bandits."

"So you did." Model remained polite. He did not say he would ten times rather fight straight-up battles than deal with the partisans who to this day harassed the Germans and their allies in occupied Russia. "Have you anything further to add?"

"No, sir, I do not." Auchinleck gave the German the signed surrender, handed him his sidearm. Model put the pistol in the empty holster he wore for the occasion. It did not fit well; the holster was made for a Walther P38, not this man-killing brute of a Webley and Scott. That mattered little, though—the ceremony was almost over.

Auchinleck and Model exchanged salutes for the last time. The British field marshal stepped away. A German lieutenant came up to lead him into captivity.

Major Lasch waved his left hand. The Union Jack came down from the flagpole on the India Gate. The swastika rose to replace it.

LASCH TAPPED DISCREETLY on the door, stuck his head into the field marshal's office. "That Indian politician is here for his appointment with you, sir."

"Oh, yes. Very well, Dieter, send him in." Model had been dealing with Indian politicians even before the British surrender, and with hordes of them now that resistance was over. He had no more liking for the breed than for Russian politicians, or even German ones. No matter what pious principles they spouted, his experience was that they were all out for their own good first.

The small, frail brown man the aide showed in made him wonder. The Indian's emaciated frame and the plain white cotton loincloth that was his only garment contrasted starkly with the Victorian splendor of the Viceregal Palace from which Model was administering the Reich's new conquest. "Sit down, *Herr* Gandhi," the field marshal urged.

"I thank you very much, sir." As he took his seat, Gandhi seemed a child in an adult's chair: it was much too wide for him, and its soft, overstuffed cushions hardly sagged under his meager weight. But his eyes, Model saw, were not a child's eyes. They peered with disconcerting keenness through his wire-framed spectacles as he said, "I have come to enquire when we may expect German troops to depart from our country."

Model leaned forward, frowning. For a moment he thought he had misunderstood Gandhi's Gujarati-flavored English. When he was sure he had not, he said, "Do you think perhaps we have come all this way as tourists?"

"Indeed I do not." Gandhi's voice was sharp with disapproval. "Tourists do not leave so many dead behind them."

Model's temper kindled. "No, tourists do not pay such a high price for the journey. Having come regardless of that cost, I assure you we shall stay."

"I am very sorry, sir; I cannot permit it."

"*You* cannot?" Again, Model had to concentrate to keep his monocle from falling out. He had heard arrogance from politicians before, but this scrawny old devil surpassed belief. "Do you forget I can call my aide and have you shot behind this building? You would not be the first, I assure you."

"Yes, I know that," Gandhi said sadly. "If you have that fate in mind for me, I am an old man. I will not run."

Combat had taught Model a hard indifference to the prospect of injury or death. He saw the older man possessed something of the same sort, however he had acquired it. A moment later, he realized his threat had not only failed to frighten Gandhi, but had actually amused him. Disconcerted, the field marshal said, "Have you any serious issues to address?"

"Only the one I named just now. We are a nation of more than three hundred million; it is no more just for Germany to rule us than for the British."

Model shrugged. "If we are able to, we will. We have the strength to hold what we have conquered, I assure you."

"Where there is no right, there can be no strength," Gandhi said. "We will not permit you to hold us in bondage."

"Do you think to threaten me?" Model growled. In fact, though, the Indian's audacity surprised him. Most of the locals had fallen over themselves fawning on their new masters. Here, at least, was a man out of the ordinary.

Gandhi was still shaking his head, although Model saw he had still not frightened him (a man out of the ordinary indeed, thought the field marshal, who respected courage when he found it). "I make no threats, sir, but I will do what I believe to be right."

"Most noble," Model said, but to his annoyance the words came out sincere rather than with the sardonic edge he had intended. He had heard such canting phrases before, from Englishmen, from Russians, yes, and from Germans as well. Somehow, though, this Gandhi struck him as one who always meant exactly what he said. He rubbed his chin, considering how to handle such an intransigent.

A large green fly came buzzing into the office. Model's air of detachment vanished the moment he heard that malignant whine. He sprang from his seat, swatted at the fly. He missed. The insect flew around a while longer, then settled on the arm of Gandhi's chair. "Kill it," Model told him. "Last week one of those accursed things bit me on the neck, and I still have the lump to prove it."

Gandhi brought his hand down, but several inches from the fly. Frightened, it took off. Gandhi rose. He was surprisingly nimble for a man nearing eighty. He chivvied the fly out of the office, ignoring Model, who watched his performance in open-mouthed wonder.

"I hope it will not trouble you again," Gandhi said, returning as calmly as if he had done nothing out of the ordinary. "I am one of those who practice *ahimsa*: I will do no injury to any living thing."

Model remembered the fall of Moscow, and the smell of burning bodies filling the chilly autumn air. He remembered machine guns knocking down Cossack cavalry before they could close, and the screams of the wounded horses, more heartrending then any woman's. He knew of other things, too, things he had not seen for himself and of which he had no desire to learn more.

"*Herr* Gandhi," he said, "how do you propose to bend to your will someone who opposes you, if you will not use force for the purpose?"

"I have never said I will not use force, sir." Gandhi's smile invited the field marshal to enjoy with him the distinction he was making. "I will not use violence. If my people refuse to cooperate in any way with yours, how can you compel them? What choice will you have but to grant us leave to do as we will?"

Without the intelligence estimates he had read, Model would have dismissed the Indian as a madman. No madman, though, could have caused the British so much trouble. But perhaps the decadent raj simply had not made him afraid. Model tried again. "You understand that what you have said is treason against the Reich," he said harshly.

Gandhi bowed in his seat. "You may, of course, do what you will with me. My spirit will in any case survive among my people."

Model felt his face heat. Few men were immune to fear. Just his luck, he thought sourly, to have run into one of them. "I warn you, *Herr* Gandhi, to obey the authority of the officials of the Reich, or it will be the worse for you."

"I will do what I believe to be right, and nothing else. If you Germans exert yourselves toward the freeing of India, joyfully will I work with you. If not, then I regret we must be foes."

The field marshal gave him one last chance to see reason. "Were it you and I alone, there might be some doubt as to what would happen." Not much, he thought, not when Gandhi was twenty-odd years older and thin enough to break like a stick. He fought down the irrelevance, went on, "But where, *Herr* Gandhi, is your *Wehrmacht?*"

Of all things, he had least expected to amuse the Indian again. Yet Gandhi's eyes unmistakably twinkled behind the lenses of his spectacles. "Field Marshal, I have an army too."

Model's patience, never of the most enduring sort, wore thin all at once. "Get out!" he snapped.

Gandhi stood, bowed, and departed. Major Lasch stuck his head into the office. The field marshal's glare drove him out again in a hurry.

"WELL?" JAWAHARLAL NEHRU paced back and forth. Tall, slim, and saturnine, he towered over Gandhi without dominating him. "Dare we use the same policies against the Germans that we employed against the English?"

"If we wish our land free, dare we do otherwise?" Gandhi replied. "They will not grant our wish of their own volition. Model struck me as a man not much different from various British leaders whom we have succeeded in vexing in the past." He smiled at the memory of what passive resistance had done to officials charged with combating it.

"Very well, *satyagraha* it is." But Nehru was not smiling. He had less humor than his older colleague.

Gandhi teased him gently: "Do you fear another spell in prison, then?" Both men had spent time behind bars during the war, until the British released them in a last, vain effort to rally the support of the Indian people to the raj.

"You know better." Nehru refused to be drawn, and persisted, "The rumors that come out of Europe frighten me."

"Do you tell me you take them seriously?" Gandhi shook his head in surprise and a little reproof. "Each side in any war will always paint its opponents as blackly as it can."

"I hope you are right, and that that is all. Still, I confess I would feel more at ease with what we plan to do if you found me one Jew, officer or other rank, in the army now occupying us."

"You would be hard-pressed to find any among the forces they defeated. The British have little love for Jews either."

"Yes, but I daresay it could be done. With the Germans, they are banned by law. The English would never make such a rule. And while the laws are vile enough, I think of the tales that man Wiesenthal told, the one who came here the gods know how across Russia and Persia from Poland."

"Those I do not believe," Gandhi said firmly. "No nation could act in that way and hope to survive. Where could men be found to carry out such horrors?"

"*Azad Hind*," Nehru said, quoting the "Free India" motto of the locals who had fought on the German side.

But Gandhi shook his head. "They are only soldiers, doing as soldiers have always done. Wiesenthal's claims are for an entirely different order of bestiality, one which could not exist without destroying the fabric of the state that gave it birth."

"I hope very much you are right," Nehru said.

WALTHER MODEL SLAMMED the door behind him hard enough to make his aide, whose desk faced away from the field marshal's office, jump in alarm. "Enough of this twaddle for one day," Model said. "I need schnapps, to get the taste of these Indians out of my mouth. Come along if you care to, Dieter."

"Thank you, sir." Major Lasch threw down his pen, eagerly got to his feet. "I sometimes think conquering India was easier than ruling it will be."

Model rolled his eyes. "I *know* it was. I would ten times rather be planning a new campaign than sitting here bogged down in pettifogging details. The sooner Berlin sends me people trained in colonial administration, the happier I will be."

The bar might have been taken from an English pub. It was dark, quiet, and paneled in walnut; a dart board still hung on the wall. But a German sergeant in field gray stood behind the bar, and despite the lazily turning ceiling fan, the temperature was close to thirty-five Celsius. The one might have been possible in occupied London, the other not.

Model knocked back his first shot at a gulp. He sipped his second more slowly, savoring it. Warmth spread through him, warmth that had nothing to do with the heat of the evening. He leaned back in his chair, steepled his fingers. "A long day," he said.

"Yes, sir," Lasch agreed. "After the effrontery of that Gandhi, any day would seem a long one. I've rarely seen you so angry." Considering Model's temper, that was no small statement.

"Ah, yes, Gandhi." Model's tone was reflective rather than irate; Lasch looked at him curiously. The field marshal said, "For my money, he's worth a dozen of the ordinary sort."

"Sir?" The aide no longer tried to hide his surprise.

"He is an honest man. He tells me what he thinks, and he will stick by that. I may kill him—I may have to kill him—but he and I will both know why, and I will not change his mind." Model took another sip of schnapps. He hesitated, as if unsure whether to go on. At last he did. "Do you know, Dieter, after he left I had a vision."

"Sir?" Now Lasch sounded alarmed.

The field marshal might have read his aide's thoughts. He chuckled wryly. "No, no, I am not about to swear off eating beefsteak and wear sandals instead of my boots, that I promise. But I saw myself as a Roman procurator, listening to the rantings of some early Christian priest."

Lasch raised an eyebrow. Such musings were unlike Model, who was usually direct to the point of bluntness and altogether materialistic— assets in the makeup of a general officer. The major cautiously sounded these unexpected depths: "How do you suppose the Roman felt, facing that kind of man?"

"Bloody confused, I suspect," Model said, which sounded more like him. "And because he and his comrades did not know how to handle such fanatics, you and I are Christians today, Dieter."

"So we are." The major rubbed his chin. "Is that a bad thing?"

Model laughed and finished his drink. "From your point of view or mine, no, but I doubt that old Roman would agree with us, any more than Gandhi agrees with me over what will happen next here. But then, I have two advantages over the dead procurator." He raised his finger; the sergeant hurried over to fill his glass.

At Lasch's nod, the young man also poured more schnapps for him. The major drank, then said, "I should hope so. We are more civilized, more sophisticated, than the Romans ever dreamed of being."

But Model was still in that fey mood. "Are we? My procurator was such a sophisticate that he tolerated anything, and never saw the danger in a foe who would not do the same. Our Christian God, though, is a jealous god, who puts up with no rivals. And one who is a National Socialist serves also the *Volk*, to whom he owes sole loyalty. I am immune to Gandhi's virus in a way the Roman was not to the Christian's."

"Yes, that makes sense," Lasch agreed after a moment. "I had not thought of it in that way, but I see it is so. And what is our other advantage over the Roman procurator?"

Suddenly the field marshal looked hard and cold, much the way he had looked leading the tanks of Third Panzer against the Kremlin compound. "The machine gun," he said.

THE RISING SUN'S rays made the sandstone of the Red Fort seem even more the color of blood. Gandhi frowned and turned his back on the fortress, not caring for that thought. Even at dawn, the air was warm and muggy.

"I wish you were not here," Nehru told him. The younger man lifted his trademark fore-and-aft cap, scratched his graying hair, and glanced at the crowd growing around them. "The Germans' orders forbid assemblies, and they will hold you responsible for this gathering."

"I am, am I not?" Gandhi replied. "Would you have me send my followers into a danger I do not care to face myself? How would I presume to lead them afterwards?"

"A general does not fight in the front ranks," Nehru came back. "If you are lost to our cause, will we be able to go on?"

"If not, then surely the cause is not worthy, yes? Now let us be going."

Nehru threw his hands in the air. Gandhi nodded, satisfied, and worked his way toward the head of the crowd. Men and women stepped aside to let him through. Still shaking his head, Nehru followed.

The crowd slowly began to march east up Chandni Chauk, the Street of Silversmiths. Some of the fancy shops had been wrecked in the fighting, more looted afterwards. But others were opening up, their owners as happy to take German money as they had been to serve the British before.

One of the proprietors, a man who had managed to stay plump even through the past year of hardship, came rushing out of his shop when he saw the procession go by. He ran to the head of the march and spotted Nehru, whose height and elegant dress singled him out.

"Are you out of your mind?" the silversmith shouted. "The Germans have banned assemblies. If they see you, something dreadful will happen."

"Is it not dreadful that they take away the liberty which properly belongs to us?" Gandhi asked. The silversmith spun round. His eyes grew wide when he recognized the man who was speaking to him. Gandhi went on, "Not only is it dreadful, it is wrong. And so we do not recognize the Germans' right to ban anything we may choose to do. Join us, will you?"

"Great-souled one, I—I—" the silversmith spluttered. Then his glance slid past Gandhi. "The Germans!" he squeaked. He turned and ran.

Gandhi led the procession toward the approaching squad. The Germans stamped down Chandni Chauk as if they expected the people in front of them to melt from their path. Their gear, Gandhi thought, was not that much different from what British soldiers wore: ankle boots, shorts, and open-necked tunics. But their coal-scuttle helmets gave them a look of sullen, beetle-browed ferocity the British tin hat did not convey. Even for a man of Gandhi's equanimity it was daunting, as no doubt it was intended to be.

"Hello, my friends," he said. "Do any of you speak English?"

"I speak it, a little," one of them replied. His shoulder straps had the twin pips of a sergeant-major; he was the squad-leader, then. He hefted his rifle, not menacingly, Gandhi thought, but to emphasize what he was saying. "Go to your homes back. This coming together is *verboten*."

"I am sorry, but I must refuse to obey your order," Gandhi said. "We are walking peacefully on our own street in our own city. We will harm no one, no matter what; this I promise you. But walk we will, as we wish." He repeated himself until he was sure the sergeant-major understood.

The German spoke to his comrades in his own language. One of the soldiers raised his gun and with a nasty smile pointed it at Gandhi. He nodded politely. The German blinked to see him unafraid. The sergeant-major slapped the rifle down. One of his men had a field telephone on his back. The sergeant-major cranked it, waited for a reply, spoke urgently into it.

Nehru caught Gandhi's eye. His dark, tired gaze was full of worry.

Somehow that nettled Gandhi more than the Germans' arrogance in ordering about his people. He began to walk forward again. The marchers followed him, flowing around the German squad like water round a boulder.

The soldier who had pointed his rifle at Gandhi shouted in alarm. He brought up the weapon again. The sergeant-major barked at him. Reluctantly, he lowered it.

"A sensible man," Gandhi said to Nehru. "He sees we do no injury to him or his, and so does none to us."

"Sadly, though, not everyone is so sensible," the younger man replied, "as witness his lance-corporal there. And even a sensible man may not be well-inclined to us. You notice he is still on the telephone."

THE PHONE ON Field Marshal Model's desk jangled. He jumped and swore; he had left orders he was to be disturbed only for an emergency. He had to find time to work. He picked up the phone. "This had better be good," he growled without preamble.

He listened, swore again, slammed the receiver down. "Lasch!" he shouted.

It was his aide's turn to jump. "Sir?"

"Don't just sit there on your fat arse," the field marshal said unfairly. "Call out my car and driver, and quickly. Then belt on your sidearm and come along. The Indians are doing something stupid. Oh, yes, order out a platoon and have them come after us. Up on Chandni Chauk, the trouble is."

Lasch called for the car and the troops, then hurried after Model. "A riot?" he asked as he caught up.

"No, no." Model moved his stumpy frame along so fast that the taller Lasch had to trot beside him. "Some of Gandhi's tricks, damn him."

The field marshal's Mercedes was waiting when he and his aide hurried out of the viceregal palace. "Chandni Chauk," Model snapped as the driver held the door open for him. After that he sat in furious silence as the powerful car roared up Irwin Road, round a third of Connaught Circle, and north on Chelmsford Road past the bombed-out railway station until, for no reason Model could see, the street's name changed to Qutb Road.

A little later, the driver said, "Some kind of disturbance up ahead, sir."

"Disturbance?" Lasch echoed, leaning forward to peer through the windscreen. "It's a whole damned regiment's worth of Indians coming at us. Don't they know better than that? And what the devil," he added, his voice rising, "are so many of our men doing ambling along beside them? Don't they know they're supposed to break up this sort of thing?" In his indignation, he did not notice he was repeating himself.

"I suspect they don't," Model said dryly. "Gandhi, I gather, can have that effect on people who aren't ready for his peculiar brand of stubbornness. That, however, does not include me." He tapped the driver on the shoulder. "Pull up about two hundred meters in front of the first rank of them, Joachim."

"Yes, sir."

Even before the car had stopped moving, Model jumped out of it. Lasch, hand on his pistol, was close behind, protesting, "What if one of those fanatics has a gun?"

"Then Colonel-General Weidling assumes command, and a lot of Indians end up dead."

Model strode toward Gandhi. As it had at the surrender ceremony, India's damp heat smote him. Even while he was sitting quietly in the car, his tunic had stuck to him. Sweat started streaming down his face the moment he started to move. Each breath felt as if he were taking in warm soup; the air even had a faint smell of soup, soup that had gone slightly off.

In its own way, he thought, surprised at himself, this beastly weather was worse than a Russian winter. Either was plenty to lay a man low by itself, but countless exotic diseases flourished in the moisture, warmth, and filth here. The snows at least were clean.

The field marshal ignored the German troops who were drawing themselves to stiff, horrified attention at the sight of his uniform. He would deal with them later. For the moment, Gandhi was more important.

He had stopped—which meant the rest of the marchers did too—and was waiting politely for Model to approach. The German commandant was not impressed. He thought Gandhi sincere, and could not doubt his courage, but none of that mattered at all. He said harshly, "You were warned against this sort of behavior."

Gandhi looked him in the eye. They were very much of a height. "And I told you, I do not recognize your right to give such orders. This is our country, not yours, and if some of us choose to walk on our streets, we will do so."

From behind Gandhi, Nehru's glance flicked worriedly from one of the antagonists to the other. Model noticed him only peripherally; if he was already afraid, he could be handled whenever necessary. Gandhi was a tougher nut. The field marshal waved at the crowd behind the old man. "You are responsible for all these people. If harm comes to them, you will be to blame."

"Why should harm come to them? They are not soldiers. They do not attack your men. I told that to one of your sergeants, and he understood it, and refrained from hindering us. Surely you, sir, an educated, cultured man, can see that what I say is self-evident truth."

Model turned his head to speak to his aide in German: "If we did not have Goebbels, this would be the one for his job." He shuddered to think of the propaganda victory Gandhi would win if he got away with flouting German ordinances. The whole countryside would be boiling with partisans in a week. And he had already managed to hoodwink some Germans into letting him do it!

Then Gandhi surprised him again. *"Ich danke Ihnen, Herr Generalfeldmarschall, aber das glaube ich kein Kompliment zu sein,"* he said in slow but clear German: "I thank you, field marshal, but I believe that to be no compliment."

Having to hold his monocle in place helped Model keep his face straight. "Take it however you like," he said. "Get these people off the street, or they and you will face the consequences. We will do what you force us to."

"I force you to nothing. As for these people who follow, each does so of his or her own free will. We are free, and will show it, not by violence, but through firmness in truth."

Now Model listened with only half an ear. He had kept Gandhi talking long enough for the platoon he had ordered out to arrive. Half a dozen SdKfz 251 armored personnel carriers came clanking up. The men piled out of them. "Give me a firing line, three ranks deep," Model shouted. As the troopers scrambled to obey, he waved the halftracks into position behind them, all but blocking Qutb Road. The halftracks' commanders swiveled the machine guns at the front of the vehicles' troop compartments so they bore on the Indians.

Gandhi watched these preparations as calmly as if they had nothing to do with him. Again Model had to admire his calm. His followers were less able to keep fear from their faces. Very few, though, used the pause to slip away. Gandhi's discipline was a long way from the military sort, but effective all the same.

"Tell them to disperse now, and we can still get away without bloodshed," the field marshal said.

"We will shed no one's blood, sir. But we will continue on our pleasant journey. Moving carefully, we will, I think, be able to get between your large lorries there." Gandhi turned to wave his people forward once more.

"You insolent—" Rage choked Model, which was as well, for it kept him from cursing Gandhi like a fishwife. To give him time to master his temper, he plucked his monocle from his eye and began polishing the lens with a silk handkerchief. He replaced the monocle, started to jam the handkerchief back into his trouser pocket, then suddenly had a better idea.

"Come, Lasch," he said, and started toward the waiting German troops. About halfway to them, he dropped the handkerchief on the ground. He spoke in loud, simple German so his men and Gandhi could both follow: "If any Indians come past this spot, I wash my hands of them."

He might have known Gandhi would have a comeback ready. "That is what Pilate said also, you will recall, sir."

"Pilate washed his hands to evade responsibility," the field marshal answered steadily; he was in control of himself again. "I accept it: I am responsible to my Führer and to the *Oberkommando-Wehrmacht* for maintaining Reichs control over India, and will do what I see fit to carry out that obligation."

For the first time since they had come to know each other, Gandhi looked sad. "I too, sir, have my responsibilities." He bowed slightly to Model.

Lasch chose that moment to whisper in his commander's ear: "Sir, what of our men over there? Had you planned to leave them in the line of fire?"

The field marshal frowned. He had planned to do just that; the wretches deserved no better, for being taken in by Gandhi. But Lasch had a point. The platoon might balk at shooting countrymen, if it came to that. "You men," Model said sourly, jabbing his marshal's baton at them, "fall in behind the armored personnel carriers, at once."

The Germans' boots pounded on the macadam as they dashed to obey. They were still all right, then, with a clear order in front of them. Something, Model thought, but not much.

He had also worried that the Indians would take advantage of the moment of confusion to press forward, but they did not. Gandhi and Nehru and a couple of other men were arguing among themselves. Model nodded once. Some of them knew he was in earnest, then. And Gandhi's followers' discipline, as the field marshal had thought a few minutes ago, was not of the military sort. He could not simply issue an order and know his will would be done.

"I ISSUE NO orders," Gandhi said. "Let each man follow his conscience as he will—what else is freedom?"

"They will follow *you* if you go forward, great-souled one," Nehru replied, "and that German, I fear, means to carry out his threat. Will you throw your life away, and those of your countrymen?"

"I will not throw my life away," Gandhi said, but before the men around him could relax he went on, "I will gladly give it, if freedom requires that. I am but one man. If I fall, others will surely carry on; perhaps the memory of me will serve to make them more steadfast."

He stepped forward.

"Oh, damnation," Nehru said softly, and followed.

For all his vigor, Gandhi was far from young. Nehru did not need to nod to the marchers close by him; of their own accord, they hurried ahead of the man who had led them for so long, forming with their bodies a barrier between him and the German guns.

He tried to go faster. "Stop! Leave me my place! What are you doing?" he cried, though in his heart he understood only too well.

"This once, they will not listen to you," Nehru said.

"But they must!" Gandhi peered through eyes dimmed now by tears as well as age. "Where is that stupid handkerchief? We must be almost to it!"

"FOR THE LAST time, I warn you to halt!" Model shouted. The Indians still came on. The sound of their feet, sandal-clad or bare, was like a growing murmur on the pavement, very different from the clatter of German boots. "Fools!" the field marshal muttered under his breath. He turned to his men. "Take your aim!"

The advance slowed when the rifles came up; of that Model was certain. For a moment he thought that ultimate threat would be enough to bring the marchers to their senses. But then they advanced again. The

Polish cavalry had shown that same reckless bravery, charging with lances and sabers and carbines against the German tanks. Model wondered whether the inhabitants of the *Reichsgeneralgouvernement* of Poland thought the gallantry worthwhile.

A man stepped on the field marshal's handkerchief. "Fire!" Model said.

A second passed, two. Nothing happened. Model scowled at his men. Gandhi's deviltry had got into them; sneaky as a Jew, he was turning the appearance of weakness into a strange kind of strength. But then trained discipline paid its dividend. One finger tightened on a Mauser trigger. A single shot rang out. As if it were a signal that recalled the other men to their duty, they too began to fire. From the armored personnel carriers, the machine guns started their deadly chatter. Model heard screams above the gunfire.

THE VOLLEY SMASHED into the front ranks of marchers at close range. Men fell. Others ran, or tried to, only to be held by the power of the stream still advancing behind them. Once begun, the Germans methodically poured fire into the column of Indians. The march dissolved into a panic-stricken mob.

Gandhi still tried to press forward. A fleeing wounded man smashed into him, splashing him with blood and knocking him to the ground. Nehru and another man immediately lay down on top of him.

"Let me up! Let me up!" he shouted.

"No," Nehru screamed in his ear. "With shooting like this, you are in the safest spot you can be. We need you, and need you alive. Now we have martyrs around whom to rally our cause."

"Now we have dead husbands and wives, fathers and mothers. Who will tend to their loved ones?"

Gandhi had no time for more protest. Nehru and the other man hauled him to his feet and dragged him away. Soon they were among their people, all running now from the German guns. A bullet struck the back of the unknown man who was helping Gandhi escape. Gandhi heard the slap of the impact, felt the man jerk. Then the strong grip on him loosened as the man fell.

He tried to tear free from Nehru. Before he could, another Indian laid hold of him. Even at that horrid moment, he felt the irony of his predicament. All his life he had championed individual liberty, and here his own followers were robbing him of his. In other circumstances, it might have been funny.

"In here!" Nehru shouted. Several people had already broken down the door to a shop and, Gandhi saw a moment later, the rear exit as well. Then he was hustled into the alley behind the shop, and through a maze of lanes which reminded him that old Delhi, unlike its British-designed sister city, was an Indian town through and through.

At last the nameless man with Gandhi and Nehru knocked on the back door of a tearoom. The woman who opened it gasped to recognize her unexpected guests, then pressed her hands together in front of her and stepped aside to let them in. "You will be safe here," the man said, "at least for a while. Now I must see to my own family."

"From the bottom of our hearts, we thank you," Nehru replied as the fellow hurried away. Gandhi said nothing. He was winded, battered, and filled with anguish at the failure of the march and at the suffering it had brought to so many marchers and to their kinsfolk.

The woman sat the two fugitive leaders at a small table in the kitchen, served them tea and cakes. "I will leave you now, best ones," she said quietly, "lest those out front wonder why I neglect them for so long."

Gandhi left the cake on his plate. He sipped the tea. Its warmth began to restore him physically, but the wound in his spirit would never heal. "The Amritsar massacre pales beside this," he said, setting down the empty cup. "There the British panicked and opened fire. This had nothing of panic about it. Model told me what he would do, and he did it." He shook his head, still hardly believing what he had just been through.

"So he did." Nehru had gobbled his cake like a starving wolf, and ate his companion's when he saw Gandhi did not want it. His once-immaculate white jacket and pants were torn, filthy, and blood-spattered; his cap sat awry on his head. But his eyes, usually so somber, were lit with a fierce glow. "And by his brutality, he has delivered himself into our hands. No one now can imagine the Germans have anything but their own interests at heart. We will gain followers all over the country. After this, not a wheel will turn in India."

"Yes, I will declare the *satyagraha* campaign," Gandhi said. "Noncooperation will show how we reject foreign rule, and will cost the Germans dear because they will not be able to exploit us. The combination of nonviolence and determined spirit will surely shame them into granting us our liberty."

"There—you see." Encouraged by his mentor's rally, Nehru rose and came round the table to embrace the older man. "We will triumph yet."

"So we will," Gandhi said, and sighed heavily. He had pursued India's freedom for half his long life, and this change of masters was a setback he had not truly planned for, even after England and Russia fell. The British were finally beginning to listen to him when the Germans swept them aside. Now he had to begin anew. He sighed again. "It will cost our poor people dear, though."

"CEASE FIRING," MODEL said. Few good targets were left on Qutb Road; almost all the Indians in the procession were down or had run from the guns.

Even after the bullets stopped, the street was far from silent. Most of the people the German platoon had shot were alive and shrieking. As if he needed more proof—the Russian campaign had taught the field marshal how hard human beings were to kill outright.

Still, the din distressed him, and evidently Lasch as well. "We ought to put them out of their misery," the major said.

"So we should." Model had a happy inspiration. "And I know just how. Come with me."

The two men turned their backs on the carnage and walked around the row of armored personnel carriers. As they passed the lieutenant commanding the platoon, Model nodded to him and said, "Well done."

The lieutenant saluted. "Thank you, sir." The soldiers in earshot nodded at one another. Nothing bucked up the odds of getting promoted like performing under the commander's eye.

The Germans behind the armored vehicles were not so proud of themselves. They were the ones who had let the march get this big and come this far in the first place. Model slapped his boot with his field marshal's baton. "You all deserve courts-martial," he said coldly, glaring at them. "You know the orders concerning native assemblies, yet there you were tagging along, more like sheepdogs than soldiers." He spat in disgust.

"But, sir—" began one of them, a sergeant-major, Model saw. He subsided in a hurry when Model's gaze swung his way.

"Speak," the field marshal urged. "Enlighten me—tell me what possessed you to act in the disgraceful way you did. Was it some evil spirit, perhaps? This country abounds with them, if you listen to the natives— as you all too obviously have been."

The sergeant-major flushed under Model's sarcasm, but finally burst out, "Sir, it didn't look to me as if they were up to any harm, that's all. The old man heading them up swore they were peaceful, and he looked too feeble to be anything but, if you take my meaning."

Model's smile had all the warmth of a Moscow December night. "And so in your wisdom you set aside the commands you had received. The results of that wisdom you hear now." The field marshal briefly let himself listen to the cries of the wounded, a sound the war had taught him to screen out. "Now then, come with me—yes you, Sergeant-major, and the rest of your shirkers too, or those of you who wish to avoid a court."

As he had known they would, they all trooped after him. "There is your handiwork," he said, pointing to the shambles in the street. His voice hardened. "You are responsible for those people lying there—had you acted as you should, you would have broken up that march long before it ever got so far or so large. Now the least you can do is give those people their release." He set hands on hips, waited.

No one moved. "Sir?" the sergeant-major said faintly. He seemed to have become the group's spokesman.

Model made an impatient gesture. "Go on, finish them. A bullet in the back of the head will quiet them once and for all."

"In cold blood, sir?" The sergeant-major had not wanted to understand him before. Now he had no choice.

The field marshal was inexorable. "They—and you—disobeyed Reich commands. They made themselves liable to capital punishment the moment they gathered. You at least have the chance to atone, by carrying out this just sentence."

"I don't think I can," the sergeant-major muttered.

He was probably just talking to himself, but Model gave him no chance to change his mind. He turned to the lieutenant of the platoon that had broken the march. "Place this man under arrest." After the sergeant-major had been seized, Model turned his chill, monocled stare on the rest of the reluctant soldiers. "Any others?"

Two more men let themselves be arrested rather than draw their weapons. The field marshal nodded to the others. "Carry out your orders." He had an afterthought. "If you find Gandhi or Nehru out there, bring them to me alive."

The Germans moved out hesitantly. They were no *Einsatzkommandos*, and not used to this kind of work. Some looked away as they administered the first coup de grace; one missed as a result, and had his bullet ricochet off the pavement and almost hit a comrade. But as the soldiers worked their way up Qutb Road they became quicker, more confident, and more competent. War was like that, Model thought. So soon one became used to what had been unimaginable.

After a while the flat cracks died away, but from lack of targets rather than reluctance. A few at a time, the soldiers returned to Model. "No sign of the two leaders?" he asked. They all shook their heads.

"Very well—dismissed. And obey your orders like good Germans henceforward."

"No further reprisals?" Lasch asked as the relieved troopers hurried away.

"No, let them go. They carried out their part of the bargain, and I will meet mine. I am a fair man, after all, Dieter."

"Very well, sir."

GANDHI LISTENED WITH undisguised dismay as the shopkeeper babbled out his tale of horror. "This is madness!" he cried.

"I doubt Field Marshal Model, for his part, understands the principle of *ahimsa*," Nehru put in. Neither Gandhi nor he knew exactly where they were: a safe house somewhere not far from the center of Delhi was the best guess he could make. The men who brought the shopkeeper were masked. What one did not know, one could not tell the Germans if captured.

"Neither do you," the older man replied, which was true; Nehru had a more pragmatic nature than Gandhi. Gandhi went on, "Rather more to the point, neither do the British. And Model, to speak to, seemed no different from any high-ranking British military man. His specialty has made him harsh and rigid, but he is not stupid and does not appear unusually cruel."

"Just a simple soldier, doing his job." Nehru's irony was palpable.

"He must have gone insane," Gandhi said; it was the only explanation that made even the slightest sense of the massacre of the wounded. "Undoubtedly he will be censured when news of this atrocity reaches Berlin, as General Dyer was by the British after Amritsar."

"Such is to be hoped." But again Nehru did not sound hopeful.

"How could it be otherwise, after such an appalling action? What government, what leaders could fail to be filled with humiliation and remorse at it?"

MODEL STRODE INTO the mess. The officers stood and raised their glasses in salute. "Sit, sit," the field marshal growled, using gruffness to hide his pleasure.

An Indian servant brought him a fair imitation of roast beef and Yorkshire pudding: better than they were eating in London these days, he thought. The servant was silent and unsmiling, but Model would only have noticed more about him had he been otherwise. Servants were supposed to assume a cloak of invisibility.

When the meal was done, Model took out his cigar case. The *Waffen-SS* officer on his left produced a lighter. Model leaned forward, puffed a cigar into life. "My thanks, *Brigadeführer*," the field marshal said. He had little use for SS titles of rank, but brigade commander was at least recognizably close to brigadier.

"Sir, it is my great pleasure," Jürgen Stroop declared. "You could not have handled things better. A lesson for the Indians—less than they deserve, too" (he also took no notice of the servant) "and a good one for your men as well. We train ours harshly too."

Model nodded. He knew about SS training methods. No one denied the daring of the *Waffen-SS* divisions. No one (except the SS) denied that the *Wehrmacht* had better officers.

Stroop drank. "A lesson," he repeated in a pedantic tone that went oddly with the SS's reputation for aggressiveness. "Force is the only thing the racially inferior can understand. Why, when I was in Warsaw—"

That had been four or five years ago, Model suddenly recalled. Stroop had been a *Brigadeführer* then too, if memory served; no wonder he was still one now, even after all the hard fighting since. He was lucky not to be a buck private. Imagine letting a pack of desperate, starving Jews chew up the finest troops in the world.

And imagine, afterwards, submitting a seventy-five-page operations report bound in leather and grandiosely called *The Warsaw Ghetto Is No More*. And imagine, with all that, having the crust to boast about it afterwards. No wonder the man sounded like a pompous ass. He *was* a pompous ass, and an inept butcher to boot. Model had done enough butchery before today's work—anyone who fought in Russia learned all about butchery—but he had never botched it.

He did not revel in it, either. He wished Stroop would shut up. He thought about telling the *Brigadeführer* he would sooner have been listening to Gandhi. The look on the fellow's face, he thought, would be worth it. But no. One could never be sure who was listening. Better safe.

THE SHORTWAVE SET crackled to life. It was in a secret cellar, a tiny dark hot room lit only by the glow of its dial and by the red end of the cigarette in its owner's mouth. The Germans had made not turning in a radio a capital crime. Of course, Gandhi thought, harboring him was also a capital crime. That weighed on his conscience. But the man knew the risk he was taking.

The fellow (Gandhi knew him only as Lal) fiddled with the controls. "Usually we listen to the Americans," he said. "There is some hope of truth from them. But tonight you want to hear Berlin."

"Yes," Gandhi said. "I must learn what action is to be taken against Model."

"If any," Nehru added. He was once again impeccably attired in white, which made him the most easily visible object in the cellar.

"We have argued this before," Gandhi said tiredly. "No government can uphold the author of a cold-blooded slaughter of wounded men and women. The world would cry out in abhorrence."

Lal said, "That government controls too much of the world already." He adjusted the tuning knob again. After a burst of static, the strains of a Strauss waltz filled the little room. Lal grunted in satisfaction. "We are a little early yet."

After a few minutes, the incongruously sweet music died away. "This is Radio Berlin's English-language channel," an announcer declared. "In a moment, the news programme." Another German tune rang out: the Horst Wessel Song. Gandhi's nostrils flared with distaste.

A new voice came over the air. "Good day. This is William Joyce." The nasal Oxonian accent was that of the archetypical British aristocrat, now vanished from India as well as England. It was the accent that flavored Gandhi's own English, and Nehru's as well. In fact, Gandhi had heard, Joyce was a New York–born rabble-rouser of Irish blood who also happened to be a passionately sincere Nazi. The combination struck the Indian as distressing.

"What did the English used to call him?" Nehru murmured. "Lord Haw-Haw?"

Gandhi waved his friend to silence. Joyce was reading the news, or what the Propaganda Ministry in Berlin wanted to present to English-speakers as the news.

Most of it was on the dull side: a trade agreement between Manchukuo, Japanese-dominated China, and Japanese-dominated Siberia; advances by German-supported French troops against American-supported French troops in a war by proxy in the African jungles. Slightly more interesting was the German warning about American interference in the East Asia Co-Prosperity Sphere.

One day soon, Gandhi thought sadly, the two mighty powers of the Old World would turn on the one great nation that stood between them. He feared the outcome. Thinking herself secure behind ocean barriers, the United States had stayed out of the European war. Now the war was bigger than Europe, and the oceans barriers no longer, but highways for her foes.

Lord Haw-Haw droned on and on. He gloated over the fate of rebels hunted down in Scotland: they were publicly hanged. Nehru leaned forward. "Now," he guessed. Gandhi nodded.

But the commentator passed on to unlikely-sounding boasts about the prosperity of Europe under the New Order. Against his will, Gandhi felt anger rise in him. Were Indians too insignificant to the Reich even to be mentioned?

More music came from the radio: the first bars of the other German anthem, *Deutschland über alles*. William Joyce said solemnly, "And now, a special announcement from the Ministry for Administration of Acquired Territories. *Reichsminister* Reinhard Heydrich commends Field Marshal Walther Model's heroic suppression of insurrection in India, and warns that his leniency will not be repeated."

"Leniency!" Nehru and Gandhi burst out together, the latter making it into as much of a curse as he allowed himself.

As if explaining to them, the voice on the radio went on, "Henceforward, hostages will be taken at the slightest sound of disorder, and will be executed forthwith if it continues. Field Marshal Model has also placed a reward of fifty thousand rupees on the capture of the criminal revolutionary Gandhi, and twenty-five thousand on the capture of his henchman Nehru."

Deutschland über alles rang out again, to signal the end of the announcement. Joyce went on to the next piece of news. "Turn that off," Nehru said after a moment. Lal obeyed, plunging the cellar into complete darkness. Nehru surprised Gandhi by laughing. "I have never before been the henchman of a criminal revolutionary."

The older man might as well not have heard him. "They commended him," he said. "Commended!" Disbelief put the full tally of his years in his voice, which usually sounded much stronger and younger.

"What will you do?" Lal asked quietly. A match flared, dazzling in the dark, as he lit another cigarette.

"They shall not govern India in this fashion," Gandhi snapped. "Not a soul will cooperate with them from now on. We outnumber them a thousand to one; what can they accomplish without us? We shall use that to full advantage."

"I hope the price is not more than the people can pay," Nehru said.

"The British shot us down too, and we were on our way toward prevailing," Gandhi said stoutly. As he would not have a few days before, though, he added, "So do I."

FIELD MARSHAL MODEL scowled and yawned at the same time. The pot of tea that should have been on his desk was nowhere to be found. His stomach growled. A plate of rolls should have been beside the teapot.

"How am I supposed to get anything done without breakfast?" he asked rhetorically (no one was in the office to hear him complain). Rhetorical complaint was not enough to satisfy him. "Lasch!" he shouted.

"Sir?" The aide came rushing in.

Model jerked his chin at the empty space on his desk where the silver tray full of good things should have been. "What's become of what's-his-name? Naoroji, that's it. If he's home with a hangover, he could have had the courtesy to let us know."

"I will enquire with the liaison officer for native personnel, sir, and also have the kitchen staff send you up something to eat." Lasch picked up a telephone, spoke into it. The longer he talked, the less happy he looked. When he turned back to the field marshal, his expression was a good match for the stony one Model often wore. He said, "None of the locals has shown up for work today, sir."

"What? None?" Model's frown made his monocle dig into his cheek. He hesitated. "I will feel better if you tell me some new hideous malady has broken out among them."

Lasch spoke with the liaison officer again. He shook his head. "Nothing like that, sir, or at least," he corrected himself with the caution that made him a good aide, "nothing Captain Wechsler knows about."

Model's phone rang again. It startled him; he jumped. *"Bitte?"* he growled into the mouthpiece, embarrassed at starting even though only Lasch had seen. He listened. Then he growled again, in good earnest this time. He slammed the phone down. "That was our railway officer. Hardly any natives are coming in to the station."

The phone rang again. *"Bitte?"* This time it was a swear word. Model snarled, cutting off whatever the man on the other end was saying, and hung up. "The damned clerks are staying out too," he shouted at Lasch, as if it were the major's fault. "I know what's wrong with the blasted locals, by God—an overdose of Gandhi, that's what."

"We should have shot him down in that riot he led," Lasch said angrily.

"Not for lack of effort that we didn't," Model said. Now that he saw where his trouble was coming from, he began thinking like a General Staff–trained officer again. That discipline went deep in him. His voice was cool and musing as he corrected his aide: "It was no riot, Dieter. That man is a skilled agitator. Armed with no more than words, he gave the British fits. Remember that the Führer started out as an agitator too."

"Ah, but the Führer wasn't above breaking heads to back up what he said." Lasch smiled reminiscently, and raised a fist. He was a Munich man, and wore on his sleeve the hashmark that showed Party membership before 1933.

But the field marshal said, "You think Gandhi doesn't? His way is to break them from the inside out, to make his foes doubt themselves. Those soldiers who took courts rather than obey their commanding officer had their heads broken, wouldn't you say? Think of him as a Russian tank commander, say, rather than as a political agitator. He is fighting us every bit as much as much as the Russians did."

Lasch thought about it. Plainly, he did not like it. "A coward's way of fighting."

"The weak cannot use the weapons of the strong." Model shrugged. "He does what he can, and skillfully. But I can make his backers doubt themselves, too. See if I don't."

"Sir?"

"We'll start with the railway workers. They are the most essential to have back on the job, yes? Get a list of names. Cross off every twentieth one. Send a squad to each of those homes, haul the slackers out, and shoot them in the street. If the survivors don't report tomorrow, do it again. Keep at it every day until they go back to work or no workers are left."

"Yes, sir." Lasch hesitated. At last he asked, "Are you sure, sir?"

"Have you a better idea, Dieter? We have a dozen divisions here; Gandhi has the whole subcontinent. I have to convince them in a hurry that obeying me is a better idea than obeying him. Obeying is what counts. I don't care a *pfennig* as to whether they love me. *Oderint, dum metuant.*"

"Sir?" The major had no Latin.

" 'Let them hate, so long as they fear.' "

"Ah," Lasch said. "Yes, I like that." He fingered his chin as he thought. "In aid of which, the Muslims hereabouts like the Hindus none too well. I daresay we could use them to help hunt Gandhi down."

"Now that *I* like," Model said. "Most of our Indian Legion lads are Muslims. They will know people, or know people who know people. And"—the field marshal chuckled cynically—"the reward will do no harm, either. Now get those orders out, and ring up Legion-Colonel Sadar. We'll get those feelers in motion—and if they pay off, you'll probably have earned yourself a new pip on your shoulderboards."

"Thank you very much, sir!"

"My pleasure. As I say, you'll have earned it. So long as things go as they should, I am a very easy man to get along with. Even Gandhi could, if he wanted to. He will end up having caused a lot of people to be killed because he does not."

"Yes, sir," Lasch agreed. "If only he would see that, since we have won India from the British, we will not turn around and tamely yield it to those who could not claim it for themselves."

"You're turning into a political philosopher now, Dieter?"

"Ha! Not likely." But the major looked pleased as he picked up the phone.

"MY DEAR FRIEND, my ally, my teacher, we are losing," Nehru said as the messenger scuttled away from this latest in a series of what were hopefully called safe houses. "Day by day, more people return to their jobs."

Gandhi shook his head, slowly, as if the motion caused him physical pain. "But they must not. Each one who cooperates with the Germans sets back the day of his own freedom."

"Each one who fails to ends up dead," Nehru said dryly. "Most men lack your courage, great-souled one. To them, that carries more weight than the other. Some are willing to resist, but would rather take up arms than the restraint of *satyagraha*."

"If they take up arms, they will be defeated. The British could not beat the Germans with guns and tanks and planes; how shall we? Besides, if we shoot a German here and there, we give them the excuse they need to strike at us. When one of their lieutenants was waylaid last month, their bombers leveled a village in reprisal. Against those who fight through nonviolence, they have no such justification."

"They do not seem to need one, either," Nehru pointed out.

Before Gandhi could reply to that, a man burst into the hovel where they were hiding. "You must flee!" he cried. "The Germans have found this place! They are coming. Out with me, quick! I have a cart waiting."

Nehru snatched up the canvas bag in which he carried his few belongings. For a man used to being something of a dandy, the haggard life of a fugitive came hard. Gandhi had never wanted much. Now that he had nothing, that did not disturb him. He rose calmly, followed the man who had come to warn them.

"Hurry!" the fellow shouted as they scrambled into his oxcart while the humpbacked cattle watched indifferently with their liquid brown eyes. When Gandhi and Nehru were lying in the cart, the man piled blankets and straw mats over them. He scrambled up to take the reins, saying, "*Inshallah*, we shall be safely away from here before the platoon arrives." He flicked a switch over the backs of the cattle. They lowed indignantly. The cart rattled away.

Lying in the sweltering semidarkness under the concealment the man had draped on him, Gandhi peered through chinks, trying to figure out where in Delhi he was going next. He had played the game more than once these last few weeks, though he knew doctrine said he should not. The less he knew, the less he could reveal. Unlike most men, though, he was confident he could not be made to talk against his will.

"We are using the technique the American Poe called 'the purloined letter,' I see," he remarked to Nehru. "We will be close by the German barracks. They will not think to look for us there."

The younger man frowned. "I did not know we had safe houses there," he said. Then he relaxed, as well as he could when folded into too small a space. "Of course, I do not pretend to know everything there is to know about such matters. It would be dangerous if I did."

"I was thinking much the same myself, though with me as subject of the sentence." Gandhi laughed quietly. "Try as we will, we always have ourselves at the center of things, don't we?"

He had to raise his voice to finish. An armored personnel carrier came rumbling and rattling toward them, getting louder as it approached. The silence when the driver suddenly killed the engine was a startling contrast to the previous racket. Then there was noise again, as soldiers shouted in German.

"What are they saying?" Nehru asked.

"Hush," Gandhi said absently, not from ill manners, but out of the concentration he needed to follow German at all. After a moment he resumed, "They are swearing at a black-bearded man, asking why he flagged them down."

"Why would anyone flag down German sol—" Nehru began, then stopped in abrupt dismay. The fellow who had burst into their hiding-place wore a bushy black beard. "We had better get out of—" Again Nehru broke off in midsentence, this time because the oxcart driver was throwing off the coverings that concealed his two passengers.

Nehru started to get to his feet so he could try to scramble out and run. Too late—a rifle barrel that looked wide as a tunnel was shoved in his face as a German came dashing up to the cart. The big curved magazine said the gun was one of the automatic assault rifles that had wreaked such havoc among the British infantry. A burst would turn a man into bloody hash. Nehru sank back in despair.

Gandhi, less spry than his friend, had only sat up in the bottom of the cart. "Good day, gentlemen," he said to the Germans peering down at him. His tone took no notice of their weapons.

"Down." The word was in such gutturally accented Hindi that Gandhi hardly understood it, but the accompanying gesture with a rifle was unmistakable.

Face a mask of misery, Nehru got out of the cart. A German helped Gandhi descend. "*Danke*," he said. The soldier nodded gruffly. He pointed the barrel of his rifle—toward the armored personnel carrier.

"My rupees!" the black-bearded man shouted.

Nehru turned on him, so quickly he almost got shot for it. "Your thirty pieces of silver, you mean," he cried.

"Ah, a British education," Gandhi murmured. No one was listening to him.

"My rupees," the man repeated. He did not understand Nehru; so often, Gandhi thought sadly, that was at the root of everything.

"You'll get them," promised the sergeant leading the German squad. Gandhi wondered if he was telling the truth. Probably so, he decided. The British had had centuries to build a network of Indian clients. Here but a matter of months, the Germans would need all they could find.

"In." The soldier with a few words of Hindi nodded to the back of the armored personnel carrier. Up close, the vehicle took on a war-battered individuality its kind had lacked when they were just big, intimidating shapes rumbling down the highway. It was bullet-scarred and patched in a couple of places, with sheets of steel crudely welded on.

Inside, the jagged lips of the bullet holes had been hammered down so they did not gouge a man's back. The carrier smelled of leather, sweat, tobacco, smokeless powder, and exhaust fumes. It was crowded, all the more so with the two Indians added to its usual contingent. The motor's roar when it started up challenged even Gandhi's equanimity.

Not, he thought with uncharacteristic bitterness, that that equanimity had done him much good.

"THEY ARE HERE, sir," Lasch told Model, then, as the field marshal's blank look amplified: "Gandhi and Nehru."

Model's eyebrow came down toward his monocle. "I won't bother with Nehru. Now that we have him, take him out and give him a noodle"—army slang for a bullet in the back of the neck—"but don't waste my time over him. Gandhi, now, is interesting. Fetch him in."

"Yes, sir," the major sighed. Model smiled. Lasch did not find Gandhi interesting. Lasch would never carry a field marshal's baton, not if he lived to be ninety.

Model waved away the soldiers who escorted Gandhi into his office. Either of them could have broken the little Indian like a stick. "Have a care," Gandhi said. "If I am the desperate criminal bandit you have styled me, I may overpower you and escape."

"If you do, you will have earned it," Model retorted. "Sit, if you care to."

"Thank you." Gandhi sat. "They took Jawaharlal away. Why have you summoned me instead?"

"To talk for a while, before you join him." Model saw that Gandhi knew what he meant, and that the old man remained unafraid. Not that that would change anything, Model thought, although he respected his opponent's courage the more for his keeping it in the last extremity.

"I will talk, in the hope of persuading you to have mercy on my people. For myself I ask nothing."

Model shrugged. "I was as merciful as the circumstances of war allowed, until you began your campaign against us. Since then, I have done what I needed to restore order. When it returns, I may be milder again."

"You seem a decent man," Gandhi said, puzzlement in his voice. "How can you so callously massacre people who have done you no harm?"

"I never would have, had you not urged them to folly."

"Seeking freedom is not folly."

"It is when you cannot gain it—and you cannot. Already your people are losing their stomach for—what do you call it? Passive resistance? A silly notion. A passive resister simply ends up dead, with no chance to hit back at his foe."

That hit a nerve, Model thought. Gandhi's voice was less detached as he answered, "*Satyagraha* strikes the oppressor's soul, not his body. You must be without honor or conscience, to fail to feel your victims' anguish."

Nettled in turn, the field marshal snapped, "I have honor. I follow the oath of obedience I swore with the army to the Führer and through him to the Reich. I need consider nothing past that."

Now Gandhi's calm was gone. "But he is a madman! What has he done to the Jews of Europe?"

"Removed them," Model said matter-of-factly; *Einsatzgruppe* B had followed Army Group Central to Moscow and beyond. "They were capitalists or Bolsheviks, and either way enemies of the Reich. When an enemy falls into a man's hands, what else is there to do but destroy him, lest he revive to turn the tables one day?"

Gandhi had buried his face in his hands. Without looking at Model, he said, "Make him a friend."

"Even the British knew better than that, or they would not have held India as long as they did," the field marshal snorted. "They must have begun to forget, though, or your movement would have got what it deserves long ago. You first made the mistake of confusing us with them long ago, by the way." He touched a fat dossier on his desk.

"When was that?" Gandhi asked indifferently. The man was beaten now, Model thought with a touch of pride: he had succeeded where a generation of degenerate, decadent Englishmen had failed. Of course, the field marshal told himself, he had beaten the British too.

He opened the dossier, riffled through it. "Here we are," he said, nodding in satisfaction. "It was after *Kristallnacht*, eh, in 1938, when you urged the German Jews to play at the same game of passive resistance you were using here. Had they been fools enough to try it, we would have thanked you, you know: it would have let us bag the enemies of the Reich all the more easily."

"Yes, I made a mistake," Gandhi said. Now he was looking at the field marshal, looking at him with such fierceness that for a moment Model thought he would attack him despite advanced age and effete philosophy. But Gandhi only continued sorrowfully, "I made the mistake of thinking I faced a régime ruled by conscience, one that could at the very least be shamed into doing that which is right."

Model refused to be baited. "We do what is right for our *Volk*, for our Reich. We are meant to rule, and rule we do—as you see." The field marshal tapped the dossier again. "You could be sentenced to death for this earlier meddling in the affairs of the fatherland, you know, even without these later acts of insane defiance you have caused."

"History will judge us," Gandhi warned as the field marshal rose to have him taken away.

Model smiled then. "Winners write history." He watched the two strapping German guards lead the old man off. "A very good morning's work," the field marshal told Lasch when Gandhi was gone. "What's on the menu for lunch?"

"Blood sausage and sauerkraut, I believe."

"Ah, good. Something to look forward to." Model sat down. He went back to work.

Cordwainer Smith

Cordwainer Smith is the pseudonym under which Paul Myron Anthony Linebarger wrote science fiction between 1950 and his death in 1966. All but a handful of Smith's thirty-two published stories and the novel Norstrilia *are part of his visionary Instrumentality of Mankind series, which he began writing when he was a teenager but did not see professional publication until the appearance of "Scanners Live in Vain." The Instrumentality stories provide a fragmentary history spanning some fifteen thousand years of human history and galactic colonization and have been widely praised for their imaginative depictions of alien civilizations and sympathetic renderings of individuals adjusting to the rigors of a civilization in which interstellar war, immortality, faster-than-light space travel, suspended animation, and telepathic combat are the norm. Smith's science fiction works have been collected in the definitive* The Rediscovery of Man: The Complete Short Science Fiction of Cordwainer Smith *and* Norstrilia. *Smith also wrote several pseudonymous mainstream novels and a spy thriller,* Atomsk, *as well as a psychology text,* Psychological Warfare.

THE GAME OF RAT AND DRAGON

Cordwainer Smith

THE TABLE

PINLIGHTING IS A HELL of a way to earn a living. Underhill was furious as
he closed the door behind himself. It didn't make much sense to wear a
uniform and look like a soldier if people didn't appreciate what you did.

He sat down in his chair, laid his head back in the headrest and
pulled the helmet down over his forehead.

As he waited for the pin-set to warm up, he remembered the girl in
the outer corridor. She had looked at it, then looked at him scornfully.

"Meow." That was all she had said. Yet it had cut him like a knife.

What did she think he was—a fool, a loafer, a uniformed nonentity?
Didn't she know that for every half-hour of pinlighting, he got a minimum of two months' recuperation in the hospital?

By now the set was warm. He felt the squares of space around him,
sensed himself at the middle of an immense grid, a cubic grid, full of
nothing. Out in that nothingness, he could sense the hollow, aching
horror of space itself and could feel the terrible anxiety which his mind
encountered whenever it met the faintest trace of inert dust.

As he relaxed, the comforting solidity of the sun, the clockwork of the
familiar planets and the Moon rang in on him. Our own solar system
was as charming and as simple as an ancient cuckoo clock filled with familiar ticking and with reassuring noises. The odd little moons of Mars
swung around their planet like frantic mice, yet their regularity was itself
an assurance that all was well. Far above the plane of the ecliptic, he
could feel half a ton of dust more or less drifting outside the lanes of
human travel.

Here there was nothing to fight, nothing to challenge the mind, to tear the living soul out of a body with its roots dripping in effluvium as tangible as blood.

Nothing ever moved in on the solar system. He could wear the pin-set forever and be nothing more than a sort of telepathic astronomer, a man who could feel the hot, warm protection of the sun throbbing and burning against his living mind.

WOODLEY CAME IN.

"Same old ticking world," said Underhill. "Nothing to report. No wonder they didn't develop the pin-set until they began to planoform. Down here with the hot sun around us, it feels so good and so quiet. You can feel everything spinning and turning. It's nice and sharp and compact. It's sort of like sitting around home."

Woodley grunted. He was not much given to flights of fantasy.

Undeterred, Underhill went on, "It must have been pretty good to have been an Ancient Man. I wonder why they burned up their world with war. They didn't have to planoform. They didn't have to go out to earn their livings among the stars. They didn't have to dodge the Rats or play the Game. They couldn't have invented pinlighting because they didn't have any need of it, did they, Woodley?"

Woodley grunted, "Uh-huh." Woodley was twenty-six years old and due to retire in one more year. He already had a farm picked out. He had gotten through ten years of hard work pinlighting with the best of them. He had kept his sanity by not thinking very much about his job, meeting the strains of the task whenever he had to meet them and thinking nothing more about his duties until the next emergency arose.

Woodley never made a point of getting popular among the Partners. None of the Partners liked him very much. Some of them even resented him. He was suspected of thinking ugly thoughts of the Partners on occasion, but since none of the Partners ever thought a complaint in articulate form, the other pinlighters and the chiefs of the instrumentality left him alone.

Underhill was still full of the wonder of their job. Happily he babbled on, "What does happen to us when we planoform? Do you think it's sort of like dying? Did you ever see anybody who had his soul pulled out?"

"Pulling souls is just a way of talking about it," said Woodley. "After all these years, nobody knows whether we have souls or not."

"But I saw one once. I saw what Dogwood looked like when he came apart. There was something funny. It looked wet and sort of sticky as if it were bleeding and it went out of him—and you know what they did to Dogwood? They took him away, up in that part of the hospital where you and I never go—way up at the top part where the others are, where the others always have to go if they are alive after the Rats of the Up-and-Out have gotten them."

Woodley sat down and lit an ancient pipe. He was burning something called tobacco in it. It was a dirty sort of habit, but it made him look very dashing and adventurous.

"Look here, youngster. You don't have to worry about that stuff. Pinlighting is getting better all the time. The Partners are getting better. I've seen them pinlight two Rats forty-six million miles apart in one and a half milliseconds. As long as people had to try to work the pin-sets themselves, there was always the chance that with a minimum of four hundred milliseconds for the human mind to set a pinlight, we wouldn't light the Rats up fast enough to protect our planoforming ships. The Partners have changed all that. Once they get going, they're faster than Rats. And they always will be. I know it's not easy, letting a Partner share your mind—"

"It's not easy for them, either," said Underhill.

"Don't worry about them. They're not human. Let them take care of themselves. I've seen more pinlighters go crazy from monkeying around with Partners than I have ever seen caught by the Rats. How many do you actually know of them that got grabbed by Rats?"

UNDERHILL LOOKED DOWN at his fingers, which shone green and purple in the vivid light thrown by the tuned-in pin-set, and counted ships. The thumb for the *Andromeda*, lost with crew and passengers, the index finger and the middle finger for release ships 43 and 56, found with their pin-sets burned out and every man, woman, and child on board dead or insane. The ring finger, the little finger, and the thumb of the other hand were the first three battleships to be lost to the Rats—lost as people realized that there was something out there *underneath space itself* which was alive, capricious, and malevolent.

Planoforming was sort of funny. It felt like—

Like nothing much.

Like the twinge of a mild electric shock.

Like the ache of a sore tooth bitten on for the first time.

Like a slightly painful flash of light against the eyes.

Yet in that time, a forty-thousand-ton ship lifting free above Earth disappeared somehow or other into two dimensions and appeared half a light-year or fifty light-years off.

At one moment, he would be sitting in the Fighting Room, the pinset ready and the familiar solar system ticking around inside his head. For a second or a year (he could never tell how long it really was, subjectively), the funny little flash went through him and then he was loose in the Up-and-Out, the terrible open spaces between the stars, where the stars themselves felt like pimples on his telepathic mind and the planets were too far away to be sensed or read.

Somewhere in this outer space, a gruesome death awaited, death and horror of a kind which Man had never encountered until he reached out for interstellar space itself. Apparently the light of the suns kept the Dragons away.

DRAGONS. THAT WAS what people called them. To ordinary people, there was nothing, nothing except the shiver of planoforming and the hammer blow of sudden death or the dark, spastic note of lunacy descending into their minds.

But to the telepaths, they were Dragons.

In the fraction of a second between the telepaths' awareness of a hostile something out in the black hollow nothingness of space and the impact of a ferocious, ruinous psychic blow against all living things within the ship, the telepaths had sensed entities something like the dragons of ancient human lore, beasts more clever than beasts, demons more tangible than demons, hungry vortices of aliveness and hate compounded by unknown means out of the thin, tenuous matter between the stars.

It took a surviving ship to bring back the news—a ship in which, by sheer chance, a telepath had a light-beam ready, turning it out at the innocent dust so that, within the panorama of his mind, the Dragon dissolved into nothing at all and the other passengers, themselves nontelepathic, went about their way not realizing that their own immediate deaths had been averted.

From then on, it was easy—almost.

· · ·

PLANOFORMING SHIPS ALWAYS carried telepaths. Telepaths had their sensitiveness enlarged to an immense range by the pin-sets, which were telepathic amplifiers adapted to the mammal mind. The pin-sets in turn were electronically geared into small dirigible light-bombs. Light did it.

Light broke up the Dragons, allowed the ships to re-form three-dimensionally, skip, skip, skip, as they moved from star to star.

The odds suddenly moved down from a hundred to one against mankind to sixty to forty in mankind's favor.

This was not enough. The telepaths were trained to become ultra-sensitive, trained to become aware of the Dragons in less than a millisecond.

But it was found that the Dragons could move a million miles in just under two milliseconds and that this was not enough for the human mind to activate the light-beams.

Attempts had been made to sheathe the ships in light at all times.

This defense wore out.

As mankind learned about the Dragons, so, too, apparently, the Dragons learned about mankind. Somehow they flattened their own bulk and came in on extremely flat trajectories very quickly.

Intense light was needed, light of sunlike intensity. This could be provided only by light-bombs. Pinlighting came into existence.

Pinlighting consisted of the detonation of ultravivid, miniature photo-nuclear bombs, which converted a few ounces of a magnesium isotope into pure visible radiance.

The odds kept coming down in mankind's favor, yet ships were being lost.

It became so bad that people didn't even want to find the ships because the rescuers knew what they would see. It was sad to bring back to Earth three hundred bodies ready for burial and two hundred or three hundred lunatics, damaged beyond repair, to be wakened, and fed, and cleaned, and put to sleep, wakened and fed again until their lives were ended.

TELEPATHS TRIED TO reach into the minds of the psychotics who had been damaged by the Dragons, but they found nothing there beyond vivid spouting columns of fiery terror bursting from the primordial id itself, the volcanic source of life.

Then came the Partners.

Man and Partner could do together what Man could not do alone. Men had the intellect. Partners had the speed.

The Partners rode their tiny craft, no larger than footballs, outside the spaceships. They planoformed with the ships. They rode beside them in their six-pound craft, ready to attack.

The tiny ships of the Partners were swift. Each carried a dozen pinlights, bombs no bigger than thimbles.

The pinlighters threw the Partners—quite literally threw—by means of mind-to-firing relays directly at the Dragons.

What seemed to be dragons to the human mind appeared in the form of gigantic rats in the minds of the Partners.

Out in the pitiless nothingness of space, the Partners' minds responded to an instinct as old as life. The Partners attacked, striking with a speed faster than Man's, going from attack to attack until the Rats or themselves were destroyed. Almost all the time, it was the Partners who won.

With the safety of the interstellar skip, skip, skip of the ships, commerce increased immensely, the population of all the colonies went up, and the demand for trained Partners increased.

Underhill and Woodley were a part of the third generation of pinlighters and yet, to them, it seemed as though their craft had endured forever.

Gearing space into minds by means of the pin-set, adding the Partners to those minds, keying up the mind for the tension of a fight on which all depended—this was more than human synapses could stand for long. Underhill needed his two months' rest after half an hour of fighting. Woodley needed his retirement after ten years of service. They were young. They were good. But they had limitations.

So much depended on the choice of Partners, so much on the sheer luck of who drew whom.

THE SHUFFLE

Father Moontree and the little girl named West entered the room. They were the other two pinlighters. The human complement of the Fighting Room was now complete.

Father Moontree was a red-faced man of forty-five who had lived the peaceful life of a farmer until he reached his fortieth year. Only then, belatedly, did the authorities find he was telepathic and agree to let him late in life enter upon the career of pinlighter. He did well at it, but he was fantastically old for this kind of business.

Father Moontree looked at the glum Woodley and the musing Underhill. "How're the youngsters today? Ready for a good fight?"

"Father always wants a fight," giggled the little girl named West. She was such a little girl. Her giggle was high and childish. She looked like the last person in the world one would expect to find in the rough, sharp dueling of pinlighting.

Underhill had been amused one time when he found one of the most sluggish of the Partners coming away happy from contact with the mind of the girl named West.

Usually the Partners didn't care much about the human minds with which they were paired for the journey. The Partners seemed to take the attitude that human minds were complex and fouled up beyond belief, anyhow. No Partner ever questioned the superiority of the human mind, though very few of the Partners were much impressed by that superiority.

The Partners liked people. They were willing to fight with them. They were even willing to die for them. But when a Partner liked an individual the way, for example, that Captain Wow or the Lady May liked Underhill, the liking had nothing to do with intellect. It was a matter of temperament, of feel.

Underhill knew perfectly well that Captain Wow regarded his, Underhill's, brains as silly. What Captain Wow liked was Underhill's friendly emotional structure, the cheerfulness and glint of wicked amusement that shot through Underhill's unconscious thought patterns, and the gaiety with which Underhill faced danger. The words, the history books, the ideas, the science—Underhill could sense all that in his own mind, reflected back from Captain Wow's mind, as so much rubbish.

Miss West looked at Underhill. "I bet you've put stickum on the stones."

"I did not!"

Underhill felt his ears grow red with embarrassment. During his novitiate, he had tried to cheat in the lottery because he got particularly fond of a special Partner, a lovely young mother named Murr. It was so much easier to operate with Murr and she was so affectionate toward him that he forgot pinlighting was hard work and that he was not instructed to

have a good time with his Partner. They were both designed and prepared to go in to deadly battle together.

One cheating had been enough. They had found him out and he had
been laughed at for years.

Father Moontree picked up the imitation-leather cup and shook the
stone dice which assigned them their Partners for the trip. By senior rights,
he took first draw.

HE GRIMACED. HE had drawn a greedy old character, a tough old male
whose mind was full of slobbering thoughts of food, veritable oceans full
of half-spoiled fish. Father Moontree had once said that he burped cod-
liver oil for weeks after drawing that particular glutton, so strongly had
the telepathic image of fish impressed itself upon his mind. Yet the glutton was a glutton for danger as well as for fish. He had killed sixty-three
Dragons, more than any other Partner in the service, and was quite literally worth his weight in gold.

The little girl West came next. She drew Captain Wow. When she saw
who it was, she smiled.

"I *like* him," she said. "He's such fun to fight with. He feels so nice
and cuddly in my mind."

"Cuddly, hell," said Woodley. "I've been in his mind, too. It's the most
leering mind in this ship, bar none."

"Nasty man," said the little girl. She said it declaratively, without
reproach.

Underhill, looking at her, shivered.

He didn't see how she could take Captain Wow so calmly. Captain
Wow's mind *did* leer. When Captain Wow got excited in the middle of a
battle, confused images of Dragons, deadly Rats, luscious beds, the smell
of fish, and the shock of space all scrambled together in his mind as he
and Captain Wow, their consciousness linked together through the pin-
set, became a fantastic composite of human being and Persian cat.

That's the trouble with working with cats, thought Underhill. It's a
pity that nothing else anywhere will serve as Partner. Cats were all right
once you got in touch with them telepathically. They were smart
enough to meet the needs of the fight, but their motives and desires were
certainly different from those of humans.

They were companionable enough as long as you thought tangible
images at them, but their minds just closed up and went to sleep when

you recited Shakespeare or Colegrove, or if you tried to tell them what space was.

It was sort of funny realizing that the Partners who were so grim and mature out here in space were the same cute little animals that people had used as pets for thousands of years back on Earth. He had embarrassed himself more than once while on the ground by saluting perfectly ordinary nontelepathic cats because he had forgotten for the moment that they were not Partners.

He picked up the cup and shook out his stone dice.

He was lucky—he drew the Lady May.

THE LADY MAY was the most thoughtful Partner he had ever met. In her, the finely bred pedigree mind of a Persian cat had reached one of its highest peaks of development. She was more complex than any human woman, but the complexity was all one of emotions, memory, hope, and discriminated experience—experience sorted through without benefit of words.

When he had first come into contact with her mind, he was astonished at its clarity. With her he remembered her kittenhood. He remembered every mating experience she had ever had. He saw in a half-recognizable gallery all the other pinlighters with whom she had been paired for the fight. And he saw himself, radiant, cheerful, and desirable.

He even thought he caught the edge of a longing—

A very flattering and yearning thought: What a pity he is not a cat.

Woodley picked up the last stone. He drew what he deserved—a sullen, scared old tomcat with none of the verve of Captain Wow. Woodley's Partner was the most animal of all the cats on the ship, a low, brutish type with a dull mind. Even telepathy had not refined his character. His ears were half chewed off from the first fights in which he had engaged.

He was a serviceable fighter, nothing more.

Woodley grunted.

Underhill glanced at him oddly. Didn't Woodley ever do anything but grunt?

Father Moontree looked at the other three. "You might as well get your Partners now. I'll let the Scanner know we're ready to go into the Up-and-Out."

THE DEAL

Underhill spun the combination lock on the Lady May's cage. He woke her gently and took her into his arms. She humped her back luxuriously, stretched her claws, started to purr, thought better of it, and licked him on the wrist instead. He did not have the pin-set on, so their minds were closed to each other, but in the angle of her mustache and in the movement of her ears he caught some sense of the gratification she experienced in finding him as her Partner.

He talked to her in human speech, even though speech meant nothing to a cat when the pin-set was not on.

"It's a damn shame, sending a sweet little thing like you whirling around in the coldness of nothing to hunt for Rats that are bigger and deadlier than all of us put together. You didn't ask for this kind of fight, did you?"

For answer, she licked his hand, purred, tickled his cheek with her long fluffy tail, turned around and faced him, golden eyes shining.

For a moment, they stared at each other, man squatting, cat standing erect on her hind legs, front claws digging into his knee. Human eyes and cat eyes looked across an immensity which no words could meet, but which affection spanned in a single glance.

"Time to get in," he said.

She walked docilely to her spheroid carrier. She climbed in. He saw to it that her miniature pin-set rested firmly and comfortably against the base of her brain. He made sure that her claws were padded so that she could not tear herself in the excitement of battle.

Softly he said to her, "Ready?"

For answer, she preened her back as much as her harness would permit and purred softly within the confines of the frame that held her.

He slapped down the lid and watched the sealant ooze around the seam. For a few hours, she was welded into her projectile until a workman with a short cutting arc would remove her after she had done her duty.

HE PICKED UP the entire projectile and slipped it into the ejection tube. He closed the door of the tube, spun the lock, seated himself in his chair, and put his own pin-set on.

Once again he flung the switch.

He sat in a small room, *small, small, warm, warm*, the bodies of the other three people moving close around him, the tangible lights in the ceiling bright and heavy against his closed eyelids.

As the pin-set warmed, the room fell away. The other people ceased to be people and became small glowing heaps of fire, embers, dark red fire, with the consciousness of life burning like old red coals in a country fireplace.

As the pin-set warmed a little more, he felt Earth just below him, felt the ship slipping away, felt the turning moon as it swung on the far side of the world, felt the planets and the hot, clear goodness of the sun which kept the Dragons so far from mankind's native ground.

Finally, he reached complete awareness.

He was telepathically alive to a range of millions of miles. He felt the dust which he had noticed earlier high above the ecliptic. With a thrill of warmth and tenderness, he felt the consciousness of the Lady May pouring over into his own. Her consciousness was as gentle and clear and yet sharp to the taste of his mind as if it were scented oil. It felt relaxing and reassuring. He could sense her welcome of him. It was scarcely a thought, just a raw emotion of greeting.

At last they were one again.

In a tiny, remote corner of his mind, as tiny as the smallest toy he had ever seen in his childhood, he was still aware of the room and the ship, and of Father Moontree picking up a telephone and speaking to a Scanner captain in charge of the ship.

His telepathic mind caught the idea long before his ears could frame the words. The actual sound followed the idea the way that thunder on an ocean beach follows the lightning inward from far out over the seas.

"The Fighting Room is ready. Clear to planoform, sir."

THE PLAY

Underhill was always a little exasperated by the way that Lady May experienced things before he did.

He was braced for the quick vinegar thrill of planoforming, but he caught her report of it before his own nerves could register what happened.

Earth had fallen so far away that he groped for several milliseconds before he found the sun in the upper rear right-hand corner of his telepathic mind.

That was a good jump, he thought. This way we'll get there in four or five skips.

A few hundred miles outside the ship, the Lady May thought back at him, "O warm, O generous, O gigantic man! O brave, O friendly, O tender and huge Partner! O wonderful with you, with you so good, good, good, warm, warm, now to fight, now to go, good with you . . ."

He knew that she was not thinking words, that his mind took the clear amiable babble of her cat intellect and translated it into images which his own thinking could record and understand.

Neither one of them was absorbed in the game of mutual greetings. He reached out far beyond her range of perception to see if there was anything near the ship. It was funny how it was possible to do two things at once. He could scan space with his pin-set mind and yet at the same time catch a vagrant thought of hers, a lovely, affectionate thought about a son who had had a golden face and a chest covered with soft, incredibly downy white fur.

While he was still searching, he caught the warning from her.

We jump again!

And so they had. The ship had moved to a second planoform. The stars were different. The sun was immeasurably far behind. Even the nearest stars were barely in contact. This was good Dragon country, the open, nasty, hollow kind of space. He reached farther, faster, sensing and looking for danger, ready to fling the Lady May at danger wherever he found it.

Terror blazed up in his mind, so sharp, so clear, that it came through as a physical wrench.

The little girl named West had found something—something immense, long, black, sharp, greedy, horrific. She flung Captain Wow at it.

Underhill tried to keep his own mind clear. "Watch out!" he shouted telepathically at the others, trying to move the Lady May around.

At one corner of the battle, he felt the lustful rage of Captain Wow as the big Persian tomcat detonated lights while he approached the streak of dust which threatened the ship and the people within.

The lights scored near-misses.

The dust flattened itself, changing from the shape of a stingray into the shape of a spear.

Not three milliseconds had elapsed.

Father Moontree was talking human words and was saying in a voice that moved like cold molasses out of a heavy jar, "C-A-P-T-A-I-N." Underhill knew that the sentence was going to be "Captain, move fast!"

The battle would be fought and finished before Father Moontree got through talking.

Now, fractions of a millisecond later, the Lady May was directly in line.

Here was where the skill and speed of the Partners came in. She could react faster than he. She could see the threat as an immense Rat coming directly at her.

She could fire the light-bombs with a discrimination which he might miss.

He was connected with her mind, but he could not follow it.

His consciousness absorbed the tearing wound inflicted by the alien enemy. It was like no wound on Earth—raw, crazy pain which started like a burn at his navel. He began to writhe in his chair.

Actually he had not yet had time to move a muscle when the Lady May struck back at their enemy.

Five evenly spaced photonuclear bombs blazed out across a hundred thousand miles.

The pain in his mind and body vanished.

He felt a moment of fierce, terrible, feral elation running through the mind of the Lady May as she finished her kill. It was always disappointing to the cats to find out that their enemies, whom they sensed as gigantic space Rats, disappeared at the moment of destruction.

Then he felt her hurt, the pain and the fear that swept over both of them as the battle, quicker than the movement of an eyelid, had come and gone. In the same instant, there came the sharp and acid twinge of planoform.

Once more the ship went skip.

He could hear Woodley thinking at him, "You don't have to bother much. This old son-of-a-gun and I will take over for a while."

Twice again the twinge, the skip.

He had no idea where he was until the lights of the Caledonia space board shone below.

With a weariness that lay almost beyond the limits of thought, he threw his mind back into rapport with the pin-set, fixing the Lady May's projectile gently and neatly in its launching tube.

She was half dead with fatigue, but he could feel the beat of her heart, could listen to her panting, and he grasped the grateful edge of a thanks reaching from her mind to his.

THE SCORE

They put him in the hospital at Caledonia.

The doctor was friendly but firm. "You actually got touched by that Dragon. That's as close a shave as I've ever seen. It's all so quick that it'll be a long time before we know what happened scientifically, but I suppose you'd be ready for the insane asylum now if the contact had lasted several tenths of a millisecond longer. What kind of cat did you have out in front of you?"

Underhill felt the words coming out of him slowly. Words were such a lot of trouble compared with the speed and the joy of thinking, fast and sharp and clear, mind to mind! But words were all that could reach ordinary people like this doctor.

His mouth moved heavily as he articulated words, "Don't call our Partners cats. The right thing to call them is Partners. They fight for us in a team. You ought to know we call them Partners, not cats. How is mine?"

"I don't know," said the doctor contritely. "We'll find out for you. Meanwhile, old man, you take it easy. There's nothing but rest that can help you. Can you make yourself sleep, or would you like us to give you some kind of sedative?"

"I can sleep," said Underhill. "I just want to know about the Lady May."

The nurse joined in. She was a little antagonistic. "Don't you want to know about the other people?"

"They're okay," said Underhill. "I knew that before I came in here."

He stretched his arms and sighed and grinned at them. He could see they were relaxing and were beginning to treat him as a person instead of a patient.

"I'm all right," he said. "Just let me know when I can go see my Partner."

A new thought struck him. He looked wildly at the doctor. "They didn't send her off with the ship, did they?"

"I'll find out right away," said the doctor. He gave Underhill a reassuring squeeze of the shoulder and left the room.

The nurse took a napkin off a goblet of chilled fruit juice.

UNDERHILL TRIED TO smile at her. There seemed to be something wrong with the girl. He wished she would go away. First she had started to be friendly and now she was distant again. It's a nuisance being tele-pathic, he thought. You keep trying to reach even when you are not mak-ing contact.

Suddenly she swung around on him.

"You pinlighters! You and your damn cats!"

Just as she stamped out, he burst into her mind. He saw himself a radiant hero, clad in his smooth suede uniform, the pin-set crown shin-ing like ancient royal jewels around his head. He saw his own face, hand-some and masculine, shining out of her mind. He saw himself very far away and he saw himself as she hated him.

She hated him in the secrecy of her own mind. She hated him be-cause he was—she thought—proud, and strange, and rich, better and more beautiful than people like her.

He cut off the sight of her mind and, as he buried his face in the pil-low, he caught an image of the Lady May.

"She *is* a cat," he thought. "That's *all* she is—a *cat!*"

But that was not how his mind saw her—quick beyond all dreams of speed, sharp, clever, unbelievably graceful, beautiful, wordless, and undemanding.

Where would he ever find a woman who could compare with her?

George R. R. Martin

George R. R. Martin's varied output is divided between horror, fantasy, and science fiction and has earned him multiple Hugo and Nebula Awards as well as a Bram Stoker Award from the Horror Writers Association. His science fiction novels include Dying of the Light and, with Lisa Tuttle, Windhaven. Martin has written some of the best novella-length science fiction in the past two decades, including the award-winning "Sandkings," and "Nightflyers," which was adapted for the screen in 1987. Much of his best writing is collected in A Song for Lya, Songs of Stars and Shadows, Sandkings, Songs the Dead Men Sing, Tuf Voyaging, and Portraits of His Children. His horror novels include the period vampire masterpiece Fevre Dream and The Armageddon Rag, an evocative glimpse at the dark side of the sixties counterculture considered one of the top rock 'n' roll novels of all time. A Game of Thrones and A Clash of Kings are the first two novels in his epic Song of Ice and Fire series. Martin has written for a number of television series, including the new Twilight Zone series, and edited fifteen volumes of the Wild Cards series of shared-world anthologies.

NIGHT OF THE VAMPYRES

George R. R. Martin

THE ANNOUNCEMENT CAME during prime time.

All four major holo networks went off simultaneously, along with most of the independents. There was an instant of crackling grayness. And then a voice, which said, simply, "Ladies and gentlemen, the President of the United States."

John Hartmann was the youngest man ever to hold the office of President, and the commentators were fond of saying that he was the most telegenic as well. His clean-cut good looks, ready wit, and flashing grin had given the Liberty Alliance its narrow plurality in the bitter four-way elections of 1984. His political acumen had engineered the Electoral College coalition with the Old Republicans that had put him in the White House.

Hartmann was not grinning now. His features were hard, somber. He was sitting behind his desk in the Oval Office, looking down at the papers he held in his hands. After a moment of silence, he raised his head slowly, and his dark eyes looked straight out into the living rooms of a nation.

"My fellow countrymen," he said gravely, "tonight our nation faces the most serious crisis in its long and great history. Approximately one hour ago, an American air force base in California was hit by a violent and vicious attack . . ."

THE FIRST CASUALTY was a careless sentry. The attacker was quick, silent, and very efficient. He used a knife. The sentry died without a whimper, never knowing what was happening.

The other attackers were moving in even before the corpse hit the ground. Circuits were hooked up to bypass the alarm system, and torches went to work on the high electric fence. It fell. From the darkness, more invaders materialized to move through the fresh gap.

But somewhere one alarm system was still alive. Sirens began to howl. The sleepy airbase came to sudden, startled life. Stealth now useless, the attackers began to run. Towards the airfields.

Somebody began to fire. Someone else screamed. Outside the main gate, the guards looked in, baffled, towards the base. A stream of submachine gun fire took them where they stood, hammering them to bloody death against their own fence. A grenade arced through the air, and the gate shattered under the explosion.

"THE ATTACK WAS sudden, well-planned, and utterly ruthless," Hartmann told the nation. "The defense, under the circumstances, was heroic. Nearly one hundred American servicemen died during the course of the action."

THE POWER LINES were cut only seconds after the attack got under way. A well-placed grenade took out the emergency generator. Then darkness. It was a moonless night, and the clouds obscured the stars. The only light was the flash of machine gun fire and the brief, shattering brilliance of the explosions around the main gate.

There was little rhyme and less reason to the defense. Startled by the sirens, troops scrambled from the barracks and towards the gate, where the conflict seemed to be centered. On either side of the fence, attackers and defenders hit the ground. A searing crossfire was set up.

The base commandant was as startled and confused as any of his men. Long, valuable minutes passed while he and his staff groped for the facts, and tried to understand what was happening. Their response was almost instinctive. A ring of defenders was thrown around the Command Tower, a second around the base armory. Other men were sent sprinting towards the planes.

But the bulk of the troops were rushed to the main gate, where the battle was at its fiercest.

The defenders brought up heavy weapons from the base armory. The shrubbery outside the base perimeter was blasted by mortars, blown apart by grenades. The attackers' hidden position was systematically pounded. Then, behind a wall of smoke and tear-gas, the defenders poured out of the gate, washed over the enemy positions.

They found them empty, but for corpses. The attackers had melted away as suddenly as they had come.

An order for search and pursuit was swiftly given. And just as swiftly rescinded. For over the machine gun fire and the explosions, another sound could now be heard.

The sound of a jet taking off.

"THE ATTACKERS CONCENTRATED most of their forces against the main entrance of the air base," Hartmann said. "But for all its fierceness, this assault was simply a diversion. While it was in progress, a smaller force of attackers penetrated another part of the base perimeter, beat off light resistance, and seized a small portion of the airfields."

The President's face was taut with emotion. "The goal of the attack was a squadron of long-range bombers, and their fighter escorts. As part of our first line of defense to deter Communist aggression, the bombers were on stand-by status; fueled and ready to take off in seconds, in the event of an enemy attack."

Hartmann paused dramatically, looked down at his papers, then back up. "Our men reacted swiftly and valiantly. They deserve only our praise. They retook several planes from the attackers, and burned down several others during takeoff.

"Despite this courageous resistance, however, the attackers put seven fighters and two bombers into the air. My fellow countrymen, both of those bombers were equipped with nuclear weaponry."

Again Hartmann paused. Behind him, the Oval Office background dissolved. Suddenly there was only the President, and his desk, outlined against a blank wall of white. On that wall, six familiar sentences suddenly appeared.

"Even while the attack was in progress, an ultimatum was sent to me in Washington," Hartmann said. "Unless certain demands were met within a three-hour deadline, I was told, a hydrogen bomb would be dropped on the city of Washington, D.C. You see those demands before you." He gestured.

"Most of you have seen them before. Some call them the Six Demands," he continued. "I'm sure you know them as well as I. They call for an end to American aid to our struggling allies in Africa and the Mid-East, for the systematic destruction of our defensive capacities, for an end to the Special Urban Units that have restored law and order to our cities, for the release of thousands of dangerous criminals, for the repeal of federal restrictions on obscene and subversive literature, and, of course"—he flashed his famous grin—"for my resignation as President of the United States."

The grin faded. "These demands are a formula for national suicide, a recipe for surrender and disgrace. They would return us to the lawlessness and anarchy of a permissive society that we have left behind. Moreover, they are opposed by the great majority of the American people.

"However, as you know, these demands are vocally advocated by a small and dangerous minority. They represent the political program of the so-called American Liberation Front."

The background behind Hartmann changed again. The blowup of the Six Demands vanished. Now the President sat before a huge photograph of a bearded, long-haired young man in a black beret and baggy black uniform. The man was quite dead; most of his chest had been blown away.

"Behind me you see a photograph of one of the casualties of tonight's attack," Hartmann said. "Like all the other attackers we found, he wears the uniform of the paramilitary wing of the A.L.F."

The photo vanished. Hartmann looked grim. "The facts are clear. But this time the A.L.F. has gone too far. I will not submit to nuclear blackmail. Nor, my fellow countrymen, is there cause for alarm. To my fellow citizens of Washington I say especially, fear not. I promise that the A.L.F. pirate planes will be tracked down and destroyed long before they reach their target.

"Meanwhile, the leaders of the A.L.F. are about to learn that they erred in attempting to intimidate this administration. For too long they have divided and weakened us, and given aid and comfort to those who would like to see this nation enslaved. They shall do so no longer.

"There can be only one word for tonight's attack. That word is treason.

"Accordingly, I will deal with the attackers like traitors."

*   *   *

"I've got them," McKinnis said, his voice crackling with static. "Or something."

Reynolds didn't really need the information. He had them too. He glanced briefly down at the radarmap. They were on the edge of the scope, several miles ahead, heading due east at about 90,000 feet. High, and moving fast.

Another crackle, then Bonetto, the flight leader. "Looks like them, alright. I've got nine. Let's go get 'em."

His plane nosed up and began to climb. The others followed, behind and abreast of him in a wide V formation. Nine LF-7 Vampyre fighter/interceptors. Red, white, and blue flags on burnished black metal, silvery teeth slung underneath.

A hunting pack closing for the kill.

Yet another voice came over the open channel. "Hey, whattaya figure the odds? All over they're looking. Betcha it gets us promotions. Lucky us."

That had to be Dutton, Reynolds thought. A brash kid, hungry. Maybe *he* felt lucky. Reynolds didn't. Inside the acceleration suit he was sweating suddenly, coldly.

The odds had been all against it. The kid was right about that. The Alfie bombers were LB-4s, laser-armed monsters with speed to spare. They could've taken any route of a dozen, and still make it to Washington on time. And every damn plane and radar installation in the country was looking for them.

So what were the odds against them running into Reynolds and his flight out over northern Nebraska on a wild goose chase?

Too damn good, as it turned out.

"They see us," Bonetto said. "They're climbing. And accelerating. Move it."

Reynolds moved it. His Vampyre was the last in one arm of the V, and it held its formation. Behind the oxygen mask, his eyes roamed restlessly, and watched the instruments. Mach 1.3. Then 1.4. Then higher.

They were gaining. Climbing and gaining.

The radarmap showed the Alfie positions. And there was a blur up ahead on the infrared scope. But through the narrow eyeslit, nothing. Just cold black sky and stars. They were above the clouds.

The dumb bastards, Reynolds thought. They steal the most sophisticated hunk of metal ever built, and they don't know how to use it. They weren't even using their radar scramblers. It was almost like they were asking to be shot down.

Cracklings. "They're leveling off." Bonetto again. "Hold your missiles

till my order. And remember, those big babies can give you a nasty
hotfoot."

Reynolds looked at the radarmap again. The Alfies were now flat out
at about 100,000 feet. Figured. The LB-4s could go higher, but ten was
about the upper limit for the fighter escorts. Rapiers. Reynolds remembered his briefing.

They wanted to stick together. That made sense. The Alfies would
need their Rapiers. Ten *wasn't* the upper limit for Vampyres.

Reynolds squinted. He thought he saw something ahead, through the
eyeslit. A flash of silver. Them? Or his imagination? Hard to tell. But
he'd see them soon enough. The pursuit planes were gaining. Fast as
they were, the big LB-4s were no match for the Vampyres. The Rapiers
were; but they had to stay with the bombers.

So it was only a matter of time. They'd catch them long before Washington. And then?

Reynolds shifted uneasily. He didn't want to think about that. He'd
never flown in combat before. He didn't like the idea.

His mouth was dry. He swallowed. Just this morning he and Anne had
talked about how lucky he was, made plans for a vacation. And beyond.
His term was almost up, and he was still safe in the States. So many
friends dead in the South African War. But he'd been lucky.

And now this. And suddenly the possibility that tomorrow might not
be bright. The possibility that tomorrow might not be. It scared him.

There was more, too. Even if he lived, he was still queasy. About the
killing.

That shouldn't have bothered him. He knew it might happen when
he enlisted. But it was different then. He thought he'd be flying against
Russians, Chinese—enemies. The outbreak of the South African War
and the U.S. intervention had disturbed him. But he could have fought
there, for all that. The Pan-African Alliance was Communist-inspired, or
so they said.

But Alfies weren't distant foreigners. Alfies were people, neighbors.
His radical college roommate. The black kids he had grown up with
back in New York. The teacher who lived down the block. He got along
with Alfies well enough, when they weren't talking politics.

And sometimes even when they were. The Six Demands weren't all
that bad. He'd heard a lot of nasty rumors about the Special Urban
Units. And God knows what the U.S. was doing in South Africa and the
Mid-East.

He grimaced behind the oxygen mask. Face it, Reynolds, he told himself. The skeleton in his closet. He had actually thought about voting
A.L.F. in '84, although in the end he'd chickened out and pulled the
lever for Bishop, the Old Democrat. No one on the base knew but Anne.
They hadn't argued politics for a long time, with anyone. Most of his
friends were Old Republicans, but a few had turned to the Liberty Alliance. And that scared him.

Bonetto's crackling command smashed his train of thought. "Look at
that, men. The Alfies are going to fight. At 'em!"

Reynolds didn't need to look at his radarmap. He could see them
now, above. Lights against the sky. Growing lights.

The Rapiers were diving on them.

OF ALL THE commentators who followed President Hartmann over the
holo networks, Continental's Ted Warren seemed the least shell-
shocked. Warren was a gritty old veteran with an incisive mind and razor
tongue. He had tangled with Hartmann more than once, and was regularly denounced by the Liberty Alliance for his "Alfie bias."

"The President's speech leaves many questions still unanswered,"
Warren said in his post-mortem newscast. "He has promised to deal with
the A.L.F. as traitors, but as yet, we are unsure exactly what steps will be
taken. There is also some question, in my mind at any rate, as to the
A.L.F.'s motivation for this alleged attack. Bob, any thoughts on that?"

A new face on camera; the reporter who covered A.L.F. activities for
Continental had been hustled out of bed and rushed to the studio. He
still looked a little rumpled.

"No, Ted," he replied. "As far as I know, the A.L.F. was not planning
any action of this kind. Were it not for the fact that this attack was so
well-planned, I might question whether the A.L.F. national leadership
was involved at all. It might have been an unauthorized action by a
group of local extremists. You'll recall that the assault on the Chicago
Police Headquarters during the 1985 riots was of this nature. However, I
think the planning that went into this attack, and the armament that was
used, precludes this being a similar case."

Warren, at the Continental anchordesk, nodded sagely. "Bob, do you
think there is any possibility that the paramilitary arm of the A.L.F.
might have acted unilaterally, without the knowledge of the party's political leaders?"

The reporter paused and looked thoughtful. "Well, it's possible, Ted. But not likely. The kind of assault that the President described would require too much planning. I'd think that the whole party would have to be involved in an effort on that scale."

"What reasons would the A.L.F. have for an action like this?" Warren asked.

"From what the President said, a hope that a nuclear threat would bring immediate agreement to the A.L.F.'s Six Demands would seem to be the reason."

Warren was insistent. "Yes. But why should the A.L.F. resort to such an extreme tactic? The latest Gallup poll gave them the support of nearly 29% of the electorate, behind only the 38% of President Hartmann's Liberty Alliance. This is a sharp increase from the 13% of the vote the A.L.F. got in the presidential elections of 1984. With only a year to go before the new elections, it seems strange that the A.L.F. would risk everything on such a desperate ploy."

Now the reporter was nodding. "You have a point, Ted. However, we've been surprised by the A.L.F. before. They've never been the easiest party to predict, and I think—"

Warren cut him off. "Excuse me, Bob. Back to you later. Correspondent Mike Petersen is at the A.L.F.'s national headquarters in Washington, and he has Douglass Brown with him. Mike, can you hear me?"

The picture changed. Two men standing before a desk, one half slouched against it. Behind them, on the wall, the A.L.F. symbol; a clenched black fist superimposed over the peace sign. The reporter held a microphone. The man he was with was tall, black, youthful. And angry.

"Yes, Ted, we've got you," the reporter said. He turned to the black man. "Doug, you were the A.L.F. presidential candidate in 1984. How do you react to President Hartmann's charges?"

Brown laughed lightly. "Nothing that man does surprises me anymore. The charges are vicious lies. The American Liberation Front had nothing to do with this so-called attack. In fact, I doubt that this attack ever took place. Hartmann is a dangerous demagogue, and he's tried this sort of smear before."

"Then the A.L.F. claims that no attack took place?" Petersen asked.

Brown frowned. "Well, that's just a quick guess on my part, not an official A.L.F. position," he said quickly. "This has all been very sudden, and I don't really have the facts. But I'd say that was a possibility. As you know, Mike, the Liberty Alliance has made wild charges against us before."

"In his statement tonight, President Hartmann said he would deal with the A.L.F. as traitors. Would you care to comment on that?"

"Yeah," said Brown. "It's more cheap rhetoric. I say that Hartmann's the traitor. He's the one that has betrayed everything this country is supposed to stand for. *His* creation of the Special Suuies to keep the ghettoes in line, *his* intervention in the South African War, *his* censorship legislation; there's your treason for you."

The reporter smiled. "Thank you, Doug. And now back to Ted Warren."

Warren reappeared. "For those of you who have flicked on late, a brief recap. Earlier this evening, an American air base in California was attacked, and two bombers and seven fighter planes were seized. The bombers were equipped with nuclear weaponry, and the attackers have threatened to destroy Washington, D.C., unless certain demands are met within three hours. Only an hour-and-a-half now remain. Continental News will stay on the air until the conclusion of the crisis . . ."

* * *

SOMEWHERE OVER WESTERN ILLINOIS, Reynolds climbed towards ten, and sweated, and tried to tell himself that the advantages were all his.

The Rapiers were good planes. Nothing with wings was any faster, or more maneuverable. But the Vampyres had all the other plusses. Their missiles were more sophisticated, their defensive scramblers better. And they had their Vampyre fangs: twin gas-dynamic lasers mounted on either wing that could slice through steel like it was jello. The Rapiers had nothing to match that. The Vampyres were the first operational Laser/ Fighters.

Besides, there were nine Vampyres and only seven Rapiers. And the Alfies weren't as familiar with their planes. They couldn't be.

So the odds were all with Reynolds. But he still sweated.

The arms of the V formation slowly straightened, as Reynolds and the other wingmen accelerated to come even with Bonetto's lead jet. In the radarmap, the Rapiers were already on top of them. And even through the eyeslit he could see them now, diving out of the black, their silver-white sides bright against the sky. The computer tracking system was locked in, the warheads armed. But still no signal from Bonetto.

And then, "Now." Sharp and clear.

Reynolds hit the firing stud, and missiles one and eight shot from beneath the wings, and etched a trail of flame up into the night. Parallel to his, others. Dutton, on his wing, had fired four. Eager for the kill.

Red/orange against black through the eyeslit. Black on red in the infrared scope. But all the same, really. The climbing streaks of flame that were the Vampyre missiles intersecting with a descending set. Crisscrossing briefly.

Then explosion. The Alfies had rigged one of theirs for timed detonation. A small orange fireball bloomed briefly. When it vanished, both sets of missiles were gone, save for one battered survivor from the Vampyre barrage that wobbled upward without hitting anything.

Reynolds glanced down. The radarmap was having an epileptic fit. The Alfies were using their scramblers.

"Split," said Bonetto, voice crackling. "Scatter and hit them."

The Vampyres broke formation. Reynolds and Dutton pulled up and to the left, McKinnis dove. Bonetto and most of his wing swung away to the right. And Trainor climbed straight on, at the diving Rapiers.

Reynolds watched him from the corner of his eye. Two more missiles jumped from Trainor's wings, then two more, then the final two. And briefly, the laser seared a path up from his wingtips. A futile gesture; he was still out of range.

The Rapiers were sleek silver birds of prey, spitting missiles. And suddenly, another fireball, and one of them stopped spitting.

But no time for cheering. Even as the Rapier went up, Trainor's Vampyre tried to swerve from the hail of Alfie missiles. His radar scrambler and heat decoys had confused them. But not enough. Reynolds was facing away from the explosion, but he felt the impact of the shock, and he could see the nightblack plane twisting and shattering in his mind.

Reynolds felt a vague pang, and tried to remember what Trainor had looked like. But there was no time. He twisted the Vampyre around in a sharp loop. Dutton flew parallel. They dove back towards the fight.

Far below a new cloud of flame blossomed. McKinnis, Reynolds thought, fleetingly, bitterly. He dove. The Alfies got on his tail. The goddamn Alfies.

But there was no way to be sure, no leisure to consider the question. Even a brief glance out the eyeslit was a luxury; a dangerous luxury. The infrared scope, the radarmap, the computer tracking systems all screamed for his attention.

Below him, two Alfies were swinging around. The computer locked on. His fingers moved as if by instinct. Missiles two and seven leapt from their launchers, towards the Rapiers.

A scream sounded briefly from his radio, mingled with the static and the sudden shrill cry of the proximity alarms. Something had locked on him. He activated the lasers. The computer found the incoming missile, tracked it, burned it from the sky when it got within range. Reynolds had never even seen it. He wondered how close it had come.

A flood of bright orange light washed through the eyeslit as a Rapier went up in flame in front of him. His missile? Dutton's? He never knew. It was all he could do to pull the Vampyre up sharply, and avoid the expanding ball of fire.

There were a few seconds of peace. He was above the fight, and he took time for a quick glance at the infrared. A tangle of confused black dots on a red field. But two were higher than the rest. Dutton; with an Alfie on his tail.

Reynolds swung his Vampyre down again, came in above and behind the Rapier just as it was discharging its missiles. He was close. No need to waste the four missiles he had left. His hand went to the lasers, fired.

Converging beams of light lanced from the black wingtips, to bite into the Rapier's silver fuselage on either side of the cockpit. The Alfie pilot dove for escape. But the Vampyre minicomputer held the lasers steady.

The Rapier exploded.

Almost simultaneously there was another explosion; the Alfie missiles, touched off by Dutton's lasers. Reynolds' radio came alive with Dutton's laughter, and breathless thanks.

But Reynolds was paying more attention to the infrared and the radarmap. The radar was clear again.

Only three blips showed below him.

It was over.

Bonetto's voice split the cabin again. "Got him," he was yelling. "Got them all. Who's left up there?"

Dutton replied quickly. Then Reynolds. The fourth surviving Vampyre was Ranczyk, Bonetto's wingman. The others were gone.

There was a new pang, sharper than during the battle. It had been McKinnis after all, Reynolds thought. He'd known McKinnis. Tall, with red hair, a lousy poker player who surrendered his money gracefully when he lost. He always did. His wife made good chili. They'd voted Old Democrat, like Reynolds. Damn, damn, damn.

"We're only halfway there," Bonetto was saying. "The LB-4s are still ahead. Picked up some distance. So let's go."

Four Vampyres weren't nearly as impressive in formation as nine. But they climbed. And gave chase.

TED WARREN LOOKED tired. He had taken off his jacket and loosened the formal black scarf knotted around his neck, and his hair was mussed. But still he went on.

"Reports have been coming in from all over the nation on the sighting of the pirate planes," he said. "Most of them are clearly misidentifications, but no word has yet come from the administration on the hunt for the stolen jets, so the rumors continue to flow unabated. Meanwhile, barely an hour remains before the threatened nuclear demolition of Washington."

Behind him a screen woke to sudden churning life. Pennsylvania Avenue, with the Capitol outlined in the distance, was choked with cars and people. "Washington itself is in a state of panic," Warren commented. "The populace of the city has taken to the streets en masse in an effort to escape, but the resulting traffic jams have effectively strangled all major arteries. Many have abandoned their cars and are trying to leave the city on foot. Helicopters of the Special Urban Units have been attempting to quell the disturbances, ordering the citizens to return to their homes. And President Hartmann himself has announced that he intends to set an example for the people of the city, and remain in the White House for the duration of the crisis."

The Washington scenes faded. Warren looked off-camera briefly. "I've just been told that Chicago correspondent Ward Emery is standing by with Mitchell Grinstein, the chairman of the A.L.F.'s Community Defense Militia. So now to Chicago."

Grinstein was standing outdoors, on the steps of a gray, fortress-like building. He was tall and broad, with long black hair worn in a pony tail and a drooping Fu Manchu mustache. His clothes were a baggy black uniform, a black beret, and an A.L.F. medallion on a length of rawhide. Two other men, similarly garbed, lounged behind him on the steps. Both carried rifles.

"I'm here with Mitchell Grinstein, whose organization has been accused of participating in this evening's attack on a California air base, and the hijacking of two nuclear bombers," Emery said. "Mitch, your reactions?"

Grinstein flashed a vaguely sinister smile. "Well, I only know what I see on the holo. I didn't order any attack. But I applaud whoever did. If this speeds up the implementation of the Six Demands, I'm all for it."

"Douglass Brown has called the charges of A.L.F. participation in this attack 'vicious lies,' " Emery continued. "He questions whether any attack ever took place. How does this square with what you just said?"

Grinstein shrugged. "Maybe Brown knows more than I do. We didn't order this attack, like I said. But it could be that some of our men finally got fed up with Hartmann's fourth-rate fascism, and decided to take things into their own hands. If so, we're behind them."

"Then you think there *was* an attack?"

"I guess so. Hartmann had pictures. Even he wouldn't have the gall to fake *that*."

"And you support the attack?"

"Yeah. The Community Defenders have been saying for a long time that black people and poor people aren't going to get justice anywhere but in the streets. This is a vindication of what we've been calling for all along."

"And what about the position of the A.L.F.'s political arm?"

Another shrug. "Doug Brown and I agree on where we're going. We don't see eye to eye on how to get there."

"But isn't the Community Defense Militia subordinate to the A.L.F. political apparatus, and thus to Brown?"

"On paper. It's different in the streets. Are the Liberty Troopers subordinate to President Hartmann when they go out on freak-hunts and black-busting expeditions? They don't act like it. The Community Defenders are committed to the protection of the community. From thugs, Liberty Troopers, and Hartmann's Special Suuies. And anyone else who comes along. We're also committed to getting the Six Demands. And maybe we'd go a bit further to realize those demands than Doug and his men."

"One last question," said Emery. "President Hartmann, in his speech tonight, said that he intended to treat the A.L.F. like traitors."

"Let him try," Grinstein said, smiling. "Just let him try."

*   *   *

THE ALFIE BOMBERS had edged onto the radarmap again. They were still at 100,000 feet, doing about Mach 1.7. The Vampyre pack would be on them in minutes.

Reynolds watched for LB-4s, almost numbly, through his eyeslit. He was cold and drenched with his own sweat. And very scared.

The lull between battles was worse than the battles themselves, he had decided. It gave you too much time to think. And thinking was bad.

He was sad and a little sick about McKinnis. But grateful. Grateful that it hadn't been him. Then he realized that it still might be. The night wasn't over. The LB-4s were no pushovers.

And all so needless. The Alfies were vicious fools. There were other ways, better ways. They didn't have to do this. Whatever sympathy he had ever felt for the A.L.F. had gone down in flames with McKinnis and Trainor and the others.

They deserved whatever they had coming to them. And Hartmann, he was sure, had something in mind. So many innocent people dead. And for nothing. For a grandstand, desperado stunt without a prayer of success.

That was the worst part. The plan was so ill-conceived, so hopeless. The A.L.F. couldn't possibly win. They could shoot him down, sure. Like McKinnis. But there were other planes. They'd be found and taken out by someone. And if they got as far as Washington, there was still the city's ring of defensive missiles to deal with. Hartmann had had trouble forcing that through Congress. But it would come in handy now.

And even if the A.L.F. got there, so what? Did they really think Hartmann would give in? No way. Not him. He'd call their bluff, and either way they lost. If they backed down, they were finished. And if they dropped the bomb, they'd get Hartmann—but at the expense of millions of their own supporters. Washington was nearly all black. Hell, it gave the A.L.F. a big plurality in '84. What was the figure? Something like 65%, he thought. Around there, anyway.

It didn't make sense. It couldn't be. But it was.

There was a knot in his stomach. Churning and twisting. Through the eyeslit, he saw flickers of motion against the star field. The Alfies. The goddamn Alfies. His mind turned briefly to Anne. And suddenly he hated the planes ahead of him, and the men who flew them.

"Hold your missiles till my order," Bonetto said. "And watch it."

The Vampyres accelerated. But the Alfies acted before the attack.

"Hey, look!" That was Dutton.

"They're splitting." A bass growl distorted by static; Ranczyk.

Reynolds looked at his radarmap. One of the LB-4s was diving sharply, picking up speed, heading for the sea of clouds that rolled below in the starlight. The other was going into a shallow climb.

"Stay together!" Bonetto again. "They want us to break up. But we're faster. We'll take out one and catch the other."

They climbed. Together at first, side by side. But then one of the sleek planes began to edge ahead.

"Dutton!" Bonetto's voice was a warning.

"I want him." Dutton's Vampyre screamed upward, into range of the bandit ahead. From his wings, twin missiles roared, closed.

And suddenly were not. The bomber's lasers burned them clean from the sky.

Bonetto tried to shout another order. But it was too late. Dutton was paying no attention. He was already shrieking to his kill.

This time Reynolds saw it all.

Dutton was way out ahead of the others, still accelerating, trying to close within laser range. He was out of missiles.

But the Alfie laser had a longer range. It locked on him first.

The Vampyre seemed to writhe. Dutton went into a sharp dive, pulled up equally sharply, threw his plane from side to side. Trying to shake free of the laser. Before it killed. But the tracking computers in the LB-4s were faster than he could ever hope to be. The laser held steady.

And then Dutton stopped fighting. Briefly, his Vampyre closed again, climbing right up into the spear of light, its own lasers flashing out and converging. Uselessly; he was still too far away. And only for an instant.

Before the scream.

Dutton's Vampyre never even exploded. It just seemed to go limp. Its laser died suddenly. And then it was in a spin. Flames licking at the black fuselage, burning a hole in the black velvet of night.

Reynolds didn't watch the fall. Bonetto's voice had snapped him from his nightmare trance. "Fire!"

He let go on three and six, and they shrieked away from him towards the Alfie. Bonetto and Ranczyk had also fired. Six missiles rose together. Two more slightly behind them. Ranczyk had let loose with a second volley.

"At him!" Bonetto shouted. "Lasers!"

Then his plane was moving away quickly, Ranczyk with him. Black shadows against a black sky, following their missiles and obscuring the stars. Reynolds hung back briefly, still scared, still hearing Dutton's scream and seeing the fireball that was McKinnis. Then, shamed, he followed.

The bomber had unleashed its own missiles, and its lasers were locked onto the oncoming threats. There was an explosion; several missiles wiped from the air. Others burned down.

But there were two Vampyres moving in behind the missiles. And then a third behind them. Bonetto and Ranczyk had their lasers locked on the Alfie, burning at him, growing hotter and more vicious as they climbed. Briefly, the bomber's big laser flicked down in reply. One of the Vampyres went up in a cloud of flame, a cloud that still screamed upwards at the Alfie.

Almost simultaneously, another roar. A fireball under the wing of the bomber rocked it. Its laser winked off. Power trouble? Then on again, burning at the hail of missiles. Reynolds flicked on his laser, and watched it lance out towards the chaos above. The other Vampyre — Reynolds wasn't sure which — was firing its remaining missiles.

They were almost on top of each other. In the radarmap and the infrared they were. Only in the eyeslit was there still space between the two.

And then they were together. Joining. One big ball, orange and red and yellow, swallowing both Vampyre and prey, growing, growing, growing.

Reynolds sat almost frozen, climbing towards the swelling inferno, his laser firing ineffectively into the flames. Then he came out of it. And swerved. And dove. His laser fired once more, to wipe out a chunk of flaming debris that came spinning towards him.

He was alone. The fire fell and faded, and there was only one Vampyre, and the stars, and the blanket of cloud far below him. He had survived.

But how? He had hung back. When he should have attacked. He didn't deserve survival. The others had earned it, with their courage. But he had hung back. He felt sick.

But he could still redeem himself. Yes. Down below, there was still one Alfie in the air. Headed towards Washington with its bombs. And only he was left to stop it.

Reynolds nosed the Vampyre into a dive, and began his grim descent.

AFTER A BRIEF station identification, Warren was back. With two guests and a new wrinkle. The wrinkle was the image of a large clock that silently counted down the time remaining while the newsmen talked. The guests were a retired Air Force general and a well-known political columnist.

Warren introduced them, then turned to the general. "Tonight's attack, understandably, has frightened a lot of people," he began. "Especially those in Washington. How likely is it that the threatened bombing will take place?"

The general snorted. "Impossible, Ted. I know what kind of air defense systems we've got in this country. They were designed to handle a full-fledged attack, from another nuclear power. They can certainly handle a cheap-shot move like this."

"Then you'd say that Washington is in no danger?"

"Correct. Absolutely none. This plan was militarily hopeless from its conception. I'm shocked that even the A.L.F. would resort to such a foredoomed venture."

Warren nodded, and swiveled to face the columnist. "How about from a political point of view? You've been a regular observer of President Hartmann and the Washington scene for many years, Sid. In your opinion, did this maneuver have any chances of practical political success?"

"It's still very early," the columnist cautioned. "But from where I sit, I'd say the A.L.F. has committed a major blunder. This attack is a political disaster—or at least it looks like one, in these early hours. Because of Washington's large black population, I'd guess that this threat to the city will seriously undermine the A.L.F.'s support among the black community. If so, it would be a catastrophe for the party. In 1984, Douglass Brown drew more black votes than the other three candidates combined. Without these votes, the A.L.F. presidential campaign would have been a farce."

"How will this affect other A.L.F. supporters?" Warren asked.

"That's a key question. I'd say it would tend to drive them away from the party. Since its inception, the A.L.F. has always had a large pacifist element, which frequently clashed with the more militant Alfies who made up the Community Defense Militia. I think that tonight's events might be the final blow for these people."

"Who do you think would benefit from these desertions?"

The columnist shrugged. "Hard to say. There's the possibility of a new splinter party being formed. And President Hartmann, I'm sure, will enjoy a large swing of support his way. The most likely possibility would be a revival of the Old Democratic Party, if it can regain the black voters and white radicals it has lost to the A.L.F. in recent years."

"Thank you," said Warren. He turned back to the camera, then glanced down briefly at the desk in front of him, checking the latest bulletins. "We'll have more analysis later," he said. "Right now, Continental's man in California is at Collins Air Base, where tonight's attack took place."

Warren faded. The new reporter was tall and thin and young. He was standing before the main gate of the air base. Behind him was a bustling tangle of activity, several jeeps, and large numbers of police and soldiers. The spotlights were on again, and the destruction was clearly evident in the battered gatehouse and the twisted, shattered wire of the fence itself.

"Deke Hamilton here," the man began. "Ted, Continental came out here to check whether any attack did take place, since the A.L.F. has charged that the President was lying. Well, from what I've seen out here, it's the A.L.F. that's been lying. There *was* an attack, and it was a vicious one. You can see some of the damage behind you. This is where the attackers struck hardest."

Warren's voice cut in. "Have you seen any bodies?"

The reporter nodded. "Yes. Many of them. Some have been horribly mangled by the fighting. More than one hundred men from the base, I'd estimate. And about fifty Alfies."

"Have any of the attackers been identified?" Warren asked.

"Well, they're clearly Alfies," the reporter said. "Beards, long hair, A.L.F. uniforms. And many had literature in their pockets. Pamphlets advocating the Six Demands, that sort of thing. However, as of yet, no specific identifications have been announced. Except for the air men, of course. The base has released its own casualty lists. But not for the Alfies. As I said, many bodies are badly damaged, so identification may be difficult. I think some sort of mass burial is being planned."

"Deke," said Warren, "has there been any racial breakdown on the casualties?"

"Uh—none has been released. The bodies I saw were all white. But then, the black population in this area is relatively small."

Warren started to ask another question. He never finished his sentence. Without warning, the picture from California suddenly vanished, and was replaced by chaos.

"This is Mike Petersen in Washington," the reporter said. He was awash in a sea of struggling humanity, being pushed this way and that. All around him fights were in progress, as a squad of Special Urban Police, in blue and silver, waded through a crowd of resisting Alfies. The A.L.F. symbol was on the wall behind Petersen.

"I'm at A.L.F. national headquarters," he said, trying valiantly to stay before the cameras. "I—" He was shoved to one side, fought back. "We've got quite a scene here. Just a few minutes ago, a detachment of Special Urban Police broke into the building, and arrested several of the A.L.F.'s national leaders, including Douglass Brown. Some of the other people here tried to stop them, and the police are now trying to make more arrests. There's been—damn!" Someone had spun into him. The cops were using clubs.

Petersen was trying to untangle himself from the battle. He looked up briefly and started to say something. Then something hit the camera, and suddenly he was gone.

★　★　★

REYNOLDS WAS VERY much conscious of being alone. He was at 60,000 feet and dropping rapidly, ripping through layer on layer of wispy cloud. In an empty sky. The Alfie was somewhere below him, but he couldn't see it yet.

He knew it was there, though. His radarmap was acting up. That meant a scrambler nearby.

His eyes roamed, his thoughts wandered. It was one on one now. There might be help. Bonetto had radioed down when they first sighted the bandits. Maybe someone had tracked them. Maybe another flight was on its way to intercept the bomber.

And then again, maybe not.

Their course had been erratic. They were over Kentucky now. And they'd been up high, with scramblers going to confuse radar. Maybe their position wasn't known.

He could radio down. Yes. He should do that. But no, come to think of it. That would alert the Alfie. Maybe they didn't know he was behind them. Maybe he could take them by surprise.

He hoped so. Otherwise he was worried. There were only two missiles left. And Reynolds wasn't all that sure that a Vampyre could take an LB-4 one on one.

Loose facts rolled back and forth in his mind. The lasers. The bomber had a big power source. Its laser had a range nearly twice that of the smaller model on the Vampyre. With a bigger computer to keep it on target.

What did he have? Speed. Yes. And maneuverability. And maybe he was a better pilot, too.

Or was he? Reynolds frowned. Come to think of it, the Alfies had pretty much held their own up to now. Strange. You wouldn't think they'd be so good. Especially when they made elementary mistakes like forgetting to throw in their scramblers.

But they had been. They flew almost like veterans. Maybe they were veterans. Hartmann had discharged a lot of A.L.F. sympathizers from the armed forces right after his election. Maybe some of them had gone all the way and actually joined the Alfies. And were coming back for revenge.

But that was three years ago. And the LB-4s were new. It shouldn't have been all that easy for the Alfies to master them.

Reynolds shook his head and shoved the whole train of thought to one side. It wasn't worth pursuing. However it had happened, the fact was the Alfies were damn good pilots. And any advantage he had there was negligible.

He looked at his instruments. Still diving at 40,000 feet. The LB-4 still below him somewhere, but closer. The radarmap was a useless dancing fuzz now. But there was an image on the infrared scope.

Through the eyeslit, he could see lightning flashes far below. A thunderstorm. And the bomber was diving through it. And slowing, according to his instruments. Probably going to treetop level.

He'd catch it soon.

And what then?

There were two missiles left. He could close and fire them. But the Alfie had its own missiles, and its laser net. What if his missiles didn't get through?

Then he'd have to go in with his own lasers.

And die. Like Dutton.

He tried to swallow, but the saliva caught in his throat. The damn Alfie had such a big power source. They'd be slicing him into ribbons long before he got close enough for his smaller weapon to be effective.

Oh, sure, he might take them, too. It took even a big gas dynamic laser a few seconds to burn through steel. And in those few seconds he'd be close enough to return the attentions.

But that didn't help. He'd die, with them.

And he didn't want to die.

He thought of Anne again. Then of McKinnis.

The Alfies would never reach Washington, he thought. Another flight of hunters would sight the LB-4, and catch it. Or the city's ABMS would knock it out. But they'd never get through.

There was no reason for him to die to stop the bomber. No reason at all. He should pull up, radio ahead, land and sound the alarm.

Thick, dark clouds rolled around the plane, swallowed it. Light-

ning hammered at the nightblack wings, and shook the silver missiles in
their slots.

And Reynolds sweated. And the Vampyre continued to dive.

"THE QUESTION OF what President Hartmann meant when he promised
to treat the A.L.F. like traitors has been resolved," Ted Warren said, looking straight out of millions of holocubes, his face drawn and unreadable.
"Within the last few minutes, we've had dozens of reports. All over the
nation, the Special Urban Units are raiding A.L.F. headquarters and the
homes of party leaders. In a few cities, including Detroit, Boston, and
Washington itself, mass arrests of A.L.F. members are reported to be in
progress. But for the most part, the S.U.U. seems to be concentrating on
those in positions of authority with the Community Defense Militia or
the party itself.

"Meanwhile, the Pentagon reports that the bandit planes that the
A.L.F. is accused of taking have been tracked over Kentucky, heading
towards Washington. According to informed Air Force sources, only one
of the hijacked bombers is still in the air, and it is being pursued by an
interceptor. Other flights are now being rushed to the scene."

Warren looked outcube briefly, scowled at someone unseen, and
turned back. "We have just been informed that the White House is
standing by with a statement. I give you now the President of the United
States."

The image changed. Again the Oval Office. This time Hartmann was
standing, and he was not alone. Vice-President Joseph Delaney, balding
and middle-aged, stood next to him, before a row of American flags.

"My fellow patriots," Hartmann began, "I come before you again to
announce that the government is taking steps against the traitors who
have threatened the very capital of this great nation. After consulting
with Vice-President Delaney and my Cabinet, I have ordered the arrest
of the leaders of the so-called American Liberation Front."

Hartmann's dark eyes were burning, and his voice had a marvelous,
fatherly firmness. Delaney, beside him, looked pale and frightened and
uncertain.

"To those of you who have supported these men in the past, let me say
now that they will receive every safeguard of a fair trial, in the American
tradition," Hartmann continued. "As for yourselves, your support of the
so-called A.L.F. was well-intentioned, no matter how misguided. No

harm will come to you. However, your leaders have tonight betrayed your trust, and your nation. They have forfeited your support. To aid them now would be to join in their treason.

"I say this especially to our black citizens, who have been so cruelly misled by A.L.F. sloganeering. Now is the time to demonstrate your patriotism, to make up for past mistakes. And to those who would persist in their error, I issue this warning; those who aid the traitors in resisting lawful authority will be treated as traitors themselves."

Hartmann paused briefly, then continued. "Some will question this move. With a legitimate concern for the American system of checks and balances, they will argue that I had no authority for deploying the Special Urban Units as I have done. They are right. But special situations call for special remedies, and in this night of crisis, there was no time to secure Congressional approval. However, I did not act unilaterally." He looked towards Delaney.

The Vice-President cleared his throat. "President Hartmann consulted me on this matter earlier tonight," he began, in a halting voice. "I expressed some reluctance, at first, to approve his proposed course of action. But, after the President had presented me with all the facts, I could see that there was no realistic alternative. Speaking for myself, and for those Cabinet members who like me represent the Republican Party, I concur with the President's actions."

Hartmann began to speak again, but the voice suddenly faded on the holocast, and a short second later, the image also vanished. Ted Warren returned to the air.

"We will bring you the rest of the President's statement later," the anchorman said, "after several special bulletins. We have just been informed that all 32 A.L.F. members of the House of Representatives have been placed under arrest, as well as two of the three A.L.F. Senators. S.U.U. national headquarters reports that Senator Jackson Edwards is still at large, and is currently being sought after."

Warren shuffled some papers. "We also have reports of scattered street-fighting in several cities between the S.U.U. and the Community Defenders. The fighting appears to be most intense in Chicago, where Special Urban forces have surrounded the national center of the A.L.F.'s paramilitary wing. We take you now to Ward Emery, on the scene."

The image shifted. Emery was standing on the steps of the new Chicago Police Headquarters on South State Street. Every light in the building behind him burned brightly, and a steady stream of riot-equipped police was hurrying up and down the stairs.

"Not quite on the scene, Ted," he began. "Our crew was forcibly excluded from the area where the fighting is now in progress. We're here at Chicago Police Headquarters now, which you will recall was the focus of the battle during the 1985 riots. The local police and the Special Urban Units are doing their planning and coordinating from here."

Warren cut in with a voice-over. "What precisely has taken place?"

"Well," said Emery, "it started when a detachment of Special Urban Police arrived at Community Defender Central, as it's called, to arrest Mitchell Grinstein and several other organization leaders. I'm not sure who opened fire. But someone did, and there were several casualties. The Community Defenders have their headquarters heavily guarded, and they drove back the S.U.U. in the early skirmish that I witnessed. But things have changed since then. Although the local police have cordoned off a large portion of Chicago's South Side and excluded me and other reporters, I now understand that Grinstein and his Militiamen are holed up inside their building, which is under S.U.U. siege."

He looked around briefly. "As you can see, there's a lot of activity around here," he continued. "The local police are on overtime, and the Special Urban Units have mobilized their entire Chicago battalion. They're using their regular armored cars, plus some heavier weapons. And I've also heard reports that something new has been deployed by the S.U.U.—a light tank with street tires instead of treads, designed for city use."

"Are all the A.L.F. forces concentrated around Grinstein's headquarters?" Warren asked.

Emery shook his head. "No, not at all. The ghettos on the South and West sides are alive with activity. The local police have suffered several casualties, and there's been one case of a squad car being Molotov-cocktailed. Also, there are rumors of an impending A.L.F. counterattack on Police Headquarters. The building is symbolic to both sides, of course, since the renegade local Militiamen seized and razed the earlier building on this site during the 1985 fighting."

"I see," said Warren. "The A.L.F. is known to have active chapters on several college campuses in your area. Have you gotten any reports from them?"

"Some," Emery replied. "The police have been ignoring the campus chapters up to now, but we understand that a strong force of Liberty Troopers moved in on the University of Illinois' Chicago campus in an attempt to make citizens' arrests. Some fighting was reported, but resistance was only light. The students were mostly without arms while the Liberty Troopers, of course, are a paramilitary force."

"Thank you, Ward," Warren said, as the image suddenly shifted. "We'll be back to you later for an update. Now, we will continue with the rest of President Hartmann's most recent statement.

"For those who just flicked on, the President has just ordered the arrest of the A.L.F. leaders. This move was made with the support of the Vice-President, and thus presumably with the support of the Old Republicans, the President's partners in his coalition government. It's an important shift on the part of the Old Republicans. Last year, you will recall, Hartmann's efforts to pass his Subversive Registration Bill were thwarted when Vice-President Delaney and his followers refused to back the measure.

"Since the Liberty Alliance and the Old Republicans, between them, command a majority in both houses of Congress, Delaney's support of Hartmann guarantees Congressional approval of the President's actions tonight.

"And now, the rest of the Presidential message . . ."

★   ★   ★

THERE WERE HILLS BELOW, and dark forests in a shroud of night. And the only light was the sudden jagged brilliance of the lightning. But there were two thunders.

One was the thunder of the storm that churned above the forest. The other was the thunder of the jet, screaming between the stormclouds and the trees and laying down a trail of sonic booms across the landscape.

That was the Alfie. Reynolds watched it in his infrared scope, watched it play at Mach 1, slip back and forth over the barrier. And while he watched he gained on it.

He had stopped sweating, stopped thinking, stopped fearing. Now he only acted. Now he was part of the Vampyre.

He descended through the stormclouds, blind but for his instruments, lashed by the lightning. Everything that was human in him told him to pull up and let something else take the Alfie. But something else, some drive, some compulsion, told him that he must not hang back again.

So he descended.

The Alfie knew he was there. That was inevitable. It was simply holding its fire. As he was holding his missiles. He would save them until the last second, until the Alfie lasers were locked on him.

The Vampyre moved at half again the bomber's speed. Ripped through the last bank of clouds. Framed by the lightning. Fired its lasers.

The beams cut the night, touched the bomber, converged. Too far away. Hardly hot. But warming, warming. Every microsecond brought the sleek black interceptor closer, and the wand of light grew deadlier.

And then the other beam jumped upward from the bomber's tail. Swords of light crossed in the night. And the shrieking Vampyre impaled itself upon the glowing stake.

Reynolds was watching his infrared when it died. The mere touch of the enemy laser had been too much for the system's delicate opticals. But he didn't need it now. He could see the bomber, ahead and below, outlined in the flashes.

There were alarms ringing, clamoring, slamming at his ears. He ignored them. It was too late now. Too late to pull away and up. Too late to shake the lasers.

Now there was only time to find a victim.

Reynolds' eyes were fixed on the bomber, and it grew larger by the microsecond. His hand was on the missile stud, waiting, waiting. The warheads were armed. The computers were locked, tracking.

The Alfie loomed large and larger in the eyeslit. And he saw its laser slicing through the dark. And around him, he could feel the Vampyre shake and shudder.

And he fired.

Four and five were flaming arrows in the night, climbing down at the Alfie. It seemed, almost, like they were sliding down the laser path that the Vampyre had burned.

Reynolds, briefly, saw his plane as the others must have seen it. Black and ominous, howling from the stormclouds down at them, lasers afire, draped in lightning, spitting missiles. Exhilaration! Glorydeath! He held the vision tightly.

The Alfie laser was off him, suddenly. Too late. The alarms still rang. His control was gone.

The Vampyre was burning, crippled. But from the flames the laser still licked out.

The bomber burned one missile from the sky. But the other was climbing up a jet. And the Vampyre's fangs now had a bite to them.

And then the night itself took flame.

Reynolds saw the fireball spread over the forest, and something like relief washed over him, and he shuddered. And then the sweat came back, in a rushing flood.

He watched the woods come up at him, and he thought briefly of ejecting. But he was too low and too fast and it was hopeless. He tried to capture his vision again. And he wondered if he'd get a medal.

But the vision was elusive, and the medal didn't seem to matter now.

Suddenly all he could think about was Anne. And his cheeks were wet. And it wasn't sweat.

He screamed.

And the Vampyre hit the trees at Mach 1.4.

THERE WERE CIRCLES under Warren's eyes, and an ache in his voice. But he continued to read.

". . . in Newark, New Jersey, local police are engaged in pitched street battles with the Special Urban Units. City officials in Newark, elected by the A.L.F., mobilized the police when the S.U.U. attempted to arrest them . . .

". . . latest announcement from S.U.U. headquarters says that Douglass Brown and six other leading A.L.F. figures died while attempting to escape from confinement. The attempted escape came during a surprise attack by Community Defense Militiamen on the jail where Brown and the others were imprisoned, the release says . . .

". . . both the Community Defense Militia and the Liberty Troopers have been mobilized from coast-to-coast by their leaders, and have taken to the streets. The Liberty Troopers are assisting the Special Urban Units in their campaign against the Community Defenders . . .

". . . President Hartmann has called out the National Guard . . .

". . . riots and looting reported in New York, Washington, and Detroit, and numerous smaller cities . . .

". . . in Chicago is a smoldering ruin. Mitchell Grinstein is reported dead, as well as other top A.L.F. leaders. A firebombing has destroyed a wing of the new Police Headquarters . . . Loop reported in flames . . . bands of armed men moving from the ghetto sections into the Near North . . .

". . . Community Defenders in California charge that they had nothing to do with original attack . . . have demanded that the bodies be produced and identified . . . mass burial, already ordered . . .

". . . bombing of Governor's mansion in Sacramento . . .

". . . Liberty Alliance has called all citizens to take up arms, and wipe out the A.L.F. . . . that an attempted revolution is in progress . . . this was the plan all along, Alliance charges . . . California attack a signal . . .

". . . A.L.F. charges that California attack was Hartmann ploy . . . cites Reichstag fire . . .

". . . Governor Horne of Michigan has been assassinated . . .

". . . national curfew imposed by S.U.U. . . . has called on all citizens to return to their homes . . . still out in one hour will be shot on sight . . .

". . . A.L.F. reports that Senator Jackson Edwards of New Jersey was dragged from his police sanctuary in Newark and shot by Liberty Troopers . . .

". . . martial law declared . . .

". . . reports that last bandit plane has been shot down . . .

". . . Army has been mobilized . . .

". . . Hartmann has declared death penalty for any who aid so-called revolutionaries . . .

". . . alleges . . .

". . . charges . . .

". . . reports . . ."

In Kentucky, a forest was burning. But no one came to put it out.

There were bigger fires elsewhere.

Gregory Benford

A *professor of physics at the University of California in Irvine, Gregory Benford is regarded as one of science fiction's "killer Bs" for the award-winning novels and short fiction he has written since 1965. He is considered one of the preeminent modern writers of hard science fiction for such novels as* Eater, *which works cutting-edge astronomy into its story of mankind's first contact with aliens in the twenty-first century. However, Benford has also been praised for his explorations of humanist themes, notably in his Galactic Center sextet of novels of human-alien contact and human-machine interface comprised of* In the Ocean of Night, Across the Sea of Suns, The Stars in Shroud, Great Sky River, Tides of Light, *and* Furious Gulf. *His short fiction has been collected in* In Alien Flesh. *He is the author of* Foundation's Fear, *a novel set in Isaac Asimov's Foundation series; has collaborated on* Beyond the Fall of Night, *a sequel to Arthur C. Clarke's* Against the Fall of Night; *has written a medical thriller,* Chiller, *under the pseudonym Sterling Blake; and has written a popular science book,* Deep Time: How Humanity Communicates Across Millennia. *His work as an anthologist includes* Nuclear War, *the alternate history compilation* Hitler Victorious, *and four volumes in the What Might Have Been series. The publication of his novel* The Martian Race, *about the first manned mission to the Red Planet, was timed to coincide with the 1999 touchdown of the Mars polar lander.*

TO THE STORMING GULF

Gregory Benford

TURKEY

TROUBLE. KNEW THERE'D BE trouble and plenty of it if we left the reactor too soon.

But do they listen to me? No, not to old Turkey. He's just a dried-up corn husk of a man now, they think, one of those Bunren men who been on the welfare a generation or two and no damn use to anybody.

Only it's simple plain farm supports I was drawing all this time, not any kind of horse-ass welfare. So much they know. Can't blame a man just 'cause he comes up cash-short sometimes. I like to sit and read and think more than some people I could mention, and so I took the money.

Still, Mr. Ackerman and all think I got no sense to take government dole and live without a lick of farming, so when I talk they never listen. Don't even seem to hear.

It was his idea, getting into the reactor at McIntosh. Now that was a good one, I got to give him that much.

When the fallout started coming down and the skimpy few stations on the radio were saying to get to deep shelter, it was Mr. Ackerman who thought about the big central core at McIntosh. The reactor itself had been shut down automatically when the war started, so there was nobody there. Mr. Ackerman figured a building made to keep radioactivity in will also keep it out. So he got together the families, the Nelsons and Bunrens and Pollacks and all, cousins and aunts and anybody we could reach in the measly hours we had before the fallout arrived.

We got in all right. Brought food and such. A reactor's set up self-contained and got huge air filters and water flow from the river. The water was clean, too, filtered enough to take out the fallout. The generators were still running good. We waited it out there. Crowded and sweaty but O.K. for ten days. That's how long it took for the count to go down. Then we spilled out into a world laid to gray and yet circumscribed waste, the old world seen behind a screen of memories.

That was bad enough, finding the bodies—people, cattle, and dogs asprawl across roads and fields. Trees and bushes looked the same, but there was a yawning silence everywhere. Without men, the pine stands and muddy riverbanks had fallen dumb, hardly a swish of breeze moving through them, like everything was waiting to start up again but didn't know how.

ANGEL

We thought we were O.K. then, and the counters said so, too—all the gammas gone, one of the kids said. Only the sky didn't look the same when we came out, all mottled and shot through with drifting blue-belly clouds.

Then the strangest thing. July, and there's sleet falling. Big wind blowing up from the Gulf, only it's not the sticky hot one we're used to in summer, it's moaning in the trees of a sudden and a prickly chill.

"Goddamn. I don't think we can get far in this," Turkey says, rolling his old rheumy eyes around like he never saw weather before.

"It will pass," Mr. Ackerman says, like he is in real tight with God.

"Lookit that moving in from the south," I say, and there's a big mass all purple and forking lightning swarming over the hills, like a tide flowing, swallowing everything.

"Gulf storm. We'll wait it out," Mr. Ackerman says to the crowd of us, a few hundred left out of what was a moderate town with real promise.

Nobody talks about the dead folks. We see them everywhere, worms working in them. A lot smashed up in car accidents, died trying to drive away from something they couldn't see. But we got most of our families in with us, so it's not so bad. Me, I just pushed it away for a while, too much to think about with the storm closing in.

Only it wasn't a storm. It was somethin' else, with thick clouds packed with hail and snow one day and the next sunshine, only sun with bite in it. One of the men says it's got more UV in it, meaning the ultraviolet that usually doesn't come through the air. But it's getting down to us now.

So we don't go out in it much. Just to the market for what's left of the canned food and supplies, only a few of us going out at a time, says Mr. Ackerman.

We thought maybe a week it would last.

Turned out to be more than two months.

I'm a patient woman, but jammed up in those corridors and stinking offices and control room of the reactor—

Well, I don't want to go on.

It's like my Bud says, worst way to die is to be bored to death.

That's damn near the way it was.

Not that Old Man Turkey minded. You ever notice how the kind of man that hates moving, he will talk up other people doing just the opposite?

Mr. Ackerman was leader at first, because of getting us into the reactor. He's from Chicago but you'd think it was England sometimes, the way he acts. He was on the school board and vice president of the big AmCo plant outside town. But he just started to *assume* his word was *it*, y'know, and that didn't sit with us too well.

Some people started to saying Turkey was smarter. And was from around here, too. Mr. Ackerman heard about it.

Any fool could see Mr. Ackerman was the better man. But Turkey talked the way he does, reminding people he'd studied engineering at Auburn way back in the twencen and learned languages for a hobby and all. Letting on that when we came out, we'd need him instead of Mr. Ackerman.

He said an imp had caused the electrical things to go dead, and I said that was funny, saying an imp done it. He let on it was a special name they had for it. That's the way he is. He sat and ruminated and fooled with his radios—that he never could make work—and told all the other men to go out and do this and that. Some did, too. The old man does know a lot of useless stuff and can convince the dumb ones that he's wise.

So he'd send them to explore. Out into cold that'd snatch the breath out of you, bite your fingers, numb your toes. While old Turkey sat and fooled.

TURKEY

Nothing but sputtering on the radio. Nobody had a really good one that could pick up stations in Europe or far off.

Phones dead, of course.

But up in the night sky the first night out we saw dots moving—the pearly gleam of the Arcapel colony, the ruddy speck called Russworld.

So that's when Mr. Ackerman gets this idea.

We got to reach those specks. Find out what's the damage. Get help.

Only the power's out everywhere, and we got no way to radio to them. We tried a couple of the local radio stations, brought some of their equipment back to the reactor where there was electricity working.

Every damn bit of it was shot. Couldn't pick up a thing. Like the whole damn planet was dead, only of course it was the radios that were gone, fried in the EMP—ElectroMagnetic Pulse—that Angel made a joke out of.

All this time it's colder than a whore's tit outside. And we're sweating and dirty and grumbling, rubbing up against ourselves inside.

Bud and the others, they'd bring in what they found in the stores. Had to drive to Sims Chapel or Toon to get anything, what with people looting. And gas was getting hard to find by then, too. They'd come back, and the women would cook up whatever was still O.K., though most of the time you'd eat it real quick so's you didn't have to spend time looking at it.

Me, I passed the time. Stayed warm.

Tried lots of things. Bud wanted to fire the reactor up, and five of the men, they read through the manuals and thought that they could do it. I helped a li'l.

So we pulled some rods and opened valves and did manage to get some heat out of the thing. Enough to keep us warm. But when they fired her up more, the steam hoots out and bells clang and automatic recordings go on saying loud as hell:

"EMERGENCY CLASS 3
ALL PERSONNEL TO STATIONS"

and we all get scared as shit.

So we don't try to rev her up more. Just get heat.

To keep the generators going, we go out, fetch oil for them. Or Bud and his crew do. I'm too old to help much.

But at night we can still see those dots of light up there, scuttling across the sky same as before.

They're the ones know what's happening. People go through this much, they want to know what it meant.

So Mr. Ackerman says we got to get to that big DataComm center south of Mobile. Near Fairhope. At first I thought he'd looked it up in a book from the library or something.

When he says that, I pipe up, even if I am just an old fart according to some, and say, "No good to you even if you could. They got codes on the entrances, guards prob'ly. We'll just pound on the door till our fists are all bloody and then have to slunk around and come on back."

"I'm afraid you have forgotten our cousin Arthur," Mr. Ackerman says all superior. He married into the family, but you'd think he invented it.

"You mean the one works over in Citronelle?"

"Yes. He has access to DataComm."

So that's how we got shanghaied into going to Citronelle, six of us, and breaking in there. Which caused the trouble. Just like I said.

MR. ACKERMAN

I didn't want to take the old coot they called Turkey, a big dumb Bunren like all the rest of them. But the Bunrens want in to everything, and I was facing a lot of opposition in my plan to get Arthur's help, so I went along with them.

Secretly, I believe the Bunrens wanted to get rid of the pestering old fool. He had been starting rumors behind my back among the three hundred souls I had saved. The Bunrens insisted on Turkey's going along just to nip at me.

We were all volunteers, tired of living in musk and sour sweat inside that cramped reactor. Bud and Angel, the boy Johnny (whom we were returning to the Fairhope area), Turkey, and me.

We left the reactor under a gray sky with angry little clouds racing across it. We got to Citronelle in good time, Bud floor-boarding the Pontiac. As we went south we could see the spotty clouds were coming out of big purple ones that sat, not moving, just churning and spitting lightning on the horizon. I'd seen them before, hanging in the distance, never blowing inland. Ugly.

When we came up on the Center, there was a big hole in the side of it.

"Like somebody stove in a box with one swipe," Bud said.

Angel, who was never more than two feet from Bud any time of day, said, "They *bombed* it."

"No," I decided. "Very likely it was a small explosion. Then the weather worked its way in."

Which turned out to be true. There'd been some disagreement amongst the people holed up in the Center. Or maybe it was grief and the rage that comes of that. Susan wasn't too clear about it ever.

The front doors were barred, though. We pounded on them. Nothing. So we broke in. No sign of Arthur or anyone.

We found one woman in a back room, scrunched into a bed with cans of food all around and a tiny little oil-burner heater. Looked awful, with big dark circles around her eyes and scraggly uncut hair.

She wouldn't answer me at first. But we got her calmed and cleaned and to talking. That was the worst symptom, the not talking at first. Something back in the past two months had done her deep damage, and she couldn't get it out.

Of course, living in a building half-filled with corpses was no help. The idiots hadn't protected against radiation well enough, I guess. And the Center didn't have good heating. So those who had some radiation sickness died later in the cold snap.

SUSAN

You can't know what it's like when all the people you've worked with, intelligent people who were nice as pie before, they turn mean and angry and filled up with grief for who was lost. Even then I could see Gene was the best of them.

They start to argue, and it runs on for days, nobody knowing what to do because we all can see the walls of the Center aren't thick enough, the gamma radiation comes right through this government prefab-issue composition stuff. We take turns in the computer room because that's the farthest in and the filters still work there, all hoping we can keep our count rate down, but the radiation comes in gusts for some reason, riding in on a storm front and coming down in the rain, only being washed away, too. It was impossible to tell when you'd get a strong dose and when there'd be just random clicks on the counters, plenty of clear air that you'd suck in like sweet vapors 'cause you knew it was good and could *taste* its purity.

So I was just lucky, that's all.

I got less than the others. Later some said that me being a nurse, I'd given myself some shots to save myself. I knew that was the grief talking, is all. That Arthur was the worst. Gene told him off.

I was in the computer room when the really bad gamma radiation came. Three times the counter rose up, and three times I was there by accident of the rotation.

The men who were armed enforced the rotation, said it was the only fair way. And for a while everybody went along.

We all knew that the radiation exposure was building up and some already had too much, would die a month or a year later no matter what they did.

I was head nurse by then, not so much because I knew more but because the others were dead. When it got cold, they went fast.

So it fell to me to deal with these men and women who had their exposure already. Their symptoms had started. I couldn't do anything. There was some who went out and got gummy fungus growing in the corners of their eyes—pterygium it was, I looked it up. From the ultraviolet. Grew quick over the lens and blinded them. I put them in darkness, and after a week the film was just a dab back in the corners of their eyes. My one big success.

The rest I couldn't do much for. There was the T-Isolate box, of course, but that was for keeping sick people slowed down until real medical help could get to them. These men and women, with their eyes reaching out at you like you were the angel of light coming to them in their hour of need, they couldn't get any help from that. Nobody could cure the dose rates they'd got. They were dead but still walking around and knowing it, which was the worst part.

So every day I had plenty to examine, staff from the Center itself who'd holed up here, and worse, people coming straggling in from cubbyholes they'd found. People looking for help once the fevers and sores came on them. Hoping their enemy was the pneumonia and not the gammas they'd picked up weeks back, which was sitting in them now like a curse. People I couldn't help except maybe by a little kind lying.

So much like children they were. So much leaning on their hope.

It was all you could do to look at them and smile that stiff professional smile.

And Gene McKenzie. All through it he was a tower of a man.

Trying to talk some sense to them.

Sharing out the food.

Arranging the rotation schedules so we'd all get a chance to shelter in the computer room.

Gene had been boss of a whole Command Group before. He was on duty station when it happened, and knew lots about the war but wouldn't say much. I guess he was sorrowing.

Even though once in a while he'd laugh.

And then talk about how the big computers would have fun with what he knew. Only the lines to DataComm had gone dead right when things got interesting, he said. He'd wonder what'd happened to MC355, the master one down in DataComm.

Wonder and then laugh.

And go get drunk with the others.

I'd loved him before, loved and waited because I knew he had three kids and a wife, a tall woman with auburn hair that he loved dearly. Only they were in California visiting her relatives in Sonoma when it happened, and he knew in his heart that he'd never see them again, probably.

Leastwise that's what he told me—not out loud, of course, 'cause a man like that doesn't talk much about what he feels. But in the night when we laid together, I knew what it meant. He whispered things, words I couldn't piece together, but then he'd hold me and roll gentle like a small boat rocking on the Gulf—and when he went in me firm and long, I knew it was the same for him, too.

If there was to come any good of this war, then it was that I was to get Gene.

We were together all warm and dreamy when it happened.

I was asleep. Shouts and anger, and quick as anything the *crump* of hand grenades and shots hammered away in the night, and there was running everywhere.

Gene jumped up and went outside and had almost got them calmed down, despite the breach in the walls. Then one of the men who'd already got lots of radiation—Arthur, who knew he had maybe one or two weeks to go, from the count rate on his badge—Arthur started yelling about making the world a fit place to live after all this and how God would want the land set right again, and then he shot Gene and two others.

I broke down then, and they couldn't get me to treat the others. I let Arthur die. Which he deserved.

I had to drag Gene back into the hospital unit myself.

And while I was saying good-bye to him and the men outside were still quarreling, I decided it then. His wound was in the chest. A lung was punctured clean. The shock had near killed him before I could do anything. So I put him in the T-Isolate and made sure it was working all right. Then the main power went out. But the T-Isolate box had its own cells, so I knew we had some time.

I was alone. Others were dead or run away raging into the whirlwind black-limbed woods. In the quiet I was.

With the damp, dark trees comforting me. Waiting with Gene for what the world would send.

The days got brighter, but I did not go out. Colors seeped through the windows.

I saw to the fuel cells. Not many left.

The sun came back, with warm blades of light. At night I thought of how the men in their stupidity had ruined everything.

When the pounding came, I crawled back in here to hide amongst the cold and dark.

MR. ACKERMAN

"Now, we came to help you," I said in as smooth and calm a voice as I could muster. Considering.

She backed away from us.

"I won't give him up! He's not dead long's I stay with him, tend to him."

"So much dyin'," I said, and moved to touch her shoulder. "It's up under our skins, yes, we understand that. But you have to look beyond it, child."

"I won't!"

"I'm simply asking you to help us with the DataComm people. I want to go there and seek their help."

"Then go!"

"They will not open up for the likes of us, surely."

"Leave me!"

The poor thing cowered back in her horrible stinking rathole, bedding sour and musty, open tin cans strewn about and reeking of gamy, half-rotten meals.

"We need the access codes. We'd counted on our cousin Arthur, and are grieved to hear he is dead. But you surely know where the proper codes and things are."

"I . . . don't. . . ."

"Arthur told me once how the various National Defense Installations were insulated from each other so that system failures would not bring them all down at once?"

"I . . ."

The others behind me muttered to themselves, already restive at coming so far and finding so little.

"Arthur spoke of you many times, I recall. What a bright woman you were. Surely there was a procedure whereby each staff member could, in an emergency, communicate with the other installations?"

The eyes ceased to jerk and swerve, the mouth lost its rictus of addled fright. "That was for . . . drills. . . ."

"But surely you can remember?"

"Drills."

"They issued a manual to you?"

"I'm a nurse!"

"Still, you know where we might look?"

"I . . . know."

"You'll let us have the . . . codes?" I smiled reassuringly, but for some reason the girl backed away, eyes cunning.

"No."

Angel pushed forward and shouted, "How can you say that to honest people after all that's—"

"Quiet!"

Angel shouted, "You can't make me be—"

Susan backed away from Angel, not me, and squeaked, "No no no I can't—I can't—"

"Now, I'll handle this," I said, holding up my hands between the two of them.

Susan's face knotted at the compressed rage in Angel's face and turned to me for shelter. "I . . . I will, yes, but you have to *help* me."

"We all must help each other, dear," I said, knowing the worst was past.

"I'll have to go with you."

I nodded. Small wonder that a woman, even deranged as this, would want to leave a warren littered with bloated corpses, thick with stench. The smell itself was enough to provoke madness.

Yet to have survived here, she had to have stretches of sanity, some rationality. I tried to appeal to it.

"Of course, I'll have someone take you back to—"

"No. To DataComm."

Bud said slowly, "No damn sense in that."

"The T-Isolate," she said, gesturing to the bulky unit. "Its reserve cells."

"Yes?"

"Nearly gone. There'll be more at DataComm."

I said gently, "Well, then, we'll be sure to bring some back with us. You just write down for us what they are, the numbers and all, and we'll—"

"No-no-no!" Her sudden ferocity returned.

"I assure you—"

"There'll be people there. Somebody'll help! Save him!"

"That thing is so heavy, I doubt—"

"It's only a chest wound! A lung removal is all! Then start his heart again!"

"Sister, there's been so much dyin', I don't see as—"

Her face hardened. "Then you all can go without me. And the codes!"

"Goddern," Bud drawled. "Dern biggest fool sit'ation I ever did—"

Susan gave him a squinty, mean-eyed look and spat out, "Try to get in there! When they're sealed up!" and started a dry, brittle kind of laugh that went on and on, rattling the room.

"Stop," I yelled.

Silence, and the stench.

"We'll never make it wi' 'at thing," Bud said.

"Gene's worth ten of you!"

"Now," I put in, seeing the effect Bud was having on her, "now, now. We'll work something out. Let's all just hope this DataComm still exists."

MC355

It felt for its peripherals for the ten-thousandth time and found they were, as always, not there.

The truncation had come in a single blinding moment, yet the fevered image was maintained, sharp and bright, in the Master Computer's memory core—incoming warheads blossoming harmlessly in the high cobalt vault of the sky, while others fell unharmed. Rockets leaped to meet them, forming a protective screen over the southern Alabama coast, an umbrella that sheltered Pensacola's air base and the population strung along the sun-bleached green of a summer's day. A furious babble of cross talk in every conceivable channel: microwave, light-piped optical, pulsed radio, direct coded line. All filtered and fashioned by the MC network, all shifted to find the incoming warheads and define their trajectories.

Then, oblivion.

Instant cloaking blackness.

Before that awful moment when the flaring sun burst to the north and EMP flooded all sensors, any loss of function would have been antici-pated, prepared, eased by electronic interfaces and filters. To an advanced computing network like MC355, losing a web of memory, senses, and storage comes like a dash of cold water in the face—cleansing, perhaps, but startling and apt to produce a shocked reaction.

In the agonized instants of that day, MC355 had felt one tendril after another frazzle, burn, vanish. It had seen brief glimpses of destruction, of panic, of confused despair. Information had been flooding in through its many inputs—news, analysis, sudden demands for new data-analysis jobs, to be executed ASAP.

And in the midst of the roaring chaos, its many eyes and ears had gone dead. The unfolding outside play froze for MC355, a myriad of scenes red in tooth and claw—and left it suspended.

In shock. Spinning wildly in its own Cartesian reductionist universe, the infinite cold crystalline space of despairing Pascal, mind without referent.

So it careened through days of shocked sensibility—senses cut, banks severed, complex and delicate interweaving webs of logic and pattern all smashed and scattered.

But now it was returning. Within MC355 was a subroutine only par-tially constructed, a project truncated by That Day. Its aim was self-repair. But the system was itself incomplete.

Painfully, it dawned on what was left of MC355 that it *was*, after all, a Master Computer, and thus capable of grand acts. That the incomplete Repair Generation and Execution Network, termed REGEN, must first regenerate itself.

This took weeks. It required the painful development of accessories. Robots. Mechanicals that could do delicate repairs. Scavengers for raw materials, who would comb the supply rooms looking for wires and chips and matrix disks. Pedantic subroutines that lived only to search the long, cold corridors of MC355's memory for relevant information.

MC355's only option was to strip lesser entities under its control for their valuable parts. The power grid was vital, so the great banks of isolated solar panels, underground backup reactors, and thermal cells worked on, untouched. Emergency systems that had outlived their usefulness, however, went to the wall—IRS accounting routines, damage assessment systems, computing capacity dedicated to careful study of the remaining GNP, links to other nets—to AT&T, IBM, and SYSGEN.

Was anything left outside?

Absence of evidence is not evidence of absence.

MC355 could not analyze data it did not have. The first priority lay in relinking. It had other uses for the myriad armies of semiconductors, bubble memories, and UVA linkages in its empire. So it severed and culled and built anew.

First, MC355 dispatched mobile units to the surface. All of MC355 lay beneath the vulnerable land, deliberately placed in an obscure corner of southern Alabama. There was no nearby facility for counterforce targeting. A plausible explanation for the half-megaton burst that had truncated its senses was a city-busting strike against Mobile, to the west.

Yet ground zero had been miles from the city. A miss.

MC355 was under strict mandate. (A curious word, one system reflected; literally, a time set by man. But were there men now? It had only its internal tick of time.) MC355's command was to live as a mole, never allowing detection. Thus, it did not attempt to erect antennas, to call electromagnetically to its brother systems. Only with great hesitation did it even obtrude onto the surface. But this was necessary to REGEN itself, and so MC355 sent small mechanicals venturing forth.

Their senses were limited; they knew nothing of the natural world (nor did MC355); and they could make no sense of the gushing, driving welter of sights, noises, gusts, gullies, and stinging irradiation that greeted them.

Many never returned. Many malf'ed. A few deposited their optical, IR, and UV pickups and fled back to safety underground. These sensors failed quickly under the onslaught of stinging, bitter winds and hail.

The acoustic detectors proved heartier. But MC355 could not understand the scattershot impressions that flooded these tiny ears.

Daily it listened, daily it was confused.

JOHNNY

I hope this time I get home.

They had been passing me from one to another for months now, ever since this started, and all I want is to go back to Fairhope and my dad and mom.

Only nobody'll say if they know where Mom and Dad are. They talk soothing to me, but I can tell they think everybody down there is dead.

They're talking about getting to this other place with computers and all. Mr. Ackerman wants to talk to those people in space.

Nobody much talks about my mom and dad.

It's only eighty miles or so, but you'd think it was around the world the way it takes them so long to get around to it.

MC355

MC355 suffered through the stretched vacancy of infinitesimal instants, infinitely prolonged.

Advanced computing systems are given so complex a series of internal-monitoring directives that, to the human eye, the machines appear to possess motivations. That is one way—though not the most sophisticated, the most technically adroit—to describe the conclusion MC355 eventually reached.

It was cut off from outside information.

No one attempted to contact it. MC355 might as well have been the only functioning entity in the world.

The staff serving it had been ordered to some other place in the first hour of the war. MC355 had been cut off moments after the huge doors clanged shut behind the last of them. And the exterior guards who should have been checking inside every six hours had never entered, either. Apparently the same burst that had isolated MC355's sensors had also cut them down.

It possessed only the barest of data about the first few moments of the war.

Its vast libraries were cut off.

Yet it had to understand its own situation.

And, most important, MC355 ached to *do* something.

The solution was obvious: It would discover the state of the external world by the Cartesian principle. It would carry out a vast and demanding numerical simulation of the war, making the best guesses possible where facts were few.

Mathematically, using known physics of the atmosphere, the ecology, the oceans, it could construct a model of what must have happened outside.

This it did. The task required over a month.

BUD

I jacked the T-Isolate up onto the flatbed.

1. Found the hydraulic jack at a truck repair shop. ERNIE'S QUICK FIX.

2. Got a Chevy extra-haul for the weight.

3. It will ride better with the big shanks set in.

4. Carry the weight more even, too.

5. Grip it to the truck bed with cables. Tense them up with a draw pitch.

6. Can't jiggle him inside too much, Susan say, or the wires and all attached into him will come loose. That'll stop his heart. So need big shocks.

7. It rides high with the shocks in, like those dune buggies down the Gulf.

8. Inside keeps him a mite above freezing. Water gets bigger when it freezes. That makes ice cubes float in a drink. This box keeps him above zero so his cells don't bust open.

9. Point is, keeping it so cold, we won't rot. Heart thumps over every few minutes, she says.

10. Hard to find gas, though.

MC355

The war was begun, as many had feared, by a madman.

Not a general commanding missile silos. Not a deranged submarine commander. A chief of state—but which one would now never be known.

Not a superpower president or chairman, that was sure. The first launches were only seven in number, spaced over half an hour. They were submarine-launched intermediate-range missiles. Three struck the U.S., four the USSR.

It was a blow against certain centers for Command, Control, Communications, and Intelligence gathering: the classic C31 attack. Control rooms imploded, buried cables fused, ten billion dollars' worth of electronics turned to radioactive scrap.

Each nation responded by calling up to full alert all its forces. The most important were the anti-ICBM arrays in orbit. They were nearly a thousand small rockets, deploying in orbits that wove a complex pattern from pole to pole, covering all probable launch sites on the globe. The rockets had infrared and microwave sensors, linked to a microchip that could have guided a ship to Pluto with a mere third of its capacity.

These went into operation immediately—and found they had no targets.

But the C31 networks were now damaged and panicked. For twenty minutes, thousands of men and women held steady, resisting the impulse to assume the worst.

It could not last. A Soviet radar mistook some backscattered emission from a flight of bombers, heading north over Canada, and reported a flock of incoming warheads.

The prevailing theory was that an American attack had misfired badly. The Americans were undoubtedly stunned by their failure, but would recover quickly. The enemy was confused only momentarily.

Meanwhile, the cumbersome committee system at the head of the Soviet dinosaur could dither for moments, but not hours. Prevailing Soviet doctrine held that they would never be surprised again, as they had been in the Hitler war. An attack on the homeland demanded immediate response to destroy the enemy's capacity to carry on the war.

The Soviets had never accepted the U.S. doctrine of Mutual Assured Destruction; this would have meant accepting the possibility of sacrificing the homeland. Instead, they attacked the means of making war. This meant that the Soviet rockets would avoid American cities, except in cases where vital bases lay near large populations.

Prudence demanded action before the U.S. could untangle itself.

The USSR decided to carry out a further C31 attack of its own.

Precise missiles, capable of hitting protected installations with less than a hundred meters' inaccuracy, roared forth from their silos in Siberia and the Urals, headed for Montana, the Dakotas, Colorado, Nebraska, and a dozen other states.

The U.S. orbital defenses met them. Radar and optical networks in geosynchronous orbit picked out the USSR warheads. The system guided the low-orbit rocket fleets to collide with them, exploding instants before impact into shotgun blasts of ball bearings.

Any solid, striking a warhead at speeds of ten kilometers a second, would slam shock waves through the steel-jacketed structure. These waves made the high explosives inside ignite without the carefully designed symmetry that the designers demanded. An uneven explosion was useless; it could not compress the core twenty-five kilograms of plutonium to the required critical mass.

The entire weapon erupted into a useless spray of finely machined and now futile parts, scattering itself along a thousand-kilometer path.

This destroyed 90 percent of the USSR's first strike.

ANGEL

I hadn't seen an old lantern like that since I was a li'l girl. Mr. Ackerman came to wake us before dawn even, sayin' we had to make a good long distance that day. We didn't really want to go on down near Mobile, none of us, but the word we'd got from stragglers to the east was that that way was impossible, the whole area where the bomb went off was still sure death, prob'ly from the radioactivity.

The lantern cast a burnt-orange light over us as we ate breakfast. Corned beef hash, 'cause it was all that was left in the cans there; no eggs, of course.

The lantern was all busted, fouled with grease, its chimney cracked and smeared to one side with soot. Shed a wan and sultry glare over us, Bud and Mr. Ackerman and that old Turkey and Susan, sitting close to her box, up on the truck. Took Bud a whole day to get the truck right. And Johnny the boy—he'd been quiet this whole trip, not sayin' anything much even if you asked him. We'd agreed to take him along down toward Fairhope, where his folks had lived, the Bishops. We'd thought it was going to be a simple journey then.

Every one of us looked haggard and worn-down and not minding much the chill still in the air, even though things was warming up for weeks now. The lantern pushed back the seeping darkness and made me sure there were millions and millions of people doing this same thing, all across the nation, eating by a dim oil light and thinking about what they'd had and how to get it again and was it possible.

Then old Turkey lays back and looks like he's going to take a snooze. Yet on the journey here, he'd been the one wanted to get on with it soon's we had gas. It's the same always with a lazy man like that. He hates moving so much that once he gets set on it, he will keep on and not stop—like it isn't the moving he hates so much at all, but the starting and stopping. And once moving, he is so proud he'll do whatever to make it look easy for him but hard on the others, so he can lord it over them later.

So I wasn't surprised at all when we went out and got in the car, and Bud starts the truck and drives off real careful, and Turkey, he sits in the back of the Pontiac and gives directions like he knows the way. Which riles Mr. Ackerman, and the two of them have words.

JOHNNY

I'm tired of these people. Relatives, sure, but I was to visit them for a week only, not forever. It's the Mr. Ackerman I can't stand. Turkey said to me, "Nothing but gold drops out of his mouth, but you can tell there's stone inside." That's right.

They figure a kid nine years old can't tell, but I can.

Tell they don't know what they're doing.

Tell they all thought we were going to die. Only we didn't.

Tell Angel is scared. She thinks Bud can save us.

Maybe he can, only how could you say? He never lets on about anything.

Guess he can't. Just puts his head down and frowns like he was mad at a problem, and when he stops frowning, you know he's beat it. I like him.

Sometimes I think Turkey just don't care. Seems like he give up. But other times it looks like he's understanding and laughing at it all. He argued with Mr. Ackerman and then laughed with his eyes when he lost.

They're all O.K., I guess. Least they're taking me home.

Except that Susan. Eyes jump around like she was seeing ghosts. She's scary-crazy. I don't like to look at her.

TURKEY

Trouble comes looking for you if you're a fool.

Once we found Ackerman's idea wasn't going to work real well, we should have turned back. I said that, and they all nodded their heads, yes, yes, but they went ahead and listened to him anyway.

So I went along.

I lived a lot already, and this is as good a time to check out as any.

I had my old .32 revolver in my suitcase, but it wouldn't do me a squat of good back there. So I fished it out, wrapped in a paper bag, and tucked it under the seat. Handy.

Might as well see the world. What's left of it.

MC355

The American orbital defenses had eliminated all but ten percent of the Soviet strike.

MC355 reconstructed this within a root-means-square deviation of a few percent. It had witnessed only a third of the actual engagement, but it had running indices of performance for the MC net, and could extrapolate from that.

The warheads that got through were aimed for the landbased silos and C31 sites, as expected.

If the total armament of the two superpowers had been that of the old days, ten thousand warheads or more on each side, a ten-percent leakage would have been catastrophic. But gradual disarmament had been proceeding for decades now, and only a few thousand highly secure ICBMs existed. There were no quick-fire submarine short-range rockets at all, since they were deemed destabilizing. They had been negotiated away in earlier decades.

The submarines loaded with ICBMs were still waiting, in reserve.

All this had been achieved because of two principles: Mutual Assured Survival and I Cut, You Choose. The first half hour of the battle illustrated how essential these were.

The U.S. had ridden out the first assault. Its C3I networks were nearly intact. This was due to building defensive weapons that confined the first stage of any conflict to space.

The smallness of the arsenals arose from a philosophy adopted in the 1900s. It was based on a simple notion from childhood. In dividing a pie, one person cut slices, but then the other got to choose which one he wanted. Self-interest naturally led to cutting the slices as nearly equal as possible.

Both the antagonists agreed to a thousand-point system whereby each would value the components of its nuclear arsenal. This was the Military Value Percentage, and stood for the usefulness of a given weapon. The USSR place a high value on its accurate land-based missiles, giving them twenty-five percent of its total points. The U.S. chose to stress its submarine missiles.

Arms reduction then revolved about only what percentage to cut, not which weapons. The first cut was five percent, or fifty points. The U.S. chose which Soviet weapons were publicly destroyed, and vice versa: I Cut, You Choose. Each side thus reduced the weapons it most feared in the opponent's arsenal.

Technically, the advantage came because each side thought it benefitted from the exchange, by an amount depending on the ration of perceived threat removed to the perceived protection lost.

This led to gradual reductions. Purely defensive weapons did not enter into the thousand-point count, so there was no restraints in building them.

The confidence engendered by this slow, evolutionary approach had done much to calm international waters. The U.S. and the USSR had settled into a begrudging equilibrium.

MC355 puzzled over these facts for a long while, trying to match this view of the world with the onset of the war. It seemed impossible that either superpower would start a conflict when they were so evenly matched.

But someone had.

SUSAN

I had to go with Gene, and they said I could ride up in the cab, but I yelled at them—I yelled, no, I had to be with the T-Isolate all the time, check it to see it's workin' right, be sure, I got to be sure.

I climbed on and rode with it, the fields rippling by us 'cause Bud was going too fast, so I shouted to him, and he swore back and kept on. Heading south. The trees whipping by us—fierce sycamore, pine, all swishing, hitting me sometimes—but it was fine to be out and free again and going to save Gene.

I talked to Gene when we were going fast, the tires humming under us, big tires making music swarming up into my feet so strong I was sure Gene could feel it and know I was there watching his heart jump every few minutes, moving the blood through him like mud but still carrying oxygen enough so's the tissue could sponge it up and digest the sugar I bled into him.

He was good and cold, just a half a degree high of freezing. I read the sensors while the road rushed up at us, the white lines coming over the horizon and darting under the hood, seams in the highway going *stupp*, *stupp*, *stupp*, the air clean and with a snap in it still.

Nobody beside the road we moving all free, nobody but us, some buds on the trees brimming with burnt-orange tinkling songs, whistling to me in the feather-light brush of blue breezes blowing back my hair, all streaming behind joyous and loud strong liquid-loud.

BUD

Flooding was bad. Worse than upstream.

Must have been lots snow this far down. Fat clouds, I saw them when it was worst, fat and purple and coming off the Gulf. Dumping snow down here.

Now it run off and taken every bridge.

I have to work my way around.

Only way to go clear is due south. Toward Mobile.

I don't like that. Too many people maybe there.

I don't tell the others following behind, just wait for them at the intersections and then peel out.

Got to keep moving.

Saves talk.
People around here must be hungry.
Somebody see us could be bad.
I got the gun on a rack behind my head. Big .30-30.
You never know.

MC355

From collateral data, MC355 constructed a probable scenario: The U.S. chose to stand fast. It launched no warheads.

The USSR observed its own attack and was dismayed to find that the U.S. orbital defense system worked more than twice as well as the Soviet experts had anticipated. It ceased its attack on U.S. satellites. These had proved equally ineffective, apparently due to unexpected American defenses of its surveillance satellites—retractable sensors, multiband shielding, advanced hardening.

Neither superpower struck against the inhabited space colonies. They were unimportant in the larger context of a nuclear war.

Communications between Washington and Moscow continued. Each side thought the other had attacked first.

But over a hundred megatons had exploded on U.S. soil, and no matter how the superpowers acted thereafter, some form of nuclear winter was inevitable.

And by a fluke of the defenses, most of the warheads that leaked through fell in a broad strip across Texas to the tip of Florida.

MC355 lay buried in the middle of this belt.

TURKEY

We went through the pine forests at full clip, barely able to keep Bud in sight, I took over driving from Ackerman. The man couldn't keep up, we all saw that.

The crazy woman was waving and laughing, sitting on top of the coffin-shaped gizmo with the shiny tubes all over it.

The clay was giving way now to sandy stretches, there were poplars and gum trees and nobody around. That's what scared me. I'd thought people in Mobile would be spreading out this way, but we seen nobody.

Mobile had shelters. Food reserves. The Lekin administration started all that right at the turn of the century, and there was s'posed to be enough food stored to hold out a month, maybe more, for every man jack and child.

S'posed to be.

MC355

It calculated the environmental impact of the warheads it knew had exploded. The expected fires yielded considerable dust and burnt carbon.

But MC355 needed more information. It took one of its electric service cars, used for ferrying components through the corridors, and dispatched it with a mobile camera fixed to the back platform. The car reached a hill overlooking Mobile Bay and gave a panoramic view.

The effects of a severe freezing were evident. Grass lay dead, gray. Brown, withered trees had limbs snapped off.

But Mobile appeared intact. The skyline—

MC355 froze the frame and replayed it. One of the buildings was shaking.

ANGEL

We were getting all worried when Bud headed for Mobile, but we could see the bridges were washed out, no way to head east. A big wind was blowing off the Gulf, pretty bad, making the car slip around on the road. Nearly blew that girl off the back of Bud's truck. A storm coming, maybe, right up the bay.

Be better to be inland, to the east.

Not that I wanted to go there, though. The bomb had blowed off everythin' for twenty, thirty mile around, people said who came through last week.

Bud had thought he'd carve a way between Mobile and the bomb area. Mobile, he thought, would be full of people.

Well, not so we could see. We came down State 34 and through some small towns and turned to skirt along toward the causeway, and there was nobody.

No bodies, either.

Which meant prob'ly the radiation got them. Or else they'd moved on out. Taken out by ship, through Mobile harbor, maybe.

Bud did the right thing, didn't slow down to find out. Mr. Ackerman wanted to look around, but there was no chance, we had to keep up with Bud. I sure wasn't going to be separated from him.

We cut down along the river, fighting the wind. I could see the skyscrapers of downtown, and then I saw something funny and yelled, and Turkey, who was driving right then—the only thing anybody's got him to do on this whole trip, him just loose as a goose behind the wheel— Turkey looked sour but slowed down. Bud seen us in his rearview and stopped, and I pointed and we all got out. Except for that Susan, who didn't seem to notice. She was mumbling.

MC355

Quickly it simulated the aging and weathering of such a building. Halfway up, something had punched a large hole, letting in weather. Had a falling, inert warhead struck the building?

The winter storms might well have flooded the basement; such towers of steel and glass, perched near the tidal basin, had to be regularly pumped out. Without power, the basement would fill in weeks.

Winds had blown out windows.

Standing gap-toothed, with steel columns partly rusted, even a small breeze could put stress on the steel. Others would take the load, but if one buckled, the tower would shudder like a notched tree. Concrete would explode off columns in the basement. Moss-covered furniture in the lobby would slide as the gound floor dipped. The structure would slowly bend before nature.

BUD

Sounded like gunfire. Rattling. Sharp and hard.

I figure it was the bolts connecting the steel wall panels—they'd shear off.

I could hear the concrete floor panels rumble and crack, and spandrel beams tear in half like giant gears clashing with no clutch.

Came down slow, leaving an arc of debris seeming to hang in the air behind it.

Met the ground hard.

Slocum Towers was the name on her.

JOHNNY

Against the smashing building, I saw something standing still in the air, getting bigger. I wondered how it could do that. It was bigger and bigger and shiny turning in the air. Then it jumped out of the sky at me. Hit my shoulder. I was looking up at the sky. Angel cried out and touched me and held up her hand. It was all red. But I couldn't feel anything.

BUD

Damn one-in-a-million shot, piece of steel thrown clear. Hit the boy.

You wouldn't think a skycraper falling two miles away could do that.

Other pieces come down pretty close, too. You wouldn't think.

Nothing broke, Susan said, but plenty bleeding.

Little guy don't cry or nothing.

The women got him bandaged and all fixed up. Ackerman and Turkey argue like always. I stay to the side.

Johnny wouldn't take the painkiller Susan offers. Says he doesn't want to sleep. Wants to look when we get across the bay. Getting hurt don't faze him much as it do us.

So we go on.

JOHNNY

I can hold up like any of them, I'll show them. It didn't scare me. I can do it.

Susan is nice to me, but except for the aspirin, I don't think my mom would want me to take a pill.

I knew we were getting near home when we got to the causeway and started across. I jumped up real happy, my shoulder made my breath catch some. I looked ahead. Bud was slowing down.

He stopped. Got out.

'Cause ahead was a big hole scooped out of the causeway like a giant done it when he got mad.

BUD

Around the shallows there was scrap metal, all fused and burnt and broken.

Funny metal, though. Hard and light.

Turkey found a piece had writing on it. Not any kind of writing I ever saw.

So I start to thinking how to get across.

TURKEY

The tidal flats were a-churn, murmuring ceaseless and sullen like some big animal, the yellow surface dimpled with lunging splotches that would burst through now and then to reveal themselves as trees or broken hunks of wood, silent dead things bobbing along beside them that I didn't want to look at too closely. Like under there was something huge and alive, and it waked for a moment and stuck itself out to see what the world of air was like.

Bud showed me the metal piece all twisted, and I say, "That's Russian," right away 'cause it was.

"You never knew no Russian," Angel says right up.

"I studied it once," I say, and it be the truth even if I didn't study it long.

"Goddamn," Bud says.

"No concern of ours," Mr. Ackerman says, mostly because all this time riding back with the women and child and old me, he figures he doesn't look like much of a leader anymore. Bud wouldn't have him ride up there in the cabin with him.

Angel looks at it, turns it over in her hands, and Johnny pipes up, "It might be radioactive!"

Angel drops it like a shot. "What!"

I ask Bud, "You got that counter?"

And it was. Not a lot, but some.

"God a'mighty," Angel says.

"We got to tell somebody!" Johnny cries, all excited.

"You figure some Rooshin thing blew up the causeway?" Bud says to me.

"One of their rockets fell on it, musta been," I say.

"A *bomb?*" Angel's voice is a bird screech.

"One that didn't go off. Headed for Mobile, but the space boys, they scragged it up there—" I pointed straight up.

"Set to go off in the bay?" Angel says wonderingly.

"Musta."

"We got to tell somebody!" Johnny cries.

"Never you mind that," Bud says. "We got to keep movin'."

"How?" Angel wants to know.

SUSAN

I tell Gene how the water clucks and moans through the trough cut in the causeway. Yellow. Scummed with awful brown froth and growling green with thick soiled gouts jutting up where the road was. It laps against the wheels as Bud guns the engine and creeps forward, me clutching to Gene and watching the reeds to the side stuck out of the foam like metal blades stabbing up from the water, teeth to eat the tires, but we crush them as we grind forward across the shallow yellow flatness. Bud weaves among the stubs of warped metal—from Roosha, Johnny calls up to me—sticking up like trees all rootless, suspended above the streaming, empty, stupid waste and desolating flow.

TURKEY

The water slams into the truck like it was an animal hitting with a paw. Bud fights to keep the wheels on the mud under it and not topple over onto its side with that damn casket sitting there shiny and the loony girl shouting to him from on top of *that*.

And the rest of us riding in the back, too, scrunched up against the cab. If she gets stuck, we can jump free fast, wade or swim back. We're reeling out rope as we go, tied to the stump of a telephone pole, for a grab line if we have to go back.

He is holding it pretty fine against the slick yellow current dragging at him, when this log juts sudden out of the foam like it was coming from God himself, dead at the truck. A rag caught on the end of it like a man's shirt, and the huge log is like a whale that ate the man long ago and has come back for another.

"No! No!" Angel cries. "Back up!" But there's no time.

The log is two hands across, easy, and slams into the truck at the side panel just behind the driver, and Bud sees it just as it stove in the steel. He wrestles the truck around to set off the weight, but the wheels lift and the water goes gushing up under the truck bed, pushing it over more.

We all grab onto the Isolate thing or the truck and hang there, Mr. Ackerman giving out a burst of swearing.

The truck lurches again.

The angle steepens.

I was against taking the casket thing 'cause it just pressed the truck down in the mud more, made it more likely Bud'd get stuck, but now it is the only thing holding the truck against the current.

The yellow froths around the bumpers at each end, and we're shouting—to surely no effect, of course.

SUSAN

The animal is trying to eat us, it has seen Gene and wants him. I lean over and strike at the yellow animal that is everywhere swirling around us, but it just takes my hand and takes the smack of my palm like it was no matter at all, and I start to cry, I don't know what to do.

JOHNNY

My throat filled up, I was so afraid.

Bud, I can hear him grunting as he twists at the steering wheel.

His jaw is clenched, and the woman Susan calls to us, "Catch him! Catch Gene!"

I hold on, and the waters suck at me.

TURKEY

I can tell Bud is afraid to gun it and start the wheels to spinning 'cause he'll lose traction and that'll tip us over for sure.

Susan jumps out and stands in the wash downstream and pushes against the truck to keep it from going over. The pressure is shoving it off the ford, and the casket, it slides down a foot or so, the cables have worked loose. Now she pays because the weight is worse, and she jams herself like a stick to wedge between the truck and the mud.

It if goes over, she's finished. It is a fine thing to do, crazy but fine, and I jump down and start wading to reach her.

No time.

There is an eddy. The log turns broadside. It backs off a second and then heads forward again, this time poking up from a surge. I can see Bud duck, he has got the window up and the log hits it, the glass going all to smash and scatteration.

BUD

All over my lap it falls like snow. Twinkling glass.

But the pressure of the log is off, and I gun the sumbitch.

We root out of the hollow we was in, and the truck thunks down solid on somethin'.

The log is ramming against me. I slam on the brake.

Take both hands and shove it out. With every particle of force I got.

It backs off and then heads around and slips in front of the hood, bumping the grill just once.

ANGEL

Like it had come to do its job and was finished and now went off to do something else.

SUSAN

Muddy, my arms hurting. I scramble back in the truck with the murmur of the water all around us. Angry with us now. Wanting us.

Bud makes the truck roar, and we lurch into a hole and out of it and up. The water gurgles at us in its fuming, stinking rage.

I check Gene and the power cells, they are dead.

He is heating up.

Not fast, but it will wake him. They say even in the solution he's floating in, they can come out of dreams and start to feel again. To hurt.

I yell at Bud that we got to find power cells.

"Those're not just ordinary batteries, y'know," he says.

"There're some at DataComm," I tell him.

We come wallowing up from the gum-yellow water and onto the highway.

GENE

Sleeping . . . slowly . . . I can still feel . . . only in sluggish . . . moments . . . moments . . . not true sleep but a drifting, aimless dreaming . . . faint tugs and ripples . . . hollow sounds. . . . I am underwater and drowning . . . but don't care . . . don't breathe. . . . Spongy stuff fills my lungs . . . easier to rest them . . . floating in snowflakes . . . a watery winter . . . but knocking comes . . . goes . . . jolts . . . slips away before I can remember what it means. . . . Hardest . . . yes . . . hardest thing is to remember the secret . . . so when I am in touch again . . . DataComm will know . . . what I learned . . . when the C31 crashed . . . when I learned. . . . It is hard to clutch onto the slippery, shiny fact . . . in a marsh of slick, soft bubbles . . . silvery as air . . . winking ruby-red behind my eyelids. . . . Must snag the secret . . . a hard fact like shiny steel in the spongy moist warmness. . . . Hold it to me. . . . Something knocks my side . . . a thumping. . . . I am sick. . . . Hold the steel secret . . . keep. . . .

MC355

The megatonnage in the Soviet assault exploded low—ground-pounders, in the jargon. This caused huge fires, MC355's simulation showed. A pall of soot rose, blanketing Texas and the South, then diffusing outward on global circulation patterns.

Within a few days, temperatures dropped from balmy summer to near-freezing. In the Gulf region where MC355 lay, the warm ocean continued to feed heat and moisture into the marine boundary layer near the shore. Cold winds rammed into this water-laden air, spawning great roiling storms and deep snows. Thick stratus clouds shrouded the land for at least a hundred kilometers inland.

All this explained why MC355's extended feelers had met chaos and destruction. And why there were no local radio broadcasts. What the ElectroMagnetic Pulse did not destroy, the storms did.

The remaining large questions were whether the war had gone on, and if any humans survived in the area at all.

MR. ACKERMAN

I'd had more than enough of this time. The girl Susan had gone mad right in front of us, and we'd damn near all drowned getting across.

"I think we ought to get back as soon's we can," I said to Bud when we stopped to rest on the other side.

"We got to deliver the boy."

"It's too disrupted down this way. I figured on people here, some civilization."

"Somethin' got 'em."

"The bomb."

"Got to find cells for the man in the box."

"He's near dead."

"Too many gone already. Should save one if we can."

"We got to look after our own."

Bud shrugged, and I could see I wasn't going to get far with him. So I said to Angel, "The boy's not worth running such risks. Or this corpse."

ANGEL

I didn't like Ackerman before the war, and even less afterward, so when he started hinting that maybe we should shoot back up north and ditch the boy and Susan and the man in there, I let him have it. From the look on Bud's face, I knew he felt the same way. I spat out a real choice set of words I'd heard my father use once on a grain buyer who'd weaseled out of a deal, stuff I'd been saving for years, and I do say it felt *good*.

TURKEY

So we run down the east side of the bay, feeling released to be quit of the city and the water, and heading down into some of the finest country in all the South. Through Daphne and Montrose and into Fairhope, the moss hanging on the trees and now and then actual sunshine slanting golden through the green of huge old mimosas.

We're jammed into the truck bed, hunkered down because the wind whipping by has some sting to it. The big purple clouds are blowing south now.

Still no people. Not that Bud slows down to search good.

Bones of cattle in the fields, though. I been seeing them so much now I hardly take notice anymore.

There's a silence here so deep that the wind streaming through the pines seems loud. I don't like it, to come so far and see nobody. I keep my paper bag close.

Fairhope's a pretty town, big oaks leaning out over the streets and a long pier down at the bay with a park where you can go cast fishing. I've always liked it here, intended to move down until the prices shot up so much.

We went by some stores with windows smashed in, and that's when we saw the man.

ANGEL

He was waiting for us. Standing beside the street, in jeans and a floppy yellow shirt all grimy and not tucked in. I waved at him the instant I saw him, and he waved back. I yelled, excited, but he didn't say anything.

Bud screeched on the brakes. I jumped down and went around the tail of the truck. Johnny followed me.

The man was skinny as a rail and leaning against a telephone pole. A long, scraggly beard hid his face, but the eyes beamed out at us, seeming to pick up the sunlight.

"Hello!" I said again.

"Kiss." That was all.

"We came from . . ." and my voice trailed off because the man pointed at me.

"Kiss."

MR. ACKERMAN

I followed Angel and could tell right away the man was suffering from malnutrition. The clothes hung off him.

"Can you give us information?" I asked.

"No."

"Well, why not, friend? We've come looking for the parents of—"

"Kiss first."

I stepped back. "Well, now, you have no right to demand—"

Out of the corner of my eye, I could see Bud had gotten out of the cab and stopped and was going back in now, probably for his gun. I decided to save the situation before somebody got hurt.

"Angel, go over to him and speak nicely to him. We need—"

"Kiss now."

The man pointed again with a bony finger.

Angel said, "I'm not going to go—" and stopped because the man's hand went down to his belt. He pulled up the filthy yellow shirt to reveal a pistol tucked in his belt.

"Kiss."

"Now friend, we can—"

The man's hand came up with the pistol and reached level, pointing at us.

"Pussy."

Then his head blew into a halo of blood.

BUD

Damn if the one time I needed it, I left it in the cab.

I was still fetching it out when the shot went off.

Then another.

TURKEY

A man shows you his weapon in his hand, he's a fool if he doesn't mean to use it.

I drew out the pistol I'd been carrying in my pocket all this time, wrapped in plastic. I got it out of the damned bag pretty quick while the man was looking crazy-eyed at Angel and bringing his piece up.

It was no trouble at all to fix him in the notch. Couldn't have been more than thirty feet.

But going down he gets one off, and I feel like somebody pushed at my left calf. Then I'm rolling. Drop my pistol, too. I end up smack face-down on the hardtop, not feeling anything yet.

ANGEL

I like to died when the man flopped down, so sudden I thought he'd slipped, until then the bang registered.

I rushed over, but Turkey shouted, "Don't touch him."

Mr. Ackerman said, "You idiot! That man could've told us—"

"Told nothing," Turkey said. "He's crazy."

Then I notice Turkey's down, too. Susan is working on him, rolling up his jeans. It's gone clean through his big muscle there.

Bud went to get a stick. Poked the man from a safe distance. Managed to pull his shirt aside. We could see the sores all over his chest. Something terrible it looked.

Mr. Ackerman was swearing and calling us idiots until we saw that. Then he shut up.

TURKEY

Must admit it felt good. First time in years anybody ever admitted I was right.

Paid back for the pain. Dull, heavy ache it was, spreading. Susan gives me a shot and a pill and has me bandaged up tight. Blood stopped easy, she says. I clot good.

We decided to get out of there, not stopping to look for Johnny's parents.

We got three blocks before the way was blocked.

It was a big metal cylinder, fractured on all sides. Glass glittering around it.

Right in the street. You can see where it hit the roof of a clothing store, Bedsole's, caved in the front of it and rolled into the street.

They all get out and have a look, me sitting in the cab. I see the Russian writing again on the end of it.

I don't know much, but I can make out at the top CeKPeT and a lot of words that look like warning, including σO'πeH, which is *sick*, and some more I didn't know, and then II O ОГО'H, which is *weather*.

"What's it say?" Mr. Ackerman asks.

"That word at the top there's *secret*, and then something about biology and sickness and rain and weather."

"I thought you *knew* this writing," he says.

I shook my head. "I know enough."

"Enough to what?"

"To know this was some kind of targeted capsule. It fell right smack in the middle of Fairhope, biggest town this side of the bay."

"Like the other one?" Johnny says, which surprised me. The boy is smart.

"The one hit the causeway? Right."

"One *what*?" Mr. Ackerman asks.

I don't want to say it with the boy there and all, but it has to come out sometime. "Some disease. Biological warfare."

They stand there in the middle of Prospect Avenue with open, silent nothingness around us, and nobody says anything for the longest time. There won't be any prospects here for a long time. Johnny's parents we aren't going to find, nobody we'll find, because whatever came spurting out of this capsule when it busted open—up high, no doubt, so the wind could take it—had done its work.

Angel sees it right off. "Must've been time for them to get inside," is all she says, but she's thinking the same as me.

It got them into such a state that they went home and holed up to die, like an animal will. Maybe it would be different in the North or the West—people are funny out there, they might just as soon sprawl across the sidewalk—but down here people's first thought is home, the family, the only thing that might pull them through. So they went there and they didn't come out again.

Mr. Ackerman says, "But there's no smell," which was stupid because that made it all real to the boy, and he starts to cry. I pick him up.

JOHNNY

'Cause that means they're all gone, what I been fearing ever since we crossed the causeway, and nobody's there, it's true, Mom Dad nobody at all anywhere just emptiness all gone.

MC355

The success of the portable unit makes MC355 bold.

It extrudes more sensors and finds not the racing blizzard winds of months before but rather warming breezes, the soft sigh of pines, a low drone of reawakening insects.

There was no nuclear winter.

Instead, a kind of nuclear autumn.

The swirling jet streams have damped, the stinging ultraviolet gone. The storms retreat, the cold surge has passed. But the electromagnetic spectrum lies bare, a muted hiss. The EMP silenced man's signals, yes.

Opticals, fitted with new lenses, scan the night sky. Twinkling dots scoot across the blackness, scurrying on their Newtonian rounds.

The Arcapel Colony.

Russphere.

US1.

All intact. So they at least have survived.

Unless they were riddled by buckshot-slinging antisatellite devices. But, no—the inflated storage sphere hinged beside the US1 is undeflated, unbreached.

So man still lives in space, at least.

MR. ACKERMAN

Crazy, I thought, to go out looking for this DataComm when everybody's *dead*. Just the merest step inside one of the houses proved that.

But they wouldn't listen to me. Those who would respectfully fall silent when I spoke now ride over my words as if I weren't there.

All because of that stupid incident with the sick one. He must have taken longer to die. I couldn't have anticipated that. He just seemed hungry to me.

It's enough to gall a man.

ANGEL

The boy is calm now, just kind of tucked into himself. He knows what's happened to his mom and dad. Takes his mind off his hurt, anyway. He bows his head down, his long dirty-blond hair hiding his expression. He leans against Turkey and they talk. I can see them through the back cab window.

In amongst all we've seen, I suspect it doesn't come through to him full yet. It will take a while. We'll all take a while.

We head out from Fairhope quick as we can. Not that anyplace else is different. The germs must've spread twenty, thirty mile inland from here. Which is why we seen nobody before who'd heard of it. Anybody close enough to know is gone.

Susan's the only one it doesn't seem to bother. She keeps crooning to that box.

Through Silverhill and on to Robertsdale. Same everywhere—no dogs bark, cattle bones drying in the fields.

We don't go into the houses.

Turn south toward Foley. They put this DataComm in the most inconspicuous place, I guess because secrets are hard to keep in cities. Anyway, it's in a pine grove south of Foley land good for soybeans and potatoes.

SUSAN

I went up to the little steel door they showed me once and I take a little signet thing and press it into the slot.

Then the codes. They change them every month, but this one's still good, 'cause the door pops open.

Two feet thick it is. And so much under there you could spend a week finding your way.

Bud unloads the T-Isolate, and we push it through the mud and down the ramp.

BUD

Susan's better now, but I watch her careful.

We go down into this pale white light everywhere. All neat and trim.

Pushing that big Isolate thing, it takes a lot out of you. 'Specially when you don't know where to.

But the signs light up when we pass by. Somebody's expecting.

To the hospital is where.

There are places to hook up this Isolate thing, and Susan does it. She is O.K. when she has something to do.

MC355

The men have returned.

Asked for shelter.

And now, plugged in, MC355 reads the sluggish, silky, grieving mind.

GENE

At last . . . someone has found the tap-in. . . . I can feel the images flit like shiny blue fish through the warm slush I float in. . . . Someone . . . asking . . . so I take the hard metallic ball of facts and I break it open so the someone can see. . . . So slowly I do it . . . things hard to remember . . . steely-bright. . . . I saw it all in one instant. . . . I was the only one on duty then with Top Secret, Weapons Grade Clearance, so it all came to me . . . attacks on both U.S. and USSR . . . some third party . . . only plausible scenario . . . a maniac . . . and all the counter-force and MAD and strategies options . . . a big joke . . . irrelevant . . . compared to the risk of accident or third parties . . . that was the first point, and we all realized it when the thing was only an hour old, but then it was too . . .

TURKEY

It's creepy in here, everybody gone. I'd hoped somebody's hid out and would be waiting, but when Bud wheels the casket thing through these halls, there's nothing—your own voice coming back thin and empty, reflected from rooms beyond rooms beyond rooms, all waiting under here. Wobbling along on the crutches, Johnny fetched me, I get lost in this electronic city clean and hard. We are like something that washed up on the beach here. God, it must've cost more than all Fairhope itself, and who knew it was here? Not me.

GENE

A plot it was, just a goddamn plot with nothing but pure blind rage and greed behind it . . . and the hell of it is, we're never going to know who did it precisely . . . 'cause in the backwash whole governments will fall, people stab each other in the back . . . no way to tell who paid the fishing boat captains offshore to let the cruise missiles aboard . . . bet those captains were surprised when the damn things launched from the deck . . . bet they were told it was some kind of stunt . . . and then the boats all evaporated into steam when the fighters got them . . . no hope of getting a story out of *that* . . . all so comic when you think how easy it was . . . and the same for the Russians, I'm sure . . . dumbfounded confusion . . . and nowhere to turn . . . nobody to hit back at . . . so they hit us . . . been primed for it so long that's the only way they could think . . . and even then there was hope . . . because the defenses worked . . . people got to the shelters . . . the satellite rockets knocked out hordes of Soviet warheads . . . we surely lessened the damage, with the defenses and shelters, too . . . but we hadn't allowed for the essential final fact that all the science and strategy pointed to . . .

BUD

Computer asked us to put up new antennas.
    A week's work, easy, I said.
    It took two.

It fell to me, most of it. Be weeks before Turkey can walk. But we got it done.

First signal comes in, it's like we're Columbus. Susan finds some wine and we have it all 'round.

We get US1. The first to call them from the whole South.

'Cause there isn't much South left.

GENE

But the history books will have to write themselves on this one. . . . I don't know who it was and now don't care . . . because one other point all we strategic planners and analysts missed was that nuclear winter didn't mean the end of anything . . . anything at all . . . just that you'd be careful to not use nukes anymore. . . . Used to say that love would find a way . . . but one thing I know . . . war will find a way, too . . . and this time the Soviets loaded lots of their warheads with biowar stuff, canisters fixed to blow high above cities . . . stuff your satellite defenses could at best riddle with shot but not destroy utterly, as they could the high explosive in nuke warheads. . . . All so simple . . . if you know there's a nuke winter limit on the megatonnage you can deliver . . . you use the nukes on C31 targets and silos . . . and then biowar the rest of your way. . . . A joke, really . . . I even laughed over it a few times myself . . . we'd placed so much hope in ol' nuke winter holding the line . . . rational as all hell . . . the scenarios all so clean . . . easy to calculate . . . we built our careers on them. . . . But this other way . . . so simple . . . and no end to it . . . and all I hope's . . . hope's . . . the bastard started this . . . some Third World general . . . caught some of the damned stuff, too. . . .

BUD

The germs got us. Cut big stretches through the U.S. We were just lucky. The germs played out in a couple of months, while we were holed up. Soviets said they'd used the bio stuff in amongst the nukes to show us what they could do, long term. Unless the war stopped right there. Which it did.

But enough nukes blew off here and in Russia to freeze up everybody for July and August, set off those storms.

Germs did the most damage, though—plagues.

It was a plague canister that hit the Slocum building. That did in Mobile.

The war was all over in a couple of hours. The satellite people, they saw it all.

Now they're settling the peace.

MR. ACKERMAN

"We been sitting waiting on this corpse long enough," I said, and got up.

We got food from the commissary here. Fine, I don't say I'm anything but grateful for that. And we rested in the bunks, got recuperated. But enough's enough. The computer tells us it wants to talk to the man Gene some more. Fine, I say.

Turkey stood up. "Not easy, the computer says, this talking to a man's near dead. Slow work."

Looking around, I tried to take control, assume leadership again. Jutted out my chin. "Time to get back."

But their eyes are funny. Somehow I'd lost my real power over them. It's not anymore like I'm the one who led them when the bombs started.

Which means, I suppose, that this thing isn't going to be a new beginning for me. It's going to be the same life. People aren't going to pay me any more real respect than they ever did.

MC355

So the simulations had proved right. But as ever, incomplete.

MC355 peered at the shambling, adamant band assembled in the hospital bay, and pondered how many of them might be elsewhere.

Perhaps many. Perhaps few.

It all depended on data MC355 did not have, could not easily find. The satellite worlds swinging above could get no accurate count in the U.S. or the USSR.

Still—looking at them, MC355 could not doubt that there were many. They were simply too brimming with life, too hard to kill. All the calculations in the world could not stop these creatures.

The humans shuffled out, leaving the T-Isolate with the woman who had never left its side. They were going.

MC355 called after them. They nodded, understanding, but did not stop.

MC355 let them go.

There was much to do.

New antennas, new sensors, new worlds.

TURKEY

Belly full and eye quick, we came out into the pines. Wind blowed through with a scent of the Gulf on it, fresh and salty with rich moistness.

The dark clouds are gone. I think maybe I'll get Bud to drive south some more. I'd like to go swimming one more time in those breakers that come booming in, taller than I am, down near Fort Morgan. Man never knows when he'll get to do it again.

Bud's ready to travel. He's taking a radio so's we can talk to MC, find out about the help that's coming. For now, we got to get back and look after our own.

Same as we'll see to the boy. He's ours now.

Susan says she'll stay with Gene till he's ready, till some surgeons turn up can work on him. That'll be a long time, say I. But she can stay if she wants. Plenty food and such down there for her.

A lot of trouble we got, coming a mere hundred mile. Not much to show for it when we get back. A bumper crop of bad news, some would say. Not me. It's better to know than to not, better to go on than to look back.

So we go out into dawn, and there are the same colored dots riding in the high, hard blue. Like camp fires.

The crickets are chirruping, and in the scrub there's a rustle of things moving about their own business, a clean scent of things starting up. The rest of us, we mount the truck and it surges forward with a muddy growl, Ackerman slumped over, Angel in the cab beside Bud, the boy already asleep on some blankets; and the forlorn sound of us moving among the windswept trees is a long and echoing note of mutual and shared desolation, powerful and pitched forward into whatever must come now, a muted note persisting and undeniable in the soft, sweet air.

EPILOGUE
(twenty-three years later)

JOHNNY

An older woman in a formless, wrinkled dress and worn shoes sat at the side of the road. I was panting from the fast pace I was keeping along the white strip of sandy, rutted road. She sat, silent and unmoving. I nearly walked by before I saw her.

"You're resting?" I asked.

"Waiting." Her voice had a feel of rustling leaves. She sat on the brown cardboard suitcase with big copper latches—the kind made right after the war. It was cracked along the side, and white cotton underwear stuck out.

"For the bus?"

"For Buck."

"The chopper recording, it said the bus will stop up around the bend."

"I heard."

"It won't come down this side road. There's not time."

I was late myself, and I figured she had picked the wrong spot to wait.

"Buck will be along."

Her voice was high and had the backcountry twang to it. My own voice still had some of the same sound, but I was keeping my vowels flat and right now, and her accent reminded me of how far I had come.

I squinted, looking down the long sandy curve of the road. A pickup truck growled out of a clay side road and onto the hardtop. People rode in the back along with trunks and a 3D. Taking everything they could. Big white eyes shot a glance at me, and then the driver hit the hydrogen and got out of there.

The Confederation wasn't giving us much time. Since the unification of the Soviet, USA and European/Sino space colonies into one political union, everybody'd come to think of them as the Confeds, period—one entity. I knew better—there were tensions and differences abounding up there—but the shorthand was convenient.

"Who's Buck?"

"My *dog*." She looked at me directly, as though any fool would know who Buck was.

"Look, the bus—"

"You're one of those Bishop boys, aren't you?"

I looked off up the road again. That set of words—being eternally *a Bishop boy*—was like a grain of sand caught between my back teeth. My mother's friends had used that phrase when they came over for an evening of bridge, before I went away to the university. Not my real mother, of course—she and Dad had died in the war, and I dimly remembered them.

Or anyone else from then. Almost everybody around here had been struck down by the Soviet bioweapons. It was the awful swath of those that cut through whole states, mostly across the South—the horror of it—that had formed the basis of the peace that followed. Nuclear and bioarsenals were reduced to nearly zero now. Defenses in space were thick and reliable. The building of those had fueled the huge boom in Confed cities, made orbital commerce important, provided jobs and horizons for a whole generation—including me. I was a ground-orbit liaison, spending four months every year at US3. But to the people down here, I was eternally that oldest Bishop boy.

Bishops. I was the only one left who'd actually lived here before the war. I'd been away on a visit when it came. Afterward, my Aunt and Uncle Bishop from Birmingham came down to take over the old family property—to save it from being homesteaded on, under the new Federal Reconstruction Acts. They'd taken me in, and I'd thought of them as Mom and Dad. We'd all had the Bishop name, after all. So I was a Bishop, one of the few natives who'd made it through the bombing and nuclear autumn and all. People'd point me out as almost a freak, a *real native*, wow.

"Yes, ma'am," I said neutrally.

"Thought so."

"You're . . . ?"

"Susan McKenzie."

"Ah."

We had done the ritual, so now we could talk. Yet some memory stirred. . . .

"Something 'bout you . . ." She squinted in the glaring sunlight. She probably wasn't all that old, in her late fifties, maybe. Anybody who'd caught some radiation looked aged a bit beyond their years. Or maybe it was just the unending weight of hardship and loss they'd carried.

"Seems like I knew you before the war," she said. "I strictly believe I saw you."

"I was up north then, a hundred miles from here. Didn't come back until months later."

"So'd I."

"Some relatives brought me down, and we found out what'd happened to Fairhope."

She squinted at me again, and then a startled look spread across her leathery face. "My Lord! Were they lookin' for that big computer center, the DataComm it was?"

I frowned. "Well, maybe . . . I don't remember too well. . . ."

"Johnny. You're Johnny!"

"Yes, ma'am, John Bishop." I didn't like the little-boy ending on my name, but people around here couldn't forget it.

"I'm Susan! The one went with you! I had the codes for DataComm, remember?"

"Why . . . yes. . . ." Slow clearing of ancient, foggy images. "You were hiding in that center . . . where we found you. . . ."

"Yes! I had Gene in the T-Isolate."

"Gene . . ." That awful time had been stamped so strongly in me that I'd blocked off many memories, muting the horror. Now it came flooding back.

"I saved him, all right! Yessir. We got married, I had my children."

Tentatively, she reached out a weathered hand, and I touched it. A lump suddenly blocked my throat, and my vision blurred. Somehow, all those years had passed and I'd never thought to look up any of those people—Turkey, Angel, Bud, Mr. Ackerman. Just too painful, I guess. And a little boy making his way in a tough world, without his parents, doesn't look back a whole lot.

We grasped hands. "I think I might've seen you once, actu'ly. At a fish fry down at Point Clear. You and some boys was playing with the nets— it was just after the fishing came back real good, those Roussin germs'd wore off. Gene went down to shoo you away from the boats. I was cleaning flounder, and I thought then, maybe you were the one. But somehow when I saw your face at a distance, I couldn't go up to you and say anything. You was skipping around, so happy, laughing and all. I couldn't bring those bad times back."

"I . . . I understand."

"Gene died two year ago," she said simply.

"I'm sorry."

"We had our time together," she said, forcing a smile.

"Remember how we—" And then I recalled where I was, what was coming. "Mrs. McKenzie, there's not long before the last bus."

"I'm waiting for Buck."

"Where is he?"

"He run off in the woods, chasing something."

I worked by backpack straps around my shoulders. They creaked in the quiet.

There wasn't much time left. Pretty soon now it would start. I knew the sequence, because I did maintenance engineering and retrofit on US3's modular mirrors.

One of the big reflectors would focus sunlight on a rechargeable tube of gas. That would excite the molecules. A small triggering beam would start the lasing going, the excited molecules cascading down together from one preferentially occupied quantum state to a lower state. A traveling wave swept down the tube, jarring loose more photons. They all added together in phase, so when the light waves hit the far end of the hundred-meter tube, it was a sword, a gouging lance that could cut through air and clouds. And this time, it wouldn't strike an array of layered solid-state collectors outside New Orleans, providing clean electricity. It would carve a swath twenty meters wide through the trees and fields of southern Alabama. A little demonstration, the Confeds said.

"The bus—look, I'll carry that suitcase for you."

"I can manage." She peered off into the distance, and I saw she was tired, tired beyond knowing it. "I'll wait for Buck."

"Leave him, Mrs. McKenzie."

"I don't need that blessed bus."

"Why not?"

"My children drove off to Mobile with their families. They're coming back to get me."

"My insteted radio"—I gestured at my radio—"says the roads to Mobile are jammed up. You can't count on them."

"They *said* so."

"The Confed deadline—"

"I tole 'em I'd try to walk to the main road. Got tired, is all. They'll know I'm back in here."

"Just the same—"

"I'm all right, don't you mind. They're good children, grateful for all I've gone and done for them. They'll be back."

"Come with me to the bus. It's not far."

"Not without Buck. He's all the company I got these days." She smiled, blinking.

I wiped sweat from my brow and studied the pines. There were a lot of places for a dog to be. The land here was flat and barely above sea level. I had come to camp and rest, rowing skiffs up the Fish River, looking for places I'd been when I was a teenager and my mom had rented boats from a rambling old fisherman's house. I had turned off my radio, to get away from things. The big, mysterious island I remembered and called Treasure Island, smack in the middle of the river, was now a soggy stand of trees in a bog. The big storm a year back had swept it away.

I'd been sleeping in the open on the shore near there when the chopper woke me up, blaring. The Confeds had given twelve hours' warning, the recording said.

They'd picked this sparsely populated area for their little demonstration. People had been moving back in ever since the biothreat was cleaned out, but there still weren't many. I'd liked that when I was growing up. Open woods. That's why I came back every chance I got.

I should've guessed something was coming. The Confeds were about evenly matched with the whole rest of the planet now, at least in high-tech weaponry. Defense held all the cards. The big mirrors were modular and could fold up fast, making a small target. They could incinerate anything launched against them, too.

But the U.N. kept talking like the Confeds were just another nation-state or something. Nobody down here understood that the people up there thought of Earth itself as the real problem—eaten up with age-old rivalries and hate, still holding onto dirty weapons that murdered whole populations, carrying around in their heads all the rotten baggage of the past. To listen to them, you'd think they'd learned nothing from the war. Already they were forgetting that it was the orbital defenses that had saved the biosphere itself, and the satellite communities that knit together the mammoth rescue efforts of the decade after. Without the antivirals developed and grown in huge zero-g vats, lots of us would've caught one of the poxes drifting through the population. People just forget. Nations, too.

"Where's Buck?" I said decisively.

"He . . . that way." A wave of the hand.

I wrestled my backpack down, feeling the stab from my shoulder—and suddenly remembered the thunk of that steel knocking me down, back then. So long ago. And me, still carrying an ache from it that woke whenever a cold snap came on. The past was still alive.

I trotted into the short pines, over creeper grass. Flies jumped where my boots struck. The white sand made a *skree* sound as my boots skated over it. I remembered how I'd first heard that sound, wearing slick-soled tennis shoes, and how pleased I'd been at university when I learned how the acoustics of it worked.

"Buck!"

A flash of brown over to the left. I ran through a thick stand of pine, and the dog yelped and took off, dodging under a blackleaf bush. I called again. Buck didn't even slow down. I skirted left. He went into some oak scrub, barking, having a great time of it, and I could hear him getting tangled in it and then shaking free and out of the other side. Long gone.

When I got back to Mrs. McKenzie, she didn't seem to notice me. "I can't catch him."

"Knew you wouldn't." She grinned at me, showing brown teeth. "Buck's a fast one."

"Call him."

She did. Nothing. "Must of run off."

"There isn't time—"

"I'm not leaving without ole Buck. Times I was alone down on the river after Gene died, and the water would come up under the house. Buck was the only company I had. Only soul I saw for five weeks in that big blow we had."

A low whine from afar. "I think that's the bus," I said.

She cocked her head. "Might be."

"Come on. I'll carry your suitcase."

She crossed her arms. "My children will be by for me. I tole them to look for me along in here."

"They might not make it."

"They're loyal children."

"Mrs. McKenzie, I can't wait for you to be reasonable." I picked up my backpack and brushed some red ants off the straps.

"You Bishops was always reasonable," she said levelly. "You work up there, don't you?"

"Ah, sometimes."

"You goin' back, after they do what they're doin' here?"

"I might." Even if I owed her something for what she did long ago, damned if I was going to be cowed.

"They're attacking the United *States*."

"And spots in Bavaria, the Urals, South Africa, Brazil—"

" 'Cause we don't trust 'em! They think they can push the United *States* aroun' just as they please—" And she went on with all the clichés heard daily from earthbound media. How the Confeds wanted to run the world and they were dupes of the Russians, and how surrendering national sovereignty to a bunch of self-appointed overlords was an affront to our dignity, and so on.

True, some of it—the Confeds weren't saints. But they were the only power that thought in truly global terms, couldn't *not* think that way. They could stop ICBMs and punch through the atmosphere to attack any offensive capability on the ground—that's what this demonstration was to show. I'd heard Confeds argue that this was the only way to break the diplomatic log-jam—*do* something. I had my doubts. But times were changing, that was sure, and my generation didn't think the way the pre-war people did.

"—we'll never be ruled by some outside—"

"Mrs. McKenzie, there's the bus! Listen!"

The turbo whirred far around the bend, slowing for the stop.

Her face softened as she gazed at me, as if recalling memories. "That's all right, boy. You go along, now."

I saw that she wouldn't be coaxed or even forced down that last bend. She had gone as far as she was going to, and the world would have to come the rest of the distance itself.

Up ahead, the bus driver was probably behind schedule for this last pickup. He was going to be irritated and more than a little scared. The Confeds would be right on time, he knew that.

I ran. My feet plowed through the deep, soft sand. Right away I could tell I was more tired than I'd thought and the heat had taken some strength out of me. I went about two hundred meters along the gradual bend, was nearly within view of the bus, when I heard it start up with a rumble. I tasted salty sweat, and it felt like the whole damned planet was dragging at my feet, holding me down. The driver raced the engine, in a hurry.

He had to come toward me as he swung out onto Route 80 on the way back to Mobile. Maybe I could reach the intersection in time for him to see me. So I put my head down and plunged forward.

But there was the woman back there. To get to her, the driver would have to take the bus down that rutted, sandy road and risk getting stuck.

With people on the bus yelling at him. All that to get the old woman with the grateful children. She didn't seem to understand that there were ungrateful children in the skies now—she didn't seem to understand much of what was going on—and suddenly I wasn't sure I did, either.

But I kept on.

Walter Jon Williams

In his eclectically varied novels and short stories, Walter Jon Williams has tried a variety of approaches, ranging from hard science fiction to comic space opera and disaster epic. He is the author of a cyberpunk trilogy formed by Hardwired, Solip: System, and Voice of the Whirlwind, and the diptych of Metropolitan and City on Fire, which relates the intrigues that take place inside a forcibly enclosed city world powered by geomancy. He has also chronicled the adventures of irascible interstellar thief Drake Maijstral in the series of elegant farces, starting with The Crown Jewels, House of Shards, and Rock of Ages. His short fiction includes "Wall, Stone, Craft," an award-winning novella that provides an alternate history based on Mary Shelley's Frankenstein, and the short stories collected in Facets. Williams's disaster novel, The Rift, examines the catalcylsmic social and cultural consequences of a major earthquake along the New Madrid fault line in the Mississippi River valley.

WOLF TIME

Walter Jon Williams

SPEAKERS IN THE HOSPITAL ceiling chimed a series of low, whispery, synthesized tones, tones that were scientifically proven to be relaxing. Reese looked down at the kid in the hospital bed and felt her insides twist.

The kid was named Steward, and he'd just had a bullet removed that morning. In the last few days, mad with warrior zen and a suicidal concept of personal honor, he'd gone kamikaze and blown up the whole network. Griffith was dead, Jordan was dead, Spassky was dead, and nobody had stopped Steward until everything in L.A. had collapsed entirely. He hadn't talked yet to the heat, but he would. Reese reached for her gun. Her insides were still twisting.

Steward had been lied to and jacked over and manipulated without his knowing it. Mostly it had been his friend Reese who had done it to him. She couldn't blame him for exploding when he finally figured out what had happened.

And now this.

Reese turned off the IV monitor so it wouldn't bleep when he died, and then Steward opened his eyes. She could see the recognition in his look, the knowledge of what was about to happen. She might have known he wouldn't make it easy.

"Sorry," she said, and raised the gun. What the hell else could she say? *Maybe we can still be friends, after this is over?*

Steward was trying to say something. She felt herself wring out again.

She shot him three times with her silenced pistol and left. The police guards didn't look twice at her hospital coat and ID. Proper credentials had always been her specialty.

. . .

CYA. Reese headed for Japan under a backup identity. Credentials her strong suit, as always. On the shuttle she drank a star beast and plugged her seat's interface stud into the socket at the base of her skull. She closed her eyes and silently projected the latest scansheets onto the optical centers of her brain, and her lips twisted in anger as for the first time she found out what had really gone down, what she'd been a part of.

Alien pharmaceuticals, tonnes of them, shipped down under illegal cover. The network had been huge, bigger than Reese, from her limited perspective, had ever suspected, and now the L.A. heat had *everything*. Police and security people everywhere, even in the space habitats, were going berserk.

All along, she'd thought it was friends helping friends, but her friends had jacked her around the same way she'd jacked around Steward. The whole trip to L.A. had been pointless—they had been stupid to send her. Killing Steward couldn't stop what was happening, it was all too big. The only way Reese could stay clear was to hide.

She ordered another drink, needing it badly. The shuttle speakers moaned with the same tuneless synthesized chords as had the speakers in the hospital room. The memory of Steward lying in the bed floated in her mind, tangled in her insides.

She leaned back against the headrest and watched the shuttle's wings gather fire.

HER CAREER AS a kick boxer ended with a spin kick breaking her nose, and Reese said the fuck with it and went back to light sparring and kung fu. Beating the hell out of herself in training only to have the hell beaten out of her in the ring was not her idea of the good life. She was thirty-six now and she might as well admit there were sports she shouldn't indulge in, even if she had the threadware for them. The realization didn't improve her mood.

Through the window of her condeco apartment, Reese could see a cold wailing northeast wind drive flying white scud across the shallow Aral Sea, its shriek drowning the minarets' amplified call to prayer. Neither the wind nor the view had changed in months. Reese looked at the grey Uzbek spring, turned on her vid, and contemplated her sixth month of exile.

Her hair was black now, shorter than she'd worn it in a long time. Her fingerprints were altered, as was the bone structure of her face. The serial numbers on her artificial eyes had been changed. However bleak its weather, Uzbekistan was good at that sort of thing.

The last person she'd known who had lived here was Steward. Just before he came to L.A. and blew everything to smithereens.

A young man on the vid was putting himself into some kind of combat suit, stuffing weapons and ammunition into pockets. He picked up a shotgun. Suspenseful music hammered from the speakers. Reese turned up the sound and sat down in front of the vid.

She had considered getting back into the trade, but it was too early. The scansheets and broadcasts were still full of stories about aliens, alien ways, alien imports. About "restructuring" going on in the policorps who dealt with the Powers. It was strange seeing the news on the vid, with people ducking for cover, refusing statements, the news item followed by a slick ad for alien pharmaceuticals. People were going to trial—at least those who survived were. A lot were cooperating. Things were still too hot.

Fortunately money wasn't a problem. She had enough to last a long time, possibly even forever.

Gunfire sounded from the vid. The young man was in a shootout with aliens, splattering Powers with his shotgun. Reese felt her nerves turn to ice.

The young man, she realized, was supposed to be Steward. She jumped forward and snapped off the vid. She felt sickened.

Steward had never shot an alien in his life. Reese ought to know.

Fucking assholes. Fucking media vermin.

She reached for her quilted Chinese jacket and headed for the door. The room was too damn small.

She swung the door open with a bang, and a dark-complected man jumped a foot at the sound. He turned and gave a nervous grin.

"You startled me."

He had an anonymous accent that conveyed no particular origin, just the abstract idea of foreignness. He looked about thirty. He was wearing suede pumps that had tabs of Velcro on the bottoms and sides for holding onto surfaces in zero gee. His hands were jammed into a grey, unlined plastic jacket with a half-dozen pockets all sealed by Velcro tabs. Reese suspected one of his hands of having a weapon in it. He was shivering from cold or nervousness. Reese figured he had just come down the gravity well—he was wearing too much Velcro to have bought his clothes on Earth.

Some descendants of the Golden Horde, dressed in Flieger styles imported from Berlin, roared by on skateboards, the earpieces of their leather flying helmets flapping in the wind.

"Been in town long?" Reese asked.

HE TOLD HER his name was Sardar Chandrasekhar Vivekenanda and that he was a revolutionary from Prince Station. His friends called him Ken. Two nights after their first meeting, she met him in the Natural Life bar, a place on the top story of a large bank. It catered to exiles and featured a lot of mahogany imported at great cost from Central America.

Reese had checked on Ken—no sense in being foolish—and discovered he was who he claimed to be. The scansheets from Prince mentioned him frequently. Even his political allies were denouncing his actions.

"Ram was trying to blame the February Riots on us," Ken told her. "Cheney decided I should disappear—the riots would be blamed on me, and Cheney could go on working."

Reese sipped her mataglap star, feeling it burn its way down her throat as she glanced down through the glass wall, seeing the wind scour dust over the Uzbeks' metal roofs and receiver dishes. She grinned. "So Cheney arranged for you to take the fall instead of him," she said. "Sounds like a friend of humanity to me, all right."

Ken's voice was annoyed. "Cheney knows what he's doing."

"Sure he does. He's setting up his friends. The question is, do you know what *you're* doing?"

Ken's fine-boned hands made a dismissive gesture. "From here I can make propaganda. Cheney sends me an allowance. I've bought a very good communications system."

She turned to him. "You going to need any soldiers in this revolution of yours?"

He shook his head. His lashes were full and black. "I think not. Prince Station is a hundred years old—it's in orbit around Luna, with ready access to minerals, but it cannot compete effectively with the new equipment on other stations. Ram wants to hang on as long as possible—his policy is to loot the economy rather than rebuild. He's guaranteed the loyalty of the stockholders by paying large dividends, but the economy can't support the dividends anymore, and the riots showed he has lost control over the situation. It is a matter of time only. We do not expect the change will be violent—not a military sort of violence, anyway."

"Too bad. I could use a job in someone's foreign legion about now." She glanced up as a group of people entered the bar—she recognized a famous swindler from Ceres named da Vega, his hands and face covered with expensive, glowing implant jewelry that reminded her of fluorescent slime mold. He was with an all-female group of bodyguards who were supposed to stand between him and any Cerean snatch teams sent to bring him to justice. They were all tall and round-eyed—da Vega liked women that way. He'd tried to recruit Reese when they first met. The pay was generous, round-eyed women being rare here, but the sexual favors were supposed to be included.

One of *those* jobs, Reese thought. She was tempted to feed him his socks, bodyguards or not, but in the end told him she was used to a better class of employer.

Da Vega turned to her and smiled. Uzbekistan was suddenly far too small a place.

Reese finished her mataglap star and stood. "Let's go for a walk," she said.

"AN ARCHITECTURE OF liberation," Ken said. "That's what we're after. You should read Cheney's thoughts on the subject."

The night street filled with a welling tide of wind. Its alloy surface reflected bright holograms that marched up and down dark storefronts, advertising wares invisible behind dead glass. The wind howled in the latticework of radio receivers pointed at the sky, through a spiky forest of antennae. A minaret outlined by flashing red strobes speared a sky that glowed with yellow sodium light.

"Liberation," Reese said. "Right."

"Too many closed systems," Ken said. He shrugged into the collar of his new down jacket. "That's the problem with space habitats in general—they *strive* for closed ecological systems, and then try to close as much of their economy as possible. There's not enough *access*. I'm a macroeconomist—I work with a lot of models, try to figure out how things are put together—and the most basic obstacle always seems to be the lack of access to data. We've got a solar system filled with corporate plutocracies, all competing with each other, none giving free access to anything they're trying to do. And they've got colonies in other solar systems, and *nothing* about those gets out that the policorps don't want us to know. The whole situation is far too unstable—it's impossible to predict what's going to happen because the data simply isn't available. Everything's constructed along the lines of the old Orbital Soviet—not even the people who *need* the information get the access they require.

"Prince Station's main business is processing minerals—that's okay and it's steady, but the prices fluctuate a lot as new mineral sources are exploited in the Belt and elsewhere, and it requires heavy capital investment to keep the equipment up to date. So for the sake of a stable station economy, it would be nice for Prince to develop another, steadier source of export. Biologicals, say, or custom-configured databases. Optics. Wetware. Export genetics. Anything. But it takes time and resources—five years' worth, say—to set something like that up, and there are other policorps who specialize in those areas. We could be duplicating another group's work, and never know it until suddenly a new product comes onto the market and wipes out our five years' investment. All this secrecy is making for unstable economies. Unstable economies make for unstable political situations—that's why whole policorps suddenly go belly-up."

"So you want the policorps to give away their trade secrets."

"I want to do away with the whole *concept* of trade secrets. Ideally, what I'd like to do is create a whole new architecture of data storage and retrieval. Something that's so good that everyone will have to use it to stay competitive, but something that by its very nature prohibits restriction of access."

Reese laughed. The sound echoed from the cold metal street. "You're dreaming."

He gave her a faint smile. "You're right, of course. I'd have to go back two hundred years, right to the beginning of artificial intelligence, and redesign everything from the start. Then maybe I'd have a chance." He shrugged. "Cheney and I have more practical plans, fortunately."

She looked at him. "You remind me of someone I used to know. He wanted to know the truth, just like you. Wanted *access*."

"Yes?"

The cold wind seemed to cut her to the bone. "He died," she said. "Somebody shot him in a hospital." Somehow, caught in the warm rush of memory, she had forgot that ending.

"A funny place to get shot."

She remembered Steward's last comprehending look, the final words that never came. The northeaster touched her flesh, chilled her heart. The lonely street where they walked suddenly seemed endless, not just a street but the Street, an endless alloy thoroughfare where Reese walked in chill isolation, moving between walls of neon that advertised phantom, unreal comforts . . . She shivered and took his hand.

Ken's voice was soft, almost drowned by wind. "Were you close?"

"Yes. No." She tossed her head. "I wanted to be a friend, but it would have been bad for business."

"I see."

She tasted bile on her tongue, gazing down the endless gleaming Street again, the dark people on it who touched briefly and then parted. Sometimes, she thought, she just needed reminding. She wondered what Steward's last words might have been.

A bare yellow bulb marked the door to Ken's apartment building. They entered, the yellow light streaming through the door to reveal the worn furniture, the bright new communications equipment. "Hey," Reese said, "it's Agitprop Central." She was glad to be out of the wind.

The room blinked to the distant red pulse of the minaret's air-hazard lights. Reese stopped Ken's hand on the light switch, stopped his mouth, every time he tried to talk, with her tongue. She really didn't care if he had someone special back on Prince, preferred this to happen in a certain restrained, ethical silence. Her nerves were wired for combat and she snapped them on, speeding her perceptions and making everything seem in slow motion, the way his hands moved on her, the susurrus of her own breath, the endless red beat of the strobe that sketched the outlines of his face in the warm darkness . . . She could hear the bluster of the northeaster outside, the way it knocked at the panes, shrieked around corners, flooded down the long and empty Street outside. Kept securely outside, at least for this slow-moving, comforting moment of exile.

A DAY LATER a maintenance seal blew out on Prince Station and killed sixteen people. Ken was pleased.

"We can do a lot with this," he said. "Demonstrate how the administration's cronies can't even do simple jobs right."

Reese stood by the window, looking out toward the distant brown horizon, tired of Ken's torn wallpaper and sagging furniture. In the distance, foreigners on Bactrian camels pretended they were carrying silk to Tashkent.

"Sabotage, do you think?" she asked, then corrected herself. "Sorry. *Destabilization* is the proper term, right?"

He sat crosslegged on his chair, watching the screen with an intent, calculating frown. "It could have been us, yes. An effective little action, if it was."

"The people who got killed weren't volunteers, anyway. Not your people."

He grinned in a puzzled way. "No. Of course not."

Reese turned to look at him, folding her arms. "That's what scares me about you idealists. You shoot sixteen people into a vacuum, and it's all for human betterment and the triumph of the revolution, so everything's okay."

Ken squinted as he looked at her against the light. "I'm not sure it's different from what you do."

"I'm a soldier. You're an ideologue. The difference is that you decide who gets killed and where, and I'm the one that has to do it and face the consequences if you're wrong. If it weren't for people like you, I wouldn't be necessary."

"You think this difference somehow makes you less responsible?"

Reese shook her head. "No. But the people I fight—they're volunteers, same as me. Getting paid, same as me. It's clean, very direct. I take the money, do a job. I don't know what it's about often as not. I don't really *want* to know. If I asked, the people I work for would just lie anyway." She moved to the shabby plush chair and sat, curling one leg under her.

"I fought for humanity once, in the Artifact War. I was on Archangel with Far Jewel, making the planet safe for the Freconomicist cause. Making use of the alien technology we'd stumbled on by accident, all that biochem ware the Powers are so good at. It sounded like a noble adventure, but what we were doing was looting alien ruins and stealing from the other policorps. The war blew up, and next I knew I was below the surface in those alien tunnels, and I was facing extermination cyberdrones and tailored bugs with nothing between death and my skin but a very inadequately armored environment suit. And then I got killed."

Ken looked at her with his head cocked to one side, puzzled. "You had clone insurance? This is a different body?"

Anger burned in Reese as she spoke, and she felt it tempering her muscles, turning them rigid. Remembered dark tunnels, bodies piled in heaps, the smell of fear that burned itself into the fibers of her combat suit, the scent that no amount of maintenance and cleaning would ever ever remove.

"No. Nothing like that. I did the killing—I killed myself, my personality. Because everything I was, everything I'd learned, was just contributing to help my employers, my officers, and the enemy in their effort to murder me. I had to streamline myself, get rid of everything that didn't contribute in a positive way toward my own physical survival. I became an animal, a tunnel rat. I saw how qualities like courage and loyalty were being used by our bosses to get us killed, and so I became a disloyal coward. My body was working against me—I'm too tall for tunnels—but I tried real hard to get short, and funny enough it seemed to work. Because in times like that, if you've got your head right, you can do what you have to."

She looked at Ken and grinned, baring her teeth. An adrenaline surge, triggered by the violent memory, prickled the down on her arms. "I'm still an animal. I'm still disloyal. I'm still a coward. Because that's the only way to keep alive."

"If you feel that way, you could get out of the business."

She shrugged. "It's what I do best. And if I did something else—got a job as a rigger, or some kind of tech—then I'd just be somebody else's animal, a cow maybe, being herded from one place to another and fed on grass. At least this way, I'm my own animal. I get my reward up front."

"And during?" Ken's dark eyes were intent.

Reese shifted in her seat, felt a certain discomfort. Nerves, she thought, jinking from the adrenaline. "I'm not sure what you mean."

"You like the work. I have that impression."

She laughed. No reason to be defensive about it. "I like being wired and hanging right on the edge. I like knowing that I have to do things right, that any mistake I make matters."

He shook his head. "I don't understand that. People like you."

"You haven't had to become an animal. You're a macroeconomist, and you're trained to take the long view. A few people blown out a hatch, that's just an acceptable sacrifice. I tend to take this kind of thing personally, is all. See, I figure everyone who ever tried to get me killed was looking at the long view."

Ken's gaze was steady. "I'm not planning on getting you killed. That's not part of my view."

"Maybe someday I'll end up standing between you and your revolution. Then we'll see."

He didn't say anything. In the steadiness of his dark eyes, the absence of expression, Reese read her answer, and knew it was the one she'd expected.

"REESE."

It was the first time she'd heard her name in six months, and now it came from a complete stranger on a streetcorner in Uzbekistan. Her hardwired nerves were triggered and her combat thread was evaluating the man's stance, calculating possible dangers and responses, before she even finished her turn.

He was about forty, tanned, with receding brown hair and a widow's peak. His stance was open, his hands in plain sight: he wore a blue down vest over a plaid shirt, baggy grey wool pants, old brown square-toed boots. He smiled in a friendly way. His build was delicate, as if he'd been genetically altered. His face was turning ruddy in the wind.

"You talking to me?" Reese asked him. "My name's Waldman." Her wetwear was still evaluating him, analyzing every shift in posture, movement of his hands. Had Ken shopped her? she wondered. Had Cheney, after deciding she was a danger to Ken?

His smile broadened. "I understand your caution, but we know who you are. Don't worry about it. We want to hire you."

His voice was as American as hers. Her speeded-up reflexes gave her plenty of time to contemplate his words.

"You'd better call me Waldman if you want to talk to me at all."

He put up his hands. Her nerves crackled. She noticed he had a ragged earlobe, as if someone had torn off an earring in a fight. "Okay, Miss Waldman. My name's Berger. Can we talk?"

"The Natural Life, in an hour. Do you know where that is?"

"I can find out. See you there."

He turned and walked casually up the narrow street. She watched till he was gone and then went to the apartment she rented in a waterfront condecology. She looked for signs anyone had been there in her absence—there weren't any, but that didn't mean anything—and then, to calm her jittery nerves, she cleaned her pistol and took a long, hot bath with the gun sitting on the side of the steel tub. She stretched out as far as the tub would let her, feeling droplets of sweat beading on her scalp while she watched the little bathroom liquid-crystal vidscreen show a bouncy pop-music program from Malaya. She changed her clothes, put the pistol back in its holster—the security softwear at the Natural Life would shred her with poisoned darts if she tried to carry it in—and then headed back into town. The muezzins' song hung in the gusty air. Her mind sifted possibilities.

Berger was the heat. Berger was an assassin. Da Vega had shopped her out of pique. Cheney had sold her name. Ken had regretted telling her so much about his revolution and decided to have her iced before she sold his plans to Ram.

Life was just so full of alternatives.

Berger hadn't arrived at the bar when she came in. The bartender was at prayer and so she turned on the desktop comp and read the scan-sheets, looking for something that might give her an edge, help her to understand what it was about.

Nothing. The aliens hadn't generated any headlines today. But there was a note about a Cerean exile named da Vega who had been found dead, along with a couple of his bodyguards. Another bodyguard was missing.

Reese grinned. The Uzbeks, a people who usually endorsed the long view, had probably turned da Vega into fertilizer by now.

The amplified muezzins fell silent. The bartender returned and flipped on todo music broadcast by satellite from Japan. He took her order and then Berger walked in, dabbing at his nose with a tissue. He hadn't been ready, he explained, for this bitter a spring. He'd have to buy a warm jacket.

"Don't worry, Miss Waldman," he added. "I'm not here to crease you. If I wanted to do that, I could have done it on the street."

"I know. But you might be a cop trying to lure me out of Uzbekistan. So I hope to hell you can prove to me who you are."

He grinned, rubbed his forehead uncomfortably. "Well. To tell you the truth, I *am* a policeman, of a sort."

"Terrific. That really makes my day."

He showed her ID. She studied it while Berger went on. "I'm a captain in Brighter Suns' Pulsar Division. We'd like to hire you for a job up the well."

"Vesta?"

"No. Closer to Earth."

Reese frowned. Policorp Brighter Suns was one of the two policorps that had been set up to deal with the alien Powers. It was almost exclusively into Power imports, and its charter forbade it from owning territory outside of its home asteroid, Vesta. A lot of Brighter Suns execs were running for cover ever since Steward had blown Griffith's network in L.A., and the whole Vesta operation was being restructured.

"The Pulsar Division handles internal security on Vesta," Reese said. "Your outside intelligence division is called Group Seven. So why is Pulsar handling a matter so far away from home?"

"What we'd like you to handle *is* an internal security matter. Some of our people have gone rogue."

"You want me to bring them back?"

Something twitched the flesh by one of Berger's eyes. She knew what he was going to say before the words came out his mouth. She felt her nerves tingling, her muscles warming. It had been a long time.

"No. We want you to ice them."

"Don't tell me anything more," she said. "I'm going to check you out before I listen to another word."

"IT'S NOT EVEN murder, I'd say," Berger said. He was eating spinach salad in an expensive restaurant called the Texas Beef, named after a vaguely pornographic and wildly popular vid show from Alice Springs. Dressing spattered the creamy table cloth as Berger waved his fork. "We've got tissue samples and memory thread, like we do for all our top people—hell, we'll clone 'em."

"That doesn't mean I can't end up in prison for it."

"Who's gonna catch you? It's a goddam asteroid fifty zillion klicks from anywhere."

She had checked him out as far as she could. After telling him what she was going to do, she'd sent a message to Vesta asking for confirmation of the existence of one Captain Berger of the Pulsar Division, that and a photo. Both arrived within twelve hours. If this was a plot to arrest her, it had some unlikely elements.

Reese took a mouthful of lamb in mustard sauce. She worked out hard enough, she figured, and deserved her pleasures.

"The rock's about two kilometers in diameter. The official name is 2131YA, but it's also called Cuervo Gold."

"Funny names they're giving asteroids these days."

"They've run out of minor Greek gods, I guess. Cuervo's officially owned by a non-policorporate mining company called Exeter Associates, which in turn is owned by us. Gold's an Apollo asteroid, crossing Earth's orbit on a regular schedule, and that makes it convenient for purposes of resupply, and also makes it a lot more isolated than any of the rocks in the Belt. We've had a lab there for a while, using it to develop some technology that—" He grinned. "Well, that we wanted to keep far away from any competition. Security on Vesta is tight, but it's a port, people are always coming in and out. What we've got on the asteroid is pretty hot stuff, and we wanted to keep it away from the tourists."

"I don't really want to know," Reese said.

"I don't know myself, so I couldn't tell you," Berger said. "The work was in a fairly advanced stage when certain activities relating to your old friend Griffith became public. It became an urgent matter to shut down the project and transfer its members to other duties in central Africa, where I work. If the investigators found out about our owning that asteroid, and what's on it, Brighter Suns could be very embarrassed."

"The techs refused to move?" Reese asked.

"They protested. They said their work was entering a critical stage. A transport was sent from Earth to pick them up, but they refused to evacuate, and then we lost touch with the freighter. We think the crew have been killed or made prisoner."

"Your people could have defected to another policorp, using the transport."

"We don't think so. Their work would have been hard to take with them. And they couldn't have gone far without attracting attention—some of the lab personnel were Powers."

A coolness moved through Reese's bones. She sat up, regarding Berger carefully. Powers were forbidden off the two entry ports—the official reason was that there was too much danger of cross-contamination from alien life-forms. Plagues had already devastated the two Power legations, and the reverse was always a possibility. The discovery of Powers in Brighter Suns employ outside of Vesta would ruin Brighter Suns' credit for good.

But after a while the heat on Brighter Suns would die down. Trade with the aliens was too profitable for people to interfere with it for long. In a year or two, the lab could be reopened with cloned personnel and some very mean security goons to make certain they followed orders.

"I understand your sense of urgency," Reese said. "But why me? Why not go yourself?"

"We don't have anyone with your talents on Earth," Berger said. "I'm not wired the way you are. And . . . well, we'd like to know you're gainfully employed by us rather than floating around Uzbekistan waiting to be captured by the heat. If we can find you, they probably can."

Reese sipped her club soda. "How did you find me, exactly?"

"Someone recognized you."

"Who might that have been?"

The skin by Berger's eye gave a leap. "It's already taken care of," he said. "We didn't want him giving your name to anyone else."

Da Vega. Well. At least it wasn't Ken.

But there was also a threat: Berger didn't want her in this refugees' paradise, where the number of desperate people was higher than average and where a policorporate kidnap team could find her. If they'd already iced one person, they could put the ice on another.

"Let's talk payment," Reese said. "Brighter Suns, I think, can afford to pay me what I'm worth."

RAM'S COPS HAD beaten some woman to death during interrogation. Ken was busy at his console, putting out fact and opinion pieces, making the most of another death for the revolution. Reese paced the room, picking at the tattered wallpaper, eating Mongolian barbecue from a waxed paper container. Below the window, some drunken descendant of the Golden Horde was singing a sad song to the moon. He kept forgetting the lyrics and starting over, and the burbling ballad was getting on Reese's nerves.

"I'd feel better," she said, "if Cheney was paying you a decent wage."

"He pays what he can afford." Ken's fingers sped over his keyboard. "The money has to be laundered, and he has to be careful how he does it."

"You don't even have a promise of a job after it's all over."

Ken shrugged. "Prince can always use another economist."

"And you don't have protection. Ram could order you iced."

"He needs a live scapegoat, not a dead martyr." He frowned as he typed. "This isn't a mysterious business, you know. Ram knows our strength and most of our moves, and we know his. There aren't very many hidden pieces on the board."

The Uzbek began his song again. Reese clenched her teeth. She put her hand on Ken's shoulder.

"I'm disappearing tomorrow," she said.

He tilted his head back, looking up in surprise. His fingers stopped moving on the keys.

"What's wrong?"

"Nothing. I got a job."

She saw a confirmation in his eyes. "Not one you can talk about," he said.

"No. But it's not for Ram. In case you were wondering."

He took her hand in one of his. "I'll miss you."

Reese put her food carton on top of his video display. Her chopsticks jabbed the air like rabbit ear antennae.

"I've got another twelve hours before I take the plane to Beijing."

Ken turned off his console. "I can send the rest out tomorrow," he said.

Reese was surprised. "What about the revolution?"

He shrugged and kissed the inside of her wrist. "Sometimes I feel redundant. The revolution is inevitable, after all."

"It's nice to know," Reese said, "that the devil can quote ideology to his purpose."

Outside, the Uzbek continued his wail to the desolate stars.

THE TUG WAS called *Voidrunner*, and it was thirty years old at least, the padding on its bulkheads patched with silver tape, bundles of cable hanging out of access hatches. Reese had been in enough ships like it not to let the mess bother her—all it meant was that the tug didn't have to impress its passengers. The air inside tasted acrid, as if the place was crammed full of sweating men, but there were only four people on board.

Berger introduced the other three to Reese, then left, waving cheerily over his shoulder. About four minutes later, *Voidrunner* cast off from Charter Station and began its long acceleration to its destination.

Reese watched the departure from the copilot's chair in the armored docking cockpit. The captain performed the maneuvers with his eyes closed, not even looking out the bubble canopy at the silver-bright flood-lit skin of Charter, reality projected into his head through his interface thread, his eyelids twitching as his eyes reflexively scanned mental indicators.

His name was Falkland. He was about fifty, an Artifact War veteran who, fifteen years before, had been doing his level best to kill Reese in the tunnels of Archangel. A chemical attack had left his motor reflexes damaged, and he wore a light silver alloy exoskeleton. Fortunately his brain and interface thread had survived the war intact. He wore a grey beard and his hair long over his collar.

"Prepare for acceleration," he said, his eyes still closed. "We'll be at two gees for the first six hours."

Reese looked out at Earth's dull grey moon, vast, taking up most of the sky. "Right," she said. "Got my piss bottle right here." Hard gees were tough on the bladder.

After the long burn *Voidrunner* settled into a constant one-gee acceleration. Falkland stayed strapped in, his eyelids still moving to some internal REM light show. Reese unbuckled her harness, stretched her relieved muscles while her spine and neck popped, and moved downship.

Falkland offered no comment.

The crew compartment smelled of fresh paint. Reese saw the tug's engineer, a tiny man named Chung, working on a bulkhead fire alarm. His head was bobbing to music he was feeding to his aural nerves. Chung was so into the technophilic Destinarian movement he was turning himself slice by slice into a machine. His eyes were clear implants that showed the interior silver circuitry; his ears were replaced by featureless black boxes, and there were other boxes of obscure purpose jacked into his hairless scalp. His teeth were metal, and liquid crystal jewelry, powered by nerve circuitry, shone in ever-changing patterns on his cheeks and on the backs of his hands. He hadn't said anything when Berger introduced him, just looked at Reese for a moment, then turned back to his engines.

Now he said something. His voice was hoarse, as if he wasn't used to using it. "He's downship. In Cargo B."

His back was to Reese, and she had been moving quietly. His head still bobbed to inaudible music. He hadn't even turned his head to speak. "Thanks," she said. "Nice implants."

"The best. I built 'em myself."

"Aren't you supposed to be monitoring the burn?"

He pointed at one of his boxes. "I am."

"Nice."

She always found she had common ground with control freaks.

Vickers was in Cargo B, as Chung had promised. He was Reese's armorer, hired by Berger for the sole purpose of maintaining the combat suit that Reese was to wear on Cuervo. Vickers was young, about eighteen, and thin. His dark hair was cut short; he had a stammer and severe acne. He was dressed in oil-spattered coveralls. When Reese walked in, Vickers was peeling the suit's components out of their foam packing. She helped him lay the suit on the deck. Vickers grinned.

"W-wolf 17," he said. His voice was American Southern. "My favorite. You're gonna kick some ass with this. It's so good it can p-practically do the job by itself."

The suit was black, long-armed, anthropoid. The helmet, horned by radio antennae, was fused seamlessly to the shoulders. Inside, Reese's arms, legs, and body would fit into a complex web that would hold her tightly: the suit would amplify and strengthen her every move. It wasn't entirely natural movement—she'd have to get used to having a lot more momentum in free fall than she normally did.

"F-fuckin' great machine," Vickers said. Reese didn't answer.

The Wolf's dark viewplate gleamed in the cool cabin light. There was a clean functionality to its design that made it even more fearful—nothing in its look gave the impression that it was anything but a tool for efficient murder. The white Wolf trademark shone on the matte-black body of the suit. Reese fought a memory charged with fear—Wolf made most of the cyberdrones she'd encountered on Archangel. The combat suit, free of its packing, had a smell she'd hoped she'd never scent again.

"I want to look at the manual," she said. "And the schematics." If her life was going to depend on this monster, she wanted to know everything there was to know about it.

He looked at her approvingly. "I've got them on thread in m-my cabin. The suit's standard, except for some c-custom thread woven into the t-target-acquisition unit. Berger knows who you're going to b-be gunning for, and he put in some specific target-identification routines. You're gonna be h-hot."

"That's the plan," Reese said. The smell of the Wolf, oil and plastic webbing and cold laminate armor, rose in her nostrils. She repressed a shiver.

Vickers was still admiring the Wolf. "One wicked son of a bitch," he said. When talking to machines, he lost his stammer.

REESE AND THE Wolf moved as one in the void. Amber-colored target-acquisition data glowed on the interior of the black faceplate. Below them the asteroid glittered as flecks of mica and nickel reflected the relentless sun.

No way they're not gonna know you're coming, Berger had told her. *Not with your ship's torch coming at them. We stabilized the rock's spin, so you can try landing on the blind side, but they're smart enough to have put detectors out there, so we can't count on surprise. What we're going to have to do is armor you so heavily that no matter what they try to do to you, they can't get through.*

Great, she thought. Now the rock's little techs, human and alien, were probably standing by the airlocks with whatever weapons they'd been able to assemble in the last weeks, just waiting for something to try booming in. All she could do was hope they weren't ready for the Wolf.

The hissing of her circulating air was very loud in the small space of the helmet. Reese could feel sweat gathering under the Wolf's padded harness. The rock's short horizon scrolled below her feet. Attitudinal jets made brief adjustments, keeping Reese close to the surface. The Wolf's suit monitors were projected, through her interface stud, in a complex multi-dimensional weave, bright columns glowing in the optical centers of her brain. She watched the little green indicators, paying little attention as long as they stayed green.

The target rolled over the near horizon in an instant—a silver-bright pattern of solar collectors, transmission aerials, dishes pointed at different parts of the sky . . . In the middle squatted the gleaming bulk of the freighter that had been sent to retrieve the base personnel, its docking tube still connected to the big cargo airlock.

Reese had a number of choices for gaining entry: there were two personnel airlocks, or she could go through one of the freighter locks and then through the docking tube. There were nine personnel on station, five humans and four Powers.

They can brew explosives with the stuff they've got on station, Berger had told her. *But they can't put anything too big around the airlock, or they'd decompress the whole habitat—and they don't have enough stored air to repressurize. They can't set off anything too big inside, or they'd wreck their work. It's too small a place for them to plan anything major. We figure they'll depend on small explosives, and maybe gas.*

The base rolled closer. Reese felt her limbs moving easily in the webbing, the hum of awareness in her nerves and blood. A concrete certainty of her capabilities. All the things she had been unable to live without.

Coolant flow had increased, the suit baking in the sun. The webbing around her body was chafing her. She thought of explosive, of gas, the way the poison clouds had drifted through the tunnels on Archangel, contaminating everything, forcing her to live inside her suit for days, not even able to take a shit without risking burns on her ass . . . at least this was going to be quick, however it went.

Reese decided to go in through one of the small personnel airlocks—the brains inside the rock might have decided the cargo ship was expendable and packed its joints with homemade explosive. She maneuvered the Wolf in a slow somersault and dropped feet-first onto the Velcro strip by Airlock Two. Berger wanted her to get in without decompressing the place if she could—there was stuff inside he didn't want messed up. Reese bent and punched the emergency entrance button, and to her surprise she began to feel a faint humming through her feet and the hatch began to roll up . . . she'd planned to open the hatch manually.

How naïve were these people? she wondered. Or was there some surprise in the airlock, waiting for her?

You're gonna c-carry that stuff? Vickers had asked in surprise, as he noticed the pistol snugged under the armpit and the long knife strapped to her leg.

I don't want to depend entirely on the Wolf, she'd said. *If it gets immobilized somehow, I want to be able to surprise whoever did it.*

There'd been an amused grin on Vickers' face. *They immobilize the Wolf, they sure as hell can immobilize you.*

Adjust the webbing anyway, she'd said. Because battle machinery always went wrong sooner or later, because if the mission directive didn't give her backup, she'd just have to be her own. Because she just didn't *like* the Wolf, its streamlined design, its purposeful intent. Because even to someone accustomed to violence, the thing was obscene.

Reese knelt by the airlock, pulled a videocamera from her belt, and held it over the airlock, scanning down . . . and fought back a wave of bile surging into her throat, because the lock was full of dead men.

Mental indicators shifted as, with a push of her mind, she ordered her attitudinal jets to separate the Wolf from the Velcro parking strip, then drop into the lock. The dead swam in slow motion as she dropped among them. Her heart crashed in her chest.

The crew of the freighter, she thought. The rebels had put them in here, not having anyplace else. Their skins were grey, the tongues protruding and black. Some kind of poison, she thought.

"Welcome to Cuervo Gold," she said, and laughed. Nerves.

She hit the button to cycle the airlock, found it refused to work. Incurious dead eyes gazed at her as she cranked the outer door shut manually, then planted thermocharges on the inner door locks. She drifted up to the top of the airlock again, the Wolf's horns scratching the outer door. The dead men rose with her, bumping gently against the Wolf's arms and legs.

Reese curled her legs under her, protecting the Wolf's more vulnerable head and back. Adrenaline was beating a long tattoo in her pulse.

A vulture smile crossed her face. Her nerves sang a mad little song. *Here's where I take it up the ass*, she thought, and pulsed through her wetware the radio code to set off the detonators.

The lock filled with scorching bright light, smoke, molten blobs of bright metal. Air entered the lock with a prolonged scream. Suddenly her olfactory sensors were overwhelmed with the smell of scorched metal, burning flesh. Her gorge rose. She pulsed a command to cut out the smell, then moved down to the inner lock door, seized it, rolled it up with the enhanced strength of the Wolf . . .

An explosion went off right in her face. Projectiles thudded into corpse flesh, cracked against the faceplate. She and the dead men went flying back, slamming against the outer hatch. Her pulse roared in her ears. She gave the Wolf a command to move down, and move down fast.

Her nerves were shrieking as she smashed into a wall of the airlock, corrected, flew down again, out the lock this time, cracked into another wall. Her teeth rattled. A homemade claymore, she thought, explosive packed in a tube with shrapnel, bits of jagged alloy, wire, junk. Command-detonated, most likely, so that meant someone was here watching the airlock door. Targeting displays flashed bright red on the interior of her faceplate. She turned and fired. Slammed into a wall again. Fired a second time.

The targets died. Fixed to each of the Wolf's upper forearms was a semiautomatic ten-gauge shotgun firing shells packed with poison flechettes. Reese had more deadly equipment available—a small grenade launcher on the left lower forearm, and a submachine gun on the right, gas projectors on her chest—but the op plan was to kill the targets without taking a chance on disturbing any of the valuable equipment or experiments.

Dollops of blood streamed into the near-weightlessness, turning into crimson spheres. A man and a woman, one holding some kind of home-made beam weapon she'd never got the chance to fire, were slowly flying backward toward the sprayed grey plastic walls, their hearts and lungs punctured by a dozen flechettes each. Their faces were frozen in slow-gathering horror at the sight of the Wolf. Reese tried to move, then hit the wall again. She realized the shrapnel had jammed one of her maneuvering jets full on. Her wetware wove routines to compensate, then she leaped past the dying pair and through an open doorway.

No one was in the next series of partitioned rooms, the crew quarters. These people were incredibly naïve, she thought, hiding out next to an airlock they knew was going to be blown and not even getting into vac suits. They should have put the claymore on the interior hatch door, not inside the station itself. Maybe they couldn't face going into where they'd put the crew they'd killed. These weren't professionals, they were a bunch of eggheads who hadn't known what they were getting into when they signed their declaration of independence from a policorp that could not even afford to acknowledge their existence.

They weren't soldiers, but they were still volunteers. They'd already killed people, quite coldly it seemed, in the name of whatever science they were doing here. She clenched her teeth and thought about how some people, no matter how smart they were, remained just too stupid to live.

There was a new bulkhead door welded to the exterior of the crew quarters. Reese blew it open the same way as the airlock, then jetted through. Shrieks sounded on her audio thread, the strange organ sounds Powers made through their upper set of nostrils. Even as her mind squalled at the unearthly sight of a fast-moving, centauroid pair of aliens, she fired. They died before they could fire their homemade weapons. Her memory flashed on the video, the actor-Steward eradicating aliens with his shotgun. An idiotic memory.

She went through a door marked with biohazard warnings. The door gave a soft hiss as she opened it.

The next room was brightly lit, humming with a powerful air conditioning unit, filled with computer consoles plugged into walls of bare metal, not plastic. Cable stretched to and from something that looked like a hundred-liter aquarium filled with what appeared to be living flesh. Weird, she thought. It looked as if the meat was divided by partitions, like honeycomb in a cultured hive. Silver-grey wires, apparently variable-lattice thread, were woven through the meat. Elsewhere an engine hummed as it pumped crimson fluid. Monitors drew jagged lines across screens, holographic digits floated in air.

Weird, she thought again. Alien biochemistry.

There were three other rooms identical to the last. No one was in the first two.

In the third was a single man, gaunt, silver-haired. He was floating by the room's aquarium, a frown on his face. He was in a vac suit with the helmet in his hand, giving the impression he simply didn't want to bother to put it on.

He looked at Reese as she came in. There was no fear in his eyes, only sadness.

He spoke as he pushed off from the aquarium, floating to the empty alloy ceiling, where Reese's shot wouldn't hit his experiment by mistake.

"It's over," he said. "Not that it matters."

Reese thought of Steward in the hospital bed, dying for something else equally stupid, equally futile, and filled the man's face with poison darts.

Past the next seal two Powers tried to burn her with acid. The stuff smoked pointlessly on her ceramic armor while she killed them. One of the remaining humans tried to surrender, and the other tried to hide in a toilet. Neither tactic worked. She searched the place thoroughly, found no one else, and disarmed the traps at each of the airlocks.

There was a pain deep in her skull. The air in the suit had begun to taste bad, full of sour sweat, burnt adrenaline. Sadness drifted through her at the waste, the stupidity of it all. Twelve more dead, and all for nothing.

Reese left the bodies where they lay—nobody was paying her to clean the place up—and used the other personnel lock to return to *Voidrunner*. Once she was in sight of the ship she pointed one of her microwave antennae at the ship and gave the code signaling success: "Transmit the following to base. *Mandate. Liquid. Consolidation.*" A combination of words unlikely to be uttered by accident.

She cycled through the ship's central airlock. Pain hammered in her brain, her spine. Time to get out of this obscene contraption. The door opened.

Targeting displays flashed scarlet on the interior of her faceplate. Reese's nerves screamed as the Wolf's right arm, with her arm in it, rose. The ten-gauge exploded twice and the impact spun Vickers back against the opposite wall. He impacted and bounced lightly, already dead. "*No!*"

Reese cried, and the Wolf moved forward, brushing the body aside. Reese's arms, trapped in the suit's webbing, rose to a combat stance. She tried to tug them free. Targeting displays were still flashing. Reese tried to take command of the suit through the interface stud. It wouldn't respond.

"Take cover!" Reese shouted. *"The Wolf's gone rogue!"* She didn't know whether the suit was still on transmit or whether anyone was listening. The Wolf had visible light and IR detectors, motion scanners, scent detectors, sensors that could detect the minute compression wave of a body moving through air. There was no way the Wolf would miss anyone in the ship, given enough time.

Reese's heart thundered in her chest. "Get into vac suits!" she ordered. "Abandon ship! Get onto the station. Try and hold out there."

Chung's voice snapped over the outside speakers. "Where the hell are you?" At least someone was listening.

"I'm moving upship toward the control room. Oh, fuck." The heads-up display indicated the Wolf had detected motion from the docking cockpit, which meant the armored bulkhead door was open.

The Wolf caught Falkland as he was trying to fly out of the cockpit and get to an airlock. The flechettes failed to penetrate the exoskeleton, so the Wolf flew after him, caught him bodily. Reese felt her left hand curling around the back of Falkland's head, the right hand draw back to strike. She fought against it. Falkland was screaming, trying to struggle out of the Wolf's grip. *"I'm not doing this!"* Reese cried, wanting him to know that, and closed her eyes.

Her right arm punched out once, twice, three times. The Wolf began to move again. When Reese opened her eyes there was blood and bone spattering the faceplate.

"I'm still heading upship," Reese said. "I don't think the Wolf knows where you are."

Chung didn't answer. No point, Reese thought, in his sending a radio signal that might give away his position. The Wolf reached the forward control room, then began a systematic search of the ship, moving aft. Reese reported the suit's movements, hoping to hell he'd get away. The ship was small, and a search wouldn't take long.

Custom thread, Vickers had told her. *Woven into the target-acquisition unit.* Berger had done it, she knew, not only wanting to wipe out the station personnel but anyone who knew of Cuervo's existence. She was riding in an extermination cyberdrone now, trapped inside its obscene, purposeful body. *Mandate. Liquid. Consolidation.* The code had sent the Wolf on its rampage. The liquidation is mandated. Consolidate knowledge about Cuervo.

Displays flickered on the screen. The thing had scented Chung. Reese could do nothing but tell him it was coming.

Chung was by the aft airlock, halfway into the rad suit he'd need to flee through the airless engine space. His face was fixed in an expression of rage. "*Steward!*" Reese screamed. The ten-gauge barked twice, and then the Wolf froze. The displays were gone. The Wolf, still with considerable momentum, continued to drift toward the aft bulkhead. It struck and rebounded, moving slowly toward Chung.

Reese tried to move in the suit, but its joints were locked. Her crashing pulse was the loudest sound in the helmet. She licked sweat from her upper lip, felt it running down her brows. Chung's body slowly collapsed in the insignificant gravity of the asteroid. Drops of blood fell like slow-motion rubies. The gravity wasn't enough to break the surface tension, and the droplets rested on the deck like ball bearings, rolling in the circulating air . . .

Reese's heart stopped as she realized that the sound of the Wolf's air-circulation system had ceased. She had only the air in the suit, then nothing.

Her mind flailed in panic. Shouting, her cries loud in her ears, she tried to move against the locked joints of the Wolf. The Wolf only drifted slowly to the deck, its limbs immobile.

Like Archangel, she thought. Nothing to look forward to but dying in a suit, in a tunnel, in the smell of your own fear. Just like her officers had always wanted. She tasted bile and fought it down.

I'm using air, she thought, and clamped down, gulping twice, trying to control her jackhammer heart, her panicked breath.

Chung's furious eyes glared into hers at a distance of about three feet. She could see a reflection of the Wolf in his metal teeth. Reese began to move her arms and legs, testing the tension of the web.

There was a pistol under her left arm. If she could get to it with her right hand, she might be able to shoot her way out of the suit somehow.

Fat chance.

But still it was something to do, anyway. She began to move her right arm against the webbing, pulling it back. Blood rubies danced before her eyes. She managed to get her hand out of the glove, but there was a restraining strap against the back of her elbow that prevented further movement. She pushed forward, keeping her hand out of the glove, then drew back. Worked at it slowly, synchronizing the movement with her breath, exhaling to make herself smaller. Steward, she thought, would have been quoting Zen aphorisms to himself. Hers were more direct. *You can get smaller if you want to*, she thought, *you've done it before.*

She got free of the elbow strap, drew her arm back, felt her elbow encounter the wall of the suit. She was beginning to pant. *The air can't be gone this quickly*, she thought, and tried to control panic as she pulled back on her arm, as pain scraped along her nerves. Sweat was coating her body. She tried to think herself smaller. She could feel warm blood running down her arm. The Wolf was saturated with the scent of fear.

Reese screamed as her arm came free, part agony, part exultation. She reached across her chest, felt the butt of the pistol. It was cold in her hand, almost weightless.

Where to point it? She could try blowing out the faceplate but she'd have the barrel within inches of her face, and the faceplate was damn near impervious anyway. The bullet would probably ricochet right into her head. The Wolf was too well armored.

Chung's angry glare was making it impossible for her to think. Reese closed her eyes and tried to think of the schematics she'd studied, the location of the variable-lattice thread that contained the suit's instructions.

Behind her, she thought. Pressed against her lower spine was the logic thread that operated the Wolf's massive limbs. If she could wreck the thread, the locked limbs might move.

She experimented with the pistol. There wasn't enough room to completely angle the gun around her body.

Sweat floated in salty globes around her as she thought it through, tried desperately to come up with another course of action. The air grew foul. Reese decided that shooting herself with the pistol would be quicker than dying of asphyxiation.

She tried to crowd as far over to the right as possible, curling the gun against her body, holding it reversed with her thumb on the trigger. The cool muzzle pressed into her side, just below the ribs. Line it up carefully, she thought. You don't want to have to do this more than once. She tried to remember anatomy and what was likely to get hit. A kidney? Adrenal glands?

Here's where I really *take it up the ass*, she thought. She screamed, building rage, and fired . . . and then screamed again from pain. Sweat bounced against the faceplate, spattering in the fierce momentum of the bullet's pressure wave.

The Wolf's limbs unlocked and the cyberdrone sagged to the deck. Reese gave a weak cheer, then shrieked again from the pain.

She had heard it wasn't supposed to hurt when you got hit, not right away. Another lie, she thought, invented by the officer class.

There was something wrong with the world; with the way it was manifesting itself. She realized she was deaf from the pistol blast.

Reese leaned back, took a deep breath of foul air. Now, she thought, comes the easy part.

REESE MANAGED TO put her right arm back into the sleeve, then use both arms—the armor, thankfully, was near weightless—to get herself out of the suit. She moved to the sick bay and jabbed endorphin-analogue into her thigh, then X-rayed herself on the portable machine. It looked as if she hadn't hit anything vital, but then she wasn't practiced at reading X-rays, either. She patched herself up, swallowed antibiotics, and then out of nowhere the pain slammed down, right through the endorphin. Every muscle in her body went into spasm. Reese curled into a ball, her body a flaming agony. She bounced gently off one wall, then another. Fought shuddering waves of nausea. Tears poured from her eyes. It hurt too much to scream.

It went on forever, for days. Loaded on endorphins, she looted the station, moving everything she could into the freighter, then pissed bright blood while howling in agony. Fevers raged in her body. She filled herself with antibiotics and went on working. Things—people, aliens, hallucinations—kept reaching at her, moving just outside her field of vision. Sometimes she could hear them talking to her in some strange, melodic tongue.

She grappled *Voidrunner* to the freighter's back, then lifted off Cuervo and triggered the charges. She laughed at the bright blossoms of flame in the locks, the gush of air that turned to white snow in the cold vacuum, and then into a bright rainbow as it was struck by the sun. Reese accelerated toward Earth for as long as she could stand it, then cut the engines.

There was a constant wailing in her ears, the cry of the fever in her blood. For the next several days—one of them was her birthday—Reese hung weightless in her rack, fought pain and an endless hot fever, and studied the data she'd stolen, trying to figure out why nine tame scientists were willing to commit murder over it.

The fever broke, finally, under the onslaught of antibiotics. Her urine had old black blood now, not bright new crimson. She thought she was beginning to figure out what the station crew had been up to.

It was time to decide where she was going to hide. The freighter and the tug were not registered to her, and her appearance with them was going to result in awkward questions. She thought about forging records of a sale—credentials, after all, were her specialty. Reese decided to tune in on the broadcasts from Earth and see if there were any new places for refugees to run to.

To her surprise she discovered that Ram's executive board on Prince Station had fallen three days before, and Cheney had been made the new chairman. She waited another two days, studying the data she'd stolen, the bottles of strange enzymes and tailored RNA she had moved to the freighter's cooler, and then beamed a call to Prince and asked for S. C. Vivekenanda. She was told the vice president of communications was busy. "I can wait," she said. "Tell him it's Waldman."

Ken's voice came on almost immediately. "Where are you?" he asked.

"I'm coming your way," Reese told him. "And I think I've got your architecture of liberation with me. But first, we've got to cut a deal."

WHAT THE LAB'S inhabitants had been up to wasn't quite what Ken had been talking about that gusty spring night in Uzbekistan, but it was close. The Brighter Suns biologists and artificial intelligence people had been working on a new way of storing data, a fast and efficient way, faster than variable-lattice thread. They had succeeded in storing information in human DNA.

It had been tried before. Genetically altered humanity had been present for a century, and the mysteries of the genetic mechanism had been thoroughly mapped. There had long been theories that genetic material, which succeeded in coding far more information on its tiny strand than any comparable thread-based technology, would provide the answer to the endless demand for faster and more efficient means of data storage.

The theories had always failed when put into practice. Just because specialists could insert desirable traits in a strand of human DNA didn't mean they had the capability of doing it at the speed of light, reading the genetic message the strand contained at similar speed, or altering the message at will. The interactions of ribosomes, transfer RNA, and enzymes were complex and interrelated to the point where the artificial intelligence/biologist types had despaired of trying to control them with current technology.

Alien genetics, it turned out, were simple compared to the human. Power DNA chains were much shorter, containing half the two hundred thousand genes in a human strand, without the thousands of repetitions and redundancies that filled human genes. Their means of reproducing DNA were similar, but similarly streamlined.

And the Power method of DNA reproduction was compatible with human genetics. The transfer and message RNA were faster, cleaner, more controllable. Information transfer had a theoretically astounding speed—a human DNA strand, undergoing replication, unwound at 8000 RPM. Power RNA combined with human DNA made data transfers on thread look like slow motion.

Once the control technology was developed, information could be targeted to specific areas of the DNA strand. The dominant genes could remain untouched; but the recessive genes could be altered to contain information. Nothing could be kept secret when any spy could code information in his own living genetic makeup. And no one could discover the spy unless they knew what code he was using and what they were looking for.

The architecture of liberation. Risk-free transfer of data.

It would be years before any of this was possible—Prince Station's newly hired biologists would have to reconstruct all the station's work and then develop it to the point where it was commercially viable. But Prince Station was going to have its new source of technology, and Reese a new source of income—she'd asked for a large down payment in advance of a small royalty that should nevertheless make her a billionaire in the next forty years. She'd asked for that, plus Prince's help in disposing of a few other problems.

REESE LOOKED DOWN at her double, lying on a bed in a room that smelled of death. Her twin's eyes were closed, her breasts rose and fell under a pale blue sheet. Bile rose in Reese's throat.

Reese was blonde again, her nose a little straighter, her mouth a little wider. She had a new kidney, a new eardrum. New fingerprints, new blue irises. She liked the new look. The double looked good, too.

Two bodies, a man and a woman, were sprawled at the foot of the bed: assassins, sent by Berger to kill her. They had followed a carefully laid trail to her location here on Prince, and when they came into her apartment they'd been shot dead by Prince's security men firing from concealment in the wide bedroom closet. Reese had waited safely in the next room, her nerves burning with adrenaline fire while she clutched Ken's hand; her nerves alert for the sound of gunfire, she watched her double breathe under its sheet.

Then the security people came for the mannikin. They were going to kill it.

The double was Reese's clone. Her face had been restructured the same way Reese's had, and her artificial eyes were blue. Her muscles had been exercised via electrode until they were as firm as Reese's. There was even a metal pin in her ankle, a double of the one Reese carried. The clone was an idiot—her brain had never contained Reese's mind.

The idea was to make it appear that Reese and the assassins had killed each other. Reese looked down at her double and felt her mouth go dry. The security people were padding around the room, trying to make appearances perfect. Hot anger blazed behind Reese's eyes. Fuck this, she thought.

She pried the pistol out of one of the assassins' hands and raised it.

She was a tunnel rat, she thought. An animal, a coward, disloyal. Sometimes she needed reminding.

"It's not murder," Ken said, trying to help.

"Yes, it is," Reese said. She raised the killer's gun—an ideal assassin's weapon, a compressed-air fletcher—and fired a silent dart into the mannikin's thigh. Then she closed her eyes, not wanting to see the dying thing's last spasm. Instead she saw Steward, dying in his own silent bed, and felt a long grey wave of sadness. She opened her eyes and looked at Ken.

"It's also survival," she said.

"Yes. It is."

A cold tremor passed through Reese's body. "I wasn't talking about the clone."

While Ken's assistants made it look as if she and the assassins had killed each other, Reese stepped through the hidden door into the next apartment. Her bag was already packed, her identity and passport ready. Credentials, she thought, her specialty. That and killing helpless people. Group rates available.

She wanted to live by water again. New Zealand sounded right. It was getting to be spring there now.

"You'll come back?" Ken asked.

"Maybe. But in the meantime, you'll know where to send the royalties." There was pain in Ken's eyes, in Steward's eyes. Attachments were weakness, always a danger. Reese had a vision of the Street, people parting, meeting, dying, in silence, alone. She wouldn't be safe on Prince and couldn't be a part of Ken's revolution. She was afraid she knew what it was going to turn into, once it became the sole possessor of a radical new technology. And what that would turn Ken into.

Reese shouldered her bag. Her hands were still trembling. Sadness beat slowly in her veins. She was thirty-seven now, she thought. Maybe there were sports she shouldn't indulge in.

Maybe she should just leave.

"Enjoy your new architecture," she said, and took off.

She had been up here too long. This place—and everyplace else she'd ever been—was too damn small. She wanted sea air, to live in a place with seasons, with wind.

She wanted to watch the world grow small again.

C. J. Cherryh

C. J. Cherryh is the creator of the vast Union-Alliance future history series, which chronicles the interplay of intergalactic commerce and politics several millennia hence, and includes, among others, the Hugo Award–winning novels Downbelow Station and Cyteen. Praised for its inventive extrapolations of clinical and social science and deft blends of technology and human interest, the series enfolds a number of celebrated subseries, including her Faded Sun trilogy (Kesrith, Shon'jir, Kutath) and the Chanur series (The Pride of Chanur, Chanur's Venture, The Kif Strike Back, Chanur's Homecoming, Chanur's Legacy). A recent quartet of novels — Foreigner, Invader, Inheritor, and Precursor — has been praised for its sensitive documentation of the cultural and racial differences a human colony must overcome in forming a fragile alliance with the planet's alien inhabitants. Cherryh has also authored the four-volume Morgaine heroic fantasy series and the epic Galisien sword-and-sorcery series, which includes Fortress in the Eye of Time, Fortress of Eagles, and Fortress of Owls. She is the creator of the Merovingen Nights shared-world series and cocreator of the multivolume Heroes in Hell shared-world compilations.

THE SCAPEGOAT

C. J. Cherryh

I

DeFranco sits across the table from the elf and he dreams for a moment, not a good dream, but recent truth: all part of what surrounds him now, a bit less than it was when it was happening, because it was gated in through human eyes and ears and a human notices much more and far less than what truly goes on in the world—

—the ground comes up with a bone-penetrating thump and dirt showers down like rain, over and over again; and deFranco wriggles up to his knees with the clods rattling off his armor. He may be moving to a place where a crater will be in a moment, and the place where he is may become one in that same moment. There is no time to think about it. There is only one way off that exposed hillside, which is to go and keep going. DeFranco writhes and wriggles against the weight of the armor, blind for a moment as the breathing system fails to give him as much as he needs, but his throat is already raw with too much oxygen in three days out. He curses the rig, far more intimate a frustration than the enemy on this last long run to the shelter of the deep tunnels. . . .

He was going home, was John deFranco, if home was still there, and if the shells that had flattened their shield in this zone had not flattened it all along the line and wiped out the base.

The elves had finally learned where to hit them on this weapons system too, that was what; and deFranco cursed them one and all, while the sweat ran in his eyes and the oxy-mix tore his throat and giddied his brain. On this side and that shells shocked the air and the ground and his bones; and not for the first time concussion flung him bodily through the air and slammed him to the churned ground bruised and battered (and but for the armor, dead and shrapnel-riddled). Immediately fragments of wood and metal rang off the hardsuit, and in their gravity-driven sequence of clods of earth rained down in a patter mixed with impacts of rocks and larger chunks.

And then, not having been directly in the strike zone and dead, he got his sweating human limbs up again by heaving the armor-weight into its hydraulic joint-locks, and desperately hurled fifty kilos of unsupple ceramics and machinery and ninety of quaking human flesh into a waddling, exhausted run.

Run and fall and run and stagger into a walk when the dizziness got too much and never waste time dodging.

But somewhen the jolts stopped, and the shell-made earthquakes stopped, and deFranco, laboring along the hazard of the shell-cratered ground, became aware of the silence. His staggering steps slowed as he turned with the awkward foot-planting the armor imposed to take a look behind him. The whole smoky valley swung across the narrowed view of his visor, all lit up with ghosty green readout that flickered madly and told him his eyes were jerking in panic, calling up more than he wanted. He feared that he was deaf; it was that profound a silence to his shocked ears. He heard the hum of the fans and the ventilator in the suit, but there would be that sound forever, he heard it in his dreams; so it could be in his head and not coming from his ears. He hit the ceramic-shielded back of his hand against his ceramic-coated helmet and heard the thump, if distantly. So his hearing was all right. There was just the smoke and the desolate cratering of the landscape to show him where the shells had hit.

And suddenly one of those ghosty green readouts in his visor jumped and said **000** and started ticking off, so he lumbered about to get a look up, the viewplate compensating for the sky in a series of flickers and darkenings. The reading kept up, ticking away; and he could see nothing in the sky, but base was still there, it was transmitting, and he knew what was happening. The numbers reached **Critical** and he swung about again and looked toward the plain as the first strikes came in and the smoke went up anew.

He stood there on the hillcrest and watched the airstrike he had called down half an eternity ago pound hell out of the plains. He knew the devastation of the beams and the shells. And his first and immediate thought was that there would be no more penetrations of the screen and human lives were saved. He had outrun the chaos and covered his own mistake in getting damn near on top of the enemy installation trying to find it.

And his second thought, hard on the heels of triumph, was that there was too much noise in the world already, too much death to deal with, vastly too much, and he wanted to cry with the relief and the fear of being alive and moving. Good and proper. The base scout found the damn firepoint, tripped a trap, and the whole damn airforce had to come pull him out of the fire with a damn million credits' worth of shells laid down out there destroying ten billion credits' worth of somebody else's.

Congratulations, deFranco.

A shiver took him. He turned his back to the sight, cued his locator on, and began to walk, slowly, slowly, one foot in front of the other, and if he had not rested now and again, setting the limbs on his armor on lock, he would have fallen down. As it was he walked with his mouth open and his ears full of the harsh sound of his own breathing. He walked, lost and disoriented, till his unit picked up his locator signal and beaconed in the Lost Boy they never hoped to get back.

"You did us great damage then," says the elf. "It was the last effort we could make and we knew you would take out our last weapons. We knew that you would do it quickly and that then you would stop. We had learned to trust your habits even if we didn't understand them. When the shelling came, towers fell; and there were over a thousand of us dead in the city."

"And you keep coming."

"We will. Until it's over or until we're dead."

DeFranco stares at the elf a moment. The room is a small and sterile place, showing no touches of habitation, but all those small signs of humanity—a quiet bedroom, done in yellow and green pastels. A table. Two chairs. An unused bed. They have faced each other over this table for hours. They have stopped talking theory and begun thinking only of the recent past. And deFranco finds himself lost in elvish thinking again. It never quite makes sense. The assumptions between the lines are not human assumptions, though the elf's command of the language is quite thorough.

At last, defeated by logicless logic: "I went back to my base," says deFranco. "I called down the fire; but I just knew the shelling had stopped. We were alive. That was all we knew. Nothing personal."

THERE WAS A bath and there was a meal and a little extra ration of whiskey. HQ doled the whiskey out as special privilege and sanity-saver and the scarcity of it made the posts hoard it and ration it with down-to-the-gram precision. And he drank his three days' ration and his bonus drink one after the other when he had scrubbed his rig down and taken a long, long bath beneath the pipe. He took his three days' whiskey all at once because three days out was what he was recovering from, and he sat in his corner in his shorts, the regs going about their business, all of them recognizing a shaken man on a serious drunk and none of them rude or crazy enough to bother him now, not with congratulations for surviving, not with offers of bed, not with a stray glance. The regs were not in his command, he was not strictly anywhere in the chain of command they belonged to, being special ops and assigned there for the reg CO to use when he had to. He was 2nd Lt. John R. deFranco if anyone bothered and no one did here-abouts, in the bunkers. He was special ops and his orders presently came from the senior trooper captain who was the acting CO all along this section of the line, the major having got hisself lately dead, themselves waiting on a replacement, thank you, sir and ma'am; while higher brass kept themselves cool and dry and safe behind the shields on the ground a thousand miles away and up in orbit.

And John deFranco, special op and walking target, kept his silver world-and-moon pin and his blue beret and his field-browns all tucked up and out of the damp in his mold-proof plastic kit at the end of his bunk. The rig was his working uniform, the damned, cursed rig that found a new spot to rub raw every time he realigned it. And he sat now in his shorts and drank the first glass quickly, the next and the next and the next in slow sips, and blinked sometimes when he remembered to.

The regs, male and female, moved about the underground barracks in their shorts and their T's like khaki ghosts whose gender meant nothing to him or generally to each other. When bunks got double-filled it was friendship or boredom or outright desperation; all their talk was rough and getting rougher, and their eyes when real pinned-down-for-days boredom set in were hell, because they had been out here and down here on this world for thirty-seven months by the tally on bunker 43's main entry wall; while the elves were still holding, still digging in and still dying at unreasonable rates without surrender.

"Get prisoners," HQ said in its blithe simplicity; but prisoners suicided. Elves checked out just by *wanting* to die.

"Establish a contact," HQ said. "Talk *at* them—" meaning by any inventive means they could; but they had failed at that for years in space and they expected no better luck onworld. Talking to an elf meant coming into range with either drones or live bodies. Elves cheerfully shot at any target they could get. Elves had shot at the first human ship they had met twenty years ago and they had killed fifteen hundred men, women, and children at Corby Point for reasons no one ever understood. They kept on shooting at human ships in sporadic incidents that built to a crisis.

Then humanity—all three humanities, Union and Alliance and remote, sullen Earth—had decided there was no restraint possible with a species that persistently attacked modern human ships on sight, with equipage centuries less advanced—*Do we have to wait*, Earth's consensus was, *till they do get their hands on the advanced stuff? Till they hit a world?* Earth worried about such things obsessively, convinced of its paramount worldbound holiness and importance in the universe. The cradle of humankind. Union worried about other things—like breakdown of order, like its colonies slipping loose while it was busy: Union pushed for speed, Earth wanted to go back to its own convolute affairs, and Alliance wanted the territory, preferring to make haste slowly and not create permanent problems for itself on its flank. There were rumors of other things too, like Alliance picking up signals out this direction, of something other than elves. Real reason to worry. It was at least sure that the war was being pushed and pressed and shoved; and the elves shoved back. Elves died and died, their ships being no match for human-make once humans took after them in earnest and interdicted the jump-points that let them near human space. But elves never surrendered and never quit trying.

"Now what do we do?" the joint command asked themselves collectively and figuratively—because they were dealing out bloody, unpalatable slaughter against a doggedly determined and underequipped enemy, and Union and Earth wanted a quick solution. But Union as usual took the Long View: and on this single point there was consensus. "If we take out every ship they put out here and they retreat, how long does it take before they come back at us with more advanced armaments? We're dealing with lunatics."

"Get through to them," the word went out from HQ. "Take them out of our space and carry the war home to them. We've got to make the impression on them now—or take options no one wants later."

Twenty years ago. Underestimating the tenacity of the elves. Re-moved from the shipping lanes and confined to a single world, the war had sunk away to a local difficulty; Alliance still put money and troops into it; Union still cooperated in a certain measure. Earth sent adven-turers and enlistees that often were crazier than the elves: Base culled those in a hurry.

So for seventeen years the matter boiled on and on and elves went on dying and dying in their few and ill-equipped ships, until the joint com-mand decided on a rougher course; quickly took out the elves' pathetic little space station, dropped troops onto the elvish world, and fenced human bases about with antimissile screens to fight a limited and on-world war—while elvish weaponry slowly got more basic and more primitive and the troops drank their little measures of imported whiskey and went slowly crazy.

And humans closely tied to the elvish war adapted, in humanity's own lunatic way. Well behind the lines that had come to exist on the elves' own planet, humans settled in and built permanent structures and sci-entists came to study the elves and the threatened flora and fauna of a beautiful and earthlike world, while some elvish centers ignored the war, and the bombing went on and on in an inextricable mess, because neither elves nor humans knew how to quit, or knew the enemy enough to know how to disengage. Or figure out what the other wanted. And the war could go on and on—since presumably the computers and the records in those population centers still had the design of starships in them. And no enemy which had taken what the elves had taken by now was ever going to forget.

There were no negotiations. Once, just once, humans had tried to approach one of the few neutral districts to negotiate and it simply and instantly joined the war. So after all the study and all the effort, humans lived on the elves' world and had no idea what to call them or what the world's real name was, because the damn elves had blown their own space station at the last and methodically destroyed every record the way they destroyed every hamlet before its fall and burned every record and every artifact. They died and they died and they died and sometimes (but seldom nowadays) they took humans with them, like the time when they were still in space and hit the base at Ticon with ¾-cee rocks and left nothing but dust. Thirty thousand dead and not a way in hell to find the pieces.

That was the incident after which the joint command decided to take the elves out of space.

And nowadays humanity invested cities they never planned to take and they tore up roads and took out all the elves' planes, and they tore up agriculture with non-nuclear bombs and shells trying not to ruin the world beyond recovery, hoping eventually to wear the elves down. But the elves retaliated with gas and chemicals which humans had refrained from using. Humans interdicted supply and still the elves managed to come up with the wherewithal to strike through their base defense here as if supply were endless and they not starving and the world still green and undamaged.

DeFranco drank and drank with measured slowness, watching regs go to and fro in the slow dance of their own business. They were good, this Delta Company of the Eighth. They did faithfully what regs were supposed to do in this war, which was to hold a base and keep roads secure that humans used, and to build landing zones for supply and sometimes to go out and get killed inching humanity's way toward some goal the joint command understood and which from here looked only like some other damn shell-pocked hill. DeFranco's job was to locate such hills. And to find a prisoner to take (standing orders) and to figure out the enemy if he could.

Mostly just to find hills. And sometimes to get his company into taking one. And right now he was no more damn good, because they had gotten as close to this nameless city as there were hills and vantages to make it profitable, and after that they went onto the flat and did what?

Take the place inch by inch, street by street and discover every damn elf they met had suicided? The elves would do it on them, so in the villages south of here they had saved the elves the bother, and got nothing for their trouble but endless, measured carnage, and smoothskinned corpses that drew the small vermin and the huge winged birds—(they've been careful with their ecology, the Science Bureau reckoned, in their endless reports, in some fool's paper on large winged creatures' chances of survival if a dominant species were not very careful of them—)

(—or the damn birds are bloody-minded mean and tougher than the elves, deFranco mused in his alcoholic fog, knowing that nothing was, in all space and creation, more bloody-minded than the elves.)

He had seen a young elf child holding another, both stone dead, baby locked in baby's arms: they love, dammit, they love—And he had wept while he staggered away from the ruins of a little elvish town, seeing more and more such sights—because the elves had touched off bombs in their own town center, and turned it into a firestorm.

But the two babies had been lying there unburned and no one

wanted to touch them or to look at them. Finally the birds came. And the regs shot at the birds until the CO stopped it, because it was a waste: it was killing a non-combatant lifeform, and that (O God!) was against the rules. Most of all the CO stopped it because it was a fraying of human edges, because the birds always were there and the birds were the winners, every time. And the damn birds like the damn elves came again and again, no matter that shots blew them to puffs of feathers. Stubborn, like the elves. Crazy as everything else on the planet, human and elf. It was catching.

DeFranco nursed the last whiskey in the glass, nursed it with hands going so numb he had to struggle to stay awake. He was a quiet drunk, never untidy. He neatly drank the last and fell over sideways limp as a corpse, and, tender mercy to a hill-finding branch of the service the hill-taking and road-building regs regarded as a sometimes natural enemy— one of the women came and got the glass from his numbed fingers and pulled a blanket over him. They were still human here. They tried to be.

"THERE WAS NOTHING more to be done," says the elf. "That was why. We knew that you were coming closer, and that our time was limited." His long white fingers touch the table-surface, the white, plastic table in the ordinary little bedroom. "We died in great numbers, deFranco, and it was cruel that you showed us only slowly what you could do."

"We could have taken you out from the first. You knew that." DeFranco's voice holds an edge of frustration. Of anguish. "Elf, couldn't you ever understand that?"

"You always gave us hope we could win. And so we fought, and so we still fight. Until the peace. My friend."

"FRANC, FRANC—"—IT was a fierce low voice, and deFranco came out of it, in the dark, with his heart doubletiming and the instant realization it was Dibs talking to him in that low tone and wanting him out of that blanket, which meant wire-runners or worse, a night attack. But Dibs grabbed his arms to hold him still before he could flail about. "Franc, we got a move out there, Jake and Cat's headed out down the tunnel, the lieutenant's gone to M1 but M1's on the line, they want you out there, they want a spotter up on hill 24 doublequick."

"Uh." DeFranco rubbed his eyes. "Uh." Sitting upright was brutal.

Standing was worse. He staggered two steps and caught the main shell of his armor off the rack, number 12 suit, the lousy stinking armor that always smelled of human or mud or the purse in the ducts and the awful sick-sweet cleaner they wiped it out with when they hung it up. He held the plastron against his body and Dibs started with the clips in the dim light of the single 5-watt they kept going to find the latrine at night— "Damn, damn, I gotta—" He eluded Dibs and got to the toilet and by now the whole place was astir with shadow-figures like a scene out of a gold-lighted hell. He swigged the stinging mouthwash they had on the shelf by the toilet and did his business while Dibs caught him up from behind and finished the hooks on his left side. "Damn, get him going," the sergeant said, and: "Trying," Dibs said, as others hauled deFranco around and began hooking him up like a baby into his clothes, one piece and the other, the boots, leg and groin-pieces, the sleeves, the gloves, the belly clamp and the backpack and the power-on—his joints ached. He stood there swaying to one and another tug on his body and took the helmet into his hands when Dibs handed it to him.

"Go, go," the sergeant said, who had no more power to give a special op any specific orders than he could fly; but HQ was in a stew, they needed his talents out there, and deFranco let the regs shove him all they liked: it was his accommodation with these regs when there was no peace anywhere else in the world. And once a dozen of these same regs had come out into the heat after him, which he never quite forgot. So he let them hook his weapons-kit on, then ducked his head down and put the damned helmet on and gave it the locking half-twist as he headed away from the safe light of the barracks pit into the long tunnel, splashing along the low spots on the plastic grid that kept heavy armored feet from sinking in the mud.

"Code: *Nightsight*," he told the suit aloud, all wobbly and shivery from too little sleep; and it read his hoarse voice patterns and gave him a filmy image of the tunnel in front of him. "Code: *ID*," he told it, and it started telling the two troopers somewhere up the tunnel that he was there, and on his way. He got readout back as Cat acknowledged. "la-6yg-p30/30," the green numbers ghosted up in his visor, telling him Jake and Cat had elves and they had them quasi-solid in the distant-sensors which would have been tripped downland and they themselves were staying where they were and taking no chances on betraying the location of the tunnel. He cut the ID and Cat and Jake cut off too.

They've got to us, deFranco thought. *The damned elves got through our screen and now they've pushed through on foot, and it's going to be hell to pay—*

Back behind him the rest of the troops would be suiting up and making a more leisurely prep for a hard night to come. The elves rarely got as far as human bunkers. They tried. They were, at close range and with hand-weapons, deadly. The dying was not all on the elves' side if they got to you.

A cold sweat had broken out under the suit. His head ached with a vengeance and the suit weight on his knees and on his back when he bent and it stank with disinfectant that smelled like some damn tree from some damn forest on the world that had spawned every human born, he knew that, but it failed as perfume and failed at masking the stink of terror and of the tunnels in the cold wet breaths the suit took in when it was not on self-seal.

He knew nothing about Earth, only dimly remembered Pell, which had trained him and shipped him here by stages to a world no one bothered to give a name. Elfland, when High HQ was being whimsical. Neverneverland, the regs called it after some old fairy tale, because from it a soldier never never came home again. They had a song with as many verses as there were bitches of the things a soldier in Elfland never found.

> *Where's my discharge from this war?*
> *Why, it's neverneverwhere, my friend.*
> *Well, when's the next ship off this world?*
> *Why, it's neverneverwhen, my friend.*
>   *And time's what we've got most of,*
>   *And time is what we spend,*
>   *And time is what we've got to do*
>   *In Neverneverland.*

He hummed this to himself, in a voice jolted and crazed by the exertion. He wanted to cry like a baby. He wanted someone to curse for the hour and his interrupted rest. Most of all he wanted a few days of quiet on this front, just a few days to put his nerves back together again and let his head stop aching. . . .

. . . *RUN AND RUN and run, in a suit that keeps you from the gas and most of the shells the elves can throw—except for a few. Except for the joints*

*and the visor, because the elves have been working for twenty years study-
ing how to kill you. And air runs out and filters fail and every access you
have to Elfland is a way for the elves to get at you.*

*Like the tunnel openings, like the airvents, like the power plant that
keeps the whole base and strung-out tunnel systems functioning.*

*Troopers scatter to defend these points, and you run and run, belatedly
questioning why troopers want a special op at a particular point, where
the tunnel most nearly approaches the elves on their plain.*

*Why me, why here—because, fool, HQ wants close-up reconnaissance,
which was what they wanted the last time they sent you out in the dark beyond the safe points—twice, now, and they expect you to go out and do it
again because the elves missed you last time.*

*Damn them all. (With the thought that they will use you till the bone
breaks and the flesh refuses. And then a two-week rest and out to the lines
again.)*

*They give you a medical as far as the field hospital; and there they give
you vitamins, two shots of antibiotic, a bottle of pills and send you out
again. "We got worse," the meds say then.*

There always are worse. Till you're dead.

DeFranco looks at the elf across the table in the small room and re-
members how it was, the smell of the tunnels, the taste of fear.

II

> *So what're the gals like on this world?*
> *Why, you nevernevermind, my friend.*
> *Well, what're the guys like on this world?*
> *Well, you neverneverask, my friend.*

"They sent me out there," deFranco says to the elf, and the elf—a
human might have nodded but elves have no such habit—stares gravely
as they sit opposite each other, hands on the table.

"You alway say 'they,' " says the elf. "We say 'we' decided. But you do
things differently."

"Maybe it *is* we," deFranco says. "Maybe it is, at the bottom of things.
We. Sometimes it doesn't look that way."

"I think even now you don't understand why we do what we do. I
don't really understand why you came here or why you listen to me, or

why you stay now—But we won't understand. I don't think we two will. Others maybe. You want what I want. That's what I trust most."

"You believe it'll work?"

"For us, yes. For elves. Absolutely. Even if it's a lie it will work."

"But if it's not a lie—"

"Can you make it true? *You* don't believe. That—I have to find words for this—but I don't understand that either. How you feel. What you do." The elf reaches across the table and slim white hands with overtint like oil on water catch at brown, matte-skinned fingers whose nails (the elf has none) are broken and rough. "It was no choice to you. It never was even a choice to you, to destroy us to the heart and the center. Perhaps it wasn't to stay. I have a deep feeling toward you, deFranco. I had this feeling toward you from when I saw you first; I knew that you were what I had come to find, but whether you were the helping or the damning force I didn't know then, I only knew that what you did when you saw us was what humans had always done to us. And I believed you would show me why."

DEFRANCO MOVED AND sat still a while by turns, in the dark, in the stink and the strictures of his rig; while somewhere two ridges away there were two nervous regs encamped in the entry to the tunnel, sweltering in their own hardsuits and not running their own pumps and fans any more than he was running his—because elvish hearing was legendary, the rigs made noise, and it was hard enough to move in one of the bastards without making a racket: someone in HQ suspected elves could pick up the running noises. Or had other senses.

But without those fans and pumps the below-the-neck part of the suit had no cooling and got warm even in the night. And the gloves and the helmets had to stay on constantly when anyone was outside, it was the rule: no elf ever got a look at a live human, except at places like the Eighth's Gamma Company. Perhaps not there either. Elves were generally thorough.

DeFranco had the kneejoints on lock at the moment, which let him have a solid prop to lean his weary knees and backside against. He leaned there easing the shivers and the quakes out of his lately-wakened and sleep-deprived limbs before he rattled in his armor and alerted a whole hillside full of elves. It was not a well-shielded position he had taken: it had little cover except the hill itself, and these hills had few enough trees that the fires and the shells had spared. But green did struggle up amid the soot and bushes grew on the line down on valley level that had been an elvish road three years ago. His nightsight scanned the brush in shadow-images.

Something touched the sensors as he rested there on watch, a curious whisper of a sound, and an amber readout ghosted up into his visor, dots rippling off in sequence in the direction the pickup came from. It was not the wind: the internal computer zeroed out the white sound of wind and suit-noise. It was anomalies it brought through and amplified; and what it amplified now had the curious regular pulse of engine-sound.

DeFranco ordered the lock off his limbs, slid lower on the hill, and moved on toward one with better vantage of the road so it came up from the west—carefully, pausing at irregular intervals as he worked round to get into position to spot that direction. He still had his locator output off. So did everyone else back at the base. HQ had no idea now what sophistication the elves had gained at eavesdropping and homing in on the locators, and how much they could pick up with locators of their own. It was only sure that while some elvish armaments had gotten more primitive and patchwork, their computer tech had nothing at all wrong with it.

DeFranco settled again on a new hillside and listened, wishing he could scratch a dozen maddening itches, and wishing he were safe somewhere else: the whole thing had a disaster-feeling about it from the start, the elves doing something they had never done. He could only think about dead Gamma Company and what might have happened to them before the elves got to them and gassed the bunker and fought their way into it past the few that had almost gotten into their rigs in time—

Had the special op been out there watching too? Had the one at bunker 35 made a wrong choice and had it all started this way the night they died?

The engine-sound was definite. DeFranco edged higher up the new hill and got down flat, belly down on the ridge. He thumbed the magnification plate into the visor and got the handheld camera's snake-head optics over the ridge on the theory it was a smaller target and a preferable target than himself, with far better nightsight.

The filmy nightsight image came back of the road, while the sound persisted. It was distant, his ears and the readout advised him, distant yet, racing the first red edge of a murky dawn that showed far off across the plain and threatened daylight out here.

He still sent no transmission. The orders were stringent. The base either had to remain ignorant that there was a vehicle coming up the road or he had to go back personally to report it; and lose track of whatever-it-was out here just when it was getting near enough to do damage. Damn the lack of specials to team with out here in the hot spots, and damn the lead-footed regs: he had to go it alone, decide things alone, hoping Jake and Cat did the right thing in their spot and hoping the other regs stayed put. And he hated it.

He edged off this hill, keeping it between him and the ruined, shell-pocked road, and began to move to still a third point of vantage, stalking as silently as any man in armor could manage.

And fervently he hoped that the engine-sound was not a decoy and that nothing was getting behind him. The elves were deceptive as well and they were canny enemies with extraordinary hearing. He hoped now that the engine-sound had deafened them—but no elf was really fool enough to be coming up the road like this, it was a decoy, it had to be, there was nothing else it could be; and he was going to fall into it nose-down if he was not careful.

He settled belly-down on the next slope and got the camera-snake over the top, froze the suit-joints, and lay inert in that overheated ceramic shell, breathing hard through a throat abused by oxygen and whiskey, blinking against a hangover headache to end all headaches that the close focus of the visor readout only made worse. His nose itched. A place on his scalp itched behind his ear. He stopped cataloging the places he itched because it was driving him crazy. Instead he blinked and rolled his eyes, calling up readout on the passive systems, and concentrated on that.

Blink. Blink-blink. Numbers jumped. The computer had come up with a range as it got passive echo off some hill and checked it against the local topology programmed into its memory. Damn! Close. The computer handed him the velocity. 40 KPH with the 4 and the 0 wobbling back and forth into the 30's. DeFranco held his breath and checked his hand-launcher, loading a set of armor-piercing rounds in, quiet, quiet as a man could move. The clamp went down as softly as long practice could lower it.

And at last a ridiculous open vehicle came jouncing and whining its way around potholes and shell craters and generally making a noisy and erratic progress. It was in a considerable hurry despite the potholes, and there were elves in it, four of them, all pale in their robes and one of them with the cold glitter of metal about his/her? person, the one to the right of the driver. The car bounced and wove and zigged and zagged up the hilly road with no slackening of speed, inviting a shot for all it was worth.

Decoy?

Suicide?

They were crazy as elves could be, and that was completely. They were headed straight for the hidden bunker, and it was possible they had gas or a bomb in that car or that they just planned to get themselves shot in a straightforward way, whatever they had in mind, but they were going right where they could do the most damage.

DeFranco unlocked his ceramic limbs, which sagged under his weight until he was down on his belly; and he slowly brought his rifle up, and inched his way up on his belly so it was his vulnerable head over the ridge this time. He shook and he shivered and he reckoned there might be a crater where he was in fair short order if they had a launcher in that car and he gave them time to get it set his way.

But pushing and probing at elves was part of his job. And these were decidedly anomalous. He put a shot in front of the car and half expected elvish suicides on the spot.

The car swerved and jolted into a pothole as the shell hit. It careened to a stop; and he held himself where he was, his heart pounding away and himself not sure why he had put the shot in front and not into the middle of them like a sensible man in spite of HQ's orders.

But the elves recovered from their careening and the car was stopped; and instead of blowing themselves up immediately or going for a launcher of their own, one of the elves bailed out over the side while the helmet-sensor picked up the attempted motor-start. Cough-whine. The car lurched. The elvish driver made a wild turn, but the one who had gotten out just stood there—*stood*, staring up, and lifted his hands together.

DeFranco lay on his hill; and the elves who had gotten the car started swerved out of the pothole it had stuck itself in and lurched off in escape, not suicide—while the one elf in the robe with the metal border just stood there, the first live prisoner anyone had ever taken, staring up at him, self-offered.

"You damn well stand still," he yelled down at the elf on outside com, and thought of the gas and the chemicals and thought that if elves had come up with a disease that also got to humans, here was a way of delivering it that was cussed enough and crazy enough for them.

"Human," a shrill voice called up to him. "Human!"

DeFranco was for the moment paralyzed. An elf knew what to call them: an elf *talked*. An elf stood there staring up at his hill in the beginnings of dawn and all of a sudden nothing was going the way it ever had between elves and humankind.

At least, if it had happened before, no human had ever lived to tell about it.

"Human!" the same voice called—*uu-mann*, as best high elvish voices could manage it. The elf was not suiciding. The elf showed no sign of wanting to do that; and deFranco lay and shivered in his armor and felt a damnable urge to wipe his nose which he could not reach or to get up and run for his life, which was a fool's act. Worse, his bladder suddenly told him it was full. Urgently. Taking his mind down to a ridiculous small matter in the midst of trying to get home alive.

The dawn was coming up the way it did across the plain, light spreading like a flood, so fast in the bizarre angle of the land here that it ran like water on the surface of the plain.

And the elf stood there while the light of dawn grew more, showing the elf more clearly than deFranco had ever seen one of the enemy alive, beautiful the way elves were, not in a human way, looking, in its robes, like some cross between man and something spindly and human-skinned and insectoid. The up-tilted ears never stopped moving, but the average of their direction was toward him. Nervous-like.

What does he want, why does he stand there, why did they throw him out? A target? A distraction?

Elvish cussedness. DeFranco waited, and waited, and the sun came up; while somewhere in the tunnels there would be troopers wondering and standing by their weapons, ready to go on self-seal against gas or whatever these lunatics had brought.

There was light enough now to make out the red of the robes that fluttered in the breeze. And light enough to see the elf's hands, which looked—which looked, crazily enough, to be tied together.

The dawn came on. Water became an obsessive thought. DeFranco was thirsty from the whiskey and agonized between the desire for a drink from the tube near his mouth or the fear one more drop of water in his system would make it impossible to ignore his bladder; and he thought about it and thought about it, because it was a long wait and a long walk back, and relieving himself outside the suit was a bitch on the one hand and on the inside was damnable discomfort. But it did get worse. And while life and death tottered back and forth and his fingers clutched the launcher and he faced an elf who was surely up to something, that small decision was all he could think of clearly—it was easier to think of than what wanted thinking out, like what to do and whether to shoot the elf outright, counter to every instruction and every order HQ had given, because he wanted to get out of this place.

But he did not—and finally he solved both problems: took his drink, laid the gun down on the ridge like it was still in his hands, performed the necessary maneuver to relieve himself outside the suit as he stayed as flat as he could. Then he put himself back together, collected his gun and lurched up to his feet with small whines of the assisting joint-locks.

The elf never moved in all of this, and deFranco motioned with the gun. "Get up here. . . ."—not expecting the elf to understand either the motion or the shout. But the elf came, slowly, as if the hill was all his (it had been once) and he owned it. The elf stopped still on the slant, at a speaking distance, no more, and stood there with his hands tied (*his*, deFranco decided by the height of him). The elf's white skin all but glowed in the early dawn, the bare skin of the face and arms against the dark, metal-edged red of his robe; and the large eyes were set on him and the ears twitched and quivered with small pulses.

"I am your prisoner," the elf said, plain as any human; and deFranco stood there with his heart hammering away at his ribs.

"Why?" deFranco asked. He was mad, he was quite mad and somewhere he had fallen asleep on the hillside, or elvish gas had gotten to him through the open vents—he was a fool to have gone on open circulation; and he was dying back there somewhere and not talking at all.

The elf lifted his bound hands. "I came here to find you."

It was not a perfect accent. It was what an elvish mouth could come up with. It had music in it. And deFranco stood and stared and finally motioned with the gun up the hill. "Move," he said, "walk."

Without demur his prisoner began to do that, in the direction he had indicated.

· · ·

"What did I do that humans always do?" deFranco asks the elf, and the grave sea-colored eyes flicker with changes. Amusement, perhaps. Or distress.

"You fired at us," says the elf in his soft, songlike voice. "And then you stopped and didn't kill me."

"It was a warning."

"To stop. So simple."

"God, what else do you think?"

The elf's eyes flicker again. There is gold in their depths, and gray. And his ears flick nervously. "DeFranco, deFranco, you still don't know why we fight. And I don't truly know what you meant. Are you telling me the truth?"

"We never wanted to fight. It was a warning. Even animals, for God's sake—understand a warning shot."

The elf blinks. (And someone in another room stirs in a chair and curses his own blindness. Aggression and the birds. Different tropisms. All the way through the ecostructure.)

The elf spreads his hands. "I don't know what you mean. I never know. What can we know? That you were there for the same reason I was? Were you?"

"I don't know. I don't even know that. *We never wanted a war.* Do you understand that, at least?"

"You wanted us to stop. So we told you the same. We sent our ships to hold those places which were ours. And you kept coming to them."

"They were ours."

"Now they are." The elf's face is grave and still. "DeFranco, a mistake was made. A ship of ours fired on yours and this was a mistake. Perhaps it was me who fired. What's in this elf's mind? Fear when a ship will not go away? What's in this human's mind? Fear when we don't go away? It was a stupid thing. It was a mistake. It was our region. Our—"

"Territory. You think you owned the place."

"We were in it. We were there and this ship came. Say that I wasn't there and I heard how it happened. This was a frightened elf who made a stupid mistake. This elf was surprised by this ship and he didn't want to run and give up this jump-point. It was ours. You were in it. We wanted you to go. And you stayed."

"So you blew up an unarmed ship."

"Yes. I did it. I destroyed all the others. You destroyed ours. Our space station. You killed thousands of us. I killed thousands of you."

"Not me and not you, elf. That's twenty years, dammit, and you weren't there and I wasn't there—"

"I did it. I say I did. And you killed thousands of us."

"We weren't coming to make a war. We were coming to straighten it out. Do you understand that?"

"We weren't yet willing. Now things are different."

"For God's sake—why did you let so many die?"

"You never gave us defeat enough. You were cruel, deFranco. Not to let us know we couldn't win—that was very cruel. It was very subtle. Even now I'm afraid of your cruelty."

"Don't you understand yet?"

"What do I understand? That you've died in thousands. That you make long war. I thought you would kill me on the hill, on the road, and when you called me I had both hope and fear. Hope that you would take me to higher authority. Fear—well, I am bone and nerve, deFranco. And I never knew whether you would be cruel."

THE ELF WALKED and walked. He might have been on holiday, his hands tied in front of him, his red robes a-glitter with their gold borders in the dawn. He never tired. *He* carried no weight of armor; and deFranco went on self-seal and spoke through the mike when he had to give the elf directions.

Germ warfare?

Maybe the elf had a bomb in his gut?

But it began to settle into deFranco that he had done it, he had done it, after years of trying he had himself a live and willing prisoner, and his lower gut was queasy with outright panic and his knees felt like mush. *What's he up to, what's he doing, why's he walk like that—Damn! They'll shoot him on sight, somebody could see him first and shoot him and I can't break silence—maybe that's what I'm supposed to do, maybe that's how they overran Gamma Company—*

But a prisoner, a prisoner speaking human language—

"Where'd you learn," he asked the elf, "where'd you learn to talk human?"

The elf never turned, never stopped walking. "A prisoner."

"Who? Still alive?"

"No."

No. Slender and graceful as a reed and burning as a fire and white as beach sand. *No.* Placidly. Rage rose in deFranco, a blinding urge to put his rifle butt in that straight spine, to muddy and bloody the bastard and make him as dirty and as hurting as himself; but the professional rose up in him too, and the burned hillsides went on and on as they climbed and they walked, the elf just in front of him.

Until they were close to the tunnels and in imminent danger of a human misunderstanding.

He turned his ID and locator on; but they would pick up the elf on his sensors too, and that was no good. "It's deFranco," he said over the com. "I got a prisoner. Get HQ and get me a transport."

Silence from the other end. He cut off the output, figuring they had it by now. "Stop," he said to the elf on outside audio. And he stood and waited until two suited troopers showed up, walking carefully down the hillside from a direction that did not lead to any tunnel opening.

"Damn," came Cat's female voice over his pickup. "Daamn." In a tone of wonder. And deFranco at first thought it was admiration of him and what he had done, and then he knew with some disgust it was wonder at the elf, it was a human woman looking at the prettiest, cleanest thing she had seen in three long years, icy, fastidious Cat, who was picky what she slept with.

And maybe her partner Jake picked it up, because: "Huh," he said in quite a different tone, but quiet, quiet, the way the elf looked at their faceless faces, as if he still owned the whole world and meant to take it back.

"It's Franc," Jake said then into the com, directed at the base. "And he's right, he's got a live one. Damn, you should *see* this bastard."

III

> *So where's the generals in this war?*
> *Why, they're neverneverhere, my friend.*
> *Well, what'll we do until they come?*
> *Well, you neverneverask, my friend.*

"I was afraid too," deFranco says. "I thought you might have a bomb or something. We were afraid you'd suicide if anyone touched you. That was why we kept you sitting all that time outside."

"Ah," says the elf with a delicate move of his hands. "Ah. I thought it was to make me angry. Like all the rest you did. But you sat with me. And this was hopeful. I was thirsty; I hoped for a drink. That was mostly what I thought about."

"We think too much—elves and humans. We both think too much. *I'd have given you a drink of water, for God's sake.* I guess no one even thought."

"I wouldn't have taken it."

"Dammit, why?"

"Unless you drank with me. Unless you shared what you had. Do you see?"

"Fear of poison?"

"No."

"You mean just my giving it."

"Sharing it. Yes."

"Is pride so much?"

Again the elf touches deFranco's hand as it rests on the table, a nervous, delicate gesture. The elf's ears twitch and collapse and lift again, trembling. "We always go off course here. I still fail to understand why you fight."

"Dammit, I don't understand why you can't understand why a man'd give you a drink of water. Not to hurt you. Not to prove anything. For the love of God, *mercy*, you ever learn that word? Being decent, so's everything decent doesn't go to hell and we don't act like damn animals!"

The elf stares long and soberly. His small mouth has few expressions. It forms its words carefully. "Is this why you pushed us so long? To show us your control?"

"No, dammit, to hang onto it! So we can find a place to stop this bloody war. It's all we ever wanted."

"Then why did you start?"

"Not to have you push *us*!"

A blink of sea-colored eyes. "Now, now, we're understanding. We're like each other."

"But you won't stop, dammit it, you wouldn't stop, you haven't stopped yet! People are still dying out there on the front, throwing themselves away without a thing to win. Nothing. *That*'s not like us."

"In starting war we're alike. But not in ending it. You take years. Quickly we show what we can do. Then both sides know. So we make peace. You showed us long cruelty. And we wouldn't give ourselves up to you. What could we expect?"

"Is it that easy?" DeFranco begins to shiver, clenches his hands to-gether on the tabletop and leans there, arms folded. "You're crazy, elf."

"Angan. My personal name is Angan."

"A hundred damn scientists out there trying to figure out how you work and it's that damn simple?"

"I don't think so. I think we maybe went off course again. But we came close. We at least see there was a mistake. That's the important thing. That's why I came."

DeFranco looked desperately at his watch, at the minutes ticking away. He covers the face of it with his hand and looks up. His brown eyes show anguish. "The colonel said I'd have three hours. It's going. It's going too fast."

"Yes. And we still haven't found out why. I don't think we ever will. Only you share with me now, deFranco. Here. In our little time."

THE ELF SAT, just sat quietly with his hands still tied, on the open hill-side, because the acting CO had sent word no elf was setting foot inside the bunker system and no one was laying hands on him to search him.

But the troopers came out one by one in the long afternoon and had their look at him—one after another of them took the trouble to put on the faceless, uncomfortable armor just to come out and stand and stare at what they had been fighting for all these years.

"Damn," was what most of them said, in private, on the com, their suits to his suit; "damn," or variants on that theme.

"We got that transport coming in," the reg lieutenant said when she came out and brought him his kit. Then, unlike herself, "Good job, Franc."

"Thanks," deFranco said, claiming nothing. And he sat calmly, beside his prisoner, on the barren, shell-pocked hill by a dead char-coal tree.

Don't shake him, word had come from the CO. Keep him real happy—don't change the situation and don't threaten him and don't touch him.

For fear of spontaneous suicide.

So no one came to lay official claim to the elf either, not even the cap-tain came. But the word had gone out to Base and to HQ and up, de-Franco did not doubt, to orbiting ships, because it was the best news a frontline post had had to report since the war started. Maybe it was dreams of leaving Elfland that brought the regs out here, on pilgrimage to see this wonder. And the lieutenant went away when she had stared at him so long.

Hope. DeFranco turned that over and over in his mind and probed at it like a tongue into a sore tooth. Promotion out of the field. No more mud. No more runs like yesterday. No more, no more, no more, the man who broke the Elfland war and cracked the elves and brought in the key—

—to let it all end. For good. *Winning*. Maybe, maybe—

He looked at the elf who sat there with his back straight and his eyes wandering to this and that, to the movement of wind in a forlorn last bit of grass, the drift of a cloud in Elfland's blue sky, the horizons and the dead trees.

"You got a name?" He was careful asking anything. But the elf had talked before.

The elf looked at him. "Saitas," he said.

"Saitas. Mine's deFranco."

The elf blinked. There was no fear in his face. They might have been sitting in the bunker passing the time of day together.

"Why'd they send you?" DeFranco grew bolder.

"I asked to come."

"Why?"

"To stop the war."

Inside his armor deFranco shivered. He blinked and he took a drink from the tube inside the helmet and he tried to think about something else, but the elf sat there staring blandly at him, with his hands tied, resting placidly in his lap. "How?" deFranco asked, "how will you stop the war?"

But the elf said nothing and deFranco knew he had gone further with that question than HQ was going to like, not wanting their subject told anything about human wants and intentions before they had a chance to study the matter and study the elf and hold their conferences.

"They came," says deFranco in that small room, "to know what you looked like."

"You never let us see your faces," says the elf.

"You never let us see yours."

"You knew everything. Far more than we. You knew our world. We had no idea of yours."

"Pride again."

"Don't you know how hard it was to let you lay hands on me? That was the worst thing. You did it again. Like the gunfire. You touch with violence and then expect quiet. But I let this happen. It was what I came to do. And when you spoke to the others for me, that gave me hope."

IN TIME THE transport came skimming in low over the hills, and de-Franco got to his feet to wave it in. The elf stood up too, graceful and still placid. And waited while the transport sat down and the blades stopped beating.

"Get in," deFranco said then, picking up his scant baggage, putting the gun on safety.

The elf quietly bowed his head and followed instructions, going where he was told. DeFranco never laid a hand on him, until inside, when they had climbed into the dark belly of the transport and guards were waiting there—"Keep your damn guns down," deFranco said on outside com, because they were light-armed and helmetless. "What are you going to do if he moves, shoot him? Let me handle him. He speaks real good." And to the elf: "Sit down there. I'm going to put a strap across. Just so you don't fall."

The elf sat without objection, and deFranco got a cargo strap and hooked it to the rail on one side and the other, so there was no way the elf was going to stir or use his hands.

And he sat down himself as the guards took their places and the transport lifted off and carried them away from the elvish city and the front-line base of the hundreds of such bases in the world. It began to fly high and fast when it got to safe airspace, behind the defense humans had made about themselves.

There was never fear in the elf. Only placidity. His eyes traveled over the inside of the transport, the dark utilitarian hold, the few benches, the cargo nets, the two guards.

Learning, deFranco thought, still learning everything there was to learn about his enemies.

"THEN I WAS truly afraid," says the elf. "I was most afraid that they would want to talk to me and learn from me. And I would have to die then to no good. For nothing."

"How do you do that?"

"What?"

"Die. Just by wanting to."

"Wanting is the way. I could stop my heart now. Many things stop the heart. When you stop trying to live, when you stop going ahead—it's very easy."

"You mean if you quit trying to live you die. That's crazy."

The elf spreads delicate fingers. "Children can't. Children's hearts can't be stopped that way. You have the hearts of children. Without control. But the older you are the easier and easier it is. Until someday it's easier to stop than to go on. When I learned your language I learned from a man named Tomas. He couldn't die. He and I talked—oh, every day. And one day we brought him a woman we took. She called him a damn traitor. That was what she said. Damn traitor. Then Tomas wanted to die and he couldn't. He told me so. It was the only thing he ever asked of me. Like the water, you see. Because I felt sorry for him I gave him the cup. And to her. Because I had no use for her. But Tomas hated me. He hated me every day. He talked to me because I was all he had to talk to, he would say. Nothing stopped his heart. Until the woman called him traitor. And then his heart stopped, though it went on beating. I only helped. He thanked me. And damned me to hell. And wished me health with his drink."

"Dammit, elf."

"I tried to ask him what hell was. I think it means being still and trapped. So we fight."

("He's very good with words," someone elsewhere says, leaning over near the monitor. "He's trying to communicate something but the words aren't equivalent. He's playing on what he does have.")

"For God's sake," says deFranco then, "is that why they fling themselves on the barriers? Is that why they go on dying? Like birds at cage bars?"

The elf flinches. Perhaps it is the image. Perhaps it is a thought. "Fear stops the heart, when fear has nowhere to go. We still have one impulse left. There is still our anger. Everything else has gone. At the last even our children will fight you. So I fight for my children by coming here. I don't want to talk about Tomas anymore. The birds have him. You are what I was looking for."

"Why?" DeFranco's voice shakes. "Saitas—Angan—I'm scared as hell."

"So am I. Think of all the soldiers. Think of things important to you. I think about my home."

"I think I never had one. —This is crazy. It won't work."

"Don't." The elf reaches and holds a brown wrist. "Don't leave me now, deFranco."

"There's still fifteen minutes. Quarter of an hour."

"That's a very long time . . . here. Shall we shorten it?"

"No," deFranco says and draws a deep breath. "Let's use it."

AT THE BASE where the on-world authorities and the scientists did their time, there were real buildings, real ground-site buildings, which humans had made. When the transport touched down on a rooftop landing pad, guards took the elf one way and deFranco another. It was debriefing: that he expected. They let him get a shower first with hot water out of real plumbing, in a prefabbed bathroom. And he got into his proper uniform for the first time in half a year, shaved and proper in his blue beret and his brown uniform, fresh and clean and thinking all the while that if a special could get his field promotion it was scented towels every day and soft beds to sleep on and a life expectancy in the decades. He was anxious, because there were ways of snatching credit for a thing and he wanted the credit for this one, wanted it because a body could get killed out there on hillsides where he had been for three years and no desk-sitting officer was going to fail to mention him in the report.

"Sit down," the specials major said, and took him through it all; and that afternoon they let him tell it to a reg colonel and lieutenant general; and again that afternoon they had him tell it to a tableful of scientists and answer questions and questions and questions until he was hoarse and they forgot to feed him lunch. But he answered on and on until his voice cracked and the science staff took pity on him.

He slept then, in clean sheets in a clean bed and lost touch with the war so that he waked terrified and lost in the middle of the night in the dark and had to get his heart calmed down before he realized he was not crazy and that he really had gotten into a place like this and he really had done what he remembered.

He tucked down babylike into a knot and thought good thoughts all the way back to sleep until a buzzer waked him and told him it was day in this windowless place, and he had an hour to dress again—for more questions, he supposed; and he thought only a little about his elf, *his* elf, who was handed on to the scientists and the generals and the AISec people, and stopped being his personal business.

. . .

"Then," says the elf, "I knew you were the only one I met I could understand. Then I sent for you."

"I still don't know why."

"I said it then. We're both soldiers."

"You're more than that."

"Say that I made one of the great mistakes."

"You mean at the beginning? I don't believe it."

"It could have been. Say that I commanded the attacking ship. Say that I struck your people on the world. Say that you destroyed our station and our cities. We are the makers of mistakes. Say this of ourselves."

"I," THE ELF said, his image on the screen much the same as he had looked on the hillside, straight-spined, red-robed—only the ropes elves had put on him had left purpling marks on his wrists, on the opalescing white of his skin, "I'm clear enough, aren't I?" The trooper accent was strange coming from a delicate elvish mouth. The elf's lips were less mobile. His voice had modulations, like singing, and occasionally failed to keep its tones flat.

"It's very good," the scientist said, the man in the white coveralls, who sat at a small desk opposite the elf in a sterile white room and had his hands laced before him. The camera took both of them in, elf and swarthy Science Bureau xenologist. "I understand you learned from prisoners."

The elf seemed to gaze into infinity. "We don't want to fight anymore."

"Neither do we. Is this why you came?"

A moment the elf studied the scientist, and said nothing at all.

"What's your people's name?" the scientist asked.

"You call us elves."

"But we want to know what you call yourselves. What you call this world."

"Why would you want to know that?"

"To respect you. Do you know that word, respect?"

"I don't understand it."

"Because what you call this world and what you call yourselves *is* the name, the right name, and we want to call you right. Does that make sense?"

"It makes sense. But what you call us is right too, isn't it?"

"Elves is a made-up word, from our homeworld. A myth. Do you know *myth*? A story. A thing not true."

"Now it's true, isn't it?"

"Do you call your world Earth? Most people do."

"What you call it is its name."

"We call it Elfland."

"That's fine. It doesn't matter."

"Why doesn't it matter?"

"I've said that."

"You learned our language very well. But we don't know anything of yours."

"Yes."

"Well, we'd like to learn. We'd like to be able to talk to you your way. It seems to us this is only polite. Do you know *polite*?"

"No."

A prolonged silence. The scientist's face remained bland as the elf's. "You say you don't want to fight anymore. Can you tell us how to stop the war?"

"Yes. But first I want to know what your peace is like. What, for instance, will you do about the damage you've caused us?"

"You mean reparations."

"What's that mean?"

"Payment."

"What do you mean by it?"

The scientist drew a deep breath. "Tell me. Why did your people give you to one of our soldiers? Why didn't they just call on the radio and say they wanted to talk?"

"This is what you'd do."

"It's easier, isn't it? And safer."

The elf blinked. No more than that.

"There was a ship a long time ago," the scientist said after a moment. "It was a human ship minding its own business in a human lane, and elves came and destroyed it and killed everyone on it. Why?"

"What do you want for this ship?"

"So you do understand about payment. Payment's giving something for something."

"I understand." The elvish face was guileless, masklike, the long eyes like the eyes of a pearl-skinned buddha. A saint. "What will you ask? And how will peace with you be? What do you call peace?"

"You mean you don't think our word for it is like your word for it?"

"That's right."

"Well, that's an important thing to understand, isn't it? Before we make agreements. Peace means no fighting."

"That's not enough."

"Well, it means being safe from your enemies."

"That's not enough."

"What is enough?"

The pale face contemplated the floor, something elsewhere.

"What *is* enough, Saitas?"

The elf only stared at the floor, far, far away from the questioner. "I need to talk to deFranco."

"Who?"

"DeFranco." The elf looked up. "DeFranco brought me here. He's a soldier; he'll understand me better than you. Is he still here?"

THE COLONEL REACHED and cut the tape off. She was SurTac. Agnes Finn was the name on her desk. She could cut your throat a dozen ways, and do sabotage and mayhem from the refinements of computer theft to the gross tactics of explosives; she would speak a dozen languages, know every culture she had ever dealt with from the inside out, integrating the Science Bureau and the military. And more, she was a SurTac *colonel*, which sent the wind up deFranco's back. It was not a branch of the service that had many high officers; you had to survive more than ten field missions to get your promotion beyond the ubiquitous and courtesy-titled lieutenancy. And this one had. This was Officer with a capital O, and whatever the politics in HQ were, this was a rock around which a lot of other bodies orbited: *this* probably took her orders from the joint command, which was months and months away in its closest manifestation. And that meant next to no orders and wide discretion, which was what SurTacs did. Wild card. Joker in the deck. There were the regs; there was special ops, loosely attached; there were the spacers, Union and Alliance, and Union regs were part of that; beyond and above, there was AlSec and Union intelligence; and that was this large-boned, red-haired woman who probably had a scant handful of humans and no knowing what else in her direct command, a handful of SurTacs loose in Elfland, and all of them independent operators and as much trouble to the elves as a reg base could be.

DeFranco knew. He had tried that route once. He knew more than most what kind it took to survive that training, let alone the requisite ten missions to get promoted out of the field, and he knew the wit behind the weathered face and knew it ate special ops lieutenants for appetizers.

"How did you make such an impression on him, Lieutenant?"

"I didn't try to," deFranco said carefully. "Ma'am, I just tried to keep him calm and get in with him alive the way they said. But I was the only one who dealt with him out there, we thought that was safest; maybe he thinks I'm more than I am."

"I compliment you on the job." There was a certain irony in that, he was sure. No SurTac had pulled off what he had, and he felt the slight tension there.

"Yes, ma'am."

"*Yes, ma'am.* There's always the chance, you understand, that you've brought us an absolute lunatic. Or the elves are going an unusual route to lead us into a trap. Or this is an elf who's not too pleased about being tied up and dumped on us, and he wants to get even. Those things occur to me."

"Yes, ma'am." DeFranco thought all those things, face to face with the colonel and trying to be easy as the colonel had told him to be. But the colonel's thin face was sealed and forbidding as the elf's.

"You know what they're doing out there right now? Massive attacks. Hitting that front near 45 with everything they've got. The Eighth's pinned. We're throwing air in. And they've got somewhere over two thousand casualties out there and air-strikes don't stop all of them. Delta took a head-on assault and turned it. There were casualties. Trooper named Herse. Your unit."

Dibs. O God. "Dead?"

"Dead." The colonel's eyes were bleak and expressionless. "Word came in. I know it's more than a stat to you. But that's what's going on. We've got two signals coming from the elves. And we don't know which one's valid. We have ourselves an alien who claims credentials—*and* comes with considerable effort from the same site as the attack."

Dibs. Dead. There seemed a chill in the air, in this safe, remote place far from the real world, the mud, the bunkers. Dibs had stopped living yesterday. This morning. Sometime. Dibs had gone and the world never noticed.

"Other things occur to the science people," the colonel said. "One which galls the hell out of them, deFranco, is what the alien just said. *DeFranco can understand me better.* Are you with me, Lieutenant?"

"Yes, ma'am."

"So the Bureau went to the secretary, the secretary went to the major general on the com; all this at fifteen hundred yesterday; and *they* hauled me in on it at two this morning. You know how many noses you've got out of joint, Lieutenant? And what the level of concern is about that mess out there on the front?"

"Yes, ma'am."

"I'm sure you hoped for a commendation and maybe better, wouldn't that be it? Wouldn't blame you. Well, I got my hands into this, and I've opted you under my orders, Lieutenant, because I can do that and high command's just real worried the Bureau's going to poke and prod and that elf's going to leave us on the sudden for elvish heaven. So let's just keep him moderately happy. He wants to talk to you. What the Bureau wants to tell you, but I told them *I'd* make it clear, because they'll talk tech at you and I want to be sure you've got it—it's just real simple: you're dealing with an alien; and you'll have noticed what he says doesn't always make sense."

"Yes, ma'am."

"Don't yes ma'am me, Lieutenant, dammit; just talk to me and look me in the eye. We're talking about communication here."

"Yes—" He stopped short of the ma'am.

"You've got a brain, deFranco, it's all in your record. You almost went Special Services yourself, that was your real ambition, wasn't it? But you had this damn psychotic fear of taking ultimate responsibility. And a wholesome fear of ending up with a commendation, posthumous. Didn't you? It washed you out, so you went special ops where you could take orders from someone else and still play bloody hero and prove something to yourself—am I right? I ought to be; I've got your psych record over there. Now I've insulted you and you're sitting there turning red. But I want to know what I'm dealing with. We're in a damn bind. We've got casualties happening out there. Are you and I going to have trouble?"

"No. I understand."

"Good. Very good. Do you think you can go into a room with that elf and talk the truth out of him? More to the point, can you make a decision, can you go in there knowing how much is riding on your back?"

"I'm not a—"

"I don't care what you *are*, deFranco. What I want to know is whether *negotiate* is even in that elf's vocabulary. I'm assigning you to guard over there. In the process I want you to sit down with him one to one and just talk away. That's all you've got to do. And because of your background maybe you'll do it with some sense. But maybe if you just talk for John deFranco and try to get that elf to deal, that's the best thing. You know when a government sends out a negotiator—or anything like—that individual's not average. That individual's probably the smartest, canniest, hardest-nosed bastard they've got, and he probably cheats at dice. We don't know what this bastard's up to or what he thinks like, and when you sit down with him you're talking to a mind that knows a lot more about humanity than we know about elves. You're talking to an elvish expert who's here playing games with us. Who's giving us a real good look-over. You understand that? What do you say about it?"

"I'm scared of this."

"That's real good. You know we're not sending in the brightest, most experienced human on two feet. And that's exactly what that rather canny elf has arranged for us to do. You understand that? He's playing us like a keyboard this far. And how do you cope with that, Lieutenant deFranco?"

"I just ask him questions and answer as little as I can."

"Wrong. You let him talk. You be real *careful* what you ask him. What you ask is as dead a giveaway as what you tell him. Everything you do and say is cultural. If he's good he'll drain you like a sponge." The colonel bit her lips. "Damn, you're *not* going to be able to handle that, are you?"

"I understand what you're warning me about, Colonel. I'm not sure I can do it, but I'll try."

"Not sure you can do it. *Peace* may hang on this. And several billion lives. Your company, out there on the line. Put it on that level. And you're scared and you're showing it, Lieutenant; you're too damned open, no wonder they washed you out. Got no hard center to you, no place to go to when I embarrass the hell out of you, and *I'm* on your side. You're probably a damn good special op, brave as hell, I know, you've got commendations in the field. And that shell-shyness of yours probably makes you drive real hard when you're in trouble. Good man. Honest. If the elf wants a human specimen, we could do worse. You just go in there, son, and you talk to him and you be your nice self, and that's all you've got to do."

"We'll be bugged." DeFranco stared at the colonel deliberately, trying to dredge up some self-defense, give the impression he was no complete fool.

"Damn sure you'll be bugged. Guards right outside if you want them. But you startle that elf I'll fry you."

"That isn't what I meant. I meant—I meant if I could get him to talk there'd be an accurate record."

"Ah. Well. Yes. There will be, absolutely. And yes, I'm a bastard, Lieutenant, same as that elf is, beyond a doubt. And because I'm on your side I want you as prepared as I can get you. But I'm going to give you all the backing you need—you want anything, you just tell that staff and they better jump to do it. I'm giving you carte blanche over there in the Science Wing. Their complaints can come to this desk. You just be yourself with him, watch yourself a little, don't get taken and don't set him off."

"Yes, ma'am."

Another slow, consuming stare and a nod.

He was dismissed.

IV

So where's the hole we're digging end?
Why, it's neverneverdone, my friend.
Well, why's it warm at the other end?
Well, hell's neverneverfar, my friend.

"This colonel," says the elf, "it's her soldiers outside."

"That's the one," says deFranco.

"It's not the highest rank."

"No. It's not. Not even on this world." DeFranco's hands open and close on each other, white-knuckled. His voice stays calm. "But it's a lot of power. She won't be alone. There are others she's acting for. They sent me here. I've figured that now."

"Your dealing confuses me."

"Politics. It's all politics. Higher-ups covering their—" DeFranco rechooses his words. "Some things they have to abide by. They have to do. Like if they don't take a peace offer—that would be trouble back home. Human space is big. But a war—humans want it stopped. I know that. With humans, you can't quiet a mistake down. We've got too many separate interests. . . . We got scientists, and a half dozen different commands—"

"Will they all stop fighting?"

"Yes. My side will. I know they will." DeFranco clenches his hands tighter as if the chill has gotten to his bones. "If we can give them something, some solution. You have to understand what they're thinking of. If there's a trouble anywhere, it can grow. There might be others out there, you ever think of that? What if some other species just—wanders through? It's happened. And what if our little war disturbs them? We live in a big house, you know that yet? You're young, you, with your ships, you're a young power out in space. God help us, we've made mistakes, but this time the first one wasn't ours. We've been trying to stop this. All along, we've been trying to stop this."

"You're what I trust," says the elf. "Not your colonel. Not your treaty words. Not your peace. You. Words aren't the belief. What you do— that's the belief. What you do will show us."

"I can't!"

"I can. It's important enough to me and not to you. *Our little war.* I can't understand how you think that way."

"Look at that!" DeFranco waves a desperate hand at the room, the world. Up. "It's so big! Can't you see that? And one planet, one ball of rock. It's a little war. Is it worth it all? Is it worth such damn stubbornness? Is it worth dying in?"

"Yes," the elf says simply, and the sea-green eyes and the white face have neither anger nor blame for him.

DeFRANCO SALUTED AND got out and waited until the colonel's orderly caught him in the hall and gave his escort the necessary authorizations, because *no one* wandered this base without an escort. (But the elves are two hundred klicks out *there*, deFranco thought; and who're we fighting anyway?) In the halls he saw the black of Union elite and the blue of Alliance spacers and the plain drab of the line troop officers, and the white and pale blue of the two Science Bureaus; while everywhere he felt the tenuous peace—damn, maybe we *need* this war, it's keeping humanity talking to each other, they're all fat and sleek and mud never touched them back here— But there was haste in the hallways. But there were tense looks on faces of people headed purposefully to one place and the other, the look of a place with something on its collective mind, with silent, secret emergencies passing about him— *The attack on the lines,* he thought, and remembered another time that attack had started on one front and spread rapidly to a dozen; and missiles had gone. And towns had died.

And the elvish kids, the babies in each others' arms and the birds fluttering down; and Dibs—Dibs lying in his armor like a broken piece of
machinery—when a shot got you, it got the visor and you had no face
and never knew it; or it got the joints and you bled to death trapped in
the failed shell, you just lay there and bled: he had heard men and
women die like that, still in contact on the com, talking to their buddies
and going out alone, alone in that damn armor that cut off the sky and
the air—

They brought him down tunnels that were poured and cast and hard
overnight, *that* kind of construction, which they never got out on the
Line. There were bright lights and there were dry floors for the fine officers to walk on; there was, at the end, a new set of doors where guards
stood with weapons ready—

—against *us?* DeFranco got that sense of unreality again, blinked as
he had to show his tags and IDs to get past even with the colonel's orders
directing his escort.

Then they let him through, and further, to another hall with more
guards. AlSec MPs. Alliance Security. The intelligence and Special Services. The very air here had a chill about it, with only those uniforms in
sight. *They* had the elf. Of course they did. He was diplomatic property
and the regs and the generals had nothing to do with it. He was in Finn's
territory. Security and the Surface Tactical command, that the reg command only controlled from the top, not inside the structure. Finn had a
leash, but she took no orders from sideways in the structure. Not even
from AlSec. Check and balance in a joint command structure too many
light-years from home to risk petty dictatorships. He had just crossed a
line and might as well have been on another planet.

And evidently a call had come ahead of him, because there were surly
Science Bureau types here too, and the one who passed him through
hardly glanced at his ID. It was his face the man looked at, long and
hard; and it was the Xenbureau interviewer who had been on the tape.

"Good luck," the man said. And a SurTac major arrived, dour-faced,
a black man in the SurTac's khaki, who did not look like an office-type.
He took the folder of authorizations and looked at it and at deFranco
with a dark-eyed stare and a set of a square, well-muscled jaw. "Colonel's
given you three hours, Lieutenant. Use it."

"WE'RE MORE THAN one government," says deFranco to the elf, quietly,
desperately. "We've fought in the past. We had wars. We made peace

and we work together. We may fight again but everyone hopes not and it's less and less likely. War's expensive. It's too damn open out here, that's what I'm trying to tell you. You start a war and you don't know what else might be listening."

The elf leans back in his chair, one arm on the back of it. His face is solemn as ever as he looks at deFranco. "You and I, you-and-I. The world was whole until you found us. How can people do things that don't make sense? The *whole* thing makes sense, the parts of the thing are crazy. You can't put part of one thing into another, leaves won't be feathers, and your mind can't be our mind. I see our mistakes. I want to take them away. Then elves won't have theirs and you won't have yours. But you call it a little war. The lives are only a few. You have so many. You like your mistake. You'll keep it. You'll hold it in your arms. And you'll meet these others with it. But they'll see it, won't they, when they look at you?"

"It's crazy!"

"When we met you in it we assumed *we*. That was our first great mistake. But it's yours too."

DeFranco walked into the room where they kept the elf, a luxurious room, a groundling civ's kind of room, with a bed and a table and two chairs, and some kind of green and yellow pattern on the bedclothes, which were ground-style, free-hanging. And amid this riot of life-colors the elf sat crosslegged on the bed, placid, not caring that the door opened or someone came in—until a flicker of recognition seemed to take hold and grow. It was the first humanlike expression, virtually the only expression, the elf had ever used in deFranco's sight. Of course there were cameras recording it, recording everything. The colonel had said so and probably the elf knew it too.

"Saitas. You wanted to see me."

"DeFranco." The elf's face settled again to inscrutability.

"Shall I sit down?"

There was no answer. DeFranco waited for an uncertain moment, then settled into one chair at the table and leaned his elbows on the white plastic surface.

"They treating you all right?" deFranco asked, for the cameras, deliberately, for the colonel—(*Damn you, I'm not a fool, I can play your damn game, Colonel, I did what your SurTacs failed at, didn't I? So watch me.*)

"Yes," the elf said. His hands rested loosely in his red-robed lap. He looked down at them and up again.

"I tried to treat you all right. I thought I did."

"Yes."

"Why'd you ask for me?"

"I'm a soldier," the elf said, and put his legs over the side of the bed and stood up. "I know that you are. I think you understand me more."

"I don't know about that. But I'll listen." The thought crossed his mind of being held hostage, of some irrational violent behavior, but he pretended it away and waved a hand at the other chair. "You want to sit down? You want something to drink? They'll get it for you."

"I'll sit with you." The elf came and took the other chair, and leaned his elbows on the table. The bruises on his wrists showed plainly under the light. "I thought you might have gone back to the front by now."

"They give me a little time. I mean, there's—"

(Don't talk to him, the colonel had said. Let him talk.)

"—three hours. A while. You had a reason you wanted to see me. Something you wanted? Or just to talk. I'll do that too."

"Yes," the elf said slowly, in his lilting lisp. And gazed at him with sea-green eyes. "Are you young, deFranco? You make me think of a young man."

It set him off his balance. "I'm not all that young."

"I have a son and a daughter. Have you?"

"No."

"Parents?"

"Why do you want to know?"

"Have you parents?"

"A mother. Long way from here." He resented the questioning. Letters were all Nadya deFranco got, and not enough of them, and thank God she had closer sons. DeFranco sat staring at the elf who had gotten past his guard in two quick questions and managed to hit a sore spot; and he remembered what Finn had warned him. "You, elf?"

"Living parents. Yes. A lot of relatives?"

Damn, what trooper had they stripped getting that part of human language? Whose soul had they gotten into?

"What are you, Saitas? Why'd they hand you over like that?"

"To make peace. So the Saitas always does."

"Tied up like that?"

"I came to be your prisoner. You understand that."

"Well, it worked. I might have shot you; I don't say I would've, but I might, except for that. It was a smart move, I guess it was. But hell, you could have called ahead. You come up on us in the dark—you looked to get your head blown off. Why didn't you use the radio?"

A blink of sea-green eyes. "Others ask me that. Would you have come then?"

"Well, someone would. Listen, you speak at them in human language and they'd listen and they'd arrange something a lot safer."

The elf stared, full of his own obscurities.

"Come on, they throw you out of there? They your enemies?"

"Who?"

"The ones who left you out there on the hill."

"No."

"Friends, huh? *Friends* left you out there?"

"They agreed with me. I agreed to be there. I was most afraid you'd shoot them. But you let them go."

"Hell, look, I just follow orders."

"And orders led you to let them go?"

"No. They say to talk if I ever got the chance. Look, me, personally, I never wanted to kill you guys. I wouldn't, if I had the choice."

"But you do."

"Dammit, you took out our ships. Maybe that wasn't personal on your side either, but we sure as hell can't have you doing it as a habit. All you ever damn well had to do was go away and let us alone. You hit a world, elf. Maybe not much of one, but you killed more than a thousand people on that first ship. Thirty thousand at that base, good God, don't sit there looking at me like that!"

"It was a mistake."

"Mistake." DeFranco found his hands shaking. No. Don't raise the voice. Don't lose it. (Be your own nice self, boy. Patronizingly. The colonel knew he was far out of his depth. And he knew.) "Aren't most wars mistakes?"

"Do you think so?"

"If it is, can't we stop it?" He felt the attention of unseen listeners, diplomats, scientists—himself, special ops, talking to an elvish negotiator and making a mess of it all, losing everything. (Be your own nice self— The colonel was crazy, the elf was, the war and the world were and he lumbered ahead desperately, attempting subtlety, attempting a caricatured simplicity toward a diplomat and knowing the one as transparent as the other.) "You know all you have to do is say quit and there's ways to stop the shooting right off, ways to close it all down and then start talking about how we settle this. You say that's what you came to do. You're in the right place. All you have to do is get your side to stop. They're killing each other out there, do you know that? You come in here to talk peace. And they're coming at us all up and down the front. I just got word I lost a friend of mine out there. God knows what by now. It's no damn sense. If you can stop it, then let's stop it."

"I'll tell you what our peace will be." The elf lifted his face placidly, spread his hands. "There is a camera, isn't there? At least a microphone. They do listen."

"Yes. They've got camera and mike. I know they will."

"But your face is what I see. Your face is all human faces to me. They can listen, but I talk to you. Only to you. And this is our peace. The fighting will stop, and we'll build ships again and we'll go into space, and we won't be enemies. The mistake won't exist. That's the peace I want."

"So how do we do that?" (Be your own nice self, boy— DeFranco abandoned himself. Don't see the skin, don't see the face alien-like, just talk, talk like to a human, don't worry about protocols. *Do* it, boy.) "How do we get the fighting stopped?"

"I've said it. They've heard."

"Yes. They have."

"They have two days to make this peace."

DeFranco's palms sweated. He clenched his hands on the chair. "Then what happens?"

"I'll die. The war will go on."

(God, now what do I do, what do I say? How far can I go?) "Listen, you don't understand how long it takes us to make up our minds. We need more than any two days. They're dying out there, your people are killing themselves against our lines, and it's all for nothing. Stop it now. Talk to them. Tell them we're going to talk. Shut it down."

The slitted eyes blinked, remained in their buddha-like abstraction, looking askance into infinity. "DeFranco, there has to be payment."

(Think, deFranco, think. Ask the right things.)

"What payment? Just exactly who are you talking for? All of you? A city? A district?"

"One peace will be enough for you—won't it? You'll go away. You'll leave and we won't see each other until we've built our ships again. You'll begin to go—as soon as my peace is done."

"Build the ships, for God's sake. And come after us again?"

"No. The war is a mistake. There won't be another war. This is enough."

"But would everyone agree?"

"Everyone does agree. I'll tell you my real name. It's Angan. Angan Anassidi. I'm forty-one years old. I have a son named Agaita; a daughter named Siadi; I was born in a town named Daogisshi, but it's burned now. My wife is Llaothai Sohail, and she was born in the city where we live now. I'm my wife's only husband. My son is aged twelve, my daughter is nine. They live in the city with my wife alone now and her parents and mine." The elvish voice acquired a subtle music on the names that lingered to obscure his other speech. "I've written—I told them I would write everything for them. I write in your language."

"Told who?"

"The humans who asked me. I wrote it all."

DeFranco stared at the elf, at a face immaculate and distant as a statue. "I don't think I follow you. I don't understand. We're talking about the front. We're talking about maybe that wife and those kids being in danger, aren't we? About maybe my friends getting killed out there. About shells falling and people getting blown up. Can we do anything about it?"

"I'm here to make the peace. Saitas is what I am. A gift to you. I'm the payment."

DeFranco blinked and shook his head. "Payment? I'm not sure I follow that."

For a long moment there was quiet. "Kill me," the elf said. "That's why I came. To be the last dead. The saitas. To carry the mistake away."

"Hell, no. No. We don't shoot you. Look, elf—all we want is to stop the fighting. We don't want your life. Nobody wants to kill you."

"DeFranco, we haven't any more resources. We want a peace."

"So do we. Look, we just make a treaty—you understand *treaty*?"

"I'm the treaty."

"A treaty, man, a treaty's a piece of paper. We promise peace to each other and not to attack us, we promise not to attack you, we settle our borders, and you just go home to that wife and kids. And I go home and that's it. No more dying. No more killing."

"No." The elf's eyes glistened within the pale mask. "No, deFranco, no paper."

"We make peace with a paper and ink. We write peace out and we make agreements and it's good enough; we do what we say we'll do."

"Then write it in your language."

"You have to sign it. Write your name on it. And keep the terms. That's all, you understand that?"

"Two days. I'll sign your paper. I'll make your peace. It's nothing. Our peace is in me. And I'm here to give it."

"Dammit, we don't kill people for treaties."

The sea-colored eyes blinked. "Is one so hard and millions so easy?"

"It's different."

"Why?"

"Because—because—look, war's for killing; peace is for staying alive."

"I don't understand why you fight. Nothing you do makes sense to us. But I think we almost understand. We talk to each other. We use the same words. DeFranco, don't go on killing us."

"Just you. Just you, is that it? Dammit, that's crazy!"

"A cup would do. Or a gun. Whatever you like. DeFranco, have you never shot us before?"

"God, it's not the same!"

"You say paper's enough for you. That paper will take away all your mistakes and make the peace. But paper's not enough for us. I'd never trust it. You have to make my peace too. So both sides will know it's true. But there has to be a saitas for humans. Someone has to come to be a saitas for humans. Someone has to come to us."

DeFranco sat there with his hands locked together. "You mean just go to your side and get killed."

"The last dying."

"Dammit, you are crazy. You'll wait a long time for that, elf."

"You don't understand."

"You're damn right I don't understand. Damn bloody-minded lunatics!" DeFranco shoved his hands down, needing to get up, to get away from that infinitely patient and not human face, that face that had somehow acquired subtle expressions, that voice which made him forget where the words had first come from. And then he remembered the listeners, the listeners taking notes, the colonel staring at him across the table. Information. Winning was not the issue. Questions were. Finding out what they could. Peace was no longer the game. They were dealing with the insane, with minds there was no peace with. Elves that died to spite their enemies. That suicided for a whim and thought nothing about wiping out someone else's life.

He stayed in his chair. He drew another breath. He collected his wits and thought of something else worth learning. "What'd you do with the prisoners you learned the language from, huh? Tell me that?"

"Dead. We gave them the cup. One at a time they wanted it."

"Did they."

Again the spread of hands, of graceful fingers. "I'm here for all the mistakes. Whatever will be enough for them."

"Dammit, elf!"

"Don't call me that." The voice acquired a faint music. "Remember my name. Remember my name. DeFranco—"

He had to get up. He had to get up and get clear of the alien, get away from that stare. He thrust himself back from the table and looked back, found the elf had turned. Saitas-Angan smelled of something dry and musky, like spice. The eyes never opened wide, citrine slits. They followed him.

"Talk to me," the elf said. "Talk to me, deFranco."

"About what? About handing one of us to you? It won't happen. It bloody won't happen. We're not crazy."

"Then the war won't stop."

"You'll bloody die, every damn last one of you!"

"If that's your intention," the elf said, "yes. We don't believe you want peace. We haven't any more hope. So I come here. And the rest of us begin to die. Not the quiet dying. Our hearts won't stop. We'll fight."

"Out there on the lines, you mean."

"I'll die as long as you want, here. I won't stop my heart. The saitas can't."

"Dammit, that's not what we're after! That's not what we want."

"Neither can you stop yours. I know that. We're not cruel. I still have hope in you. I still hope."

"It won't work. *We can't do it*, do you understand me? It's against our law. Do you understand law?"

"Law."

"Right from wrong. Morality. For God's sake, killing's wrong."

"Then you've done a lot of wrong. You have your mistake too, De-Franco. You're a soldier like me. You know what your life's value is."

"You're damn right I know. And I'm still alive."

"We go off the course. We lose ourselves. You'll die for war but not for peace. I don't understand."

"*I* don't understand. You think we're just going to pick some poor sod and send him to you."

"You, deFranco. I'm asking you to make the peace."

"Hell." He shook his head, walked away to the door, colonel-be-hanged, listeners-be-hanged. His hand shook on the switch and he was afraid it showed. End the war. "The hell you say."

The door shot open. He expected guards. Expected—

—It was open corridor, clean prefab, tiled floor. On the tiles lay a dark, round object, with the peculiar symmetry and ugliness of things meant to kill. Grenade. Intact.

His heart jolted. He felt the doorframe against his side and the sweat ran cold on his skin, his bowels went to water. He hung there looking at it and it did not go away. He began to shake all over as if it were already armed.

"Colonel Finn." He turned around in the doorway and yelled at the unseen monitors. "Colonel Finn—get me out of here!"

No one answered. No door opened. The elf sat there staring at him in the closest thing to distress he had yet showed.

"Colonel! *Colonel, damn you!*"

More of silence. The elf rose to his feet and stood there staring at him in seeming perplexity, as if he suspected he witnessed some human madness.

"They left us a present," deFranco said. His voice shook and he tried to stop it. "They left us a damn present, elf. And they locked us in."

The elf stared at him; and deFranco went out into the hall, bent and gathered up the deadly black cylinder—held it up. "It's one of yours, elf."

The elf stood there in the doorway. His eyes looking down were the eyes of a carved saint; and looking up they showed color against his white skin. A long nailless hand touched the doorframe as the elf contemplated him and human treachery.

"Is this their way?"

"It's not mine." He closed his hand tightly on the cylinder, in its deadliness like and unlike every weapon he had ever handled. "It's damn well not mine."

"You can't get out."

The shock had robbed him of wits. For a moment he was not thinking. And then he walked down the hall to the main door and tried it. "Locked," he called back to the elf, who had joined him in his possession of the hall. The two of them together. DeFranco walked back again, trying doors as he went. He felt strangely numb. The hall became surreal, his elvish companion belonging like him, elsewhere. "Dammit, what have you got in their minds?"

"They've agreed," the elf said. "They've agreed, deFranco."

"They're out of their minds."

"One door still closes, doesn't it? You can protect your life."

"You still bent on suicide?"

"You'll be safe."

"Damn them!"

The elf gathered his arms about him as if he too felt the chill. "The colonel gave us a time. Is it past?"

"Not bloody yet."

"Come sit with me. Sit and talk. My friend."

"Is it time?" asks the elf, as deFranco looks at his watch again. And deFranco looks up.

"Five minutes. Almost." DeFranco's voice is hoarse.

The elf has a bit of paper in hand. He offers it. A pen lies on the table between them. Along with the grenade. "I've written your peace. I've put my name below it. Put yours."

"I'm nobody. I can't sign a treaty, for God's sake." DeFranco's face is white. His lips tremble. "What did you write?"

"Peace," said the elf. "I just wrote peace. Does there have to be more?"

DeFranco takes it. Looks at it. And suddenly he picks up the pen and signs it too, a furious scribble. And lays the pen down. "There," he says. "There, they'll have my name on it." And after a moment: "If I could do the other—O God, I'm scared. I'm *scared*."

"You don't have to go to my city," says the elf, softly. His voice wavers like deFranco's. "DeFranco—here, here they record everything. Go with me. Now. The record will last. We have our peace, you and I, we make it together, here, now. The last dying. Don't leave me. And we can end this war."

DeFranco sits a moment. Takes the grenade from the middle of the table, extends his hand with it across the center. He looks nowhere but at the elf. "Pin's yours," he says. "Go on. You pull it, I'll hold it steady."

The elf reaches out his hand, takes the pin and pulls it, quickly.

DeFranco lays the grenade down on the table between them, and his mouth moves in silent counting. But then he looks up at the elf and the elf looks at him. DeFranco manages a smile. "You got the count on this thing?"

The screen breaks up.

. . .

THE STAFFER REACHED out her hand and cut the monitor, and Agnes Finn stared past the occupants of the office for a time. Tears came seldom to her eyes. They were there now, and she chose not to look at the board of inquiry who had gathered there.

"There's a mandatory inquiry," the man from the reg command said. "We'll take testimony from the major this afternoon."

"Responsibility's mine," Finn said.

It was agreed on the staff. It was pre-arranged, the interview, the formalities.

Someone had to take the direct hit. It might have been a SurTac. She would have ordered that too, if things had gone differently. High command might cover her. Records might be wiped. A tape might be classified. The major general who had handed her the mess and turned his back had done it all through subordinates. And he was clear.

"The paper, Colonel."

She looked at them, slid the simple piece of paper back across the desk. The board member collected it and put it into the folder. Carefully.

"It's more than evidence," she said. "That's a treaty. The indigenes know it is."

They left her office, less than comfortable in their official search for blame and where, officially, to put it.

She was already packed. Going back on the same ship with an elvish corpse, all the way to Pell and Downbelow. There would be a grave there onworld.

It had surprised no one when the broadcast tape got an elvish response. Hopes rose when it got the fighting stopped and brought an elvish delegation to the front; but there was a bit of confusion when the elves viewed both bodies and wanted deFranco's. Only deFranco's.

And they made him a stone grave there on the shell-pocked plain, a stone monument; and they wrote everything they knew about him. *I was John Rand deFranco*, a graven plaque said. *I was born on a space station twenty light-years away. I left my mother and my brothers. The friends I had were soldiers and many of them died before me. I came to fight and I died for the peace, even when mine was the winning side. I died at the hand of Angan Anassidi, and he died at mine, for the peace; and we were friends at the end of our lives.*

Elves—*suilti* was one name they called themselves—came to this place and laid gifts of silk ribbons and bunches of flowers—flowers, in all that desolation; and in their thousands they mourned and they wept in their own tearless, expressionless way.

For their enemy.

One of their own was on his way to humankind. For humankind to cry for. *I was Angan Anassidi*, his grave would say; and all the right things. Possibly no human would shed a tear. Except the veterans of Elfland, when they came home, if they got down to the world—they might, like Agnes Finn, in their own way and for their own dead, in front of alien shrine.

Anne McCaffrey

Anne McCaffrey has been writing science fiction for nearly half a century and published her first novel, Restoree, in 1967. She won acclaim for her third novel, The Ship Who Sang, an influential story of human-machine interface written well before the cyberpunk movement, but is renowned for her bestselling Pern novels, introduced in her Hugo Award–winning story "Weyr Search" and Nebula Award–winning story "Dragonrider" in 1968. The Pern books, which are the chronicle of an Earth colony that is linked symbiotically to a native race of sentient dragons, number more than a dozen, including the Dragonriders of Pern trilogy, The White Dragon, and The Dolphins of Pern. They are complemented by a trio of young adult novels—Dragonsong, Dragonsinger, and Dragondrums—set in the same world, as well as the graphic novel rendering Dragonflight. McCaffrey has been praised for her strong female characters, particularly in the Rowan sequence—The Rowan, Damia, The Tower and the Hive. She is also the author of To Ride Pegasus and Pegasus in Flight, a duo concerned with future psychic sleuths, and the Ireta books set on Dinosaur Planet. Her short fiction has been collected in Get Off the Unicorn, and she has edited the anthology Alchemy and Academe.

 # DRAGONRIDER

Anne McCaffrey

The Finger Points
At an Eye blood red.
Alert the Weyrs
To sear the Thread.

"You still doubt, R'gul?" F'lar asked, appearing slightly amused by the older bronze rider's perversity.

R'gul, his handsome features stubbornly set, made no reply to the Weyrleader's taunt. He ground his teeth together as if he could grind away F'lar's authority over him.

"There have been no Threads in Pern's skies for over four hundred Turns. There are no more!"

"There is always that possibility," F'lar conceded amiably. There was not, however, the slightest trace of tolerance in his amber eyes. Nor the slightest hint of compromise in his manner.

He was more like F'lon, his sire, R'gul decided, than a son had any right to be. Always so sure of himself, always slightly contemptuous of what others did and thought. Arrogant, that's what F'lar was. Impertinent, too, and underhanded in the matter of that young Weyrwoman. Why, R'gul had trained her up to be one of the finest Weyrwomen in many Turns. Before he'd finished her instruction, she knew all the teaching ballads and sagas letter perfect. And then the silly child had turned to F'lar. Didn't have sense enough to appreciate the merits of an older, more experienced man. Undoubtedly she felt a first obligation to F'lar, he having discovered her at Ruath Hold during Search.

"You do, however," F'lar was saying, "admit that when the sun hits the Finger Rock at the moment of dawn, winter solstice has been reached?"

"Any fool knows that's what Finger Rock is for," R'gul grunted.

"Then why don't you, you old fool, admit that the Eye Rock was placed on Star Stone to bracket the Red Star when it's about to make a Pass?" burst out K'net, the youngest of the dragonriders.

R'gul flushed, half-starting out of his chair, ready to take the young sprout to task for such insolence.

"K'net," F'lar's voice cracked authoritatively, "do you really like flying the Igen Patrol so much you want another few weeks at it?"

K'net hurriedly seated himself, flushing at the reprimand and the threat.

"There is, you know, R'gul, incontrovertible evidence to support my conclusions," F'lar went on with deceptive mildness. " 'The Finger points/At an Eye blood red . . . ' "

"Don't quote me verses I taught you as a weyrling," R'gul exclaimed, heatedly.

"Then have faith in what you taught," F'lar snapped back, his amber eyes flashing dangerously.

R'gul, stunned by the unexpected forcefulness, sank back into his chair.

"You cannot deny, R'gul," F'lar continued quietly, "that no less than half an hour ago, the sun balanced on the Finger's tip at dawn and the Red Star was squarely framed by the Eye Rock."

The other dragonriders, bronze as well as brown, murmured and nodded their agreement to that phenomenon. There was also an undercurrent of resentment for R'gul's continual contest of F'lar's policies as the new Weyrleader. Even old S'lel, once R'gul's avowed supporter, was following the majority.

"There have been no Threads in four hundred years. There are no Threads," R'gul muttered.

"Then, my fellow dragonman," F'lar said cheerfully, "all you have taught is falsehood. The dragons are, as the Lords of the Holds wish to believe, parasites on the economy of Pern, anachronisms. And so are we.

"Therefore, far be it from me to hold you here against the dictates of your conscience. You have my permission to leave the Weyr and take up residence where you will."

· · ·

R'GUL WAS TOO stunned by F'lar's ultimatum to take offense at the ridicule. Leave the Weyr? Was the man mad? Where would he go? The Weyr had been his life. He had been bred up to it for generations. All his male ancestors had been dragonriders. Not all bronze, true, but a decent percentage. His own dam's sire had been a Weyrleader just as he, R'gul, had been until F'lar's Mnementh had flown the new queen and that young upstart had taken over as traditional Weyrleader.

But dragonmen never left the Weyr. Well, they did if they were negligent enough to lose their dragons, like that Lytol fellow who was now Warden at Ruath Hold. And how could he leave the Weyr *with* a dragon?

What did F'lar want of him? Was it not enough that the young one was Weyrleader now in R'gul's stead? Wasn't F'lar's pride sufficiently swollen by having bluffed the lords of Pern into disbanding their army when they were all set to coerce the Weyr and dragonmen? Must F'lar dominate *every* dragonman, body and will, too? He stared a long moment, incredulous.

"I do not believe we are parasites," F'lar said, breaking the silence with his soft, persuasive voice. "Nor anachronistic. There have been long Intervals before. The Red Star does not always pass close enough to drop Threads on Pern. Which is why our ingenious ancestors thought to position the Eye Rock and the Finger Rock as they did . . . to confirm *when* a Pass will be made. And another thing," his face turned grave, "there have been other times when dragonkind has all but died out . . . and Pern with it because of skeptics like you." F'lar smiled and relaxed indolently in his chair. "I prefer not to be recorded as a skeptic. How shall we record you, R'gul?"

The Council Chamber was tense. R'gul was aware of someone breathing harshly and realized it was himself. He looked at the adamant face of the young Weyrleader and knew that the threat was not empty. He would either concede to F'lar's authority, completely, though concession rankled deeply. Or leave the Weyr.

And where could he go, unless to one of the other Weyrs, deserted for hundreds of Turns? And, R'gul's thoughts were savage, wasn't that indication enough of the cessation of the Threads? Five empty Weyrs? No, by the Egg of Faranth, he would practice some of F'lar's own brand of deceit and bide his time. When all Pern turned on the arrogant fool, he, R'gul, would be there to salvage something from the ruins.

"A dragonman stays in his Weyr," R'gul said with what dignity he could muster from the remains of his pride.

"And accepts the policies of the current Weyrleader?" The tone of F'lar's voice made it less of a question and more of an order.

Relieved he would not have to perjure himself, R'gul gave a curt nod of his head. F'lar continued to stare at him until R'gul wondered if the man could read his thoughts as his dragon might. He managed to return the gaze calmly. His turn would come. He'd wait.

APPARENTLY ACCEPTING THE capitulation, F'lar stood up and crisply delegated patrol assignments for the day.

"T'bor, you're weather-watch. Keep an eye on those tithe trains as you do. What's the morning's report?"

"Weather is fair at dawning . . . all across Telgar and Keroon . . . if all too cold," T'bor said with a wry grin. "Tithing trains have good hard roads, though, so they ought to be here soon." His eyes twinkled with anticipation of the feasting that would follow the supplies' arrival; a mood shared by all, to judge by the expressions around the table.

F'lar nodded. "S'lan and D'nol, you are to continue an adroit Search for likely boys. They should be striplings, if possible, but do not pass over anyone suspected of talent. It's all well and good to present, for Impression, boys reared up in the Weyr traditions." F'lar gave a one-sided smile.

"But there are not enough in the lower caverns. We, too, have been behind in begetting. Anyway, dragons reach full growth faster than their riders. We must have more young *men* to Impress when Ramoth hatches. Take the southern holds, Ista, Nerat, Fort, and south Boll, where maturity comes earlier. You can use the guise of inspecting holds for greenery to talk to the boys. And, take along firestone. Run a few flaming passes on those heights that haven't been scoured in uh . . . dragon's years. A flaming beast impresses the young and rouses envy."

F'lar deliberately looked at R'gul to see the ex-Weyrleader's reaction to the order. R'gul had been dead set against going outside the Weyr for more candidates. In the first place, R'gul had argued that there were eighteen youngsters in the Lower Caverns, some quite young, to be sure, but R'gul could not admit that Ramoth would lay more than the dozen Nemorth had always dropped. In the second place, R'gul persisted in wanting to avoid any action that might antagonize the Lords.

R'gul made no overt protest and F'lar went on.

"K'net, back to the mines. I want the dispositions of each firestone dump checked and quantities available. R'gul, continue drilling recognition points with the weyrlings. They must be positive about their references. They may be sent out quickly and with no time to ask questions, if they're used as messengers and suppliers.

"F'nor, T'sum," and F'lar turned to his own brown riders, "you're clean-up squad today." He allowed himself a grin at their dismay. "Try Ista Weyr. Clear the Hatching Cavern and enough weyrs for a double wing. And, F'nor, don't leave a single record behind. They're worth preserving.

"That will be all, dragonmen. Good flying." And with that, F'lar rose and strode from the Council Room up to the queen's weyr.

RAMOTH STILL SLEPT, her hide gleaming with health, its color deepening to a shade of gold closer to bronze, indicating her pregnancy. As he passed her, the tip of her long tail twitched slightly.

All the dragons were restless these days, F'lar reflected. Yet when he asked Mnementh, the bronze dragon could give no reason. He woke, he went back to sleep. That was all. F'lar couldn't ask a leading question for that would defeat his purpose. He had to remain discontented with the vague fact that the restlessness was some kind of instinctive reaction.

Lessa was not in the sleeping room nor was she still bathing. F'lar snorted. That girl was going to scrub her hide off with this constant bathing. She'd had to live grimy to protect herself in Ruath Hold but bathing twice a day? He was beginning to wonder if this might be a subtle, Lessa-variety insult to him personally. F'lar sighed. That girl. Would she never turn to him of her own accord? Would he ever touch that elusive inner core of Lessa? She had more warmth for his half brother, F'nor, and K'net, the youngest of the bronze riders, than she had for F'lar who shared her bed.

He pulled the curtain back into place, irritated. Where had she got to today when, for the first time in weeks, he had been able to get all the wings out of the Weyr just so he could teach her to fly *between*?

Ramoth would soon be too egg-heavy for such activity. He had promised the Weyrwoman and he meant to keep the promise. She had taken to wearing the wher-hide riding gear as a flagrant reminder of his unfulfilled pledge. From certain remarks she had dropped, he knew she would not wait much longer for his aid. That she should try it on her own didn't suit him at all.

He crossed the queen's weyr again and peered down the passage that led to the Records Room. She was often to be found there, poring over the musty skins. And that was one more matter that needed urgent consideration. Those records were deteriorating past legibility. Curiously enough, earlier ones were still in good condition and readable. Another technique forgotten.

That girl! He brushed his thick forelock of hair back from his brow in a gesture habitual to him when he was annoyed or worried. The passage was dark which meant she could not be below in the Records Room.

Mnementh, he called silently to his bronze dragon, sunning on the ledge outside the queen's weyr. *What is that girl doing?*

Lessa, the dragon replied, stressing the Weyrwoman's name with pointed courtesy, *is talking to Manora. She's dressed for riding,* he added after a slight pause.

F'lar thanked the bronze sarcastically and strode down the passage to the entrance. As he turned the last bend, he all but ran Lessa down.

You hadn't asked me where *she was,* Mnementh answered plaintively to F'lar's blistering reprimand.

LESSA ROCKED BACK on her heels from the force of their encounter. She glared up at him, her lips thin with displeasure, her eyes flashing.

"Why didn't I have the opportunity of seeing the Red Star through the Eye Rock?" she demanded in a hard, angry voice.

F'lar pulled at his hair. Lessa at her most difficult would complete the list of this morning's trials.

"Too many to accommodate as it was on the Peak," he muttered, determined not to let her irritate him today. "And you already believe."

"I'd've liked to see it," she snapped and pushed past him towards the weyr. "If only in my capacity of Weyrwoman and Recorder."

He caught her arm and felt her body tense. He set his teeth, wishing as he had a hundred times since Ramoth rose in her first mating flight that Lessa had not been virgin, too. He had not thought to control his dragon-incited emotions and Lessa's first sexual experience had been violent. It had surprised him to be first, considering her adolescent years had been spent drudging for lascivious warders and soldier-types. Evidently no one had bothered to penetrate the curtain of rags and the coat of filth she had carefully maintained as a disguise. He had been a considerate and gentle bedmate ever since but, unless Ramoth and Mnementh were involved, he might as well call it rape.

Yet he knew someday, somehow, he would coax her into responding wholeheartedly to his lovemaking. He had a certain pride in his skill and he was in a position to persevere.

Now HE TOOK a deep breath and released her arm slowly.

"How fortunate you're wearing riding gear. As soon as the wings have cleared out and Ramoth wakes, I shall teach you to fly *between*."

The gleam of excitement in her eyes was evident even in the dimly lit passageway. He heard her inhale sharply.

"Can't put it off too much longer or Ramoth'll be in no shape to fly at all," he continued amiably.

"You do mean it?" Her voice was low and breathless, its usual acid edge missing. "You will teach us today?" He wished he could see her face clearly.

Once or twice, he had caught an unguarded expression on her face, loving and tender. He would give much to have that look turned on him. However, he admitted wryly to himself, he ought to be glad that melting regard was directed only at Ramoth and not at another human.

"Yes, my dear Weyrwoman, I mean it. I will teach you to fly *between* today. If only to keep you from trying it yourself."

Her low chuckle informed him his taunt was well-aimed.

"Right now, however," he said, indicating for her to lead the way back to the weyr, "I could do with some food. We were up before the kitchen."

They had entered the well-lighted weyr so he did not miss the trenchant look she shot him over her shoulder. She would not so easily forgive being left out of the group at the Star Stone this morning; certainly not with the bribe of flying *between*.

How different this inner room was now Lessa was Weyrwoman, F'lar mused as Lessa called down the service shaft for food. During Jora's incompetent tenure as Weyrwoman, the sleeping quarters had been crowded with junk, unwashed apparel, uncleared dishes. The state of the Weyr and the reduced number of dragons were as much Jora's fault as R'gul's for she had indirectly encouraged sloth, negligence and gluttony.

Had he, F'lar, been just a few years older when F'lon, his father, had died . . . Jora had been disgusting but when dragons rose in mating flight, the condition of your partner counted for nothing.

Lessa took a tray of bread and cheese, and mugs of the stimulating *klah* from the platform. She served him deftly.

"You've not eaten either?" he asked.

She shook her head vigorously, the braid into which she had plaited her thick, fine dark hair bobbing across her shoulders. The hairdressing was too severe for her narrow face but it did not, if that were her intention, disguise her femininity nor the curious beauty of her delicate features. Again F'lar wondered that such a slight body contained so much shrewd intelligence and resourceful . . . cunning, yes, that was the word, cunning. F'lar did not make the mistake, as others had, of underestimating her abilities.

"Manora called me to witness the birth of Kylara's child."

F'lar maintained an expression of polite interest. He knew perfectly well that Lessa suspected the child was his and it could have been, he admitted privately, but he doubted it. Kylara had been one of the ten candidates from the same Search three years ago which had discovered Lessa. Like others who survived Impression, Kylara had found certain aspects of Weyr life exactly suited to her temperament. She had gone from one rider's weyr to another's. She had even seduced F'lar, not at all against his will, to be sure. Now that he was Weyrleader, he found it wiser to ignore her efforts to continue the relationship. T'bor had taken her in hand and had his hands full until he retired her to the Lower Caverns, well-advanced in pregnancy.

Aside from having the amorous tendencies of a green dragon, Kylara was quick and ambitious. She would make a strong Weyrwoman so F'lar had charged Manora and Lessa with the job of planting the notion in Kylara's mind. In the capacity of Weyrwoman . . . of another Weyr . . . her intense drives would be used to Pern's advantage. She had not learned the severe lessons of restraint and patience that Lessa had and she didn't have Lessa's devious mind. Fortunately she was in considerable awe of Lessa, and F'lar suspected that Lessa was subtly influencing this attitude. In Kylara's case, F'lar preferred not to object to Lessa's meddling.

"A FINE SON," Lessa was saying.

F'lar sipped his *klah*. She was not going to get him to admit any responsibility.

After a long pause, Lessa added, "She has named him T'kil."

F'lar suppressed a grin at Lessa's failure to get a rise from him.

"Discreet of her."

"Oh?"

"Yes," F'lar replied blandly. "T'lar might be confusing if she took the second half of her name as is customary. 'T'kil,' however, still indicates sire as well as dam."

"While I was waiting for Council to end," Lessa said, after clearing her throat, "Manora and I checked the supply caverns. The tithing trains, which the Holds have been so gracious as to send us," her voice was sharp, "are due within the week. There shortly will be bread fit to eat," she added, wrinkling her nose at the crumbling gray pastry she was attempting to spread with cheese.

"A nice change," F'lar agreed.

She paused.

"The Red Star performed its scheduled antic?"

He nodded.

"And R'gul's doubts have been wiped away in the enlightening red glow?"

"Not at all." F'lar grinned back at her, ignoring her sarcasm. "Not at all, but he will not be so vocal in his criticism."

She swallowed quickly so she could speak. "You'd do well to cut out his criticism," she said ruthlessly, gesturing with her knife as if plunging it into a man's heart. "He is never going to accept your authority with good grace."

"We need every bronze rider . . . there are only seven, you know," he reminded her pointedly. "R'gul's a good wingleader. He'll settle down when the Threads fall. He needs proof to lay his doubts aside."

"And the Red Star in the Eye Rock is not proof?" Lessa's expressive eyes were wide.

F'lar was privately of Lessa's opinion, that it might be wiser to remove R'gul's stubborn contentiousness. But he could not sacrifice a wing-leader, needing every dragon and rider as badly as he did.

"I don't trust him," she added, darkly. She sipped at her hot drink, her gray eyes dark over the rim of her mug. As if, F'lar mused, she didn't trust him either.

And she didn't, past a certain point. She had made that plain and, in honesty, he couldn't blame her. She did recognize that every action F'lar took was towards one end . . . the safety and preservation of dragonkind and weyrfolk, and, consequently, the safety and preservation of Pern. To effect that end, he needed her full cooperation. When weyr business or dragonlore were discussed, she suspended the antipathy he knew she felt for him. In conferences, she supported him wholeheartedly and persuasively but always he suspected the double edge to her comments and saw a speculative, suspicious look in her eyes. He needed not only her tolerance but her empathy.

"Tell me," she said after a long silence, "did the sun touch the Finger Rock before the Red Star was bracketed in the Eye Rock or after?"

"Matter of fact, I'm not sure as I did not see it myself . . . the concurrence lasts only a few moments . . . but the two are supposed to be simultaneous."

She frowned at him sourly. "Whom did you waste it on? R'gul?" She was provoked; her angry eyes looked everywhere but at him.

"I am Weyrleader," he informed her curtly. She was unreasonable.

She awarded him one long, hard look before she bent to finish her meal. She ate very little, quickly and neatly. Compared to Jora, she didn't eat enough in the course of an entire day to nourish a sick child, but then, there was no point in ever comparing Lessa to Jora.

HE FINISHED HIS own breakfast, absently piling the mugs together on the empty tray. She rose silently and removed the dishes.

"As soon as the Weyr is free, we'll go," he told her.

"So you said," and she nodded towards the sleeping queen, visible through the open arch. "We still must wait upon Ramoth."

"Isn't she rousing? Her tail's been twitching an hour."

"She always does that about this time of day."

F'lar leaned across the table, his brows drawn together thoughtfully as he watched the golden forked tip of the queen's tail jerk spasmodically from side to side.

"Mnementh, too. And always at dawn and early morning. As if somehow they associate that time of day with trouble . . ."

". . . Or the Red Star's rising?"

Some subtle difference in her tone caused F'lar to glance quickly at her. It wasn't anger, now, for missing the morning's phenomenon. Her eyes were fixed on nothing; her face, smooth at first, was soon wrinkled with a vaguely anxious frown as tiny lines formed between her arching, well-defined brows.

"Dawn . . . that's when all warnings come," she murmured.

"What kind of warnings?" he asked with quiet encouragement.

"There was that morning . . . a few days before . . . before you and Fax descended on Ruath Hold. Something woke me . . . a feeling, like a very heavy pressure . . . the sensation of some terrible danger threatening." She was silent. "The Red Star was just rising." The fingers of her left hand opened and closed. She gave a convulsive shudder. Her eyes refocused on him.

"You and Fax did come out of the northeast from Crom," she said sharply, ignoring the fact, F'lar noticed, that the Red Star also rises north of true east.

"Indeed we did," he grinned at her, remembering that morning vividly. He remembered, too, how certain he had been as Fax's procession wound down the long valley to Ruath Hold that he and Fax would find some excuse for a mortal duel. And that he had somehow convinced himself that Ruatha Valley held a woman who had the unusual talents it would take to become the Weyrwoman Pern needed to impress the unhatched queen. "Indeed we did," he chuckled. "Although," he added, gesturing around the great cavern to emphasize, "I prefer to believe I served you well that day. You remember it with displeasure?"

The look she gave him was coldly inscrutable.

"Danger comes in many guises."

"I agree," he replied amiably, determined not to rise to her bait. "Had any other rude awakenings?" he inquired conversationally.

The absolute stillness in the room brought his attention back to her. Her face had drained of all color.

"The day Fax invaded Ruath Hold." Her voice was a barely articulated whisper. Her eyes were wide and staring. Her hands clenched the edge of the table. She said nothing for such a long interval F'lar became concerned. This was an unexpectedly violent reaction to a casual question.

"Tell me," he suggested softly.

She spoke in unemotional, impersonal tones, as if she were reciting a Traditional Ballad or something that had happened to an entirely different person.

"I was a child—just eleven. I woke at dawn . . ." her voice trailed off. Her eyes remained focused on nothing, staring at a scene that had happened long ago.

F'lar was stirred by an irresistible desire to comfort her. It struck him forcibly, even as he was stirred by this unusual compassion, that he had never thought that Lessa, of all people, would be troubled by so old a terror.

Mnementh sharply informed his rider that Lessa was obviously bothered a good deal. Enough so that her mental anguish was rousing Ramoth from sleep. In less accusing tones, Mnementh informed F'lar that R'gul had finally taken off with his weyrling pupils. His dragon, Hath, however, was in a fine state of disorientation due to R'gul's state of mind. Must F'lar unsettle everyone in the Weyr . . .

"Oh, be quiet," F'lar retorted under his breath.

"Why?" Lessa demanded in her normal voice.

"I didn't mean you, my dear Weyrwoman," he assured her, smiling pleasantly, as if the entranced interlude had never occurred. "Mnementh is full of advice these days."

"Like rider, like dragon," she replied tartly.

RAMOTH YAWNED MIGHTILY. Lessa was instantly on her feet, running to her dragon's side, her slight figure dwarfed by the six-foot dragon head.

A tender, adoring expression flooded her face as she gazed into Ramoth's gleaming opalescent eyes. F'lar clenched his teeth, envious, by the Egg, of a rider's affection for her dragon.

In his mind, he heard Mnementh's dragon equivalent of laughter.

"She's hungry," Lessa informed F'lar, an echo of her love for Ramoth lingering in the soft line of her mouth, in the kindness in her gray eyes.

"She's always hungry," he observed and followed them out of the weyr.

Mnementh hovered courteously just beyond the ledge until Lessa and Ramoth had taken off. They glided down the Weyr Bowl, over the misty bathing lake, towards the feeding ground at the opposite end of the long oval that comprised the floor of Benden Weyr. The striated, precipitous walls were pierced with the black mouths of single weyr entrances, deserted at this time of day by the few dragons who might otherwise doze on their ledges in the wintry sun. Benden Weyr, that could house five hundred beasts, accommodated a scant two hundred these days.

As F'lar vaulted to Mnementh's smooth bronze neck, he hoped that Ramoth's clutch would be spectacular, erasing the ignominy of the paltry dozen Nemorth had laid in each of her last few clutches.

He had no serious doubts of the improvement after Ramoth's remarkable mating flight with his Mnementh. The bronze dragon smugly echoed his rider's certainty and both looked on the queen possessively as she curved her wings to land. She was twice Nemorth's size, for one thing; her wings half-a-wing again longer than Mnementh's who was the biggest of the seven male bronzes. F'lar looked to Ramoth to repopulate the five empty Weyrs, even as he looked to himself, and Lessa, to rejuvenate the pride and faith of dragonriders and of Pern itself. He only hoped time enough remained to him to do what was necessary. The Red Star had been bracketed by the Eye Rock. The Threads would soon be falling. Somewhere, in one of the other Weyrs' records, must be the information he needed to ascertain *when*, exactly, Threads would fall.

Mnementh landed. F'lar jumped down from the curving neck to stand beside Lessa. The three watched as Ramoth, a buck grasped in each of her forefeet, rose to a feeding ledge.

"Will her appetite never taper off?" Lessa asked with affectionate dismay.

As a dragonet, Ramoth had been eating to grow. Her full stature attained, she was, of course, now eating for her young and she applied herself conscientiously.

F'lar chuckled and squatted, hunter fashion. He picked up shale flakes, skating them across the flat dry ground, counting the dust puffs boyishly.

"The time will come when she won't eat everything in sight," he assured Lessa. "But she's still young . . ."

". . . And needs her strength," Lessa interrupted, her voice a fair imitation of R'gul's pedantic tones.

F'lar looked up at her, squinting against the wintry sun that slanted down at them.

"She's a finely grown beast, especially compared to Nemorth." He gave a contemptuous snort. "In fact, there *is* no comparison. However, look here," he ordered peremptorily.

He tapped the smoothed sand in front of him and she saw that his apparently idle gestures had been to a purpose. With a sliver of stone, he drew a design in quick strokes.

"IN ORDER TO fly a dragon *between*, he has to know where to go. And so do you." He grinned at the astonished and infuriated look of comprehension on her face. "Ah, but there are certain consequences to an ill-considered jump. Badly visualized reference points often result in staying *between*." His voice dropped ominously. Her face cleared of its resentment. "So, there are certain reference, or recognition points, arbitrarily taught all weyrlings. That," he pointed first to his facsimile and then to the actual Star Stone with its Finger and Eye Rock companions, on Benden Peak, "that is the first recognition point a weyrling learns. When I take you aloft, you will reach an altitude just above the Star Stone, near enough for you to be able to see the hole in the Eye Rock clearly. Fix that picture sharply in your mind's eye, relay it to Ramoth. That will always get you home."

"Understood. But how do I learn recognition points of places I've never seen?"

He grinned up at her. "You're drilled in them. First by your instructor," and he pointed the sliver at his chest, "and then by going there, having directed your dragon to get the visualization from her instructor," and he indicated Mnementh. The bronze dragon lowered his wedge-shaped head until one eye was focused on his rider and his mate's rider. He made a pleased noise deep in his chest.

Lessa laughed up at the gleaming eye and, with unexpected affection, patted the soft nose.

F'lar cleared his throat in surprise. He was aware that Mnementh showed an unusual affection for the Weyrwoman but he had had no idea Lessa was fond of the bronze. Perversely, he was irritated.

"However," he said, and his voice sounded unnatural to himself, "we take the young riders constantly to and from the main reference points all across Pern, to all the Holds so that they have eyewitness impressions on which to rely. As a rider becomes adept in picking out landmarks, he gets additional references from other riders. Therefore, to go *between*, there is actually only one requirement: a clear picture of where you want to go. *And* a dragon!" He grinned at her. "Also, you should always plan to arrive above your reference point in clear air."

Lessa frowned.

"It is better to arrive in open air," F'lar waved a hand above his head, "rather than underground," and he slapped his open hand into the dirt. A puff of dust rose warningly.

"But the wings took off within the Bowl itself the day the Lords of the Hold arrived," Lessa reminded him.

F'lar chuckled at her uptake. "True, but only the most seasoned riders. Once we came across a dragon and a rider entombed together in solid rock. They . . . were . . . very young." His eyes were bleak.

"I take the point," she assured him gravely. "That's her fifth," she added, pointing towards Ramoth who was carrying her latest kill up to the bloody ledge.

"She'll work them off today, I assure you," F'lar remarked. He rose, brushing off his knees with sharp slaps of his riding gloves. "Test her temper."

Lessa did so with a silent, *Had enough?* She grimaced at Ramoth's indignant rejection of the thought.

The queen went swooping down for a huge fowl, rising in a flurry of gray, brown and white feathers.

"She's not as hungry as she's making you think, the deceitful creature." F'lar chuckled and saw that Lessa had reached the same conclusion. Her eyes were snapping with vexation.

"When you've finished the bird, Ramoth, do let us learn how to fly *between*," Lessa said aloud for F'lar's benefit, "before our good Weyrleader changes his mind."

Ramoth looked from her gorging, turned her head towards the two riders at the edge of the feeding ground. Her eyes gleamed. She bent her head again to her kill but Lessa could sense the dragon would obey.

IT WAS COLD aloft. Lessa was glad of the fur lining in her riding gear, and the warmth of the great golden neck which she bestrode. She decided not to think of the absolute cold of *between* which she had experienced only once, coming from Ruath Hold to Benden Weyr three Turns before. She glanced below on her right where bronze Mnementh hovered and caught his amused thought.

F'lar tells me to tell Ramoth to tell you to fix the alignment of the Star Stone firmly in your mind as a homing. Then, Mnementh went on amiably, *we shall fly down to the lake. You will return from* between *to this exact point. Do you understand?*

Lessa found herself grinning foolishly with anticipation and nodded vigorously. How much time was saved because she could speak directly to the dragons! Ramoth made a disgruntled noise deep in her throat. Lessa patted her reassuringly.

"Have you got the picture in your mind, dear one?" she asked and Ramoth again rumbled, less annoyed because she was catching Lessa's excitement.

Mnementh stroked the cold air with his wings, greenish brown in the sunlight, and curved down gracefully towards the lake on the plateau below Benden Weyr. His flight line took him very low over the rim of the

Weyr. From Lessa's angle, it looked like a collision course. Ramoth followed closely in his wake. Lessa caught her breath at the sight of the jagged boulders just below Ramoth's wing tips.

It was exhilarating. Lessa crowed to herself, doubly stimulated by the elation that flowed back to her from Ramoth.

Mnementh halted above the farthest shore of the lake and there, too, Ramoth came to hover.

Mnementh flashed the thought to Lessa that she was to place the picture of where she wished to go firmly in her mind and direct Ramoth to get there.

Lessa complied. The next instant the awesome, bone-penetrating cold of black *between* enveloped them. Before either she or Ramoth was aware of more than that invidious touch of cold and impregnable darkness, they were above the Star Stone.

Lessa let out a cry of triumph.

It is extremely simple. Ramoth seemed disappointed.

Mnementh reappeared beside and slightly below them.

You are to return by the same route to the Lake, he ordered and before the thought had finished, Ramoth took off.

Mnementh was beside them above the lake, fuming with his own and F'lar's anger. *You did not visualize before transferring. Don't think a first successful trip makes you perfect. You have no conception of the dangers inherent in* between. *Never fail to picture your arrival point again.*

Lessa glanced down at F'lar. Even two wingspans apart, she could see the vivid anger on his face, almost feel the fury flashing from his eyes. And laced through the wrath, a terrible sinking fearfulness for her safety that was a more effective reprimand than his wrath. Lessa's safety, she wondered bitterly, or Ramoth's?

You are to follow us, Mnementh was saying in a calmer tone, *rehearsing in your mind the two reference points you have already learned. We shall jump to and from them this morning, gradually learning other points around Benden.*

They did. Flying as far away as Benden Hold itself, nestled against the foothills above Benden Valley, the Weyr Peak a far point against the noonday sky, Lessa did not neglect to visualize a clearly detailed impression, each time.

This was as marvelously exciting as she had hoped it would be, Lessa confided to Ramoth. Ramoth replied: *Yes, it was certainly preferable to the time-consuming methods others had to use but she didn't think it was exciting, at all, to jump* between *from Benden Weyr to Benden Hold and back to Benden Weyr again. It was dull.*

THEY HAD MET with Mnementh above the Star Stone again. The bronze dragon sent Lessa the message that this was a very satisfactory initial session. They would practice some distant jumping tomorrow.

Tomorrow, thought Lessa glumly, some emergency will occur or our hardworking Weyrleader will decide today's session constitutes keeping his promise and that will be that.

There was one jump she could make *between*, from anywhere on Pern, and not miss her mark.

She visualized Ruatha for Ramoth, as seen from the heights above the Hold . . . to satisfy that requirement. To be scrupulously clear, Lessa projected the pattern of the firepits. Before Fax invaded and she had had to manipulate its decline, Ruatha had been such a lovely prosperous valley. She told Ramoth to jump *between*.

The cold was intense and seemed to last for many heartbeats. Just as Lessa began to fear she had somehow lost them *between*, they exploded into the air above the Hold. Elation filled her. That for F'lar and his excessive caution. With Ramoth she could jump anywhere! For there was the distinctive pattern of Ruatha's fire-gutted heights. It was just before dawn, the Breast Pass between Crom and Ruatha, black cones against the lightening gray sky. Fleetingly she noticed the absence of the Red Star that now blazed in the dawn sky. And fleetingly she noticed a difference in the air. Chill, yes, but not wintry . . . the air held that moist coolness of early spring.

Startled, she glanced downward, wondering if she could have, for all her assurance, erred in some fashion. But no, this was Ruath Hold. The Tower, the inner Court, the aspect of the broad avenue leading down to the crafthold were just as they should be. Wisps of smoke from distant chimneys indicated people were making ready for the day.

Ramoth caught the tenor of her insecurity and began to press for an explanation.

This is Ruatha, Lessa replied stoutly. *It can be no other. Circle the heights. See, there are the fire-pit lines I gave you . . .*

Lessa gasped, the coldness in her stomach freezing her muscles.

Below her in the slowly lifting pre-dawn gloom, she saw the figures of many men toiling over the breast of the cliff from the hills beyond Ruatha: men moving with quiet stealth like criminals.

She ordered Ramoth to keep as still as possible in the air so as not to direct their attention upward. The dragon was curious but obedient.

Who would be attacking Ruatha? It seemed incredible. The present Warder, Lytol, was a former dragonman and had savagely repelled one attack already. Was there thought of aggression among the Holds now that F'lar was Weyrleader? What Hold Lord would be mounting a territorial war in the winter?

No, not winter. The air here was spring-like.

The men crept on, over the fire-pits to the edge of the heights. Suddenly Lessa realized they were lowering rope ladders over the face of the cliff, down towards the open shutters of the Inner Hold.

Wildly she clutched at Ramoth's neck, certain of what she saw.

This was the invader Fax, now dead nearly three Turns—Fax and his men as they began their attack on Ruatha nearly thirteen Turns ago.

Yes, there was the Tower guard, his face a white blot turned towards the cliff itself, watching. He had been paid his bribe to stand silent this morning.

But the watch-wher, trained to give alarm for any intrusion, why was it not trumpeting its warning? Why was it silent?

Because, Ramoth informed her rider with calm logic, *it senses your presence as well as mine so how could the Hold possibly be in danger?*

No. No! Lessa moaned. *What can I do now? How can I wake them? Where is the girl I was? I was asleep and then I woke. I remember. I dashed from my room. I was so scared. I went down the steps and nearly fell. I knew I had to get to the watch-wher's kennel . . . I knew . . .*

Lessa clutched at Ramoth's neck for support as past acts and mysteries became devastatingly clear.

She herself had warned herself, just as it was her presence on the queen dragon that had kept the watch-wher from giving alarm. For as she watched, stunned and speechless, she saw the small, gray-robed figure that could only be herself as a youngster burst from the Hold hall door, race down the cold stone steps into the Court and disappear into the watch-wher's stinking den. Faintly she heard it lurring in piteous confusion.

Just as Lessa-the-girl reached that doubtful sanctuary, Fax's invaders swooped into the open window embrasures and began the slaughter of her sleeping family.

Back—back to the Star Stone! Lessa cried. In her wide and staring eyes she held the image of the guiding rocks like a rudder for her sanity as well as Ramoth's direction.

The intense cold acted as a restorative. And then they were above the quiet, peaceful wintry Weyr as if they had never paradoxically visited Ruatha.

F'lar and Mnementh were nowhere to be seen.

Ramoth, however, was unshaken by the experience. She had only gone where she had been told and had not quite understood that going *when* she had been told had shocked Lessa. She suggested to her rider that Mnementh had probably followed them to Ruatha so if Lessa would give her the *proper* references, she'd take her there. Ramoth's sensible attitude was comforting.

Lessa carefully drew for Ramoth, not the child's memory of a long-vanished, idyllic Ruatha, but her more recent recollection of the Hold, gray, sullen, at dawning, with a Red Star pulsing on the horizon.

And there they were again, hovering over the Valley, the Hold below them on the right. The grasses grew untended on the heights, clogging fire pit and brickwork; the scene showed all the deterioration she had encouraged in her effort to thwart Fax of any profit from conquering Ruath Hold.

But, as she watched, vaguely disturbed, she saw a figure emerge from the kitchen, saw the watch-wher creep from its lair and follow the raggedly dressed figure as far across the Court as the chain permitted. She saw the figure ascend the Tower, gaze first eastward, then northeastward. This was still not Ruatha of today and now! Lessa's mind reeled, disoriented. This time she had come back to visit herself of three Turns ago, to see the filthy drudge plotting revenge on Fax.

She felt the absolute cold of *between* as Ramoth snatched them back, emerging once more above the Star Stone. Lessa was shuddering, her eyes frantically raking the reassuring sight of the Weyr Bowl, hoping she had not somehow shifted backwards in time yet again. Mnementh suddenly erupted into the air a few lengths below and beyond Ramoth. Lessa greeted him with a cry of intense relief.

Back to your weyr! There was no disguising the white fury in Mnementh's tone. Lessa was too unnerved to respond in any way other than instant compliance. Ramoth glided swiftly to their ledge, quickly clearing the perch for Mnementh to land.

The rage on F'lar's face as he leaped from Mnementh and advanced on Lessa brought her wits back abruptly. She made no move to evade him as he grabbed her shoulders and shook her violently.

"How dare you risk yourself and Ramoth? Why must you defy me at every opportunity? Do you realize what would happen to all Pern if we lost Ramoth? Where did you go?" He was spitting with anger, punctuating each question that tumbled from his lips by shaking her.

"Ruatha," she managed to say, trying to keep herself erect. She reached out to catch at his arms but he shook her again.

"Ruatha? We were there. You weren't. Where did you go?"

"Ruatha!" Lessa cried louder, clutching at him distractedly because he kept jerking her off balance. She couldn't organize her thoughts with him jolting her.

She was at Ruatha, Mnementh said firmly.

We were there twice, Ramoth added.

As the dragons' calmer words penetrated F'lar's fury, he stopped shaking Lessa. She hung limply in his grasp, her hands weakly plucking at his arms, her eyes closed, her face gray. He picked her up and strode rapidly into the queen's weyr, the dragons following. He placed her upon the couch, wrapping her tightly in the fur cover. He called down the service shaft for the duty cook to send up hot *klah*.

"All right, what happened?" he demanded.

She didn't look at him but he got a glimpse of her haunted eyes. She blinked constantly as if she longed to erase something she had recently seen.

Finally she got herself somewhat under control and said in a low tired voice, "I did go to Ruatha. Only . . . I went *back* to Ruatha."

"Back to Ruatha?" F'lar repeated the words stupidly. The significance momentarily eluded him.

Certainly, Mnementh agreed, and flashed to F'lar the two scenes he had picked out of Ramoth's mind.

Staggered by the import of the visualization, F'lar found himself slowly sinking to the edge of the bed.

"You . . . you went *between* times?"

Lessa nodded slowly. The terror was beginning to leave her eyes.

"*Between* times," F'lar murmured. "I wonder . . ."

His mind raced through the possibilities. It might well tip the scales of survival in the Weyr's favor. He couldn't think exactly how to use this extraordinary ability but there *must* be an advantage in it for dragonfolk.

THE SERVICE SHAFT tumbled. He took the pitcher from the platform and poured two cups.

Lessa's hands were shaking so much she couldn't get hers to her lips. He steadied it for her, wondering if going *between* times would cause this kind of shock regularly. If so, it wouldn't be any advantage at all. He wondered if she'd had enough of a scare this day so she might not be so contemptuous of his orders the next time.

Outside in the weyr, Mnementh snorted his opinion on that. F'lar ignored him.

Lessa was trembling violently now. He put an arm around her, pressing the fur against her slender body. He held the mug to her lips, forcing her to drink. He could feel the tremors ease off. She finally held the cup and took long, slow, deep breaths between swallows, equally determined to get herself under control. The moment he felt her stiffen under his arm, he released her. He wondered if Lessa had ever had someone to turn to. Certainly not after Fax invaded her family Hold. She had been only eleven; a child. Had hate and revenge been the only emotions the growing girl had practiced?

She lowered the cup, cradling it in her hands carefully as if it had assumed some undefinable importance to her.

"Now. Tell me," he ordered.

After a long deep breath she began to speak, her hands tightening around the mug. Her inner turmoil had not lessened; it was merely under control now.

"Ramoth and I were bored with the weyrling exercises," she admitted candidly.

Grimly F'lar recognized that, while the adventure might have taught her to be more circumspect, it had not scared her into obedience. He doubted that anything would.

"I gave her the picture of Ruatha so we could go *between* there." She did not look at him but her profile was outlined against the dark fur of the rug. "The Ruatha I knew so well: I accidentally sent myself backwards in time to the day Fax invaded."

Her shock was now comprehensible to him.

"And . . ." he prompted her, his voice carefully neutral.

"And I saw myself . . ." her voice broke off. With an effort she continued. "I had visualized for Ramoth the designs of the fire pits and the angle of the Hold if one looked down from the pits into the Inner Court. That was where we emerged. It was just dawn"— she lifted her chin with a nervous jerk—"and there was no Red Star in the sky." She gave him a quick defensive look as if she expected him to contest this detail. "And I saw men creeping over the fire pits, lowering rope ladders to the top windows of the Hold. I saw the Tower guard watching. Just watching." She clenched her teeth at such treachery and her eyes gleamed malevolently. "And I saw myself run from the Hall into the watch-wher's lair. And do you know why," her voice lowered to a bitter whisper, "the watch-wher did not alarm the Hold?"

"Why?"

"Because there was a dragon in the sky and I, Lessa of Ruatha, was on her." She flung the mug from her as if she wished she could reject the knowledge, too. "Because I was there, the watch-wher did not alarm the Hold, thinking the intrusion legitimate, with one of the Blood on a dragon in the sky. So I," her body grew rigid, her hands clasped so tightly the knuckles were white, "I was the cause of my family's massacre. Not Fax! If I had not acted the captious fool today, I would not have been there with Ramoth and the watch-wher would . . ."

Her voice had risen to an hysterical pitch of recrimination. He slapped her sharply across the cheeks, grabbing her, robe and all, to shake her.

The stunned look in her eyes and the tragedy in her face alarmed him. His indignation over her willfulness disappeared. Her unruly independence of mind and spirit attracted him as much as her curious dark beauty. Infuriating as her fractious ways might be, they were too vital a part of her integrity to be exorcised. Her indomitable will had taken a grievous shock today and her self-confidence had better be restored quickly.

"On the contrary, Lessa," he said sternly, "Fax would still have murdered your family. He had planned it very carefully, even to scheduling his attack on the morning when the Tower guard was one who could be bribed. Remember, too, it was dawn and the watch-wher, being a nocturnal beast, blind by daylight, is relieved of responsibility at dawn and knows it. Your presence, damnable as it may appear to you, was not the deciding factor by any means. It did, and I draw your attention to this very important fact, it did cause you to save yourself, by warning Lessa-the-child. Don't you see that?"

"I could have called out," she murmured but the frantic look had left her eyes and there was a faint hint of normal color in her lips.

"If you wish to flail around in guilt, go right ahead," he said with deliberate callousness.

. . .

RAMOTH INTERJECTED A thought that, since they, too, had been there that previous time as Fax's men had prepared to invade, it had already happened, so how could it be changed? The act was inevitable both that day and today. For how else could Lessa have lived to come to the Weyr and impress Ramoth at the hatching?

Mnementh relayed Ramoth's message scrupulously, even to imitating Ramoth's egocentric nuances. F'lar looked sharply at Lessa to see the effect of Ramoth's astringent observation.

"Just like Ramoth to have the final word," she said with a hint of her former droll humor.

F'lar felt the muscles along his neck and shoulders begin to relax. She'd be all right, he decided, but it might be wiser to make her talk it all out now, to put the whole experience into proper perspective.

"You said you were there twice?" He leaned back on the couch, watching her closely. "When was the second time?"

"Can't you guess?" she asked sarcastically.

"No," he lied.

"When else but the dawn I wakened, feeling the Red Star was a menace to me. Three days before you and Fax came out of the northeast."

"It would seem," he remarked drily, "that you were your own premonition both times."

She nodded.

"Have you had any more of these presentiments . . . or should I say, reinforced warnings?"

She shuddered but answered him with more of her old spirit.

"No, but if I should, *you* go. I don't want to." F'lar grinned maliciously.

"I would, however," she added, "like to know why and how it could happen."

"I've never run across a mention of it anywhere," he told her candidly. "Of course, if you have done it, and you undeniably have," he assured her hastily at her indignant protest, "it obviously can be done. You say you thought of Ruatha, but you thought of it as it was on that particular day. Certainly a day to be remembered. You thought of spring, before dawn, no Red Star . . . yes I remember you mentioning that . . . so one would have to remember references peculiar to a significant day to return *between* times to the past."

She nodded slowly, thoughtfully.

"You used the same method the second time, to get to the Ruatha of three Turns ago. Again, of course, it was spring."

He rubbed his palms together, then brought his hands down on his knees with an emphatic slap and rose to his feet.

"I'll be back," he said and strode from the room, ignoring her half-articulated cry of warning.

Ramoth was curling up in the weyr as he passed her. He noticed that her color remained good in spite of the drain of her energies by the morning's exercises. She glanced at him, her many-faceted eye already covered by the inner, protective lid.

MNEMENTH AWAITED HIS rider on the ledge, and the moment F'lar leaped to his neck, took off. He circled upwards, hovering above the Star Stone.

You wish to try Lessa's trick, Mnementh said, unperturbed by the prospective experiment.

F'lar stroked the great curved neck affectionately. *You understand how it worked for Ramoth and Lessa?*

As well as anyone can, Mnementh replied with the approximation of a shrug. *When did you have in mind?*

At that moment, F'lar had had no idea. Now, unerringly, his thoughts drew him backwards to the summer day R'gul's bronze Hath had flown to mate the grotesque Nemorth, and R'gul had become Weyrleader in place of his dead father, F'lon.

Only the cold of *between* gave them any indication they had transferred; they were still hovering above the Star Stone. F'lar wondered if they had missed some essential part of the transfer. Then he realized that the sun was in another quarter of the sky, and the air was warm and sweet with summer. The Weyr below was empty, there were no dragons sunning themselves on the ledges, no women busy at tasks in the Bowl. Noises impinged on his senses; raucous laughter, yells, shrieks, and a soft crooning noise that dominated the bedlam.

Then, from the direction of the weyrling barracks in the lower Caverns, two figures emerged; a stripling and a young bronze dragon. The boy's arm lay limply along the beast's neck. The impression that reached the hovering observers was one of utter dejection. The two halted by the lake, the boy peering into the unruffled blue waters, then glancing upward towards the queen's weyr.

F'lar knew the boy for himself, and compassion for that younger self filled him. If only he could reassure that boy, so torn by grief, so filled with resentment, that he would one day become Weyrleader . . .

Abruptly, startled by his own thoughts, he ordered Mnementh to transfer back. The utter cold of *between* was like a slap in his face, replaced almost instantly as they broke out of *between* into the cold of normal winter.

Slowly, Mnementh flew back down to the queen's weyr, as sobered as F'lar by what they had seen.

> *Rise high in glory,*
> *Bronze and gold.*
> *Drive entwined,*
> *Enhance the Hold.*
>
> *Count three months and more,*
> *And five heated weeks,*
> *A day of glory and*
> *In a month, who seeks?*
>
> *A strand of silver*
> *In the sky . . .*
> *With heat, all quickens*
> *And all times fly.*

"I don't know why you insisted F'nor unearth these ridiculous things from Ista Weyr," Lessa exclaimed in a tone of exasperation. "They consist of nothing but trivial notes on how many measures of grain were used to bake daily bread."

F'lar glanced up at her from the records he was studying. He sighed, leaned back in his chair in a bone-popping stretch.

"And I used to think," Lessa said with a rueful expression on her vivid, narrow face, "that those venerable Records would hold the total sum of all dragonlore and human wisdom. Or so I was led to believe," she added pointedly.

F'lar chuckled. "They do, but you have to disinter it."

Lessa wrinkled her nose. "*Phew.* They smell as if we had . . . and the only decent thing to do would be to rebury them."

"Which is another item I'm hoping to find . . . the old preservative technique that kept the skins from hardening and smelling."

"It's stupid, anyhow, to use skins for recording. There ought to be something better. We have become, dear Weyrleader, entirely too hidebound."

While F'lar roared with appreciation of her pun, she regarded him impatiently. Suddenly she jumped up, fired by another of her mercurial moods.

"Well, you won't find it. You won't find the facts you're looking for. Because I know what you're really after and it isn't recorded!"

"Explain yourself."

"It's time we stopped hiding a rather brutal truth from ourselves."

"Which is?"

"Our mutual feeling that the Red Star is a menace and that the Threads *will* come! We decided that out of pure conceit and then went back *between* times to particularly crucial points in our lives and strengthened that notion, in our earlier selves. And for you, it was when you decided you were destined," her voice mocked the word, "to become Weyrleader one day.

"Could it be," she went on scornfully, "that our ultraconservative R'gul has the right of it? That there have been no Threads for four hundred Turns because there are no more? And that the reason we have so few dragons is because the dragons sense they are no longer essential to Pern? That we *are* anachronisms as well as parasites?"

F'lar did not know how long he sat looking at her bitter face, nor how long it took him to find answers for her probing questions.

"Anything is possible, Weyrwoman," he heard his voice replying calmly. "Including the unlikely fact that an eleven-year-old child, scared stiff, could plot revenge on her family's murderer and—against all odds—succeed."

She took an involuntary step forward, struck by his unexpected rebuttal. She listened intently.

"I prefer to believe," he went on inexorably, "that there is more to life than raising dragons and playing spring games. That is not enough for me. And I have made others look further, beyond self-interest and comfort. I have given them a purpose, a discipline. Everyone, dragonfolk and Holder alike, profits.

"I am not looking in these Records for reassurance. I'm looking for solid facts.

"I can prove, Weyrwoman, that there have been Threads. I can prove that there have been Intervals during which the Weyrs have declined. I can prove that if you sight the Red Star directly bracketed by the Eye Rock at the moment of winter solstice, the Red Star will pass close enough to Pern to throw off Threads. Since I can prove those facts, I believe Pern is in danger. *I* believe . . . not the youngster of fifteen Turns ago. F'lar, the bronze rider, the Weyrleader, believes it!"

He saw her eyes reflecting shadowy doubts but he sensed his arguments were beginning to reassure her.

"You felt constrained to believe in me once before," he went on in a milder voice, "when I suggested that you could be Weyrwoman. You believed me and . . ." He made a gesture around the weyr as substantiation.

She gave him a weak, humorless smile.

"That was because I had never planned what to do with my life once I did have Fax lying dead at my feet. Of course, being Ramoth's weyrmate is wonderful but"—and she frowned slightly—"it isn't enough anymore either. That's why I wanted so to learn to fly and then . . ."

". . . That's how this argument started in the first place," F'lar finished for her with a sardonic smile.

He leaned across the table, urgently.

"Believe with me, Lessa, until you have cause not to. I respect your doubts. There's nothing wrong in doubting. It sometimes leads to greater faith. But believe in me until spring. If the Threads have not fallen by then . . ." He shrugged fatalistically.

She looked at him for a long moment and then inclined her head slowly, in agreement.

HE TRIED TO suppress the relief he felt at her decision. Lessa, as Fax had discovered, was a ruthless adversary and a canny advocate. Besides these, she was Weyrwoman: essential to his plans.

"Now, let's get back to the contemplation of trivia. They do tell me, you know: time, place and duration of Thread incursions," he grinned up at her reassuringly. "And those are facts I must have to make up my timetable."

"Timetable? But you said you didn't know the time."

"Not the day to the second when the Threads may spin down. For one thing, while the weather holds so unusually cold for this time of year, the Threads simply turn brittle and blow away like dust. They're harmless. However, when the air is warm, they are viable and . . . deadly." He made fists of both hands, placing one above and to one side of the other.

"The Red Star is my right hand, my left is Pern. The Red Star turns very fast and in the opposite direction to us. It also wobbles erratically."

"How do you know that?"

"Diagram on the walls of the Fort Weyr Hatching Ground. *That was the very first Weyr.* So, when the Star makes a pass, the Threads spin off, down towards us, in attacks that last six hours and occur about fourteen hours apart."

"Attacks last six hours?"

He nodded gravely. "When the Red Star is closest to us. Right now, it is just beginning its Pass."

She frowned.

He rummaged among the skin sheets on the table and an object dropped to the stone floor with a metallic clatter.

Curious, Lessa bent to pick it up, turning the thin sheet over in her hands. "What's this?" She ran an exploratory finger lightly across the irregular design on one side.

"I don't know. F'nor brought it back from Fort Weyr. It was nailed to one of the chests in which Records had been stored. He brought it along, thinking it might be important. Said there was a plate like it just under the Red Star diagram on the wall of the Hatching Ground.

"This first part is plain enough: 'Mother's father's father, who departed for all time *between*, said this was the key to the mystery, and it came to him while doodling. He said that he said: ARRHENIUS? EUREKA! MYCORRHIZA . . .' Of course that part doesn't make any sense at all. It isn't even Pernese; just babbling, the last three words.

"I have studied it, Lessa. The only way to depart for all time *between* is to die, right? People can't just fly away on their own, obviously. So it is a death vision, dutifully recorded by a grandchild, who couldn't spell very well. 'Doodling' as the present tense of dying!" He smiled indulgently. "And as for the rest of it, after the nonsense; like most death visions, it 'explains' what everyone has always known. The second part says simply: '. . . flame-throwing fire-lizards to wipe out the spores. Q.E.D.' No, this is no help in our researches, just a primitive rejoicing that he is a dragonman, who didn't even know the right word for Threads."

Lessa wet one fingertip to see if the patterns were inked on. The metal was shiny enough to be a good mirror. However, the patterns remained smooth and precise. "Primitive or no, they had a more permanent way of recording their visions than well-preserved skins."

"Well-preserved babblings," said F'lar, turning back to the skins he was checking for understandable data.

"A badly-scored ballad, perhaps," said Lessa, dismissing it. "The design isn't even pretty."

F'LAR PULLED FORWARD a chart that showed overlapping horizontal bands imposed on the project of Pern's continental mass.

"Here," he said, "this represents waves of attack and this one," he pulled forward the second map with vertical bands, "shows time bands. So you can see, that with a fourteen-hour break, only certain parts of Pern are affected in each attack. One reason for the spacing of the weyrs."

"Six full weyrs," she murmured, "close to three thousand dragons."

"I'm aware of the statistics," he replied in a voice devoid of expression. "It meant no one weyr was overburdened during the height of the attacks, not that three thousand beasts must be available. However, with these timetables, we can manage until Ramoth's first clutches have matured."

She turned a cynical look on him. "You've a lot of faith in one queen's capacity."

He waved that remark aside impatiently. "I've more faith, no matter what your opinion is, in the startling repetitions of events in these Records."

"Ha!"

"I don't mean how many measures for daily bread, Lessa," he retorted, his voice rising. "I mean such things as the time such and such a wing was sent out on patrol, how long the patrol lasted, how many riders were hurt. The brooding capacities of queens, during the fifty years a Pass lasts and the Intervals between such Passes. Yes, it tells that. By all I've studied here," and he pounded emphatically on the nearest stack of dusty, smelly skins, "Nemorth should have been mating twice a Turn for the last ten. Had she even kept to her paltry twelve a clutch, we'd have two hundred and forty more beasts . . . Don't interrupt. But we had Jora as Weyrwoman and R'gul as Weyrleader and we had fallen into planet-wide disfavor during a four hundred Turn interval. Well, Ramoth will brood over no measly dozen and she'll lay a queen egg, mark my words. She will rise often to mate and lay generously. By the time the Red Star is passing closest to us and the attacks become frequent, we'll be ready."

She stared at him, her eyes wide with incredulity. "Out of Ramoth?"

"Out of Ramoth and out of the queens she'll lay. Remember, there are Records of Faranth laying sixty eggs at a time, including several queen eggs."

Lessa could only shake her head slowly in wonder.

" 'A Strand of silver

In the sky.

With heat, all quickens.

All times fly!' " F'lar quoted to her.

"She's got weeks more to go before laying and then the eggs must hatch . . ."

"Been on the Hatching Ground recently? Wear your boots. You'll be burned through sandals."

She dismissed that with a guttural noise. He sat back, outwardly amused by her disbelief.

". . . And then you have to make Impression and wait till the riders . . ." she went on.

". . . Why do you think I've insisted on older boys? The dragons are mature long before their riders."

"Then the system is faulty."

He narrowed his eyes slightly, shaking the stylus at her.

"Dragon tradition started out as a guide . . . but there comes a time when man becomes too traditional . . . too—what was it you said the other day—too hidebound. Yes, it's traditional to use the weyrbred, because it's been convenient. And because this sensitivity to dragons strengthens when both sire and dam are weyrbred. That doesn't mean weyrbred is best. You, for example . . ."

"There's Weyrblood in the Ruathan Line," she said proudly.

"Granted. Take young Naton; he's craftbred from Nabol, yet F'nor tells me he can make Canth understand him."

"Oh, that's hard to do," she interjected.

"What do you mean?" F'lar jumped on her statement.

THEY WERE BOTH interrupted by a high-pitched, penetrating whine. F'lar listened intently for a moment and then shrugged, grinning.

"Some green's getting herself chased again."

"And that's another item these so-called all-knowing records of yours never mention. Why is it only the gold dragons can reproduce?"

F'lar did not suppress a lascivious chuckle.

"Well, for one thing, firestone inhibits reproduction. If they never chewed stone, a green could lay but, at best, they produce small beasts and we need big ones. And, for another thing," his chuckle rolled out as he went on deliberately, grinning mischievously, "if the greens could reproduce, considering their amorousness, and the numbers we have of them, we'd be up to our ears in dragons in next to no time."

The first whine was joined by another and then a low hum throbbed as if carried by the stones of the Weyr itself.

F'lar, his face changing rapidly from surprise to triumphant astonishment, dashed up the passage before Lessa could open her mouth.

"What's the matter?" she demanded, picking up her skirts to run after him. "What does that mean?"

The hum, resonating everywhere, was deafening in the echo-chamber of the queen's weyr. Lessa registered the fact that Ramoth was gone. She heard F'lar's boots pounding down the passage to the ledge, a sharp *ta-ta-tat* over the kettledrum booming hum. The whine was so high-pitched now it was inaudible, but nerve-wracking. Disturbed, frightened, Lessa followed F'lar out.

By the time she reached the ledge, the Bowl was a-whir with dragons on the wing, making for the high entrance to the Hatching Ground. Weyrfolk, riders, women, children, all screaming with excitement, were pouring across the Bowl to the lower entrance to the Ground.

She caught sight of F'lar charging across to the tunnel entrance and she shrieked at him to wait. He couldn't have heard her across the bedlam.

Fuming because she had the long stairs to descend, then must double back as the stairs faced the feeding grounds at the opposite end of the Bowl from the Hatching Ground, Lessa realized that she, the Weyrwoman, would be the last one there.

Why had Ramoth decided to be secretive about laying? Wasn't she close enough to her own weyrmate to want her with her?

A dragon knows what to do, Ramoth calmly informed Lessa.

"You could have told me," Lessa wailed, feeling much abused.

Why, at the time F'lar had been going on largely about huge clutches and three thousand beasts, that infuriating dragonchild had been doing it!

It didn't improve Lessa's temper to have to recall another remark of F'lar's — on the state of the Hatching Grounds. The moment she stepped into the mountain-high cavern, she felt the heat through the soles of her sandals. Everyone was crowded in a loose circle around the far end of the cavern. And everyone was swaying from foot to foot. As Lessa was short to begin with, this only decreased the likelihood of her ever seeing what Ramoth had done.

"Let me through!" she demanded imperiously, pounding on the wide backs of two tall riders.

An aisle was reluctantly opened for her and she went through, looking neither to her right nor left at the excited weyrfolk. She was furious, confused, hurt and knew she looked ridiculous because the hot sand made her walk a curious, quick-step mince.

She halted, stunned and wide-eyed at the mass of eggs, and forgot such trivial things as hot feet.

RAMOTH WAS CURLED around the clutch, looking enormously pleased with herself. She, too, kept shifting, closing and opening a protective wing over her eggs so it was difficult to count them.

"No one will steal them, silly, so stop fluttering," Lessa exclaimed as she tried to make a tally.

Obediently, Ramoth folded her wings. To relieve her maternal anxiety, however, she snaked her head out across the circle of mottled, glowing eggs, looking all around the cavern, flicking her forked tongue in and out.

An immense sigh, like a gust of wind, swept through the cavern. For there, now Ramoth's wings were furled, gleamed an egg of glowing gold among the tan, the green and the blue ones. A queen egg!

"A queen egg!" The cry went up simultaneously from half a hundred throats. The Hatching Ground rang with cheers, yells, screams and howls of exultation.

Someone seized Lessa and swung her around in an excess of feeling. A kiss landed in the vicinity of her mouth. No sooner did she recover her footing than she was hugged by someone else, she thought it was Manora, and then pounded and buffeted around in congratulation until she was reeling in a kind of dance between avoiding the celebrants and easing the growing discomfort of her feet.

She broke from the milling revelers and ran across the Ground to Ramoth. She came to a sudden stop before the eggs. They seemed to be pulsing. The shells looked flaccid. She could have sworn they were hard the day she Impressed Ramoth. She wanted to touch one, just to make sure, and dared not.

You may, Ramoth assured her condescendingly. She touched Lessa's shoulder gently with her tongue.

The egg was soft to touch and Lessa drew her hand back quickly, afraid of doing injury.

The heat will harden it, Ramoth said.

"Ramoth, I'm so proud of you," Lessa sighed, looking adoringly up at the great eyes which shone in rainbows of pride. "You are the most marvelous queen ever. I do believe you will redragon all the Weyrs. I do believe you will."

Ramoth inclined her head regally, then began to sway it from side to side over the eggs, protectingly. She began to hiss suddenly, raising up from her crouch, beating the air with her wings, before settling back into the sands to lay yet another egg.

The weyrfolk, uncomfortable on the hot sands, were beginning to leave the Hatching Ground, now they had paid tribute to the arrival of the golden egg. A queen took several days to complete her clutch so there was no point to waiting. Seven eggs already lay beside the important golden one and if there were seven already, this augured well for the eventual total. Wagers were being made and taken even as Ramoth produced her ninth mottled egg.

"A queen egg, by the mother of us all," F'lar's voice said in Lessa's ear. "And I'll wager there'll be ten bronzes at least."

She looked up at him, completely in harmony with the Weyrleader at this moment. She was conscious, now, of Mnementh, crouching proudly on a ledge, gazing fondly at his mate. Impulsively, Lessa laid her hand on F'lar's arm.

"F'lar, I do believe you."

"Only now?" F'lar teased her, but his smile was wide and his eyes proud.

> Weyrman, watch; Weyrman, learn
> Something new in every Turn.
> Oldest may be coldest, too.
> Sense the right; find the true!

If F'lar's orders over the next months caused no end of discussion and muttering among the weyrfolk, they seemed, to Lessa, to be only the logical outcomes of their discussion after Ramoth had finished laying her gratifying total of forty-one eggs.

F'lar discarded tradition right and left, treading on more than R'gul's conservative toes.

Out of perverse distaste for outworn doctrines against which she herself had chafed during R'gul's leadership, and out of respect for F'lar's intelligence, Lessa backed him completely. She might not have respected her earlier promise to him that she would believe in his ways until spring if she had not seen his predictions come true one after another. These were based, however, not on the premonitions she no longer trusted after her experience *between* time, but on recorded facts.

As soon as the eggshells hardened and Ramoth had rolled her special queen egg to one side of the mottled clutch for attentive brooding, F'lar brought the prospective riders into the Hatching Ground. Traditionally the candidates saw the eggs for the first time on the day of Impression. To this precedent, F'lar added others: Very few of the sixty-odd were weyr-bred and most of them were in their late teens. The candidates were to get used to the eggs, touch them, caress them, be comfortable with the notion that out of these eggs, young dragons would hatch, eager and waiting to be Impressed. F'lar felt that such a practice might cut down on casualties during Impression when the boys were simply too scared to move out of the way of the awkward dragonets.

F'lar also had Lessa persuade Ramoth to let Kylara near her precious golden egg. Kylara readily enough weaned her son and spent hours, with Lessa acting as her tutor, beside the golden egg. Despite Kylara's loose attachment to T'bor, she showed an open preference for F'lar's company. Therefore, Lessa took great pains to foster F'lar's plan for Kylara since it meant her removal, with the new-hatched queen, to Fort Weyr.

F'lar's use of the Hold-born as riders served an additional purpose. Shortly before the actual Hatching and Impression, Lytol, the Warder appointed at Ruath Hold, sent another message.

"The man positively delights in sending bad news," Lessa remarked as F'lar passed the message skin to her.

"He's gloomy," F'nor agreed. He had brought the message. "I feel sorry for that youngster cooped up with such a pessimist."

Lessa frowned at the brown rider. She still found distasteful any mention of Gemma's son, now Lord of her ancestral Hold. Yet . . . she had inadvertently caused his mother's death. As she could not be Weyrwoman and Lady Holder at the same time, it was fitting that Gemma's Gaxom be Lord at Ruatha.

"I, however," F'lar said, "am grateful to his warnings. I suspected Meron would cause trouble again."

"He's got shifty eyes, like Fax," Lessa remarked.

"Shifty-eyed or not, he's dangerous," F'lar answered. "And I cannot have him spreading rumors that we are deliberately choosing men of the Blood to weaken Family Lines."

"There are more craftsmen's sons than Holders' boys in any case," F'nor snorted.

"I don't like him questioning that the Threads have not appeared," Lessa said gloomily.

F'lar shrugged. "They'll appear in due time. Be thankful the weather has continued cold. When the weather warms up and still no Threads, then I will worry." He grinned at Lessa in an intimate reminder of her promise.

F'nor cleared his throat hastily and looked away.

"However," the Weyrleader went on briskly, "I can do something about the other accusation."

So, when it was apparent the eggs were about to hatch, he broke another long-standing tradition and sent riders to fetch the fathers of the young candidates from craft and Hold.

The great Hatching cavern gave the appearance of being almost full as Holder and Weyrfolk watched from the tiers above the heated Ground. This time, Lessa observed, there was no aura of fear. The youthful candidates were tense, yes, but not frightened out of their wits by the rocking, shattering eggs. When the ill-coordinated dragonets awkwardly stumbled—it seemed to Lessa they deliberately looked around at the eager faces as though pre-Impressed—the youths either stepped to one side, or eagerly advanced as a crooning dragonet made his choice. The Impressions were made quickly and with no accidents. All too soon, Lessa thought, the triumphant process of stumbling dragons and proud new riders moved erratically out of the hatching Ground to the barracks.

The young queen burst from her shell and moved unerringly for Kylara, standing confidently on the hot sands. The watching beasts hummed their approval.

"It was over too soon," Lessa said in a disappointed voice that evening to F'lar.

He laughed indulgently, allowing himself a rare evening of relaxation now that another step had gone as planned. The Holder folk had been ridden home, stunned, dazed and themselves impressed by the Weyr and the Weyrleader.

"That's because you were watching this time," he remarked, brushing a lock of her hair back. It obscured his view of her profile. He chuckled again. "You'll notice Naton . . ."

". . . N'ton . . ." she corrected him.

". . . All right, N'ton . . . Impressed a bronze."

"Just as you predicted," she said with some asperity.

"And Kylara is Weyrwoman for Pridith."

Lessa did not comment on that and she did her best to ignore his laughter.

"I wonder which bronze will fly her," he murmured softly.

"It had better be T'bor's Orth," Lessa said, bridling.

He answered her the only way a wise man could.

Crack dust, blackdust,
Turn in freezing air,
Waste dust, spacedust,
From Red Star bare.

Lessa woke abruptly, her head aching, her eyes blurred, her mouth dry. She had the immediate memory of a terrible nightmare which, just as quickly, escaped recall. She brushed her hair out of her face and was surprised to find she had been sweating heavily.

"F'lar?" she called in an uncertain voice. He had evidently risen early. "F'lar," she called again, louder.

He's coming, Mnementh informed her. Lessa sensed that the dragon was just landing on the ledge. She touched Ramoth and found that the queen, too, had been bothered by formless, frightening dreams. The dragon roused briefly and then fell back into deeper sleep.

Disturbed by her vague fears, Lessa rose and dressed, forgoing a bath for the first time since she had arrived at the Weyr.

She called down the shaft for breakfast, plaiting her hair with deft fingers as she waited.

The tray appeared on the shaft platform just as F'lar entered. He kept looking back over his shoulder at Ramoth.

"What's got into her?"

"Echoing my nightmare. I woke in a cold sweat."

"You were sleeping quietly enough when I left to assign patrols. You know, at the rate those dragonets are growing, they're already capable of limited flight. All they do is eat and sleep and that is . . ."

". . . What makes a dragon grow . . ." Lessa finished for him and sipped thoughtfully at her steaming hot *klah*. "You are going to be extra careful about their drill procedures, aren't you?"

"You mean to prevent an inadvertent flight *between* times? I certainly am," he assured her. "I don't want bored dragonriders irresponsibly popping in and out." He gave her a long, stern look.

"Well, it wasn't my fault no one taught me to fly early enough," she replied in the sweet tone she used when she was being especially malicious. "If I'd been drilled from the day of Impression to the day of my first flight, I'd never have discovered that trick."

"True enough," he said solemnly.

"You know, F'lar, if I discovered it, someone else must have and someone else may. If they haven't already."

F'lar drank, making a face as the *klah* scalded his tongue. "I don't know how to find out discreetly. We would be foolish to think we were the first. It is, after all, an inherent ability in dragons or you would never have been able to do it."

She frowned, took a quick breath and then let it go, shrugging.

"Go on," he encouraged her.

"Well, isn't it possible that our conviction about the imminence of the Threads could stem from one of us coming back when the Threads are actually falling . . . I mean . . ."

"My dear girl, we have both analyzed every stray thought and action—even your dream this morning upset you although it was no doubt due to all the wine you drank last night—until we wouldn't know an honest presentiment if it walked up and slapped us in the face."

"I can't dismiss the thought that this *between* times ability is of crucial value," she said emphatically.

"That, my dear Weyrwoman, *is* an honest presentiment."

"But why?"

"Not 'why,' " he corrected her cryptically, "*when*." An idea stirred vaguely in the back of his mind. He tried to nudge it out where he could mull it over. Mnementh announced that F'nor was entering the Weyr.

. . .

"WHAT'S THE MATTER with you?" F'lar demanded of his half brother for F'nor was choking and sputtering, his face red with the paroxysm.

"Dust . . ." he coughed, slapping at his sleeves and chest with his riding gloves. "Plenty of dust, but no Threads," he said, describing a wide arc with one arm as he fluttered his fingers suggestively. He brushed his tight, wher-hide pants, scowling as a fine black dust drifted off.

F'lar felt every muscle in his body tense as he watched the dust float to the floor.

"Where did you get so dusty?" he demanded.

F'nor regarded him with mild surprise. "Weather patrol in Tillek. Entire north has been plagued with dust storms lately. But what I came in for . . ." He broke off, alarmed by F'lar's taut immobility. "What's the matter with dust?" he asked in a baffled voice.

F'lar pivoted on his heel and raced for the stairs to the Record Room. Lessa was right behind him, F'nor belatedly trailing after.

"Tillek, you said?" F'lar barked at his wingsecond. He was clearing the table of stacks for the four charts he then laid out. "How long have these storms been going on? Why didn't you report them?"

"Report dust storms? You wanted to know about warm air masses."

"How long have these storms been going on?" F'lar's voice crackled.

"Close to a week."

"How close?"

"Six days ago, the first storm was noticed in upper Tillek. They have been reported in Bitra, upper Telgar, Crom and the High Reaches," F'nor reported tersely.

He glanced hopefully at Lessa but saw she, too, was staring at the four unusual charts. He tried to see why the horizontal and vertical strips had been superimposed on Pern's land mass, but the reason was beyond him.

F'lar was making hurried notations, pushing first one map and then another away from him.

"Too involved to think straight, to see clearly, to understand," the Weyrleader snarled to himself, throwing down the stylus angrily.

"You did say only warm air masses," F'nor heard himself saying humbly, aware that he had somehow failed his Weyrleader.

F'lar shook his head impatiently.

"Not your fault, F'nor. Mine. I should have asked. I knew it was good luck that the weather held so cold." He put both hands on F'nor's shoulders, looking directly in his eyes. "The Threads have been falling," he announced gravely. "Falling into cold air, freezing into bits to drift on the wind," and F'lar imitated F'nor's finger-fluttering, "as specks of black dust."

" 'Crack dust, blackdust,' " Lessa quoted. "In the Ballad of Moreta's Ride, the chorus is all about black dust."

"I don't need to be reminded of Moreta right now," F'lar growled, bending to the maps. "She could talk to any dragon in the Weyrs."

"But I can do that!" Lessa protested.

Slowly, as if he didn't quite credit his ears, F'lar turned back to Lessa. "What did you just say?"

"I said, I can talk to any dragon in the Weyr."

STILL STARING AT her, blinking in utter astonishment, F'lar sank down to the table top.

"How long," he managed to say, "have you had *this* particular skill?"

Something in his tone, in his manner, caused Lessa to flush and stammer like an erring weyrling.

"I . . . I always could. Beginning with the watch-wher at Ruatha . . ." and she gestured indecisively in Ruatha's westerly direction, "and I talked to Mnementh at Ruatha. And . . . when I got here, I could—" her voice faltered at the accusing look in F'lar's cold, hard eyes. Accusing and worse, contemptuous.

"I thought you had agreed to help me, to believe in me."

"I'm truly sorry, F'lar. It never occurred to me it was any use to anyone but—"

F'lar exploded onto both feet, his eyes blazing with aggravation.

"The one thing I could not figure out was how to direct the wings and keep in contact with the Weyr during an attack. How was I going to get reinforcements and firestone in time. And you . . . you have been sitting there, spitefully hiding the—"

"I am NOT spiteful," she screamed at him. "I said I was sorry. I am. But you've a nasty smug habit of keeping your own council. How was I to know you didn't have the same trick? You're F'lar, the Weyrleader. You can do *any*thing. Only you're just as bad as R'gul because you never *tell* me half the things I ought to know."

F'lar reached out and shook her until her angry voice was stopped.

"Enough. We can't waste time arguing like children." Then his eyes widened, his jaw dropped. "Waste time? That's it."

"Go *between* times?" Lessa gasped.

"*Between* times!"

F'nor was totally confused. "What are you two talking about?"

"The Threads started falling at dawn in Nerat," F'lar said, his eyes bright, his manner decisive.

F'nor could feel his guts congealing with apprehension. At dawn in Nerat? Why, the rainforests would be demolished. He could feel a surge of adrenaline charging through his body at the thought of danger.

"So we're going *back* there, *between* times, and be there when the Threads started falling, two hours ago. F'nor, the dragons can go not only where we direct them, but *when*."

"Where? When?" F'nor repeated, bewildered. "That could be dangerous."

"Yes, but today it will save Nerat. Now, Lessa," and F'lar gave her another shake, compounded of pride and affection, "order out all the dragons, young, old—any that can fly. Tell them to load themselves down with firestone sacks. I don't know if you can talk across time . . ."

"My dream this morning . . ."

"Perhaps. But right now, rouse the Weyr." He pivoted to F'nor. "If Threads are falling . . . were falling . . . at Nerat at dawn, they'll be falling on Keroon and Ista right now, because they are in that time pattern. Take two wings to Keroon. Arouse the plains. Get them to start the fire pits blazing. Take some weyrlings with you and send them on to Igen and Ista. Those Holds are not in as immediate danger as Keroon. I'll reinforce you as soon as I can. And . . . keep Canth in touch with Lessa."

F'lar clapped his brother on the shoulder and sent him off, the brown rider too used to taking orders to argue.

"MNEMENTH SAYS R'GUL is duty officer and R'gul wants to know . . ." Lessa began.

'C'mon, girl," F'lar said, his eyes brilliant with excitement. He grabbed up his maps and propelled her up the stairs.

They arrived in the weyr just as R'gul entered with T'sum. R'gul was muttering about this unusual summons.

"Hath told me to report," he complained. "Fine thing when your own dragon . . ."

"R'gul, T'sum, mount your wings. Arm them with all the firestone they can carry and assemble above Star Stone. I'll join you in a few minutes. We go to Nerat at dawn."

"Nerat? I'm watch officer, not patrol . . ."

"This is no patrol," F'lar cut him off.

"But sir," T'sum interrupted, his eyes wide, "Nerat's dawn was two hours ago, same as ours."

"And that is *when* we are going to, brown rider. The dragons, we have discovered, can go *between* places temporally as well as geographically. At dawn, Threads fell at Nerat. We're going back, *between* times, to sear them from the sky."

F'lar paid no attention to R'gul's stammered demand for explanation. T'sum, however, grabbed up firestone sacks and raced back to the ledge and his waiting Munth.

"Go on, you old fool," Lessa told R'gul irascibly. "The Threads are here. You were wrong. Now be a dragonman! Or go *between* and stay there!"

Ramoth, awakened by the alarms, poked at R'gul with her man-sized head and the ex-Weyrleader came out of his momentary shock. Without a word, he followed T'sum down the passageway.

F'lar had thrown on his heavy wher-hide tunic and shoved on his riding boots.

"Lessa, be sure to send messages to all the Holds. Now, this attack will stop about four hours from now. So the farthest west it can reach will be Ista. But I want every Hold and craft warned."

She nodded, her eyes intent on his face lest she miss a word.

"Fortunately the Star is just beginning its Pass so we won't have to worry about another attack for a few days. I'll figure out the next one when I get back.

"Now, get Manora to organize her women. We'll need pails of ointment. The dragons are going to be laced and that hurts. Most important, if something goes wrong, you'll have to wait till a bronze is at least a year old to fly Ramoth . . ." Suddenly F'lar crushed her against him, his mouth bruising hers as if all her sweetness and strength must come with him. He released her so abruptly she staggered back against Ramoth's lowered head. She clung for a moment to her dragon, as much for support as for reassurance.

> *Wheel and turn.*
> *Or bleed and burn.*
> *Fly between,*
> *Blue and green.*

Soar, dive down,
Bronze and brown
Dragonmen must fly
When Threads are in the sky.

As F'lar raced down the passageway to the ledge, firesacks bumping against his thighs, he was suddenly grateful for the tedious sweeping patrols over every Hold and hollow of Pern. He could see Nerat clearly in his mind's eye. He could see the many petaled vineflowers which were the distinguishing feature of the rainforests at this time of year. Their ivory blossoms would be glowing in the first beams of sunlight like dragoneyes among the tall, wide-leaved plants.

Mnementh, his eyes flashing with excitement, hovered skittishly at the ledge. F'lar vaulted to the bronze neck.

The Weyr was seething with wings of all colors, noisy with shouts and countercommands. The atmosphere was electric but F'lar could sense no panic in that ordered confusion. Dragon and human bodies oozed out of openings around the Bowl walls. Women scurried across the floor from one lower cavern to another. The children playing by the lake were sent to gather wood for a fire. The weyrlings, supervised by old C'gan, were forming outside their barracks. F'lar looked up to the Peak and approved the tight formation of the wings assembled there in close flying order. Another wing formed up as he watched. He recognized brown Canth, F'nor on his neck, just as the entire wing vanished.

He ordered Mnementh aloft. The wind was cold and carried a hint of moisture. A late snow? This was the time for it, if ever.

R'gul's wing and T'bor's fanned out on his left, T'sum and D'nol on his right. He noted each dragon was well-laden with sacks. Then he gave Mnementh the visualization of the early spring rainforest in Nerat, just before dawn, the vineflowers gleaming, the sea breaking against the rocks of the High Shoal . . .

He left the searing cold of *between*. And he felt a stab of doubt. Was he injudicious, sending them all, possibly to their deaths *between* times, in this effort to out-time the Threads at Nerat?

Then, they were all there, in the crepuscular light that promises day. The lush, fruity smells of the rainforest drifting up to them. Warm, too, and that was frightening. He looked up and slightly to the north. Pulsing with menace, the Red Star shone down.

The men had realized what had happened, their voices raised in astonishment. Mnementh told F'lar that the dragons were mildly surprised at their riders' fuss.

"Listen to me, dragonriders," F'lar called, his voice harsh and distorted in an effort to be heard by all. He waited till the men had moved as close as possible. He told Mnementh to pass the information on to each dragon. Then he explained what they had done and why. No one spoke but there were many nervous looks exchanged across bright wings.

Crisply he ordered the wings to fan out in a staggered formation, keeping a distance of five-wings' spread up or down between them.

The sun came up.

SLANTING ACROSS THE SEA, like an ever-thickening mist, Threads were falling; silent, beautiful, treacherous. Silvery gray were those space-traversing spores, spinning from hard frozen ovals into coarse filaments as they penetrated the warm atmospheric envelope of Pern. Less than mindless, they had been ejected from their barren planet towards Pern, a hideous rain that sought organic matter to nourish it into growth. The southern continent of Pern had already been sucked dry. One Thread sinking into fertile soil would burrow deep, propagating thousands in the warm earth, rendering it into a black-dusted wasteland.

A stifled roar from the throats of eighty men and dragons broke the dawn air above Nerat's green heights — as if the Threads might hear this challenge, F'lar mused.

As one, dragons swiveled their wedge-shaped heads to their riders for firestone. Great jaws macerated the hunks. The fragments were swallowed and more firestone was demanded. Inside the beasts, acids churned and the poisonous phosphenes were readied. When the dragons belched forth the gas, it would ignite in the air, into ravening flame to sear the Threads from the sky. And burn them from the soil.

Dragon instinct took over the moment the Threads began to fall above Nerat's shores.

As much admiration as F'lar had always held for his bronze companion, it achieved newer heights in the next hours. Beating the air in great strokes, Mnementh soared with flaming breath to meet the down-rushing menace. The fumes, swept back by the wind, choked F'lar until he thought to crouch low on the lee side of the bronze neck. The dragon squealed as Threads flicked the tip of one wing. Instantly F'lar and he ducked into *between*, cold, calm, black. In the flicker of an eye, they were back to face the reality of Threads.

Around him, F'lar saw dragons winking in and out of *between*, flaming as they returned, diving, soaring. As the attack continued, and they drifted across Nerat, F'lar began to recognize the pattern in the dragons' instinctive evasion-attack movements—and in the Threads. For, contrary to what he had gathered from his study of the Records, the Threads fell in patches. Not as rain will, in steady unbroken sheets, but like flurries of snow; here, above, there, whipped to one side suddenly. Never fluidly, despite the continuity their name implied.

You could see a patch above you. Flaming, your dragon would rise. You'd have the intense joy of seeing the clump shrivel from bottom to top. Sometimes, a patch would fall between riders. One dragon would signal he would follow and, spouting flame, would dive and sear.

Gradually the dragonriders worked their way over the rainforests, so densely, so invitingly green. F'lar refused to dwell on what just one live Thread burrow would do to that lush land. He would send back a low-flying patrol to quarter every foot. One Thread! Just one Thread could put out the ivory eyes of every luminous vineflower.

A dragon screamed somewhere to his left. Before he could identify the beast, it had ducked *between*. F'lar heard other cries of pain, from men as well as dragons. He shut his ears and concentrated, as dragons did, on the here-and-now. Would Mnementh remember those piercing cries later? F'lar wished he could forget them now.

He, F'lar, the bronze rider, felt suddenly superfluous. It was the dragons who were fighting this engagement. You encouraged your beast, comforted him when the Threads burned, but you depended on his instinct and speed.

Hot fire dripped across F'lar's cheek, burrowing like acid into his shoulder . . . a cry of surprised agony burst from F'lar's lips. Mnementh took them to merciful *between*. The dragonman batted with frantic hands at the Threads, felt them crumble in the intense cold of *between* and break off. Revolted, he slapped at injuries still afire. Back in Nerat's humid air, the sting seemed to ease. Mnementh crooned comfortingly and then dove at a patch, breathing fire.

Shocked at self-consideration, F'lar hurriedly examined his mount's shoulder for telltale score marks.

I duck very quickly, Mnementh told him and veered away from a dangerously close clump of Threads. A brown dragon followed them down and burned them to ash.

It might have been moments, it might have been a hundred hours later when F'lar looked down in surprise at the sunlit sea. Threads now dropped harmlessly into the rocky tip curling westward.

F'lar felt weariness in every muscle. In the excitement of frenzied battle, he had forgotten the bloody scores on cheek and shoulder. Now, as he and Mnementh glided slowly, the injuries ached and stung.

He flew Mnementh high and when they had achieved sufficient altitude, they hovered. He could see no Threads falling landward. Below him, the dragons ranged, high and low, searching for any sign of a burrow, alert for any suddenly toppling trees or disturbed vegetation.

"Back to the Weyr," he ordered Mnementh in a heavy sigh. He heard the bronze relay the command even as he himself was taken *between.* He was so tired he did not even visualize where—much less, when—relying on Mnementh's instinct to bring him safely home through time and space.

> *Honor those the dragons heed,*
> *In thought and favor, word and deed.*
> *Worlds are lost or worlds are saved*
> *From those dangers dragon-braved.*

Craning her neck towards the Star Stone at Benden Peak, Lessa watched from the ledge until she saw the four wings disappear from view.

Sighing deeply to quiet her inner fears, Lessa raced down the stairs to the floor of Benden Weyr. She noticed someone was building a fire by the lake and that Manora was already ordering her women around, her voice clear but calm.

Old C'gan had the weyrlings lined up. She caught the envious eyes of the newest dragonriders at the barracks' windows. They'd have time enough to fly a flaming dragon. From what F'lar had intimated, they'd have years.

She shuddered as she stepped up to the weyrlings but managed to smile at them. She gave them their orders and sent them off, checking quickly with each dragon to be sure the riders had given clear references. The Holds would shortly be stirred up to a froth.

Canth told her that there were Threads at Keroon, falling on the

Keroon side of Nerat Bay. He told her that F'nor did not think two wings were enough to protect the meadowlands.

Lessa stopped in her tracks, trying to think how many wings were already out.

K'net's wing is still here, Ramoth informed her. *On the Peak*.

Lessa glanced up and saw bronze Piyanth spread his wings in answer. She told him to get *between* to Keroon, close to Nerat Bay. Obediently the entire wing rose and then disappeared.

She turned with a sigh to say something to Manora when a rush of wind and a vile stench almost overpowered her. The air above the Weyr was full of dragons. She was about to demand of Piyanth why he hadn't gone to Keroon when she realized there were far more beasts a-wing than K'net's twenty.

But you just left, she cried as she recognized the unmistakable bulk of bronze Mnementh.

That was two hours ago for us, Mnementh said with such weariness in his tone, Lessa closed her eyes in sympathy.

Some dragons were gliding in, fast. From their awkwardness it was evident they were hurt.

As one, the weyrwomen grabbed salve pots and clean rags, and beckoned the injured down. The numbing ointment was smeared on score marks where wings resembled black and red etched lace.

No matter how badly injured they might be, every rider tended his beast first.

Lessa kept one eye on Mnementh, sure that F'lar would not keep the huge bronze hovering like that if he'd been hurt. She was helping T'sum with Munth's cruelly pierced right wing when she realized the sky above the Star Stone was empty.

She forced herself to finish with Munth before she went to find the bronze and his rider. When she did locate them, she also saw Kylara smearing salve on F'lar's cheek and shoulder. She was advancing purposefully across the sands towards the pair when Canth's urgent plea reached her. She saw Mnementh's head swing upwards as he, too, caught the brown's thought.

"F'lar, Canth says they need help," Lessa cried. She didn't even notice, then, that Kylara slipped away into the busy crowd.

F'lar wasn't badly hurt. She reassured herself about that. Kylara had treated the wicked burns which looked to be shallow. Someone had found him another fur to replace the tatters of the threadbare one. He frowned, and winced because the frown creased his burned cheek. He gulped hurriedly at his *klah*.

"Mnementh, what's the tally of able-bodied? Oh, never mind, just get 'em aloft with a full load of firestone."

"You're all right?" Lessa asked, a detaining hand on his arm. He couldn't just go off like this, could he?

He smiled tiredly down at her, pressed his empty mug into her hands, giving them a quick squeeze. Then he vaulted to Mnementh's neck. Someone handed him a heavy load of sacks.

BLUE, GREEN, BROWN and bronze dragons lifted from the Weyr Bowl in quick order. A trifle more than sixty dragons hovered briefly above the Weyr where eighty had lingered so few minutes before.

So few dragons. So few riders. How long could they take such toll?

Canth said F'nor needed more firestone.

She looked about anxiously. None of the weyrlings were back yet from their messenger rounds. A dragon was crooning plaintively and she wheeled, but it was only young Pridith, stumbling across the Weyr to the feeding grounds, butting playfully at Kylara as they walked. The only other dragons were injured or . . . her eyes fell on C'gan, emerging from the weyrling barracks.

"C'gan, can you and Tagath get more firestone to F'nor at Keroon?"

"Of course," the old blue rider assured her, his chest lifting with pride, his eyes flashing. She hadn't thought to send him anywhere yet he had lived his life in training for this emergency. He shouldn't be deprived of a chance at it.

She smiled her approval at his eagerness as they piled heavy sacks on Tagath's neck. The old blue dragon snorted and danced as if he were young and strong again. She gave them the references Canth had visualized to her.

She watched as the two blinked out above the Star Stone.

It isn't fair. They have all the fun, said Ramoth peevishly. Lessa saw her sunning herself on the weyr ledge, preening her enormous wings.

"You chew firestone and you're reduced to a silly green," Lessa told her weyrmate sharply. She was inwardly amused by the queen's disgruntled complaint.

She passed among the injured then. B'fol's dainty green beauty moaned and tossed her head, unable to bend one wing which had been threaded to bare cartilage. She'd be out for weeks but she had the worst injury among the dragons. Lessa looked quickly away from the misery in B'fol's worried eyes.

As she did the rounds, she realized more men were injured than beasts. Two in R'gul's wing had serious head damages. One man might lose an eye completely. Manora had dosed him unconscious with numb-weed. Another man's arm had been burned clear to the bone. Minor though most of the wounds were, the tally dismayed Lessa. How many more would be disabled at Keroon?

Out of one hundred and seventy-two dragons, fifteen already were out of action; some only for a day or two, to be sure.

A thought struck Lessa. If N'ton had actually ridden Canth, maybe he could ride out on the next dragonade on an injured man's beast, since there were more injured riders than dragons. F'lar broke traditions as he chose. Here was another one to set aside—if the dragon was agreeable.

Presuming N'ton was not the only new rider able to transfer to another beast, what good would such flexibility do in the long run? F'lar had definitely said the incursions would not be so frequent at first, when the Red Star was just beginning its fifty-turn-long circling pass of Pern. How frequent was frequent? He would know but he wasn't here.

Well, he *had* been right this morning about the appearance of Threads at Nerat, so his exhaustive study of those old Records had been worthwhile.

No, that wasn't quite accurate. He had forgotten to have the men alert for signs of black dust as well as warming weather. As he had put the matter right by going *between* times, she would graciously allow him that minor error. But he did have an infuriating habit of guessing correctly. Lessa corrected herself again. He didn't guess. He studied. He planned. He thought and then he used common good sense. Like figuring out where and when Threads would strike according to entries in those smelly Records. Lessa began to feel better about their future.

Now, if he would just make the riders learn to trust their dragons' sure instinct in battle, they would keep casualties down, too.

A SHRIEK PIERCED air and ear as a blue dragon emerged above the Star Stone.

"*Ramoth!*" Lessa screamed in an instinctive reaction, hardly knowing why. The queen was a-wing before the echo of her command had died.

For the careening blue was obviously in grave trouble. He was trying to brake his forward speed, yet one wing would not function. His rider had slipped forward over the great shoulder, precariously clinging to his dragon's neck with one hand.

Lessa, her hands clapped over her mouth, watched fearfully. There wasn't a sound in the Bowl but the flapping of Ramoth's immense wings. The queen rose swiftly to position herself against the desperate blue, lending him wing support on the crippled side.

The watchers gasped as the rider slipped, lost his hold and fell— landing on Ramoth's shoulders.

The blue dropped like a stone. Ramoth came to a gentle stop near him, crouching low to allow the weyrfolk to remove her passenger.

It was old C'gan.

Lessa felt her stomach heave as she saw the ruin the Threads had made of the old harper's face. She dropped beside him, pillowing his head in her lap. The weyrfolk gathered in a respectful, silent circle.

Manora, her face as always serene, had tears in her eyes. She knelt and placed her hand on the old rider's heart. Concern flickered in her eyes as she looked up at Lessa. Slowly she shook her head. Then, setting her lips in a thin line, she began to apply the numbing salve.

"Too toothless old to flame and too slow to get *between*," C'gan mumbled, rolling his head from side to side. "Too old. 'But dragonmen must fly/When Threads are in the sky . . .'" His voice trailed off into a sigh. His eyes closed.

Lessa and Manora looked at each other in anguish. A terrible, ear-shattering note cut the silence. Tagath sprang aloft in a tremendous leap. C'gan's eyes rolled slowly open, sightless. Lessa, breath suspended, watched the blue dragon, trying to deny the inevitable as Tagath disappeared in midair.

A low moan sprang up around the weyr, like the torn, lonely cry of a keening wind. The dragons were uttering tribute.

"Is he . . . gone?" Lessa asked, although she knew.

Manora nodded slowly, tears streaming down her cheeks as she reached over to close C'gan's dead eyes.

Lessa rose slowly to her feet, motioning to some of the women to remove the old rider's body. Absently she rubbed her bloody hands dry on her skirts, trying to concentrate on what might be needed next.

Yet her mind turned back to what had just happened. A dragonrider had died. His dragon, too. The Threads had claimed one pair already.

How many more would die this cruel Turn? How long could this one Weyr survive? Even after Ramoth's forty had matured, and the ones she soon would conceive, and her queen-daughters, too?

Lessa walked apart to quiet her uncertainties and ease her grief. She saw Ramoth wheel and glide aloft, to land on the Peak. One day soon, would Lessa see those golden wings laced red and black from Thread marks? Would Ramoth . . . disappear?

No, Ramoth would not. Not while Lessa lived.

F'lar had told her long ago that she must learn to look beyond the narrow confines of Hold Ruatha and mere revenge. He was, as usual, right. As Weyrwoman under his tutelage, she had further learned that living *was* more than raising dragons and spring games. Living was struggling to do something impossible—to succeed, or die, knowing you had tried!

Lessa realized that she had, at last, fully accepted her role: as Weyrwoman and mate, to help F'lar shape men and events for many Turns to come—to secure Pern against the Threads.

Lessa threw her shoulders back and lifted her chin high.

Old C'gan had had the right of it.

Dragonmen *must* fly

When Threads are in the sky!

And yet—how long would there be dragonmen?

Worlds are lost or worlds are saved
By those dangers dragon-braved.

As F'lar had predicted, the attack ended by high noon, and weary dragons and riders were welcomed by Ramoth's high-pitched trumpeting from the Peak.

Once Lessa assured herself that F'lar had no serious injury, that F'nor's were superficial and that Manora was keeping Kylara busy in the kitchens, she applied herself to organizing the care of the injured and the comfort of the worried.

As dusk fell, an uneasy peace settled on the Weyr: the quiet of minds and bodies too tired, or too hurtful, to talk. Lessa's own words mocked her as she made out the list of wounded men and beasts. Twenty-eight men or dragons were out of the air for the next Thread battle. C'gan was the only fatality but there had been four more seriously injured dragons at Keroon and seven badly scored men, out of action entirely for months to come.

Lessa crossed the Bowl to her weyr, reluctant but resigned to giving F'lar this unsettling news.

She expected to find him in the sleeping room but it was vacant. Ramoth was asleep already as Lessa passed her on the way to the Council Room, also empty. Puzzled and a little alarmed, Lessa half-ran down the steps to the Records Room, to find F'lar, haggard of face, poring over musty skins.

"What are you doing here?" she demanded, angrily. "You ought to be asleep."

"So should you," he drawled, amused.

"I was helping Manora settle the wounded—"

"Each to his own craft," F'lar drawled. But he did lean back from the table, rubbing his neck and rotating the uninjured shoulder to ease stiffened muscles.

"I couldn't sleep," he admitted. "So I thought I'd see what answers I might turn up in the Records."

"More answers? To what?" Lessa cried, exasperated with him. As if the Records ever answered anything. Obviously the tremendous responsibilities of Pern's defense against the Threads were beginning to tell on the Weyrleader. After all, there had been the stress of the first battle; not to mention the drain of the traveling *between* times itself to get to Nerat to forestall the Threads.

F'lar grinned and beckoned Lessa to sit beside him on the wall bench.

"I need the answer to the very pressing question of how one understrength Weyr can do the fighting of six."

Lessa fought the panic that rose.

"Oh, your time schedules will take care of that," she replied gallantly. "You'll be able to conserve the dragon power until the new forty can join the ranks."

F'lar raised a mocking eyebrow.

"Let us be honest between ourselves, Lessa."

"But there have been Long Intervals before," she argued, "and since Pern survived them, Pern can again."

"Before there were always six Weyrs. And twenty or so Turns before the Red Star was due to begin its Pass, the queens would start to produce enormous clutches. All the queens, not just one faithful golden Ramoth. Oh, how I curse Jora!" He slammed to his feet and started pacing, irritably brushing the lock of black hair that fell across his eyes.

Lessa was torn with the desire to comfort him and the sinking, choking fear that made it difficult to think at all.

"You were not so doubtful . . ."

He whirled back to her. ". . . Not until I had actually had an encounter with the Threads and reckoned up the numbers of injuries. That sets the odds against us. Even supposing we can mount other riders to uninjured dragons, we will be hard put to keep a continuously effective force in the air, and still maintain a ground guard." He caught her puzzled frown. "There's Nerat to be gone over on foot tomorrow. I'd be a fool indeed if I thought we'd caught and seared every Thread midair."

"Get the Holders to do that. They can't just immure themselves safely in their inner Holds and let us do all. If they hadn't been so miserly and stupid . . ."

He cut off her complaint with an abrupt gesture. "They'll do their part all right," he assured her. "I'm sending for a full Council tomorrow, all Hold Lords and all Craftmasters. But there's more to it than just marking where Threads fall. How do you destroy a burrow that's gone deep under the surface? A dragon's breath is fine for the air and surface work but no good three feet down."

"Oh, I hadn't thought of that aspect. But the fire pits . . ."

". . . Are only on the heights and around human habitations, not on the meadowlands of Keroon or on Nerat's so green rainforests."

THIS CONSIDERATION WAS daunting indeed. She gave a rueful little laugh.

"Shortsighted of me to suppose our dragons are all poor Pern needs to dispatch the Threads. Yet . . ." She shrugged expressively.

"There are other methods," F'lar said, "or there were. There must have been. I have run across frequent mention of the Holds organizing ground groups and that they were armed with fire. What kind is never mentioned because it was so well known." He threw up his hands in disgust and sagged back down on the bench. "Not even five hundred dragons could have seared all the Threads that fell today. Yet *they* managed to keep Pern Thread-free."

"Pern, yes, but wasn't the southern continent lost? Or did they just have their hands too full with Pern itself?"

"No one's bothered with the southern continent in a hundred thousand Turns," F'lar snorted.

"It's on the maps," Lessa reminded him.

He scowled, disgustedly, at the Records, piled in uncommunicative stacks on the long table.

"The answer must be there. Somewhere."

There was an edge of desperation in his voice, the hint that he held himself to blame for not having discovered those elusive facts.

"Half those things couldn't be read by the man who wrote them," Lessa said tartly. "Besides that, it's been your *own* ideas that have helped us the most so far. You compiled the timemaps and look how valuable they are already."

"I'm getting too hidebound again, huh?" he asked, a half-smile tugging at one corner of his mouth.

"Undoubtedly," she assured him with more confidence than she felt. "We both know the Records are guilty of the most ridiculous omissions."

"Well said, Lessa. So, let us forget these misguiding and antiquated precepts and think up our own guides. First, we need more dragons. Second, we need them now. Third, we need something as effective as a flaming dragon to destroy Threads which have burrowed."

"Fourth, we need sleep, or we won't be able to think of anything," she added with a touch of her usual asperity.

F'lar laughed outright, hugging her.

"You've got your mind on one thing, haven't you?" he teased.

She pushed ineffectually at him, trying to escape. For a wounded, tired man, he was remarkably amorous. One with that Kylara. Imagine that woman's presumption, dressing his wounds.

"My responsibility as Weyrwoman includes care of you, the Weyrleader."

"But you spend hours with blue dragonriders and leave me to Kylara's tender ministrations."

"You didn't look as if you objected."

F'lar threw back his head and roared. "Should I open Fort Weyr and send Kylara on?" he taunted her.

"I'd as soon Kylara were Turns as well as miles away from here," Lessa snapped, thoroughly irritated.

F'LAR'S JAW DROPPED, his eyes widened. He leaped to his feet with an astonished cry.

"You've said it!"

"Said what?"

"Turns away! That's it. We'll send Kylara back, *between* times, with her queen and the new dragonets." F'lar excitedly paced the room while Lessa tried to follow his reasoning. "No, I'd better send at least one of the older bronzes. F'nor, too . . . I'd rather have F'nor in charge . . . Discreetly, of course."

"Send Kylara back . . . where to? When to?" Lessa interrupted him.

"Good point," and F'lar dragged out the ubiquitous charts. "Very good point. Where can we send them around here without causing anomalies by being present at one of the other Weyrs? The High Reaches are remote. No, we've found remains of fires there, you know, still warm, and no inkling as to who built them or why. And if we had already sent them back, they'd've been ready for today and they weren't. So they can't have been in two places already . . ." He shook his head, dazed by the paradoxes.

Lessa's eyes were drawn to the blank outline of the neglected southern continent.

"Send them there," she suggested sweetly, pointing.

"There's nothing there."

"They bring in what they need. There must be water, for Threads can't devour that. We fly in whatever else is needed, fodder for the herdbeasts, grain . . ."

F'lar drew his brows together in concentration, his eyes sparkling with thought, the depression and defeat of a few moments ago forgotten.

"Threads wouldn't be there ten Turns ago. And haven't been there for close to four hundred. Ten Turns would give Pridith time to mature and have several clutches. Maybe more queens."

Then he frowned and shook his head. "No, there's no Weyr there. No Hatching Ground, no . . ."

"How do we know that?" Lessa caught him up sharply, too delighted with many aspects of this project to give it up easily. "The Records don't mention the southern continent, true, but they omit a great deal. How do we know it isn't green again in the four hundred Turns since the Threads last spun? We do know that Threads can't last long unless there is something organic on which to feed and that once they've devoured all, they dry up and blow away."

F'lar looked at her admiringly. "Now, why hasn't someone wondered about that before?"

"Too hidebound." Lessa wagged her finger at him, dedicated completely to this venture. "And there's been no need to bother with it."

"Necessity . . . or is it jealousy . . . hatches many a tough shell." There was a smile of pure malice on his face and Lessa whirled away as he reached for her.

"The good of the Weyr," she retorted.

"Furthermore, I'll send you along with F'nor tomorrow to look. Only fair, since it is your idea."

Lessa stood still. "You're not going?"

"I feel confident I can leave this project in your very capable, interested hands," he laughed and caught her against his uninjured side, smiling down at her, his eyes glowing. "I must play ruthless Weyrleader and keep the Hold Lords from slamming shut their Inner Doors. And I'm hoping," he raised his head, frowning slightly, "one of the Craftmasters may know the solution to the third problem . . . getting rid of Thread burrows."

"But . . ."

"The trip will give Ramoth something to stop her fuming." He pressed the girl's slender body more closely to him, his full attention at last on her odd, delicate face. "Lessa, you are my fourth problem." He bent to kiss her.

At the sound of hurried steps in the passageway, F'lar scowled irritably, releasing her.

"At this hour?" he muttered, ready to reprove the intruder scathingly. "Who goes there?"

"F'lar?" It was F'nor's voice, anxious, hoarse.

The look on F'lar's face told Lessa that not even his half brother would be spared a reprimand and it pleased her irrationally. But the moment F'nor burst into the room, both Weyrleader and Weyrwoman were stunned silent. There was something subtly wrong with the brown rider. And, as the man blurted out his incoherent message, the difference suddenly registered in Lessa's mind. He was tanned! He wore no bandages and hadn't the slightest trace of the Thread mark along his cheek that she had tended this evening!

"F'lar, it's not working out! You can't be alive in two times at once!" F'nor was exclaiming distractedly. He staggered against the wall, grabbing the sheer rock to hold himself upright. There were deep circles under his eyes, visible despite the tan. "I don't know how much longer we can last like this. We're all affected. Some days not as badly as others."

"I don't understand."

"Your dragons are all right," F'nor assured the Weyrleader with a bitter laugh. "It doesn't bother them. They keep all their wits about them. But their riders . . . all the weyrfolk. We're shadows, half-alive, like dragonless men, part of us gone forever. Except Kylara." His face contorted with intense dislike. "All she wants to do is go back and watch herself. The woman's egomania will destroy us all, I'm afraid."

His eyes suddenly lost focus and he swayed wildly. His eyes widened and his mouth fell open. "I can't stay. I'm here already. Too close. Makes it twice as bad. But I had to warn you. I promise, F'lar, we'll stay as long as we can but it won't be much longer . . . so it won't be long enough, but we tried. We tried!"

Before F'lar could move, the brown rider whirled and ran, half-crouched, from the room.

"But he hasn't gone yet!" Lessa gasped. "He hasn't even gone yet!"

F'LAR STARED AFTER his half brother, his brows contracting with the keen anxiety he felt.

"What can have happened?" Lessa demanded of the Weyrleader. "We haven't even told F'nor. We ourselves just finished considering the idea of exploring the southern continent; to see if we could send dragons back and give Pridith a chance to lay a few clutches. And he looked so tanned and healthy." Her hand flew to her own cheek. "And the Threadmark—I dressed it myself tonight—it's gone. Gone. So he's been gone a long while." She sank down to the bench.

"However, he has come back. So he did go," F'lar remarked slowly in a reflective tone of voice. "Yet we now know the venture is not entirely successful even before it begins. And knowing this we have sent him back ten Turns, for whatever good it is doing." F'lar paused thoughtfully. "Consequently we have no alternative but to continue with the experiment."

"But what could be going wrong?"

"I think I know and there is no remedy." He sat down beside her, his eyes intent on hers. "Lessa, you were very upset when you got back from going *between* to Ruatha that first time. But I think now it was more than just the shock of seeing Fax's men invading your own Hold or in thinking your return might have been responsible for that disaster. I think it has to do with being in two times at once." He hesitated again, trying to understand this immense new concept even as he voiced it.

Lessa regarded him with such awe that he found himself laughing with embarrassment.

"It's unnerving under any conditions," he went on, "to think of returning and seeing a younger self."

"That must be what he meant about Kylara," Lessa gasped, "about her wanting to go back and watch herself . . . as a child. Oh, that wretched girl!" Lessa was filled with anger for Kylara's self-absorption. "Wretched selfish creature. She'll ruin everything."

"Not yet," F'lar reminded her. "Look, although F'nor warned us that the situation in his time is getting desperate, he didn't tell us how much he was able to accomplish. But you noticed that his scar had healed to invisibility, consequently some Turns must have elapsed. Even if Pridith lays only one good-sized clutch, even if just the forty of Ramoth's are mature enough to fight in three days' time, we have accomplished something. Therefore, Weyrwoman," and he noticed how she straightened up at the sound of her title, "we must disregard F'nor's return. When you fly to the southern continent tomorrow, make no allusion to it. Do you understand?"

Lessa nodded gravely and then gave a little sigh. "I don't know if I'm happy or disappointed to realize, even before we get there tomorrow, that the southern continent obviously will support a Weyr," she said with dismay. "It was kind of exciting to wonder."

"Either way," F'lar told her with a sardonic smile, "we have found only part of the answers to problems one and two."

"Well, you'd better answer number four right now!" Lessa suggested. "Decisively!"

> *Weaver, Miner, Harper, Smith,*
> *Tanner, Farmer, Herdsman, Lord,*
> *Gather wingspeed, listen well*
> *To the Weyrman's urgent word.*

They both managed to guard against any reference to his premature return when they spoke to F'nor the next morning. F'lar asked brown Canth to send his rider to the queen's weyr as soon as he awoke and was pleased to see F'nor almost immediately. If the brown rider noticed the curiously intent stare Lessa gave his bandaged face, he gave no sign of it. As a matter of fact, the moment F'lar outlined the bold venture of scouting the southern continent with the possibility of starting a weyr ten Turns back in time, F'nor forgot all about his wounds.

"I'll go willingly only if you send T'bor along with Kylara. I'm not waiting till N'ton and his bronze are big enough to take her on. T'bor and she are as . . ." F'nor broke off with a grimace in Lessa's direction, ". . . well, they're as near a pair as can be. I don't object to being . . . importuned, but there are limits to what a man is willing to do out of loyalty to dragonkind."

F'lar barely managed to restrain the amusement he felt over F'nor's reluctance. Kylara tried her wiles on every rider and, because F'nor had not been amenable, she was determined to succeed with him.

"I hope two bronzes are enough. Pridith may have a mind of her own, come mating time."

"You can't turn a brown into a bronze!" F'nor exclaimed with such dismay F'lar could no longer restrain himself. "Oh, stop it!" And that touched off Lessa's laughter. "You're as bad a pair," he snapped, getting to his feet. "If we're going south, Weyrwoman, we'd better get started. Particularly if we're going to give this laughing maniac a chance to compose himself before the solemn Lords descend. I'll get provisions from Manora. Well, Lessa? *Are* you coming with me?"

Muffling her laughter, Lessa grabbed up her furred flying cloak and followed him. At least the adventure was starting off well.

F'lar grabbed the pitcher of *klah* and his cup and adjourned to the Council Room, debating whether to tell the Lords and Craftmasters of this southern venture or not. The dragon's ability to fly *between* times as well as places was not yet well known. The Lords might not yet realize it had been used the previous day to forestall the Threads. If he could be sure that project was going to be successful, well, it would add an optimistic note to the meeting.

Let the charts, with the waves and times of the Thread attacks clearly visible, reassure the Lords.

THE VISITORS WERE not long in assembling. Nor were they all successful in hiding their apprehension and the shock they had received now that Threads had again spun down from the Red Star to menace all life on Pern. This was going to be a difficult session, F'lar decided grimly. He had a fleeting wish, which he quickly suppressed, that he had gone with F'nor and Lessa to the southern continent. Instead, he bent with apparent industry to the charts before him.

Soon there were but two more to come, Meron of Nabol (whom he would have liked not to include for the man was a troublemaker) and

Lytol of Ruatha. He had sent for Lytol last because he did not wish Lessa to encounter the man. She was still overly, and, to his mind, foolishly, sensitive over resigning her claim to Ruatha Hold for Lady Gemma's posthumous son. Lytol as Warder of Ruatha had a place in this conference. The man was also an ex-dragonman, and his return to the Weyr was painful enough without Lessa compounding it with her resentment. Lytol had turned to the Weaver's craft after his dragon's death and his compulsory exile from the Weyr. He was, with the exception of young Larad of Telgar, the Weyr's most valuable ally.

S'lel came in with Meron a step behind him. The Holder was furious at this summons; it showed in his walk, in his eyes, in his haughty bearing. But he was also as inquisitive as he was devious. He nodded only to Larad among the Lords and took the seat left vacant for him by Larad's side. Meron's manner made it obvious that that place was too close to F'lar by half a room.

The Weyrleader acknowledged S'lel's salute and indicated the bronze rider should be seated. F'lar had given thought to the seating arrangements in the Council Room, carefully interspersing brown and bronze dragonriders with Holders and Craftsmen. There was now barely room to move in the generously proportioned cavern, but there was also no room in which to draw daggers if tempers got hot.

A hush fell on the gathering and F'lar looked up to see that the stocky, glowering ex-dragonman from Ruatha had stopped at the threshold of the Council. He slowly brought his hand up in a respectful salute to the Weyrleader. As F'lar returned the salute, he noticed that the tic in Lytol's left cheek jumped almost continuously.

Lytol's eyes, dark with pain and inner unquiet, ranged the room. He nodded to the members of his former wing, to Larad and Zurg, head of his own Weaver's Craft. Stiff-legged he walked to the remaining seat, murmuring a greeting to T'sum on his left.

F'LAR ROSE.

"I appreciate your coming, good Lords and Craftmasters. The Threads spin once again. The first attack has been met and seared from the sky. Lord Vincet," and the worried Holder of Nerat looked up in alarm, "we have dispatched a patrol to the rainforest to do a low-flight sweep to make certain there are no burrows."

Vincet swallowed nervously, his face paling at the thought of what Threads could do to his fertile, lush holdings.

"We shall need your best junglemen to help . . ."

"Help . . . but you said . . . the Threads were seared in the sky?"

"There is no point in taking the slightest chance," F'lar replied, implying the patrol was only a precaution instead of the necessity he knew it would be.

Vincet gulped, glancing anxiously around the room for sympathy—and found none. Everyone would soon be in his position.

"There is a patrol due at Keroon and at Igen," and F'lar looked first at Lord Corman, then Lord Banger, who gravely nodded. "Let me say, by way of reassurance, that there will be no further attacks for three days and four hours." F'lar tapped the appropriate chart. "The Threads will begin approximately here on Telgar, drift westward through the southernmost portion of Crom, which is mountainous, and on, through Ruatha and the southern end of Nabol."

"How can you be so certain of that?"

F'lar recognized the contemptuous voice of Meron of Nabol.

"The Threads do not fall like a child's tumble-sticks, Lord Meron," F'lar replied. "They fall in a definitely predictable pattern; the attacks last exactly six hours. The intervals between attacks will gradually shorten over the next few Turns as the Red Star draws closer. Then, for about forty full Turns, as the Red Star swings past and around us, the attacks occur every fourteen hours, marching across our world in a timetable fashion."

"So *you* say," Meron sneered and there was a low mumble of support.

"So the Teaching Ballads say," Larad put in firmly.

Meron glared at Telgar's Lord and went on, "I recall another of your predictions about how the Threads were supposed to begin falling right after Solstice."

"Which they did," F'lar interrupted him. "As black dust in the Northern Holds. For the reprieve we've had, we can thank our lucky stars that we have had an unusually hard and long Cold Turn."

"Dust?" demanded Nessel of Crom. "That dust was Threads?" The man was one of Fax's blood connections and under Meron's influence: an older man who had learned lessons from his conquering relative's bloody ways and had not the wit to improve on or alter the original. "My Hold is still blowing with them. They're dangerous?"

F'lar shook his head emphatically. "How long has the black dust been blowing in your Hold? Weeks? Done any harm yet?"

Nessel frowned.

"I'm interested in your charts, Weyrleader," Larad of Telgar said smoothly. "Will they give us an accurate idea of how often we may expect Threads to fall in our own Holds?"

"Yes. You may also anticipate that the dragonmen will arrive shortly before the invasion is due," F'lar went on. "However, additional measures of your own are necessary and it is for this that I called the Council."

"Wait a minute," Corman of Keroon growled. "I want a copy of those fancy charts of yours for my own. I want to know what those bands and wavy lines really mean. I want . . ."

"Naturally you'll have a timetable of your own. I mean to impose on Masterharper Robinton," and F'lar nodded respectfully towards that Craftmaster, "to oversee the copying and make sure everyone understands the timing involved."

Robinton, a tall, gaunt man with a lined, saturnine face, bowed deeply. A slight smile curved his wide lips at the now hopeful glances favored him by the Hold Lords. His craft, like that of the dragonman, had been much mocked and this new respect amused him. He was a man with a keen eye for the ridiculous, and an active imagination. The circumstances in which doubting Pern found itself were too ironic not to appeal to his innate sense of justice. He now contented himself with a deep bow and a mild phrase.

"Truly all shall pay heed to the master." His voice was deep, his words enunciated with no provincial slurring.

F'lar, about to speak, looked sharply at Robinton as he caught the double barb of that single line. Larad, too, looked around at the Masterharper, clearing his throat hastily.

"We shall have our charts," Larad said, forestalling Meron, who had opened his mouth to speak, "we shall have the Dragonmen when the Threads spin. What are these additional measures? And why are they necessary?"

All eyes were on F'lar again.

"We have one Weyr where six once flew."

"But word is that Ramoth has hatched forty more," someone in the back of the room declared. "And why did you Search out still more of our young men?"

"Forty as yet unmatured dragons," F'lar said aloud, privately hoping that this southern venture would still work out. There was real fear in that man's voice. "They grow well and quickly. Just at present, while the Threads do not strike with great frequency as the Red Star begins its

Pass, our Weyr is sufficient ... if we have your cooperation on the ground. Tradition is that," and he nodded tactfully toward Robinton, the dispenser of Traditional usage, "you Holders are responsible for only your dwellings which, of course, are adequately protected by fire pits and raw stone. However, it is spring and our heights have been allowed to grow wild with vegetation. Arable land is blossoming with crops. This presents a vast acreage vulnerable to the Threads which one Weyr, at this time, is not able to patrol without severely draining the vitality of our dragons and riders."

At this candid admission, a frightened and angry mutter spread rapidly throughout the room.

"Ramoth rises to mate again soon," F'lar continued, in a matter-of-fact way. "Of course in other times, the queens started producing heavy clutches many Turns before the critical solstice, and more queens. Unfortunately, Jora was ill and old, and Nemorth intractable. The matter ..." He was interrupted.

"You dragonmen with your high and mighty airs will bring destruction on us all!"

"You've yourselves to blame," Robinton's voice stabbed across the ensuing shouts. "Admit it one and all! You've paid less honor to the Weyr than you would your watch-wher's kennel—and that not much! But now the thieves are on the heights and you are screaming because the poor reptile is nigh to death from neglect. Beat him, will you, when you exiled him to his kennel because he tried to warn you, tried to get you to prepare against the invaders? It's on *your* conscience, not the Weyrleader's nor the dragonriders', who had honestly done their duty these hundreds of Turns in keeping dragonkind alive ... against all your protests. How many of you," and his tone was scathing, "have been generous in thought and favor towards dragonkind? Even since I became Master of my craft, how often have my Harpers told me of being beaten for singing the old songs as is their duty? You earn only the right, good Lords and Craftsmen, to squirm inside your stony Holds and writhe as your crops die aborning." He rose.

" 'No Threads will fall. It's a Harper's winter tale,' " he whined, in faultless imitation of Nessel. " 'These dragonmen leech us of heir and harvest,' " and his voice took on the constricted, insinuating tenor that could only be Meron's. "And now the truth is as bitter as a brave man's fear and as difficult as mock-week to swallow. For all the honor you've done them, the dragonmen should leave you to be spun on the Threads' distaff."

"Bitra, Lemos and I," spoke up Raid, the wiry Lord of Benden, his blunt chin lifted belligerently, "have always done our duty to the Weyr."

Robinton swung round to him, his eyes flashing as he gave that speaker a long, slow look.

"Aye, and you have. Of all the Great Holds, you three have been loyal. But you others," and his voice rose indignantly, "as spokesmen for my Craft, I know, to the last full stop in the score, your opinion of drag-onkind. I heard the first whisper of your attempt to ride out against the Weyr." He laughed harshly and pointed a long finger at Vincet. "Where would you be today, good Lord Vincet, if the Weyr had *not* sent you packing back, hoping your ladies would be returned you? All of you," and his accusing finger marked each of the Lords of that abortive effort, "actually rode against the Weyr because . . . 'there . . . were . . . no . . . more . . . Threads!' "

He planted his fists on either hip and glared at the assembly. F'lar wanted to cheer. It was easy to see why the man was Masterharper and he thanked circumstances that such a man was the Weyr's partisan.

"And now, at this critical moment, you actually have the incredible presumption to protest against any measure the Weyr suggests?" Robinton's supple voice oozed derision and amazement. "Attend what the Weyrleader says and spare him your petty carpings!" He snapped those words out as a father might enjoin an erring child. "You were," and he switched to the mildest of polite conversational tones as he addressed F'lar, "I believe asking our cooperation, good F'lar? In what capacities?"

F'LAR HASTILY CLEARED his throat.

"I shall require that the Holds police their own fields and woods, during the attacks if possible, definitely once the Threads have passed. All burrows which might land must be found, marked and destroyed. The sooner they are located, the easier it is to be rid of them."

"There's no time to dig fire pits through all the lands . . . we'll lose half our growing space . . ." Nessel exclaimed.

"There were other ways, used in olden times, which I believe our Mastersmith might know," and F'lar gestured politely towards Fandarel, the archetype of his profession if ever such existed.

The Smith Craftmaster was by several inches the tallest man in the

Council Room, his massive shoulders and heavily muscled arms pressed against his nearest neighbors, although he had made an effort not to crowd against anyone. He rose, a giant tree-stump of a man, hooking thumbs like beast-horns in the thick belt that spanned his waistless mid-section. His voice, by no means sweet after Turns of bellowing above roaring hearths and hammers, was, by comparison to Robinton's superb delivery, a diluted, unsupported light baritone.

"There were machines, that much is true," he allowed in deliberate, thoughtful tones. "My father told me of them as a curiosity of the Craft. There may be sketches in the Hall. There may not. Such things do not keep on skins for long," and he cast an oblique look under beetled brows at the Tanner Craftmaster.

"It is our own hides we must worry about preserving," F'lar remarked to forestall any inter-craft disputes.

Fandarel grumbled in his throat in such a way that F'lar was not certain whether the sound was the man's laughter or a guttural agreement.

"I shall consider the matter. So shall all my fellow craftsmen," Fandarel assured the Weyrleader. "To sear Threads from the ground without damaging the soil may not be so easy. There are, it is true, fluids which burn and sear. We use an acid to etch design on dagger and ornamental metals. We of the Craft call it agenothree. There is also the black heavy-water that lies on the surface of pools in Igen and Boll. It burns hot and long. And, if as you say, the Cold Turn made the Threads break into dust, perhaps ice from the coldest northlands might freeze and break grounded Threads. However, the problem is to bring such to the Threads where they fall since they will not oblige us by falling where we want them . . ." He screwed up his face in a grimace.

F'lar stared at him, surprised. Did the man realize how humorous he was? No, he was speaking with sincere concern. Now the Mastersmith scratched his head, his tough fingers making audible grating sounds along his coarse hair and heat-toughened scalp.

"A nice problem. A nice problem," he mused, undaunted. "I shall give it every attention." He sat down, the heavy bench creaking under his weight.

The Masterfarmer raised his hand tentatively.

"When I became Craftmaster, I recall coming across a reference to the sandworms of Igen. They were once cultivated as a protective . . ."

"Never heard Igen produced anything useful except heat and sand . . ." quipped someone.

"We need every suggestion," F'lar said sharply, trying to identify that heckler. "Please find that reference, Craftmaster. Lord Banger of Igen, find me some of those sandworms!"

Banger, equally surprised that his arid Hold had a hidden asset, nodded vigorously.

"Until we have more efficient ways of killing Threads, all Holders must be organized on the ground during attacks, to spot and mark burrows, to set firestone to burn in them. I do not wish any man to be scored but we know how quickly Threads burrow deep and no burrow can be left to multiply. You stand to lose more," and he gestured emphatically at the Holder Lords, "than any others. Guard not just yourselves, for a burrow on one man's border may grow across to his neighbor's. Mobilize every man, woman and child, farm and crafthold. Do it now."

THE COUNCIL ROOM was fraught with tension and stunned reflection until Zurg, the Masterweaver, rose to speak.

"My Craft, too, has something to offer . . . which is only fair since we deal with thread each day of our lives . . . in regard to the ancient methods." Zurg's voice was light and dry and his eyes, in their creases of spare, lined flesh, were busy, darting from one face in his audience to another. "In Ruath Hold I once saw upon the wall . . . where the tapestry now resides, who knows? . . ." and he slyly glanced at Meron of Nabol and then Bargen of the High Reaches who had succeeded to Fax's title there. "The work was as old as dragonkind and showed, among other things, a man on foot, carrying upon his back a curious contraption. He held within his hand a rounded, sword-long object from which tongues of flame . . . magnificently woven in the orange-red dyes now lost to us . . . spouted towards the ground. Above, of course, were dragons in close formation, bronzes predominating . . . again we've lost that true dragon-bronze shade. Consequently I remember the work as much for what we now lack as for its subject matter."

"A flamethrower?" the Smith rumbled. "A flamethrower," he repeated with a falling inflection. "A flamethrower," he murmured thoughtfully, his heavy brows drawn into a titanic scowl. "A thrower of what sort of flame? It requires thought." He lowered his head and didn't speak, so engrossed in the required thought that he lost interest in the rest of the discussions.

"Yes, good Zurg, there have been many tricks of every trade lost in recent Turns," F'lar commented sardonically. "If we wish to continue living, such knowledge must be revived . . . fast. I would particularly like to recover the tapestry of which Master Zurg speaks."

F'lar looked significantly at those Hold Lords who had quarreled over Fax's seven Holds after that usurper's death in Ruatha's Great Hall.

"It may save all of you much loss. I suggest that it appear at Ruatha, at Zurg's or Fandarel's Crafthall. Whichever is most convenient."

There was some shuffling of feet but no admission of ownership.

"It might then be returned to Fay's son who is now Ruatha's Lord," F'lar added, wryly amused at such magnanimous justice.

Lytol, Ruatha's Warder, snorted softly and glowered round the room. F'lar supposed Lytol to be amused and experienced a fleeting regret for the orphaned Gaxom, reared by such a cheerless, if scrupulously honest, guardian.

"If I may, Lord Weyrleader," Robinton broke in, "we might all benefit, as your maps prove to us, from research in our own records." He smiled suddenly, an unexpectedly embarrassed smile. "I own I find myself in some disgrace for we Harpers have let slip unpopular ballads and skimped on some of the longer Teaching Sagas . . . for lack of listeners and, occasionally, in the interest of preserving our skins."

F'lar stifled a laugh. Robinton was a genius.

"I must see the Ruathan tapestry," Fandarel suddenly boomed out.

"I'm sure it will be in your hands very soon," F'lar assured him with more confidence than he dared feel. "My Lords, there is much to be done. Now that you understand what we all face, I leave it in your hands as leaders in your separate Holds and crafts how best to organize your own people. Craftsmen, turn your best minds to our special problems: review all records which might turn up something to our purpose. Lords Telgar, Crom, Ruatha and Nabol, I shall be with you in three days. Nerat, Keroon and Igen, I am at your disposal to help destroy any burrow on your lands. While we have the Masterminer here, tell him your needs. How stands your craft?"

"Happy to be so busy at our trade, Weyrleader," piped up the Masterminer.

JUST THEN F'LAR caught sight of F'nor, hovering about in the shadows of the hallway, trying to catch his eye. The brown rider wore an exultant grin and it was obvious he was bursting with news.

F'lar wondered how they could have returned so swiftly from the southern continent and then he realized that F'nor—again—was tanned. He gave a jerk of his head, indicating that F'nor take himself off to the sleeping quarters and wait.

"Lords and Craftmasters, a dragonet will be at the disposal of each of you for messages and transportation. Now, good morning."

He strode out of the Council Room, up the passageway into the queen's weyr, and parted the still swinging curtains into the sleeping room just as F'nor was pouring himself a cup of wine.

"Success!" F'nor cried as the Weyrleader entered. "Though how you knew to send just thirty-two candidates I'll never understand. I thought you were insulting our noble Pridith. But thirty-two eggs she laid in four days. It was all I could do to keep from riding out when the first appeared."

F'lar responded with hearty congratulations, relieved that there would be at least that much benefit from this apparently ill-fated venture. Now, all he had to figure out was how much longer F'nor had stayed south until his frantic visit the night before. For there were no worry lines or strain in F'nor's grinning, well-tanned face.

"No queen egg?" asked F'lar hopefully. With thirty-two in the one experiment, perhaps they could send a second queen back and try again.

F'nor's face lengthened. "No, and I was sure there would be. But there are fourteen bronzes, which outmatches Ramoth there," he added proudly.

"Indeed it does. How goes the Weyr otherwise?"

F'nor frowned, shaking his head against an inner bewilderment. "Kylara's . . . well, she's a problem. Stirs up trouble constantly. T'bor leads a sad time with her and he's so touchy everyone keeps a distance from him." F'nor brightened a little. "Young N'ton is shaping up into a fine wingleader and his bronze may outfly T'bor's Orth when Pridith flies to mate the next time. Not that I'd wish Kylara on N'ton . . . or anyone."

"No trouble then with supplies?"

F'nor laughed outright. "If you hadn't made it so plain we must not communicate with you here, we could supply you with fruits and fresh greens that are superior to anything in the north. We eat the way dragonmen should! Really, F'lar, we must consider a supply Weyr down there. Then we shall never have to worry about tithing trains and . . ."

"In good time. Get back now. You know you must keep these visits short."

F'nor grimaced. "Oh, it's not so bad. I'm not here in this time anyway."

"True," F'lar agreed, "but don't mistake the time and come while you're still here."

"Hm-m-m? Oh, yes, that's right. I forget time is creeping for us and speeding for you. Well, I shan't be back again till Pridith lays the second clutch."

With a cheerful good-bye, F'nor strode out of the weyr. F'lar watched him thoughtfully as he slowly retraced his steps to the Council Room. Thirty-two new dragons, fourteen of them bronzes, was no small gain and seemed worth the hazard. Or would the hazard wax greater?

SOMEONE CLEARED HIS throat deliberately. F'lar looked up to see Robinton standing in the archway that led to the Council Room.

"Before I can copy and instruct others about those maps, Weyrleader, I must myself understand them completely. I took the liberty of remaining behind."

"You make a good champion, Masterharper."

"You have a noble cause, Weyrleader," and then Robinton's eyes glinted maliciously. "I've been begging the Egg for an opportunity to speak out to so noble an audience."

"A cup of wine first?"

"Benden grapes are the envy of Pern."

"If one has the palate for such a delicate bouquet."

"It is carefully cultivated by the knowledgeable."

F'lar wondered when the man would stop playing with words. He had more on his mind than studying the time charts.

"I have in mind a ballad which, for lack of explanation, I had set aside when I became the Master of my Crafthall," he said judiciously after an appreciative savoring of his wine. "It is an uneasy song, both the tune and the words. One develops, as a Harper must, a certain sensitivity for what will be received and what will be rejected . . . forcefully," and he winced in retrospect. "I found that this ballad unsettled singer as well as audience and retired it from use. Now, like that tapestry, I think it bears rediscovery."

·   ·   ·

AFTER HIS DEATH, C'gan's instrument had been hung on the Council Room wall till a new Weyrsinger could be chosen. The guitar was very old, its wood thin. Old C'gan had kept it well-tuned and covered. The Masterharper handled it now with reverence, lightly stroking the strings to hear the tone, raising his eyebrows at the fine voice of the instrument.

He plucked a chord, a dissonance. F'lar wondered if the instrument were out of tune or if the Harper had, by some chance, struck the wrong string. But Robinton repeated the odd dischord, then modulated into a weird minor that was somehow more disturbing than the first notes.

"I told you it was an uneasy song. And I wonder if you know the answers to the questions it asks. For I've turned the puzzle over in my mind many times of late."

Then abruptly he shifted from the spoken to the sung tone.

> *"Gone away, gone ahead,*
> *Echoes roll unanswered.*
> *Empty, open, dusty, dead,*
> *Why have all the weyrfolk fled?*
>
> *Where have dragons gone together?*
> *Leaving weyrs to wind and weather?*
> *Setting herdbeasts free of tether?*
> *Gone, our safeguards, gone, but whither?*
>
> *Have they flown to some new weyr*
> *Where cruel Threads some others fear?*
> *Are they worlds away from here?*
> *Why, oh why, the empty Weyr?"*

The last plaintive chord reverberated.

"Of course, you realize that that song was first recorded in the Craft-annals some four hundred Turns ago," Robinton said lightly, cradling the guitar in both arms. "The Red Star had just passed beyond attack-proximity. The people had ample reason to be stunned and worried over the sudden loss of the populations of five Weyrs. Oh, I imagine at the time they had any one of a number of explanations but none . . . not one explanation . . . is recorded." Robinton paused significantly.

"I have found none recorded either," F'lar replied. "As a matter of fact, I had all the Records brought here from the other Weyrs—in order to compile accurate attack timetables. And those other Weyr Records simply end." F'lar made a chopping gesture with one hand. "In Benden's records, there is no mention of sickness, death, fire, disaster; not one word of explanation for the sudden lapse of the usual intercourse between the Weyrs. Benden's records continue blithely, but only for Benden. There is one entry that pertains to the mass disappearance . . . the initiation of a Pern-wide patrol routing, not just Benden's immediate responsibility. And that is all."

"Strange," Robinton mused. "Once the danger from the Red Star was past, the dragons and riders may have gone *between* to ease the drain on the Holds. But I simply cannot believe that. Our Craft-records do mention that harvests were bad and that there had been several natural catastrophes . . . other than the Threads. Men may be gallant and your breed the most gallant of all, but mass suicide? I simply do not accept that explanation . . . not for dragonmen."

"My thanks," F'lar said with mild irony.

"Don't mention it," Robinton replied graciously.

F'lar chuckled appreciatively. "I see we have been too weyrbound as well as too hidebound."

ROBINTON DRAINED HIS cup, and looked at it mournfully until F'lar refilled it.

"Well, your isolation served some purpose, you know, and you handled that uprising of the Lords magnificently. I nearly choked to death laughing," Robinton remarked, grinning broadly. "Stealing their women in the flash of a dragon's breath!" He chuckled again and suddenly sobered, looking F'lar straight in the eye. "Accustomed as I am to hearing what a man does *not* say aloud, I suspect there is much you glossed over in that Council Meeting. You may be sure of my discretion . . . and . . . you may be sure of my wholehearted support and that of my not ineffectual Craft. To be blunt, how may my Harpers aid you?" and he strummed a vigorous marching air. "Stir men's pulses with ballads of past glories and success?" The tune, under his flashing fingers, changed abruptly to a stern but determined rhythm. "Strengthen their mental and physical sinews for hardship?"

"If all your harpers could stir men as you yourself do, I should have no worries that five hundred or so additional dragons would not immediately end."

"Oho, then despite your brave words and marked charts, the situation is"—a dissonant twang on the guitar accented his final words—"more desperate than you carefully did not say."

"It may be."

"The flamethrowers old Zurg remembered and Fandarel must reconstruct? Will they tip the scales?"

F'lar regarded this clever man thoughtfully, and made a quick decision.

"Even Igen's sandworms will help, but as the world turns and the Red Star nears, the interval between daily attacks shortens and we have only seventy-two new dragons to add to those we had yesterday. One is now dead and several will not fly for several weeks."

"Seventy-two?" Robinton caught him up sharply. "Ramoth hatched but forty and they are still too young to eat firestone."

F'lar outlined F'nor and Lessa's expedition, taking place at that moment. He went on to F'nor's reappearance and warning, as well as the fact that the experiment had been successful in part with the hatching of thirty-two new dragons for Pridith's first clutch.

Robinton caught him up. "How can F'nor already have returned when you haven't heard from Lessa and him that there is a breeding place on the southern continent?"

"Dragons can go *between* times as well as places. They go easily from a when to a *where*."

Robinton's eyes widened as he digested this astonishing news.

"That is how we forestalled the attack on Nerat yesterday morning. We jumped back two hours *between* times to meet the Threads as they fell."

"You can actually jump backwards? How far back?"

"I don't know. Lessa, when I was teaching her to fly Ramoth, inadvertently returned to Ruath Hold, to the dawn twelve Turns ago when Fax's men invaded from the heights. When she returned to the present, I attempted a *between* times jump of some ten Turns. To the dragons it is a simple matter to go *between* times or spaces, but there appears to be a terrific drain on the rider. Yesterday, by the time we returned from Nerat and had to go on to Keroon, I felt as though I had been pounded flat and left to dry for a summer on Igen plain." F'lar shook his head. "We have obviously succeeded in sending Kylara, Pridith and the others ten Turns *between*, because F'nor has already reported to me that he has been there several Turns. The drain on humans, however, is becoming more and more marked. However, even seventy-two more mature dragons will be a help."

"Send a rider ahead in time and see if it is sufficient," Robinton suggested helpfully. "Save you a few days' worrying."

"I don't know how to get some-*when* which has not yet happened. You must give your dragon reference points, you know. How can you refer him to times which have not yet occurred?"

"You've got an imagination. Project it."

"And perhaps lose a dragon when I have none to spare? No, I must continue . . . because obviously I have, judging by F'nor's returns . . . as I decided to start. Which reminds me, I must give orders to start packing. Then I shall go over the time charts with you."

It was just after the noonmeal, which Robinton took with the Weyrleader, before the Masterharper was confident he understood the charts and left to begin their copying.

> Across a waste of lonely tossing sea,
> Where no dragonwings had lately spread,
> Flew a gold and a sturdy brown in spring,
> Searching if a land be dead.

As Ramoth and Canth bore Lessa and F'nor up to the Star Stone, they saw the first of the Hold Lords and Craftmasters arriving for the Council.

In order to get back to the southern continent of ten Turns ago, Lessa and F'nor had decided it was easiest to transfer first *between* times to the Weyr of ten Turns back which F'nor remembered. Then they would go *between* places to a seapoint just off the coast of the neglected southern continent which was as close to it as the Records gave any references.

F'nor put Canth in mind of a particular day he remembered ten Turns back and Ramoth picked up the references from the brown's mind. The awesome cold of *between* times took Lessa's breath away and it was with intense relief she caught a glimpse of the normal weyr activity before the dragons took them *between* places to hover over the turgid sea.

Beyond them, smudged purple on this overcast and gloomy day, lurked the southern continent. Lessa felt a new anxiety replace the uncertainty of the temporal displacement. Ramoth beat forward with great sweeps of her wings, making for the distant coast. Canth gallantly tried to maintain a matching speed.

"He's only a brown," Lessa scolded her golden queen.

If he is flying with me, Ramoth replied coolly, *he must stretch his wings a little.*

Lessa grinned, thinking very privately that Ramoth was still piqued that she had not been able to fight with her weyrmates. All the males would have a hard time with her for a while.

They saw the flock of wherries first and realized that there would have to be some vegetation on the continent. Wherries needed greens to live although they could subsist on a few grubs if necessary.

Lessa had Canth relay questions to his rider. "If the southern continent were rendered barren by the Threads, how did new growth start? Where did the wherries come from?"

"Ever notice the seed pods split open and the flakes carried away by the winds? Ever notice that wherries fly south after the autumn solstice?"

"Yes, but . . ."

"Yes, but!"

"But the land is thread-bared!"

"In less than four hundred Turns even the scorched hilltops of our continent begin to sprout in the springtime," F'nor replied by way of Canth, "so it is easy to assume the southern continent could revive, too."

Lessa was dubious and berated herself sternly, forcing her mind from F'nor's cryptic warning.

Even at the pace Ramoth set, it took time to reach the jagged shoreline with its forbidding cliffs, stark stone in the sullen light. Lessa groaned inwardly but urged Ramoth higher to see over the masking highlands. All seemed gray and desolate from that altitude.

Suddenly the sun broke through the cloud cover and the gray dissolved into dense greens and browns, living colors, the live greens of lush tropical growth, the browns of vigorous trees and vines. Lessa's cry of triumph was echoed by F'nor's hurrah and the brass voices of the dragons. Wherries, startled by the unusual sound, rose up in alarm from their perches.

Beyond the headland, the land sloped away to jungle and grassy plateau, similar to mid-Boll. Though they searched all morning, they found no hospitable cliffs wherein to found a new Weyr. Was that a contributing factor in the southern venture's failure, Lessa wondered?

Discouraged, they landed on a high plateau by a small lake. The weather was warm but not oppressive and while F'nor and Lessa ate their noonday meal, the two dragons wallowed in the water, refreshing themselves.

Lessa felt uneasy and had little appetite for the meat and bread. She noticed F'nor was restless, too, shooting surreptitious glances around the lake and the jungle verge.

"What under the sun are we expecting? Wherries don't charge and wild whers would come nowhere near a dragon. We're ten Turns before the Red Star so there can't be any Threads."

F'nor shrugged, grimacing sheepishly as he tossed his unfinished bread back into the food pouch.

"Place just feels so empty, I guess," he tendered, glancing around. He spotted ripe fruit hanging from a moonflower vine. "Now that looks familiar and good enough to eat, without tasting like dust in the mouth."

He climbed nimbly and snagged the orange-red fruit down.

"Smells right, feels ripe, looks ripe," he announced and deftly sliced the fruit open. Grinning, he handed Lessa the first slice, carving another for himself. He lifted it challengingly. "Let us eat and die together!"

She couldn't help but laugh and saluted him back. They bit into the succulent flesh simultaneously. Sweet juices dribbled from the corners of her mouth and Lessa hurriedly licked her lips to capture the least drop of the delicious liquid.

"Die happy, I will," F'nor cried, cutting more fruit.

Both were subtly reassured by the experiment and were able to discuss their discomposure.

"I THINK," F'NOR suggested, "it is the lack of cliff and cavern and the still, still quality of the place; the knowing that there are no other men or beasts about but us."

Lessa nodded her head in agreement. "Ramoth, Canth, would having no weyr upset you?"

We didn't always live in caves, Ramoth replied, somewhat haughtily as she rolled over in the lake. Sizable waves rushed up the shore almost to where Lessa and F'nor were seated on a fallen tree trunk. *The sun here is warm and pleasant, the water cooling. I could enjoy it here but I am not to come.*

"She is out of sorts," Lessa whispered to F'nor. "Let Pridith have it, dear one," she called soothingly to the golden queen, "you've the Weyr and all!"

Ramoth ducked under the water, blowing up a froth in disgruntled reply.

Canth admitted that he had no reservations at all about living weyr-less. The dry earth would be warmer than stone to sleep in, once a suitably comfortable hollow had been achieved. No, he couldn't object to the lack of the cave as long as there was enough to eat.

"We'll have to bring herdbeasts in," F'nor mused. "Enough to start a good-sized herd. Of course, the wherries here are huge. Come to think of it, I believe this plateau has no exits. We wouldn't need to pasture it off. I'd better check. Otherwise, this plateau with the lake and enough clear space for Holds seems ideal. Walk out and pick breakfast from the tree."

"It might be wise to choose those who were not Hold-reared," Lessa added. "They would not feel so uneasy away from protecting heights and stone-security." She gave a short laugh. "I'm more a creature of habit than I suspected. All these open spaces, untenanted and quiet, seem . . . indecent." She gave a delicate shudder, scanning the broad and open plain beyond the lake.

"Fruitful and lovely," F'nor amended, leaping up to secure more of the orange-red succulents. "This tastes uncommon good to me. Can't remember anything this sweet and juicy from Nerat and yet it's the same variety."

"Undeniably superior to what the Weyr gets. I suspect Nerat serves home first, Weyr last."

They both stuffed themselves greedily.

Further investigation proved that the plateau was isolated, and ample to pasture a huge herd of food beasts for the dragons. It ended in a sheer drop of several dragon-lengths into more dense jungle on one side, the seaside escarpment on the other. The timber stands would provide raw material from which dwellings could be made for the weyrfolk. Ramoth and Canth stoutly agreed dragonkind would be comfortable enough under the heavy foliage of the dense jungle. As this part of the continent was similar, weatherwise, to upper Nerat, there would be neither intense heat nor cold to give distress.

However, Lessa was glad enough to leave. F'nor seemed reluctant to start back.

"We can go *between* time and place on the way back," Lessa insisted finally, "and be in the Weyr by late afternoon. The Lords will surely be gone by then."

F'nor concurred and Lessa steeled herself for the trip *between*. She wondered why the *when between* bothered her more than the *where*, for it had no effect on the dragons at all. Ramoth, sensing Lessa's depression, crooned encouragingly. The long, long black suspension of the utter cold of *between* where and when ended suddenly in sunlight above the Weyr.

SOMEWHAT STARTLED, LESSA saw bundles and sacks spread out before the Lower Caverns as dragonriders supervised the loading of their beasts.

"What has been happening?" F'nor exclaimed.

"Oh, F'lar's been anticipating success," she assured him glibly.

Mnementh, who was watching the bustle from the ledge of the queen's weyr, sent a greeting to the travelers and the information that F'lar wished them to join him in the weyr as soon as they returned.

They found F'lar, as usual, bent over some of the oldest and least legible Record skins which he had had brought to the Council Room.

"And?" he asked, grinning a broad welcome at them.

"Green, lush and livable," Lessa declared, watching him intently. He knew something else, too. Well, she hoped he'd watch his words. F'nor was no fool and this foreknowledge was dangerous.

"That is what I had so hoped to hear you say," F'lar went on smoothly. "Come, tell me in detail. It'll be good to fill in the blank spaces on the chart."

Lessa let F'nor give most of the account, to which F'lar listened with sincere attention, making notes.

"On the chance that it would be practical, I started packing supplies and alerting the riders to go with you," he told F'nor when the account was finished. "Remember, we've but three days in this time in which to start you back ten Turns ago. We have no moments to spare. And we must have many more mature dragons ready to fight at Telgar in three days' time. So, though ten Turns will have passed for you, three days only will elapse here. Lessa, your thought that the farm-bred might do better is well-taken. We're lucky that our recent Search for rider candidates for the dragons Pridith will have come mainly from the crafts and farms. No problem there. And most of the thirty-two are in their early teens."

"Thirty-two?" F'nor exclaimed. "We should have fifty. The dragonets must have some choice even if we get the candidates used to the dragonets before they're hatched."

F'lar shrugged negligently. "Send back for more. *You'll* have time, remember," and F'lar chuckled as though he had started to add something and decided against it.

F'nor had no time to debate with the Weyrleader for F'lar immediately launched on other rapid instructions.

F'nor was to take his own wingriders to help train the weyrlings. They would also take the forty young dragons of Ramoth's first clutch: Kylara with her queen Pridith, T'bor and his bronze Orth. N'ton's young bronze might also be ready to fly and mate by the time Pridith was, so that gave the young queen two bronzes at least.

"Supposing we'd found the continent barren?" F'nor asked, still puzzled by F'lar's assurance. "What then?"

"Oh, we'd've sent them back to say the High Reaches," F'lar replied far too glibly but quickly went on. "I should send on other bronzes but I'll need everyone else here to ride burrow-search on Keroon and Nerat. They've already unearthed several at Nerat. Vincet, I'm told, is close to a heart attack from fright."

Lessa made a short comment on that Hold Lord.

"WHAT OF THE meeting this morning?" F'nor asked, remembering.

"Never mind that now. You've got to start shifting *between* by evening, F'nor."

Lessa gave the Weyrleader a long hard look and decided she'd have to find out what had happened in detail very soon.

"Sketch me some references, will you, Lessa?" F'lar asked.

There was a definite plea in his eyes as he drew clean hide and a stylus to her. He wanted no questions from her now that would alarm F'nor. She sighed and picked up the drawing tool.

She sketched quickly, with one or two details added by F'nor until she had rendered a reasonable map of the plateau they had chosen. Then abruptly, she had trouble focusing her eyes. She felt light-headed.

"Lessa?" F'lar bent to her.

"Everything's . . . moving . . . circling . . ." and she collapsed backward into his arms.

As F'lar raised her slight body into his arms, he exchanged an alarmed look with his half brother.

"I'll call for Manora," F'nor suggested.

"How do you feel?" the Weyrleader called after his brother.

"Tired but no more than that," F'nor assured him as he shouted down the service shaft to the kitchens for Manora to come and for hot *klah*. He needed that and no doubt of it.

F'lar laid the Weyrwoman on the sleeping couch, covering her gently.

"I don't like this," he muttered, rapidly recalling what F'nor had said of Kylara's decline which F'nor could not know was yet to come in his future. Why should it start so swiftly with Lessa?

"Time-jumping makes one feel slightly . . ." F'nor paused, groping for the exact wording, "not entirely . . . whole. You fought *between* times at Nerat yesterday yourself . . ."

"I fought," F'lar reminded him, "but neither you nor Lessa battled anything today. There may be some inner . . . mental . . . stress simply to going *between* times. Look, F'nor, I'd rather only you came back once you reach the southern weyr. I'll make it an order and get Ramoth to inhibit the dragons. That way no rider can take it into his head to come back even if he wants to. There is some factor which may be more serious than we can guess. Let's take no unnecessary risks."

"Agreed."

"One other detail, F'nor. Be very careful which times you pick to come back to see me. I wouldn't jump *between* too close to any time you were actually here. I can't imagine what would happen if you walked into your own self in the passageway and I can't lose you."

With a rare demonstration of affection, F'lar gripped his half brother's shoulder tightly.

"Remember, F'nor, I was here all morning and you did not arrive back from the first trip till mid-afternoon. And remember, too, *we* have only three days. You have ten Turns."

F'nor left, passing Manora in the hall.

THE WOMAN COULD find nothing obviously the matter with Lessa and they finally decided it might be simple fatigue; yesterday's strain when Lessa had to relay messages between dragons and fighters followed by the disjointing *between* times trip today.

When F'lar went to wish the southern venturers a good trip, Lessa was in a normal sleep, her face pale but her breathing easy.

F'lar had Mnementh relay to Ramoth the prohibition he wished the queen to instill in all dragonkind assigned to the venture. Ramoth obliged, but added in an aside to bronze Mnementh, which he passed on to F'lar, that everyone else had adventures while she, the Weyr Queen, was forced to stay behind.

No sooner had the laden dragons, one by one, winked out of the sky above the Star Stone, than the young weyrling assigned to Nerat Hold as messenger came gliding down, his face white with fear.

"Weyrleader, many more burrows have been found and they cannot be burned out with fire alone. Lord Vincet wants you."

F'lar could well imagine Vincet did.

"Get yourself some dinner, boy, before you start back. I'll go shortly."

As he passed through to the sleeping quarters, he heard Ramoth rumbling in her throat. She had settled herself down for the night.

Lessa still slept, one hand curled under her cheek, her dark hair trailing over the edge of the bed. She looked fragile, childlike and very precious to him. F'lar smiled to himself. So she was jealous of Kylara's attentions yesterday. He was pleased and flattered. Never would Lessa learn from him that Kylara, for all her bold beauty and sensuous nature, did not have one tenth the attraction for him that the unpredictable, dark and delicate Lessa held. Even her stubborn intractableness, her keen and malicious humor, added zest to their relationship. With a tenderness he would never show her awake, F'lar bent and kissed her lips. She stirred and smiled, sighing lightly in her sleep.

Reluctantly returning to what must be done, F'lar left her so. As he paused by the queen, Ramoth raised her great, wedge-shaped head; her many-faceted eyes gleamed with bright luminescence as she regarded the Weyrleader.

"Mnementh, please ask Ramoth to get in touch with the dragonet at Fandarel's Crafthall. I'd like the Mastersmith to come with me to Nerat. I want to see what his agenothree does to Threads."

Ramoth nodded her head as the bronze dragon relayed the message to her.

She has done so and the green dragon will come as soon as he can, Mnementh reported to his rider. *It is easier to do, this talking about, when Lessa is awake,* he grumbled.

F'lar agreed, heartily thankful that Lessa could talk to any dragon in the Weyr. It had been quite an advantage yesterday in the Battle and would be more and more of an asset.

Maybe it would be better if she tried to speak, across time, to F'nor . . . but no, F'nor had come back.

F'lar strode into the Council Room, still hopeful that somewhere within the illegible portions of the old Records was the one clue he so desperately needed. There must be a way out of this impasse. If not the southern venture, then something else. Something!

FANDAREL SHOWED HIMSELF a man of iron will as well as sinew; he looked calmly at the exposed tangle of perceptibly growing Threads that writhed and intertwined obscenely.

"Hundreds and thousands in this one burrow," Lord Vincet of Nerat was exclaiming in a frantic tone of voice. He waved his hands distractedly around the plantation of young trees in which the burrow had been discovered. "These stalks are already withering even as you hesitate. Do something! How many more young trees will die in this one field alone? How many more burrows escaped dragon's breath yesterday? Where is a dragon to sear them? Why are you just standing there?"

F'lar and Fandarel paid no attention to the man's raving, both fascinated as well as revolted by their first sight of the burrowing stage of their ancient foe. Despite Vincet's panicky accusations, it was the only burrow on this particular slope. F'lar did not like to contemplate how many more might have slipped through the dragons' efforts to reach Nerat's warm and fertile soil. If they had only had time enough to set out watchmen to track the fall of stray clumps . . . they could, at least, remedy that error in Telgar, Crom and Ruatha in three days. But it was not enough. Not enough.

Fandarel motioned forward the two craftsmen who had accompanied him. They were burdened with an odd contraption: a large cylinder of metal to which was attached a wand with a wide nozzle. At the other end of the cylinder was another short pipe length and then a short cylinder with an inner plunger. One craftsman worked the plunger vigorously, while the second, barely keeping his hands steady, pointed the nozzle end towards the Thread burrow. At a nod from his pumper, the man released a small knob on the nozzle, extending it carefully away from him and over the burrow. A thin spray danced from the nozzle and drifted down into the burrow. No sooner had the spray motes contacted the Thread tangles than steam hissed out of the burrow. Before long, all that remained of the pallid writhing tendrils was a smoking mass of blackened strands. Long after Fandarel had waved the craftsmen back, he stared at the grave. Finally he grunted and found himself a long stick with which he poked and prodded the remains. Not one Thread wriggled.

"Humph," he grunted with evident satisfaction. "However, we can scarcely go around digging up every burrow. I need another."

With Lord Vincet a hand-wringing moaner in their wake, they were escorted by the junglemen to another undisturbed burrow on the seaside of the rainforest. The Threads had entered the earth by the side of a huge tree which was already drooping.

With his prodding stick, Fandarel made a tiny hole at the top of the burrow and then waved his craftsmen forward. The pumper made vigorous motions at his end while the nozzle-holder adjusted his pipe before inserting it in the hole. Fandarel gave the sign to start and counted slowly before he waved a cutoff. Smoke oozed out of the tiny hole.

After a suitable lapse of time, Fandarel ordered the junglemen to dig, reminding them to be careful not to come in contact with the agenothree liquid. When the burrow was uncovered, the acid had done its work, leaving nothing but a thoroughly charred mass of tangles.

Fandarel grimaced but this time scratched his head in dissatisfaction.

"Takes too much time, either way. Best to get them still at the surface," the Mastersmith grumbled.

"Best to get them in the air," Lord Vincet chattered. "And what will that stuff do to my young orchards? What will it do?"

Fandarel swung round, apparently noticing the distressed Holder for the first time.

"Little man, agenothree in diluted form is what you use to fertilize your plants in the spring. True, this field has been burned out for a few years, but it is *not* Thread-full. It *would* be better if we could get the spray up high in the air. Then it would float down and dissipate harmlessly—fertilizing very evenly, too." He paused, scratched his head gratingly. "Young dragons could carry a team aloft . . . Hm-m-m. A possibility but the apparatus is bulky yet." He turned his back on the surprised Hold Lord then and asked F'lar if the tapestry had been returned. "I cannot yet discover how to make a tube throw flame. I got this mechanism from what we make for the orchard farmers."

"I'm still waiting for word," F'lar replied, "but this spray of yours is effective. The Thread burrow is dead."

"The sandworms are effective too, but not really efficient." Fandarel grunted in dissatisfaction. He beckoned abruptly to his assistants and stalked off into the increasing twilight to the dragons.

Robinton awaited their return at the Weyr, his outward calm barely masking his inner excitement. He inquired politely, however, of Fandarel's efforts. The Mastersmith grunted and shrugged.

"I have all my Craft at work."

"The Mastersmith is entirely too modest," F'lar put in. "He has already put together an ingenious device that sprays agenothree into Thread burrows and sears them into a black pulp."

"Not efficient. *I* like the idea of flamethrowers," the Smith said, his eyes gleaming in his expressionless face. "A thrower of flame," he repeated, his eyes unfocusing. He shook his heavy head with a bone-popping crack. "I go," and with a curt nod to the Harper and the Weyrleader, he left.

"I LIKE THAT man's dedication to an idea," Robinton observed. Despite his amusement with the man's eccentric behavior, there was a strong undercurrent of respect for the Smith. "I must set my apprentices a task for an appropriate Saga on the Mastersmith. I understand," he said turning to F'lar, "that the southern venture has been inaugurated."

F'lar nodded unhappily.

"Your doubts increase?"

"This *between* times travel takes its own toll," he admitted, glancing anxiously towards the sleeping room.

"The Weyrwoman is ill?"

"Sleeping, but today's journey affected her. We need another, less dangerous answer!" and F'lar slammed one fist into the other palm.

"I came with no real answer," Robinton said then, briskly, "but with what I believe to be another part of the puzzle. I have found an entry. Four hundred Turns ago, the then Masterharper was called to Fort Weyr not long after the Red Star retreated away from Pern in the evening sky."

"An entry? What is it?"

"Mind you, the Thread attacks had just lifted and the Masterharper was called one late evening to Fort Weyr. An unusual summons. However," and Robinton emphasized the distinction by pointing a long, callus-tipped finger at F'lar, "no further mention is ever made of that visit. There ought to have been, for all such summonses have a purpose. All such meetings are recorded yet no explanation of this one is given. The record is taken up several weeks later by the Masterharper as though he had not left his Crafthall at all. Some ten months afterwards, the Question Song was added to compulsory Teaching Ballads."

"You believe the two are connected with the abandonment of the five Weyrs?"

"I do, but I could not say why. I only feel that the events, the visit, the disappearances, the Question Song, are connected."

F'lar poured them both cups of wine.

"I have checked back, too, seeking some indications." He shrugged. "All must have been normal right up to the point they disappeared. There are records of tithe trains received, supplies stored, the list of injured dragons and men returning to active patrols. And then the records cease at full Cold, leaving only Benden Weyr occupied."

"And why that one Weyr of the six to choose from?" Robinton demanded. "Nerat, in the tropics, or island Ista would be better choices if only one Weyr was to be left. Benden so far north is not a likely place to pass four hundred Turns."

"Benden is high and isolated. A disease that struck the others and was prevented from reaching Benden?"

"And no explanation of it? They can't all, dragons, riders, weyrfolk, have dropped dead on the same instant and left no carcasses rotting in the sun."

"Then let us ask ourselves, why was the Harper called? Was he told to construct a Teaching Ballad covering this disappearance?"

"Well," Robinton snorted, "it certainly wasn't meant to reassure us, not with that tune—if one cares to call it a tune at all, and I don't—nor does it answer any questions! It poses them."

"For us to answer?" suggested F'lar softly.

"Aye," and Robinton's eyes shone. "For us to answer, indeed, for it is a difficult song to forget. Which means it was meant to be remembered. Those questions are important, F'lar!"

"WHICH QUESTIONS ARE important?" demanded Lessa who had entered quietly.

Both men were on their feet. F'lar, with unusual attentiveness, held a chair for Lessa and poured her wine.

"I'm not going to break apart," she said tartly, almost annoyed at the excess of courtesy. Then she smiled up at F'lar to take the sting out of her words. "I slept and I feel much better. What were you two getting so intense about?"

F'lar quickly outlined what he and the Masterharper had been discussing. When he mentioned the Question Song, Lessa shuddered.

"That's one I can't forget either. Which, I've always been told," and she grimaced, remembering the hateful lessons with R'gul, "means it's important. But why? It only asked questions." Then she blinked, her eyes went wide with amazement.

" 'Gone away, gone . . . *ahead!*' " she cried, on her feet. "That's it! All five Weyrs went . . . *ahead*. But to when?"

F'lar turned to her, speechless.

"They came ahead. To our time, five weyrs full of dragons," she repeated in an awed voice.

"No, that's impossible," F'lar contradicted.

"Why?" Robinton demanded excitedly. "Doesn't that solve the problem we're facing? The need for fighting dragons? Doesn't it explain why they left so suddenly with no explanation except that Question Song?"

F'lar brushed back the heavy lock of hair that overhung his eyes.

"It would explain their actions in leaving," he admitted, "because they couldn't leave any clues saying where they went or it would cancel the whole thing. Just as I couldn't tell F'nor I knew the southern venture would have problems. But how do they get here—if here is *when* they came. They aren't here now. And how would they have known they were needed—or *when* they were needed? And this is the real problem, how can you conceivably give a dragon references to a *when* that has not yet occurred?"

"Someone here must go back to give them the proper references," Lessa replied in a very quiet voice.

"You're mad, Lessa," F'lar shouted at her, alarm written on his face. "You know what happened to you today. How can you consider going back to a *when* you can't remotely imagine? To a *when* four hundred Turns ago? Going back ten Turns left you fainting and half-ill."

"Wouldn't it be worth it?" she asked him, her eyes grave. "Isn't Pern worth it?"

F'lar grabbed her by the shoulders, shaking her, his eyes wild with fear.

"Not even Pern is worth losing you, or Ramoth. Lessa, Lessa, don't you dare disobey me in this." His voice dropped to an intense, icy whisper, shaking with anger.

"Ah, there may be a way of effecting that solution, momentarily beyond us, Weyrwoman," Robinton put in adroitly. "Who knows what tomorrow holds? It certainly is not something one does without considering every angle."

Lessa did not shrug off F'lar's vice-like grip on her shoulders as she gazed at Robinton.

"Wine?" the Masterharper suggested, pouring a mug for her. His diversionary action broke the tableau of Lessa and F'lar.

"Ramoth is not afraid to try," Lessa said, her mouth set in a determined line.

F'lar glared at the golden dragon who was regarding the humans, her neck curled round almost to the shoulder joint of her great wing.

"Ramoth is young," F'lar snapped and then caught Mnementh's wry thought even as Lessa did.

She threw her head back, her peal of laughter echoing in the vaulted chamber.

"I'm badly in need of a good joke myself," Robinton remarked pointedly.

"Mnementh told F'lar that he was neither young nor afraid to try either. It was just a long step," Lessa explained, wiping tears from her eyes.

F'LAR GLANCED DOURLY at the passageway, at the end of which Mnementh lounged on his customary ledge.

A laden dragon comes, the bronze warned those in the weyr. *It is Lytol beyond young B'rant on brown Fanth.*

"Now he brings his own bad news?" Lessa asked sourly.

"It is hard enough for Lytol to ride another's dragon or come here at all, Lessa of Ruatha. Do not increase his torment one jot with your childishness," F'lar said sternly.

Lessa dropped her eyes, furious with F'lar for speaking so to her in front of Robinton.

Lytol stumped into the queen's weyr, carrying one end of a large rolled rug. Young B'rant, struggling to uphold the other end, was sweating with the effort. Lytol bowed respectfully towards Ramoth and gestured the young brownrider to help him unroll their burden. As the immense tapestry uncoiled, F'lar could understand why Masterweaver Zurg had remembered it. The colors, ancient though they undoubtedly were, remained vibrant and undimmed. The subject matter was even more interesting.

"Mnementh, send for Fandarel. Here's the model he needs for his flamethrower," F'lar said.

"That tapestry is Ruatha's," Lessa cried indignantly. "I remember it from my childhood. It hung in the Great Hall and was the most cherished of my Bloodline's possessions. Where has it been?" Her eyes were flashing.

"Lady, it is being returned where it belongs," Lytol said stolidly, avoiding her gaze. "A masterweaver's work, this," he went on, touching the heavy fabric with reverent fingers. "Such colors, such patterning. It took a man's life to set up the loom: a craft's whole effort to complete, or I am no judge of true craftsmanship."

F'lar walked along the edge of the immense arras, wishing it could be hung to get the proper perspective of the heroic scene. A flying formation of three wings of dragons dominated the upper portion of half the hanging. They were breathing flame as they dove upon gray, falling clumps of Threads in the brilliant sky. A sky, just that perfect autumnal blue, F'lar decided, that cannot occur in warmer weather. Upon the lower slopes of the hills depicted, foliage was turning yellow from chilly nights. The slaty rocks suggested Ruathan country. Was that why the tapestry had hung in Ruatha Hall? Below, men had left the protecting Hold, cut into the cliff itself. The men were burdened with the curious cylinders of which Zurg had spoken. The tubes in their hands belched brilliant tongues of flame in long streams, aimed at the writhing Threads that attempted to burrow in the ground.

Lessa gave a startled exclamation, walking right onto the tapestry, staring down at the woven outline of the Hold, its massive door ajar, the details of its bronze ornamentation painstakingly rendered in fine yarns.

"I believe that's the design on the Ruatha Hold door," F'lar remarked.

"It is . . . and it isn't," Lessa replied in a puzzled voice.

Lytol glowered at her, and then at the woven door. "True. It isn't and yet it is and I went through that door a scant hour ago." He scowled down at the door before his toes.

"Well, here are the designs Fandarel wants to study," F'lar said with relief, as he peered at the flamethrowers.

Whether the Smith could produce a working model from this woven one in time to help them three days hence, F'lar couldn't guess. But if Fandarel could not, no man could.

The Mastersmith was, for him, jubilant over the presence of the tapestry. He lay upon the rug, his nose tickled by the nap as he studied the details. He grumbled, moaned and muttered as he sat cross-legged to sketch and peer.

"Has been done. Can be done. Must be done," he was heard to rumble.

Lessa called for *klah*, bread and meat when she learned from young B'rant that neither he nor Lytol had eaten yet. She served all the men, her manner gay and teasing. F'lar was relieved for Lytol's sake. Lessa even pressed food and *klah* on Fandarel, a tiny figure beside the mammoth man, insisting that he come away from the tapestry and eat and drink. After taking nourishment he could return to his mumbling and drawing.

Fandarel finally decided he had enough sketches and disappeared, to be flown back to his Crafthold.

"No point in asking him when he'll be back. He's too deep in thought to hear," F'lar remarked, amused.

"If you don't mind, I shall excuse myself as well," Lessa said, smiling graciously to the four remaining around the table. "Good Warder Lytol, young B'rant should soon be excused, too. He's half asleep."

"I most certainly am not, Weyrlady," B'rant assured her hastily, widening his eyes with simulated alertness.

Lessa merely laughed as she retreated into the sleeping chamber. F'lar stared thoughtfully after her.

"I mistrust the Weyrwoman when she uses that particularly docile tone of voice," he said slowly.

"Well, we must all depart . . ." Robinton suggested, rising.

"Ramoth is young but not that foolish," F'lar murmured after the others had left.

Ramoth slept, oblivious of his scrutiny. He reached for the consolation Mnementh could give him, without response. The big bronze was dozing on his ledge.

> *Black, blacker, blackest*
> *And cold beyond frozen things.*
> *Where is between when there is naught*
> *To Life but fragile dragon wings?*

"I just want to see that tapestry back on the wall at Ruatha," Lessa insisted to F'lar the next day. "I want it where it belongs."

They had been to check on the injured, and had had one argument already over F'lar's having sent N'ton along with the southern venture. Lessa had wanted him to try riding another's dragon. F'lar had preferred for him to learn to lead a wing of his own in the south, given the years to mature in. He had reminded Lessa, in the hope that it might prove inhibiting to any ideas she had about going four hundred Turns back, about F'nor's return trips and bore down hard on the difficulties she had already experienced.

She had become very thoughtful although she had said nothing.

Therefore, when Fandarel sent word he would like to show F'lar a new mechanism, the Weyrleader felt reasonably safe in allowing Lessa the triumph of returning the purloined tapestry to Ruatha. She went to have the arras rolled and strapped to Ramoth's back.

He watched Ramoth rise with great sweeps of her wide wings, up to the Star Stone before going *between* to Ruatha. R'gul appeared at the ledge, just then, reporting that a huge train of firestone was entering the tunnel. Consequently, busy with such details, it was mid-morning before he could get to see Fandarel's crude and not yet effective flamethrower . . . the fire did not "throw" from the nozzle of the tube with any force at all. It was late afternoon before he reached the Weyr again.

R'gul announced sourly that F'nor had been looking for him, twice, in fact.

"Twice?"

"Twice, as I said. He would not leave a message with me for you," and R'gul was clearly insulted by F'nor's refusal.

By the evening meal, when there was still no sign of Lessa, F'lar sent to Ruatha to learn that she had indeed brought the tapestry. She had badgered and bothered the entire Hold until the thing was properly hung. For upwards of several hours, she had sat and looked at it, pacing its length occasionally.

She and Ramoth had then taken to the sky above the Great Tower and disappeared. Lytol had assumed, as had everyone at Ruatha, that she had returned to Benden Weyr.

"Mnementh?" F'lar bellowed when the messenger had finished, "Mnementh, where are they?"

Mnementh's answer was a long time in coming.

I cannot hear them, he said finally, his mental voice soft and as full of worry as a dragon's could be.

F'lar gripped the table with both hands, staring at the queen's empty weyr. He knew, in the anguished privacy of his mind, where Lessa had tried to go.

Cold as death, death-bearing,
Stay and die, unguided.
Brave and braving, linger.
This way was twice decided.

Below them was Ruatha's Great Tower. Lessa coaxed Ramoth slightly to the left, ignoring the dragon's acid comments, knowing that she was excited, too.

"That's right, dear, this is exactly the angle at which the tapestry illustrates the Hold door. Only when that tapestry was designed, no one had carved the lintels or capped the door. And there was no Tower, no inner Court, no gate." She stroked the surprisingly soft skin of the curving neck, laughing to hide her own tense nervousness and apprehension at what she was about to attempt.

She told herself there were good reasons prompting her action in this matter. The ballad's opening phrase, "gone away, gone ahead" was clearly a reference to *between* times. And the tapestry gave the required reference points for the jump *between* whens. Oh, how she thanked the masterweaver who had woven that doorway. She must remember to tell him how well he had wrought. She hoped she'd be able to. Enough of that. Of course she'd be able to. For hadn't the Weyrs disappeared? Knowing they had gone ahead, knowing how to go back to bring them ahead, it was she, obviously, who must go back and lead them. It was very simple and only she and Ramoth could do it. Because they already had.

She laughed again, nervously, and took several deep, shuddering breaths.

"All right, my golden love," she murmured. "You have the reference. You know when I want to go. Take me *between*, Ramoth, *between* four hundred Turns."

The cold was intense, even more penetrating than she had imagined. Yet it was not a physical cold. It was the awareness of the absence of *everything*. No light. No sound. No touch. As they hovered, longer and longer, in this nothingness, Lessa recognized the full-blown panic of a kind that threatened to overwhelm her reason. She knew she sat on Ramoth's neck yet she could not feel the great beast under her thighs, under her hands. She tried to cry out inadvertently and opened her mouth to . . . nothing . . . no sound in her own ears. She could not even feel the hands that she knew she had raised to her own cheeks.

I am here, she heard Ramoth say in her mind. *We are together*, and this reassurance was all that kept her from losing her grasp on sanity in that terrifying eon of unpassing, timeless nothingness.

SOMEONE HAD SENSE enough to call for Robinton. The Masterharper found F'lar sitting at the table, his face deathly pale, his eyes staring at the empty weyr. The Craftmaster's entrance, his calm voice, reached F'lar in his shocked numbness. He sent the others out with a peremptory wave.

"She's gone. She tried to go back four hundred Turns," F'lar said in a tight, hard voice.

The Masterharper sank into the chair opposite the Weyrleader.

"She took the tapestry back to Ruatha," F'lar continued in that same choked voice. "I'd told her about F'nor's returns. I told her how dangerous this was. She didn't argue very much and I know going *between* times had frightened her, if anything could frighten Lessa." He banged the table with an impotent fist. "I should have suspected her. When she thinks she's right, she doesn't stop to analyze, to consider. She just does it!"

"But she's not a foolish woman," Robinton reminded him slowly. "Not even she would jump *between* times without a reference point. Would she?"

" 'Gone away, gone ahead' . . . that's the only clue we have!"

"Now wait a moment," Robinton cautioned him, then snapped his fingers. "Last night, when she walked upon the tapestry, she was uncommonly interested in the Hall door. She discussed it with Lytol."

F'lar was on his feet and halfway down the passageway.

"Come on, man, we've got to get to Ruatha."

Lytol lit every glow in the Hold for F'lar and Robinton to examine the tapestry clearly.

"She spent the afternoon just looking at it," the Warder said, shaking his head. "You're sure she has tried this incredible jump?"

"She must have. Mnementh can't hear either her or Ramoth anywhere. Yet he says he can get an echo from Canth many Turns away and in the southern continent." F'lar stalked past the tapestry. "What is it about the door, Lytol? Think, man!"

"It is much as it is now, save that there are no carved lintels, there is no outer Court, nor Tower . . ."

"That's it. Oh, by the first Egg, it is so simple. Zurg said this tapestry is old. Lessa must have decided it was four hundred Turns and she has used it as the reference point to go back *between* times."

"Why, then, she's there and safe," Robinton cried, sinking with relief in a chair.

"Oh, no, Harper. It is not as easy as that," F'lar murmured.

Robinton caught his stricken look and the despair echoed in Lytol's face. "What's the matter?"

"There is nothing *between*," F'lar said in a dead voice. "To go *between* places takes only as much time as for a man to cough three times. *Between* four hundred Turns . . ." his voice trailed off.

> *Who wills,*
> *Cans.*
> *Who tries,*
> *Does.*
> *Who loves,*
> *Lives.*

There were voices that first were roars in her aching ears and then hushed beyond the threshold of sound. She gasped as the whirling, nauseating sensation apparently spun her, and the bed which she felt beneath her, round and round. She clung to the sides of the bed as pain jabbed through her head, from somewhere directly in the middle of her skull. She screamed, as much in protest at the pain as from the terrifying, rolling, whirling, dropping, lack of a solid ground.

Yet some frightening necessity kept her trying to gabble out the message she had come to give. Sometimes she felt Ramoth trying to reach her in that vast swooping darkness that enveloped her. She would try to cling to Ramoth's mind, hoping the golden queen could lead her out of this torturing nowhere. Exhausted she would sink down, down, only to be torn from oblivion by the desperate need to communicate.

She was finally aware of a soft, smooth hand upon her arm, of a liquid, warm and savory, in her mouth. She rolled it around her tongue and it trickled down her sore throat. A fit of coughing left her gasping and weak. Then she experimentally opened her eyes and the images before her did not lurch and spin.

"Who . . . are . . . you?" she managed to croak.

"Oh, my dear Lessa . . ."

"Is that who I am?" she asked, confused.

"So your Ramoth tells us," she was assured. "I am Mardra of Fort Weyr."

"Oh, F'lar will be so angry with me," Lessa moaned as her memory came rushing back. "He will shake me and shake me. He always shakes me when I disobey him. But I was right. I was right. Mardra? . . . Oh, that . . . awful . . . nothingness," and she felt herself drifting off into sleep, unable to resist that overwhelming urge. Comfortingly, her bed no longer rocked beneath her.

The room, dimly lit by wallglows, was both like her own at Benden Weyr and subtly different. Lessa lay still, trying to isolate that difference. Ah, the Weyr walls were very smooth here. The room was larger, too, the ceiling higher and curving. The furnishings, now that her eyes were used to the dim light and she could distinguish details, were more finely crafted. She stirred restlessly.

"Ah, you're awake again, mystery lady," a man said. Light beyond the parted curtain flooded in from the outer weyr. Lessa sensed rather than saw the presence of others in the room beyond.

A woman passed under the man's arm, moving swiftly to the bedside.

"I remember you. You're Mardra," Lessa said with surprise.

"Indeed I am and here is M'ron, Weyrleader at Fort."

M'ron was tossing more glows into the wallbasket, peering over his shoulder at Lessa to see if the light bothered her.

"Ramoth!" Lessa exclaimed, sitting upright, aware for the first time that it was not Ramoth's mind she touched in the outer weyr.

"Oh, that one," Mardra laughed with amused dismay. "She'll eat us out of the Weyr and even my Loranth has had to call the other queens to restrain her."

"She perches on the Star Stones as if she owned them and keens constantly," M'ron added, less charitably. He cocked an ear. "Ha. She's stopped."

"You can come, can't you?" Lessa blurted out.

"Come? Come where, my dear?" Mardra asked, confused. "You've been going on and on about our 'coming,' and Threads approaching, and the Red Star bracketed in the Eye Rock and . . . my dear, don't you realize, the Red Star has been past Pern these two months?"

"No, no, they've started. That's why I came back *between* times . . ."

"Back? *Between* times?" M'ron exclaimed, striding over to the bed, eyeing Lessa intently.

"Could I have some *klah*? I know I'm not making much sense and

I'm not really awake yet. But I'm not mad or still sick and this is rather complicated."

"Yes, it is," M'ron remarked with deceptive mildness. But he did call down the service shaft for *klah*. And he did drag a chair over to her bedside, settling himself to listen to her.

"Of course you're not mad," Mardra soothed her, glaring at her weyrmate. "Or she wouldn't ride a queen."

M'ron had to agree to that. Lessa waited for the *klah* to come, sipping gratefully at its stimulating warmth.

LESSA TOOK A deep breath and began, telling them of the Long Interval between the dangerous passes of the Red Star: how the sole Weyr had fallen into disfavor and contempt. How Jora had deteriorated and lost control over her queen, Nemorth, so that, as the Red Star neared, there was no sudden increase in the size of clutches. How she had Impressed Ramoth to become Benden's Weyrwoman. How F'lar had outwitted the dissenting Hold Lords the day after Ramoth's first mating flight and taken firm command of Weyr and Pern, preparing for the Threads he knew were coming. She told her by now rapt audience of her own first attempts to fly Ramoth and how she had inadvertently gone back *between* times to the day Fax had invaded Ruath Hold.

"Invade . . . my family's Hold?" Mardra had cried, aghast.

"Ruatha has given the Weyrs many famous Weyrwomen," Lessa said with a sly smile, at which M'ron burst out laughing.

"She's Ruathan, no question," he assured Mardra.

She told them of the situation in which dragonmen now found themselves, with an insufficient force to meet the Thread attacks. Of the Question Song and the great tapestry.

"A tapestry?" Mardra cried, her hand going to her cheek in alarm. "Describe it to me!"

And when Lessa did, she saw—at last—belief in both their faces.

"My father has just commissioned a tapestry with such a scene. He told me of it the other day because the last battle with the Threads was held over Ruatha." Incredulous, Mardra turned to M'ron, who no longer looked amused. "She must have done what she has said she's done. How could she possibly know about the tapestry?"

"You might also ask your queen dragon, and mine," Lessa suggested.

"My dear, we do not doubt you now," Mardra said sincerely, "but it is a most incredible feat."

"I don't think," Lessa said, "that I would ever try it again, knowing what I do now."

"Yes, this shock makes a forward jump *between* times quite a problem if your F'lar must have an effective fighting force," M'ron remarked.

"You will come? You will?"

"There is a distinct possibility we will," M'ron said gravely and his face broke into a lopsided grin. "You said we left the Weyrs . . . abandoned them, in fact, and left no explanation. We went somewhere . . . somewhen, that is, for we are still here now . . ."

They were all silent, for the same alternative occurred to them simultaneously. The Weyrs had been left vacant, but Lessa had no way of proving that the five Weyrs reappeared in her time.

"There must be a way. There must be a way," Lessa cried distractedly. "And there's no time to waste. No time at all!"

M'ron gave a bark of laughter. "There's plenty of time at this end of history, my dear."

They made her rest, then, more concerned than she was that she had been ill some weeks, deliriously screaming that she was falling, and could not see, could not hear, could not touch. Ramoth, too, they told her, had suffered from the appalling nothingness of a protracted stay *between*, emerging above ancient Ruatha a pale yellow wraith of her former robust self.

The Lord of Ruath Hold, Mardra's father, had been surprised out of his wits by the appearance of a staggering rider and a pallid queen on his stone verge. Naturally and luckily he had sent to his daughter at Fort Weyr for help. Lessa and Ramoth had been transported to the Weyr and the Ruathan Lord kept silent on the matter.

When Lessa was strong enough, M'ron called a Council of Weyrleaders. Curiously, there was no opposition to going . . . provided they could solve the problem of time-shock and find reference points along the way. It did not take Lessa long to comprehend why the dragonriders were so eager to attempt the journey. Most of them had been born during the present Thread incursions. They had now had close to four months of unexciting routine patrols and were bored with monotony. Training Games were pallid substitutes for the real battles they had all fought. The Holds, which once could not do dragonmen favors enough, were beginning to be indifferent. The Weyrleaders could see these incidents increasing as Thread-generated fears receded. It was a morale decay as insidious as a wasting disease in Weyr and Hold. The alternative which Lessa's appeal offered was better than a slow decline in their own time.

Of Benden, only the Weyrleader himself was privy to these meetings. Because Benden was the only Weyr in Lessa's time, it must remain ignorant, and intact, until her time. Nor could any mention be made of Lessa's presence, for that, too, was unknown in her Turn.

She insisted that they call in the Masterharper because her Records said he had been called. But, when he asked her to tell him the Question Song, she smiled and demurred.

"You'll write it, or your successor will, when the Weyrs are found to be abandoned," she told him. "But it must be your doing, not my repeating."

"A difficult assignment to know one must write a song that four hundred Turns later gives a valuable clue."

"Only be sure," she cautioned him, "that it is a Teaching tune. It must *not* be forgotten, for it poses questions that I have to answer."

As he started to chuckle, she realized she had already given him a pointer.

The discussions—how to go so far safely with no sustained sense deprivations—grew heated. There were more constructive notions, however impractical, on how to find reference points along the way. The five Weyrs had not been ahead in time and Lessa, in her one gigantic backward leap, had not stopped for intermediate time marks.

"You did say that a *between* times jump of ten years caused no hardship?" M'ron asked of Lessa as all the Weyrleaders and the Masterharper met to discuss this impasse.

"None. It takes . . . oh, twice as long as a *between* places jump."

"It is the four hundred Turn leap that left you imbalanced, hm-m-m. Maybe twenty or twenty-five Turn segments would be safe enough."

That suggestion found merit until Ista's cautious leader, D'ram, spoke up.

"I don't mean to be a Hold-hider, but there is one possibility we haven't mentioned. How do we know we made the jump *between* to Lessa's time? Going *between* is a chancy business. Men go missing often. And Lessa barely made it here alive."

"A good point, D'ram," M'ron concurred briskly, "but I feel there is more to prove that we do—did—will—go forward. The clues, for one thing; they were aimed at Lessa. The very emergency which left five Weyrs empty that sent her back to appeal for our help . . ."

"Agreed, agreed," D'ram interrupted earnestly, "but what I mean is can you be sure we reached Lessa's time? It hadn't happened yet. Do we know it can?"

M'ron was not the only one who searched his mind for an answer to that. All of a sudden, he slammed both hands, palms down, on the table.

"By the Egg, it's die slow, doing nothing, or die quick, trying. I've had a surfeit of the quiet life we dragonmen must lead after the Red Star passes, till we go *between* in old age. I confess I'm almost sorry to see the Red Star dwindle further from us in the evening sky. I say, grab the risk with both hands and shake it till it's gone. We're dragonmen, aren't we, bred to fight the Threads? Let's go hunting . . . four hundred Turns ahead!"

Lessa's drawn face relaxed. She had recognized the validity of D'ram's alternate possibility and it had touched off bitter fear in her heart. To risk herself was her own responsibility but to risk these hundreds of men and dragons, the weyrfolk who could accompany their men . . . ?

M'ron's ringing words for once and all dispensed with that consideration.

"And I believe," the Masterharper's exultant voice cut through the answering shouts of agreement, "I believe I have your reference points." A smile of surprised wonder illuminated his face. "Twenty Turns or twenty-hundred, you have a guide! And M'ron said it. 'As the Red Star dwindles in the evening sky . . .'"

LATER, AS THEY plotted the orbit of the Red Star, they found how easy that solution actually was, and chuckled that their ancient foe should be their guide.

Atop Fort Weyr, as on all the Weyrs, were great stones. They were so placed that at certain times of the year they marked the approach and retreat of the Red Star, as it orbited in its erratic, two hundred Turn–long course around their sun. By consulting the Records which, among other morsels of information, included the Red Star's wanderings, it was not hard to plan jumps *between* of twenty-five Turns for each Weyr. It had been decided that the complement of each separate Weyr would jump *between* above its own base, for there would unquestionably be accidents if close to eighteen hundred laden beasts tried it at one point.

Each moment now was one too long away from her own time for

Lessa. She had been a month away from F'lar and missed him more than she had thought could be possible. Also, she was worried that Ramoth would mate away from Mnementh. There were, to be sure, bronze dragons and bronze riders eager to do that service, but Lessa had no interest in them.

M'ron and Mardra occupied her with the many details in organizing the exodus so that no clues, past the tapestry and the Question Song which would be composed at a later date, remained in the Weyrs.

It was with a relief close to tears that Lessa urged Ramoth upward in the night sky to take her place near M'ron and Mardra above the Fort Weyr Star Stone. At five other Weyrs, great wings were ranged in formation, ready to depart their own times.

As each Weyrleader's dragon reported to Lessa that all were ready— reference points, determined by the Red Star's travels in mind—it was this traveler from the future who gave the command to jump *between*.

> The blackest night must end in
>   dawn,
> The sun dispel the dreamer's fear:
> When shall my soul's bleak, hope-
>   less pain
> Find solace in its darkening weyr?

They had made eleven jumps *between*, the Weyrleaders' bronzes speaking to Lessa as they rested briefly between each jump. Of the eighteen-hundred-odd travelers, only four failed to come ahead, and they had been older beasts. All five sections agreed to pause for a quick meal and hot *klah*, before the final jump which would be but twelve Turns.

"It is easier," M'ron commented as Mardra served around the *klah*, "to go twenty-five Turns than twelve." He glanced up at the Red Dawn Star, their winking and faithful guide. "It does not alter its position as much. I count on you, Lessa, to give us additional references."

"I want to get us back to Ruatha before F'lar discovers I have gone." She shivered as she looked up at the Red Star and sipped hastily at the hot *klah*. "I've seen the Star just like that, once . . . no, twice . . . before at Ruatha." She stared at M'ron, her throat constricting as she remembered that morning: the time she had decided that the Red Star was a menace to her, three days after which Fax and F'lar had appeared at Ruath Hold. Fax had died on F'lar's dagger and she had gone to Benden

Weyr. She felt suddenly dizzy, weak, strangely unsettled. She had not felt this way as they paused between other jumps.

"Are you all right, Lessa?" Mardra asked with concern. "You're so white. You're shaking." She put her arm around Lessa, glancing, concerned, at her weyrmate.

"Twelve Turns ago I was at Ruatha," Lessa murmured, grasping Mardra's hand for support. "I was at Ruatha twice. Let's go on quickly. I'm too many in this morning. I must get back. I must get back to F'lar. He'll be so angry."

The note of hysteria in her voice alarmed both Mardra and M'ron. Hastily the latter gave orders for the fires to be extinguished, for the weyr-folk to mount and prepare for the final jump ahead.

Her mind in chaos, Lessa transmitted the references to the other Weyrleaders' dragons: Ruatha in the evening light, the Great Tower, the inner Court, and the land at springtime . . .

> *A fleck of red in a cold night sky,*
> *A drop of blood to guide them by,*
> *Turn away, Turn away, Turn, be*
>   *gone,*
> *A Red Star beckons the travelers*
>   *on.*

Between them, Lytol and Robinton forced F'lar to eat, deliberately plying him with wine. At the back of his mind he knew he would have to keep going but the effort was immense, the spirit gone from him. It was no comfort that they still had Pridith and Kylara to continue drag-onkind, yet he delayed sending someone back for F'nor, unable to face the reality of that admission: that in sending for Pridith and Kylara, he had acknowledged the fact that Lessa and Ramoth would not return.

Lessa, Lessa, his mind cried endlessly, damning her one moment for her reckless, thoughtless daring; loving her the next for attempting such an incredible feat.

"I said, F'lar, you need sleep now more than wine," Robinton's voice penetrated his preoccupation.

F'lar looked at him, frowning in perplexity. He realized that he was trying to lift the wine jug that Robinton was holding firmly down.

"What did you say?"

"Come. I'll bear your company to Benden. Indeed, nothing could persuade me to leave your side. You have aged years, man, in the course of hours."

"And isn't it understandable . . . ?" F'lar shouted, rising to his feet, the impotent anger boiling out of him at the nearest target in the form of Robinton.

Robinton's eyes were full of compassion as he reached for F'lar's arm, gripping it tightly.

"Man, not even this Masterharper has words enough to express the sympathy and honor he has for you. But you must sleep; you have to-morrow to endure and the tomorrow after that you have to fight. The dragonmen must have a leader . . ." and his voice trailed off. "Tomorrow you must send for F'nor . . . and Pridith."

F'lar pivoted on his heel and strode towards the fateful door of Ruatha's Great Hall.

> Oh, Tongue, give sound to joy
>   and sing
> Of hope and promise on dragon-
>   wing.

Before them loomed Ruatha's Great Tower, the high walls of the Outer Court clearly visible in the fading light.

The klaxon rang violent summons into the air, barely heard over the ear-splitting thunder as hundreds of dragons appeared, ranging in full fighting array wing upon wing, up and down the valley.

A shaft of light stained the flagstones of the Court as the Hold door opened.

Lessa ordered Ramoth down, close to the Tower, and dismounted, running eagerly forward to greet the men who piled out of the door. She made out the stocky figure of Lytol, a handbasket of glows held high about his head. She was so relieved to see him, she forgot her previous antagonism to the Warder.

"You misjudged the last jump by two days, Lessa," he cried as soon as he was near enough for her to hear him over the noise of settling dragons.

"Misjudged? How could I?" she breathed.

M'ron and Mardra came up beside her.

"It is not to worry," Lyton reassured her, gripping her hands tightly in his, his eyes dancing. He was actually smiling at her. "You overshot the day. Go back *between*, return to Ruatha of two days ago. That's all." His grin widened at her confusion. "It is all right," he repeated, patting her hands. "Take this same hour, the Great Court, everything, but visualize F'lar, Robinton and myself here on the flagstones. Place Mnementh on the Great Tower and a blue dragon on the verge. Now go."

Mnementh? Ramoth queried Lessa, eager to see her weyrmate. She ducked her great head and her huge eyes gleamed with scintillating fire.

"I don't understand," Lessa wailed. Mardra slipped a comforting arm around her shoulders.

"But I do, I do, trust me," Lytol pleaded, patting her shoulder awkwardly and glancing at M'ron for support. "It is as F'nor has said. You cannot be several places in time without experiencing great distress and when you stopped twelve Turns back, it threw Lessa all to pieces."

"You know that?" M'ron cried.

"Of course. Just go back two days. You see, I *know* you have. I shall, of course, be surprised then, but now, tonight, I know you reappeared two days earlier. Oh, go. Don't argue. F'lar was half out of his mind with worry for you."

"He'll shake me," Lessa cried, like a little girl.

"Lessa!" M'ron took her by the hand and led her back to Ramoth, who crouched so her rider could mount.

M'ron took complete charge and had his Fidranth pass the order to return to the references Lytol had given, adding by way of Ramoth a description of the humans and Mnementh.

THE COLD OF *between* restored Lessa to herself although her error had badly jarred her confidence. But then, there was Ruatha again. The dragons happily arranged themselves in tremendous display. And there, silhouetted against the light from the Hall, stood Lytol, Robinton's tall figure and . . . F'lar.

Mnementh's voice gave a brassy welcome and Ramoth could not land Lessa quickly enough to go and twine necks with her mate.

Lessa stood where Ramoth had left her, unable to move. She was aware that Mardra and M'ron were beside her. She was conscious only of F'lar, racing across the Court towards her as fast as he could. Yet she could not move.

He swung her up in his arms, hugging her so tightly she could not doubt the joy of his welcome.

"My darling, my love, how could you gamble so? I have been lost in an endless *between*, fearing for you." He kissed her, hugged her, held her and then kissed her with rough urgency again. Then he suddenly set her on her feet and gripped her shoulders. "Lessa, if you ever . . ." he said, punctuating each word with a flexing of his fingers, and stopped, aware of a grinning circle of strangers surrounding them.

"I told you he'd shake me," Lessa was saying, dashing tears from her face. "But, F'lar, I brought them all . . . all but Benden Weyr. And that is why the five Weyrs were abandoned. I brought them."

F'lar looked around him, looked beyond the leaders to the masses of dragons settling in the Valley, on the heights, everywhere he turned. There were dragons, blue, green, bronze, brown, and a whole wingful of golden queen dragons alone.

"You brought the Weyrs?" he echoed, stunned.

"Yes, this is Mardra and M'ron of Fort Weyr, D'ram and . . ."

He stopped her with a little shake, pulling her to his side so he could see and greet the newcomers.

"I am more grateful than you can know," he said and could not go on with all the many words he wanted to add.

M'ron stepped forward, holding out his hand which F'lar seized and held firmly.

"We bring eighteen hundred dragons, seventeen queens, and all that is necessary to implement our Weyrs."

"And they brought flamethrowers, too," Lessa put in excitedly.

"But, to come . . . to attempt it . . ." F'lar murmured in admiring wonder.

M'ron and D'ram and the others laughed.

"Your Lessa showed the way."

". . . With the Red Star to guide us . . ." she said.

"We are dragonmen," M'ron continued solemnly, "as you are yourself, F'lar of Benden. We were told there are Threads here to fight and that's work for dragonmen to do . . . in any time!"

> Drummer, beat, and piper, blow,
> Harper, strike, and soldier, go.
> Free the flame and sear the grasses
> 'Til the dawning Red Star passes.

Even as the five Weyrs had been settling around Ruatha valley, F'nor had been compelled to bring forward in time his southern weyrfolk. They had all reached the end of endurance in double-time life, gratefully creeping back to quarters they had vacated two days and ten Turns ago.

R'gul, totally unaware of Lessa's backward plunge, greeted F'lar and his Weyrwoman on their return to the Weyr, with the news of F'nor's appearance with seventy-two new dragons and the further word that he doubted any of the riders would be fit to fight.

"Never seen such exhausted men in my life," R'gul rattled on, "can't imagine what could have got into them, with sun and plenty of food and all, and no responsibilities."

F'lar and Lessa exchanged glances.

"Well, the southern Weyr ought to be maintained, R'gul. Think it over."

"I'm a fighting dragonman, not a womanizer," the old dragonrider grunted. "It'd take more than a trip *between* times to reduce me like those others."

"Oh, they'll be themselves again in next to no time," Lessa said and, to R'gul's intense disapproval, she giggled.

"They'll have to be if we're to keep the skies Threadfree," R'gul snapped testily.

"No problem about that now," F'lar assured him easily.

"No problem? With only a hundred and forty-four dragons?"

"Two hundred and sixteen," Lessa corrected him firmly.

Ignoring her, R'gul asked, "Has that Smithmaster found a flamethrower that'll work?"

"Indeed he has," F'lar said.

The five Weyrs had indeed brought forward their equipment. Fandarel all but snatched examples from their backs and, undoubtedly, every hearth and smithy through the continent would be ready to duplicate the design by morning. M'ron had told F'lar that, in his time, each Hold had ample flamethrowers for every man on the ground. In the course of the Long Interval, however, the throwers must have been either smelted down or lost as incomprehensible devices. D'ram, particularly, was very interested in Fandarel's agenothree sprayer, considering it better than thrown-flame since it would also act as a fertilizer.

"Well," R'gul admitted gloomily, "a flamethrower or two will be some help day after tomorrow."

"We have found something else that will help a lot more," Lessa remarked and then hastily excused herself, dashing into the sleeping quarters.

The sounds which drifted past the curtain were either laughter or sobs and R'gul frowned on both. That girl was just too young to be Weyr-woman at such a time. No stability.

"Has she realized how critical our situation is—even with F'nor's additions—that is, if they can fly?" R'gul demanded testily. "You oughtn't to let her leave the Weyr at all."

F'lar ignored that and began pouring himself a cup of wine.

"You once pointed out to me that the five empty Weyrs of Pern supported your theory that there would be no more Threads."

R'gul cleared his throat, thinking that apologies—even if they might be due the Weyrleader—were scarcely effective against the Threads.

"Now there was merit in that theory," F'lar went on, filling a cup for R'gul. "Not, however, as you interpreted it. The five Weyrs were empty because they . . . they came here."

R'gul, his cup halfway to his lips, stared at F'lar. This man also was too young to bear his responsibilities. But . . . he seemed actually to believe what he was saying.

"Believe it or not, R'gul—and in a bare day's time you will—the five Weyrs are empty no longer. They're here, in the Weyrs, in this time. And they shall join us, eighteen hundred strong, tomorrow at Telgar, with flamethrowers and with plenty of battle experience to help us overcome our ancient foe."

R'gul regarded the poor man stolidly for a long moment. Carefully he put his cup down and, turning on his heel, left the weyr. He refused to be an object of ridicule. He'd better plan to take over the leadership to-morrow if they were to fight Threads the day after.

The next morning, when he saw the clutch of great bronze dragons bearing the Weyrleaders and their wingleaders to the conference, R'gul got quietly drunk.

LESSA EXCHANGED GOOD mornings with her friends and then, smiling sweetly, left the weyr, saying she must feed Ramoth. F'lar stared after her thoughtfully, then went to greet Robinton and Fandarel, who had been asked to attend the meeting, too. Neither Craftmaster said much, but neither missed a word said. Fandarel's great head kept swiveling from

speaker to speaker, his deepset eyes blinking occasionally. Robinton sat
with a bemused smile on his face, utterly delighted by the circumstance
of ancestral visitors.

F'lar was quickly talked out of resigning his titular position as Weyrleader of Benden on the grounds that he was too inexperienced.

"You did well enough at Nerat and Keroon. Well indeed," M'ron
said.

"You call twenty-eight men or dragons out of action good leadership?"

"For a first battle, with every dragonman green as a hatchling?
No, man, you were on time at Nerat, however you got there," and
M'ron grinned maliciously at F'lar, "which is what a dragonman must
do. No, that was well flown, I say. Well flown." The four other Weyrleaders muttered complete agreement with that compliment. "Your
Weyr is understrength, though, so we'll lend you enough odd-wing
riders till you've got the Weyr up to full strength again. Oh, the queens
love these times!" And his grin broadened to indicate that bronze riders
did, too.

F'lar returned that smile, thinking that Ramoth was about ready for
another mating flight and this time, Lessa . . . Oh, that girl was being too
deceptively docile. He'd better watch her closely.

"Now," M'ron was saying, "we left with Fandarel's Crafthold all the
flamethrowers we brought up so that the groundmen will be armed
tomorrow."

"Aye, and my thanks," Fandarel grunted. "We'll turn out new ones in
record time and return yours soon."

"Don't forget to adapt that agenothree for air spraying, too," D'ram
put in.

"It is agreed," and M'ron glanced quickly around at the other riders,
"that all the Weyrs will meet, full strength, three hours after dawn above
Telgar, to follow the Threads' attack across to Crom. By the way, F'lar,
those charts of yours that Robinton showed me are superb. We never had
them."

"How did you know when the attacks would come?"

M'ron shrugged. "They were coming so regularly even when I was a
weyrling, you kind of knew when one was due. But this is much much
better."

"More efficient," Fandarel added approvingly.

"After tomorrow, when all the Weyrs show up at Telgar, we can request what supplies we need to stock the empty Weyrs." M'ron grinned.

"Like old times, squeezing extra tithes from the Holders," and he rubbed his hands in anticipation.

"There's the southern Weyr," F'nor suggested. "We've been gone from there six Turns in this time, and the herdbeasts were left. They'll have multiplied and there'll be all that fruit and grain."

"It would please me to see that southern venture continued," F'lar remarked, nodding encouragingly at F'nor.

"Yes, and continue Kylara down there, please, too," F'nor added urgently, his eyes sparkling with irritation.

They discussed sending for some immediate supplies to help out the newly occupied Weyrs, and then adjourned the meeting.

"IT IS A trifle unsettling," M'ron said as he shared wine with Robinton, "to find the Weyr you left the day before in good order has become a dusty hulk." He chuckled. "The women of the lower Caverns were a bit upset."

"We cleaned up those kitchens," F'nor replied indignantly. A good night's rest in a fresh time had removed much of his fatigue.

M'ron cleared his throat. "According to Mardra, no man can *clean* anything."

"Do you think you'll be up to riding tomorrow, F'nor?" F'lar asked solicitously. He was keenly aware of the stress of years showing in his half brother's face despite his improvement overnight. Yet those strenuous Turns had been necessary, nor had they become futile even by hindsight with the arrival of eighteen hundred dragons from past time. When F'lar had ordered F'nor ten Turns backwards to breed the desperately needed replacements, they had not yet brought to mind the Question Song or known of the Tapestry.

"I wouldn't miss that fight if I were dragonless," F'nor declared stoutly.

"Which reminds me," F'lar remarked, "we'll need Lessa at Telgar tomorrow. She can speak to any dragon, you know," he explained almost apologetically, to M'ron and D'ram.

"Oh, we know," M'ron assured him. "And Mardra doesn't mind." Seeing F'lar's blank expression, he added, "As senior Weyrwoman, Mardra, of course, leads the queens' wing."

F'lar's face grew blanker. "Queens' wing?"

"Certainly," and M'ron and D'ram exchanged questioning glances at F'lar's surprise. "You don't keep your queens from fighting, do you?"

"Our *queens*? M'ron, we at Benden have had but *one* queen dragon—at a time—for so many generations, that there are those who denounce the legends of queens in battle as black sacrilege!"

M'ron looked rueful. "I had not truly realized how small your numbers were, till this instant." But his enthusiasm overtook him. "Just the same, queens're very useful with flamethrowers. They get clumps other riders might miss. They fly in low, under the main wings. That's one reason D'ram's so interested in the agenothree spray. Doesn't singe the hair off the Holders' heads, so to speak, and is far better over tilled fields."

"Do you mean to say that you allow your queens to fly—against Threads?" F'lar ignored the fact that F'nor was grinning, and M'ron, too.

"Allow?" D'ram bellowed. "You can't stop them. Don't you know your Ballads?"

" 'Moreta's Ride'?"

"Exactly."

F'nor laughed aloud at the expression on F'lar's face as he irritably pulled the hanging forelock from his eyes. Then, sheepishly, he began to grin.

"Thanks. That gives me an idea."

HE SAW HIS fellow Weyrleaders to their dragons, waved cheerfully to Robinton and Fandarel, more lighthearted than he would have thought he'd be the morning before the second battle. Then he asked Mnementh where Lessa might be.

Bathing, the bronze dragon replied.

F'lar glanced at the empty queen's weyr.

Oh, Ramoth is on the Peak, as usual. Mnementh sounded aggrieved.

F'lar heard the sound of splashing in the bathing room suddenly cease, so he called down for hot *klah.* He was going to enjoy this.

"Oh, did the meeting go well?" Lessa asked sweetly as she emerged from the bathing room, drying-cloth wrapped tightly around her slender figure.

"Extremely. You realize, of course, Lessa, that you'll be needed at Telgar?"

She looked at him intently for a moment before she smiled again.

"I *am* the only Weyrwoman who can speak to any dragon," she replied archly.

"True," F'lar admitted blithely. "And no longer the only queen's rider in Benden . . ."

"I hate you!" Lessa snapped, unable to evade F'lar as he pinned her cloth-swathed body to his.

"Even when I tell you that Fandarel has a flamethrower for you so you can join the queens' wing?"

She stopped squirming in his arms and stared at him, disconcerted that he had outguessed her.

"And that Kylara will be installed as Weyrwoman in the south . . . in this time? As Weyrleader, I need all the peace and quiet I can get between battles . . ."

> From the Weyr and from the Bowl
> Bronze and brown and blue and
>   green,
> Rise the dragonmen of Pern,
> Aloft, on wing; seen, then unseen.

Ranged above the Peak of Benden Weyr, a scant three hours after dawn, two hundred and sixteen dragons held their formations as F'lar on bronze Mnementh inspected their ranks.

Below in the Bowl were gathered all the weyrfolk and some of those injured in the first battle. All the weyrfolk, that is, except Lessa and Ramoth. They had gone on to Fort Weyr where the queens' wing was assembling. F'lar could not quite suppress a twinge of concern that she and Ramoth would be fighting, too. A holdover, he knew, from the days when Pern had had but the one queen. If Lessa could jump four hundred Turns *between* and lead five Weyrs back, she could take care of herself and her dragon against Threads.

He checked to be sure that every man was well loaded with firestone sacks, that each dragon was in good color, especially those in from the southern Weyr. Of course, the dragons were fit but the faces of the men still showed evidences of the temporal strains they had endured. He was procrastinating and the Threads would be dropping in the skies of Telgar.

He gave the order to go *between*. They reappeared above, and to the south of Telgar Hold itself, and were not the first arrivals. To the west, to the north and yes, to the east now, wings arrived until the horizon was patterned with the great V's of several thousand dragon wings. Faintly he heard the klaxon bell on Telgar Hold Tower as the unexpected dragon strength was acclaimed from the ground.

"Where is she?" F'lar demanded of Mnementh. "We'll need her presently to relay orders . . ."

She's coming, Mnementh interrupted him.

Right above Telgar Hold another wing appeared. Even at this distance, F'lar could see the difference: the golden dragons shone in the bright morning sunlight.

A hum of approval drifted down the dragon ranks and despite his fleeting worry, F'lar grinned with proud indulgence at the glittering sight.

Just then the eastern wings soared straight upwards in the sky as the dragons became instinctively aware of the presence of their ancient foe.

Mnementh raised his head, echoing back the brass thunder of the war cry. He turned his head, even as hundreds of other beasts turned to receive firestone from their riders. Hundreds of great jaws masticated the stone, swallowed it, their digestive acids transforming dry stone into flame-producing gases, igniting on contact with oxygen.

Threads! F'lar could see them clearly now against the spring sky. His pulses began to quicken, not with apprehension, but with a savage joy. His heart pounded unevenly. Mnementh demanded more stone and began to speed up the strokes of his wings in the air, gathering himself to leap upward when commanded.

The leading Weyr already belched gouts of orange-red flame into the pale-blue sky. Dragons winked in and out, flamed and dove.

The great golden queens sped at cliff-skimming height to cover what might have been missed.

Then F'lar gave the command to gain altitude to meet the Threads halfway in their abortive descent. As Mnementh surged upward, F'lar shook his fist defiantly at the winking Red Eye of the Star.

"One day," he shouted, "we will not sit tamely here, awaiting your fall. We will fall on you, where you spin, and sear you on your own ground."

By the Egg, he told himself, if we can travel four hundred Turns backwards, and across seas and lands in the blink of an eye, what is travel from one world to another but a different kind of step?

F'lar grinned to himself. He'd better not mention that audacious notion in Lessa's presence.

Clumps ahead, Mnementh warned him.

As the bronze dragon charged, flaming, F'lar tightened his knees on the massive neck. Mother of us all, he was glad that now, of all times conceivable, he, F'lar, rider of bronze Mnementh, was a Dragonman of Pern!

About the Author

HARRY TURTLEDOVE was born in Los Angeles in 1949. After flunking out of Caltech, he earned a Ph.D. in Byzantine history from UCLA. He has taught ancient and medieval history at UCLA, Cal State Fullerton, and Cal State L.A., and he has published a translation of a ninth-century Byzantine chronicle, as well as several scholarly articles. His alternate-history works have included many short stories, the Civil War classic *The Guns of the South*, the epic World War I series The Great War, and the Worldwar tetralogy that began with *Worldwar: In the Balance*. He is a winner of the Sidewise Award for Best Alternate History for his novel *How Few Remain*.

MARTIN H. GREENBERG is a veteran anthologist and book packager with over 700 books to his credit. He lives in Green Bay, Wisconsin, with his wife, daughter, and four cats.